THE LOST W...
BOO...

MANTLE
OF THE
WORLD RULER

KATE GATELEY

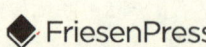
FriesenPress

One Printers Way
Altona, MB R0G 0B0,
Canada

www.friesenpress.com

Copyright © 2023 by Kate Gateley
First Edition — 2023

All rights reserved.

www.kategateley.com

Author photo by Ashley Marston Photography

Cover Design by Covet Design

No part of this publication may be reproduced in any form, or by any means, electronic or mechanical, including photocopying, recording, or any information browsing, storage, or retrieval system, without permission in writing from FriesenPress.

ISBN
978-1-03-915526-8 (Hardcover)
978-1-03-915525-1 (Paperback)
978-1-03-915527-5 (eBook)

1. FICTION, FANTASY, CONTEMPORARY

Distributed to the trade by The Ingram Book Company

For Scott,
May our rivers flow together through eternity

PROLOGUE

2018 AD

The tunnel was unlit, but Cassius's eyes were well accustomed to the shadows. And not just from today. As he'd traversed the realm between life and death in his endless search for immortality, he had become almost married to the darkness. That is, if a thing such as companionship were to his taste. But he had resembled a lone wolf more than anything in his most recent quest, primal in his wanderings and vicious in his pursuit.

He was hunting a primeval Druid magic—one so deeply rooted in darkness that it was all but forgotten. Yet somehow, he could almost feel its truth pulse through his dry veins as he navigated deeper through the fissure in the stone.

It had been a *very* long time since he had come here.

He had sworn, not just that day but ever since, that he would never return to this loathsome place again. Yet after the events in Northern Ireland, he felt he had no choice. His greatest legion of Wraiths had been lost to some unknown power the Witch had unleashed—an unexpected force that somehow decimated an entire army in one swift motion. With it, he knew he would have to retrace his steps to the Sibyl's grotto once more. Dead or not, her divining magic would have left an imprint here, and he would be a fool to ignore the significance the place had carved into his path all those years ago.

And much like last time, his hunger for immortality overpowered all else, now branching into survival.

He had mulled over in his mind what this change to their shared destiny might mean during his expedited flight out of London. Sipping deep on a glass of very expensive red wine—which he could scarcely taste over the petulance of death permeating his mouth—he had rolled it over in his mind again and again but found no respite. Yes, he was unchained from the Prophecy now, unbound and able to change tactics, but so were *they*. This created both an opening on his path and a significant roadblock.

The trouble was, he was still dying.

What he *did* know was that he would have to slip into the shadows for some time; that much was clear. No one could know where he was going or what he was searching for. As such, he had spared no expense on the luxuries he might enjoy on the way to Rome. Champagne and caviar had adorned his table, along with an endless supply of cocaine, should the mood strike. It never did anymore; he had long since lost any desire for a conventional high.

The real drug was in the Bearing magic.

On the floor of the plane had been several sedated Bearers, youthful and ripe for the picking whenever the craving should strike him. Well, he always had the craving.

Caleb and the others had procured them on short notice and, apparently, with some difficulty. But this was their job; he didn't extend gratitude towards expected behaviours from his subordinates. Bringing the women on board without fuss had unfortunately meant they had required sedation, and that just wasn't to his taste. No, he liked his quarries lucid; somehow, the screaming enhanced the experience for him. So, he had waited for them to awaken and feasted on their magic just before landing, once they could look him in the eye, fresh with terror.

Fully charged with the Bearers' gifts to him, he had climbed the mountains alone once more. The journey upward was at least as terrible as it had been back then, but it was of no consequence. If *Julia* had access to some new, unidentified power, then he must seek its counter. He knew that, alone, she couldn't be as powerful as he was, regardless of whatever this new skill was that she had obtained.

The Witch had only ever been as strong as those who surrounded her.

And indeed, the World Ruler had brandished his sword at the castle ruins, and his fools had shown up for him; the Druids had always been a thorn in Cassius's side. What he needed now was some means to strip away all those around her—those who would unfailingly show up to protect her—so that he might capture her without struggle. He couldn't risk losing more Wraiths in another direct conflict, nor could he risk his own life in the process.

The Codex Druidicus: a long-lost tome that a faceless Roman Sorcerer had dared to create, bottling ancient and volatile Druidic magics within its pages.

With that, Cassius could exact his true revenge.

Inside the mountain now, the passage continued to narrow as he slowly descended towards the abandoned chamber below. He paused for a moment to push back the bile that rose to his throat, his stomach churning with the exhaustion of a long climb. He was reminded of his last encounter with the place, and the bitch-wolf, almost two thousand years earlier. Instantly, a reflexive hot anger pounded through his fragile chest at the memory of her wretchedness. He welcomed the feeling though; the fresh rage fuelled his quest onward.

Plunging deeper into the earth, Cassius noticed an unfamiliar dampness surrounding him that hadn't been there before. Soon, he was ankle deep in lukewarm water that smelled strongly of sulfur. He vaguely recalled a well-spring in the corner of the Oracle's chamber; it had seemed inconsequential then. Perhaps it had simply risen over the decades, fed by some sort of volcanic hot spring. He wondered if he would even be able to access the chamber at all.

His nightmares had long been haunted by the vision of the Oracle, all those years ago, transforming from vile crone to howling wolf, then to *mater*, and at last, into a fragile child. He suspected this was some sort of mystical scar, an imprint she had left to punish him for all of eternity, always familiar, always nagging, and *always* beckoning him back to the dark cave in the mountain.

And now, almost two thousand years later, he had returned.

He felt the skin on the back of his neck prickle as he approached the innermost chamber. It confirmed his suspicions: There was still plenty of her magic here, despite the Prophetess having long since traversed to the Otherworld. Her spirit still guarded the place. He could feel it. He suddenly felt something deep in his belly that he hadn't for many years—*fear*.

Approaching the chamber at last, he was pleased to discover the water was only waist deep. Cautiously, he waded into the room, which now bore an eerie white glow, despite its depth so far from the sun.

Yes, she was definitely still here, in one form or another.

"Sibyl!" he called out. "I have returned victorious."

No sound came in reply, only the quiet lapping of the water surrounding him as he disturbed it with his wary motions.

"Your Prophecy no longer holds. I am unbound!"

The cave continued to mock him in silence, but he could definitely feel her residual magic. He tried a more direct approach.

"I need to find the lost source of the Druid's darkest secrets," he said in a commanding tone. "Where can I find the *Codex Druidicus?*"

For a moment, all was completely still. Even the effects of his wake seemed to pause into an unnatural, eerie calm. But then the water began to ripple, as though something large was swimming just below the surface and creating slow, narrowing circles around him.

Snakes. Panic quickly overcame him. He had always been fearful of snakes, ever since he was a small child. He wondered if this wasn't her intention, tapping into his most ancient fears.

She knew him, after all. But he had known her as well. *Intimately.*

"I'm not here to play games with you this time, Oracle! Stop this at once and give me the answers I seek!" he shouted, regaining control of his fear.

It was beastly hot in the cavern, which was a change from last time. He wondered if the water around him wasn't heating up from below, for the slow circling began to show signs of bubbling … churning … almost as if it were on the brink of boiling.

"Name your price!" he demanded.

Then a booming voice rang out against the stone walls, the voice of the Oracle, emanating from somewhere deep below. Ancient and terrible.

With the Sovereign standing tall, the World Ruler too must bear his crown,
As the Sorcerer seeks to find the grail, spear in hand, to chalice he is bound.

To reveal the lost wellspring, the Sun and Moon must accept their fate.
When the Celt accepts the mantle, the Crone too shall find her strength.

For the earthen weapons masters, and tree talkers with open sky above,
Darkness reigns where light cannot, and from its root, the land will rot.

Cassius could barely stand the heat now, the air around him having grown thick with steam, making it difficult to breathe. And the water seemed to be rising. He would need to get out of the cave quickly.

He launched himself towards the door, but the water was at his shoulders now, rising ever more rapidly towards the stone ceiling. He was being barred exit.

"Let me out, you bitch!"

He dug into his deepest recesses, where the stolen Bearing magic and his own hot rage fuelled his very existence, and forced himself up and out of the cavern.

The water followed him violently all the way up the tunnel, surging around him. Cassius swallowed much of it as he scrambled and scraped along the surrounding stone to reach the surface before it engulfed him whole. Spitting and choking now, the sulfurous tinge burning his throat and nostrils, he realized it meant to consume him.

At last, and to the testament of his own raw power, he reached the narrow recess at the top of the slope. He could smell the fresh mountain air just beyond the crevasse, and in one final push, he landed on his hands and knees just outside the grotto. Behind him, the mountain shook violently, enraged that he had escaped. And then the entrance collapsed in on itself.

She had blocked him out now for good. It was over.

Lying drenched in the Sibyl's sour fluids on the side of the mountain, Cassius began to laugh. Recounting now the last two lines of the new Prophecy—the only two that would matter to him—he knew that the Codex did indeed exist and that its secrets would mean an end to all Wielders not bent to his control. He would poison the tree from its roots using the Druid's own magic against them.

He just had to find the *Codex Druidicus*.

CHAPTER 1

Dom's reality shook around him like an earthquake as he grasped Julia from the core of his being. The situation unfolding before them was all too familiar, mirroring the origin of their curse all those years ago, with Julia's cottage fully engulfed in flames and her body limp, having collapsed into his outstretched arms. There was absolutely no way he was going to let her leave him this time, not even if it meant giving another thousand years in service to the Otherworld.

Thank God she stuck around. This time.

The previous time, so very long ago, when the Druids had sent him across to the Otherworld, he had promised its guides to protect her with all of his might, literally till death did them part and beyond. That part of the vow had been easy. In turn, they would allow her multiple chances to defeat Cassius once and for all. The hard part, however, had been keeping them both alive long enough to try.

Except for the fact there were two modern firetrucks spraying water and fire retardant all around—and of course, the gathering crowd of nosey neighbours—his feelings were eerily similar to that first time all those many years ago. And it terrified him. Out of the corner of his eye, he could see the growing horde muttering under their breath. Their voices spoke loudly in his mind about how unfortunate the timing was, with Julia having been away so long and only just returning, and wondering what the cause might have been.

"Do you think it was an electrical fire?" one whispered voice asked.

"Maybe, but Bill's been taking care of the place for her, and you know how diligent he is," someone offered.

Another person suggested, *"Maybe it was a lightning strike?"*

"Fat chance. The weather's been perfectly clear!"

Uncomfortable laughter followed.

By now, the flames easily rose two storeys high, evidently fuelled by more than wood and old plaster. Colourful licks of flame poured forth from the blown-out Tudor windows. An especially loud bang from somewhere in the attic startled the concerned observers. To the untrained eye, the magnitude of the blaze looked to be the result of a home filled with an abundance of items that could ignite; Gertie had been known as a collector of oddities, after all. To the trained eye, however, it was not only clear that the blaze was intentional but that it had been fuelled by Wraiths.

None of this mattered to Dom in the moment. Julia staying in the here-and-now was the only important thing. After a few initial moments of terror, she had slumped backwards into his arms, her breath strangely slow and calm. He stroked her hair, holding her tight to his chest.

She was here, and they were alive. "I've got you," he said.

A moment later, Dom slid his phone awkwardly from his jeans pocket and quickly texted Ronan five simple words:

Wraiths torched cottage. Action needed.

That would be enough for Ronan to set the gears in motion in Vancouver. Thank God the man was already on the coast. He always had such an uncanny knack for being exactly where he needed to be, but Dom wasn't about to complain about Ronan's dumb luck just now.

"Julia," he whispered in her ear, "we have to back up."

The firefighters were directing the onlookers to move further away so they could spray higher up into the trees. Meanwhile, local volunteers were cutting back the nearby brush with haste, creating an impromptu fire line. It was quite dry on the island, the heat of summer having been already well established. He could understand their urgency. However, he was far more worried about moving her to safety. He put his hand to her cheek; she was ice cold.

"I think she's going into shock …" he said to nobody in particular.

Soon there were hands around them, helping Dom move her to a safer location across the road. He lay her back against a mossy stump, and someone offered a sugary drink. He stared at her with a furrowed brow, deeply worried for her wellbeing.

"Dom," she said at last, teeth chattering, "we have to g-get … away f-from here—"

"I know, but I can't just sling you over my shoulder after you faint on me either. Well, I could, but I don't think they would like that." He gestured towards Bill and some other less familiar neighbours who all shared the same look of doting concern.

He had hoped to make her at least smile, but she didn't. In fact, her eyes reminded him of a small, frightened animal's, and he suddenly realized what she was truly worried about: She was about to be pulled into one of her divinations.

"Hold on, love," he said.

Suddenly, a raspy voice sounded from behind them, making them both jump.

"The suite at my place just down the road is empty for the next few days if you need somewhere to stay."

Dom didn't recognize the rail-thin older woman, but Julia seemed to and smiled appreciatively. "Thanks, Joan, that would be amazing."

Dom knew that Salt Spring Island, being a regular tourist destination, was heavily dotted with vacation rentals; he was grateful there was somewhere for them to stay even at the height of the busy summer season.

"Of course. The door is unlocked; just let yourself in whenever you like," Joan said before floating back towards the group of neighbours. Her quirky patchwork linen skirt swayed in the breeze behind her. Dom was reminded of the quilt, safely stowed in the trunk of their rental car, and took consolation that their most important possessions, the ones that *really* mattered, were still unscathed and safely out of sight.

He had insisted they bring along several important artifacts from Ireland—the ones that were allowed to leave the country anyway—including several logs and journals he had written over the years, a handful of old maps and relevant history books, and Ronan's compass, which he had borrowed once more. He'd also packed his sword. Dom had needed to stretch the truth with Canadian customs about that item, as it wasn't every day that one travelled with an ancient steel blade. His persona as a linguistic anthropologist had been especially helpful in this regard.

Looking around, his thoughts began to clear. And then his phone pinged. Ronan no doubt.

"Are you alright to move?" he asked Julia. "I need to contact the Dru— Ronan, but we should get somewhere private first."

"I can manage …" She pushed off the ground, rising slowly under her own power and taking only a moment to steady herself.

He overheard someone mention something about collecting food and clothing, and another citing the need for a community potluck to gather resources. He already knew they wouldn't be able to stay long enough to appreciate the efforts; somehow, Cassius's forces had breached the protective isle, and that meant it no longer offered safe harbour.

Perhaps he had kept her away too long, lingering at the manor house for those weeks as he recovered. Hindsight was such a fucking waste of energy.

"Okay. Let's go," Julia said. She flashed a tight smile to the group huddled together and strode confidently towards the car, settling herself into the passenger seat. To any onlooker, she would have seemed reasonably shaken up but obviously holding it together. To Dom's eyes, he could see that she was gathering every inch of strength she possessed before the imminent magical collapse to come.

He slid quickly into the driver's seat and took off, gravel spitting out behind the tires as he sped down the drive, as Julia offered him simple directions to Joan's place. Dom wondered absently if this experience was anything like driving someone to the hospital who was about to give birth but didn't share his thoughts; Julia looked like she might pass out at any moment. Plus, talking about childbearing always made her uncomfortable.

Thankfully, the suite really was only a few minutes away, privately located above a refinished barn on the back of a large, well-kept property.

"She was a friend of my grandmother's," Julia said as she exited the car, her voice distant. "A bit of a rabble-rouser, according to Gertie anyway, but harmless."

Dom raised his eyebrows in surprise; the woman's initial impression had seemed far from turbulent. Julia shrugged before leading the way up the outdoor staircase towards the entrance. He stayed close enough behind to catch her should she falter, but she managed fine enough without his support. When they reached the small landing, as promised, the door was unlocked.

Inside, they found a large open room decorated with an abundance of coastal-themed artwork and knickknacks typical for the region, no doubt to appease a particular type of bed-and-breakfast connoisseur. It was sunny and welcoming, with the only door within leading to a small bathroom. Across from a lacily adorned queen bed was a small kitchenette with a café table for two.

Julia seated herself on the frilly duvet and leaned back, eyes already closed. "Dom, I don't know how much longer I can stay here. *Conscious*, I mean …"

He was honestly shocked she had lasted this long but assumed the newly forged connectivity to her powers had allowed her to keep the magical portents from flooding in. But not for much longer.

"I understand. You'll be alright?" he asked, attempting to keep the fear from his voice. He wasn't convinced it had worked.

"I've got this," she said quietly. And then she slipped away.

Her face remained comparatively serene as her eyes tracked frantically behind her purpled lids. His heart pained at the sight. But he had made a promise to trust her magical intuition, and he meant to keep it. Her skin was still ice cold, so he gently covered her in a bobbly crocheted blanket before wandering to the kitchenette to pour himself a glass of water, which he swallowed in one extended gulp. It tasted like iron.

His body was on high alert, and he knew it would remain so until she woke. He could feel his muscles taught with the anticipation of threat. Primed for battle. His breath slowed as he took in his surroundings. While he had transported her to what was presumably a safe space, he had his doubts. Clearly the Wraiths had found a way in, and he couldn't be sure of anything right now.

He pulled out his phone to check his messages. There was one from Ronan:

Call me immediately.

The call didn't make it past the first ring before his best friend answered.

"Domhnall. Are you alright? Where's Julia?"

"We're fine. She's here. Well ... kind of. I can't really say where her mind has gotten to, but she said she needed to do this, so …"

"Right," Ronan said, hardly skipping a beat. "Well, I've got news. A boat was spotted leaving Salt Spring not too long ago, looking *highly* suspicious. I've got several of the others on it, but we don't know yet who was on board or where they're headed."

Before leaving Ireland, Dom had insisted that the Druids station lookouts on live-aboard fishing vessels near the island, out of what had seemed an abundance of caution. He had been met with slight resistance at the time, but clearly, his instincts had been correct.

"Cowards," Dom said, venom gathering on his tongue. The Wraiths had obviously only meant to deliver a message, rather than show up and fight.

"Well, that's not the most important bit."

Dom gritted his teeth. "Oh?"

As usual, Ronan waited to deliver the most poignant information until he was in control of the conversation. "Lennie says Cassius has completely disappeared off the map. We'd assumed so far that he had stayed in London but thought maybe he was heading to L.A., as several of his generals in England seem to have received promotions and were travelling west. But when his jet arrived at LAX, he wasn't with them …"

Dom was trying his best to stay focused on their conversation as he watched Julia arch and thrash on the bed, tossing her covers off. She settled into a still state again before he could reach her, but his distraction was already detected by Ronan.

"Domhnall, are you listening?"

"I am. Sorry … It's just, Julia—"

The Druid cleared his throat loudly. Dom had a distinct suspicion that Ronan was much more concerned about Julia than he was letting on; the two had forged a profound bond during the battle, the details around which he hadn't completely sussed out yet.

"I think the most important thing is to relocate the two of you. Off of that island for sure, but out of the country if you can manage it. Not anywhere you have been before though … if you can help it. I was waiting until you arrived safely to update you on this matter, but there's been a notable gathering of Wraiths over the past several days around here. They were expecting you to return to the region." Ronan let out a rueful laugh.

"Hmm …" Dom said, his thoughts firing off one by one. Staying in the region was risky, but so was relocating Julia too abruptly. They needed to go somewhere Cassius wouldn't expect, which was fairly limited considering he had Wraiths spanning the entire Western continent. Scanning the available options, he made a judgement call. "I think south. It sounds like we're going to need to do some reconnaissance in Los Angeles anyways. Can you find us somewhere to stay along the way? It can't be San Francisco though; we've definitely been there before."

"Of course. I'll arrange accommodations, and we can go from there. Give me a bit of time. You'll need to find a vehicle to cross the border. I think that's safest. No more than three days, Domhnall, and you'll need to be on the road. I don't have a good feeling about what these Wraiths are up to."

Dom nodded, though obviously Ronan couldn't see him, and then grunted.

"Great. Keep in touch then," Ronan paused. "I hope—"

"She'll be alright," Dom said, hoping he was actually telling the truth.

Ronan hung up, and Dom began to pace.

After about two hours, there came a knock at the door. Joan, he assumed.

He begrudgingly pulled on his jeans and t-shirt; it was beastly hot in the suite, and he had stripped down to naught but his boxers to survive the space. The windows were open but had offered little help in quelling the sauna-like environment.

Julia was still bone-chilled though, so his suffering was inconsequential.

"It's just little old me," Joan said. "I've brought you two a fan; you must be sweltering!" She attempted to peer over and then under Dom's arm at Julia's prone body stretched out on the bed. "The A/C unit broke last summer, and I just haven't bothered to get it fixed. I'm getting old, you see. Always so much to do around here …" Her voice was raspy as it trailed off, reminding him of newspaper being slowly shredded.

7

"Thanks, Joan," he said, putting on his most charming smile. "Julia's just lying down for a rest. She's been through a lot today. As you know."

"Of course, of course. Just let me know if there is anything else I can get you. A meal train will be arriving soon for you; Bill's arranged it. He's devastated. Blaming himself, naturally." She waved her hand absently.

As if on cue, Dom's stomach growled. He was grateful for the humble hospitality found on the island, even if it came with a bit more curiosity than he cared for at the moment.

"Oh wonderful," he said, nodding serenely while keeping Julia's body safely blocked from view. "Thanks again, Joan!"

He watched as she descended the steps and then closed the door behind himself once more.

Another painful hour passed before Julia finally settled into a deep slumber, her breath slowing at last into the all-too-familiar rhythm of exhaustion.

She had called out several times during the transcendence, his name, but also words or places he wasn't familiar with. He'd gone to her side each time, speaking soothing words even though he knew she wasn't close enough to their physical plane to hear; he only hoped his presence would serve as an anchor. At one point his mind had wandered to Agnes Sweeney—the wise woman whose consciousness Cassius had destroyed. *What must it be like to be lost within your own mind?* He forced his thoughts away from the topic.

Now that Julia was visibly asleep, he knew she was back with him. Sweaty and depleted from the afternoon's events, Dom desperately needed a shower. Taking a moment, he hastily descended the stairs towards their rental car to collect their luggage. Thankfully, both he and Julia were accustomed to travelling light, this rebirth being no exception. After quietly setting their bags near the foot of the bed and checking that she was still comfortable, he slipped into the bathroom, fresh clothes in hand, for a cold shower.

He could kill for a beer right now.

Dom kept the shower quick, afraid he might wake Julia, but when he came out, she hadn't moved an inch. Fully dressed and towelling off his hair, which was now long enough to tie back, a second knock arrived at the door.

It was Bill and the lawyer, Joe Linder.

"Dom! I wish we were meeting again in less unpleasant circumstances," Joe said, shaking his hand fervently.

Bill nodded silently, holding out a case of Lucky Lager beer.

Dom grinned broadly at the offering and gestured them down the steps, moving towards a shaded patio behind the barn. He flipped over a round log to set their drinks on. Popping the top of a cold, sweaty can Bill had handed him as they descended the steps, he quickly drained two-thirds of the beer and set it on the log.

"Julia's sleeping," he said, not inviting further discussion. She would rouse in her own time and not a moment sooner, if he had his way about it. Thankfully, the pair of men were amenable.

"I'm so sorry this happened," Bill said, looking pained as they settled onto several vibrantly painted Adirondack chairs that surrounded an empty metal firepit.

"Stop there, Bill," Dom said, holding up his broad hands. "We know you've taken beautiful care of the place. You can't help when something like this happens—sometimes it's just an act of God, you know? But Julia knows Gertie would have only wanted her to be safe. And I'm just glad it didn't happen while we were asleep."

"The timing feels so strange," Bill said, wringing his dusty red ball cap in his small hands. "I spoke to the fire chief. We can't think of anything that would have ignited the flames. However, Gertie *was* a bit of a collector ..."

His tone was honest and not the slightest bit accusatory. Dom leaned back in the chair, crossing an ankle over his knee while noticing both men eyeing his muscular frame.

"Are you a rugby player, Dom?" Joe asked, raising his eyebrows at Dom's shorter-than-average shorts.

In truth, Dom had always been a bit vain about his powerful legs, but all of the younger warriors had been, back *when* he had come from. He chuckled and gestured for Bill to pass him another beer; he was extremely thirsty. "You could say that. I was, in my younger days at least ..."

He spent the next forty-five minutes regaling them with lighthearted stories about his days spent playing rugby in Ireland, some of which were true, though the majority were careful fabrications riding just close enough to the truth that they sounded believable. Dom had always been an excellent storyteller, which suited his needs far more often than he cared to admit.

"I'm not sure what our next move will be—now that the cottage is gone, of course." He paused for effect. "We'd planned to take a trip down the American coastline before summer's end. I'm guessing we will just push that forward a bit."

It was imperative they weren't suspicious about how fast they would have to leave. These two men were solid, and he needed them on his side if they were to slip away mostly unnoticed, but you never knew who might be feeding information to the other side.

Dom and Julia hadn't actually discussed much past their summer plans, let alone what might transpire over the next six months between now and the winter solstice.

"That sounds like a positive alternative," Joe said, waving happily at a silver sedan that had just pulled up in the driveway. "I have to admit, we've all been a little unsure about what Julia would end up doing with the house. But this certainly wasn't on the list!"

"I had been looking forward to having you both around for a while," Bill said. Dom was taken aback by his sincerity, and he felt the corners of his mouth pull upwards without effort.

Exiting their car, two middle-aged women and a teenage girl in noisy flip-flops crunched up the drive, arms laden with aluminum trays and several grocery bags.

"This should do you for a time," Bill said, looking relieved.

"You're too kind!" Dom said, hopping up to gratefully accept the goods. "Won't you join us?"

"No, no. We're just passing through. Send our condolences to Julia, though," one woman said. Clearly the mother of the teenager, she was struggling to hide her smirk at the look on her daughter's face, which had turned beet red at the sight of Dom rising from his chair.

"You didn't tell me your names," Dom said, quickly oozing with charm.

The other woman spoke. "I'm Carol. And this is Janet and her daughter, Kennedy."

Dom recalled Julia saying something last winter about Carol being another overly nosey neighbour. The scrutiny scrawled across her face only confirmed it.

"Lovely to meet you all. And thanks *so* very much!"

All three women beamed at him before turning on their heels to go. His two companions took this as a cue to leave as well and made their excuses, with Bill handing him a card with the phone number for the fire chief. "When she's ready, she'll need to call for the official report. The sooner the better."

"And don't forget to deal with the insurance too, before you go," Joe added as an afterthought over his shoulder.

After waving them off, Dom hauled the food up the steps in one trip. Crossing the threshold of the suite, he found that Julia was no longer on the bed. His heart pounded rapidly in his chest, and he almost dropped everything when she spoke.

"Dom, is that you?" she called out from the bathroom. Breathing in a sigh of relief, he could smell soapy floral notes floating through the air; she had to be feeling fairly well if she was able to shower.

"It is! And good news, I've got food."

She stepped out of the bathroom wearing only a towel, her long hair sopping wet on her shoulders. Her eyes were still strangely distant, with dark prominent circles underneath them, but she smiled at the sight of him.

"Julia." He hastily set the food down on the floor and strode through the hot room towards her, his arms outstretched. As usual, he was staggered by her raw beauty, and even now, he eyed her figure hungrily.

"I'm alright, Dom. Really," she said, leaning into his hug momentarily before pushing back with playful accusation. "But it's fucking *boiling* in here! Why didn't you open any windows?"

He laughed.

She was definitely still his Julia, despite having just spent the better part of three hours upon the astral plane. He watched as she eyed the shoddy box fan Joan had sourced for them, which was doing a decidedly piss-poor job at circulating the air.

"You must have been dying in here," she said sympathetically.

"Oh, don't worry about me. I went outside for a bit. Had a beer with the lads."

She cocked her head. "The lads?"

"Bill and Joe stopped by. But I suppose I could've opened a few more windows before I went down. You were just so cold lying there; I didn't want to make it worse for you, while you were …"

Her face dropped slightly as she looked deep into his eyes, tracing her slender fingers along his arms. His flesh rose to her touch.

"I'm not ready to talk about it just yet," she said, obviously referencing what she had seen, or experienced, while away.

He kissed her gently on the forehead. "I understand. Come, let's eat! You must be starving!"

"Well, we both know *you* are," Julia said, offering him a heart-stopping grin.

He watched as she pulled on some simple black underwear followed by a pair of denim shorts. Braless, she slid one of his old t-shirts over her head and tied the bottom hem into a knot at her left hip. She had recently claimed it as her own, and as usual, the effect of her wearing his clothes stirred something rather primal within him. However, he kept his thoughts to himself.

Shoulder to shoulder, they rustled through the bags of food on the floor in an attempt to find something they could heat without too much effort, as the suite had only a toaster oven for cooking.

"Hmm …" Dom said, suddenly serious as he peeled back the foil on what looked to be a freezer-burnt vegetarian lasagna. "I'm not sure how this is going to go."

She chuckled, leaning into him affectionately.

His heart pounded in his throat at her touch. Perhaps he was just imagining it in the moment, but there was increased gravity between them today that hadn't been there before. Or at least, not for many, *many* years. It was a youthful feeling he hadn't experienced since she'd first crossed his path in a small village near the River Shannon in eleventh-century Ireland.

"Aha!" she proclaimed, unearthing a bundle of cheese, cured meat, and olives. "Much better!"

"For you, maybe. I'm so hungry I could eat a horse!" Dom stood and started to fiddle with the toaster oven, swearing under his breath at its obvious inadequacies. Suddenly, she was behind him, arms wrapped tightly around his middle.

He felt his abs and lower back clench at the impact. "Wha—"

"I love you, Domhnall," Julia said. "So much. And I don't say it enough, but you're *literally* the only thing keeping me tethered to the earth right now.

I feel so … disjointed. The visions … but with you here, I'm safe. And whole. And I just …"

She was crying.

He turned towards her and took her face in his hands, struggling to find the words to comfort her. He too had experienced the gambit of emotions today. He brushed away her tears before leaning in and kissing her deeply. She tasted like toothpaste.

"Would you believe me if I told you that you have the same effect on me?" he asked, staring into her bleary eyes. "I thought I was going to lose you today, and … I don't think I would have survived it this time."

"I'm still here," she said, leaning her tall frame against his. Silently, he cried too.

He still wasn't entirely sure she knew the spell she cast on him, especially now that her hand in their destiny had launched them onto an entirely new path. In fact, despite everything that had happened, for the first time in a millennium, he was allowing himself to have real hope.

She truly was a miracle.

"Dom?" she asked after a time.

"Hmm?"

She chuckled. "Your stomach is growling at me."

"Oh. That it is," he said, joining in her laughter.

They did their best to cobble together a late-day meal before settling into bed. It wasn't the most satiating meal, but Dom's exhaustion finally caught up to him and rest soon took precedence. His eyelids were as heavy as lead while she lay quietly curled in his arms.

"You should sleep, Dom. Honestly."

"Are you sure?" he asked, concerned about leaving her in such a vulnerable state.

"Yes. I'll wake you if I need you. And besides, tomorrow is a big day!"

He peered at her through one groggy eye. "Oh?"

"It's the oldest we've ever been!" she said, and he could feel her smile grow against his chest.

"Every day is the oldest we've ever been—"

"You know what I mean. The longest we've ever been together … or whatever."

He knew what she meant. "You're right. Happy Solstice, Julia."

"Happy Solstice," she said.

He slept then, heavy and dreamless. He woke several times to her tossing and turning, but for the most part, the night was quiet.

The following morning, Julia spoke to the fire chief.

In the end, they suspected it was more than likely a short on the back of Gertie's old refrigerator. Dom knew that wasn't true. But now that the protection spell was down, the Druidic watchmen Ronan had placed had managed to sneak onto the property, sight unseen, to doctor the findings overnight. Both he and Ronan could find no reasonable alternative, and it was better than a finding of arson at any rate, magical or not.

"That thing should have been replaced years ago," a gruff-sounding man named Byron had told her, his familiar tone intimating that he was someone who had been well acquainted with Gertie at some point in time. "But otherwise, it seemed a lot of old stuff ignited at once."

Dom sat quietly through the conversation. Julia had insisted it be held on speakerphone in case she missed anything important; she didn't feel steady with her own mind just yet.

"I'm sorry, Dom. I feel so useless. My thoughts are so scattered ... even my memories leading up to the fire aren't clear."

"It's alright, love. I completely understand."

He felt like he had said that a lot over the past twenty-four hours, but it really was no concern to him. All of this landed firmly within his wheelhouse: crisis management and quick logistics. He only hoped he could buy her the time she needed in order to feel settled once more.

Thanks to the Druids, the insurance claim would be simple. As soon as the report declared the cause of the fire to be an electrical fault, all she had to do was make the call and set the wheels in motion. Once the physical debris was cleaned up, she would list the property for sale.

"Are you still sure you want to sell?" Dom asked, following the conversation with the fire chief. He shifted onto his side under the frilly bedclothes.

"I am. With the protection spell gone ... I just don't feel safe here anymore."

She eyed the door momentarily before sinking back into the same dark look she had been struggling to conceal all morning. He knew she hadn't slept much the night before, and so he was doing his best to keep them restful for one more day.

Despite this, he was positively frantic to get moving. "Tomorrow, if you're ready, we should leave."

She nodded in agreement.

Dom spoke to Ronan on the phone for close to an hour, working through each leg of their journey, ever grateful for his friend's unwavering support. That afternoon, it was arranged that they would ferry back to Vancouver Island and hook up with one of the Druids, Sean, in Victoria. After sorting some expedited visas—thanks in this case to Lennie's connections—they would then board a ferry to the United States. Ronan had assured them that, each step of the way, they would have a Druid overwatch, seen or unseen. Julia, still exhausted and foggy headed, had been agreeable to every element of the plan.

The only matter she had any opinion on was their transport.

"We should get something small and discreet," Dom said, struggling to hide his disappointment at the idea.

"Don't be ridiculous," she said, unexpectedly running her hand along his inner thigh. "We need something comfortable that you'll *actually* fit in."

"Oh? And what do you suggest then?" he asked, surprised by her change in tone.

The late-day sun was pouring brightly into the suite, but thankfully, a cross breeze had kept the room from reaching the sauna-like levels it had yesterday. They had spent the majority of the day in bed, peaceful in their cocoon, but it was still a bit too warm to be called comfortable.

"Hmm …" she said, hopping on top of him playfully and tilting her head. "What about a truck? Nothing *too* big though."

Her own truck, which had been hardly reliable for any real journey, was damaged beyond repair in the fire.

"I want whatever you want …" he said, his voice trailing off as she leaned back, still straddling him.

Citing the heat, she removed her thin t-shirt. Her hair had taken on the humidity, tumbling down her chest in full, gorgeous auburn waves. She tugged at it momentarily, lifting it from the back of her neck. The skin on her breasts was flushed pink, but her nipples were hard despite the heat.

"I need a haircut," she said as she looked at him, doe-eyed. "And so do you."

She leaned in and ran her fingers through his mane, which could almost be described as curly now with all the heat.

"Do I?" He raised one eyebrow before roaring like a lion.

She laughed into his chest.

And then they made love.

He still wasn't convinced she was entirely present at all times yet, the reverberations of the powerful visions still clearly pulling at her psyche. However, as she was leading the charge, he happily agreed to whatever she asked of him. It had always been this way, seeking each other out physically to ground themselves fully in *this* reality.

Any further plans could wait until tomorrow.

CHAPTER 2

I knew I wouldn't recall many details from the time between the fire and our cross-border journey. It wasn't that I wasn't *present* but more like I was carrying through the motions without forming any memory. Dom had taken natural control of the situation as he deftly pivoted towards our still-developing plans.

And for the most part, I didn't mind.

"Ronan's arranged a beach house for us in Oregon," he said as we approached the international ferry terminal in Victoria's downtown inner harbour for the mid-afternoon sailing. "There's a solid group of Druids located along the coast who ... Well, he figures this is our safest bet for now. And I agree."

I nodded in silence. I had been struggling to pay attention to our plans ever since they were laid out to me, and it was still a struggle today, even as he repeated them. I kept dissociating at unpredictable intervals. Magical transcendence followed by significant sleep deprivation had that effect on a girl.

"We're taking a vacation together. I think we are also, probably, newly engaged," he added, but his sentiment seemed purely procedural. "That will solidify our narrative."

I stared at him, perplexed.

"Narrative?"

"I just mean … you're not exactly solid right now, love. It's easier if we have a clear story when we go through customs. There's no way to know who might be watching. And we *do* stick out a bit to begin with …"

He eyed me with the same strained look he had been giving me all day while running his fingers through his newly shorn hair. We had both agreed it would be wise to freshen up before the voyage south; we were a bit travel worn. He looked impossibly handsome now, of course, with his tidy beard and casually coifed hair. Even with my haircut, there was no real way of hiding my memorable tresses without dying them. I pulled my hair back self-consciously into a ponytail.

"Alright. It's the truth anyways, at least at some point in our timeline." I sighed. "And easier than telling them we're running from a group of maniacal Wraiths hell-bent on vengeance."

His expression faltered slightly, but he looked mostly appeased.

Since arriving back at the cottage and finding it in flames, I had spiralled in-and-out of a steady state. The initial shock of flames had been enough to knock us both to the ground. But once I realized I wouldn't be leaving this physical plane, as I had so long ago, that's when the real fun had started. More accurately, I was catapulted into a series of violent visions and jagged-edged portents that I'd had no choice but to let run their course. Just before the end of my journey, something entirely worse had pooled into my divinations: a truth I wasn't yet ready to discuss openly with Dom.

"Are you ready?" he asked as the border guard approached the vehicle ahead of ours.

Even then, I was struggling to stick with the present moment. I thought of the quilt, rolled up unassumingly in its canvas bag on the back seat, before handing my passport to Dom on the driver's side. He had conceded to leaving the ancient weaponry behind, with Sean agreeing to send Dom's sword back to him at a later date when things weren't so … tense. I knew Dom wasn't comfortable with the choice, but it would reduce our chance of delay.

I nodded. "Ready as I'll ever be."

His eyes bulged then. "Oh! Hold on! I've got something for you."

Struggling in his jeans pocket for a moment, he held out his hand towards me.

"A Claddagh ring," he said.

Sitting daintily on his broad palm was a golden ring, boasting a detailed pair of hands cradling a crowned heart. I had seen many iterations of these before, but this one was much simpler and far more beautiful than any I had yet encountered.

"Oh, wow! Dom …" I said, honestly shocked at his timing.

"Can't be engaged without a ring," he said, beaming.

I gulped. "Right."

I had actually considered wearing the replicated talisman, currently draped around my neck, as the sign of our commitment. Not that those kinds of formalities had ever really mattered. Something much greater bonded us to one another on this earthly plane and beyond.

Yet, something about *this* gesture caused me to blush deep crimson. It wasn't butterflies in my stomach causing the heat to rise in my cheeks, though, but the embarrassment of being caught off guard.

"Sorry, love, I had actually hoped to give it to you under different circumstances, but needs being what they are …" he said, placing it on my ring finger. "You point the heart towards yourself when it belongs to someone."

There was a knock on our window, and I was suddenly *very* overwhelmed. Dom, of course, was as cool as a cucumber.

"She finally said yes!" he said, causing even the painfully serious border guard to crack a slight smile in the face of Dom's unadulterated joy.

Thankfully, we passed through the rigmarole with ease. At the end, the border guard placed some arbitrarily blue ticket under our windshield wiper before Dom scooted up to the customs desk to have our passports scanned.

"Be right back!" Dom said happily.

While he was gone, panic set in.

I placed the backs of my hands on my heated cheeks and forced myself to take several slow, deep breaths. Was this the point of his timing for the ring? If so, the result had been exactly as he had intended, effectively snapping me out of my dreamlike state and pouring some life into my pallid face, at least for a few moments.

However, I also felt suddenly and deeply hurt.

I watched as he returned to the truck, blissfully unaware that he had crossed a line.

"You've never been much of an actor," Dom said, seating himself in the driver's seat once more. "Not that we're doing anything wrong, but the way you've ... *existed* ... for the last few days might have signalled something different. A genuine reaction is always the most truthful!"

He was right in one aspect at least. Despite some careful makeup application, I still bore the deep purple marks under each eye evident of someone who hadn't slept for days. Frankly, I looked miserable, and it wouldn't have been hard to jump to the conclusion that I was being led from the country under duress. But still, the fact that he was right about my appearance stung.

I spun the ring around on my finger; it was a perfect fit. The bastard.

"I see. Truthful."

"You don't have to wear it, if you don't want to."

A potential eruption was building inside of me. "No, no. I'll wear it."

He nodded, visibly pleased. It seemed he was so comfortable running "narratives" that he'd forgotten I was a real person with feelings. Suddenly, I couldn't hold back any longer.

"Honestly, Dom? That was *really* manipulative. And what if it had triggered a vision?" I asked, turning to face him while fighting back hot tears. I wasn't used to my emotions swinging about so wildly.

Confusion bloomed across his face, followed by what I assumed was shame as he looked away hastily. "You're right. I shouldn't have done it like that. But I've never given you one like that before, so I figured it would be alright."

I rolled my eyes in a sarcastic look that clearly said, *"Ooh, well in that case."*

"Julia, please, I'm sorry. I didn't think you'd be so upset. It wasn't my intention to lie to you, just to surprise you at the right moment so it looked—"

"It's lovely, Dom. Really. I'm sorry for overreacting. I'm just ... tired." I didn't feel comforted in the least by his defensiveness but had bigger worries to contend with.

He grimaced and rolled his shoulders back several times before putting the truck into drive; it was time to follow the queue onto the ferry.

"Do you think you might be able to rest while we travel?" he asked tentatively once we were parked below deck.

I released a slow yawn before leaning my face against the cool window. "I hope so."

He nodded silently.

MANTLE OF THE WORLD RULER

Once on land, we would immediately hit the coastal route southward. And by sleeping discreetly in the truck overnight somewhere along the way, with any luck, we would arrive in Florence, Oregon, by mid-morning, undetected by any Wraiths stateside. It wasn't a long drive, all things considered, and Dom assured me he was more than capable of the task. I knew he was exhausted from all that had happened since our return to Canada, although right now, I wasn't feeling particularly sorry for him.

Slumped against the passenger door, my mind attempted to recollect the events from earlier in the day. I was suddenly curious whether Dom had bought the ring this morning, or if he had in fact brought it all the way from Ireland.

Instantly, I was mad at myself for caring so much about the damn thing anyway.

Earlier in the day, upon our arrival in Victoria, both Dom and our Druidic escort—a fellow by the name of Sean Walsh—had deftly facilitated our needs. Ronan, meanwhile, had remained in Vancouver, pulling strings from just across the water. I barely had to think as we went through the motions, which I now regretted. Sean was a man of few words, evidently prescribing to the anonymity school of Druidry. Mysterious nature aside, he *had* made it easy for us to run errands before delivering us to the car dealership at noon.

We had decided on a four-door Toyota Tacoma, which I was pleased with. However, as we were buying it new off the lot, we didn't have a lot of choice when it came to colour.

"White?"

Dom cringed. "That's all they've got. Well, that or something called 'inferno,' but that doesn't feel very discreet to me. And perhaps a bit *too soon*, if you take my meaning." The man couldn't resist a clever joke.

I had hoped for a nice silver or charcoal, but at least colour didn't affect performance. It felt surreal to have the kind of money stashed away to buy a brand-new vehicle with cash—yet another perk of life with Dom, I supposed. Plus, cash reduced our risk of being traced.

21

Once purchased, we bid our silent friend adieu. He placed several sandbags in the truck bed, though I knew they didn't actually contain regular sand. Instead, they contained enchantments that would hopefully help keep us from being tracked. There was no guarantee that the Druid guards along the way wouldn't lose us, so it was a good insurance policy.

Sean reminded me of Ronan a bit, only slightly older and less forbidding at first glance.

"Thank you, Sean. *Go n-éirí an bóthar leat,*" Dom said, handing the man his sword for safekeeping on this side of the border. No doubt they would bring it to him as soon they had a chance to conceal and smuggle it properly. The Druids knew the importance of the blade to Dom.

Sean nodded silently, clasping Dom's arm in a firm embrace before taking off. Wordless undercurrents often surged between Dom and our allies that I couldn't fully grasp, but I got the sense that this particular man was one of the more powerful Wielders in the area.

Clearly, we had been delegated a top-notch escort, in addition to whatever other watchful, allied eyes followed us.

Parked now below deck on the ferry, I felt foolish for not asking more questions about him; I was still very intrigued by the greater Druid network. However, in the current circumstances, I wasn't nearly curious enough to launch into a conversation with Dom about it. His jaw was set in a straight line as he leaned back into his seat with his eyes closed, arms crossed on his broad chest. But I knew he wasn't actually sleeping.

Shockingly, I actually did sleep, curled up in the passenger seat, for almost our entire journey from the border through Washington State, my body finally succumbing to the overpowering exhaustion that had plagued it for days. I knew we stopped at some point for Dom to rest but barely remembered the experience. I slid out of the truck to pee in the ditch and curled back up without a word. When I woke again, we were parked in a questionable-looking port town whose name I didn't catch, waiting for a grocery store to open.

I was stiff, hungry, and desperately in need of a real washroom. But I also felt clearer and more alive than I had in days; it was time to swap drivers and carry on.

Dom had been hesitant to leave my side for even a moment on our journey, but his own growling stomach and lavatory needs had at last overwhelmed his sense of duty. He hastily ventured to the grocery store across the parking lot for provisions while I relieved myself and pumped gas. He returned with several full bags full of food in what could only be described as record time.

"I'm still sorry about the colour," Dom said, gesturing to our white truck. "I know you had your heart set on something a little bit ... *cooler.*"

"I'll survive," I said, fitting the gas cap. These were the first real words we had spoken to each other since our spat on the ferry, and I realized how much I missed hearing his voice.

He held out his groceries, grinning with childlike pride.

"Impressive. Did you jog through the store?"

"Pretty much," he said. "But I wasn't sure what you would want, so I got chicken—"

I groaned, and he barked out a laugh.

"*Sandwiches.* Chicken sandwiches. You think I'd mess up the interior with a whole bird?"

"I wouldn't put it past you," I said, smiling genuinely for the first time in days.

I hopped into the driver's seat, and he handed me a bottle of water and half of a limp sandwich. I gobbled it down gratefully, chasing down the day-old bread with the cool liquid. Dom was actually quite fond of our new ride, so much so that I caught him silently scrutinizing the crumbs that fell on my lap while I quickly scarfed back my "breakfast."

"I like the navigation on this one," he said, gesturing towards the dashboard screen as we took off. "Although I still have a very hard time believing technology like this is even real."

"Is it like *The Jetsons* for you?" I asked with a playful wink.

"Go ahead and laugh, Julia! But it's not always easy to keep up with everything."

"I'm not laughing *at* you, I promise," I said (a half-truth).

Our new truck really was slick, purring gratefully to life at the push of a button. Soon we were on the road again, and Dom, who had been determined to stay awake and keep me company, nodded off within fifteen minutes.

I didn't mind. In fact, it felt good to finally be in charge of something again.

Taking great pleasure in the act, I put our new ride through its paces as we rounded each bend or climbed a new hill. Two hands on the wheel, the yellow gold ring gleamed brightly on my finger with each tactical movement, I was surprised at how much I liked the look of it on my hand and blushed once more in spite of myself. I had never considered marriage seriously in this version of my life. My own romantic history had always been patchy. Since meeting Dom, however, it felt like I had skipped over the consideration stage, effectively launching into an exciting and deeply complicated new life in one fell swoop.

Wraiths, curses, and Sorcery. It still felt so surreal. Yet here I was, barrelling south with my centuries-old lover fast asleep in the seat beside me, arms crossed protectively across his chest. His breath rasped quietly; his head was cocked at an awkward angle. He looked terribly uncomfortable. I admired his ability to fall asleep anywhere, no doubt a learned skill from many years of sleeping on the road.

Looking out the rear-view mirror, I felt surprisingly unthreatened as I kept an eye out for any vehicles that might be following us. I had abandoned my phone in the glove box when we'd departed Victoria and so had no real way of receiving advanced warnings from the Druids, should it be necessary. I assumed Dom's was in working order, though, and trusted that Ronan would contact us if something came up.

After about an hour, Dom stirred. We were crossing the long bridge over the Columbia River into Astoria, Oregon.

"As usual, I'm impressed with the marvels of humankind," he said with an inward yawning breath as he adjusted his seat upright. It was an impressive bridge, to be sure, starting low and gradually climbing into a high cantilever span for boat passage before spiralling into a 360-degree off-ramp. Dom stared out the window in awe.

We drove in silence for a few more minutes, quietly passing through the city as Dom groggily gained his bearings. "Sorry about that, Julia. I dozed off for a bit there—"

"Dom, I've been thinking," I said, cutting him off. "I want to stop at Cannon Beach."

He furrowed his brow. We had agreed to no stops unless absolutely necessary until we were safely in Florence at the designated safe spot, but I had visited this particular beach on a childhood trip with Gertie and my mother, and it was far too spectacular for Dom to miss.

"I don't know, love—"

"Oh, come on! We've been given a chance to *actually* live our life! Or whatever version of our life this is …" My voice faltered at the look on his face, and I took a deep breath. "Please?"

He paused for a moment, mental wheels turning furiously. "I don't like that it feels like you have to beg me for the things you want. It feels wrong, and it's one of the things that needs to change."

If this was the beginning of an apology, I gratefully accepted. "Excellent!"

Deep in my subconscious magical core, I was still battling the new darkness I had unearthed after the fire; shadowed memories stormed away violently within me. However, the outer parts of me simply craved some time spent in the sunshine with my lover.

We arrived at the beach shortly thereafter, the coastline unfolding spectacularly before us. It was early enough in the morning to find the shore still relatively quiet but for a few early morning runners and dog walkers.

"Now that's a sight to behold!" Dom exclaimed as we descended onto the sand.

Haystack Rock stood boldly just off the shoreline, spectacular in its stature against the misty morning sky. The sun was only just beginning to burn through the haze. I paused, closing my eyes peacefully in its early soft rays.

Dom intertwined his fingers into my own, and I leaned into his solid frame.

"Look, Julia. I'm really sorry," he said simply. "When I'm … afraid … I feel the need to control everything."

"Afraid?" I opened my eyes once more as he turned me to face him.

"Terrified, actually. Do you have any idea how worried I've been about you?"

"Well, yeah, but when I didn't disappear … I thought that was it." I felt guilty now for not taking the time to consider the weight of his side of the story. On the other hand, he had also been going about like everything was hunky-dory.

"I've always been a good actor. Or liar, more accurately. But … it can't go on like this. It's eating me alive."

He took my left hand in his own and gently pulled the ring off.

"Dom, wait—"

"Give me a chance to get this right," he said, his grey-blue eyes pleading. Watching him tuck the ring back safely into his front pocket, I felt surprisingly torn to lose possession of it.

Together, we walked slowly towards the water, Dom stopping once to scratch a sopping-wet yellow Labrador who charged up to greet us. The dog squeaked its ball several times before Dom threw it athletically back in the direction of its owner.

"I miss the dogs," he said, smiling at the enthusiastic pup.

"Have you heard from Thomas at all?" I asked. Dom had made the decision to leave his—*our*—dogs in our friend Thomas's care while he healed following the battle in Northern Ireland. Thankfully, it was a mutually beneficial agreement: Thomas and the dogs adored each other.

"I have actually. When the Druids found out the cottage was alight, Thomas, Peggy, and some others returned with the dogs to help Morgan fortify the estate." He paused, and when he continued, his tone was reassuring. "But all is well … Don't worry. It seems it was only the cottage they wanted to target. The dogs also seemed keen to stay with Morgan, so Thomas left them there."

I felt guilty for not having considered the greater threats unfolding all around us in the aftermath of the midsummer blaze. Not only had Peggy lost her partner, Malcolm, during a fight that was *directly* instigated by Dom and me, but now she was having to attend to the needs of our estate while we were gone. It was hard enough to ask Morgan, our groundskeeper, to care for it all, let alone our friends.

"And the others?"

"I spoke briefly with Ronan last night on the phone; nothing new to report. He's relieved we will get there today though. Lennie's sent a few emails. Mostly just status reports, information we might eventually need in Los Angeles down the line. Nothing too important … unless you want me to elaborate?"

Ronan and Lennie were Dom's most important generals and with that came regular correspondence. However, I had forgotten that we would only be stopping in Florence for a handful of weeks before setting off again on yet another mission further south. I wished desperately for a chance to *actually* slow down.

"No, not right now. Thanks, though," I said, appreciative at least for his consideration.

Reaching the shoreline at last, I kicked off my sandals and tossed my keys on top of them, realizing sadly that, apart from the fob for the new truck, the remaining keys were to Gertie's cottage and my old vehicle, all utterly useless now.

Pushing my pain aside, I waded barefoot into the cool water as I slowly breathed in the salty sea air. A calm breeze rippled across my face as the frothy waves lapped against my ankles. I loosened my hair from its tie to let it flow unbound around me.

"Do you know that I can actually feel it now? The raw magic of the sea? It's like I finally speak its language …" The momentary sadness I had felt seconds earlier all but dissipated in the gentle waves licking my fingertips. Instead, a deep swell gathered within my core, hearth-fire heartily ablaze as I raised my hands out towards the tide. I felt at ease by the shoreline. The magic here was alive, and I felt a powerfully intuitive connection to it, almost as if it fed directly into my Bearing core. I felt the channel of the tide radiate from all parts of me.

Dom didn't reply.

I looked over my shoulder to discover that he was standing several paces back, mouth agape. All around me, droplets of water were gathered into a shimmering sphere, catching light in the early morning sun as they twinkled around me. Heart pounding at the sight, I dropped my arms hastily, and the droplets fell, returning to the sea.

Shit. Had anyone seen that? I hadn't even realized what I was doing. I expected Dom to scold me for drawing so much attention to us, ultimately dragging me back to the car for a quick escape. What he offered instead was a gigantic, joyful smile.

"Incredible!"

Quickly tucking his cellphone and keys into his shoes, he rolled his jeans midway up his calves before joining me in the low breakers. Before long, he was splashing around, playful as a puppy and soaking wet.

"Is this our shower for the day then?" I asked as Dom scooped a handful of water and threw it in my direction.

"Sure!" he yelped, tossing himself fully into the water, clothes and all.

I laughed heartily and conceded to joining him in his saltwater bathtub. Our water fight quickly escalated, and it was not just because we each needed a shower. I had felt little connection to myself and my own magic since the cottage had burned down, and had been hesitant to reach into myself, afraid that I might not find much of anything. And Dom knew it too.

It wasn't just the water that washed over the both of us now. It was relief.

CHAPTER 3

Our foray onto Cannon Beach brightened both of our moods immensely. Dom and I happily chatted the whole way back to the truck, laughing arm-in-arm like the lovers we were. Much of the previous day's frustration had washed away in the ocean. It was just so *easy* to be around him when things were light. I wondered, for what must have been the thousandth time, what life might have been like if we hadn't been tied up into this whole Prophecy mess in the first place.

We took advantage of the beachside change rooms before departing. I towelled my hair off as I walked across the gravel parking lot, eyeing Dom, who was at the truck already, quickly transferring the small gold ring from his soggy jeans pocket into the recesses of his bag.

"Do you want to drive or shall I?" I asked.

"It's up to you, love!" he said, smiling innocently as he zipped the duffle shut.

I hopped lightheartedly into the driver's seat.

The Oregon coastline was as ecstatic in spirit as we were over the final leg of our journey. I was enamoured with the high cliffs and sandy beaches as we wound our way along the coastline. Dom exclaimed at regular intervals about the impeccable beauty beyond our windows.

"I could live in a place like this," he said. I mused on how the sunny, windswept shoreline reminded me wholeheartedly of him.

"Or maybe even a vacation home," I said, playing along.

He nodded in agreement.

"Where *do* you want to settle down when this is all over?" I asked. Over the past months, I had barely dared to dream of questions like this, let alone voice them out loud. Yet something about the energy of the morning felt accepting of this line of communication.

"Hmm. I think I would miss Ireland too much to be away for very long," he said after a time. "But I *would* love to travel a bit. Just for fun, you know? I've actually always wanted to visit Spain."

He was right; this life had rarely allowed room for leisure and never once the Prophecy was in play. "You've … *we've* … never been there?"

"We haven't, and it's funny because I think it would really suit the both of us!" he said with a laugh.

I pictured the two of us embracing the night at one of Ibiza's famous beach clubs, sweaty, drunk, and purely ecstatic. "I like the sound of this plan!" I said, and over the next half-hour, we discussed what the perfect vacation might look like for us, had we the time, energy, and *safety*.

"We're maybe a bit old for a vacation like that though," he said with a chuckle. "I do want a quiet life in the end."

"Me too …" I said, lingering on the words. "We've lived plenty of life already."

He let out a low chuckle before our bubble burst with an ominous text from Ronan.

"Ah shit!" he said, reading it; he reached back to rifle through the contents of the back seat, his shoulder pushing into me.

"Dom, what is it?"

He pulled out Ronan's compass, which was spinning frantically. The highway had recently descended inland from its cliff-side traverse, which meant we were now passing through a more populated area.

"Wraiths."

"What! Where? What do we do?"

My heart pounded forcibly into my throat.

"Dom?"

He held his mobile to his ear, waiting impatiently for Ronan to pick up. "Just keep driving."

MANTLE OF THE WORLD RULER

Ronan answered, and the two shared a speedy exchange, switching between Irish and English seamlessly before Dom hung up. He swore loudly.

"It looks like there's a Conventos somewhere near here, but Ronan thinks it's unrelated to our travel. Lennie has contacts in the area, and apparently they're monitoring the situation."

Now that he mentioned it, I *could* feel a significant change in energy as we got further from the shore, but I'd thought it was just my Bearing magic disconnecting from the tides. Now, the hair on my arms stood on end, and I could feel a familiar anxiety in the pit of my stomach as Dom's phone went off again.

"Lennie? … I can barely hear you," he said, pausing to listen for a few moments. "Ah, shit."

I kept my focus on the road as Dom rummaged once more through his bag, withdrawing a newer-looking map with handwritten dark lines across its face.

"Where did you get that?" I asked; the map was unfamiliar to me.

"Sean," he said, "but it's from Ronan."

As usual, I was surprised by his leanings toward non-technological planning but then remembered how useless our phones would be in areas of heavy magic. Naturally, they had expected this possibility and were fully prepared. I looked towards the dash; the truck's navigation display was suddenly going haywire, as if on cue.

"Don't worry about it," Dom said, while I held down several buttons on the console in an attempt to restart the system. Before being cut off, Lennie had dictated some coordinates; Dom was using his thumb and pinky finger to draw a distance between them.

"We can stick to this road, I think. They're meeting further to the east, so we should be able to pass by undetected."

"As long as I can keep my shit under control," I said, only half joking. I thought back to the strange experience with the water droplets on the beach; I still had absolutely no idea how I had managed it.

"Right," he said, folding up the map and shoving it into the recess in the passenger door, and looking sure of himself.

"Are we close?"

"Very. Once we get through this Wraith garbage," he said, gesturing in the assumed direction of the magical disturbance. "The Druids have placed protective spells around the beach house, so we should be shrouded once we cross through."

Our life really *was* a perpetual yo-yo between limitless joy and inconceivable danger.

I attempted to steady my breath, thinking back to the blissful smile on Dom's face at the beach only hours before. However, the dark magic reminded me of our battle on the seaside, and I struggled to remain calm.

Sensing my need for assurance, Dom reached across and touched my thigh. His hand was warm and instantly soothing. "It'll be alright, Julia. The Knaves are on it."

"Knaves? That sounds sinister."

Something about the name was vaguely familiar, but I couldn't quite place it. I'd known there were other Wielder sects, of course, but Knaves were a mystery to me. Perhaps the Druids didn't take to them.

"It isn't really. Well … actually, they're Wielder friends of Lennie's, so maybe a *bit* sinister," he said with a chuckle. "But they are on the same side as us, even if they aren't aligned with the Druids."

Bingo.

As yet another mysterious arm of the cause was revealing itself to me; my curiosity was staved off by the continued sense of dread I felt in my Bearing core as we passed through the "Wraith garbage." The compass continued to whirl uncontrollably on Dom's outstretched palm.

"Can you feel it?" he asked.

"Definitely," I said, braking at a stop sign. "Which—"

"Turn left. Then we go on for another few miles before we go right again."

I stared at him in disbelief. "How do you know?"

He tapped his temple and winked conspiratorially.

"Why do I even ask?" I shook my head. I thought again of his fingers on the map moments earlier and now appreciated the precision he wielded. He really was incredible when it came to directions, and I relaxed a little, knowing I was in the best possible hands. Within minutes, the Wraith darkness dropped entirely, replaced by the familiar tug of Druidic magic. It was calm and welcoming, like a soft summer breeze.

"Ooh, that's better," I said and stretched my back tall in the driver's seat, twisting slightly to relieve some of the tension.

Still holding the compass in his right hand, Dom removed his left hand from my thigh and directed me to the right once more as we turned into a residential area. Lining the narrow streets were colourful vacation cottages, their doors and gardens adorned with nautical art while proud American flags flapped softly in the breeze. We were definitely getting closer to the ocean once again; its pull was growing stronger with each passing mile.

The trees swayed above us as we pulled into the driveway of our final destination. The location was secluded and instantly welcoming. There were no homes between us and the shoreline, but the ocean still remained out of sight behind dunes and brush.

"Well, this is nice," I said, hopping out of the truck and stretching my arms above my head; I had been carrying a lot more tension in my body than I'd realized. Suddenly, Dom's arms were around me, his own relief palpable as he lifted me up, spinning us around once in jubilant celebration. My back cracked loudly.

"Oh God! I'm sorry, Julia," he said with a smile as he plopped me back down.

"I'm fine," I said, joining him in his mirth. "Just getting old."

"You're telling me!" he said as he launched into his own set of stretches, lunging deep. I wondered how long we would continue to take such detailed notice of our continued existence together in this newest timeline.

For Dom in particular, I knew it was a perpetual fixture in his mind.

Quickly unloading our luggage, he excused himself and headed towards the bathroom. I was grateful for a moment alone to gain my bearings as I explored our new accommodations. Wholly unfamiliar with the space, I didn't expect any visions to arise, but one could never be too sure.

The house was well loved and modest, yet still large enough to host a cozy family or two. On the main floor was the primary bedroom and bath, as well as a full-sized kitchen and dining area. It also hosted a broad living room, its comfortable furniture facing out the two-story windows towards the shoreline. I could see from where I stood that the ocean lay beyond a long thicket of low-growing, windswept trees. I wondered if the view would be better from above.

33

Looking up to the second floor, two open-concept bedroom nooks were barely visible along a mezzanine that ran the length of the building, one placed on each end and each containing its own double bed. In between them was what I assumed to be another bathroom. I climbed the carpeted stairs, and indeed, the view *was* improved. I continued to feel little magical disturbance around me, apart from the Druidic energy that I had already grown accustomed to while in Ireland.

Several bookshelves lined the walls of the first sleeping nook, and I noticed a pamphlet sticking out from between two old novels that read *Oregon Dunes National Recreation Area*. Something about the image on the front struck me, and for a moment, I could almost feel the sand between my toes and the smell of saltwater engulfed my senses. In my mind's eye, a storm grew overhead, and I could see myself standing facing the sea, fully alight in my power.

Slam!

I started at the sound of Dom rustling around in the kitchen cupboards below and knocked over a stack of old DVDs with my elbow. But my heart raced more from the glimpse of the vision I had just encountered than the sudden noise. I took several deep breaths before descending the stairs to greet him.

"I'm really impressed," I said as I joined him.

"The Druids wouldn't let us down," he said, beckoning me towards the fridge.

To both of our pleasure, it was also fully stocked with food and drink.

"How on earth did you manage all this on such short notice?"

"Ronan called in a favour," he said as he cracked open a cold beer and handed it to me. "Plus, we didn't want to be fussing about with food like always. We're supposed to be in hiding for a time, after all."

"I don't know if *we* do the fussing," I said with a laugh, bumping into him playfully with my hip. He ran his fingers affectionately down my back. It looked like Dom had, once again, worked his ordinary magic to make our experience extraordinary. I wasn't complaining.

We exited the kitchen onto a sunny deck on the south side of the rental. A sweet wooden swing hung from a solid wood pergola, and we hopped on awkwardly, Dom slopping beer onto his shorts in the process.

He shrugged, hardly bothered. "This really is a lovely place."

"It is," I said serenely.

We swung for a time, peaceful in each other's quiet company. Dom stretched his arm across the back of the swing, and I snuggled in, resting my head on his well-built shoulder. The midday sun was hot on our faces, however, and we soon relocated to a shady pair of deck chairs.

Dom leaned back casually, finishing his beer in one large gulp. I was deeply envious of his natural ability to relax when times were quiet; it was obviously a skill borne from navigating so many cresting waves of crisis followed by short peaceful lulls. Yet, as much as I wanted to fully relax in the space, the vision upstairs had reminded me that true rest was a luxury I could not yet afford.

At the most basic level, I knew the purpose of our secured location was to buy us time to start deciphering the quilt. So, I felt anxious to begin that work. But there were also the secrets I had been carrying with me since Gertie's cottage had burned to the ground, their chorus practically screaming to be spoken aloud. The time had finally come to share that truth.

"Hey, Dom ... how far around us have the Druid's drawn the perimeter?"

In the moment, he was wholly distracted by several shorebirds passing overhead. It reminded me humorously of the Labrador we had met on the beach earlier in the day. Dom, too, I expected.

"Sorry, what was that?"

"The perimeter. How far can we travel from here before being potentially exposed?"

I thought of the manor house, with its sprawling grounds and clear boundaries well known to all of its inhabitants.

"Hmm ... let me get the map," he said before hopping up, perhaps less athletically than usual.

Within seconds, he returned, spreading the now crumpled paper onto the surface of the deck. "I think it actually covers us farther south, along the shoreline. Ronan's drawn it here in red." He pointed to an oblong band of permanent marker that circled several miles around our current location.

"Oh good." I immediately recognized the dune park within the perimeter. I tapped my finger gently at its centre. "Let's go there now ... please."

"Now?" he asked, confused. "We just got here." He was no doubt looking forward to kicking his feet up, and I didn't blame him. Yet something about the energy of that specific location was calling out to me. It was a sensation I didn't yet understand, but my inner fire had practically roared when I saw the pamphlet upstairs, a sign I would be foolhardy to ignore.

I dreaded what was about to come out of my mouth. "I saw a brochure for it upstairs and then I had a … divination. Or something. I'm not sure. But I think it's important we go there. Because … well, there's something I need to tell you."

I had his full attention now. "Oh?"

"I'm sorry I didn't tell you sooner. But I think I heard a new … Prophecy," I said, the word practically strangling me as it left my voice box. "When I was … there. After the fire."

He stared at me in disbelief. "Why didn't you—"

"I wanted to wait until we were safe. Didn't want anyone to overhear."

He shook his head as if to wake from a dream, clearly as horrified as I was. When he didn't wake, he spoke low and deep. "You were wise to wait."

I closed my eyes as if to aid in remembrance, but it was unnecessary—the lines of the new Prophecy were burned painfully into my every waking thought. I stared at him, preferring his princely image over what I had encountered during my transcendence.

He shifted to kneel in front of me, taking my hand into his own and kissing it slowly in an ancient yet familiar gesture. "Tell me what you need me to do."

We quickly gathered our things and climbed into the truck. Its navigation technology continued to be spotty amidst all of the free-Wielding magics that surrounded us. Dom drove the reasonably short distance to the entrance of the park, which thankfully required little effort to find. High clouds gathered ominously overhead during our quick trip, and so we found ourselves passing more people exiting the park than arriving. It was exactly as I had seen it.

"Where do we go now?" he asked.

I pointed ahead. "Keep driving."

We continued on through the body of the park, passing thrill seekers driving dune buggies and boldly sand surfing. It was obviously a very popular tourist destination, but we weren't here for leisure.

"The road will narrow soon and take us further out onto the dunes," I said, feeling surprisingly sure of my own directions.

Dom nodded minutely; message received. We drove in silence for a time, but I could practically hear the gears shifting in his head as he carefully navigated the well-paved roads towards the more rugged portion of the park. Between us and the expansive ocean lay a tall ridge of sand, dotted with patches of dune grass.

"Park us there," I said, pointing towards an upcoming lot. We had passed several like it along the way, but something felt significant about this particular spot.

The truck shuddered to a stop, and Dom looked over at me, his eyes serious. "Lead the way."

We couldn't see the beach beyond from where we stood, the dune's massive prominence completely obscuring the view. I pulled my hair back into a tight ponytail before beginning the ascent up a narrow trail; I knew instinctively that it would lead directly from the base of the parking lot over to the other side.

The wind started to pick up, the air thick with a strange pre-storm essence that left me feeling distinctly unsettled. This was *definitely* the place. I climbed up carefully, slipping several times and cursing myself for not wearing my running shoes. Dom followed behind with natural ease.

By the time we reached the top, the clouds had gathered in a looming spectacle, shadowing ominously over the now completely empty beach below.

"Julia ... what is this place?" Dom asked, scarcely hiding his apprehension. A great bald eagle soared low along the breakers, dipping low several times before taking off skyward as it released a heart-stopping cry.

"It's so thin ..." I said, my voice trailing off. Suddenly, I could feel the overriding power surging from the tide, calling out to me:

"It's time, dear one. I am here."

She was here, my moon mother, holding me close in tender embrace. She knew me, and I her. I breathed a long sigh of relief before taking off down the dune trail towards the sodden beach below. Behind, I could feel the warmth of Dom's sun essence as I slid awkwardly down the sand, landing on my bum several times without grace. He didn't laugh or offer help; he too felt the power of place and followed the direction of the higher powers.

By the time we reached the bottom of the slope, the waves had grown almost ten-fold in stature. I removed my shoes, casting them aside in favour of finding ground. I had barely considered the four elements and directions, but my inner magic firmly pushed in its own direction. I strode onward, confidence building as a sense of stillness formed around me amidst the tumult. After several more paces, I turned to discover Dom falling behind as he struggled to cross the veiled threshold between the safety of the dunes and the raw, roiling power of the sea. It was almost as if the air was thick around him. He dipped his shoulder low and barely inched forward. As for myself, I felt no struggle, passing through as smooth as a tumbled stone as I reached the water at last.

"Julia!" he cried, as he fell to his knees.

He was even further behind now, wiping the back of his arm across his brow as the sand and spit slashed around him, chapping his face pitilessly. I knew that any normal man would have failed to crest the dune entirely, let alone been able to descend to the shoreline. Yet, *Domhnall Mac Brien* persisted. Now, however, he was being violently barred passage, and I felt a deep calm settle within me.

"Leave him," I said, my voice commanding, mighty as the sea itself. Dom's eyes shot towards me, frightened and reverent at once. The assaulting forces dropped immediately, and he sank into the softness of my magic. Around us, the wind and water raged onward, but within the sphere of my protection, there was only calm.

Dom remained on his knees, shoulders drooping in relief as I slowly stepped towards him across the cold sand. I placed my chilled hands around his windswept head, brushing his hair back gently from his battered face. Despite everything, his skin was still warm to my touch.

He looked up, his breath hitching slightly as he sighed, fighting back a tidal wave of emotion. "Why are we here?"

Taking a deep breath of my own, I replied—not with my voice, but speaking directly into his mind, just as Agnes had done with me all those weeks ago. Somehow, I knew I could manage it today, though I had never before.

With the Sovereign standing tall, the World Ruler too must bear his crown,
As the Sorcerer seeks to find the grail, spear in hand, to chalice he is bound.

To reveal the lost wellspring, the Sun and Moon must accept their fate.
When the Celt accepts the mantle, the Crone too shall find her strength.

MANTLE OF THE WORLD RULER

For the earthen weapons masters, and tree talkers with open sky above,
Darkness reigns where light cannot, and from its root, the land will rot.

As I spoke wordlessly to him, I knitted in the images of what I had seen: of his destiny and mine, woven together in our continuing battle against Cassius. My path had never felt clear in the past, which I had now come to understand was limited by our curses. But now, I knew there was a future. Our future. And the price we would pay would be dire if we ignored the call. This new Prophecy was commanding Dom to step into his own divine, balanced power, just as I had been called to do.

At last, I fell to the ground before him, sobbing and patently unsure of what came next.

"Diviner," Dom said in astonishment before crashing into his own breaker of sobs. I wrapped my arms around him, and we stayed there for a time … whole.

And terrified.

CHAPTER 4

"Look, Julia. I've been thinking," Dom said as we tucked into bed early one evening. Somehow, an entire week had already passed since our arrival at the beach house.

"Oh?" I stifled a yawn as I placed my open novel on my chest.

"It's about the new Prophecy." He set his own book on the bedside table and rolled onto his side, placing his head on his hand. We had been attempting to practise some semblance of "normalcy" during our new daily routine, but even something as simple as reading in bed side-by-side seemed to pose a challenge.

I nodded, drawing in breath as he finished his thought.

"I just don't think we can interpret it entirely as written." He abruptly adjusted himself into a seated position, hands slowly drawing in his heels towards his groin, knees falling outward as he bent into a deep stretch. "Or as *seen*, I suppose … well, you know what I mean. Anyway. Even though my name—Domhnall—directly translates to 'World Ruler,' I have no intention of leading or ruling anyone, or anything, really, apart from myself."

I let out a long exhalation as I eyed his muscular frame; he was fidgety and visibly conflicted. I sensed his need for comfort as he flexed his shoulders back and rocked his neck from side to side before wrapping his arms around his knees with a groan. I sat up easily beside him and nudged close, gently tracing my fingertips over the scars across his naked back. Carried over through many lifetimes, their whitened lines were now scattered visibly against his lightly sun-kissed skin. I thought of my own scar from Cassius's spear, which was still dark and prominent despite Ronan's deft hand in its healing.

"Hmm ..." I said, taking a moment to ponder my response.

Instead of discussing the new Prophecy or diving straight into research, we had found ourselves wandering towards the beach every day. It was perfect and had felt like the intuitive thing to do, allowing ourselves time to settle in before cracking everything wide open. I'd also sensed he had been harbouring resistance against the new Prophecy from the moment I shared it. His grief had been palpable, and I hadn't wished to push him on the matter, knowing all too well what it felt like to have your apparent destiny thrust upon you without time for consideration.

"Well ... it *was* thinking differently that saved our lives back in May," I offered at last, noting a visible relaxation ripple through his body as I spoke and stroked his skin. The same thoughts had also crossed *my* mind. Going against expectations had been precisely what had changed our fate for the better. We would be foolish to take the new Prophecy *too* literally.

"So, you agree with me then?" he asked, turning towards me, eyes surprisingly hopeful.

"I think it's too early to know exactly *what* it means," I said, offering small reassurance. "But I'm glad to know how you feel about it, and I agree that you're in charge of your own destiny. That's really important."

"That didn't really answer my question." He chuckled unexpectedly as he turned towards me. "You would have made a good lawyer, I think. Or perhaps a politician?"

I snorted while shoving him playfully, and together we flopped back onto the bed, abandoning our books for a more physical release.

♛

The following morning, I finally unpacked the quilt.

"I have no fucking clue what I'm doing," I said to Dom as he peered curiously over at me. We'd decided to turn the long dining table into a research desk, and he was currently seated on the other side with several maps spread before him and his silver laptop.

"Well, you'll know better than I do," he said with a kind smile.

"Gee, thanks." I returned my attention to the unusual textile.

It felt strangely light today and easy to manipulate as I spread it over the back of a plush armchair in the adjacent living room. I closed my eyes as I traced my palms over the different sections but was met with the same protective magic as always.

"I just don't understand it. I thought that, after what happened in Ireland, I would be able to tease it apart somehow."

"Well, don't beat yourself up over it. You've only just begun! And besides, we've got lots to be getting on with if you need a break," he said, waving his hand in mock enticement towards a stack of supremely dull-looking documents and textbooks he had arranged to have delivered.

"No thanks," I said, and plunked myself on top of the quilt, annoyed before even really starting.

"Suit yourself."

I leaned back and listened in silence as Dom typed loudly in his usual methodical style. Ronan had sent another email, no doubt. Letting out a sigh, I tried not to be *too* irritated with Dom as he bemoaned the ergonomics of his computer while hammering at his keyboard. I didn't have the heart to tell him it was more than likely a user error as the laptop was practically brand new.

Absently, I cast my gaze upwards towards the mezzanine and the bookshelves beyond. I hadn't been upstairs since we'd first arrived. Suddenly, something slid off the third shelf and thumped onto the floor. I lurched forward, causing a beleaguered Dom to pause in his task and look up.

"Julia, what is it?"

"So weird … I think something just fell off that bookshelf."

I stood, my gaze fixed on the second floor as I padded across the faded living room carpet, Dom following at my heels. I paused at the bottom of the stairs, causing him to almost walk into me. "Seriously, Dom? It's probably nothing."

"I needed the break anyway," he said. "Ronan and Lennie are fighting about something stupid and want me involved … and I'd really rather not."

"Hmm …" I said, distracted.

We climbed the stairs quickly but were deflated when, at the top, we discovered nothing but a small book lying innocently on the floor.

"Bit of an overreaction," I said, crouching low. "Sorry."

"Well, what book is it?" he asked, clearly attuned to a life spent with magic users. There was often more than met the eye with any unusual occurrence.

I picked up the volume, which turned out to be a guidebook for visiting Santa Cruz and Big Sur, California. Turning it over in my hand once to glance at the back cover, I stood slowly and handed it over to Dom. "What do you think?"

He flipped through the pages once, causing a well-worn bookmark to tumble to the floor. I leaned over and picked it up; it bore a single name on it, handwritten in blue pen: *Bernadette Smith.*

"Looks like Bernadette wanted to visit Big Sur," I said, eyeing the unassuming bookmark. There was nothing particularly remarkable about it, merely a rough scissor-cut piece of brown cardboard adequate for the job.

Holding it across my open palm, I closed my eyes instinctively and was instantly rewarded with a vision. In my mind's eye, I could see the glimmering Californian coastline and a small log cabin on the mountainside with a chimney emitting plumes of colourful smoke. A Bearer lived there. I was certain. Suddenly walking *through* the vision, I approached the cabin and rapped on the door three times.

A voice called from somewhere unseen: *"I've been waiting for you, Julia. I can help you."*

I paused. "Who are you?"

"Bernadette, obviously," she said, kind laughter ringing through my ears as I returned to the current moment. The sensation was surreal but not altogether unnerving. Bernadette, whoever she was, had invited me into the vision, and I had accepted—and had been transported there with her. This was distinctly unlike my other visions, where I was simply thrust into them. Nor was it like my encounters with Agnes Sweeney or Aisling, who each had forced their way into my mind with their own versions of a Send.

Opening my eyes, I found I was still standing before the bookshelf. But I could feel my cheeks had flushed significantly, as if I were recovering from spinning around one too many times. "Dom … who owns this house?"

He was holding me by the elbow and slightly red-faced himself, never having become fully comfortable with my intermittent breaks from reality. "Uh ... you know, I'm not entirely sure. Ronan said the Druids sourced it, but he was certain it was the safest possible location for us. I didn't really question it. Should we leave?"

"Hmm ..." I took the travel guide back from him and slid Bernadette's page marker back in. "No, it's fine. But I think we need to go here." I wriggled the book at him.

"Okay. I don't see why not. When?"

"Not yet, I don't think. We have some work to do here still, and obviously, this was meant to be one of our stops along the way. Bernadette must have stopped here too," I said, gesturing towards the bookshelf. Twice now, the house had provided me with magical guideposts, and I knew better than to ignore the significance of the fact.

"Maybe sometime after Ronan and Lennie arrive?" Dom suggested as he turned for the stairs. "We can stop on the way to Los Angeles. Lennie's certain we are going to be needed down there on reconnaissance by the fall."

The current plan was for us to spend the next six months along the Canadian and American western coastlines, as that seemed to be the mostly logical place that Cassius—or at least *signs* of Cassius—might show up. I had my doubts, but our sources confirmed that his Los Angeles stronghold was somewhere he'd visited regularly over the past few years. And we had to start somewhere. Thankfully, Lennie and Ronan were set to join us sometime in August. We needed all the help we could get.

"Sounds great," I said as I tucked the small book into my back pocket. "What were they fighting about anyways?"

"Oh ... same as usual. Old ways conflicting with new ideas." He paused. "Though if I'm honest, Ronan's been a bit of a miserable bastard. Anything he doesn't agree with, big or small, seems to explode into a huge fight. Lennie's looking like the agreeable one these days, and that's saying something."

I snorted, following behind. "And they want you to mediate?"

He sighed heavily. "Something like it." There was evidently much more that went unsaid, but he left it at that. "You ready to get to work?"

"Only if I have to," I said, dropping the topic.

44

Still, I had a sense that Ronan's change in behaviour had little to do with Lennie and everything to do with what we'd been through together in Northern Ireland.

Five days later, we finally came up for air. So far, our research had mostly consisted of Dom continuing to plot points correlated to our shared history across a large map and me attempting to divine if they held any significance for my present magical development. If our experience at the cottage taught us anything, it was that there was clearly danger in returning to the places we had been before; no doubt Cassius would have had our history under scrutiny as well.

To add to the mounting pile of homework, we decided to simultaneously log significant historical events that might point us in the right direction. Or any direction at all, really. Dom started from the beginning of our timelines, while I opted to start backwards from 1968.

It was unsurprisingly dull work.

"Where are you?" I asked, rubbing my eyes late one afternoon. The sun was still beaming brightly outside, and it felt almost sinful to be inside working this hard.

"Bogged down somewhere near the end of the Middle Ages," he said, not looking up from the massive volume before him. I admired his uncanny ability to focus over long stretches.

"I'm still in the nineteenth century," I said. "Honestly though, I'm *so* bored." Frankly, the entire thing felt rather fruitless, despite our best intentions. As yet, the only thing that felt clear at all on the path ahead was a trip to Big Sur to meet Bernadette Smith.

"You know what? I'm tired too," Dom said, snapping his book shut. "How about a walk?" It was only four o'clock.

I raised heavily skeptical eyebrows at him. "Is that what we do when we're tired?"

"I meant I'm tired of *this*."

"Oh, great! Me too!" I hopped up enthusiastically.

He laughed in his low, deep rumble. "Should we maybe just go down to the beach? I don't feel like going far ... I just want to be outside, really."

"Worried you're starting to lose your tan with all this studiousness?" I asked playfully as I pushed my chair in.

"You might say so."

We gathered our things, which had been sitting in a neglected pile by the front entrance. I rolled up two freshly laundered beach towels on top of several warm beers that had remained hidden in the bottom of my backpack over the past few weeks. Stepping into the bedroom, I wriggled into my one-piece swimsuit, followed by a loose white tank-top, a pair of athletic shorts, and a cheap pair of gas station sunglasses. Dom donned his trunks quickly before muttering something about getting food from the kitchen. He met me outside almost ten minutes later, where I was sitting quietly under the oak tree.

"All ready?" he asked and tucked several wrapped sandwiches into the top of my pack; I had wondered what had been taking him so long.

"Yup!" I said, hopping up and striding towards the narrow path between us and the shoreline.

The trail itself was eerily dim, dipping low through a coastal marshland of knotted trees and boggy patches. It wasn't a long walk, but something about this in-between space made me slightly apprehensive. We'd found upon our arrival that several of the makeshift bridges leading over murkier sections had been badly broken. It had initially added to the eerie effect. Thankfully, Dom had taken it upon himself to repair them almost immediately, which was reassuring for our passage today. That said, I still breathed a sigh of relief when we reached the edge of the covered trail and transitioned onto several large mounds of sand dotted with dune grass.

Dom was uncharacteristically silent in my wake, and I turned around more than once to ensure he was still following. Naturally, he had always been close behind, but he bore a distant look on his face.

"Is the research bringing up bad memories for you?" I asked as I took off my flip-flops to carry in my hand. I had wondered if the task might dredge up some hard memories when he'd first suggested it all the way back at *Caisleán na Spéirmhná*, our home in Ireland.

"Hmm?" he asked, his mind clearly off on a different tangent. He raised his hand to his brow to block the sun, and I found it strange that he had left his sunglasses behind; Dom just wasn't someone who came ill-equipped, even for something as simple as eyewear.

"Like ... is any of the research triggering?"

"Oh, no. Not entirely. Some of it maybe, but nothing groundbreaking. I was just thinking about something that came up today though ... something that happened between us when we were in medieval Ireland."

I turned to look at him briefly, instantly curious.

CHAPTER 5

We walked in silence for another minute before climbing a final large sand dune, arriving face-to-face with the ocean at last. The late afternoon sun was serene and welcoming across the open Oregon coastline. I could feel the presence of the moon waiting to rise, although we wouldn't see her face for hours.

Below, the beach was practically empty, most of the tourists and cottage-goers having returned to their accommodations for the night. We saw a father with a "played-out" child fast asleep on his shoulder, and I smiled as he somehow managed to haul several beach chairs and a cooler bag all at once without disturbing the sleeping girl. Someone I assumed to be the mother was farther down the beach, convincing an older sibling that it was indeed time to leave.

"We'll be back tomorrow," I heard her say on the breeze, but she was met with only tears in reply.

"Oh, come on," Dom said quietly so that only I could hear. "Five more minutes, please, Mum?" My heart melted at the look on his face.

We traversed the beach to our favourite spot, laying out our towels in unison before either of us spoke again. Dom removed his grey t-shirt and plunked himself down, stretching out his long legs and bracing himself on his elbows, partially reclined. I slid off my shorts and pulled my top over my head. I had tied my hair back into a tight bun; it was always so hot on my shoulders in the sun.

"Bathing beauty," he said, beaming up at me. I only had one swimsuit in my possession; the rest had burned in Gertie's fire. Thankfully, it was my favourite: simple, black, and just the right cut.

I winked. "Speak for yourself." I eyed his broad chest decorated in golden curls that glinted in the sun's rays. I still stood by what I'd said many moons ago: Looks like his *should* be criminal.

"I want to tell you a story," he said.

I cracked open a beer and handed it to him, saying apologetically, "It's warm." I lowered myself down beside him. "And I'm all ears."

"Well, I think you'll like this tale," he said, taking a big swig followed by a grimace. "Eugh! That's terrible."

I chuckled and decided against opening my own can.

"We've talked plenty about the *original* circumstances of us wanting to run away together," he said. "I suppose that was maybe our first attempt at marriage. And I've told you the story about being married for Canadian citizenship, back in the late sixties."

I grinned wickedly. "Yes, I remember that one."

He smiled back, but then his face grew serious. "Well, the thing is ... although I've always wanted to, I've never really gotten it right, you know? Not how I would have liked it, anyway. And not how you would have liked it either, I don't think."

"Got what right, exactly?" I asked. Not for the first time since arriving in Oregon, I witnessed his notable efforts to voice his true feelings. Unlike most other topics, where he was almost always loquacious, these efforts took him a little more effort to sort through.

"Marriage, a wedding ... all that. We've tried it so many times, but I think ... because it's always been squashed under the pressure of the original timeline, it always felt so ..."

"Rushed?"

"Partly, but also kind of ... pointless? I mean—No, not like that," he said quickly, seeing the colour rise in my cheeks, "but we're bonded together in so many other ways, it always felt ... frivolous, maybe? I think that's why I fucked it up so royally when we were boarding the ferry. I just have a habit of expecting it to be disappointing for you. And for me too, actually."

I thought of the beautiful ring he had taken back from me, not for the first time that day even, and wondered what had become of it. "I wasn't *entirely* disappointed."

He looked out towards the water awkwardly and absently swigging beer again. This was followed by another grunt of disgust and him dumping it out in full beside him. "For *fuck's* sake."

I snorted out a laugh.

He waved his hand, not truly bothered. "Anyway … we used to fight a lot," he said with a chuckle. "But I'm guessing that comes as no surprise. Everyone did back then, not just us. And the time I was reminded of today, while researching, was when we found ourselves together in the 1330s near Kilkenny."

I wrapped my arms around my knees, giving my full attention to him; I adored it when Dom dove into storytelling mode.

"Now … this was a time when the medieval world was essentially ruled by violence, politics, and famine—the Black Death arrived only two decades later. Also, the first woman accused of heresy and Witchcraft in Ireland had been burned at the stake only a few years previously. So, that was obviously a fun plot twist for us to arrive to," he added sarcastically.

"Fuck …" I said.

"Indeed. Essentially, fanatical bishops were at war with the more financially powerful Anglo-Norman families. *Those* families were at war not only with each other but also with the remaining Irish-Gaelic people who had taken to the hills and were trying at every opportunity to reclaim the land and rights they had lost. One of the results, naturally, was deep suspicion between all those in power—there was a lot of demon hunting going on, real or no. And ultimately, the following centuries would prove some of the most damaging in the history of Witches throughout Europe."

"Sounds like a great time to get engaged," I said dryly.

"You're right; the timing was terrible! Especially when the bride-to-be was a magic user and the groom was fully aligned with the Druidic enemies of the church," he said with a dark laugh. "Anyway, we found each other, and as you can imagine, times were tough. Cassius was meddling with both the aristocratic families and the church throughout Leinster—he had always been a deft hand at upsetting power and claiming it for his own. I, of course, had been following his moves for a short time already—both keeping an eye on him and looking for you. You, meanwhile, were doing the same."

I was suddenly confused. "Wait, I thought I would have still remembered you at this point in time, and that I would have come and found you at the tomb."

"Ah, but you *did* remember. And the last time, you *had* come to me. However, you still hadn't actually left Ireland in any of your regenerations yet, so we decided to get clever and change tactics with our next opportunity, being that things had become pretty predictable by now. You see, in those days, Cassius would always be in roughly the same area as you, regardless of where you were born, being that your destinies were ... *are* ... so closely woven, I imagine. It's not something we've ever been able to really explain."

I shuddered at the thought; Dom also looked momentarily disturbed.

He waved his hand once more, pulling himself back on track. "Basically, near the end of our previous cycle in the late 1200s, we agreed that the *next time* the curse was set in motion—and I was 'reborn'—you would keep yourself hidden while watching out for Cassius, until I worked my way towards wherever you were. You had full access to your powers then, remember, so were well-suited to protect yourself. And you also remembered me. Plus, the Druids were already proving to be immensely helpful in our plight. Come to think of it, this was likely the time when we fully forged our long-term relationship with them."

"Incredible," I said under my breath. The depth of our alliance with the Druids spanned centuries.

"It is," he said, nodding. "Another fact we had to consider was that travel was quite tedious then. And since you had already developed a knack for popping up all over the island, we decided it might be easier if, this time, we had a planned strategy from the start, for the sake of efficiency."

"Wow. We must have been really committed to the secrecy of it all to agree to be apart from each other."

"We were! But don't forget the map we were working with was also much smaller than what we're working with now. North American colonization and the growth of the 'modern world' is what's broadened the scope between you and Cassius. This obviously changed things for us significantly later on … but I digress."

I could tell he wasn't ready to tell those stories yet, the ones where I'd begun to forget and he'd struggled to find me. I nodded encouragingly, and he continued.

"As we had planned, I found you. Perhaps a bit later than anticipated due to all of the political turmoil throughout the land, but there you were. All graceful long limbs and brilliant hair … I was always so staggered by your beauty." He gazed at me affectionately. "Still am."

Several seagulls flew overhead, emitting squawking cries. Their fellows down the shoreline appeared to have discovered someone's discarded lunch.

"Likewise, no doubt," I said, looking back at him with a love that had spanned centuries. I leaned over to kiss him deeply. The interlude was brief, however, as I could tell he was more than itching to finish his story.

"Mmm … Where was I? … Ah, right … So! Thankfully, you had yet to be forced into any marriage before you remembered our story; it was after your mother's passing when you were eighteen. Truthfully, the fact that you were a peasant girl *and* pagan also helped; you weren't like the women in the middle and upper classes who were often forced into marriage at the ripe age of fifteen for the sake of political alliances—"

"Ew! Really?" Then a thought dawned on me. "Wait, was I *ever* married off in those early days before the curse was set in motion? Like, as a teenager?"

"No, and that has always been the funny thing. I honestly think destiny has always made sure of that. Protected you, essentially, until the curse went into full effect upon your mother's death."

I stared at him and gulped. Although he knew about them, we didn't discuss the partners I had found throughout my twenties during the regenerations where I had forgotten us.

"Regarding the age though … it's one of those point-of-reference things that just made sense at the time. It's obviously completely inappropriate now, but early political marriages were just a part of life back then."

"Still though … it's brutal to imagine."

"And in many cases, it was." He leaned back, pausing in thought. "You know, it's hard to remember the roots of exactly *why* we were attempting a conventional marriage in the first place, even then. You had obviously avoided it thus far, and I was a relative stranger to anyone in the area, so whether I did or didn't marry you wasn't of any consequence really. Not to mention that we could have just pretended. The time we shared before needing to fight Cassius once more was far more important than any scrutiny we might have faced from the church.

"But I suppose we were very concerned with 'fitting in' back in those days. A young man and woman sharing their quarters along the road like we were doing wasn't well looked upon, unless you were in wedlock, of course. And since we were attempting to work our way into the community to gain knowledge of where Cassius actually *was* and who he was working with, I think it ultimately became part of our 'super-spy' attempts to defeat him. Perhaps it was even an act of survival. If you could blend in as an Anglo-Norman, you were less likely to face persecution from those in power. We surely thought it would allow us time to continue our work without interruption."

"Sounds complicated," I said, almost in disbelief. I had learned practically nothing of medieval Ireland in any of my studies, so I had to take his word for it. Not to mention the fact that, with ancient memories like this, unless I had an anchor or reference point to draw upon, it had so far been rare for me to have any visions accompanying these stories.

"Long story short, we finally organized ourselves enough to get married in 1332 in the St. Canice's Cathedral in Kilkenny. Essentially *the* Catholic church of the region—if you wanted people to know you were being wed, that is."

"Feels like a pretty big church for a marriage between people like us."

"Oh, it was. But I think, by that point, we wanted Cassius to know *precisely* where we were, to mock him and maybe even draw him out of hiding. We were rather grandiose in those days, as you can imagine."

"I find that hard to believe," I said teasingly as I thought of Dom's outgoing personality to this day.

"Naturally, we fought about the feasibility of the plan. You were still not entirely convinced it was a good idea to draw attention to ourselves in the first place, but I wished for nothing more than to … to *handle* you—for lack of a better word—in public without bringing you shame or drawing attention. Not that your height and auburn hair helped matters," he said with a wink. "But I was rather possessive in those days and wasn't fond of other men's advances either. I think, at my core, I still wanted a wife tucked into my arm and, more importantly, into my bed."

"Sounds pretty conventional to me," I said, still trying my best to parachute my modern mind into the fourteenth century with understanding. I puzzled and then laughed. "Surely, we didn't *abstain?*"

He barked out a laugh. "Oh, fuck, of course not! But like I said, the root causes for our wish to be wed have always been complicated and influenced not only by our story but also the time period we were thrust into."

I nodded; it really *was* more complicated than I had comprehended when Dom had given me the Claddagh ring at the ferry.

"Anyway! We had debated the date and location for weeks before we finally settled on it. And the church, for its part, had already been in disrepair for some time and was being fixed, apparently funded through some forced act of penance from a wealthier family connected to the diose—"

"I think I see where this is going," I said, suddenly anticipating what would come next as a vague memory of crumbling stone entered my psyche.

"Oh no, you beat me to the punch!" he said excitedly and quickly finished his story. "The day before the wedding, the bell tower collapsed and crushed much of the church along with it! Boom! The end. No wedding."

I laughed in semi-shock. "What horrible timing!"

"No doubt." He shook his head in latent disbelief before suddenly falling serious. "You really can't make this shit up; I assure you."

He looked out towards the ocean for a moment, his verbose storytelling grinding to an abrupt halt. I waited patiently as I knew he was now sorting through some complicated emotions.

After a time, he spoke, eyes still seaward. "I guess what I'm trying to say … in an extremely drawn-out way as usual … is that, if we *were* to do it this time around, I would want to do it right. For *us*. With clear reasoning and intention behind it. Not motivated by lies and espionage, or the fear of Cassius … or hindered by the possibility of churches collapsing around us either." He turned his frame towards me as he emitted a shy chuckle. "And certainly not because it's the 'way things are always done!' I do understand that it's an antiquated idea …"

I nodded, understanding at last. "Dom—"

"So, of course ... it's really only if you wanted it too," he finished, staring straight at me as he blurted out the last words.

As I wound my cool fingers into his much warmer ones, I noticed that his sand-encrusted palm was much sweatier than usual. This temperature difference between us had always provided a unique sensation; it felt like coming home. Suddenly, I breathed easier than I had in weeks. "I think what happened at the ferry—while it wasn't ideal—made me realize that I *do* actually want it. To be married to you. If you'll marry me, that is."

The most magnificent smile I had ever witnessed spread across his face. "Was that a proposal?"

"Oh, shit ... I guess it was," I blushed crimson and pushed my sunglasses back onto my head to return his gaze in full.

He turned towards me on his knees, awkwardly twisting his towel in the process and covering it in dry sand. He took both of my hands into his and brushed his lips across my knuckles, his whiskers tickling them slightly. "Well then ... the answer is *yes*. There's nothing I want more than to marry you, Julia Harrison."

Completely alone on the beach now but for the shorebirds, we kissed long and hard, blissful in the infinity of the moment. As our lips broke, I saw that a scattering of water droplets had gathered in a perfect orb around us, creating a twinkling halo of light as the sun caught itself in the display.

"How do you *do* that?" he asked, laughing heartily as they sprinkled down upon us; I wasn't able to maintain the spectacle for long, but I hadn't really tried to either. It was in brief moments like these that I felt most aligned—with myself, the sea, and my lover. My past, present, and future.

"No clue," I said, pausing to think for a moment about other things. Feminism to me meant the power of choice to change one's name ... or not. And I wanted to change mine. "And it'll be *O'Brien*. Harrison holds no meaning for me. And let's be real, every time I'm reborn, I have a different last name anyway. I've almost always been an O'Brien, haven't I?"

"You have. But it would be an honour to make it official once more."

It wasn't the perfect proposal—in fact, I wasn't entirely sure it could be officially labelled one at all. It was more of a long story followed by an intuitive thrust into the unknown. But even that felt perfect in itself ... and very much *us*.

"So, where's the ring?" I asked.

"Oh!" Dom said before digging around in my backpack for a moment. He handed me a wrapped sandwich. "It's in there."

"In the *sandwich?*" I said, stuck between shock and laughter.

"No, not *in* the sandwich. But my trunks don't have any pockets, and I didn't want to lose it on the way here. I've had it hidden in the kitchen since we arrived, but I couldn't figure out how to get it out of the house just now. It's inside the wrappings. Do you think I would have let you choke on the thing?" He laughed.

I peeled back the neatly folded wax paper and found the gold Claddagh sitting tucked into a tiny slit in the thick brown bread. No wonder he had lingered so long in the kitchen; this was precision work.

He picked it up and brushed any residual crumbs off before gently sliding it onto my finger, this time with the bottom of the heart pointing out. "There. It really does look lovely on you."

"You put it on the other way," I said, noticing that the bottom of the heart was pointing away this time.

"Well, this time we're properly engaged. We'll flip it when we have a *real* wedding."

I looked down at my hand, heart utterly happy. "It's perfect."

Dom took a large bite of his chicken-salad sandwich, chewing contentedly. A look of joy lingered on his face, which I assumed was only partly due to satiation.

"I'll have the other one," I said, realizing my own gnawing hunger.

He handed it to me, mouth muffled with another bite. "Sorry, I should have brought champagne or something."

I took an eager bite and promptly choked on a chunk of chicken.

"Christ, are you alright?" Dom said as he patted me hard on the back.

Throat clearing after several moments of coughing, I burst into a fit of giggles before flopping back onto the sand. "I think I'll survive."

It felt amazing to just be living life, in the moment, informal marriage proposal and all. I felt so grounded, whole, and safe. Finishing his final bite, he rested his head softly on my belly. It was a beautifully loving gesture, but I suspected it was also indicative of another subconscious wish of his.

We would have to discuss that at a later date.

CHAPTER 6

I had almost forgotten that my thirty-first birthday was fast approaching, what with all of the research, our official engagement, and simply enjoying life. Meanwhile, Dom was positively vibrating over the fact that he would get to spend my actual birthday with me.

"I don't think we've spent your birthday together in ..." he counted on his fingers for a moment, "over a thousand years!"

I laughed awkwardly. "We're clearly long overdue. But honestly, Dom, I'm not really into big celebrations. It's always just felt like a lot of pressure to be happy on a day I usually hope passes quickly."

He waved his hand in the air. "Don't be ridiculous. This is an *extra*-special birthday."

"Alright then." I eyed him suspiciously.

He was definitely up to something, but what was the worst he could do? It's not like we knew anyone here anyway, and Ronan and Lennie weren't due to join us until the end of the month. Meanwhile, any local Druids had kept their distance. Likely he had something special planned for just the two of us, which sounded perfect.

When I was small, I used to spend weeks building up hope and excitement around my birthday, only to be met with disappointment. It was the one day a year where I would let my guard down, momentarily pausing from chronic attempts to control the emotional climate around me to stay safe. I didn't feel that same need with Dom, so just maybe, this one would truly be about *me*.

This year, August eighth landed on a Wednesday—not that this meant all that much to either of us at the moment. It was strange to be operating outside of the typical workweek, but I had quickly grown to prefer it.

"The five-day workweek is such a *new* concept that I still struggle to wrap my head around it," Dom said in the days leading up to my birthday. "Usually, I can ignore when the latest ideas feel awkward and just adapt—occupational hazard and all—but the 'nine-to-five' thing has never sat right with me. It's very odd."

I laughed. "Yeah, but it's better than people working themselves to the bone seven days a week, isn't it?" I was thinking back to my research around when we had been "here" during the industrial revolution in the 1800s.

He grinned knowingly. "Well, I think my point of reference reaches back a *touch* farther than that."

Dom was the kind of man who rose with the sun, preferring to live as his needs or his body bid him. If he *was* going to lie in bed past dawn, there had better be a good reason, which usually involved desires of a more carnal nature. It also explained why he was so quickly frustrated with the arbitrary schedules of society or when waylaid by unexpected modern inconveniences like his uncooperative computer. Dom was happiest when he could follow his gut, more often in the direction of his next meal, or focus on a task without interruption. In fact, he had almost unbelievable motivation when something fully aligned with his interest, as had been shown by his diligent research around our history.

And so, it came as no surprise to wake on the morning of my birthday alone. Rolling over, my ears immediately pricked at the sound of Dom loudly banging around in the kitchen, no doubt preparing us some elaborate breakfast. I felt a magnitude of appreciation that, throughout our countless regenerations, Dom had always taken my well-being to heart, placing my needs high on his list of priorities.

I stretched my legs and back before heading to the bathroom. Timing being what it was, I had my period. But Dom wasn't the kind of man to grumble about such things. Maybe this was also because of his ancient mindset—or perhaps he just wasn't an asshole? Regardless, I was still somewhat disappointed that sex wasn't likely to be as vigorous as it had been as of late. I thought back fondly to the previous weeks alone together at the vacation house and smiled in spite of myself. It *had* been good, but surely a few days off to rest would do us some good too. Although I wasn't entirely sure if Dom actually had an off switch.

"Julia? Are you up?"

"Yep," I said, pulling a sweater over my thin tank top before exiting the bedroom; summer or not, I was often chilled in the morning.

"Oh wow!" I exclaimed as I entered the kitchen.

Naturally, Dom had pulled out all of the stops today, creating some kind of muffin-tin pastry-cup Eggs Florentine combination. It looked and smelled delicious.

"I found it online!" he said, proud as punch.

"Well, look at you go," I said, coming up beside him and smacking his butt playfully.

He pulled me into a tender kiss, "Happy birthday, love."

"Thanks," I said, genuinely grateful for the first time in a very long time that it was, indeed, my birthday.

Dom was momentarily distracted by his phone. I assumed he was checking for any final recipe steps. Returning my gaze to breakfast, I noticed he had made far more than we needed for just the two of us.

"You feeling extra hungry this morning?"

He didn't respond. Suddenly, there was a loud knock at the door.

"Dom?" I immediately started panicking.

He smiled broadly. "Don't worry. It's your birthday!"

"I know!" I said, struggling to catch up.

He grinned mischievously. "You had better answer that then."

I looked over my outfit for a moment, disappointed that Dom hadn't given me a heads up that I might like to have a shower this morning, or even wear bra. Another knock came as I rushed to the door. Turning the handle, I screamed loudly at the sight on the threshold.

"Ronan! Lennie!"

"Happy Birthday, Julia," Ronan said, his Dublin lilt pleasing to my ears.

"Many happy returns!" Lennie said, his particular British accent sounding posh as usual.

I'd missed hearing their voices.

"Surprise!" Dom said, behind me; he placed his arms around me in a reverse bear-hug. "I told you it was going to be a good day."

"You turkey!" I said, not knowing what else to say.

I wasn't usually one for surprises, but my mood soared at the face of such dear friends.

"We've brought food ... and *drink,*" Ronan said with a wink as he gestured towards a box containing twelve non-descript bottles of wine. Knowing him, they were likely very fancy.

With only the Range Rover in the driveway, parked beside our truck, it was clear that Lennie had travelled down with Ronan. I found myself concerned about how their trip south had gone.

"The Conventos ... Did you come across it?"

"We did," Lennie said, grinning with unexpected pleasure.

Ronan looked uneasy. "We can talk more about that later," he said, clapping his hands together, drawing the attention back to me. "We've brought gifts for the birthday girl!"

"Oh, wow! You didn't have to," I said, blushing.

Dom kissed me loudly on the cheek before sneaking back to the kitchen to finish plating breakfast. He hollered over his shoulder, "Hope you're hungry!"

"Starved," Lennie said as he handed me a flat, long-ish box wrapped in dark purple tissue paper, its weight considerable. "This is for you."

It was nice to share space with Lennie when he wasn't acting extremely inconvenienced or, worse, intentionally goading Dom. I had a feeling that was still to come, however.

Ronan handed me a large shopping bag, neatly stuffed with folded tissue in the top. "Hope it fits!"

We gathered at the small breakfast table in the kitchen just as Dom was pouring thick and delicious yellow hollandaise sauce all over his pastry creations.

"Are you going to open your gifts?" he asked sweetly, gesturing towards the presents I had just plunked on the table.

"You smug bastard," Ronan said. "What did *you* get her then?"

"I bought her a truck and an engagement ring, thank you very much," Dom said, but I knew damn well he was hiding something else.

"Let's see it then." Ronan reached out for my left hand.

I smiled broadly, still surprised at how much I liked the look of it.

"Very pretty," he said. "Congratulations you two … again?"

Dom laughed. "We like to repeat things a bit around here. But it's the first time *this* time."

Lennie spoke up, already impatient with their banter. "Open mine first."

I peeled back the paper to discover a matte-emerald-green box within. Lennie grinned broadly, with Dom looking temporarily concerned.

Within, I discovered a long, slightly curved knife. Or was it a dagger? Regardless, it was stunning. Topped with a silver cross-guard, the handle was made of red hardwood, from which jutted a strangely golden-tinged blade. I could tell immediately that it was endowed with some kind of magic, but I was not yet familiar with what it might be. Below it in the box was a leather sheath that I assumed could be strapped to the wearer's leg for its safekeeping.

"Wow, Lennie. This is incredible," I said, stunned.

"It's from the order of the Knaves. I've been spending a bit more time with them as of late."

Ronan shifted in his chair before taking a large bite of pastry and egg.

Many times, I had gone over the conversation between the three of us on that fateful day on the tower. I still hadn't fully divulged the entirety of the scenario to Dom. Not because I felt any guilt in the matter, but I was worried for Ronan, concerned that Dom wouldn't take kindly to his best friend agreeing to murder his fiancée.

I actually had planned to tell Dom the whole story before they were expected to join us, but as they had arrived in a surprise visit, that timeframe was now completely botched. Furthermore, the longer I went without telling him, the harder it got. I eyed the ring on my finger, feeling guilty. I would tell Dom the whole story the next time we were alone.

"I'll teach you how to use it later if you like," Lennie said, pouring himself a cup of coffee, completely oblivious to the surprised looks on the faces of Dom and Ronan. Then he started casually flipping through his phone; certainly, many things *had* remained the same.

Ronan's gift was a gorgeous powder-blue linen dress, its quality instantly notable. Eyeing its dimensions, it was also likely a perfect fit, loose and long and just right for hot summer nights on the Oregon coast.

"Picked it up on Robson Street before we left Vancouver. Domhnall told me you've been spending a lot of time at the beach," Ronan said.

Dom beamed at his friend, but there was something behind the smile that caused me to double my resolve to tell him the truth.

"Wow, thanks Ronan. It's so luxurious!"

We chatted happily through the remainder of breakfast, with Ronan and Dom clearing plates and washing up. It was pleasant to hear the two of them laughing together, catching up on all that had been missed. I excused myself to shower and put on something other than pajamas. I had no idea what else Dom had planned for the day but no doubt there would be some kind of itinerary.

Pulling on my shorts in our bedroom, a soft knock soon came at the door. "Love? It's me."

I turned and smiled at Dom keenly as he crossed the threshold; it was already turning out to be a pleasant birthday. "Hi, you."

"Sorry if a surprise isn't what you wanted. But I thought it might be nice to celebrate your special day with an *actual* party."

"It's wonderful," I said, planting a kiss on his scratchy cheek. His hair and beard had grown out considerably since his sheering in Victoria over a month ago, which in my opinion, far better suited his character; I liked him a bit woolly.

"I've got a few more things planned but nothing too strenuous," he said with a wink. I thought of the tourists we had witnessed wildly riding dune buggies across the dunes and worried that his definition of *strenuous* was perhaps much different than my own.

I took a deep breath; this was my moment to tell Dom about the pact Ronan and I, and ultimately Lennie, had made atop the battlement.

"Hey, so ... I just want to clear up—"

Suddenly, he crouched down and pulled out a brown rectangular package from under the bed, which he then slid towards me excitedly. It was tied simply with red and white string.

"It's a bit fancier than the one you used in the sixties," he said, visibly eager for me to open the gift immediately.

I sat down on the floor beside him and carefully undid the wrappings. Inside was a camera. "Oh, Dom, what a good idea!"

"It has all the bells and whistles without being too fancy, at least according to the fella I spoke to over the phone."

He must have had it sent here discreetly. Leave it to Dom to find the perfect gift.

"I have no idea how to use one this complicated," I said.

"I've no doubt you'll figure it out. Happy birthday, love."

I was thrilled but also distinctly sidelined from my plans to convey necessary details to Dom.

"These bedrooms don't have any doors!" I heard Ronan call out, laughing audibly from upstairs. "Good thing I didn't bring a date."

"You? Bring a date? That's a laugh!" Lennie replied, ribbing Ronan from his own doorless bedroom nook up in the mezzanine.

Dom couldn't resist bounding upstairs to join the fun, leaving me to inspect my new gift alone. It was sophisticated, but within a few minutes, I was fairly certain I would be able to at least point-and-click my way through whatever adventures Dom had planned for the day.

To my delight, this meant spending the entirety of the afternoon at the beach, frolicking in the surf and enjoying pleasant company. Having found a frisbee in one of the hall closets, Lennie and I sat back to enjoy watching Dom and Ronan throw increasingly more difficult passes to one another, diving dramatically in their more and more frequently failed attempts.

"They never really stop, do they?" I asked.

"No. Honestly, I'm tired just watching," Lennie said as he stretched out onto his back. We shared in a giggle as the two Celts eventually ended up tossing the disc too far into the ocean to retrieve safely without being pulled out to sea themselves.

"Looks like it's game over, boys!" I called out.

"Ah, *fuck*—that's on you, Ronan!" Dom said, chuckling to himself as he walked towards us and reached for his towel. I smiled broadly; he was magnificent.

They all were really. It was a perfect afternoon.

Having enjoyed a plenitude of beers and laughter in the sunshine, the four of us returned from the beach happy, sandy, and in my case, mildly sunburnt. Dom's skin had bronzed to an almost ambient glow over the past several weeks on the coast, but my own had never been amenable to quite this much sun.

"I'm hopping in with the birthday girl," Dom said, winking at me. "For the sake of conserving water, of course."

I snorted.

Another moment had presented itself for me to discuss with Dom the finer details from my time on the battlements with Ronan and Lennie, but he stopped suddenly in his tracks.

"Oh wait, I forgot. It's not a good time for you," he said out of earshot of the others. "Sorry, love. I'll go start on dinner and shower quick later before we all sit down."

Warmed from the heat of the day and alcohol, I found it hard to argue; I felt desperate for the sensation of cool water on my angry shoulders. I knew he had a big meal planned, so no doubt this was the more sensible decision anyway.

I revelled in the soothing trickle down my back; with my head under the showerhead, I wondered if maybe my worries were overblown. After all, the day had been so consistently upbeat there should be no reason to bring up the battle at all; it was a dark topic and hardly birthday dinner conversation. I would tell Dom the whole tale soon; I decided to keep conflict to a minimum on my "special day."

Mindful of my tender shoulders, I changed into the new dress from Ronan. It fit precisely as anticipated: fashionably loose and extremely comfortable. I knotted my wet hair into a tight bun on top of my head, keeping my reddened shoulders bare—protected as much as possible from any contact, apart from the thin tied straps—and joined Dom and Ronan out on the deck. Something smelled delicious.

"What's for dinner?" I asked as Dom extended a cool glass of white wine in my direction. I accepted it gratefully.

He had kept our meal a secret all day, but I presumed some form of high-quality meat was involved. Smoke was emitting heartily from a small barbeque on the corner of the deck, confirming my suspicions.

"Surf 'n' turf!" Dom said excitedly before jabbing his thumb in the direction of a plastic tub, which I presumed contained some form of live sea life. There was also a massive silver stockpot with a flat lid perched atop an outdoor propane burner.

"Where did *these* come from?" I asked, peering into the bin. Four large crabs peered beadily from its depth, waving their clawed arms slowly about, patently unaware of their fate.

"Friends of Lennie dropped them off," Ronan said, and I detected slight annoyance in his tone. Then he beamed at me. "The dress fits great!"

I twirled around once before sitting down on the shadier side of the deck. "Thanks!"

"Very nice," Dom said nonchalantly before turning his focus towards the grill once more, which had suddenly flared bright orange.

I took a big swig of wine. "Where *is* Lennie?"

"Showering now, I presume," Ronan said. "He was a bit … sidetracked by one of his *lady* friends earlier."

I could see Dom's shoulders shake in silent laughter as he tended to the steaks. "Sidetracked! That's one word for it."

"Oh, really?" I said but was unable to press for further details before Lennie joined us again.

"Smells great, Dom," Lennie said, in uncharacteristically high spirits. "Water's boiling. Time for the crab, I think?"

"Sure. The steak needs to rest anyway."

I was heartened to see Dom and Lennie continuing to work together side-by-side without chaffing at each other too badly. I wondered how long it would actually last.

"How's your summer been, Ronan?" I asked, turning my attention to him as the other two faced-off with the crabs.

"It's been interesting, now that you mention it." He turned his frame towards me, his eyes lighting up. "I've made some significant strides on my Wraith regeneration research since the battle. I've been meaning to pick your brain a bit about that, about what happened when you stepped off the edge. Not tonight, of course, but—"

"Oh, really? Alright." I was shocked at how quickly we'd arrived at the topic. I was also surprised at how uncomfortable I felt about the momentary flicker of obsession I detected across his features—a sight that set off alarm bells.

It must be the alcohol, right?

Feigning distraction, I eyed Dom, who was squealing delightedly as he tossed the final crab into the salted water. Lennie shook his head as if he were a complete lunatic.

"Haven't you ever cooked crab before?" I called out, chuckling as I rose from my chair to peer down into the boiling water. "I can help if you like."

"Oh, I have," he said, smiling brightly. "But something about these little bastards makes me a bit squeamish."

"I see that." I rubbed his back affectionately, the effects of the wine already dancing through my veins, and rested my head on his shoulder. Dom hadn't showered yet and smelled salty and warm. The scent took me back to the fateful day of our first seminar, when I could feel his essence all around me even before walking into Totem Field Studios.

Ronan and Lennie ducked inside, citing the need to prep a salad and refill their drinks. I set down my empty glass near the barbeque and put my arms around Dom's neck, feeling suddenly romantic.

"The crabs need another seven or eight minutes," he said, eyeing the pot dreamily over my shoulder.

"I'm sorry ... Was that supposed to be seductive?"

A cheeky expression spread across his face as his voice dropped into a low purr, catching my drift. "They'll also need to ... cool down ... before we clean them."

He grabbed my ass and pulled me close, murmuring something about wild crustaceans in my ear; it was too much. I burst out into a fit of laughter. "Fuck, I love you," I said once my giggles subsided.

His eyes clouded in distant memory. "And I've loved you for such a long time. *De réir a chéile a thógtar na caisleáin.*" Now he definitely *was* being romantic.

"Mm ... What does that mean?" I asked, pushing myself suggestively into his solid frame. I still didn't understand him when he spoke in his native tongue, no matter how hard I tried. He looked at me adoringly as my heartbeat pounded loudly in my throat, inner fire blissfully ablaze.

"The direct translation is, 'castles are built gradually.' But it's more like saying, 'Rome wasn't built in a day,'" Ronan said loudly from behind, effectively deflating the moment.

Lennie grabbed my glass to refill it. "I think that one sounds better in Irish, Dom."

It wasn't like Ronan to push in like this, and I blinked slowly through furrowed brows. Indeed, *both* men seemed completely unconcerned to have interrupted the tender moment. Dom made a rude gesture towards the pair of them before we sat down on the edge of the deck to clean the crabs. It wasn't a hard task, but hopefully, many hands would also make for light work. I was starving.

"Speaking of castles," Lennie said as we began, deftly popping the back shell off the crab with a silver kitchen knife, "I really do mean to teach you to use the blade I got you, Julia. You don't want to find yourself in another moment like up on the ramparts."

My stomach dropped. Now really wasn't the time for this discussion.

"It's true. I won't always be there to finish the job," Ronan said somewhat flippantly; he was perhaps a bit drunker than the rest of us. Frankly, he had been a bit off since his arrival, but I had not yet determined the reason for it.

"What do you mean, 'finish the job?'" Dom asked, his voice strangely steady as he violently cracked off several crab legs at once.

"Surely, Julia told you about the … pact?" Lennie said, realization dawning that perhaps he had opened a door that had been meant to remain shut. "Ah …"

I let out a slow breath. It's not like I hadn't told Dom about the two of them witnessing my internal struggle at the end and what it had taken for me to rise above. However, I had struggled to name the actual act of making a pact; something subconscious had held me back. Dom, however, knew immediately what we spoke of as his gaze snapped between me and Ronan.

"For fuck's sakes, Dom," Ronan said hotly. "What was I supposed to do? She was completely defenseless!"

I felt a spike of anger at Ronan's changing tone. "Hey!" I stood abruptly, crab guts splattering my new dress. "Let me speak for my—"

"What did you *just* say?" Dom growled, his gaze fixed terrifyingly on his best friend. Then he erupted. "We *discussed* this, Ronan! How many times did I tell you not to make *those* kinds of promises!"

Ronan stood to face Dom head on, clearly unafraid of his lumbering friend. "So, I was just supposed to let her be dragged off and tortured as the rest of us lay dying on the battlefield? Great idea! Some *craic*," he said sardonically.

Lennie chimed in, his British accent almost comically mild in comparison to the two angry Irishmen. "You weren't there, Dom. There wasn't really any other choice available to us—"

"Stay out of this, Lennie!" Dom barked. He turned on Ronan once more. "Do you have any idea what could have happened if she were to die by *your* hand?"

"But I didn't," I said loudly. "And that's why we're all here now, in case you hadn't noticed."

Dom spun towards me, shoulders heaving in exasperation. "Don't you understand, Julia? If *he* had killed you, the curse ... the Prophecy ... it could have been altered *forever!*"

"A torturous death for the sake of your *fucking* curses?" Ronan said, his own anger piquing. "Not on *my* watch!"

I realized then what Dom was implying. Combined, both the curses and Prophecy bore specific parameters that allowed for our continued rebirth *together*. If Ronan had entered into the equation, even with something so simple as ending my life pre-emptively, a drastically different outcome might have resulted. Magic was funny like that.

The two Celts stood braced to fight, Dom's knuckles clenched, and his white teeth bared as Ronan exhaled heavily through his long nose. Lennie backed away from the fray, wisely scuttling the tray of freshly cleaned crabs out of harm's reach in the same motion. Ronan's stubbornness would be his downfall; while he was powerful in his own right, it was clear who would rise victorious in a physical altercation. Yet somehow, I also couldn't see him stooping so low as to break his Druidic vow and Wield magic against Dom, either. Ronan was about to lose miserably, and I wasn't sure their relationship could recover if Dom beat the pulp out of his best friend on my behalf.

"Ronan, that's *exactly* what you were supposed to do …" I said, my voice dropping along with my sinking heart, "exactly what you were supposed to let happen." I looked to Dom as yet another layer of his complicated and grief-laden existence was exposed to me.

My words broke the spell.

Dom released his fists and turned slowly towards me, rolling his shoulders back simultaneously. *"Fuck.* I'm so sorry, Julia, I—"

"No, wait. Let's talk about this somewhere else," I said, eyeing the harsh angle at which Ronan's jaw was now protruding from his face. Both men clearly needed space to cool down. Not to mention that I didn't want to have this particular conversation with Ronan or Lennie listening anyway.

I took Dom by the hand and skirted around to the front of the house; his grasp was as warm as his boiling blood. Under the comforting shade of the white oak, I dropped his hand and turned to face him head on, absently realizing that where we now stood was indeed a *thin place*. "I should have told you about it. Fully. I honestly don't know why I didn't … I guess I was afraid you'd be angry with me."

"Angry?" he asked, visibly surprised.

He glanced back in the direction of Ronan and Lennie, nostrils flaring in residual aggravation. I looked down; I was covered in crustacean innards and had likely ruined the dress. I drew my eyes back up. "I'm really sorry."

Without warning, he launched into a (slightly tipsy) speech. "Unfortunately, they're right. I did leave you unprepared and tasked Ronan to protect you instead of supporting you to protect yourself. I know that was a mistake now, and I was a fool to think otherwise. But what I'm most angry about is that the self-righteous bastard took your life into his hands after I explicitly told him not to. There is such thing as duty, and I thought I could trust *Ronan,* at least, to uphold that. My request to him should have been honour bound."

With barely a pause for breath, he continued. "You know that there's more to my understanding of the Otherworld than I'm comfortable sharing with him. It's honestly the whole reason I shy away from working too closely with the Druids in the first place. You've seen that now, with the new Prophecy. There's much more to it all than meets the eye.

"All those years ago, when I chose love over a chance at dominion, I named my path. And time and time again, that choice has allowed me to be close to an infinite source of power—your power—which is more incredible than anything I could have dreamed of in my life, and I witnessed my *own father* rise to become the greatest High King Ireland would ever see! I've *seen* greatness in action. And I know the stakes. But don't you see, Julia? It's always been you. Through it all, my duty is to *you*. And I'll be damned if anyone gets in the way of that."

Something about his posture in the moment, the way he stood firmly braced and voice ringing clear, reminded me distinctly of an ancient leader, a great leader, contrary to his opposing message. He was naturally fit to rule, much like his father, and was *very much* a hero.

I felt a cold finger of fear run down my spine. "And now the new Prophecy is asking you to accept the opposite ... to step into *your* power," I said.

"It is. And I've already told you that's *not fucking* happening. We've got to stay focused and figure out what the quilt means ... retrace our steps so that you can find the tools you need to access the memories, all that ...". He stifled an unexpected yawn; the day was feeling suddenly long. "*That's* our mission. Otherwise, there's no rest."

I knew all too well what he meant. The burden of our repeated rebirths continued to be immensely heavy for the pair of us; whatever hopes we had of a time of respite in this new chapter of our life together would surely have to wait.

"I understand. You're kind of like a recovering chronic hero," I said, collecting his broad palms into my slender hands.

"Perhaps I am." He barked out a laugh before furrowing his brow. "But also—if I'm honest—something's off with Ronan. He's looking at you differently, and I'm not sure I like it."

"What?" I was surprised he would mention it, but he wasn't wrong. "Dom ... you know you have nothing to worry about."

He shifted his weight slightly. "Of course not, and I'm sure it's just him fixating on the fact you might hold the answers he needs for his research—you're useful to him now, you know—but there's also how fucking magnetic you are these days too—"

"*Magnetic?*"

"Like … the power about you. Something's changed. Or rather, you're not hiding it so much anymore. And people are noticing. They're drawn to you. And that makes me feel … envious, I suppose? It's silly. I know."

"You're not silly." I ran my fingers through his salt-crusted hair, massaging his temples with my thumbs. He pressed into my fingertips, moaning low in pleasure.

"You're the most remarkable woman I've ever encountered."

I snorted again. "Even if I'm covered in crab guts?"

He grinned, sniffing deeply in my direction. "Even then."

"Did you want to hop into the shower together before we join them again?"

"*Absolutely*, I do."

Apparently, it wasn't the first confrontation of this type between the two friends and not likely to be the last. Dom informed me hours after the "almost fight" that most conflicts of this calibre had occurred *long* before I was in the picture, when they were both "younger men."

"How does that even work?" I asked as he wrapped his solid frame around me, tucking into bed for the night. He smelled strongly like whisky and a little bit like birthday cake.

"What do you mean?"

"Well … like … you're *old*."

He dug his fingers playfully into my ribs, and I shrieked louder than I probably should have with houseguests about.

"Mind who you're calling old, Julia soon-to-be O'Brien!" he said through a vibrating laugh. "And I don't know. I might be ancient, but in my mind, and in my body, well … I guess I still act my age most of the time."

"Oh *really*?"

He ground his hips against me. "I do. Is that a problem for you?"

I yawned before rolling over to face him and laughed. "No. It's not. But I do picture you as an older man sometimes. What your body would look like … Actually, it's more your face than anything. Is that weird?"

He paused for a moment. "I've long wished to watch your body change through the years, Julia; you know that. And there's something incredibly sexy about it. A mature woman, fully in her power—"

"*Mature* woman?" I said, retaliating with my own tickles; I felt very young, all things considered. I was also far more drunk that I realized.

After our shower earlier, Dom and I had rejoined the others on the deck and masked our discomfort with perhaps a little too much birthday frivolity in the form of an expensive bottle of whisky Ronan had brought, which Dom drank heartily in what I assumed was retaliation.

"You know what I mean! I'm going to enjoy growing old with you. Happy birthday, love," he said and kissed me sloppily on my forehead.

I basked for a brief moment in his sweet sentiment. And within minutes of my silence, he was fast asleep, his breath audible as his body relaxed into an inebriated slumber.

"Goodnight," I said quietly.

In the moonlight, I traced the lines of his peaceful face with my sleepy eyes, imagining once more what he might look like with deeper crow's feet and gently greying hair. I could see him smiling at a room full of friends he's known for many years, yet still never losing sight of me across the table. It felt warm and real, but I wasn't entirely sure if it was a vision or a simply a wish.

I let out a long sigh. There was just so much still between us and that chapter of our lives that it was hard most days to even dare to dream.

CHAPTER 7

The following day was business as usual. I awoke to find Dom and Ronan chatting pleasantly in the kitchen, hot coffee and breakfast at the ready. It would seem "the lads" were very well equipped to move on from what had quite nearly been a damaging physical altercation.

"Morning," I said, yawning groggily and sliding into the room wearing a pair of old slippers I had found in the hall closet. I was significantly hungover. "Where's Lennie?"

Dom grinned. "He's taking a phone call. *Outside.*"

Ronan raised his eyebrows, indicating that the call was with a person of note.

I attempted to push my chair back using my foot, my hands already greedily cradling the steaming cup of coffee Dom had poured for me. He gave me big kiss on the cheek and pulled out my chair for me instead.

"Did you sleep well?"

The answer was no. I had passed out for the first half of the night from drink, and then in the latter half, my dreams had been disturbed by the new Prophecy echoing so loudly in my mind that I could barely stay asleep. "Mostly."

He looked momentarily concerned, adeptly reading the words between the lines. I pressed my cup to my lips and locked eyes with him in reassurance.

The door opened, and Lennie returned, cheeks flushed. "Morning, Julia."

"Was that Wren?" Ronan asked. Clearly, he knew her too. Now I was more than curious about this new woman in Lennie's life.

"It was. She's going to come by this week, I think. With some of the others."

Ronan abruptly pushed himself back from the table and cleared his plate. He spoke again with his back turned. "Is that absolutely necessary—"

"Why not? I'd like to meet her," Dom interjected.

"No, not *her*. I mean the others," Ronan said, turning to face us once more. Evidently, I was missing some significant notes on whatever was happening between Lennie, Ronan, and the Knaves. Dom too looked slightly perplexed.

"Why would it be a problem, Ronan?" Lennie asked, but his voice was strangely controlled and had a slight pitch to it, as if to prod him.

"It's not," Ronan replied as he gruffly left the room.

I helped myself to a slice of toast and two wedges of cut orange. I eyed the breakfast sausage with skepticism, my stomach quite uneasy still from the night before.

"Hair of the dog, Julia?" Lennie asked as he dumped the remaining swill down the sink from the discarded beer bottles from the night before.

"No. Thanks," I said flatly. He laughed.

"I think you'll like Wren, Julia. She's from Seattle, and she's a Wielder. Close to our age."

I chewed my piece of toast slowly; it was going down alright so far. I eyed the sausages once more before deciding wholeheartedly against them. "Cool. I'm looking forward to it."

Dom smiled peaceably. "Care to enlighten us on Ronan's issue with the other guests you've invited?"

Lennie rolled his eyes. "It's the same shit we've been fighting about all summer. He doesn't think the Knaves follow enough of a *moral code*. That they're irresponsible with their magic or some other preposterous thing. I think he just doesn't want to put his research at risk. But it's ridiculous! They want to find a way to defeat the Wraiths just as badly as the Druids."

"Are there a lot of Wraiths down here?" I asked, my stomach turning at the thought. I pushed my plate back.

"They're rampant! A much heavier population than in Canada. The Knaves have done a hell of a job keeping them at bay, despite what the local Druids would tell you."

Dom snorted. "I can only imagine."

I looked between the two men, surprised at the thinly veiled kinship developing between them.

"Is that who's giving you leads from L.A.?" I asked.

"Yes. Which reminds me …"

Lennie pulled out his laptop from his bag, which had been concealed below the table, and immediately became immersed in his work. Dom raised his eyebrows as if to say, *"I guess that's the end of that conversation,"* and turned his attention towards me.

"Are you feeling alright? You've barely eaten."

"Not everyone eats their way through a hangover, Dom," Ronan said, returning to the room once more, wearing running shoes, athletic shorts, and a quick-dry t-shirt. "You still up for that run?"

Dom stared at me, not yet releasing his concern. "I am … as long as Julia's alright."

"Oh my Goddess, you guys! I'm just hungover," I said, laughing in slight embarrassment. "Go! Please. Get out of my sight. You're far too … *perky* for me right now."

Without another word, the seemingly superhuman Celts were off sprinting down the road, pushing each other well past a stomach-able limit of exertion. Perhaps it only mocked the flavour of physical battle, but I was glad at least that they had each other in their lunacy. Indeed, Dom had been grumbling over the past several weeks about his fitness dropping below his personal standards despite the accumulating equipment he'd ordered.

I left Lennie in the kitchen and returned to our bed on the main floor. Unfortunately, I felt far too shitty to fall asleep. Listening to an obnoxiously loud ticking clock on the wall across from me that featured the native wildflowers of Oregon State, I lay still for a time, alone with my thoughts. Today we would share the new Prophecy with Ronan and Lennie; they deserved to know the latest from the Otherworld. And I was anxious for more information about the Knaves, who were proving to be a real bone in Ronan's craw.

I finally dozed off only to be jarred awake by the slamming kitchen door and loud, combative voices. I rolled out of bed and dragged myself to the kitchen, hoping that no new confrontations were afoot. Instead, I discovered both men with massive grins on their faces, despite the fact they were completely drenched in sweat and looking notably unwell.

Lennie spoke without popping his head up. "So, who was sick first?"

"Fucking hell!" Dom said through heavy breathing, lips pulled back and teeth bared in strained exhaustion. "It was me, but only because Ronan's such a stubborn bastard."

Ronan wiped his pale forehead with the bottom of his shirt, looking equally diminished. "I think that makes me the victor."

Dom snorted before downing two full glasses of water. "Right."

"Careful you don't puke again," I added, noticing the splotchy hue developing on Dom's face. "Cold shower?"

"Yes, *please!*" he said, running his right hand through his sweaty hair, causing it to stand up spectacularly on end. He moved to reach his arm around me as we exited the kitchen together, and I squealed, leaping just out of his grasp.

"Ew! You're so sweaty! Don't touch me!"

He grinned mischievously. "Oh, it's like that, is it?"

I took off at a run but was caught almost instantly into a giant, sweaty bear-hug. He smelled like exertion and raw masculine essence; it was intoxicating being near him when he was using his body precisely as it was designed, even if the sensation of his cooling sweat was slightly gross. He kissed me once with a growl before pulling me into the bathroom and closing the door loudly behind us.

"Are you feeling any better?" he asked, still panting as he pulled his soaked grey t-shirt over his head. As usual, the visual was stupendous.

"Not really, but I'll take a nap this afternoon and be fine."

"Ah. I keep forgetting you're still bleeding too. You *must* be tired."

"I am," I said, smiling appreciatively at his concern.

"It's no matter, love. I'm not exactly up for much right now anyway—that bastard just didn't stop running and fast too! Fuck. He's kept up training."

"Well, I'm glad you have someone here to motivate you again."

"Oh, you motivate me plenty," he said, gripping his hand possessively on my backside. "I'm desperate for a wash though."

He climbed into the cool shower, with me following shortly thereafter, once he had turned the water back up to a reasonable warmth. Something about showering together simply for the purpose of becoming clean felt like a significant developmental milestone in our coupledom. We really *were* growing older together.

Always quick to shower, he soon climbed out and towelled himself off as I lingered behind, cranking the heat up further and basking in the steamy atmosphere.

"It's too hot in here for me, love. I'll catch you outside."

"Sounds good!" I shouted through the steam, but he was already gone. I stayed a little while longer before feeling guilty for taking all of the hot water from Ronan. He was ex-military though; surely, he could handle a cold shower from time to time.

I wrapped a towel around myself and dragged my feet slowly to the bedroom. Still damp and mostly naked, I gave in to my exhaustion and curled up under the sheets. Within moments, I was fast asleep.

———

"Julia," Dom said, gently brushing back waves of unruly hair from my face. "Hmm?"

"You've been asleep for almost two hours. I just wanted to make sure you didn't want to get up."

"Shit, sorry." I wiped the drool from my cheek. I felt significantly better than I had several hours before, albeit extremely groggy.

"It's fine, love," Dom said as he lay down casually beside me. He was wearing a soft white t-shirt, which contrasted with his warmly tanned biceps. "Really though, are you alright? Yesterday was … a lot. I'm so sorry it took such a turn."

"I'm not really surprised, to be honest," I said with a smile and drew in a slow breath through my nose. Stretching with my arms above my head and all the way down to my toes, I rolled onto my back as my towel spread open to expose my breasts.

Dom's eyes widened slightly. "Oh—"

I smiled seductively; I was abnormally horny when I was hungover.

"Domhnall! Are you coming or what?" Ronan hollered from somewhere beyond the threshold of our bedroom.

Dom groaned, pushing himself up off the bed begrudgingly. "I think I like having house guests a lot less than I used to."

"Told you so," I said, quickly pulling my towel around myself once more and sitting up. "I miss our bed in Ireland."

"Me too. This one's much too small. And lumpy," Dom said, eyeing the mattress with perhaps more accusation than it deserved.

"Okay, Goldilocks," I said, but I completely agreed. We had made the best of our stay in Oregon, and certainly the accommodations had suited our needs, but I knew we both longed for a curated space of our own and a sense of *place*. When we would achieve that level of comfort, however, was another question altogether. I pushed the thought from my mind.

"Where are you going anyway?" I asked, distracted by Lennie and Ronan's loud bickering coming from the hallway.

"The lads want to go to the grocery store. Lennie doesn't like the coffee we picked, and Ronan isn't happy with the state of our vegetables either."

"Losers," I said. "Can't you stay?" I was pouting, but only half pretending to be disappointed.

"Hmm," he said, furrowing his brow in an internal debate. Without another word, he slid from the bed and left the room, announcing loudly that he was going to stay behind with me; they could figure out the predicament on their own.

"Are they mad at us?" I asked, raising one eyebrow when he returned. He dived dramatically onto the bed beside me, causing me to flop onto my side towards him, towel completely askew.

"You know what? I don't really care," he said, grinning mischievously as he nuzzled into my chest; evidently, he had plans for us that didn't involve debating about the weight and price of organic produce in an American grocery store.

♥

Later that afternoon, I returned to the group at last. My well-being felt significantly improved since my dire hangover at breakfast. Dom had once again left the bedroom sometime while I slept, and so I found all three men settled in the living room together, arguing about something new. This time, at least, it wasn't serious.

"You can't honestly tell me that you think the dress is blue," Lennie said, shoving his computer towards Dom to display what I instantly recognized as a viral photo from several years previous. "It's clearly gold and white!"

"No way. It's black and blue!" Dom said, reaching out from his reclined position and tapping at Lennie's screen. Lennie immediately wiped it with his sleeve.

Ronan laughed along with them, though I noticed he didn't take a side.

Seeing that I was at last awake, Dom rose from the couch to greet me. "Julia," he said, his voice unabashed in its fondness.

Lennie and Ronan were seated in a pair of adjacent armchairs and nodded in my direction before diverting their attention towards other things. I had come to notice that they openly ignored Dom when he was being demonstratively loving towards me, which seemed slightly childish on their part. Dom really wasn't over the top in his adoration, simply comfortable in his own skin and unafraid to show it. It was more likely they were both uncomfortable with intimacy.

I stretched my arms above my head and yawned before leaning in for a kiss and wrapping my arms over his shoulders. Dom was the only partner with whom I had ever felt comfortable with public displays of affection, more than likely due to his sheer authenticity around the matter.

"Did you manage to solve the world's problems while I slept? Or am I still needed around here?" I asked the room at large. Dom and I settled onto the couch together, him seated and me stretched out leaning against his solid frame.

"Do you honestly think these two fools are getting anywhere without us?" Lennie asked as he lithely bolted in the direction of the kitchen towards a loudly whistling kettle.

Ronan rolled his eyes and returned to the stack of papers before him, which he had been shuffling loudly. He was wearing reading glasses, which was new. Before long, Lennie returned with an over-encumbered tray carrying a large teapot, cups, and several different brown-paper packages of cookies and pastries, no doubt spoils from their voyage to the grocer. Dom leapt up to clear Lennie's computer from the tabletop as I scooped several books out of the way.

"Tea, Julia?" Lennie asked.

"Mm. Yes please." I helped him sort the tray between us and sat back down. Dom absently trailed his fingers down my spine as I leaned forward, causing me to involuntarily arch my back at his touch. He chuckled at my reaction as I gripped his thigh affectionately.

Ronan's eyes shot from his paperwork towards us momentarily and then back to the tea. "I'll have some. No sugar though."

Lennie rolled his eyes and finished pouring. Dom passed, opting for the large glass of water on the table beside him; he must have been more hungover than he was letting on. That or he was just as nervous as I was to tell the others about the new Prophecy.

"Well, we best cut to the chase," Dom announced suddenly. "Julia heard ... or 'saw' ... a new Prophecy."

I had only just raised the cup to my lips for my first sip of tea. "Ah, thanks, Dom." I set my cup back down and took a deep breath as all eyes turned on me.

"Sorry," Dom said sheepishly, but I knew he simply meant to get on with it; he never was one to wait when action was needed.

I shared the new Prophecy with the other two men. And as expected, the reviews were mixed.

"This is brilliant!" Lennie remarked, clapping his hands loudly. I wasn't used to this level of animation from someone usually so guarded. Dom looked about, as surprised as I felt.

"Um ... care to elaborate?" Dom asked, transitioning rapidly from confusion to visible suspicion as he stared at Lennie. I noticed Ronan's knuckles whiten around his teacup.

Lennie stood, clearly unable to keep his body still. "I've been saying for months that the Knaves would play an integral part in this fight. And this proves it."

Dom puzzled. "How does this prove anything?"

"Don't you see? *For the earthen weapons masters, and tree talkers with open sky above ...* ' You're meant to lead them!" Lennie said, his voice rising excitedly. He walked to the back of his chair and placed his hands on it to steady himself. *"'The World Ruler too must bear his crown'!"*

"Maybe ..." I said, still puzzling over much of the new Prophecy's meaning myself. It was interesting to see which parts Lennie latched onto; for my own part, I was still caught on the eerie last line: *"Darkness reigns where light cannot, and from its root, the land will rot."*

Whatever the hell that meant.

"I'm not entirely sure young Domhnall here has any interest in leading anyone," Ronan said, snorting. "He's made *that* quite plain over the years."

Dom tensed where he sat. "I'm not sure anyone but *me* gets to decide what I—"

"Hold on," I said, interrupting. "What do you mean about the earthen weapons masters? The 'tree talkers' obviously references the Druids, but ..." My voice trailed off in uncertainty, and I held up my hand to stem the volcano that was about to erupt between the two Celts. Dom relaxed only slightly, just enough to settle back onto the couch. Ronan continued to look miserable.

Lennie turned his gaze on me. "The Knaves specialize in metallurgy. Weapons specifically. But also, alchemy and all that. That blade I gave you for your birthday isn't meant for cutting up apples. And you'll recall the pair of gold knives I had on the ramparts? Those weren't for chopping salad either." He sounded rather pompous.

I recalled the image of Lennie running towards Ronan and me in Northern Ireland, curved blades flashing beside him as he sprinted across the stone walkway. The sight had been utterly breathtaking. And if I was honest, otherworldly. "So, are they imbibed with magic or something?" I asked, thinking of the gorgeous blade he had gifted me, which was currently sitting unassumingly on my bedside table.

"Sort of," Lennie said, poised to launch into more detail.

Suddenly, Ronan was standing. "It's a rather grey area of Wielding, Julia. The Knaves mine ore and graphite, and other precious metals, to alchemize their creations, but they aren't particularly mindful about returning the magic to the earth either. To be so focused on industry instead of the earth—"

"That's bullshit, and you know it," Lennie said, keeping his attention on me and Dom. "Think of it more like a long-term loan. The Knaves have found a way to harness the Wielding magic and place it into their weaponry.

It's still elemental and so no different than the Druids' pouches, really ... They just don't expire so quickly."

"And surely the blades can also be smelted into new forms too," Dom said clearly keeping up. "I mean, do you think we didn't recycle and reforge blades when they broke back in the day?"

Lennie nodded enthusiastically. "It keeps the Wielding magic external to the user, for the most part. It's quite unlike the Wraiths, where they draw it *inward* to harness its uses, which ultimately destroys them."

"Fascinating," I said. Dom nodded, also impressed.

Ronan was also unable to keep still for the discussion—albeit for a very different reason than Lennie—and had migrated to the window. Looking out, his face was sullen. "You have no idea what you're talking about Lennie. Absolutely no clue. And it's all so bloody dangerous!"

"Why don't you just tell us how you *really* feel, Ronan," Lennie said, no longer hiding his defensiveness. Evidently, he had folded into the ranks of the Knaves easily.

"Without taking care of the magic," Ronan said, turning to face Lennie head on and taking two long strides in his direction, "you risk destroying yourselves in the process, and *all* of us, with your stupidity!"

"Who says we aren't taking care of the magic?" Lennie asked, his voice slick as silver. "It's not like the Druids don't pull magic inward—*infusing* themselves with it. It's a lot like the Wraiths, if I'm being completely honest. You just rely on your long-held *duty* to return it to the earth. But what happens when that slips, Ronan? I haven't forgotten about Malcolm's sacrifice, and I don't feel like what the Knaves are doing with their magic comes even *close* to that level of danger."

Ronan slammed his mug down onto a side table, causing it to fall over awkwardly into a neighbouring armchair. I shot my hand out to stop the cup with my magic but, as usual, was only able to diminish the liquid, not break its fall. Sometimes I didn't even know why I bothered. Wielding magic just didn't manifest for me the way it seemed to for other Witches. Dom stilled me with his hand. Rapt, he was watching their discussion with an unusual look on his face.

"Ask your friends!" Ronan yelled. *"You* might be responsible with this form of Wielding, but what I saw from them when they took out that

Conventos several days ago was far from sensible. They were fighting like a pack of Wraiths themselves!"

Ever since the events on the precipice, Ronan had seemed more agitated when it came to *how* magic was used, grilling me on more than one occasion following the battle about what exactly I'd done. To which, of course, I still had no clear answer. However, his reaction now felt extreme; I couldn't blame Lennie for being defensive.

While Ronan's body movements were uncharacteristically erratic, Lennie stood completely still, controlled like a venomous snake set to strike. "What about their fighting didn't you like, Ronan? That they did what they needed to do to get the job done, fighting from their hearts instead of always having to think everything through from every *fucking* angle before striking?"

"They're reckless," Ronan said.

Dom rolled his shoulders back several times; this was one of the many disputes he had been forced to mediate over email all summer, and his patience was growing thin. Lennie and Ronan continued to bicker for another several minutes, circling around the same argument without making any headway.

At last, Dom reached his breaking point. "Would you two just *shut the fuck up* for a moment! I can't even think!"

The room fell silent as he rose to his feet. The shift in the dynamic was instantly palpable. Lennie looked appeased, if not slightly relieved, as he wasn't a leader by nature. Despite the regular chafing between him and Ronan, the pair clearly knew where they stood. I expected Ronan to react with anger, as he had been so prone to over the past several days, but he too showed signs of compliance. At Dom's words, he ran his hand over his stubbled chin and looked out the window once more.

I sat stock still, feeling neither relief nor compliance in my own body. Rather, I felt an unexpected well of pride. Dom truly was the World Ruler, even if he didn't yet recognize it in himself.

"The fact of the matter is that we need all the resources we can muster if we hope to defeat Cassius, wherever the fuck he is right now. Not to mention that we can assume he's also heard the new Prophecy, since it includes *him* as well," Dom said, his face darkening as he made eye contact with me. "I, for one, am not pleased with his inclusion: *'As the Sorcerer seeks to find the grail, spear in hand, to chalice he is bound ...'* Julia's fate is still tied to his."

Silence blanketed the room. I felt a chill finger run down my spine.

"We're wasting precious time here, bickering about details and methods," Dom said, his voice gravelly. "You know damn well that Cassius is busy coming up with his own 'methods' and isn't letting anyone trip him up in the process either."

"I think, the more help we can get, the better," I said quietly.

His body relaxed at my words. "I'd like to go for a walk, Julia. Care to join me?"

"I'd love to."

CHAPTER 8

Lennie's Knave friends arrived five days later in a massive dually pickup, towing an equally huge RV trailer behind it. Realistically, the beach house wasn't large enough to accommodate everyone without us practically piling on top of each other, so this had been a wise choice, even if it *was* a bit of a monstrosity.

I appreciated the practicality of the Knaves already.

It had been hilarious to watch the three men gather outside as a fellow named Stuart Haak deftly reversed the trailer into a narrow gravel driveway along the west side of the house; I wasn't entirely sure the parking spot was meant for a rig that large. I decided to greet the newcomers from afar and remained on the deck. I was decidedly nervous to be around this unfamiliar group of Wielders and wondered how well me and my still emerging Bearing magic would mix with them.

Thankfully, I quickly discovered that I had absolutely nothing to worry about.

Everyone clapped loudly for Stuart's solid effort as he jumped out of the truck and gave us all a low bow. He was quickly followed by three others who emerged from the truck's interior: all women. I felt instant relief wash over me; there had been far too much "lad energy" in the house for my liking over the past week.

I was thrilled to finally meet Wren, who wasn't anything like I had expected—though, in all fairness, I likely hadn't given Lennie enough credit. Somehow, I had pictured him dating someone as closed off as, or maybe even more pretentious than, he was. Perhaps even another MI6 type with a penchant for mystery. Wren was anything but. She was vibrant and welcoming and wholly confident in her own skin. All of that wasn't to say that she *couldn't* be a secret agent, but she was pretty much the polar opposite of Lennie in terms of her energy.

I was beginning to understand how he'd fallen for her so rapidly over the past few months. He absolutely glowed in her presence.

"I'm so glad you're here," I heard him say sweetly as he pulled her into an embrace before kissing her behind the ear. Their fresh love was instantly tangible on the summer breeze.

Wren Sylvester was shorter, like Lennie, though with a softer figure. She wore her chestnut hair shoulder length with fashionably cut bangs. Her left arm was decorated with an intricate sleeve tattoo that featured colourful flora and fauna, along with some imagery I recognized from one of Gertie's tarot decks. She also wore a shiny silver nose ring.

She practically oozed fun and coolness.

"Me too. Where's Julia?" she said, instantly homing in on my presence. "Oh! She *is* powerful!"

"Just like I told you," Lennie said happily as he led Wren towards me.

Dom arrived at my side at the same moment, eager to greet Lennie's new partner as well.

"Welcome!" he said happily.

"It's so great to *finally* meet you," I said, smiling broadly. It felt like a bit of an exaggerated statement on my part, as she and Lennie had apparently only been together for a short while, not to mention that I had only really known of her existence for a little over a week, but with the way Lennie had spoken about her so far, it felt like they had known each other for a lifetime.

Destiny was funny like that.

"Likewise!" she said, and pulled me into a warm hug, thus confirming her status as a "West Coaster." Wren gave Dom a quick hug too before leaning back, grinning widely at the pair of us. "We've been waiting to meet you both for quite some time."

Noticing the confused look on my face, Lennie caught me up. "There are Seers among the Knaves too. A little bit different than the Druids. Not really so much 'divining' as dream interpretation, but still …"

"Well, we're definitely not as powerful as Bearers when it comes to the Sight," Wren said modestly, "but we can extrapolate a bit from what we do see. Like you two, for example. You've been in my dreams for years, in one form or another."

"Poor you," Dom said with a wink. I gave him a quick shove.

For my part, however, I was instantly intrigued. I had never met another Bearer who carried even remotely similar Divining "talents" to mine, let alone a Wielder with *any* form of the Sight in their repertoire. Perhaps she would be able to share some of her methods with me. Or at the very least, commiserate with me after a deeply troubled night's sleep.

"Wait … Did you already know about the new Prophecy then, since you've been dreaming about me and Dom?" I asked, eyeing Lennie suspiciously. I could feel Dom shift uncomfortably beside me and took his hand into my own to steady him.

"Sort of," Lennie said, deferring back to Wren.

"Not in the same detail, and there were no words like what you saw. But several of us have been dreaming of the World Ruler and the Sovereign for years. But divining is a funny thing. You know how it is," she said, offering me a wink. "When Lennie filled me in after your discussion from the other day though, I knew that *this* was what it had all meant!" Her eyes flickered briefly towards Dom, who had turned his attention away from the discussion.

Across the lawn, Ronan and Stuart were speaking animatedly beside the truck; although, from where I stood, it didn't seem entirely friendly.

"Is everything okay over there?" I asked, looking over Lennie's and Wren's heads and across the lawn; Dom and I were both notably taller than the pair of them. I wondered if Ronan and Stuart's dispute was about the Knaves' delayed arrival. They were originally supposed to join us at the beach house earlier in the morning, but something had held them up—a "something" that Lennie had been hesitant to elaborate on further with Ronan in the same room.

"Who cares? Those two have it out for each other," a fair-haired woman said, popping up from behind Wren. She had short-cropped hair and a handful of freckles scattered across her smiling face, and wore denim overall shorts with a purple crop top that gave her a distinctly summery flare. She also looked like she could kick some serious ass when it came down to it. "I'm Alanna."

I shook her hand, which was cool to the touch, like mine. "Nice to meet you."

"I think Stuart gets a kick out of it," a third woman said, appearing at Alanna's side with a quick wave. "I'm Shereen, by the way." She was taller than the other two women, with brown skin and wavy black hair that she wore in a messy knot on the top of her head. This feature added to her illusion of height when she stood next to them, although I still was notably taller than the entire trio.

Shereen Osman and Alanna Carter were also quite clearly a couple, the gravity between the two of them unmistakable as they wove their hands together affectionately.

"Are you all from Seattle?" I asked, recalling what Lennie had told me about Wren; I noticed that Alanna's and Shereen's accents also sounded similar to mine.

"The three of us are," Alanna said, gesturing towards Wren and Shereen. "We all met at university—which was already kind of random—and then we stumbled upon the fact we were all Wielders one weekend at a dorm party!"

"It's a great story; we'll have to tell it to you later," Wren said, turning her attention towards Ronan and Stuart, whose conversation was now heating up into a fully fledged argument. "Excuse me for a second, everyone," she said happily.

She exchanged quiet words with the two men, who both buttoned up immediately; I knew then that we were going to be *great* friends. She and Stuart returned to the group, the latter arriving with a big grin across his face.

"That bastard really has it out for me!" he said, shaking his head. He had pale skin framed by a dark, tidy beard and spoke with a unique accent.

"Where is your accent from?" I asked, puzzled. "It's not Kiwi."

"Our Julia here's a linguist," Dom said, winking at me once before reaching out to shake Stuart's hand. "Unlike me."

"Hardly," I said. "But I do have a *real* linguistics degree."

MANTLE OF THE WORLD RULER

Despite not understanding my jab at Dom, Stuart let out a hearty laugh that sounded much older than the face accompanying it. "South African. I'm from Pretoria though, so you're right, the accent is similar to a New Zealander. But also ... different? There is a lot of different accents where I'm from."

I smiled with a nod. "Cool. I like it."

"Can I get anyone a beer? Or something harder?" Dom asked, shifting naturally into the role of host.

"Me, please!" Wren said; the others nodded in agreement, with only Alanna passing.

"We were thinking of having a barbeque tonight," Lennie said, following Dom's lead.

"Ah, excellent. I've been craving a good *braai,*" Stuart said eagerly. Soon he, Dom, and Lennie were launched into a discussion about the merits of lighter fluid on charcoal and getting it up to temperature for cooking as much meat as possible.

"What's the secret then?" I heard Lennie ask.

"You hold your hand over the coals for about five seconds," Stuart said conspiratorially with a wink. Soon, the three of them were cracking open cold beers and chatting happily, making a surprisingly natural trio.

Leaving them to it, I looked at Ronan instead. He was keeping his distance, plainly harbouring a residual grudge from their interactions a week before in the Conventos raid, not to mention whatever had just happened across the lawn. He had always been an argumentative person, but it was so unusual to see him in constant conflict with literally everyone he came across; he enjoyed a social gathering as much as anyone else. I hoped he and Dom could at least stay on positive terms throughout the evening; they had only just patched things up.

"Ronan and Stuart really got into it last week," Shereen offered quietly, noticing the direction of my gaze. "Honestly though? It barely matters over what. It was dumb. Wren had things well in hand."

"Neither Lennie nor Ronan have spoken to us about it since," I said, "but I can still tell something's off."

"It was awesome," Alanna said, her eyes glazing over as she remembered the raid. "We cleared them out entirely."

I wasn't used to speaking with a Wielder who took pleasure in direct combat; the Druids were so consistently spiritual, if not remorseful after a battle.

"So, what's Ronan's issue then?"

"I have no idea," Wren said, joining Alanna, Shereen, and me in the four deck chairs. "He did just as much damage as the rest of us. Maybe he's feeling guilty? Which he shouldn't be, obviously. But he and Stuart clashed on how the magic was *handled.*"

I watched as Ronan approached the group of men staring down into the charcoal grill. Dom put his arm around Ronan's shoulder and gave him a quick shake of welcome. I relaxed slightly. "Ronan's been off this summer. I haven't known him long enough to guess exactly why but …"

"I've known him for a little while," Wren said. "The Seattle Knaves have come up to Vancouver on occasion to help, and vice versa with the Druids. Last week wasn't the first time we've crossed paths. I know Sean and Graham too. Have you met them yet?"

I watched as Ronan migrated back into things once more, grinning along with the rest of them at last. "I've met Sean briefly, but not Graham."

"Graham Barron? He's a riot," Shereen offered. "But it's Lindsey you'll want to watch out for. She's a force. She and Ronan were apparently a thing once, a *very* long time ago. But she left him in the dust."

"I honestly can't picture them together," Alanna said as she lit a joint.

I looked towards the four men: two Knaves, a Druid, and an otherworldly Celt. There was clearly a unique dynamic forming, much like the one I was in with the three Wielders seated around me.

"Is Lindsey from Seattle too?" I asked.

"No, she's Scottish, like Graham. Spends a fair bit of time in Vancouver though—she's got family there. Honestly, the Knaves and Druids are more alike than they are different. But a lot of Druids seem to struggle to accept that," Alanna said wistfully as she offered me a hoot, which I gratefully accepted.

"I honestly didn't even know you all existed," I said and grinned awkwardly.

"It's no matter. We're all on the same side in the long run," Wren said, adding brightness to Alanna's contemplative tone. She looked towards the group of men, who now seemed relaxed and happy.

"Tell us more about yourself, Julia," Shereen said, and soon we were laughing and chatting happily about growing up on the West Coast.

In the end, the Knaves were truly delightful company. They brought with them a boatload of energy and passion, and I could now easily see why Lennie had fallen in line with them. My inner hearth burned keen and bright throughout the evening, and despite the continued lack of Bearers, I felt a fast kinship with the group of Knaves who had joined our inner ranks.

The following morning, we set to work. It was quickly apparent that, just as the Knaves enjoyed a good party, they were equally as diligent about their purpose. "Work hard, play hard" would serve as a fitting mission statement for them.

"We'll need to get you caught up on what's been happening in L.A.," Wren said to Dom as she procured her large tablet and placed it in front of him at the kitchen table. The two of them clearly spoke the same language when it came to group dynamics. However, Wren openly expressed her lack of knowledge about classical battle tactics and gladly sought Dom's help. "I want to pick your brain on a few things. Lennie said you would be able to help." She sat down beside him, fully engaged.

"Oh, let's have a look then," Dom said, feigning hesitation. Soon the pair had launched into an exploration of a draft plan to infiltrate one of Cassius's major strongholds. The tower, which apparently sat in the heart of Downtown Los Angeles, housed several of his satellite "shadow corporations," and since his disappearance, this was where most of the action seemed to be happening—or at least, where the majority of his known underlings were currently stationed. Most notably, a Wraith by the name of Caleb, who was apparently nearly as evil as The Child of Rome himself.

Lennie was seated across from Dom at the table, wearing his usual noise-cancelling headphones while typing away furiously on his laptop. I had to commend him for adapting to the activity of the Oregon house; it was a far cry from the solitude found in the quiet corners of our Ireland home when he'd visited us there.

Suddenly, I felt shaky about what my expected role would be in today's endeavours. To no one's surprise, Dom was a natural addition to the group. Everyone seemed so dynamic today, each of them carrying out their unspoken, preassigned roles—even Ronan, who remained as dedicated to his research as ever. But where did I, the quilt examination, and my shoddy Bearing magic fit in to it all?

I felt comparably stagnant.

"Julia," Stuart said tentatively, "did you want to join us outside for some weapons training? Lennie mentioned you had shown an interest."

I looked up from my second cup of coffee that morning, surprised to be included. "Sure! But ... I'll warn you, I'm a complete novice."

Alanna chuckled. "Don't worry. I can already tell you'll be a natural. With a reach like that, how could you not be?" she said, stretching out her shorter arms in example.

"Julia used to be quite skilled with a dagger. You'd all be wise to watch your backs once she catches on," Dom said, his eyes remaining on task as a familiar cheeky grin spread across his face; I made a mental note to ask him more about this comment when we were in private. Truthfully, I had reasonably assumed that, at some point in my various histories, I had fought in close quarters, but I doubted any of it would come to light in the here and now.

I was effectively starting from scratch.

"Don't worry, Julia. Stuart's an expert with a dagger," Shereen said. "You're learning from the best."

Ronan, who had already been up for hours working on his own research, had the unfortunate timing of walking into the kitchen precisely as those words were uttered. He snorted, then immediately turned on his heel, exiting the room as quickly as he had arrived. I knew that he was also strong with a dagger, as I had witnessed at the battle, but no doubt their tactics would be wholly different in play.

"The blade Lennie gave you is a great one to start with," Stuart said, opening the door and gesturing for our exit.

"Oh, you've seen it?" I asked, leaving the shade of the kitchen and stepping out into the early morning sunshine. I had brought the unusual dagger to breakfast with me, expecting rightly that it would come up at some point in the conversation.

"I have actually," Stuart said with a broad grin, "since I made it. I'm not just good at using fires to cook meat. I'm actually considered a 'master of the forge' amongst the Knaves. I've studied for years in both the composition and use of our weapons."

"Fascinating," I said, turning my own blade over in my hand. It nestled perfectly in my palm and was light as a feather.

"Our craft was born during the industrial age," he said, "which explains why the Druids are so averse to it: It flies in the face of everything they stand for."

"Well, *some* Druids," Shereen clarified, tossing her eyes towards the house. "The more open-minded ones are fine with it. And look at Lennie. He actually prefers it. Not that he *considers* himself a Druid, I suppose, but his parents were, obviously. He said something the other day about how much more sustainable being a Knave *actually* is."

Stuart nodded. "It's become a bit of a lost art over the past century, weapons forging. With humankind's need for more modern armaments taking over, our original makers lost their means to 'keep the lights on,' as you say, so the skill dwindled in parallel. We're working to bring it back though. Our kind have taken over a lot of the graphite mines that shut down in the early nineties. And Shereen's actually just started working with the forge too."

"He's taken me on as an apprentice," she said happily. "I like working with my hands."

Beside us, Alanna dropped down a heavy-looking wooden crate she had just hauled over from the back of Stuart's truck. She really was extremely strong. As she removed the lid, I was practically blinded by the gold and silver weapons within. Blinking several times, I realized it wasn't just the sun's reflection that was causing the effect; they were imbued with magic.

"Incredible," I said, slightly bleary-eyed. I stepped closer to peer inside the box as my eyes adjusted. It contained a handful of blades in all different shapes and sizes. I looked up at Stuart, who was now wearing sunglasses, evidently having anticipated the effect.

"Sorry, I should have warned you," he said with a laugh. "Some of this batch 'adds light to the dark,' so they would have activated while inside the closed box."

My mind was immediately flooded with questions so I started with what I thought was the simplest one of all. "So ... how do you know which blade is for you?"

"Starting with the hardest question first!" Stuart said. "I like your style!"

Whoops.

"Essentially ... know your power, know your blade." He reached for a magnificent-looking short sword with ripples of silver and gold throughout its blade; it reminded me somewhat of Damascus steel. "But most of us acquire a bit of an arsenal over time, depending on our needs."

I pondered for a moment. "Okay, so ... are they mostly used to heighten your skill then?"

"Sometimes," Alanna said. "Once you get good at using them, that's when they really sing. But more often, especially for beginners, they are used to cover a deficit."

"Sing?" I asked, puzzling further; this was some pretty specific and spectacular Wielding magic.

Stuart pulled out a pair of long golden blades with inset black stones at the end of each handle and grinned dangerously. "'Sing' is a term we use to describe when the weapon and their Wielder live up to their aligned potential. As you build in skill and connection to your chosen weapons, so does the potential for effectiveness."

"Amazing," I said.

"Another thing is that you might not have a need for that specific blade every time. Perhaps you want a pair of blades that work powerfully in unison—" He suddenly whipped his duo through the air so quickly they appeared as a blur. He paused again, looking suddenly lethal. "So, you might choose these two if you were fighting several foes at once. They're helpful because they provide extra force, which sustains the length of time you're actually able to fight."

I thought of Lennie running towards us on the ramparts, with his dual, curved golden swords, and things began to click into place. "So, do you have … recipes? Or how do you know what mix will create the desired effect *and* match with the intended Wielder?"

"That's the fun of it!" Shereen said. "It's a bit like throwing spaghetti against the wall and seeing what sticks. We have some formulations that have been passed down through the generations, but each blade has its own story in the end. So, it's a bit tricky to stick to any single set of rules."

Stuart moved his head enthusiastically, eyes alight; this was clearly his heart's calling. "Of course, there's even more to it than that, but at its base, it's all about having an awareness around your own strengths and weaknesses and building from there."

More questions blossomed on my end. "So, what about my blade? How did you choose what it and *I* needed?"

"Ah! Well, Lennie told me you don't have a lot of experience with hand-to-hand, so I riffed on that a bit to create a dagger that might help you out under pressure. Think of your weapon as an extension of yourself, not only physically but magically too. If you're needing combat skills, but don't have a lot of them, a specific design can help bridge that gap. If you *do* have the skills, then they'll only increase your power further."

I was somewhat confused, but Shereen spoke up to clarify. "So, like … you don't have a lot of close-range skills—which is fine, as it takes years of practice to master that anyways—but this blade," she said, reaching out for mine, "rarely misses its target, especially when thrown directly towards an enemy."

I wondered how they knew this, but then Alanna read my mind. "Stu took it for a bit of a test drive when we raided the Conventos. It's *definitely* good at its job," she said, raising her eyebrows.

"I've named it *Wraith Slayer*," Stuart said, completely unabashed.

I gulped.

"Right." I stared at the three of them; they all shared a strange look that could almost be described as elation around their mission. I wondered if one effect of permitting the weapons to "sing" was, in fact, euphoria.

I spent the next twenty minutes together with Stuart, Alanna, and Shereen, learning how to handle the blade properly, which started at the most basic level of learning how to safely remove and return it to a leather sheath on my calf. Next came learning how to connect to the Wielding power embedded in it, if or when I chose to thrust it into an enemy. Initially, I felt awkward and clumsy, but by the end, I was managing well enough; it would seem throwing it was a greater strength of mine than actually stabbing something at close range.

"See? Told you that you were a natural," Alanna said when I successfully managed a series of more complicated moves in succession, followed by throwing my dagger into a burlap target beside Stuart's truck. I jumped up and down in excitement.

It *did* feel good to use the blade.

Suddenly, I heard clapping from the deck, where Wren, Lennie, and Dom had finally joined us outside. Ronan was still nowhere to be seen.

Dom hopped off the deck and strode to my side. "Well done, Julia!"

"Thanks," I said and lay back onto the dry grass, breathing heavily. While I was far from considering myself "in shape" these days, wielding the blade had been exhilarating, leaving me with something like a runner's high. "How did it go inside?"

"Dom here is a genius," Wren said, taking Lennie's hand in her own.

"That's perhaps a bit of a stretch," Lennie teased, but based on the peaceable look on his face, he agreed.

I laughed, then suddenly realized how thirsty I was and also that I desperately needed the washroom. "I'll be right back," I said to Dom, kissing him on the cheek and taking off for the indoors.

Exiting the bathroom several minutes later, I lingered in the kitchen for a few moments as I gulped back a cool glass of water. I noticed through the window that Dom, Lennie, and Wren were taking their turns to check out the different blades Stuart had brought along. Unfortunately, this meant I was alone inside, effectively leaving myself open to more questioning should Ronan appear.

My intuition was irritatingly correct, as usual. Ronan's voice filled the air behind me. "Julia, if you're done out there, I'd like to pick your brain for a bit."

"Oh? Honestly, Ronan, I'm pretty tired right now. That was hard work!" I said with a laugh, an arguably poor attempt to keep things light. It wasn't *entirely* untrue; I did want to go put my feet up for a while or maybe connect with Dom once he was finished having a go at it with the blades. But I also wasn't in the mood for *this* conversation, right now.

He bristled. "You keep avoiding me. It's not like I'm eager to make you do something you don't want to do, but we *need* to talk about what happened. And what you *know.*"

I swallowed hard. He wasn't going to let this die. I stared longingly out the window at the others and let out a slow sigh. "Sorry. Is this for your research or ... what are we doing here?"

"Never mind," he said as he slammed his glass down and exited the room once more.

CHAPTER 9

Time passed quickly with the Knaves on site. However, they also brought with them such lively energy that I found myself surprisingly exhausted in their presence. The fact was, as much as I enjoyed their company, the Knaves just went a little bit harder than I was used to, almost like they vibrated on a different frequency. Their meetings would last for hours without anyone tiring out, cooking dinner was a social experience that would extend well into the evening, and someone was almost always practising blade skills loudly in the backyard during any perceived "downtime."

In Ireland, I had become accustomed to spending extended time with Wielders. But they, of course, had been Druids, who enjoyed peaceful conversation, meditation time, and pleasurably crafting simmering pots of soup to be savoured after a long walk across the hillside. Ronan, someone I would have previously described as high-strung, seemed positively placid compared to the Knaves.

Frankly, their collective arrival had been a significant adjustment to my psyche, even if I did enjoy them individually as people. Truly, they were wonderful and kind. Yet, more than once, I found myself wondering if the magic stored in their blades didn't *make* them hyper, if not restless. Frenetic, even. After all, they wore source magic literally on their hips.

I was exhausted by it.

Over time, I noticed that Stuart seemed to have boundless energy as well, particularly after a long session of blade practice outside; he just didn't seem to tire out like normal people did after strenuous exercise. Wren and Lennie would regularly sneak off outside for what I assumed were marathon sex sessions, returning long after the rest of us had gone to sleep. And while Alanna and Shereen usually went to bed early, they would be up and ready to go at the crack of dawn almost every single day.

"Dom, they just don't stop," I said to him one night as we collapsed into bed, bone-tired. "It's like one of them is always awake. Is that a *thing* for them?"

He laughed it off but didn't disagree.

As much as I liked the idea of the kind of magic that might offer continuous, renewed energy, it didn't seem to affect me the same way as it did them; if anything, it was keeping me up at night. With this theory in mind, I started storing my new blade away from our bed at night, hoping to alleviate my worsening insomnia. Though Dom jived better than I did with their energy levels, he too was getting tired out after several weeks with them as company.

"Whatever you think you need to do," he had said groggily when I slipped out of bed to relocate my blade. As usual, magic didn't affect him the same way it did me, but I had a hunch he was feeling it too, since as soon as I delivered the dagger to a spot above the fridge, he slept like an absolute baby.

Happily, on the last day of August, I found myself completely alone outside of the beach house in a rare moment of calm. No Dom, no Knaves, and no *Ronan*. Thank the Goddess. During yet another impromptu team meeting, where Lennie, Stuart, and Ronan were undoubtedly set to spar, I had quietly snuck outside in search of respite. I could feel Dom's eyes on my back as I exited the front door, but he would know where to find me if necessary.

We had already danced around the threat building in California for the better part of two weeks. On the whole, the group—or more effectively, Ronan versus everyone else—had spent far more time with the debate around the *ethics* of magic than on the actual threat at hand. While I didn't always disagree with Ronan's viewpoint, it was quickly becoming an irritating trend among our allies to get bogged down in the wrong sorts of details. Dom also shared in my frustration at the lack of actual forward momentum, but he clearly felt a growing affinity towards the Knaves as well, whether he cared to admit it or not.

With my feet intuitively leading me to the large oak tree in the front yard, I settled down onto my knees and gently ran my hands along its bark in gratitude for the peace and solitude. It was indeed a thin place, and I took a deep breath, willing the tempest within my magical core to settle.

On top of feeling somewhat claustrophobic with our current arrangements, my struggles with the heat of August had followed me all the way down to Oregon, spurring me to ponder all that had happened over the past year. A mere twelve months earlier, I had been cleaning out my grandmother's attic and preparing for my final semester at the University of British Columbia. I had no set plans for the future, let alone any recollection of who Dom was or what he meant to me. Now, I was sharing a house with a horde of Wielders and an otherworldly prince, who were debating the finer points of magical cultivation instead of focusing on a plan to defeat a relentless Sorcerer, who just so happened to also want my head on a pike. Not to mention, we *still* had no additional Bearers in our midst.

Despite the attempt to calm myself by the tree, I felt further disappointment settle into my belly.

One year ago, I had also discovered the quilt, which still managed to maintain its mystery, despite my best efforts. So many things had changed in my life, and yet a disturbing amount had remained the same. Ronan still managed to get under my skin at the best of times (big surprise), and Lennie's proclivity for fuelling conflict remained, even with Wren in the picture and his growing kinship with Dom in effect. For his part, my *fiancé*, the natural-born leader, still struggled some days to pull himself away from the centre of the action to view things from a broader perspective. I missed him when he toiled away for hours, discussing logistics with the others, even if he did try his best to approach the task with more balance than he had in the past.

"Dom, this is all starting to feel awfully familiar," I had said in the early hours one morning when he was preparing himself to argue the finer points of some very specific raiding tactic. I was decidedly grumpy from a poor night's sleep and hadn't appreciated starting my day with the déjà-vu-like experience.

"I know, I know ... I'm so sorry, Julia. I'm really trying to reprogram myself, but it's just so hard sometimes. I get so wrapped up in it all."

"You're not even a magic user," I had said irritably as I pulled the covers over my head, but then I apologized immediately for how unfair I was being. "Sorry, that was uncalled for."

"It's not your fault, love. This has been *a lot*," Dom said. "I was really starting to enjoy just having you to myself too." Then he joined me in my impromptu blanket fort with a peaceable grin, completely unoffended.

We had snuggled for a bit, attempting to distract ourselves with more primal callings, but my mind was fully awake for the day, worries in tow. "I just … I still feel so unprepared for any kind of conflict. Like, yes, I've learned some blade skills and everything—and I own *Wraith Slayer*—but it just doesn't feel like enough. I don't feel like enough."

"Of course, you're enough, love. But … don't think I haven't noticed the lack of Bearers in our midst either. Because I have, and it's obviously an issue we need to address."

He wasn't wrong.

The fact remained that my Bearing magic was untrained and unpredictable. Not even twenty-four hours before, I had been so frustrated over yet another three-hour-long meeting that had gone absolutely nowhere that I managed to shatter an entire tray of drying dishes while stepping into the kitchen for a breather. I'd thought that being around so many Wielders would allow my own version of Wielding magic to thrive, but instead, I couldn't do shit. I knew Witches didn't Wield in the same way, but this just felt embarrassing.

Alanna and Shereen had kindly helped me clean up the mess, as they too were reaching a breaking point with the circular conversations, despite their seemingly limitless energy.

"I think our time here is running out," Shereen had said. Alanna nodded solemnly.

And indeed, it was decided that the Knaves and Lennie would be moving on towards Los Angeles in the next few days to continue their recon, and Ronan would be heading south with them. He would have preferred to stick with Dom, but Dom had other ideas, responding to the suggestion with a stern *"absolutely not."* Ronan got on well enough with Wren, so he would at least have one ally for the voyage. Some Druids were already down there too, apparently, including Sean, so that was positive.

Dom and I, however, were still working out the details of our next steps. I had made it next to nowhere with the quilt, and our continued mapping and research sessions had remained as dry as the sunburnt grass beneath my feet.

Regardless, I knew it would soon be time for us to move as well.

But where? It all felt complicated, truth be told, and I just craved a moment of silence to figure out our next best steps. Attempting to push my worries aside, I closed my eyes to connect to the roots of the tree and the not-so-distant pull of the ocean beyond.

"Julia?"

Dom's voice brought me back to my senses under the coastal oak before I'd even had a chance to contemplate anything. He sounded extremely ragged. I turned slowly, noticing that he was also rather red in the cheeks.

"Oh no, what's happened?"

He gestured for me to stay seated. "Nothing. Well, no, not *nothing* ... but I needed to step out as well. You've got the right idea."

I watched as he settled down beside me, his body visibly weary. I wasn't annoyed by his interruption, despite my cravings for solitude. Dom could also be incredibly grounding for me, and so we sat in silence for a time, intuitively anchoring each other in place. Co-regulation at its finest. Above us, the clouds moved slowly, creating a brief sense of timelessness in a world where time seemed to be constantly nipping at our heels.

After a while, I spoke up. "Dom, it's time to visit Bernadette."

"I know," he said. "I was coming out here to say the same thing. And besides, I need a break from these *muppets* anyway."

I took his hand and kissed it gently. "So, it's settled then?"

"As far as these things can be." He looked up as Ronan suddenly exited the front door in a heat of anger and took off down the block running.

"What *exactly* are they after in L.A.?" I asked. "Besides gaining intel on Cassius's minions."

I already knew there were a concerning number of Wraiths gathering in and around one of Cassius's main strongholds. Moonlighting as various corporations, these groups were participating in some extremely shady doings. And that was just what was visible from the outside. Apparently, both the Knaves and Druids shared great concerns about what was happening on the inside too.

"Wren is fairly certain they're hiding something big. Perhaps some sort of new weapon or tactical force, and the Knaves want the inside scoop."

"Okay, but then I just don't understand why everyone can't seem to come to an agreement on the next steps. Shouldn't it be simpler?"

Dom shook his head ruefully. "Honestly? I think when it boils down to it, the Knaves just want a fight. It's what we keep dancing around. Ronan and the Druids believe intel is the answer, only acting offensively when it's needed. The Knaves ... well, they don't need quite so much provocation. They want any and all Wraiths wiped out."

"And what about you?" I asked, not sure I wanted to hear the answer.

"Oh Julia, you know I love a good fight as much as the rest of them. But this is reckless. We've fought too hard and too long to just run and gun ourselves into a dangerous situation—"

"I'm sorry, *'run and gun'?*" I asked, chuckling in spite of myself. My mind went towards video games and basketball, surprised by what I recognized as a wholly modern turn of phrase.

"Stuart said it—but you know what I mean. It's not the type of tactical offence I prefer. There needs to be a plan, and ..." His voice trailed off.

And leadership, I thought but didn't push the issue, since clearly, he was also sensing what we had suspected since the advent of the new Prophecy: They needed the World Ruler.

"And the other Druids?" I asked, redirecting the conversation.

"Well, we've met Sean, obviously—he's of the same mind as Ronan. Apparently, he's already on his way down to Los Angeles as we speak. And then there's also Graham and Lindsey."

"Have you met her?"

"I have," Dom said chuckling. "She's a force."

"That's what everyone keeps saying." I was curious about her, but I also self-consciously wondered what people might be saying about *me*.

"Graham is too though. He's an absolute beast. They are quite the pair in battle," Dom said.

"Are they together?"

"They're both Scottish. Cousins, I think."

"Does that automatically make them cousins?" I said, laughing.

"No, no," Dom said with a grin, "they're *actually* related."

I pondered the existence of these new Druids and found myself comforted at the idea of meeting them when we arrived further south. Hopefully, they would at least bring a calmer energy to the situation. Even strange, hyper energy aside, my intuitive Bearing magic *did* align closer to the Druids than it did the Knaves. Dom, on the other hand, seemed to really "get" the Knaves with their more forthcoming tactics. I hoped that Sean, Graham, and Lindsey would bring some tonic to the turmoil. *Balance to the force.*

"Lindsey's Ronan's ex, right?" I asked, snooping somewhat. I knew Dom loved good gossip though, despite his denials.

"She is," he said. "He was absolutely shattered when she left him apparently. It was right before I met him, and he was still a complete mess. I guess, in some fucked-up way, we were able to commiserate as bachelors in that moment ... through our shared loneliness."

"I bet," I said, pushing down the guilt I always felt at the notion of Dom being alone in his search for me. My mind wandered towards Ronan then, who had just appeared on the drive. He ignored us entirely as he skirted the house and made for the kitchen entrance. He looked lonely, and I felt for him.

What was more unsettling, however, was the part of me that knew Ronan and I also had work to do around his mission to understand how the Wraith magic truly worked. I wasn't sure how I could help but had a distinct sense that my future included it. Still, I also felt a strange sense of dread surrounding the task.

"He's really not himself right now, and I'll be glad to be rid of him for a bit," Dom said, truthfully.

"Are you finding it hard?" I asked as we stood up to make our way back towards the house. It was almost suppertime, and we were apparently on salad duty. Dom didn't really see the point of salad without added protein.

This was going to go well.

"A bit. But our friendship has always had its ups and downs, ebbs and flows. Ronan's a bit of a troubled soul, despite his shiny exterior. So, it's not like this is new or anything. He's probably just going through a phase."

I thought of Ronan's careers, cars, and general demeanour through life. "Shiny" was definitely one way to describe it. Another might be polished to the point of being hard. But I had also experienced a deep friendship from him too. Kindness even. Hell, he had even made the pact with me up on the ramparts and meant it. He was truly loyal to both to us and to the cause.

I did understand what Dom was saying though: There was an inner turmoil there that perhaps remained unaddressed. Ronan's dogged persistence also continually got in his own way. "Hmm ..."

"It's why Lindsey left him, I think. He just wasn't dealing with his shit, and she got tired of it—not for lack of effort on her part though. I think she really *did* try to help him. And I know he doesn't resent her or anything like that, even if he hates talking about it. If anything, she's a symbol of his own failure to open up," Dom said, reading my line of thought. "I hope it doesn't cause any problems in Los Angeles though."

"Do you think it will? We're all fully functioning adults here, aren't we?" I asked, realizing the apparent irony of my question as we crossed the threshold into the house.

Stuart, Wren, Alanna, and Shereen were all outside near the barbeque, laughing jovially as if nothing was wrong at all. Lennie, meanwhile, was seated at the kitchen table with his headphones on once more, pounding away furiously. Behind him, Ronan was chopping onions with equal vigour, apparently unaware of our arrival.

"No offence to the guy, but we don't exactly have time to be working through decades-old baggage when there's a fight at hand," Dom said under his breath.

"Hark who's talking," I said quietly in jest.

I realized then we were all more alike than we were different, whether we cared to admit it or not. Each of our stories were woven together, a collective tapestry of complicated, meaningful, and *emotional* moving parts.

I had been feeling like we were spinning our wheels for weeks, but perhaps that wasn't the case at all. Relationships were being fought for and forged in real time, every move pressing its influence towards our ultimate goal. Things *were* happening, it's just that transformations were often painful, and sometimes unseen.

After all, it takes a lot of pressure to turn shit into diamonds. If only this particular form of gem creation could help us find out what Cassius was really up to.

CHAPTER 10

Exiting his sleek gold Mercedes Benz E-Class, Cassius crouched down before leaning back on his heels, surveying the landscape ahead. This … *place* … was nothing like he had anticipated. In his mind, a map such as this should be kept hidden deep within the bowels of a vast fortress, somewhere out of reach to any but the most skilled tracker. Perhaps somewhere remote like Siberia or high in the mountains of Northern China. Instead, he found himself looking headlong into what could only be described as a rural American junkyard. A backwater shithole.

Covered in the scrap metal of half-buried pickup trucks, twisted greenhouse frames, and discarded oil tanks, endless acres of wasteland spread out crudely before his eyes. This really *was* the last place he'd expected to find a valuable artifact, but stranger things had happened over the course of his long life. Perhaps it served as a fortress in its own right; surely the chain-link fence topped in spiralling barbed-wire gave an impression of some sort of fortification, at least to the average man.

For him, it was a feeble attempt at discouraging trespassers.

Beyond the fence, in what he presumed to be the centre of the disaster, was a flat-topped, faded-brown trailer. From the hillside above it all, he squinted but could glean little else about the structure itself. Still, he knew without a doubt this was where the map was located, largely because it made the most sense, but more importantly, because he could *feel it*.

Placing the palm of his hand on the ground, he reached out with his senses for any nearby magic sources he might be able to tap into. He quickly discovered that the place was utterly destitute but for the map or, at the very least, its enchanted container. Yes, the map was likely guarded by some sort of feeble spell, which was serving now as more of a beacon than protection. It would be easy enough to capture the prize as there were definitely no magic users here. Yet, he would still have to be careful not to expend too much of his own magic in the process, just in case.

Each scrap of magic within him mattered now more than ever.

Breathing out loudly through his nose, Cassius used his hand on the ground to push himself back up to a standing position, his deteriorating muscles and ligaments threatening to snap as he rose and then steadied himself against his newly purchased vehicle. He wasn't used to travelling without a driver, let alone pumping his own gas, and was repelled by how frail he had become during the past two months as he followed one dead end after another in his search for the source material. The hunt for the *Codex Druidicus* and its knowledge: the power of the ancient Druids that he would turn loose on their modern counterparts. Yet, he couldn't risk any of his underlings knowing his mission—for the Wraiths were also descendants of this original darkness—so he would have to withstand the discomfort for a bit longer.

To his satisfaction, near the end of August, Cassius had discovered a lead: evidence that the book had been *intentionally* concealed hundreds of years ago. Having spent the better part of two weeks scouring old letters in a private French library, he'd discovered that details of the Codex's whereabouts had fallen into the hands of a very well-documented and prestigious family, and that this very family had a map to the Codex's hidden location and guarded it well. And so, while his mission had become that much more arduous—the map being an unexpected step in the process—he finally had some breadcrumbs to follow through the centuries.

According to the letters, once the family gleaned the importance of what the map protected—due to continued threats landing at their doorstep over the years—they had hidden it. Over time, the same family had eventually immigrated to the Americas to build their own empire, taking the map with them. It had come as no surprise to Cassius when he discovered that the family's vast fortune had collapsed; these things happened so often to weaker men, especially when they attempted to make it big in the "New World." Even as the family fell into ruin, the importance of the map was never forgotten, though its ultimate purpose was. So, utter revulsion or no, here he was in rural Louisiana, where the map apparently resided.

He walked forward several paces, gold watch glinting boldly in the sunlight. With a flick of that very wrist, he passed through the locked chain-link gates with a click. At this, several Dobermans charged eagerly towards him, jaws snapping at his unexpected arrival. However, once the beasts reached a two-metre proximity, they stopped dead in their tracks at the sight of him. As usual, his glamour didn't work on four-legged beasts. Whining in terror, they turned heel and rocketed back towards the trailer.

He showed mercy and let the beasts live; dogs had their uses, after all.

Both rats and chickens scattered at the sight of him as he delved deeper into the junkyard towards his destination. He was disgusted to spot a sow and her piglets rooting through a massive pile of ripped trash bags between a rusting school bus and a slanted outbuilding with broken windows. The associated boar lay sprawled on a shredded and stained mattress, looking bristled and menacing.

Cassius returned his eyes to the trailer ahead. He knew it was worth the discomfort of witnessing such a repugnant place; the map was priceless in its own right and would undoubtedly lead him to the Codex.

He had first heard rumours of the *Codex Druidicus* during the mid-fourteenth century in France, when the Black Death was efficiently decimating most of Europe and the rest of the world. No stranger to plagues, he had played his cards deftly and with precision as soon as word of the sickness reached his ears. In fact, during the short four-year period, he had managed to carve out a sizeable profit for himself by acquiring properties and warehousing various mercantile outfits throughout much of Western Europe. Anyone he encountered would marvel at his ability to travel throughout the realm and yet remain untouched by the buboes. He would usually swear he had no idea why he was immune and spot free, though perhaps it was just that God had smiled on him more than other men.

That, of course, was a lie.

But how does one explain to a disease-ridden street urchin begging for scraps of food between piles of dead bodies that you've been siphoning magic from Bearers for centuries to sustain an *almost* immortal existence? No, that was far too much explanation for anyone, let alone the trash that littered those streets. And so, he had continued to maintain an outward display of piety, a king among mortals, a monarch among men. He might have even felt something akin to pleasure at the sight of all of the death and chaos, if not for his constant hunger. Even then, it gnawed at him relentlessly.

And yet, this was a time period when he had also been exceptionally powerful.

Having vanquished the World Ruler and the Witch only twenty years previously in Ireland, he was just beginning to hit his stride when the plague knocked on his door. He had, of course, taken its arrival to be a good sign; any opportunity to gain footholds throughout the realm gave him a distinct advantage against the Prophecy—and brought him one step closer to immortality. If he had only known then what he did now, he might have searched for the Codex back then. But at that time, the tome and its secrets had still been a rumour. A myth. The book would have been exceedingly unlikely to help him, given how powerful he already was. Today, he saw the usefulness of it as a tool to defeat the Wielders protecting the Witch, to use their own power against them just as his Wraiths did.

Hindsight, however, was an adversary he refused to acknowledge. That seemed to be something he and the World Ruler held in common.

As he approached the dilapidated trailer, Cassius could hear foul music blasting from somewhere within. Looking down, he noticed a heap of glass bottles and beer cans outside of one of the small, filthy windows just as a gnarled hand reached out and added another can to the growing pile. He realized then it was quite possible the map had already been ruined beyond repair, regardless of its container. How could someone inhabiting *this* place keep an item of that importance safe from destruction?

He pushed the thought from his mind.

Cassius, of course, possessed several libraries worth of treasured books and artifacts—his vast collection of art alone was a valuable fortune. Most of it he had paid for outright; Cassius liked to acquire things with his own means. However, many of the pieces were technically stolen, though that depended on your definition of theft. He took great pride in the seemingly endless resources he'd had available to him throughout the centuries, but what he was seeking now would require information beyond anything he held in his dominion.

Face to face with the rusted door of the trailer, Cassius momentarily considered knocking. After all, it *was* polite. He then looked down at his knuckles, the ones that weren't cloaked in the external glamour, and thought better of himself.

"Open up," he commanded. No response came.

He spoke again, regretfully accessing precious magical stores to amplify his voice. "You will open this door at once!" He took several steps back. The dogs were still nowhere to be seen.

Soon, the door was flung open, and a visibly drunk man staggered out onto the ground before him. He wore knee-high rubber boots and a high-visibility vest. It had clearly been a long time since the man had engaged in any form of personal care. His bald-topped head was a stark contrast to the six inches of hair that hung from a line below his ears. His beard was of equal length, though it stuck out coarsely in all directions from his sideburns to his chin.

He was also missing a chunk of his nose, over which he eyed Cassius with scrutiny.

"Who the hell are you?" the man asked, slurring his words.

Cassius said nothing.

"Where the *fuck* are my dogs?" the man asked, eyes darting left and right.

In one smooth motion, Cassius reached out his hand and clenched his fist in the air, effectively collapsing the man's airways without laying a finger on him. Once the man hit the ground and finished thrashing, Cassius stepped around his lifeless form and entered the dank trailer alone.

It was somehow even more disgusting inside than he had anticipated. Cassius kept his arms close to his body as he moved from the kitchen towards a musty seating room. Beyond that was likely a bedroom, but he wouldn't need to enter the space. The map was extremely close now, but where was it hidden?

He closed his eyes momentarily and sought out the enchantment, finding it almost immediately. A hideous framed velvet painting of a kneeling child with a basket of flowers hung above a small tube television. Cassius knew the map would be tucked behind it. Pulling the painting from the wall, he smashed the glass in one swift motion and discovered a sheet of thin velum paper, rolled and tucked in the back. There it was. Fully intact and seemingly untouched by the fool who lay dead outside.

He had done his research about the place, of course. Or at least, about the family that had supposedly been handling the map for generations. The man outside was apparently "Bob" or, more specifically, Robert David Timothée Dubois, *the third*. He had inherited the land, and the atrocious painting, from his "wealthy" parents when they'd died several decades ago. Not knowing its importance, his parents had protected its secret just the same. Cassius doubted they had trusted Bob with the same information.

Hastily tucking the map into the inside of his now ill-fitting custom suit, Cassius exited the space almost as quickly as he had entered it. Stepping around the dead body without looking down, he whistled several times in quick succession. Soon, the pack of Dobermans could be seen peering around from behind the trailer, and Cassius gestured absently towards the corpse. If Bob had taken even half as good care of them as he had the land he'd inherited, they were likely *very* hungry.

Returning to his parked car, Cassius slid in and immediately ground the gears into reverse, wishing to leave the place as quickly as possible. Gravel kicked up behind him, and he felt his body strain painfully as the vehicle responded to his will. However, both his secrecy and expediency were paramount; the immediate inspection of the map could wait until he was somewhere more private.

He calmed his racing mind all the way back to the interstate. It wasn't in his nature to rush into things; after all, time had always been his to hold as he pleased, even if he wasn't fully immortal. Yet, these days, with the most recent regeneration of his enemies, things were *different*, and he now felt time biting at his heels almost as often as his gnawing hunger.

He needed a new strategy before he was chewed to pieces.

Cassius had, of course, vacillated though various plans over the past twelve months in response to his enemies' inane actions, responding accordingly based on centuries of experience. Yes, the Witch had somehow managed to thwart him at the auditorium, and then by a sheer act of providence, decimated his army on the precipice. But he now knew those to be oversights on his part. He had been too eager, too hungry, and too hasty. He had also placed too much trust in that fool Desmond, the Indovino, who had (of course) failed him miserably. If Desmond had demonstrated even a minute awareness of the power he Wielded through divination, Cassius might have kept him alive. At the very least, he could have continued to collect information from the Indovino's Sight, a legacy of the man's distant Druidic heritage.

He did not regret killing him, however.

Cassius had relied too heavily on the past when he should have turned his thinking towards the future. But that didn't matter now. The original Prophecy had been irrevocably broken, and that was all that mattered. He was now *truly* free to do as he pleased for the first time in a *very* long time, and the new Prophecy had confirmed it.

The tides had turned in his favour. And he needed to move carefully.

The fact remained that the Witch was immensely powerful. And he now suspected that rather than being his undoing, she (and any magic she carried) was in fact the key to his immortality:

As the Sorcerer seeks to find the grail, spear in hand, to chalice he is bound.

The chalice and the grail. He needed her. They were bound.

Cassius felt for his most powerful weapon, the *Spear of Longinus*. It was currently tucked away in a custom pocket along the inside of his suit jacket—couture being couture, after all. The spear contracted into a simple matte-black baton when stored, but at his touch and command, it would magically bloom at its tip into a pair of gleaming, mismatched blades. It was his greatest creation to date. Since its forging, he had kept it on his person at all times, never knowing when an opportunity might arise to siphon off more of the sweet Bearing elixir, the only thing assuring his survival at the moment. He didn't view this as a weakness though—the blades served as an extension of his own magic. Another tool towards permanent immortality. His evolution. It was part of him now.

Continuing along the highway, Cassius's mind slowed to its usual canter. Deep and contemplative, yet unrelenting.

There were three distinct problems that would need attending before he could finally capture the Witch. All of which would need to be attended to as soon as possible. As valuable as the spear was, it didn't seem to work on dear

Julia. Not yet anyway. And it was also completely useless against Wielders, other than as a stabbing weapon, of course, unless they were secretly stealing magic like Desmond was.

Yes, first he would need to deal with the Wielders: Druids and the like. Those who gathered magic externally and were the preliminary barrier between him and his prize:

For the earthen weapons masters, and tree talkers with open sky above.

The Druids—who he assumed were the *"tree talkers"* in the Prophecy—with their pathetic pouches and feeble battle skills, had always relied on their vast network and boastful cleverness to get ahead. Sheer numbers with not a lot of talent. Sometimes it was hard to believe that his Wraiths shared the same origins. To Cassius's knowledge, when the split between the Wraiths and the modern-day Druids happened centuries ago, the latter had rejected the old ways—the dark ways—and had sought a "natural connection to the earth" instead. These "tree-talking" Druids had turned their backs on the powerful rites of blood and sacrifice. And so, the division between the two was born. It was all laughable, of course. All things that are green and natural can ultimately burn.

The original Druids had also tried to hide and safeguard their secrets through their tradition of oral history. But dark magic required a firmer foundation than mere words. It needed to be locked into ancient texts and powerful grimoires, just as the unknown Roman Sorcerer had done with the Codex centuries before.

And then there were the Knaves. According to his intelligence, this newer sect of Wielders was still actively growing in numbers, particularly in North America. And while they were just another version of the same old thorn in his side, these *"earthen weapons masters"* deserved some credit, at least, for their ingenuity, if nothing else. Plus, they had learned how to use fire to their advantage, which was more than the Druids could say for themselves. He acknowledged the Knaves' forging skills, even though they were still no match for his Wraith blacksmiths. To counter the Knaves' charmed blades, he'd recently sent his Wraiths explicit instructions on how to counter their force. It might not tip the balance in their favour, but it would at least slow them down.

And, of course, neither of their skills with metallurgy were near his calibre; that type of alchemy was reserved for Sorcerers alone. But this was what he needed the book for. The Druid's own dark magic was surely the answer to the Witch's "outer guard." And now that he had the map, he was that much closer to finding the Codex, and once he had it …

Darkness reigns where light cannot, and from its root, the land will rot.

Cassius pulled over off the highway and into an abandoned parking lot. Before him, a dilapidated service station stood all alone, windows broken and boarded. This would have to do. Leaving the car running, he removed the map from his jacket and unrolled it slowly before him. It was immensely old, no doubt preserved over the centuries by the spells that bound it. Even now, away from its unsightly container, he could feel it disintegrating. The map wouldn't last long. Cassius pulled out his cellphone and attempted to take a photo of it, but all the camera produced was a white blur before momentarily malfunctioning. It was probably for the best; even *if* it managed to take a picture, it could be tapped.

Instead, he relied on a far older and more reliable skill: memorization.

It was an unusual representation, with several layers of detail reaching out to him at once. Magic had certainly been involved in its creation, and from his best guess, Bearing magic was holding it together. His hands began to shake at the need; he wouldn't last much longer.

Steadying himself, Cassius concluded that the Codex was still hidden somewhere in the Old World, which made sense. It would have been far too risky to bring it over to America before securing a safehold. Not to mention how often ships sank during the colonization eras. Judging by the disintegration of Bob's family lineage over the generations, they had never discovered the means, or motivation, to move the Codex. In the old days, there was power in knowledge. To be a keeper of valuable information gave you infinite authority. Status. In the New World, money was mistaken for power. But it was an easy distraction and a ruler of weak men. Cassius, of course, had adapted to this with ease, but that wasn't the case for most.

Squinting slightly to gather every last drop of information, it seemed he would need to combine several coordinates, like an enigma, before he could secure the final location. Now that he held the brittle parchment before him, he could see that it wasn't really a map at all. Not in the traditional sense, anyway. Punching the first set of numbers into his GPS, which (much like his hands) was barely functioning, he found himself laughing darkly.

Marrakech. Oh, this was going to be far too easy. He had spent many moons in that place and knew even its murkiest secrets. If anyone could unearth clues there, it was Cassius.

He tossed the map aside, effectively disintegrating it on impact as it hit the seat beside him; any magic that *might* have been available to him from it had long since drifted away. He hated that he noticed such a thing and how desperate he felt for it.

Just as he was about to exit the car, a rusted blue pickup truck appeared on the road. It slowed down at the sight of him and parked in the abandoned lot with his engine still running. Cassius lifted his cellphone to his ear, feigning importance. After several moments, the truck carried on. An unknown amount of time passed before Cassius realized his body had begun to waver in consciousness.

He was almost out of time.

Stepping out of his car, the engine still running, Cassius looked down with disgust at the coating of dirt on his shoes. The air around him was dry and heavy with the dust of harvest, one of his most hated times of year. Checking for any further signs of witnesses, he dragged himself towards the central bay door and peered inside.

It was, indeed, *abandoned.*

With a weak jut of his wrist, the bay door opened, squealing loudly on its seized hinges, just enough for him to fit his car through. Having used what little magic he had left within him to pry the building open, Cassius slowly returned to the Mercedes and got in. He backed it in, got out again, and closed the door, relying mostly on gravity. He shakily rounded to the trunk of the car and popped it open with the key fob. Inside was the body of a young woman, bound and gagged. She was still alive, though barely. He had forgotten about her briefly during his encounter with "Bob" and the map. Indeed, he had almost cut it too close once again, but pausing to read the map had been far too tempting to put off for long.

There was no use waking the girl, he didn't have the energy to play with his food today. Besides, she was covered in her own shit and urine. It was appalling. And so, pulling out his marvellous two-pronged spear, he slid it

115

deftly between her ribs, just as he had done with Julia in the auditorium. Instantly, Bearing magic began to pulse through him, and he felt himself begin to shake with the rush. The girl's eyes flickered briefly before she passed out for good.

He recalled watching Julia on that day, but there had been no rush. No enchanted high. She had felt empty as she left consciousness. But looking back now, that had clearly been intentional, like she had denied him access on purpose. And then there was the thing he had barely dared to admit to himself: Julia had somehow managed to suck some of his magic *back into herself*. A reverse flow through his greatest weapon. He had realized what Julia was doing almost immediately and put end to it.

But the fact remained that she had an edge on him.

And so, this was his second issue: perfecting his ability to harvest Bearing magic without the flow being reversed. All of his past victims had been helpless to him. Every. Single. One. He wasn't used to anyone fighting back once he got the spear in, so he had never needed any kind of personal protection. It was perhaps the secret to his success with the spear, but now he knew there was a chink in his armour.

Thankfully, he had Kenzie to help him repair that. The Bearer he had managed to corrupt and turn to his side had proven most useful.

Standing in the darkness of the service station, and shaking now with power instead of weakness, he pulled out his phone and dialled the first person on his speed dial. "Kenzie," he said, steadying his breathing so as to not give away his current state. If his current body could still perform the act, he would likely be experiencing a raging, and very distracting, erection right now. Not because of Kenzie, of course, but because of the magic currently surging through his veins … and the thought of what Julia's magic would feel like inside of his body. *Finally.*

He shuddered.

"Cassius!" she exclaimed. He hated her enthusiasm.

"I'm going to be in Los Angeles briefly. Tell Caleb to arrange things. I'll need to feed before I leave again. You'll be there. And ready." It wasn't a request.

He heard her breathing heavily on the other end of the line before she quietly said, "Yes, master."

He hung up the phone without a word. He knew she got something sexual out of the experience but didn't care particularly. He couldn't remember the last time he had craved any carnal relations, so it was pitiful that she believed their relationship to be an intimate one. But it was a better explanation for her than what he was really up to.

Kenzie, whom he had discovered by accident, had been the missing piece. She had been captured and contained for one of his usual feedings, but upon encountering her, he'd immediately noticed she was different. Dark. And disturbingly eager to please. Late one night in a dingy motel room, he had plunged his spear into her just like the others, but she had welcomed it. And he discovered that—in her case—the magic didn't leave her body so readily as it had the others. And it also seemed to stop when he stopped. A replenishable source.

She was the *perfect* candidate for his experiment.

Kenzie wasn't remotely as intelligent as his other generals, Caleb being his number one at the moment and arguably one of his best in many years. The man was vicious, if not to the point of being reckless. But Cassius preferred someone leading in his stead who could get the job done, no questions asked. He was as efficient as a battle axe and not afraid to use torture when needed. When it came down to it, he would eventually ask Caleb to dispatch Kenzie—whom he had been left in charge of while Cassius was away—assuming that the World Ruler and his league of fools didn't manage it first. He didn't really care how she met her end once he was done with her. Kenzie was an idiot, and he expected she would get herself caught sooner or later.

But, regardless of the circumstances, her death would be required; there was too much risk of her discovering what he was attempting to do through accessing her magic. A part of Cassius actually hated to do it, as Kenzie *had* proven immensely loyal. Unwavering, really. But she was also a woman. And a Bearer. And he would have no use for her once he had finally obtained Julia for good.

This led him to his third and most infuriating hurdle: the World Ruler.

Domhnall O'Brien had been a thorn in his side for centuries. Of course, Cassius had always managed to kill him; *that* wasn't his concern when it came to the man. Cassius knew he could overpower the World Ruler when they were both at full strength. However, he would be remiss to ignore the fact that Domhnall was also extremely resilient. Countless times they had faced one another, and every time, he had shown up with a new set of skills, adapting to each and every new environment he was reborn into as though he had never left. Yes, the gods seemed to smile on Domhnall O'Brien, but Cassius had a plan for that too. The World Ruler's greatest weakness was not only his love for Julia but also his loyalty and adoration for those he held dearest.

The key to destroying the World Ruler, once and for all, was undoubtedly through his heart.

Strength returning to his body, Cassius rolled the dead woman out of his trunk and left her on the oily floor of the abandoned shop. His trunk was filthy, but he wouldn't have need of the car for much longer. Cassius then slid into the driver's seat and blasted the shop's door open with a thrust of his knuckled fist, blowing it clear off its hinges. He took off at great speed, leaving the woman and this … place … in the dust.

CHAPTER 11

With the truck fully loaded, I was far sadder than expected to be departing from the Oregon beach house we had called home over the past few months. Sure, it had its quirks, and the Knaves had honestly worn me out, but it had also become a place of respite for all of us—a *mostly* peaceful space to transition into our new reality. That said, another part of me was also relieved to be on the move once more. Over the past several nights, my dreams had grown concerning, blurred with images of Cassius delving deeper into darkness. I wasn't even entirely sure if the dreams held real meaning, but regardless, our enemies to the south were moving pieces across the board no matter how still we sat.

Visiting Big Sur, and Bernadette, felt like the most intuitive next step.

"This is just a small visit, Dom, not a *mission*. We don't have to rush there," I had said when it was finally time to make plans to leave. Lennie and Ronan, in a rare moment of agreement, were firm in their belief that we would be wiser to make the journey to Los Angeles in a straight shot. In Dom's eyes, this only served to bolster the argument for going slower. He had lost almost all patience with the both of them, and as they weren't coming along anyway, he gave their thoughts little consideration.

In the end, we agreed to make the trip to Big Sur over two days, rather than forging onward to the point of sheer exhaustion by end of the journey, like we had on the way to Oregon. Dom continued to place the trip in the "mission" category, but I decided to let it slide.

As summer slowly transitioned into fall, we hit the road at last. I felt my body release a tension I didn't even realize I'd been harbouring. "It's just so good to be moving again!"

"So true," Dom said, taking a deep sip of takeout coffee before promptly slopping it across his pant leg. "Oy! Drive a little straighter, won't you?"

We were stopped at a red light. I laughed. "So sorry!"

While the inland route might have shortened our drive by an hour or so, Dom and I both agreed that staying as close as possible to the shoreline was our safest bet, especially since we would quickly be moving from the Druids' ring of protection. Indeed, as we travelled south from Florence towards Big Sur along the 101, it seemed that, as long as I was near the shoreline, my Bearing sense was clear and easily accessible to me. The more inland we went, the shakier I felt.

"It's not like it's not *there*, per se," I said, trying to explain the sensation as we crossed the California border. "It's more like, when I'm closer to the tides, I have a handle on what's coming next. Like … I can maybe do a better job at detecting Wraiths or any danger. Or maybe it just gives me confidence … I don't know."

Dom, who had taken over driving, nodded enthusiastically. "You don't have to convince me, love. You know what you're doing. I'm just the driver on this quest!"

Frankly, he had been almost *too* amenable on the trip so far, clearly glad for a break from Ronan and Lennie's current issues. I understood where he was coming from.

We spent the night in a city called Eureka. From there, we would be forced to turn inland for a time, so it felt like a rational checkpoint with my Bearing magic. Instead of going to the effort of setting up the truck-bed tent, air mattress, and bedding that we had picked up while in Florence, we stayed in an extremely colourful bed and breakfast in a restored Victorian-era home. It was quaint and pleasant, with the hosts decidedly hands off, just as we liked it. However, as the creaky double bed was far too cramped for our long bodies, neither of us found great sleep that night; we should have gone with the tent.

"I thought you could sleep almost anywhere," I muttered to Dom in the middle of the night. He had been tossing and turning for almost an hour.

"Apparently not. I must be getting old," he replied, rolling grumpily onto his other side. By morning, we were both groggy but eager to be on the road again.

"Need more coffee," I groaned as we pulled out onto the highway. Dom grumbled something incoherent in reply. Caffeine was a *must* today.

We opted not to stop for long in the San Francisco area, instead plunging onward towards San Jose and then over the Santa Cruz Mountains. Our logic was to continue avoiding any place we might have been before and, hopefully, any Wraiths as well.

"I'm a bit sad to not visit again though," Dom said, smiling wistfully out the passenger window. "We had a lot of fun in California. *Back then*."

"I know, but I think Ronan is right in this regard at least. Best to steer clear of anywhere Cassius might expect us to be."

Dom nodded silently in agreement.

Reaching San Jose at last, we took Highway 17 over the Santa Cruz Mountains and back towards the shoreline. The drive itself was steep as we traversed the busy mountain pass. It reminded me somewhat of the Malahat Highway between Victoria and the Cowichan Valley back on Vancouver Island, only more intense.

"I think I'm going to be sick," Dom said. No doubt, the heavily winding highway and too much coffee in his empty belly were proving a bad combination.

"Just look straight ahead," I offered, doing my best to keep the truck from turning too harshly, but it was futile.

He whined as we rounded a 180-degree turn. "That's the problem!"

Thankfully, it was a quick drive, and soon, we were descending into Santa Cruz.

The energy was decidedly different here, almost as if it were moving with intention and real excitement. I didn't know if it was the geography itself or my renewed proximity to the shoreline that was bolstering my spirits, but I was willing to take whatever I could get at this point; I too had been feeling fairly awful all day.

"Oh, I wish we could stay here for a bit," I said, smiling broadly at the sight of Monterey Bay. Alas, it was only a brief pit-stop for the bathroom, and of course, sustenance. I found Dom leaning casually on the side of the truck as I returned, heartily filling his mouth with several different kinds of street food at once.

"Hungry," he said with his mouth full, and I laughed.

"I see that. Did you get anything for me?"

He handed me foil-paper-wrapped soft taco. "Of course."

Bellies full, we were soon skirting around the bay, passing countless signs for organic farms, avocado sales, and strawberry stands along the way as we approached Carmel-by-the-Sea, known more commonly as Carmel. The air smelled strongly of the Pacific Ocean, and we could spot countless surfers playing in the breakers; this was the California I had always imagined.

"Would you ever want to try surfing?" I asked, looking at Dom in the driver's seat.

"I *have* gone surfing, actually," he said and then regaled me with stories of donning a wet suit and taking to the sea off the coast of Ireland.

"Ireland?" I asked, surprised.

"Of course! One of her best kept secrets, really. Ronan and I have gone several times actually. The waves can be *wicked.*"

"I guess that makes sense. I don't know why I hadn't thought of that—obviously, it's an island. Sounds cold, though."

"It was," he said, laughing.

Soon, we began to climb the mountains towards Big Sur. The coastline was utterly rapturous as we wound along some of the scariest, most incredible highway I had ever encountered. Several times we both remarked at the shocking lack of barriers between us and the cliffside towards the ocean.

"Jesus, Mary, and Joseph!" Dom exclaimed at one point as we hugged yet another curve at the edge of the world.

"No shit," I said in agreement; it would be *very* easy to cascade off the edge if you weren't paying enough attention.

Eventually, we turned slightly inland towards dense forest.

"I can feel we're getting close. There's something about this *place* ... "

"Mm. Good," Dom said, agreeable once more, albeit this time I could sense something different growing in his tone.

"Are you worried about me meeting with Bernadette?" I asked, shifting to face him. If our recent history was any indication, I didn't exactly have a great track record in meeting other Bearers, in terms of "successful" outcomes.

"A bit, to be honest. But I can't expect every situation to be like Agnes Sweeney, can I? If you feel good about it, then so do I." He was clearly attempting to convince himself that this was true.

I nodded, unclenching my jaw. "Thanks. This doesn't feel like a risk though. Not really. But it *does* feel important."

Indeed, the closer we got to Big Sur, the more magnificent the energy felt. All around us, great redwoods rose to the sky, ancient gatekeepers to a place that was clearly a significant portal to deeper power. There was undoubtedly something alive about the place. It was no wonder that artists, writers, and spiritual humans flocked here in droves.

Dom ran his hand though his hair, scratching his head. "My skin is tingling."

"You can feel it too?" I was suddenly curious.

He shrugged. "Looks like."

Dom's connection to the Otherworld was as mysterious as the place itself, but moments like these reminded me that he too had a deeper connection to the essence of our lives than most anyone else I knew.

"*You're a Wizard, Domhnall!*" I said, grinning wide.

"What?" he asked, the Harry Potter reference clearly lost on him.

We continued onward. Lennie's note said that Bernadette lived on the mountainside above Pfeiffer Beach, and so that was where we would stop first. However, the suggested address wasn't showing up on our navigation screen. Typical.

"Hmm." I paused. "Maybe just pull over here so I can try to sense it."

Dom obliged dutifully and nestled the long truck in a small alcove between two large roadside redwoods. I hopped out, stretching lightly onto my tiptoes as Dom exited loudly from the other side.

"You were going to visit here before I swept you away in all of this madness last winter, weren't you?" he said, approaching me from behind, arms wrapping around me in sweet embrace. "I'm glad you've finally arrived."

The forest beyond us was cool yet welcoming; indeed, it felt good to be here. We were definitely getting close to the right place. "It's alright. I honestly kind of forget about life 'before' sometimes."

"Do you think you've always been drawn here though? With or without me, maybe you've always been destined to meet Bernadette," he offered. I liked how he pronounced her name, with a bit of a lingering note on the "Bern" part.

"Maybe, but it seems like too much of a coincidence."

"Oh, come on, Julia. Stranger things have happened." He kissed my neck affectionately. "Look at me, for example. I'm the son of fucking Brian Boru!"

I turned towards him in false alarm. "You are? I had no idea!"

He barked out a laugh before dipping me low and kissing me firmly on my parted lips, his beard scratching gently. "You better believe it, *baby!*"

I burst into laughter, delighting as usual in the joy he brought me.

And then I received a message ... from Bernadette:

"Welcome, Julia! Please ask Domhnall to wait outside. I want to speak to you alone. This is Bearer's business but do ask him not to worry. You'll be back in his arms before you know it."

I was quickly discovering that, just as different Bearers had their own interpretations of magic, so did they vary in enacting a *Send*. I had never been able to communicate more than a few words at once—despite Aisling's hurried lesson and my subsequent attempts—but it seemed that the more practice you had, the more words you could deliver. I thought of the young Witch then, who had entered into our life in Ireland with a literal splash and left it just as quickly. I hoped she was safe, wherever she was.

Dom sensed my brief interruption as my mind oscillated between Bearing acquaintances old and new, and placed me back solidly on my feet. Suddenly, the alcove we had parked in shifted abruptly in our view, presenting now as a narrow driveway leading up to a small mountain cabin. Navigation be damned, we had found her home by sheer sense.

"Whoa! Can you see it?" I asked Dom.

He cocked his head slightly, closing one eye. "Kind of ... if I look at it just right."

I was relieved her protection spell was allowing Dom to at least witness where I was going, although I had no doubt that he would find passage into this place difficult if he were to actually attempt it.

"She's asked me to leave you at the truck."

Dom bristled. "Oh, has she now?"

"It's not like that. I think she would just prefer to speak to me alone. Bearer stuff, you know …" I said, sensing his understandable apprehension. "Dom … I have a good feeling about this. I promise."

He breathed in slowly through his nose, followed by an equally long exhale. Then, crossing his arms, he leaned back against the truck. "Alright."

"Thanks," I said and turned to peer down the drive once more. I suddenly felt underdressed for the event, wearing worn flip-flops and a pair of crinkly linen shorts with a thin tank top. But what does one wear when they visit a powerful Witch in the woods anyway?

Stepping forward, I expected to encounter some form of resistance, the spell perhaps wrapping around me as I breached its core. However, I felt nothing but clear passage as I slowly crunched down the path. I turned to look over my shoulder but could no longer see Dom, only forest.

"Okay, Julia," I said quietly to myself, "you can do this."

The home itself was simple, resembling many of the smaller wood cabins I had known back on Salt Spring Island. Built with hewn logs, it had several small square windows dotting the front and a simple panelled wood door. As it was in my original vision back in Florence, the chimney was emitting a pillar of multi-coloured smoke. She was home and waiting for me.

A stick of rose-scented incense was burning just outside the door, jammed into a small dark-blue ceramic pot full of sand. Taking two short steps up, I rapped on the door quietly. "Hello?"

Several seconds later, the door swung inward and revealed a taller grey-haired woman, somewhere maybe in her late sixties. She had brilliant blue eyes and a sun-kissed face, and wore simple linen slacks and a loose top, much like my own. I wasn't sure who I was expecting to find, but as soon as I saw her, she was exactly as she should be.

"Welcome!" she exclaimed, leaning back playfully from her hips. "I've been waiting a long time for you, Julia."

"I feel like I have been too ..." I said, pausing momentarily as an overwhelming sense of déjà vu flooded over me. "It's nice to finally meet you, Bernadette."

"Oh, good grief, Julia, call me Bernie," she said, patting me softly on the forearm as she led me in. I was instantly at home.

Bernie's cabin was simple, tidy, and chock full of power, almost exactly as one would expect from a Witch who had been in the trenches long enough to know the value of her own light. She didn't need to adorn the place with a plethora of artifacts to aid in her Wielding; she had plenty of Bearing magic surging within for that.

I ducked slightly as we stepped into a sunroom off the back of the cabin. There, two plush fabric chairs faced each other over a simple tea service set out across a low pine table.

"Tea?" she offered.

I *was* thirsty after our drive. "I would love some, thank you."

Sinking down into the squat seating, I watched as she busied herself preparing it for me exactly as I liked it, casual in her sense of knowing.

"Sorry about Domhnall," she said, pouring just enough cream into my cup.

"He'll survive," I said, accepting the hot mug gratefully.

She chuckled. "I have no doubt he will."

We sat for a moment, peering at each other over our cups and savouring the curls of hot steam spiralling off them; the air was humid in the forest.

"I prefer green tea myself. Jasmine. But this Earl Grey is nice too."

"It's my favourite," I said.

"I know."

A question rose to my lips. "Have we met before?"

She smiled. "We have. But you wouldn't remember."

"Because ..."

"Because I didn't want you to. It wasn't time yet."

I took another long sip of the soothing liquid. She was deliberate in her delivery, careful in her thoughts. In the past, if someone left me hanging like this, I would have felt the urge to fill the space with idle words. With Bernie, however, the waiting in between words felt oddly delicious.

MANTLE OF THE WORLD RULER

I looked out the glass of the sunroom and spotted a galvanized steel tub just beyond a short deck. I imagined Bernie sitting out there, immersed in warm water and surrounded by cool forest. It seemed perfect, and then I thought of Dom; he would love a place like this.

"He's powerful," she said, riding along on my train of thought.

"He is," I agreed.

"And you know what he needs to do, even if he hasn't accepted it yet."

Where I expected my heart to sink at her comment, my chest actually opened in complete lightness. "I do."

She smiled serenely and rose to her feet. "Good. Now, on to more prevailing matters. We need to discuss *your* path."

I watched quietly as she strode towards a large wooden armoire in the small living room beyond. It took up much of the wall, yet somehow, I suspected it was even larger on the inside. She opened it up, rustled around for a bit, and then pulled out several rolls of paper and an assortment of other items before bringing them all back to where we were sitting. She waited patiently as I hastily cleared the teapot and cups to the side.

"I'm a bit of a cartographer," she said.

"I see that," I said with a smile as she unrolled an unusual-looking map.

"But I specialize more in helping others along their journeys. I have a bit of a knack for hearing people's inner voice—their wants and needs—especially when they can't. And then I use the maps," she said, gesturing before her, "to help plot it out."

"Incredible."

She laughed. "No, not really. Just many years of practice. You know that about Bearing magic, don't you? It can't *really* be taught. The learning is in the work, not in the holding of the knowledge itself."

I thought of the lack of mentorship I'd received as a young girl when my magic was practically exploding out of me. "And what about if you had no guidance at all? Not even a foundation?"

"You didn't have 'no guidance,' Julia," she said. "You've always had yourself."

I thought for a moment, and she waited, peaceful in her silence. "I guess I've always struggled to listen to my own intuition."

She swept the curling edges back on the first map she placed down. "I know. Put your hands on here."

I reached out, cautious at first. She nodded encouragingly as I set my outstretched hands gently on the unassuming paper. It was decorated with a series of grid lines, colourful land masses, and water blobs that resembled nowhere I had ever been.

"It's not going to bite you; it's just paper," she said, easing the tension. "The magic isn't in the map anyway. It's in us. We'll build the path together, now."

CHAPTER 12

Bernie placed a see-through glass compass halfway between my thumbs. One point of the needle, which I assumed was the magnetized end, resembled an arrowhead. The other end looked distinctly like a crescent moon. I had never seen a compass like this before, but the energy coming from it felt instantly recognizable. "This feels familiar …"

"It is. Your friend Ronan actually has one of my compasses. It's a bit different than this one though."

"How—"

"I placed it in his path many years ago."

I briefly searched my knowledge for when I might have met Bernie, but there was nothing solid. I returned my thoughts to the task at hand. "But … I thought it used Wielding magic."

"Of course not. If it did, how did you think Domhnall could have managed to use it?"

In spite of my confusion, the pieces were slowly coming together. Somehow, she knew that Dom would need the compass to find me this time, as I had become almost untraceable in this modern life.

"Can I ask *how* you knew?"

"Let's just say that when I met you and Domhnall all those years ago in San Francisco, my path was altered as well. And I knew he was going to have one hell of a time finding you the next time."

"But Ronan uses the compass to detect Wraith magic," I said, still grasping for understanding.

"Yes, well, he uses it for what *he* needs it to do. Just as Dom did. It's not an exact science," she said, chuckling. "But the compasses are meant to help people find more clarity on their journeys."

I drew a slow intake of breath. Bernie moved my hands slightly and placed a short candle on the table between us. Running her beautifully aged hand overtop, she lit the flame.

"I've always been a dismal Wielder," I offered.

"Me too," she said with a grin before closing her eyes. Instinctively, I followed her lead.

Immediately, I was transported to a different place altogether. Landing with a bracing jolt, I was surprised to discover my feet had found solid ground. Bernie was there too, standing firmly at my side but *much* younger in form. Her hair was thick and blonde and pulled back into a tight ponytail. The bottom half of her hair below the ponytail was shaved in a cool "V." I assumed this was what she had looked like when I had unknowingly met her all those years ago, with a modern twist of her own invention.

"Where are we?" I asked.

"On your path."

Together, we stood on a steep cliff and faced outward across a stormy sea. The horizon was dark and menacing. I could feel a commanding surge of energy coming from somewhere within its shadowy depths. The small compass weighed heavily in the palm of my hand.

"Doesn't look like much of a path," I said, unable to resist stating the obvious.

She took me by the shoulders and slowly turned me towards the land, where an expansive, blinding light was emanating from somewhere high above. I took a moment for my eyes to adjust. The air was strange, but not in a bad way. Everything was illuminated in a glow that caused my skin to prickle. I ran my cool fingers along my forearms, which only increased the tingling sensation.

"You have a lot of wild Bearing magic within you," she said, now standing several feet away. I could see beads of sweat beginning to form on her temple; clearly, this process wasn't easy on her.

"Are you—"

She spoke over me, though there was no impatience in her tone. "It's important to understand that, in the end, we *do* design much of our own journeys. Consciously or not."

A long and winding road appeared before us that led into a gorgeous, rolling green mountain range beyond. Drawn forward instinctually, I took a small step. Suddenly, the ground shifted, and we began to rapidly travel forward; the sensation left me feeling disoriented and a bit sick to my stomach.

"The sun is here. And the moon too," she offered in comfort.

Directly above, I could feel the presence of the moon quietly urging me onward.

This is your path.

"But what about the tides?" I asked, with half a mind to turn back; the road ahead felt unsettling and unsure.

"They certainly have their draw," Bernie said, looking over her shoulder as well. She placed her hand gently on my own before speaking once more. "But remember, she's not found *only* at the sea. Although, it is nice to feel her presence so clearly, I agree. It's why I live where I do. And you as well."

I nodded.

It was true; the last few weeks I had naturally let myself be drawn to the ocean. Letting it fill and replenish me with its safety and embrace. The natural ease of its ebbs and flows was what I needed right now, but I also understood Bernie's meaning. To my left, I could see the sun seated low on the horizon, highlighting a similarly beautiful mountain range, although it was distinctly its own. Shale-grey rock faces led gradually upward to snow-capped mountaintops that sparkled wonderfully in the magnanimous light.

"Domhnall ..."

"He's been right beside you, all along. Yet clearly you see his path as his own, which is exactly as it should be," Bernie said, an admiring smile blossoming on her young face.

I thought of Dom's arms wrapped around me from behind just before I had crossed the enchanted threshold towards Bernie's cabin, and suddenly my breath caught; I missed him, even now. Turning inward, I could sense the strong, pulsing undercurrent between the sun's kingdom and my own winding path under the silver moon. While intense, it felt perfectly cohesive and eternally binding.

"Our tie …"

"They need each other, the sun and moon. But you already knew that," she added, looking ahead. "Let's continue."

The road shifted once more, and we found ourselves standing at the banks of a vast river, charged and glorious in its clear intention. I closed my eyes and took several long breaths. "I can feel the bond … It's in the lakes, and rivers, and groundwater …"

"Good. You're doing wonderfully," she said, her voice filled with pride. This caused me to open my eyes and look at her; I wasn't used to being congratulated for using my intuition.

She continued. "So, looking to the rivers … Can you feel how freely they flow between the both of you?"

I nodded slowly. I could; it was a marvel to behold, really.

"Domhnall will need to be mindful of damming any of the flow for the sake of control or fear. Water flows precisely as it means to across the landscape. Sometimes, it rushes quick, crashing loudly onto jagged rocks, and other times, it meanders silently along, eventually forming a tranquil lake. All are important processes and create the balance of life as we know it."

I thought of Dom and me, recognizing what I already knew. On this journey, we were never meant to get in each other's way. Only to stand firmly in fine balance, side-by-side.

"The World Ruler," I said.

Her face filled with pride. "And the Sovereign."

With the Sovereign standing tall, the World Ruler too must bear his crown.

Together, we turned from the river and faced down the winding path of my life map. It was eerily quiet, and I came to notice that this place boasted a strangely skewed sense of time.

"Now we face into the unknown," she said.

Suddenly, I began to worry about how long I had been away. Familiar anxiety filled my ribs as my hands grew proportionately numb. Above, the sky darkened. My voice grew shaky as I tripped over an outstretched root, hooking my foot and stumbling spectacularly forward onto my hands and knees. "What's happening?"

"Julia ..." Bernie said, her voice suddenly very far away.

Before me, I could see countless physical obstacles—thorny bracken and knotted trees ... along with gigantic rocks scattered along the way; the passage ahead was not an easy one, and I soon felt very afraid. "What do I do?"

"I think we will return now."

At once, my mind spun and I fell back abruptly into my seat in the sunroom. I spent a few short moments fighting back overwhelming nausea, but eventually the feeling passed.

"Sorry about that. Some people's maps are more tumultuous than others ... It can be hard to gain your bearings when that happens," she said, wiping the sweat from the brow of her now much older face.

"Bernie ... What *was* that?"

She looked suddenly serious. "Julia. You need to let go of the desire to unpack all of the memories ... You don't need to understand absolutely *everything* that's ever happened to you. You can lose yourself in your memories, just as you can in the ocean."

I looked up, confused.

She continued. "The memories will come back if and when you need them, and no sooner."

I thought of the quilt sitting in the back of our truck; we were still pinning most of our hopes on deciphering it. "I don't understand."

She blew out the candle and handed me the small compass before rolling up the larger map. Next, she brought out a smaller roll of charcoal-grey paper, which was completely blank. This one didn't need holding down as it settled with a strange weight across the table.

"You've created a fair few roadblocks for yourself, my dear."

"What do you mean?" I asked, sitting up straight.

"It's no matter. Everyone does it. Far too often, our biggest obstacles are the ones we inadvertently place for ourselves, and all too often using other people's carefully crafted or projected ideas." She lit a different candle, this one matte black with a brilliant flame. "More specifically, the ideas about who they *think* we are."

Within seconds, the base of the wick was welling with hot wax. Bernie quickly drizzled it across the strange dark paper, which hissed and popped as she tilted the candle this way and that.

"Hold onto the compass now."

"What—"

"It's like this," she said, gripping the top of my hand. I noticed she was wearing a gold ring with an affixed garnet gemstone. Why hadn't I noticed that before?

Precipitously, we returned together to something that resembled the map space, but instead of a vast landscape, visions played out ahead of us where we stood, shoulder-to-shoulder.

Visions from *my* life. Each one.

Glimpses of childhood traumas endured, countless losses and deaths, and every heartbreak throughout the centuries were felt all at once. I could feel the recent agony of my childhood, my dog passing, the loneliness of navigating puberty alone, and the confused sorrow of early heartbreaks. Faster and faster, the raw, agonizing memories swirled around me, culminating in a vast chasm—a chasm whose depth had been solidified with the deaths of my mother and grandmother not so long ago.

This was a place that I only visited in deepest despair.

"Why are you showing me this?" I asked, my voice shaking as tears streamed down my face.

"You see, Julia," Bernie said, her voice soothing within my mind. "Many of us carry an ocean of grief ... a tidal wave of hidden truths. Memories we can't undo or unsee. Memories that haunt us ... or sneak up on us when we least expect them. And you, because of your most ... *unique* circumstances, carry much, much more than the rest of us. Both of you do," she said, and I knew she was also referring to Dom.

At the thought of him, the visions rapidly started reaching back throughout our chronological history, each one more fragmented than the last until all I could see was dense fog spilling out before me.

"Bernie, I don't have access to these memories anymore. Not very easily, anyway."

"Do you remember what you did all those years ago to make the memories stick? And do you remember the *cost?*" she asked, but this time it wasn't with the same air of knowing she had born towards me so far. She was asking me sincerely; we needed direction for the compass.

Remembering the compass sitting in my palm, I raised it and thought about when I would have gone to the greatest length to preserve my memories.

Strangely, it wasn't the creation of the quilt at all.

In a darkened room near a large-mouthed hearth, I saw myself performing the magic required to form the tattoo on Dom's back. It must have been hundreds of years ago, based on the carved wooden furniture and lack of adequate light in the room. Yet, it wasn't so far back as the days of thatched huts and cauldron fires as I had seen once before. Dom—shirtless with his lean, muscular lines descending all the way from his broad shoulders to the tops of his powerful glutes—was bent over a low stool, jaw clenched in agony as I raised my hands high, swaying them violently through the air as I read out a dark incantation in a language I didn't understand. Shaking and drenched in sweat, the look on his face was one of both sheer torture and deepest trust. Who I was now wept for him at the sight.

The me I was then, however, was stone-cold serious. And at my feet was a book.

In my Bearing core, I could feel the strength it had taken to sustain this volume of Wielding magic, and I knew the *cost*. It was distinctly unnatural and akin to Sorcery. I sensed that the rite placed our lives in danger and betrayed all intuitive principles of both Bearing and Wielding. One wrong move, one misstep, and we would both be killed. The past me cut deeply into my palm with a blackened knife, and I gagged at the sight. Then, dripping the blood from my clenched fist, I made a slow line down Dom's spine. He arched in pain as if it were acid but remained steadfast in his resolve.

What horrors had we experienced to drive us to this place?

I watched as the trunk of the great tree, followed by the branches and roots, spread across his once bare back. Intricate limbs cascaded into what was at first a harsh circle, each line carved into his flesh as if by a blunt knife. I knew it would eventually heal into a masterpiece, yet in the moment, it was nothing short of horrific as dark blood pooled throughout the harsh design. Almost as if in slow motion, Dom bucked on his knees while emitting a howling sound I had never heard from him before, primal and transcendent in his pain. I could see both spit and blood running freely from his mouth onto the wood-planked floor below—he had bit his tongue or lip through the torment.

Dom would do (and had always done) whatever it took to protect me.

I watched as the *then* Julia shifted from a pillar of solid Bearing power to a shaking leaf as the dark magic infiltrated Dom's body. She ran her fingers through her hair. Waiting. Watching. Agonizing. And then, after what felt like ages—though probably was only a few minutes in actual time—Dom's body relaxed fully as he passed out on the floor.

It was done.

Dom's breath was shallow where he lay, but he was alive. Hot tears streamed down both versions of my cheeks at the sight of the blood and lacerated flesh on his once perfect frame. The me back then fell to the floor, sobbing and shaking, and trying to wake him.

I had to look away at the grim sight.

Instead, I glanced at the book beside us. Once open, its pages covered in harsh script and the iron-coloured droplets from Dom's back, it had now closed tightly shut of its own volition. In all my memory, I had never encountered a book such as this. While more unassuming than the usual grimoires, which were often adorned with carved symbols and ornate fixtures, this book was almost sinister in its simplicity. And it clearly had a mind of its own. Across its brown cover was a faintly embossed etching that would have reminded me of a flower or mandala if not for the dark-red, glistening spot in its centre. This was an incredibly dark, dangerous, and disturbing book.

How had we come across it? And what had we done with the book after the spell was done? Surely, we had destroyed it ... or at least hidden it somewhere.

The vision faded before I could gather any more information. I looked over at Bernie, fearing her reaction would be one of judgement or perhaps terror at what I had meddled with, but she remained steadfast. If anything, she looked unsurprised.

"There have been many dark grimoires throughout history. However, this one—the *Codex Druidicus*—is rumoured to have been one of the worst ever created. The Druid's darkest history filtered through a distorted Roman lens."

"How do you know that?" I asked, still wiping salty tears from my face.

"It's my job in this life to know things. To see things. But *how* I know isn't important right now. Keep going," she said, reminding me once more of the compass in the palm of my hand. "I can sense there's still one more memory—and book—that we need to attend to today."

We travelled backwards further through time, a blur of colourful visions surrounding us as we picked up speed towards the memory that both the compass, and my intuition, were directing us to.

We were going back to the very start.

At last, I saw the actual scene of my original mother's death—the death I already knew I had caused inadvertently over one thousand years ago. I watched as the struggle ensued, the dark magic of the original grimoire clouding each of our eyes, infecting our minds as we turned against one another—grandmother, mother, and daughter—an infinite darkness unleashed.

One after the other, just as the generations of women that followed, we fell victim to a darkness that was not our own. This was an inherited darkness created by those who wished to control us and stifle our spirituality. To either consume our magic as their own or train us to turn it against one another. I wept then, harder than I ever had, my lungs filled with a grief so ancient I feared it might consume me. This was the betrayal of our original divine magic, the consumption of the original feminine Goddess by a patriarchal God.

"It was never your fault," Bernie said in my mind as she waved her garnet-ringed hand through the air once.

My breath caught, and I dropped the compass to the ground.

We returned to the sunroom with more ease this time, the contrast between my shadows and the exhilarating daylight extreme. Outside, birds were singing along happily, oblivious to the pain I felt within; the joys of living life in the moment were suddenly all too plain.

"Have you told Domhnall about this?" she asked me.

"Not fully," I said. "I only just saw the full truth of it all when the cottage burned down at the solstice in June."

She nodded solemnly. "Sometimes memories need to be set aside. Not necessarily forgotten, just ... accepted. Stored. We must learn what we can from them—and, of course, it's utterly important to *believe* our own stories, and what happened to us—but on this journey, we eventually reach a stage when it's time to live in the *present.*"

"A bit hard for a diviner," I said ruefully.

"Think of it this way: Perhaps you've been so stuck, focused on the past, that you've never learned how to live in the moment, let alone learn how to live for the future."

"But that's the thing," I said, frustrated by my "road blocks," as she called them. "I've never been able to divine the future with any clarity either. I've experienced a few portents, dreams that came true and stuff. But nothing solid."

"Do you need to?" she asked, fighting back a slight grin.

I stood up to look out of the window into the deep forest beyond. Shimmering down through the upper canopy, the sun's rays caressed the earth, ethereal and light. "Aren't I supposed to? Isn't that my role in all of this? To figure out how to defeat Cassius once and for all? So far, I feel like I've only managed to get people that I love injured and killed. I feel this crushing guilt … *all* the time … like I'll never be good enough … or strong enough."

"You can't change what happened in the past, Julia. Nor can you influence how people perceive your actions, or the choices they'll make as a result of them. Everyone is entitled to their own lived experience, even *you*," Bernie said kindly.

I thought of all of my friends' faces on the fateful day at the precipice, and how each of them had been affected differently. I nodded.

"All you can do is listen to your inner voice—your *intuition*—and make the best choices you can with the knowledge you have at the time," she finished.

"But … I have this quilt … It feels like … like a roadmap of the past? I mean—I made it—attaching pieces cycle-by-cycle in what I *think* was an attempt to help my future self. I can feel my magic every time I pick it up, like there's a part of me embedded in every stitch. It feels important for understanding what will come next," I said, my frustration mounting. The fact that *I* had fashioned the quilt during past lives had been a cumulative realization over the last year with Dom. And with that came a sense of knowing that it was mine, and a keen awareness of its (potentially) hidden knowledge. My inability to read it, however, was infuriating. "If I could just understand it, I might be able to get us out of this mess!"

"Hmm," she said, listening quietly.

I felt like I was once again sitting in therapy, in the type of session where your counsellor is waiting for you to sort yourself out towards a conclusion you both already know.

I grappled with my emotions around the quilt for a time, eventually slumping in resignation. "If I'm completely honest ... it feels like a bit of a dead end. At least for right now."

"Maybe. Or perhaps not." She shrugged, smiling brightly. "But *certainly*, your experiences have shaped you greatly, arguably more so than any other Bearer in history. And of course, Bearers *can* leave magic behind, in and around things, which stays active for generations." She gestured towards the compass.

I nodded slowly in understanding. "Kind of like Dom's tattoo ... Somehow, using what was *clearly* dark magic, I managed to imbue enough of my own memories into its creation to re-connect myself to our past when I finally touched it again. Like an anchor."

"Exactly. And in that case, you were wise to gain insight from the messages you left there, as clearly it was worth taking a *great risk* to pass that information on to yourself. However, even that isn't a blueprint for the future. Surely what happened on the precipice taught you that much. You have the power to create something entirely different if you so choose ..."

"Perhaps the quilt was meant to force me to acknowledge the existence of my past ... that it was indeed real—all of the trials, and pain, and suffering—and that these stories throughout the generations will have influenced me in a way I may not always understand."

"But they do not diminish the power of the choices you have in your future."

I nodded, contemplating.

"When you unleashed your power back in May," she said, rolling up the dark paper hastily, almost as if she didn't want to touch it. "It was only the first step of many. And I think the same can be said for many others, as well."

I thought then of how many of us were now working together to try to defeat Cassius.

"Well, what about Ronan? He wants something from me. Wants me to help him. And ... I think I'm supposed to do it. But I'm terrified. I think—"

"His path is complicated ..." she said, then held her words for a beat, that enthralling space between words expanding once more. "I can't say for sure how that will all play out. But his story, too, must be journeyed alongside your own. And Domhnall's."

I groaned. "Oh, good Goddess. It's not going to be like some kind of fucked-up Arthur and Lancelot quest, is it?"

She paused and stared at me for a moment, slack-jawed. Then she burst out into a fit of full-belly laughter. "Oh goodness, no. That's not what I meant. It's just that we can have more than one person align with our destinies at any one point. Friends, family ... all the way into the collective. Some people's journeys run parallel to our own for longer. Others, only briefly."

"Oh. Okay. Good," I said, and half-joined her in the frivolity.

I could sense that our time together was coming to an end, and I wracked my brain for any and all questions I might be able to ask her while I had her attention.

"But what about offensive Bearing magic? Can't that be taught?"

"No, not exactly. You've been fighting for yourself your whole life, Julia. It just looks different now that you're standing in your own power. You did what you needed to do to survive as a child, and no doubt, you'll do the same now. It's simply a matter of making the right choices to follow your own path of intuition, instead of the one that others had previously laid out for you."

"Just that simple, huh?" I said, cocking my head slightly with a raised eyebrow. "And what about the new Prophecy."

"I never said I had all of the answers. But that compass is for you, and I hope it helps you along your journey." A mysterious look briefly flitted across her face.

I watched as she glided to the woodstove in her kitchen beyond and tossed the dark roll into the flames. A brilliant *whoosh!* came from the firebox, and then she turned on her heels back towards me, swaying slightly in playful movement.

"There, now I won't remember anything private," she said, removing the ring and placing it into her pocket. "The ring was for my protection. The flames are for yours."

Above the cabin, I knew that brilliantly coloured smoke would be billowing towards the heavens. She worked her magic in paper, metal, and fire.

None of this was familiar to me, yet the way she moved through her own magic with such conviction made complete sense. I eyed what looked to be a small ceramic smelting urn in the corner, and other wrought-iron tools and bellows that hung behind the woodstove.

"Thanks," I said, breathing a bit easier now that the deed was done.

She smiled again. "Domhnall will be growing restless outside. I prepared a meal for him if you wouldn't mind delivering for me."

We walked together into her small kitchen where the vast woodstove took up most of the real estate. Within a small black fridge, she pulled out a tinfoil-wrapped container of food. She handed it to me gently.

"Thanks. He will be glad of it," I said.

"I know," she replied. "It's his favourite."

CHAPTER 13

I found Dom leaning peacefully against one of the towering redwoods. He was seated between two massive roots at its base, legs outstretched and arms folded forbiddingly across his chest. His eyes were closed, but I knew he wasn't asleep. In fact, as soon as my footfalls crunched onto the outer rim of the perimeter spell, he snapped to attention. "Julia!"

My heart leapt at his gaze. "Hey!"

On his feet in a fraction of a second, he pulled me into a massive bear-hug. "Thank God! I was starting to worry!"

"Starting to?" I said with a chuckle. I fumbled the tinfoil lunch from Bernie, which fell to the forest floor.

"Well, you were gone for almost four hours."

"I was?" This was news to me. It felt like I'd been with the cartographer for maybe an hour, if not less.

He pulled back from our embrace to take the measure of me. Satisfied that I was still whole, his face grew thoughtful. "It felt okay here though. You were right. This place ... it's *different*. Time passes in an unusual way. And that's saying something, coming from me!"

He barked out a laugh, and I smiled in knowing. "I know what you mean."

"What's that?" Dom said, eyeing the package I'd dropped on the ground.

"Bernie sent you some food."

His stomach growled. *"Incredible."*

MANTLE OF THE WORLD RULER

We sat together on the truck gate in peaceful silence. Dom made his way through a gorgeous meal of roast chicken, golden potatoes, and herbed veggies. It was cold, but he didn't mind in the slightest. Watching him devour the spread, I wondered absently if roast chicken could be considered a part of your identity, because surely it was part of his. Not wanting to crowd his feast, I eventually helped myself to the gas station roast beef sandwich I had stored in a soft-sided cooler, as well as a handful of grapes.

Several moments passed as we silently ate.

Now satiated and exceptionally calm, I turned towards him, my bent knee and shin resting against his thigh. I watched as he scraped the last morsels of his surprise meal and prepared myself to deliver the abbreviated version of what had happened with Bernie. There would be plenty of time to unpack everything in detail over the coming weeks—not least of all because I was still processing everything myself—but there were some things I was dying to tell him.

"She gave me a compass," I said, handing my new trinket over to him.

He immediately inspected it, turning the compass over in his hand several times before closing his eyes. He took a deep breath through his nose. "Hmm … It reminds me of Ronan's," he said intuitively.

"Well, here's the crazy thing—she made them *both!*" I smacked his arm enthusiastically with the back of my hand.

He opened his eyes and smirked. "I can tell."

"What? How?"

"Well, obviously I'm not a magic user, so maybe they won't feel the same for me as they do for you. But it's almost like a … a hum. Or something. A lot like Ronan's. The weight, even."

"I'm kind of shocked you aren't more thrown by this not-so-coincidence." I hopped off the back of the truck to stand in front of him, placing my hands on his knees and jiggling them slightly to get his attention. "Dom, this is wild!"

He laughed heartily and smiled at me affectionately. "You know what, Julia? In the past, I might have been shocked, but with the way things have been going over the last year and a bit, I'm not sure I *can* be surprised anymore."

He spread his knees wider as I stepped forward to tuck in close to his core. Wrapping his arms around me protectively, I rested my head on his chest with a deep sigh. He was warm and smelled undeniably familiar and safe. He also smelled a bit like poultry seasoning.

"She took me *into* my memories a bit," I said. "It's kind of hard to explain, but it was really intense. Like nothing I've ever seen before. But it was also really enlightening."

Previously—*in this lifetime*—I might have been anxious to reveal that I had gained access to "core memories," worried that it might bring up more grief. Dom and I were always *so* eager for me to remember more of our lives together, but it was usually coupled with reminders of our losses as well, which wasn't easy. However, the biggest takeaway from my visit with Bernie was that I would remember what I needed to *when* I needed to.

And that was more than okay.

"Oh?" Dom said, waiting patiently to learn more. "You don't have to share anything with me that you don't want to, Julia. You know that."

I could tell that he meant it, genuinely.

"Thanks. I will eventually—it's a fair bit to unpack, and I think we're going to need to hit the road soon. But I learned two big things." I stepped back to look him in the eye. "First, I need to stop focusing so much on the past. The quilt, while it may hold answers, isn't the *only* tool I have in navigating the future. You and I … we … *our paths* are woven together regardless."

Dom nodded, clearly understanding more than I was saying out loud.

"I actually saw the night I placed the tattoo on your back. The lengths we went to …" I shuddered. "It was awful."

"It's not a memory I like to drag up very often, to be completely honest," he said.

I shook my head, still in disbelief around what I'd been capable of back then. "I don't blame you. What a horrific thing to have to endure. I'm so sorry."

"For the record, I think it was worse for you in the long run. You were depleted and sick for weeks—far longer than it took for my skin to heal and recover from the actual act. Memory carving—that's what you called it—is *very* sinister stuff. With lasting consequences. I think Ronan and the lads would refer to it as dark Druidics today. Sort of in the same vein as the stuff Malcolm was messing with before the battle in Northern Ireland. But far worse. We did what was necessary though, and I've never regretted it." Dom was still grimacing at the memory. "That being said … I'm also not keen to replicate the experience if I don't have to."

We did what was necessary.

He smiled in an attempt to soothe me. I nodded, unable yet to smile myself. Stillness surrounded us for a moment, the sheer depth of the forest cocooning us in its soft silence as we contemplated what it had taken to ensure I didn't forget about "us" entirely.

After a time, I spoke. "The book I used ... What a horrific thing. What did we do with it afterward?"

"We made sure to hide it as best we could, willing that it would never be found again. We connected with a Bearer a lot like Bernie actually, a trusted map maker. She promised to bury it far and deep ... and we trusted that. I think you were afraid to try to destroy it because of the dark magics it carried, largely because of what happened when the original grimoire burned down Grianne's cottage."

"Well, that's the second thing. It's something I've been meaning to tell you for a bit. On that horrible day—when my first curse was enacted—it was me who killed her. I saw it when Gertie's cottage burned down, and I haven't been sure how to tell you." I looked at Dom, nervous. His face remained suspiciously calm. "But it wasn't *me* me. It was the grimoire. It possessed me, them ... all of us. The darkness ... it was like an infection. Books like that ..."

Dom remained silent for a moment, and then spoke somewhat tentatively. "Were you worried I'd think poorly of you for what *really* happened?"

"Well ... sort of."

He hopped down and pulled me into a tender embrace. "Christ, Julia. That's the last thing I would do. We've made an *infinite* number of choices over the centuries. Mostly they've been good and honourable, but not always. We do what we have to do with the information we have in the moment. That's always been the line."

"That's what Bernie said too."

"Well, she's right. Plus, the whole 'cottage burning down' thing was completely out of your control. Both times."

"Was it though?" I let out a deep sigh; there was so much left to process from the visit with Bernie.

"Don't be silly, Julia—of course it was. Besides, if we're keeping score, you're *way* ahead of me on the moral-conscience count anyway. If anyone should be apologizing, it's me."

"I doubt that," I said, looking high into the canopy.

He shrugged. "Believe what you will, Julia, but you've always been the one to keep us on the straight and narrow. Not me."

"I find that hard to believe." I dropped my eyes from above and smacked him playfully on the shoulder while turning away. My mind wandered to my own rocky path that Bernie had shown me. "Straight and narrow" were the last words I would use to describe *any* of my journeys over the centuries.

"Oh, come on, Julia." He grabbed me by the shoulders to face me head on and graced me with a roguish grin. "You know I couldn't avoid trouble even if it were looking me straight in the eye!"

I giggled, staring back as hard as I could. "Certified bad boy, huh?"

"I'll be whoever you want me to be, Julia—I live to serve!"

Then he kissed me firmly on the lips.

We carried on like this for several moments, hands travelling up and down each other's bodies beside the truck as we lusted for one another unabashedly. Before long though, our energy began to shift and my thoughts along with it. I thought of the parallel cartography tracks Bernie had shown me and knew wholeheartedly that this wasn't the truth—he couldn't truly live if he were always acting in my service. Dom and I walked our own paths concurrently, at our healthiest when we were able to thrive in our own rights, side-by-side.

"Dom, I love you for exactly who you are. You don't have to be or do anything *for* me. You are your own person, with your own path. You should live for yourself first."

He smiled kindly, but his body language made it plain he wished to shift away from the vulnerable direction the new conversation was headed; I had no doubt he would have preferred we continued the hot and heavy stuff instead.

"We should really get moving," he said.

As anticipated, this would be a theme we would need to unpack over time. I changed tactics as we moved to climb back into the truck to hit the road. "Do you think it—the grimoire—still exists?"

"The *Codex Druidicus,* I believe it was called," Dom said, skirting towards the passenger seat. It was the same title Bernie had used. "No idea if it still exists, but I hope not. We only accessed one page, which was early on in its contents. Most of the book that followed was in harshly scribbled Latin and visibly sinister. I guess …" He looked suddenly guilty, perhaps because we hadn't taken its dangers seriously enough. "Well … we've always just hoped that with the advent of the modern world, relics like that would be lost in the 'annals of time.' Historical redundancy, I suppose."

"Well, you haven't been lost yet, so …" I teased him as the truck started with a purr.

"Are you calling me a *relic?*" he asked in mock (and absolute) indignation.

"If the shoe fits."

He gave me a gentle shove in return. We chatted for a time about nothing at all as we wound our way peacefully out of the forest towards our pre-booked campsite; you had to hand it to the Druids for their planning skills.

Eventually, the conversation returned to Bernie.

"I can't remember when we would have met her in San Francisco, but if she cooked like that back then"—he patted his well-satiated stomach—"I think we would have got on *swimmingly.*"

"She said we can both visit her next time," I told him. She hadn't actually said it, but I knew it hadn't really been a goodbye when I left; we would see each other again someday soon.

"Grand," Dom replied.

"Oh hey—speaking of swimming—what do you say we go down to Pfeiffer Beach for a dip before we set up our campground site?"

"Good idea, because you stink."

"I do not!"

He shook his head in mirthful disagreement as he dodged the blow from an empty water bottle I hurled at him from across the truck.

For the next several days, Dom was in incredible spirits. It almost felt as if we were on a mini vacation, if not for the fact we were just putting off joining the Knaves and Ronan in Los Angeles for a little bit longer while we splashed around in the Pacific and camped along its shores.

Not that we explicitly dreaded seeing them or anything. We had been in touch with Lennie and Wren several times via a group text chat, which almost always boosted Dom's mood. He and Wren were becoming fast friends, and not just because she liked to razz Lennie about the same things Dom did—as hilarious as that was. The fact was, Dom and Wren thought remarkably similarly. I admired the pair of them for their ability to sort through complex information with such efficiency.

However, while Dom was calculated and risk-averse, Wren bore the same heated wildness shared by the rest of the Knaves. This made him slightly uneasy, even if she was arguably the most rational of the bunch.

"Dom, do you have to work *right now*," I asked begrudgingly out the window earlier in the day when he was caught up on his phone, reading a document Wren had just emailed. We were supposed to be packing up and heading to the beach for the afternoon, and he had been lingering outside of the truck for over five minutes.

"No … I … wait. Work?" he asked in a puzzled voice while still clearly distracted by his phone.

"You know what I mean." I let out a loud sigh.

"I'm sorry. It's just that Wren is trying to convince Lennie they need to do some deeper reconnaissance at the tower without any backup. He doesn't agree, and she wants me on her side."

My phone had been going off in the group chat for several minutes already, but I was choosing to ignore it for my preference of hitting the beach. "You can't honestly think that's a good idea before we have more of a plan?" While I knew next to nothing about these types of things, my intuition was telling me that this was a bad idea.

"Of course not. It's reckless. I'm just trying to explain to her why we need to wait until we have all of the facts. Then we can act with precision, together." Dom shoved his phone into his pocket and hopped into the driver's seat. "I'm really sorry, Julia. I'll finish dealing with it later."

True to his word, Dom gave me his utmost attention for the rest of the day.

That evening, we found ourselves back at the campsite and tucking in for some drinks around the campfire. Dom had already cracked into his third or fourth beer since we'd returned, not that this made a huge difference to his disposition. According to him, American beer was "like drinking water," and while I tended to agree, I was also inclined to take it a bit slower when the only relief was found in an outhouse.

Naturally, Dom began storytelling as we settled in for the evening. I delighted in his tales about the kinds of places we used to visit when we were on the road throughout history, particularly because it felt like a common theme to what we were doing now. I found myself gazing at him affectionately as he ran his fingers through his saltwater-encrusted hair. His beard had grown substantially over the past few weeks, and frankly, he was the picture-perfect California beach boy, as far as I was concerned.

"Well, I think mostly we've slept in a lot of barns." He leaned back into his camping chair. The sun was setting low over the ocean now, with the moon coming out high above us. "Sometimes it was taverns and inns, but that was only if we were lucky. Usually, it was pretty rough ... And nothing so sophisticated as this."

He gestured at our truck. We had spent the past several nights sleeping in a pop-up tent that fit perfectly into the truck bed. Dom loved the efficiency of it, while I just appreciated being alone with him; camping with a lover had always felt so intimate to me.

And incredibly *sexy*.

"The air mattress must be a bit of an improvement," I said cheekily. Okay, that part of our sleeping arrangement wasn't the sexiest.

"They've been around for longer than you think," he said, and I would have just taken his word for it, as Dom had lived that kind of stuff, but he launched into an entire spiel around the different types of beds we would have slept on throughout history, down to some very specific details about stuffing linen sacks with different varieties of wool or straw. I didn't mind though. I felt grateful to be in nature with him once more, surrounded by fresh air and crowned in starlight.

"Should we maybe go crawl into the tavern over there?" I eventually asked, jerking my thumb towards the truck. We had been chatting for hours, and the fire had long since burned down. It truly was one of those nights I wished could have lasted forever, and I knew he felt the same. He'd had this sort of distant twinkle in his eyes since I re-emerged from Bernie's cabin. Perhaps due to nothing more than the magic of the place itself, I had the sense that Dom really enjoyed his stay in Big Sur.

It was the most tranquil I had ever seen him, in both recent and past history.

Early the following morning, Dom received a phone call. Half asleep, he rummaged around for a moment to find his cell, which had been forcibly wedged between our bed and the truck liner, cast aside during our previous evening's adventures no doubt.

"What do you mean they've been *captured?*" Dom asked, flummoxed. "Lennie was supposed to have the entire system bugged or whatever! But … why did they go in the first place? How did this happen?"

Gathering my bearings, I shifted uncomfortably on the air mattress to face Dom; there had to be a mistake. Lennie was the last person to get himself captured due to a surveillance error. And Dom had explicitly instructed Wren to wait until we arrived in L.A.

I watched as Dom's face transitioned from pale to bright red. "You're fucking kidding me!"

Ronan muttered something on the other end of the line, which I assumed was something to the effect of "No, I'm *not* fucking kidding, Domhnall," and hung up.

I stared at him for a moment, mouth open. "What's going on?"

"We have to get to L.A., and fast. Lennie and Wren have been taken by Caleb—"

"Who?" I asked, unable to place the name.

"One of Cassius's generals. But by the looks of it, they're slowly accessing all of Lennie's files. He must be in serious danger to give those passwords up. It's *critical* they don't reach Ronan's research."

Dom was clearly speaking Ronan's utterances back at me. I nodded slowly, my head spinning. "Surely though, Ronan's backed it up some other way?"

In the wrong hands, Ronan's research would be used against us.

"Do you really think that would stop someone as skilled as Lennie?"

"But why would Len—" And then it dawned on me; they weren't torturing Lennie for the passwords. There was no way he would give them up, not on his own life.

They were torturing Wren.

"Oh *shit*. Dom—"

"Do you mind if I drive?" he said, kicking off the covers and hastily unzipping the tent.

I nodded numbly; I had absolutely no wish to fumble my way through L.A.'s infamous traffic with a fuming Celt strapped in beside me telling me where to go as we raced to rescue our friends. Of course, L.A. was hours away, but the rapid onslaught of events left my head spinning and thinking a series of steps ahead.

Dom tossed on his t-shirt from the day before, along with a pair of rumpled blue jeans, before hastily taking down the tent. Meanwhile, on a small patch of grass near our campsite, I fought with all my might to force the air from our mattress. My attempt to keep the bed relatively clean was futile, since everything was going to be shoved into the back seat anyway.

Our friends were in danger, and we suddenly could not move fast enough.

"Fuck, fuck, *fuck!*" I said to no one in particular as I pulled my fleece over my head and climbed into the passenger seat in one swift motion. Waiting for Dom to return from the bathroom, I hastily ran my fingers through my hair several times in an attempt to tame it. It was still slightly salty from the day before, crunchy waves flowing outrageously in every direction as I forced it into a tight knot on top of my head.

I puzzled at the facts at hand.

Didn't Wren have some aspect of the Sight? Surely that alone should have caused her to pause and check in before making a move, perhaps seek out some kind of dream warning. Then I thought of my own unpredictability with the Sight and realized that, as much as a dream might have told her to wait, it could have also encouraged her to take a leap of faith. Divining was funny like that, which I knew better than anyone.

Suddenly, Dom appeared at the door, donning his sunglasses as he hopped into the truck. "Let's go."

We drove mostly in silence for the first hour, Dom's logistical brain clearly running endless scenarios as to how we might breach the high tower. He had seen the building plans already, since Wren had shared them with him back in Oregon. He knew the situation better than most, but that didn't help when we were still several hours away.

Ronan called several times, repeatedly annoyed when I answered instead of Dom.

"Can I speak to him?" Ronan asked shortly.

"Do the speaker phone," Dom grumbled; he had two hands on the wheel and was driving rather more aggressively than I was comfortable with.

"Holy shit—Dom!" I said as we narrowly passed a slow-moving minivan just before a freight truck honked its horn loudly at us in the oncoming lane.

"Sorry about that," he said absently as he turned his attention back to Ronan. "What do we know?"

Ronan let out a growl of exasperation before giving us a long-winded update on the situation; I could see now why Dom got so frustrated when he was on the phone with any of them.

"Get to the point, Ronan! How much time do we have? And who's there with you?"

"Stuart, Alanna, and Shereen … and then a handful of Knaves that I don't know have been coming and going from the place as well, keeping an eye on us," Ronan offered, plainly irritated. "And then Sean, Graham, and Lindsey are here for the Druids. Which is … well, it's a small number."

In my mind's eye, I could picture Ronan down there, immensely frustrated with what he had dubbed "cowboy antics" from the American Knaves and bolstered only slightly by a small group of Druids who weren't entirely on his side either by the sounds of it.

No wonder he wanted us down there as fast as humanly possible.

"And let me guess, no Bearers?" I asked, biting back my usual annoyance.

"None that I know of. Sorry, Julia. Not like they would come anyway, but it looks like you're our girl."

I frowned, immediately annoyed by his tone. Truthfully, I was unsure of how much help I would actually be in an offensive setting. I tried to remember all that the Knaves had taught me, as well as what Bernie had told me about Bearing magic being something you develop for yourself.

But was I really a Witch with a fighting disposition?

"Ronan! How much *time?*" Dom asked loudly, pulling off into a narrow gravel patch on the side of the road. I looked at him, somewhat startled and confused, but he was already hopping out and opening the rear door to dig through his duffle bag. A passing car honked loudly, swerving to avoid Dom's bold presence on the narrow shoulder. With his arms full with several rolls of paper, Dom slammed the door shut and rounded to the passenger side of the truck.

"I don't know, Dom! Not a lot! Just get your arse down here! The Knaves are out of control!" Ronan replied loudly before hanging up. I didn't think Dom heard his reply, but he probably didn't need to. No doubt the Knaves and Druids were at each other's throats; Ronan's urgency underscored the need for Dom to step in and smooth things over.

Appearing at my window, Dom gestured for me to take over driving. I didn't mind in the slightest. I felt a desperate need for something to do, and clearly Dom needed a chance to work through whatever maps and intel he could. Not to mention the fact that he had been driving like an absolute maniac so far; we were of no use to the cause if we died in a traffic incident.

Drivers now swapped, I turned on my left signal light, and we took off down the highway once more.

CHAPTER 14

The drive between Big Sur and Los Angeles would go down as one of the longest drives in history— for me anyway. Despite our relative ease of travel, and the fact that the distance between Big Sur and Los Angeles proper was really only about six hours, tensions remained high as we rocketed down the highway towards our rescue mission.

Hopefully we wouldn't be too late.

Dom spent most of the drive pouring over the floor plans Wren had printed for him, muttering to himself about this and that, jaw clenched and hair completely askew from running his hands though it so many times. Unfortunately, when we were about an hour away from our intended destination—Cassius's downtown high-rise—Dom received a text informing him that the group had changed muster points to a new location, which was considerably farther away.

"You're joking, right?" I said. "It's *literally* called the 'City of Industry?' *That's* where the Knaves keep their forge in L.A.? Ronan must be dying inside!" I laughed awkwardly in a vain attempt to keep Dom from imploding at this new turn of events.

"Ridiculous," Dom said, his cheeks reddening in anger. I wasn't sure if he was referencing the *name* of the city or that the group had relocated outside of Los Angeles city limits. Regardless, it didn't matter; he was thoroughly pissed off.

Apparently, Ronan and the others were having trouble with Wraiths patrolling the area they had staked out near the tower and were worried they might draw attention to themselves before it was time to strike. The L.A. Knaves had offered up one of their less frequently used warehouses for our purposes. The Druids (more accurately, Ronan) had dragged their feet a little, but in the end, the Knaves (mainly, Stuart) had won out.

"That's not what I told them to do. The fucking *objective*," Dom said, exhaling loudly through his teeth, "was to find a safe-house as close as possible to where we would strike."

"Well, it's not *that* far off the map I guess," I said, poking at the GPS. "And if they weren't feeling safe where they were, maybe it's for the best that they found somewhere more secure until we arrive."

Dom grunted something that sounded like, "You wouldn't understand," and went back to moodily scouring the floor plans unrolled on his lap. I resisted the urge to tell him that he was acting a bit like a teenage boy—his angst lashed out through heavy breath and rapid hand movements. Clearly though, Dom felt strongly that every moment wasted brought us one step closer to mission failure, and that included transport time. It even seemed to include just sitting still. And he wasn't wrong; time *was* of the essence.

I also got the distinct sense he was seething about having been openly disobeyed.

We drove for a while longer in silence as I pondered the evolving situation before us. Lennie and Wren had been captured in the early morning, which meant they had been out of communication with the group for at least seven or eight hours, accounting for the time it took for our side to realize they were missing in the first place.

Ronan sent several updates on continuing activity across some of Lennie's more heavily protected networks. Apparently, they had not yet accessed the core of his research, but they were trying. While unnerving, we took this as a sign that he was still alive.

Both the traffic and air pollution were heavy as we finally passed through the Los Angeles area, steadily travelling further inland and away from the ocean. I could feel the increased distance from the shoreline deep within my Bearing core, but I tried to remember what Bernie had said: The moon exists away from the sea as well.

We reached the City of Industry in the mid-afternoon, almost twenty-eight kilometres—or eighteen miles—east of our objective. It was hot in the San Gabriel Valley, the truck's thermostat registering the outside air at well above thirty degrees Celsius in the shade. Despite the air conditioning, I was glad to be wearing shorts and a t-shirt; I had long since discarded my fleece from the morning into the back seat.

The forge was apparently located somewhere near the centre of the city, if you could call it that. It reminded me more of a giant industrial park than a proper municipality. Upon our arrival, we found Ronan pacing impatiently outside. He was wearing a fitted dress-shirt and expensive-looking pants, but based on how much sweat had soaked through his top alone, he had likely been waiting outside for some time already. I could only assume the heat outside was preferable to what was going on within and with whom.

Dom quickly squeezed my hand before launching himself out of the passenger side without shutting the door, taking his bundle of papers along with him in a flurry. I hadn't even shut off the engine yet.

"Took you long enough—" I heard Ronan say, approaching the truck, but he was silenced by the look on Dom's face as he strode past him towards the door without a word. Ronan remained rooted on the spot.

I took my time getting out of the truck, intuition gently reminding me to assess the new situation for myself before entering into the fray. Feeling outward from within, I could immediately sense that the building before us was cloaked somehow. Dom had managed to enter without resistance though, so I guessed the intention was more to obscure the identity of the building than anything else.

"Where is everyone?" I asked Ronan.

"Inside. It's got a glamour on it, so it looks—"

"Yeah, I know," I said, watching out of the corner of my eye as he slipped ever-so-slightly behind me. I had become accustomed to these "hand offs" any time Dom stepped into a leadership role. I was never left without protection, but it still made me feel rather infantile. Sovereign or not, I didn't like the feeling of being babysat.

Out of concern for Lennie and Wren, however, I let it slide.

I walked slowly towards the main door, ignoring my sweaty, Ronan-shaped-shadow as I inspected the site. At first glance, it looked like a sort of industrial warehouse or shipping depot, bearing an almost identical façade to the other buildings along the same road. The whole city was effectively one giant industrial zone, which I could only imagine was making Ronan's skin crawl. This particular site was apparently manned by a group of Los Angeles Knaves, about whom I knew absolutely nothing. I assumed this must be one of the locations where they kept a forge though, based simply on the sharp scent assaulting my nostrils.

Coal dust, molten metal, and magic.

"I can smell the forge," I said, turning towards Ronan for clarification, "and *feel* it."

"The fires aren't lit," he said, sounding disgusted, "but I can feel it too. It's very intense. This is a major manufacturing hub for the Knaves."

"Oh?" I asked somewhat absently. "And what do they make?"

"Weapons," Ronan said coolly.

I sensed that he was not speaking of blades only but of something that unsettled him even more. He didn't elaborate.

With Ronan still following a step behind me, I reached the perimeter of the enchantment around the building. It felt sharp and hot on my face, like a knife.

How fitting.

Thankfully, I felt no resistance as I pushed through to the other side of the barrier. While the building before me still resembled its neighbours, it now looked considerably older. Up above, a giant smokestack stuck out rather rudely from the roof, no doubt meant to vent the great furnaces nestled within.

"It's rather a sight to behold," Ronan said haughtily.

"No kidding," I said. Together, he and I entered the building without looking back.

I had expected air conditioning, but instead, the air inside was stagnant. At least the sun wasn't beating down on our necks anymore though. Ronan directed me to follow a narrow hallway, which eventually brought us to a small cafeteria-like space, which seemed to have slightly more airflow.

I immediately spotted Dom standing at the centre of a large table, arms spread wide over the freshly unrolled floor plans before him. He looked hot, but I wasn't sure if it was due to the physical climate of the room or the emotional one. Right away, I could see that there weren't many in our ranks. Wren and Lennie's absence was notable.

"I warned them not to go in there without us," I heard Shereen say, her eyes rimmed red with tears as she looked over towards me and Ronan. Alanna had her arm around Shereen's shoulders, her own face hardened like stone. Some of our friends had listened to Dom's instruction, even if Lennie and Wren had not.

"They knew what they were doing," Stuart said, defending their choice. However, he too looked distraught.

A woman with her back to me spoke next, her Scottish accent immediately evident. "But do *we* know what we're doing? I can't make heads or tails of these plans at all. Even at this scale. It's like a bloody labyrinth in there!" she said, cocking her head to the right in an attempt to understand.

I assumed this must be Lindsey Boyd.

My suspicions were quickly confirmed as Ronan placed himself at the very opposite end of the table, pulling his sodden shirt away from himself in several quick bursts while avoiding eye contact with his ex-girlfriend. This also explained why Ronan was overdressed, as he was likely trying to make an impression of "doing well."

Sean (whom I recognized immediately) and a solid-looking man I presumed to be Graham stood flanking Lindsey on either side. She had long brown hair that she wore in a single thick, badass-looking braid. She was powerful to be sure. I could feel it.

I could also see why Ronan gave her a wide berth as tempers flared.

"I'm familiar with the layout," Dom said, his voice commanding yet soothing with its surety.

"Well, tell us what you know then, *World Ruler*," a dark-haired man said impatiently. I didn't recognize him but assumed he must be a delegate from this particular gathering of Knaves, as he wore a *very* sinister-looking blade openly on his hip. A second man stood to his left, looking equally as menacing with a slender sword strapped to his back in a black leather harness.

I didn't like their tone. Dom bristled as well, but almost imperceptibly—only so much so that I would notice. Dom's reputation had evidently preceded him, even down here; clearly word got around between the West Coast Knaves.

MANTLE OF THE WORLD RULER

"Wren shared the layout with me back in Florence and had these printed for me since ..." Dom paused. I knew that he was about to say something like *"since I hate working from a fucking screen, and she was kind enough to get them for me, despite Lennie saying she was encouraging an old Luddite in his backwards ways,"* but he didn't, letting the silence continue for a long moment instead.

Stuart cleared his throat once, while Shereen blinked back more tears.

Finally, swallowing hard and looking up to the ceiling to regain composure, Dom finished his thought. "Since she knew it might come to this."

It was no secret that Dom had grown fond of Wren during our stay in Oregon. I had the distinct impression that any friendships he forged in this life would feel different, particularly following our battle in Northern Ireland. These friendships had the potential of lasting more than several months or years. And so, I presumed that the entire situation was harder on Dom than I had perhaps given him credit for. More than he realized even. Either that or he was growing more emotive in his "old age," which I didn't mind either, current circumstances notwithstanding.

The unknown Knaves shifted on the spot, clearly uncomfortable with this unexpected display of emotion in response to their outburst.

"Do we know yet where in the building they're being held?" I asked, doing my best to steer the ship momentarily as I sidled up next to Ronan, the only empty space left around the table. Dom flickered a smile of gratitude in my direction as he brought his watery gaze down to me.

"Nope," Stuart said, lacing his fingers behind his head in frustration. "But we can assume it's somewhere almost unassailable."

Before our arrival, the others had plainly been agonizing over the plans, trying to make sense of what was located where. But to no avail. Leave it to Cassius to enlist the design of what looked to be the most complicated office tower ever built. Thankfully, I knew that Dom already had that part well sorted; these types of challenges were firmly within his wheelhouse.

I watched as he pulled out several sheets of paper, eyeing them each in turn before shaking his head. He was working his way up from the bottom floor at an agonizingly slow rate, analyzing Goddess knew what; he had literally spent the past four hours in the truck memorizing the layout already. What could there possibly be that he hadn't seen?

Everyone waited with bated breath, the unknown Knaves now looking only moderately curious.

"*Christ,*" Dom said under his breath as he reached the final sheet for inspection. He had arrived on the floor plan to a top-level executive suite, the last one in the pile. "An *atrium* too ... How very Roman of him."

I looked at him quizzically; he knew damn well there was an atrium on the top floor, as he had gone on about it for a solid ten minutes in the truck already. He cast his gaze around the room and shot me a quick glance as if to say *"Trust me."*

And then I realized what he was doing.

The group was clearly divided. The Washington Knaves were distraught and ready for blood. The Druids conversely seemed tentative, hesitant to act without more information. At best, the L.A. Knaves could be described as openly skeptical. This wasn't a unified front. And so, Dom was putting on theatrics, placing himself at their level and drawing them in before he set himself apart as their leader.

Dom ushered Lindsey and Stuart towards him, since they were obviously the leaders of their corresponding groups. He blatantly left the L.A. Knaves out, which worked well, as it bolstered them and drew them forward in rapt attention. Soon, the pair was inspecting the topmost floorplan with vigour.

From where I stood, I could see that a massive executive office took up about a third of the top floor. An open floorspace occupied the rest of the layout, with a single staircase located along the opposing wall. The atrium, as mentioned, was situated above.

"The elevator doesn't even reach that floor," Lindsey said, looking closer at the plans with dawning understanding.

"It's definitely the end of the line," Stuart said, leaning in as well.

"And the office?" the first of the two L.A. Knaves asked, fully invested now.

Suddenly, I was reminded of the vison I'd had last year on Samhain when Cassius had killed his employee for sharing insider information. In my mind's eye, I could see the room before me and knew with surety that this was the place where Cassius performed all of his "hiring and firing."

"That's Cassius's office," I said with absolute certainty. The entire table gawked at me almost comically.

"And how the hell do you know that?" the second unknown knave asked. He didn't sound angry though; if anything, I would say he was slightly impressed.

Dom eyed me carefully, waiting for my response.

"I've seen it. In a vision," I said firmly. This was my moment to bolster Dom's competence as he rallied them to his banner. "He might not be there now, but that is *one hundred and fifty percent* his office."

"Julia's right," Dom said. "It's the most fortified place, so *that* will be our target."

Alanna spoke up then. "Before they left, Lennie said Cassius was still nowhere to be seen. His general, though—Caleb—he was spotted this morning going in. Would *he* be granted access?"

I immediately appreciated that these people thought like magic users. Cassius's office wouldn't be protected by a simple security lock. Instead, it would be shielded by magic and closed from anyone but the most important individuals in his organization.

"Well, that's who their recon target was, Caleb," Stuart said. "And if he *does* have access to Cassius's office, I'm sure that's where he would've taken them."

"Those bastards can't resist the taste of power. Playing pretend while Daddy's away," Ronan added, rejoining the discussion at last. I watched Lindsey's eyes flash briefly towards him, but she made no reply.

Dom nodded once before stepping away from the table. That was enough for him, and there was no time to lose.

"Perfect. I'll take a group of Knaves up from the bottom through the loading bay. We'll have to clear every floor along the way to be sure we aren't trapped and that we don't miss Lennie and Wren either, just on an off chance. Ronan, you'll take Julia and the Druids up once we give you the signal; you're going to need to get us into the office once we reach the top. We'll take care of the Wraiths everywhere in between, so you are ensured clear passage."

"What about the civilians?" the second L.A. Knave asked.

"There won't be too many people inside. Thank fuck it's a Saturday. We can stage a gas leak or something to clear out whoever is left, cleaners or any security guards. I assume you can manage that?" Dom asked.

Both of the L.A. Knaves nodded in earnest.

With the directives that followed, Dom gave away the fact that he knew the plans inside and out. His feigned ignorance from earlier was evidently unnoticed or of no importance to any of them, now he had them in his command, and they were ready to fight.

I could feel the Knave's energy ramping up around me, exhilarated both by Dom's action-oriented directive and the magic coming from their weapons. Alanna and Shereen were both menacingly fingering the blades at their hips, while Stuart looked almost manic as he set his own singing dagger on the table between himself and Dom. To his left, the L.A. Knaves placed their own blades down in parallel, which I knew to be a promise of their allegiance, as well as the allegiance of what I hoped would be many others who were still on their way.

To my surprise, however, it was the Druids who spoke first.

"So, we can now safely assume that Wren and Lennie are being held in the most difficult room to access," Sean said, "at the very top of the tallest tower. *Grand.*" He was usually a man of few words.

Graham cracked his knuckles. "I do like a challenge."

Lindsey looked from me to Dom and grinned while raising a playful eyebrow. "We're in."

Ronan said nothing, but I could feel his energy ramping up beside me just as much as the rest.

"Sorry I didn't share my strategy with you in advance," Dom said. "I needed to see how they would all react before I made any decisions."

"I understand, and I trust you." I squeezed his hand. "It would have been difficult to show me while I was driving anyway."

Following the meeting, we had gathered in a loading bay on the south end of the Knaves' forge, where several unmarked white delivery vans were waiting for us, along with a host of unfamiliar local Knaves. They numbered approximately forty-five. From here, they would travel to another loading bay, this one at the base of Cassius's tower. To the uninitiated—regular humans going about their business downtown—the gleaming glass walls encasing this arm of Cassius's empire were allegedly unassailable purely because of its elite status. Only those who had purpose would dare enter. It was *so* Cassius.

To the magically trained eye, however, the place wreaked of Wraith magic.

"Are you going to be alright though?" I asked, my fear bubbling to the surface. "You don't have your sword or anything."

"It's no problem!" Dom said, grinning. "Sean managed to smuggle my sword over the border!" He was no longer hiding his own growing enthusiasm for the fight ahead.

"Well, that's convenient," I said, not feeling quite so keen.

Dom pulled me into a tight embrace right there on the loading dock and kissed me forcibly on top of my head. "Don't worry, Julia. If all goes to plan, with me and the Knaves leading, you won't even need to fight. We simply need you and the Druids to get us into the office—it's bound to be enchanted."

"I just hope I can help," I said, feeling my confidence slip slightly. All around me, however, the growing horde of Knaves and small group of Druids were suiting themselves up for battle. Already, each and every one of them looked formidable. That did bolster my confidence.

I had the blade from Lennie, as well as any personal protective spells my subconscious might (or might not) decide to use. I had not used any magic offensively since I had blown apart the castle in Ireland and obliterated any Wraiths near it. But I did my best to remember Bernie's message about Bearers having the power to choose how their magic could be exacted, specifically when it came to using it offensively. I could hardly think of a situation where I wanted to use my magic more than I did now ... to help friends and allies who were in trouble.

"Any tips for if I come across a Wraith?" I asked, gripping Dom as tight as possible; I hated these sorts of goodbyes.

"Kill them dead," he said. And that was that.

CHAPTER 15

The tower itself was pristine, the newest beacon to grace the L.A. skyline. Apart from the window washers working their way up the south side of the tower, it looked like a naked, raw monolith. A part of me was surprised the city had actually approved the design, since it stuck out *so* dramatically—Los Angeles didn't exactly strike me as a city looking for more skyscrapers than it already had—but I didn't find any time to consider the particulars of city planning before I was pulled forcibly back into reality.

BOOM!

That was the signal. Time to begin our ascent.

Dom and the Knaves had surrounded the building and hopefully managed to clear the lower levels before us without too many casualties. The L.A. Knaves had shown up in surprising numbers, which was heartening. From where we stood though, there was no way to know for sure what we would face once inside.

Exiting the unmarked van, I caught up to Ronan and the others at the front entrance. Several glass doors iced in polished silver invited us deceivingly into the hellscape I knew existed within. Crossing the threshold into the disguised fortress, we waded through the sharply air-conditioned entrance and past a large front desk with waterfalled marble edging and clean smooth lines.

This was definitely the place. *Spare no expense.*

Beyond the front desk, we approached the limp bodies of two unsuspecting security guards who had been overcome before a bank of six closed elevators. Looking down, I awkwardly stepped over each man; they were still breathing but heavily stunned by the borrowed and now-spent Druidic pouches. So far, the Knaves were adhering to Dom's rule: Kill no innocents.

Ahead of me, Ronan stood out in stark contrast against the white and silver lobby, dressed head-to-toe in an oppressive forest green. On both hands, he wore black leather gloves, with bracers on his forearms to protect them from what I presumed would be spell kickback. I hadn't noticed them in any previous confrontation, but now they stood out almost conspicuously. Each was intricately stamped with Celtic knotwork, no doubt imbuing the wearer with protection from the onslaught of any magical attack. He wore solid-black military boots on his feet but was otherwise only armed with his dagger, in addition to his exceptional Wielding abilities.

He had pulled out all of the stops for this particular invasion.

Apart from the sheathed golden blade from Lennie, which weighed heavily on my leg in its calf-holster, I was armed only with magic. But based on the Bearer's inferno growing within, I suddenly had a distinct sense that it would be more than enough. With each step closer to our friends, the fire raging only grew in intensity through my chest.

I just hoped Lennie and Wren were still alive.

"This way," Ronan said, leading our small group at considerable speed towards the west staircase. I now lamented the tactical decision to dismantle the power to the building and, therefore, the elevators. The act of climbing thirty-plus flights of labyrinthine staircases towards the executive suite filled me with growing dread. Although, it wasn't like we would have taken the elevators anyway.

"Here, drink this," Ronan said, handing me a small flask of foul-smelling liquid, which he produced from an inner pocket of his jacket just as we reached the first rise.

"What is it?" I asked, shocked at the unexpected offering; Ronan was going off-book.

He didn't answer and instead just held the flask towards me. I didn't notice any of the Druids drinking anything, but perhaps they had their own methods to aid the climb. Trusting Ronan's instinct, I choked back the viscous liquid. It burned horribly all the way down my throat. However, almost immediately, I felt a tingling sensation reach out bracingly through my appendages as my heart began to beat a new and powerful rhythm; I could practically feel my pupils dilate.

"For fuck's sakes, Ronan! It's like magical *speed*."

He grimaced. "It's nothing too dangerous—and besides, the Knaves have their own means of doing essentially the same thing," he said, as if to justify his own use of something he considered morally grey. "We need to get you up to the top. The effects are short lived, so let's go."

"*Bloodsbane?*" Lindsey asked from behind us, her voice bordering on accusation. Ronan shot her a scathing look. Sean and Graham made no comment, though my newfound vigour kept me from caring in the moment.

Entering the chilly stairwell lit with eerie blueish security lighting, we clamoured over several more bodies, these ones notably deceased. The enemy had evidently anticipated our arrival. The stench that greeted us here was almost unbearable, the Wraiths having left their putrid mark before us. My mind focused on Dom, cutting down foes somewhere above us, and I broke out into a mindless sprint towards the top floor.

The ascent *was*, in fact, expedited by Ronan's private brew; though, as I neared the top, I was relieved to discover the effects wearing off almost as quickly as they had begun. At one point, it bordered on an almost out-of-body experience as we planted our feet on each landing before turning yet higher, crossing to the other side of the building or leaping over dispatched Wraiths and wounded Knaves alike.

"I hope you know where we're going," I had said dazedly as I sprinted quickly through more office space towards another illogically placed set of stairs. Some crazed part of my brain made a note that this layout was *definitely* not to code. *How would anyone get out in a fire?* No one responded, and I wondered then if I had actually spoken the last words out loud or only in my head.

The others had no difficulty keeping up with my increased athleticism, however, and I knew then that my assigned Druidic guard meant to carry this task through to the end, whatever the cost. Reaching the top floor at last, I violently cast the double doors aside into the topmost floor, chest heaving and ready for action.

What we saw next took my breath away.

To my still-readjusting eyes, all was moving as if in slow motion. I could see various flashes of bright gold as the Knaves sliced through the air, arcing and colliding with the blackened steel of the Wraiths' scythes in a blurred dance across the glossy, mirror-like floor. Immediately, I could sense Wielding energy competing for domination of the space, like a rip curl in the ocean. The Wraiths were dark pools that the Knaves dove around and sliced though, carving their own offensive spells into their foes.

It was truly a work of art.

My still-drugged heart pounded a resounding thump as my eyes scanned the room for Dom. Not seeing him, I closed my eyes momentarily and was instantly able to sense and target my lover within the fray. I felt our connection tighten, and I knew he would have felt it too. Amidst the supernaturally streaked black and gold of the other combatants, his long silver blade was flying wild, effectively killing the Wraiths two-to-one over most of his Knave counterparts. He was utterly brilliant and fully fleshed in his element. I froze on the spot, admiring his magnificence.

"Julia! We *need* to find Lennie and Wren!" Ronan called from somewhere beyond my left ear. The other Druids remained silently honed.

"Right. Let's go!" I exhaled loudly before launching into the madness.

The Druids were not prepared for me to lead them into the fray, but they fell in line around me in a protective diamond formation. Shoulders back, I held my palms forward at waist height as blackened spells flew towards us. Our arrival had been noted. Similar to the interaction on the dunes in Oregon, I felt an unconscious protection spell forming from within, crackling like electricity across the surface of my skin as I pushed any combative forces away from me and my guard. Bernie was right, I had the power to decide how my magic would work for me in the moment.

And it felt amazing.

Sean was rocketing ahead of us through the magical onslaught like a steel-toed boot through a sandcastle. He was Wielding a brutal, concentrated force. He wouldn't last long before his stored magic reserves were depleted, however, and we needed to get across to the fortified office beyond fast. Reflexively, I reached my right hand forward, much like I would have when throwing my dagger, only this time it was empty. A massive surge of Bearing magic suddenly left my body. My magic shunted down through my right arm and into Sean's broad back like a tightening rope. The boost not only replenished his reserves, but bolstered his physical push forward—shuttling him at a still greater speed, like a battering ram. The group's pace quickened in our magical wake.

Ronan briefly threw me a mystified look. "How—"

The look of shock on my own face intimated *"No idea,"* and Ronan's attention was quickly drawn back into the action.

On all sides, he and the others were deflecting the deluge in their own ways, utterly impeccable in their timing. To my left, Ronan was lunging and blocking Wraith offensives as he cast his own counters outward between the blows. I knew he was bracing himself through each assault, but he remained steadfast. On my other side, Lindsey performed a similarly protective display. However, the violent spells seemed to be rolling over her like water on oilskin. I assumed Graham was still trailing us, based solely on the steady flux of expletives being hurled from behind.

At least half a dozen Wraiths lay between us and the doorway; it was going to be a battle to the very last. And then we still had to breach the enchantments surrounding the office. I narrowed my focus to who and what lay fortified ahead and tasted the sour bile of Sorcery at the back of my throat.

"He's in there! And there's someone else with him!" I shouted with surety. We knew Caleb would be here at the very least. I was unnerved, however, by the second source of darkness detected beyond.

Suddenly, a black-cloaked figure leapt through the air at Ronan from behind, knees raised and a charred sickle outstretched. Without thought, I crouched and tore the gold blade from its shin-sheath with my right hand and threw it forcibly into what I hoped were his kidneys, guiding it with magic throughout its flight. The Wraith screeched in agony before collapsing into a crumpled pile on the glossy floor.

Dom's words of advice rang through my head—*"Kill them dead"*—and I was surprised at how little remorse I felt in the act.

Ronan looked back, his eyes wide. "Thanks."

Without looking too closely, I snatched up the blade with my left hand and continued my trajectory as intended, my trusted guard holding space around me as I focused my energy forward, directing it in a cutting motion through the darkness protecting the final chamber. I heard Dom roar ferociously from somewhere unseen, the draw of his otherworldliness irresistible to the soul-sucking Wraiths. My inner fire piqued to a sea of flames. The threat to my lover pushed me over the edge, and a familiar feeling washed over me.

It's time to end this.

Sean arrived at the doors first, closely followed by Graham, who blew forcefully past and immediately began to unload his precarious cargo. I thought of Malcolm and the sacrifices he had made in creating dark Druidics; this item was no exception in its cost. I could feel the raw force contained in the deceptively small package and fervently hoped the lessons learned from Malcom's demise had allowed them to distribute the weight of its creation in a less damaging way.

As the others prepared the various components to detonate, I hovered my fingertips just beyond the face of the polished wood doors. "I can feel something beyond the protective enchantments," I said to no one in particular.

A violent force from the other side of the doors slammed hard into the right side of my ribcage before slashing all the way upwards and across my face. I let out a stifled yelp and spun sideways before hitting the floor hard on my elbows. I could feel a gash open on my cheek, stinging as hot blood spilled onto the highly polished floor. My novice protection spell had been no match against *this* kind of magic.

"Julia!" Dom's voice howled from somewhere behind me. Whether he had witnessed the blow or felt it within his own being, in a matter of seconds, he was at my side. His Knaves formed a protective semi-circle around us as the Druids continued their machinations.

"I'm alright," I said, not untruthfully. It likely looked worse than it was. I was more winded than anything, feeling suddenly sick to my stomach. However, the impact was significant enough to force us to take pause. Someone inside was clearly on the offensive. Time ground to a halt as the truth I felt within my body finally caught up to my mind.

I felt her. *Another Bearer.*

"What *was* that?" Ronan asked, helping Dom bring me to my feet.

"More like who," I said, rubbing my side tenderly. I almost couldn't believe the words about to leave my mouth. "There's a *Bearer* in there with him."

"What?" Dom said, with complete shock. He had dark blood spattered across his face and clothing like confetti; thankfully none of it was his own.

"How can that be?" Lindsey shouted, looking violent.

Stuart arrived at her side, panting heavily while holding his favourite pair of long golden blades, their handles wrapped in supple black leather. "What are you talking about?" he demanded. "Did I hear you say there was another Bearer?"

I had no idea how he could have heard me, but then I wondered if perhaps part of the Knaves weapons "singing" for them also meant heightened senses all around. Despite the newly emerging threat, the Knaves began to beat back the Wraiths, giving us a moment to regroup.

"That's what she said," Dom said loudly over the ongoing fight around us. His gaze remained on me, with a mix of concern, fear, and fury.

Wren, Lennie, and the Knaves had done extensive research on this murderous arm of Cassius's business, and not once had there been any indication of a Bearer working within the ranks. I closed my eyes and felt outwards once more. Caleb was definitely in there, his magic notably jagged, almost frenetic beyond the doors. I clenched my jaw. The other source of magic was something entirely different, like hearth fire and brimstone. A familiar boiling feeling rose within me, distinctly akin to betrayal.

I gulped. "She's—"

"Back up!" Sean called out suddenly, as he and Graham set to blast open the doors. We had no time to change tactics, only to duck for cover. Sean and Graham simultaneously launched black bundles towards several points along the base of the doors. With a series of resounding explosions, the doors and their enchantments were blown off their hinges.

"Excellent!" Graham hollered after landing hard on his butt several feet from where he'd started. Sean too had lost his balance, landing forcibly on his side to the left of where we hunched down protectively.

Dom had somehow managed to position himself between me and the explosion, taking the brunt of the energy on his back. He let out a loud, "Oof!" into my ear as he wrapped his arms around me.

The room immediately filled with dust and residue.

"Bit bigger than they planned, I think," Stuart said, laughing darkly from somewhere unseen. Closer by, Ronan scoffed but didn't disagree. Lindsey let out a delighted cackle; it would seem that, in the heat of the moment, even the Druids could get excited about offensive magic.

"Are you alright?" Dom asked, drawing my attention back to him as he breathed the words into my ear.

Still recovering from the blow I'd experienced only moments earlier, I was grateful for Dom's steady protection. "I am ... but thank you."

"Good," he said with a curt nod and turned his attention back to his surroundings while keeping an arm around me. I sensed that the existence of a dark Bearer had thrown him off considerably, presumably because we had never encountered anything like it before.

Meanwhile, the battle behind us was halted only briefly by the blast. Soon, we were accosted once more by the shrill sound of keening Knave blades as they collided with wailing Wraiths. Alanna and Shereen were still somewhere in the fight, and I swallowed hard.

"Everyone, get up!" Dom said, instinctively naming the danger gathering around us from all sides; time was of the essence.

Staggering to my feet, I had not even begun to process the aftermath of the explosion before I felt the harsh violence of Caleb's Wielding magic all around as it poured out from the previously fortified space. It was dangerous but not impenetrable, with its cracks immediately apparent to even my untrained abilities—the Druids could easily handle him. However, I also sensed an unexpected hesitation and assumed that the Wielders around me could now also detect the molten darkness emanating from within. Bearing magic. Unhinged. I watched as Ronan's and Lindsey's eyes widened; their jaws were set in a combination of fear and acceptance of destiny.

"What *is* that?" Dom asked and braced his raised sword in two hands. Clearly, he also sensed the exceptional disturbance. Before anyone could answer him, the dust finally settled, and we were greeted with a horrific sight.

On one side of the room, Lennie was magically bound to a chair before a bank of computer monitors. Caleb stood behind him with a charred sickle to his throat, grinning maliciously. Lennie was clearly battered and bruised but still very much alive. A small part of my mind was disgusted by a wave of magical déjà vu; this was precisely what I had expected to see, and I wondered if I had in fact dreamt of it before. The real shock, however, was happening on the opposite side of the room.

This image I definitely had *not* divined.

Wren was suspended in the air in front of a massive bank of windows. Her chest seemed strung to the ceiling, as her back bent in an inhuman arch. Bloody slashes traced across her skin as all four limbs swung limply below. The blood travelled smoothly down her body and dripped in a steady stream from her toes and nowhere else. The floor underneath was just concave enough to allow the rich red liquid to stream neatly into a discreet floor drain. She was visibly unconscious, if not dead already.

Out of the corner of my eye, I could see Lennie shaking violently as he clattered on the keys. Our worst suspicions came true: They were torturing Wren in order to force Lennie to gain access to hidden files. *Ronan's* files, containing his research on Wraith regeneration. And the person guilty of this horrific treachery stood casually at Wren's head.

A Bearer unlike anyone I'd met in my life.

"You're just in time," she said, her voice dripping like syrup. She wore her thin blonde hair at chin length, which only further accentuated her unusually angular jawline. Petite and immaculately dressed, she would have looked more like a cheerleading coach than a sadistic, dark Bearer, if not for the comparatively cheerless grin that spread across her face.

"What have you done?" I asked, speaking not only with my own voice but with the echo of countless Bearers that had come before me.

"Oh, I'm not done yet." She thrust her hand out into the air, claw-like. With a flick of the wrist, she cleanly broke Wren's neck without even laying a hand on her. The rapid movement was simply shocking; she could have used her Bearing magic to kill Wren in any number of ways, and we had all thought she would. But this had been maliciously intentioned, more like Sorcery than anything else.

A skill she had learned at Cassius's knee.

The collective intake of breath was audible over the fighting going on behind us, but it was soon drowned by Lennie's cry of anguish as he was confronted with the murder of his lover. I felt my own inner rage pique at the continued violence at the hands of Cassius and his minions. And at such a monstrous betrayal from my own kind.

And that was when something within me broke.

I shrieked, thrusting my arms directly in front of me as I sent out a wave of enchantment across the room. It was much like what I had created at the castle, only more focused. The effect of the magic reverberated off the windows, causing the glass to shatter spectacularly in every direction. Both Caleb and the dark Bearer hit the floor hard, and I knew immediately that the former was dead.

"You think you can use your pathetic Bearing against me?" the dark Bearer asked, pushing herself up off of the floor and scrambling towards Lennie. Contrary to her barb, she was unmistakeably weakened. Panting heavily and wiping blood from her nose, she held her hand out to Lennie just has she had with Wren. "Let me go, or he's next."

We all paused.

Caleb's binding thrall had been released now that he was dead. Freed from the chair, Lennie now hung flaccidly in the air at the hands of yet another magic user while his eyes remained locked in horror on Wren's dead body. It was as if he were frozen in time. As if all of his fight was gone, or he had simply resigned himself to join her in death.

Dom and Stuart both moved to charge forward while the Druids remained still. The result was a strange, disorganized tension pulling between the two camps. Like a stutter, only with dire consequences. Then to my dismay, they all looked towards me for direction. I froze and looked to Dom, who communicated to me in his unspoken language.

"This is a Bearer's fight. What do we do next?"

Despite the fresh rage I felt surging through every inch of my body—my control balanced on the edge of a knife—I had no interest in sacrificing Lennie as collateral damage in order to avenge my kin. This was between me and her, but Lennie didn't deserve to die for it; Wren was already one too many lost.

"Let him go," I said, stepping slightly forward. "This is between us." My voice, again, didn't feel like my own.

The grin left her face, and she faltered slightly at my advance. I was right; she was weaker than she looked after the magical blow I had dealt. But what should I do? I hesitated at the thought of attacking another Bearer, even one who'd betrayed her own. I needed a moment to think. In the slight window of time I had so graciously provided by pausing, the Bearer dropped Lennie to the ground and dove headlong out the top-floor window. It had taken only a single moment.

Fuck!

Dom and Stuart rushed to the ledge.

"She's getting away!" Dom growled.

Alanna and Shereen had finally fought their way to the doorway and were now standing in horror at the sight of Wren, broken on the floor. Lennie, barely conscious, was dragging himself across the glass, his hands and arms now bleeding profusely as he grappled to reach her lifeless form.

"Let's go!" Stuart boomed and made immediately for the stairs. With Wren's passing, he was now first in command. The Knaves who remained standing followed dutifully behind him, Alanna and Shereen included. It seemed that the Knaves had gained the upper hand in the battle, as more of them were rushing into view as we spoke.

I watched waves of both temptation and reluctance ripple through Dom's body for a fraction of a second. He then strode to my side. "Julia, we need to get out of here."

"Dom's right," Ronan said, making for the doorway. He paused. Lindsey, Graham, and Sean were attempting to pick up Lennie, who was flat out refusing to let go of Wren's body.

"We'll bring her with us, you fucking numpty!" Graham said, aggravated by the delayed exit. His accent sounded extra thick. "We've got to *go!*"

Lindsey looked nervously at the amount of blood coming from Lennie's hands and yelled for Ronan, who walked over to Lennie. He bent down in an attempt to look at his hands, but Lennie was distraught and wouldn't let him near.

"I don't have anything I can give him up here anyway," Ronan said. "It's all down in the van."

Sean shook his head in resignation. "We'll just have to haul him out."

Ronan stood once more, his frustration and mounting anxiety to leave visible in his posture. "Christ, man! We've got to *move!*" He looked to Dom.

Dom squeezed my hand once before letting go, his compassion for Lennie equally evident in his form as he approached the bereaved man. He crouched down and said something into Lennie's ear. After a long pause, Lennie rose from the ground, supported by Dom. The pair then made silently for the exit, with Dom handing me his sword and beckoning for me to follow. I guessed that, before we reached ground level, supporting his friend was going to become a two-handed job. I floated wordlessly after them.

Behind us, Graham gently lifted Wren's body. She looked tiny in his arms, and I saw that he had tears in his eyes, as did several of the others. "Easy does it, sister," he said quietly.

Throughout the office, countless Wraith bodies lay scattered amidst the detritus of battle, disintegrating, their stolen magic leaving them crippled and broken at its release. Computers, desks, and file cabinets lay strewn across the once perfectly polished floor, an odd juxtaposition between the old world and the new. I spotted a handful of Knave bodies, still warm with recently extinguished life. I fought back a disgusting feeling of relief that I didn't recognize any of them. What the hell was happening to me? I knew there was no way we would be able to retrieve them all now; their comrades would return for them if they could, but it was just another harsh reality of working for the cause.

"We should at least collect the Knave's weapons," Lindsey said, and she and Sean set to work quickly reclaiming the precious blades before our enemies could get their hands on them. I absently wondered why this would be important to a Druid but didn't have an ounce of energy left in my mind to ruminate until we were somewhere safe.

CHAPTER 16

"What the fuck was Julia supposed to do?" Dom asked angrily. He had one arm draped protectively over my knee. We sat together on a low red-leather couch at the side of the room. He leaned forward. "She barely even had a chance to *think* before that evil Witch dropped Lennie and hurled herself out the window!"

We had retreated to the L.A. Knaves' warehouse in the City of Industry, though their leaders had not joined us in this meeting. As far as they were concerned, the Knaves were mercenaries for hire in a Wielders' war. And when they found out about the dark Bearer, they'd wiped their hands clean of the lot of us. Fickle? Perhaps. But on the other hand, this was a can of worms that none of us were particularly pleased to be looking down into. I had the distinct impression they had mainly signed up to kill Wraiths, the allure of which was now satisfied.

I sat with my knees drawn close and my head in my hands, the shock of what had happened in the tower now expressing itself fully within my body. The fact was that the people who surrounded me now were all adept fighters. Meanwhile, I was still wholly unaccustomed to the harsh realities of battle; despite glimpses of my own leadership and power, borne from my emotion and anger, in that moment, I wondered if I ever would be.

The whole situation was well and truly fucked.

"I'm so sorry everyone," I said, my face still buried.

Dom tensed around me, but I sensed the move was as much caring protection as it was defence. He growled low, as if to say, *"If one more person comes at Julia, there'll be hell to pay."*

Meanwhile, I was struggling to keep up with the argument going on around me.

Since the ten of us had arrived at the hidden warehouse, I found myself shaking and fighting back waves of intense nausea. The strange smells coming from the L.A. Knaves unlit smelting fires were not helping matters in the least, and I hated to imagine what it smelled like in here when the fires were actually going. Horrible. I also felt like I was still coming down from the strange elixir I had taken, the room spinning severely anytime I moved my head too quickly or looked around.

Someone had set a pail at my feet, presumably Ronan, but I hadn't needed it just yet.

"We don't disagree with what you did at all, Julia. How could we? You were seriously impressive, snuffing Caleb out like that. But we *also* know that Lennie would have gladly died if that meant we could have caught that Bearer. And that's where the issue lies," Stuart said, but I knew his comment was directed past me and at the Druids.

"We aren't in the business of sacrificing lives, Stuart," Ronan said haughtily.

"At least not if we can help it," Sean said in agreement, while Graham nodded and folded his arms across his massive chest. Graham had taken Wren's killing the hardest of the Druids by far, which surprised me based on his hardened exterior. It just went to show that you can't judge a book by its cover.

"Or a Witch by their jacket," Gertie's voice interjected from somewhere in the beyond.

I hadn't thought of her for quite some time and wondered then what Gertie would think of the Bearer's betrayal. Surely, she would offer me some sage advice or provide an example of someone she had known on Salt Spring Island who had been "turned to the dark side" over some minor local dispute. She had warned me, after all. But the truth was, Gertie had absolutely no awareness of issues this significant or this dire. She had been—effectively—safe on her mountain, away from the harsh truths of the *real* magical world.

I opened one eye briefly, the crushing realization of how unprepared I still was for this life flashing before my eyes as I squinted at the gathered warriors all around.

It felt like the Druids and Knaves had been at it for hours, spending more energy disagreeing about the ethics of the battle than acknowledging the fact we had just unearthed a sadistic Bearer playing Sorcerer's apprentice. Apparently, her name was Kenzie Clarke. She had been completely overlooked as being a Bearer, though apparently the group did know of her as one of Cassius's generals. A little secret he had been keeping for a rainy day, perhaps?

"If you all wouldn't have paused like that, we could have maybe saved Lennie *and* caught Kenzie!" Stuart slammed his fists onto the long table in the centre of the space, pulling everyone's attention sharply back.

At the sound, I looked up abruptly, and the room lurched before me. I proceeded to empty the entire contents of my stomach into the pail that Dom had adeptly delivered to my face in attuned anticipation. No one else seemed to notice or care; maybe they were used to this type of thing post-combat? My head was positively swimming, the overwhelming emotions I was feeling manifesting as physical vertigo.

"And where were the Druids while we hunted her down?" Alanna asked.

"Easier said than done, *boy-o*," Graham said, squaring himself off with Stuart. His Scottish accent rang loud and brash over Stuart's South African one. "We had no idea what she was capable of! We had no intel! Even you have to admit, Wielding has its limits against Bearing magic. Or perhaps her magic is better described as Sorcery."

It was true. We definitely hadn't anticipated the dark Bearer, let alone that she would be so profoundly skilled, particularly at torture. I had a strong suspicion that she had learned everything she knew from Cassius. I looked towards a dark corner of the room, and my stomach plummeted and my heart hurt. Lennie sat stock still before Wren's blanket-wrapped lifeless body.

The same unbridled rage I'd felt when first discovering Kenzie's treachery burned again in my core, demanding revenge. My body began to tremble as the flames licked and snapped within, threatening to crumble any last resolve I held on to. Shock was a weak container for boiling anger.

MANTLE OF THE WORLD RULER

Dom rubbed my back instinctively, settling my inner storm slightly as Ronan's next words drew me back towards the conversation.

"It's not like Dom went after them either," he said, unexpectedly tossing Dom onto the fire with the rest of them. Either that or he was projecting his own perceived failings onto his leader instead.

The room fell silent as Dom's back straightened, but Lindsey spoke first, her own Glaswegian accent growing thicker the angrier she got. "Oh, just fuck off, Ronan! Julia just faced betrayal by one of her own kin! Do you really think that would've been the moment to abandon her? Leave it to you to forget the basic fundamentals of being *human!*"

Lindsey had remained strangely silent throughout the argument before this, seemingly caught between two minds. But now she was letting loose, and not just on Ronan. "That goes for you too, Stuart. Take a moment to *think!* There's a time for action and a time to regroup. Like Graham said, we had absolutely no idea what Kenzie was capable of. We could have gotten both Julia and Dom killed if we'd rushed in without a plan. And without them—in case you've all forgotten—we don't stand a chance in hell at defeating Cassius!"

Ronan looked furious, whereas Stuart just stared at Lindsey with a look that seemed remarkably clear, considering the confused darkness of the moment, and I could have sworn I'd just witnessed a man falling in love in real time.

"I just don't understand how we missed her," Shereen said, referencing Kenzie. She too had been quiet for most of the discussion, lost in thought as she diligently polished and cleaned the blades of her fallen comrades. Tears ran down her face as she worked; she had been one of Wren's closest friends.

"Well, that's the thing, hon. Lennie and Wren obviously detected something was wrong," Alanna said, soothing her partner. "That's why they snuck in ... to try to find out more."

"A brazen plan that almost got them *both* killed!" Ronan barked. Both women looked at him scathingly. Immediately, the others piped in, and the squabbling started all over again. And then, amidst the chaos, Lennie collapsed over Wren's body, sobbing silently.

At this, Dom reached his limit for circular discussion and witnessing his friend in pain without taking suitable action. His voice thundered over the room as he stood. "Enough! This discussion is going *nowhere!* We must band *together!* Not sit here debating what we did or didn't do!"

The others hushed. Finally, Shereen spoke, her voice deep with sorrow. "What do you propose?"

Dom paused, organizing his thoughts while regaining command of the situation. Unbeknownst to the others in the room, I knew he would lord the silence over them for several more moments as he rolled his shoulders back and bent his neck from side to side, working his way through a suitable plan in his head while waiting for everyone to orient themselves to his next words. While he used this particular skill set sparingly, I knew he had done it countless times before in our past lives. Just like his father, the legendary Brian Boru, Domhnall O'Brien was a giant among men. I let out a low sigh, willing his strength to steady me as well.

"Where I come from … *when* I came from …" he said slowly, meeting every single eye in the room before continuing, "the notion of 'kingdom' didn't translate into monarchy … at least, not in the conventional sense."

I watched as each face puzzled over his proclamation. Where was he going with this? Only Ronan looked like he expected what came next as he leaned back ever so slightly.

"And as such," he continued, "no singular king reigned, save for the High King—"

"Ard-Rí na hÉireann," Ronan said quietly, but Dom clearly didn't take it as an interruption, at least not from his most ardent general.

Nodding slightly, Dom went on. "And at his peak, the *Ard-Rí* worked to unify all kingdoms throughout the land. He started by delegating down to each provincial king below him, who then put forth their needs to the petty kings. They then led the clan chieftains, noblemen, freemen, and lastly the slaves. When he called their banners to battle, they came at once, with no questions asked. However, he did not *rule* them. They knew that they could always say no if it didn't align with their territory's needs, political or otherwise, but doing so also meant that he might not consider helping them when the time came to reciprocate. It was a delicate system based on honour, trust, and integrity, and the belief that a nation united was stronger than a host of warring factions."

From where I sat, humbled if not slightly humiliated by the barf-pail at my feet, I was again in awe at the natural command Dom held. He was simultaneously educating, encouraging, and (arguably) persuading the group before us into line. Apart from Ronan's momentary translation, not a single person spoke over him. Instead, they waited in rapt attention for his next utterance.

"By no means am I suggesting that we thrust a single person into this top role," Dom said, and I almost laughed out loud. He was clearly the perfect candidate, reluctant or no. But that was his decision to make, so I kept my mouth shut. "But we must observe the ability to work *together,* within our own *kingdoms* … towards a single cause."

Dom's voice rose as he looked towards me, adoringly. I watched in reverence as he continued to cast his spell. "That cause is to defeat Cassius and his vile rule over all that we hold dear. And if *that* cause is to be our leader, the highest call we can ultimately rely on, then *surely*, we can learn to work cohesively within our own camps. We may not see things the same way, nor will we always approach a battle with the same mindset. But we must be informed by what the greater purpose is asking us to do. We each bring our own unique gifts and talents to the table, and debating over which way is right is utterly ridiculous … In fact, it's a colossal fucking waste of time to spend valuable moments arguing with one another when we could be out there! Strategizing. Fighting. Putting the pieces into place to end Cassius's rule …"

Dom wandered back towards me, finishing his thought as he ran his fingers through his hair in visible frustration; the effect was precisely as intended. "I can't Wield … nor can I Bear. But I've sure as shit given my life to this cause enough times that I refuse to lose steam now through petty arguments between people who are on the same side of the issue! Even if most of the time I *am* a simple human when compared to the rest of you and your abilities." Finished, Dom was looking directly at me now. In fact, in this moment, he only had eyes for me.

"You're not a *simple human*, Domhnall," I said, lovingly. I could guess that the others weren't buying into this particular sentiment either. Dom truly was a singularly unique and powerful person.

"That may be so, Julia. But we all need to be okay with being different from one another." He smiled gently at me while pushing a stray hair behind my ear. "And by God, I'm fucking tired of losing the love of my life at Cassius's hands, time-and-time again. Very few of you have even the slightest notion what it's been like …"

Dom dropped slowly onto his knees before me, taking my hands into his own and kissing the tops gently. One by one, he traced each knuckle with his whiskered lips, sending violent shivers up my spine with each repeated caress. Unlike moments earlier in his speech, I knew this wasn't a calculated act. Here he was, in front of all of them, unabashedly cherishing my very existence.

The fact I was still *alive*.

My eyes trailed over Dom's head, which was now resting sideways on my lap, his gaze towards Lennie, who was collapsed devastatingly over his lost love.

"Dom's right," Lindsey said quietly after several moments of breath. Surprisingly, both Stuart and Ronan nodded in agreement. "We have to stop being on opposing sides. We're independent arms of the same body. The same mission."

Dom looked appreciatively at Lindsey. "For what it's worth … I don't disagree with the Knaves *or* the Druids. I *know* Lennie would have rather died than let Kenzie get away, especially after what he had witnessed. I would have been the same if I were him." He wove his fingers through mine. His tone had changed once more, veering now towards sadness. I squeezed back reassuringly. "But that's not what happened, and the choice for me … *for us* … at that moment in time, was to regroup with the Druids and get the hell out of there. *Alive*. I have no regrets. I would have loved to chase down and decimate the rest of the Wraiths *and* that dark Witch. But the higher cause came into play, and my decision hinged on that. Do you see?"

With that, it was as if an illusion had been lifted from the room. Perspective, at long last. A long silence hung in the air, thick with the ache of reality, before being broken by Ronan.

"So, what now?"

"We need to adjust our viewpoint. And get our shit together!" Lindsey said.

"Okay," Stuart said, "so … what do we know?"

"Wren was deeply worried about what the Wraiths were up to behind closed doors without their leader. We simply don't know enough about what these fuckers are up to in Cassius's absence. And that makes me extremely nervous. There was some other kind of magic showing up in the fight today, or am I wrong?"

"You're not wrong," Lennie said, suddenly appearing behind Stuart; evidently Dom's call to order hadn't been missed by a living soul in the room. Everyone shifted to look towards Lennie in compassion, but he now wore such a hardened mask that he was impenetrable to their sympathies. At least for the time being. "The Wraiths are changing. They're ... stronger. That's what Wren and I were after, intelligence around what *exactly* they were up to. Wren was keeping it quiet until we had something concrete, but she thought that the Knaves' weapons haven't been as effective as they should be lately—no offense, Stu—and she needed to find out why."

"Well, now we have proof," Dom said, pulling his sword from where it lay behind us across the back of the couch. I had returned it to him when we reached the bottom of the tower and loaded ourselves into the vans, where he had quickly wrapped it in a thick woven cloth. I'd thought nothing of it at the time, but in hindsight, it really wasn't like him to scurry it away like that when we weren't fully clear of the conflict. "It's ruined."

Stuart walked over and took Dom's prized weapon into his own hands, crouching onto the floor to remove the wrappings. To my surprise, Dom's sword was now cracked throughout, almost as if it were disintegrating before our very eyes.

"*Jislaaik,*" Stuart said, shaking his head in astonishment.

"I could feel the blade growing weaker the longer I fought," Dom said. "I think several more blows and it would have shattered in my hands."

"Oh, Dom, I'm so sorry," I said.

"Don't worry, love. It's not the first sword I've broken and won't be the last. Though I did like this one a fair bit."

Silence spread throughout the room. If the Wraiths were imbuing their own blades with magic, like the Knaves did, or worse, using their blades to somehow siphon off the magic the Knaves held in their own, we had a *serious* problem on our hands.

"So, that's one clear issue, but what about what happened with Kenzie?" Graham asked, tension still visibly evident in his lumbering posture.

Sean spoke, looking more aggrieved than tense. "Graham's right. How did we miss her? She added an unknown threat to the fight."

"It's true," Alanna said. "When those doors blew open, it was almost like a burst of oxygen to the Wraiths' fire."

Lennie nodded. "Well, we think ... *thought* ... that they were trying to find a way to combat whatever Julia *did*, at the castle, and they clearly haven't been idle."

"But Julia still managed to kill Caleb today?" Shereen asked, looking fearful.

"She did," Lennie said, his face growing paler yet. "But the Wraiths didn't—"

"I knew this was going to happen!" Ronan said, interrupting him. "It's why I've been so focused on my research." He stared at me accusingly. "What Julia did at the castle hasn't gone unaddressed by the other side!"

"That's exactly what they were torturing Lennie for, Ronan!" Lindsey barked, annoyed. "*Your* fucking research!" She was right, of course; Ronan's study of the Wraith regeneration was dangerous to begin with—what secrets could our enemies unlock with it in their grips? At this, the group resumed its boiling tension, Dom's verbal charm from earlier dissipating more by the second.

Ronan ignored her, his face suddenly blank as he caught up to what Lennie was saying. "The Wraiths didn't die."

My heart sank because I knew exactly what they meant. It wasn't lost on me that the only one killed by my outburst had been Caleb. There were enough Wraiths nearby that it should have killed at least a handful more. Was it all tied to Kenzie somehow? Just like I had somehow managed to "boost" Sean, was she able to protect the Wraiths around her using her own source magic? The even more confusing part was that I knew they wouldn't be giving it back. Were they using her as some sort of magical resource upon which they could draw?

At this thought, I unexpectedly dry heaved into my bucket, and Ronan rolled his eyes. Dom returned to my side and rubbed my back for several moments, looking concerned. I glared at Ronan; my disparaging stomach was definitely his fault. Whatever the hell he had given me was *not* leaving my system kindly.

"Ugh! It's the bloodsbane, Ronan! You asshole," Lindsey said, placing her palm to her forehead. She took off towards what I assumed was a kitchen area, citing the need for a tonic. At this point, I wasn't sure if she meant for me or herself.

Dom looked back and forth between me and Ronan, suddenly fuming. *"What* did you give her?"

"Nothing I didn't take willingly," I said, waving my hand passively, not wanting the conversation to veer off course. Dom stared at Ronan as if to say, *"Don't you think for one fucking minute we won't be talking about this later,"* but he remained outwardly silent.

The conversation continued for a time, debating what the Wraiths might be up to in order to counter my ability to strip the magic of their stolen power. It likely had something to do with why Kenzie was around and had risen to such a high rank; it wasn't Cassius's style to give just anyone authority, let alone a woman.

He loathed women.

"But then why did Caleb die?" Stuart asked, puffing his chest slightly. Lindsey had just returned with a full mug of something hot, and he had definitely taken notice of her return.

"Chamomile," she whispered as she handed it to me with wink. "Simple remedy."

"I don't think he was a Wraith, per se," Lennie said, "not in the sense that the others were. We think … thought … that Caleb—and now I assume Kenzie too—were actually Cassius's novices of sorts. Like he had trained them to step up for just such an occasion when he might need to go dark. He clearly didn't teach them much, but it was like Sorcery all the same."

"Evil understudies," Graham said, causing a ripple of unexpectedly macabre laughter throughout the room.

The tea was immediately helpful, sending a warm, soothing sensation down my throat and into my stomach. At last, I spoke without fear of throwing up. "I used to see a man in some of my nightmares, after the time Cassius skewered me, close by his side. But it wasn't Caleb."

"You'll have been seeing Desmond," Lennie said, and I looked at him, shocked. "Wren used to see him too in her dreams sometimes. He's dead now, apparently. Or at least that's what Caleb said at one point."

Frankly, I was shocked at how much Wren and Lennie had shared between the two of them during the comparatively short duration of their relationship. Some of this seemed important for all of us to know, but we didn't. Then again, who was I to talk? Dom and I had repeatedly "jumped in with two feet" over the past thousand years, holding nothing back in our brief unions. These kinds of connections were truly exceptional.

It made my heart hurt further still, over the depth of Lennie's loss.

"Wait … Did you learn anything of use while …" Ronan faltered slightly. On the one hand, the timing was incredibly insensitive, but on the other, it was possible that Lennie might have inadvertently gathered knowledge that might be useful to our cause.

Lennie nodded, but his face went suddenly ashen; his mask of strength wouldn't last much longer.

"Why don't we discuss it tomorrow?" Dom said, noticing Lennie's imminent collapse. "Julia isn't well, and we could all use some sleep."

Dom didn't know that I was feeling significantly better thanks to Lindsey's remedy. But indeed, the hour had grown late. And I was happy to act as the reprieve Lennie needed.

CHAPTER 17

I awoke early the next day to the sight of Dom standing shirtless, staring out the small window of our hastily rented motel room near the City of Industry. We had left for the motel late in the evening, and dawn had come quickly. The early morning light outlined his powerful frame in an almost ethereal glow, highlighting the strangeness of the space we'd been occupying since the events on the tower. Ever since …

"Is everything okay?" I asked quietly as I pushed my poorly throttled emotions down.

He remained still for a moment, and then shook his head slightly before returning to bed. He wore thin jersey pajama bottoms, and despite everything that had happened the day before, something about the way they sat on his hips caught my attention in a very primal way. I watched hungrily as he settled onto the mattress, wondering if my brain might actually be broken; surely, I shouldn't be thinking about that right now. Maybe this was just what it felt like to live fully in the spare moments between threat and safety. Between life and death.

"Morning, love. Everything's fine. I've just been thinking …"

"What were you thinking about?" I asked, snuggling in as close as I could. As always, he smelled deliciously familiar. He brushed my hair away from the both of us and rested his chin near the top of my head.

"Nothing really—okay, that's not true," he said, catching himself. "I'm just a bit … worried. I feel like a lot of pieces are moving on the board right now, but none of them seem to be in our control." I felt his jaw tense in a resigned grimace. I ran my fingers through his golden chest hair, scratching gently. He let out a low sigh.

"Well," I said, "I think your call-to-action last night will have helped some."

"Maybe." He didn't sound convinced. "It all devolved pretty quickly after that, if I'm being honest." Once Lennie had brought to our attention the undeniable truth of the Wraiths' strangely growing powers, even Dom couldn't stem the discomfort spreading among the group.

"They're a tough crowd for sure," I offered. "But we'll figure it out."

He nodded slightly.

After the adjournment of the post-battle debrief (if you could even call it that, as it was anything but brief), Ronan, Sean, Graham, and Lindsey had retired to the same motel as us, each in their respective rooms. The Knaves had apparently found other accommodations with their kin.

Dom and I both hoped this would serve as a bit of a circuit breaker between the two camps before the next stage of our plan was set into play. Not to mention the fact that it wouldn't have been a good idea to move Lennie away from Wren's body, which I guessed was being prepared for transport at this very moment.

"What time are we supposed to meet with the others?" I asked.

"Nine," he said. I looked over his shoulder at the clock and was disappointed that it was only an hour and a half away.

In truth, I barely remembered going to bed the night before, collapsing in sheer exhaustion while promising to discuss things more deeply in the morning. Neither of us had slept well. I had been plagued by nightmares concerning a certain dark Bearer and tossed and turned through most of the night. Meanwhile, Dom had clearly already been up for hours, unable to stay asleep with how much was going on in his head. I had heard him hop into the shower at one point—no doubt in an attempt to regulate his system—but it was unlikely that it had made much of a difference.

With this many loose ends needing tying, Dom was unlikely to rest at all.

I felt such a strange mix of grief, confusion, and fearful anticipation roiling within my core. These mixed with some unnamed dark feelings just below the surface that I was blatantly ignoring. I was also somehow incredibly horny, almost as if there was steam within me building pressure and begging for release. I thought of the feeling of Dom's hands and lips on my body, and shivered.

I knew I wouldn't be able to suppress these feelings for long.

Dom's body seemed taut with his own sea of emotions as he tossed himself onto his back with a low grunt. "I've suggested we meet on neutral ground this morning," he said, running his hands through his hair, which now stuck up in all directions. He laced his fingers behind his head in repose, his abdomen flexing deliciously as he held himself in position. Unable to get comfortable, he quickly rolled onto his side again, looking towards me.

If I hadn't known him better, I'd have thought he was laying it on a bit thick. It had the same effect on me regardless.

"Is Lennie going to be there?" I asked.

"No, I don't think so. He'll want to stay with Wren—" His voice caught before he finished the thought. "I'll speak with him later."

We lay on the motel mattress for a few beats, well aware of the tentative emotional space we occupied. A loud clunking somewhere outside of our room caught my attention, followed by the sound of ice cascading into a bucket and the low murmur of a man's voice. The motel wasn't the choicest of accommodations, truth be told, at least when it came to privacy.

Then out of nowhere, my chest suddenly felt hot, my jaw quivering as I struggled to keep it together. All of the choked emotions were about to escape. "Can ... can I tell you something?"

"Of course."

"It's just that I'm so ... so ... fucking *angry!*" I pushed myself up to a half-seated position, gripping the sheets in frustration, my hidden feelings too wrathful for containment. Heated tears poured down my cheeks as I looked to my lover for an anchor in the chaos. It was all just too much, and I was about to explode.

Dom's face softened in reply. "The loss of a loved one is—"

"I don't think I've ever felt so betrayed in my entire life! Kenzie ... She ... I ..." I was shaking now, rage exploding out of every pore as I struggled to speak. "That bitch! That ... evil ... absolute-heaping-pile-of-flaming-garbage-*fuck! Argh!*"

I slammed my fists onto the mattress.

Dom raised his eyebrows at the word-vomit but managed not to laugh. This was probably for the best because I might have murdered him in cold blood had he tried to make light of my anger.

"We've come across plenty of morally grey Bearers in the past," he said, "but ... that was beyond anything we've ever seen. You're right."

"That's the thing though—I don't even know *what* we've seen! I don't know who's grey and who's dark, and certainly not enough to know how to detect any of it in advance. Fuck! I'm still so disconnected from myself that I couldn't even clearly sense her presence behind the door, and then when I did—well, talk about a shock to my system! There I was, rolling in there like I had things under control and then ..." I reached my fingers to briefly touch the gash across my check. "I had no clue a Bearer could do something like that. It felt so awful. And I froze. And ..."

And she got away.

Dom sat up and gently pushed my hair behind my ear before tenderly pressing the back of his hand against my heated cheek. "Oh, love. It's alright. I know you're angry. I am too. But you can't blame yourself for what happened with Kenzie. Truly. This is like nothing we've ever encountered before. It was a shock. For *all* of us."

Since his hands were always warm, the sensation of his touch on my heated face wasn't particularly settling. I moved my own much-cooler palms to my face, and he cupped them from the outside instead. While this physical sensation was certainly more soothing, I was now met with the intensity of his gaze full on. In it, I could plainly see the familiar pools of grief, always present yet just beyond reach.

The burden he had carried with him throughout the ages.

I began to shake again as more tears poured down. "Dom? When is all of the pain going to end? The never feeling prepared ... never sitting still for long, always afraid of what will come next. And the loss! Seeing Wren like that ... Dom, I don't know what to do with these feelings. What Lennie ... what you ..."

"I don't know either, Julia," he said, a single tear rolling down his cheek and into his sandy beard. "The pain never really leaves. Not for me, anyway. You just get better at carrying it."

"He's going to need your help," I said simply though my sobs.

"I know," Dom said, and he looked away, blinking back more tears of his own with a quiet sniff.

My anger fell away then, making room for something far deeper.

Divinely attuned, Dom was suddenly kissing me forcibly on the lips, his thumb grazing painfully over my cheek where Kenzie had slashed me. And then his palm pressed against the tears on my face. I felt my body shudder at the act as something powerful surged between us, another wave of emotions that needed tending to.

It wasn't a steam valve after all—this strange feeling inside of me. It was an engine just getting started. *This* was a necessity for our survival.

I pulled my nightshirt off with one hand as I pushed Dom onto his back with the other, feeling his chest already heaving in anticipation. His cheeks flushed as his eyes darted slightly back and forth, that familiar look that always decorated his gorgeous face before he gave in fully to desire. His jaw shifted as he shoved his thumbs downward, wrenching his bottoms off.

I yanked my own underwear off in unison. My need to be completely naked against my lover was now trumping any other feelings I might be having. I ground into him as I climbed on top. "I need you inside of me," I said, my breath suddenly raspy.

I reached down to bring him along with me, but he was already there.

"Dear God ... Julia ..." he breathed through his teeth as I slid onto his very erect cock.

I relished the intensity of his entry at this angle and tossed my head back, groaning loudly with pleasure as I worked him in. Dom loved when I was vocal during sex, unabashed in my free and feminine expression. He loved to join in with his own noises too, letting out a primal growl as I continued to howl to the heavens at the depth of the feeling.

Leaning forward now that he was entirely in, I pushed his hands behind his head as I vigorously rode him. "Fuck ... Dom ... *Fuck!*"

He swore loudly several times himself before burying his face into my chest. "Jesus, Mary, and Joseph ..." he groaned.

Somewhere in the distance, I thought I heard the ice machine going outside our room again but let the thought pass. I didn't give a flying fuck if the entire world knew we were together in this moment.

When my legs got tired, Dom flipped me onto my back.

"Zeus almighty …" Dom said as he slid back in deep. "Persephone and Hades …"

It was his turn to take control. I wrapped my legs around his body and held on for dear life as he transmuted his own complicated emotions into my core, one robust thrust at a time. Arching underneath him, I raked my fingers from his shoulders to his ass and back again, clamouring to be closer still and willing this moment of raw intimacy to last forever.

"Harder," I moaned.

"Good Lord! What you do to me … *Christ,* woman!" he shouted, leaning back, pulling my leg onto his shoulder and holding on as he approached a rigorous climax: hard, deep, and loud. He gritted his teeth without breaking eye contact with me. At the sight of his unbridled passion, I let go at last and joined him in release, my body shuddering in rapt enthusiasm as I moaned to the heavens.

Hallelujah!

A shared, glorious, small death.

♛♥

Afterward, and to my surprise, I couldn't help but giggle. "You get a bit religious during sex you know … and pretty eclectic too."

"I do not," Dom said, but he was grinning broadly as he wiped sweat from his brow. "Okay, maybe. But it's only because I'm worshiping *you.*"

"And a bunch of other gods too … if I'm not mistaken."

He rolled onto his side and kissed my shoulder. "No, love. It's only ever been you. I just run out of words to use in place of your … sexual divinity when I'm riding you."

I snorted. "I don't think you can use 'sexual divinity' and 'riding you' in the same sentence and be taken seriously. Besides, wasn't it me riding *you?*"

"Why not!" he said, letting out a large breath and flashing me a cheeky smile. "And it's sort of slang in Ireland—especially in the north. Like, I would call you a 'good ride' because you're *very rideable*. Sexy, like."

"Thanks," I said, rolling my eyes.

"Whereas a *shift*, or shifting, basically means kissing with tongue." Dom winked.

"That makes no sense."

He laughed. After a few moments catching our breath, we hopped out of bed for a much-needed shower before our next meeting.

Soon we found ourselves hopping into our truck and heading to meet the Knaves once more. Since there was only three of them joining us this morning—Stuart, Alanna, and Shereen—we decided to meet on neutral ground for breakfast. The Druids went ahead to reserve seats at the closest diner. It would be easy enough to magically mask our conversation, and any heated discussions could be more easily brought to heel in a public setting anyway. That, and I was pretty sure Dom might starve to death if he didn't eat his weight in sausage, toast, and hash browns before ten a.m.

When Dom and I arrived, we found the Druids already waiting with coffees in hand, having commandeered both a booth and an adjoining table. No sign of the Knaves yet, though. Lindsey beamed happily at the sight of us, with Graham and Sean nodding pleasantly from behind their newspapers. Ronan, meanwhile, looked both expectant and miserable. I eyed the empty seat beside him uncomfortably.

"Julia! Come sit beside me," Lindsey said, and shoved Graham over towards Sean. Dom took the seat beside Ronan instead. This was probably for the best, and Ronan perked up slightly having his best friend at his side.

Sliding into the booth beside her, Lindsey gave me wink. "Does Dom do a lot of praying in the morning, Julia? Asking for a friend."

I smiled awkwardly, cheeks flushing. "You could say that. Did someone need ice for their orange juice or something?"

"No, Ronan wanted ice for Sean's leg. It hadn't healed right overnight with the magic he'd tried, so they wanted to try to take the swelling down the old-fashioned way. You should have heard him when he got back. *'That heathen's going about it like he's the feckin' Pope or something in there!'*" She was smiling as she mimicked Ronan's accent with precision. "Good for you though. Got to let off that battle stress somehow."

Lindsey had a bracing familiarity about her, but I liked it. "Well, I'm relatively new to 'post-combat-coitus,' but I would agree," I said with a grin.

"Hah! That's a good one," she said. "I'm jealous though. The only fun I had this morning was watching Ronan try to straighten a broken finger on Graham, which ended up with Ronan headbutted in the jaw, followed by a whole slew of foul language."

Sean shook his head in laughter from behind his paper. "It was pretty funny."

"It was an accident. I'm all better now, though," Graham said with a sly grin as he wiggled his fingers at me. Clearly, he also enjoyed taking the mickey out of Ronan.

"I think the Knaves suffered worse injuries than any of us though," Lindsey said, concern spreading across her brow. "Some of them are pretty beat up this morning. They really get *in* there."

"How do you know that?"

On cue, Stuart walked through the door, his arm heavily bandaged. It seemed to be leaking something foul and green that he was struggling to contain. He was followed by Alanna and Shereen several seconds later. They looked to be in slightly better shape. As expected, there was no sign of Lennie.

"*Bru*, I'm going to need you to take a look at this," Stuart said to Ronan in a surprisingly friendly and upbeat tone as he settled down at the table across from Lindsey. To be honest, I sensed Stuart was putting on a bit of a performance, playing extra nice with Ronan to whatever end.

"*I* could give that a look over," Lindsey said sardonically, shooting Ronan the kind of glance that left no one in doubt how she felt about him these days, "but apparently I'm better with dogs." I knew that she was a veterinarian and could imagine how this might have played out in her relationship with Ronan. She grinned at Stuart then, who laughed heartily.

Ronan either didn't hear her or was ignoring her completely. "Sure, Stuart, I've got my kit outside. Shall we go now?"

Stuart, who I assumed was usually the kind of person to wait until after a meal for wound cleaning, at least based on the look on his face, agreed immediately and followed Ronan outside.

"Hope they don't get into it," Lindsey said to me quietly. "Stuart was telling me this morning they had a history of conflict."

"Oh, are you two in touch?" I asked, smiling cheekily—my turn to be familiar.

She grinned. "He might have asked me for my number last night before we left … to keep in contact about all the goings on."

I knew Ronan and the other Druids stationed in Vancouver had met with some of the Washington Knaves in the past, but evidently, she and Stuart hadn't actually crossed paths yet.

"I bet," I said.

"You don't miss a beat, do you?" she said before finishing off her first cup of coffee.

"How's Lennie doing?" I asked Alanna as she and Shereen settled themselves in at our table.

"You know, it was so strange. He woke up this morning and was going on about motorcycles. Left the forge before we did. I mean, it's harmless probably, but it was a bit odd."

I shot a look at Dom, immediately suspecting that he had some sort of hand in this. But he was too busy talking animatedly to the server who had arrived to take our orders. Priorities. Ronan and Stuart were still nowhere to be seen, but the others seemed to be able to guess what they might like in a pinch.

"Did you stay at the forge then?" I asked, curious.

"We did," Shereen said. "They have several guest suites upstairs, and we wanted to connect with them before we left. Send our condolences along. They lost several of their own."

I cringed; I didn't even know their names. "I'm so sorry."

Alanna shrugged. "We all know what we signed up for. Wren, too. And even Lennie. None of us takes our role lightly in any of this, even if the Druids might think otherwise."

"Hey, don't count me in that number," Lindsey said, raising her hands. "I have plenty of respect for how you fight. That was incredible yesterday."

Shereen smiled kindly at Lindsey, while Alanna managed a grateful nod.

Our meals arrived at the same time Stuart and Ronan returned.

"Poisoned blade," Ronan said, answering the question before it was asked. The server initially gave him an odd look but continued onward with her work as if she hadn't heard a thing; my guess was this place served all sorts.

"Nothing old Rony-boy couldn't handle though!" Stuart said sitting down heavily at the table. I wondered if anyone had ever gotten away with calling him that before. It was highly doubtful. Stuart's arm did look considerably less swollen now though, so that was at least one positive.

And thankfully, the air did remain surprisingly cordial between the Druids and Knaves as the meal went on, which meant Dom's intuition to meet in a public space was correct. If anything, I think we were all glad for comfort food and company, and relished both. Time passed peacefully as we finished our breakfasts, but then it was time for the conversation to move towards more serious matters.

"Are we all ready? Ronan?" Dom said.

Ronan set a small pouch on the table and held his hand over top of it for brief moment. Within seconds it emitted a strong lemony smell. If I could guess, this was the tool we would be using to muddle our conversations from anyone who might overhear. The Druids looked unsurprised; the Knaves looked slightly impressed without comment. Trade secrets no doubt. I looked around the diner cautiously, but it appeared that none of the other patrons had noticed the smell. I made a mental note to ask Dom after if he had smelled anything either, but I assumed not because he wasn't technically a magic user.

"The way I see it, there's two things we'll need to address immediately," Dom said, leaning in so that his voice wouldn't carry too far. "First, we need to figure out what the hell happened with Kenzie's magic and how she's apparently fuelling the Wraiths—that's where Ronan comes in. He's apparently got a lead in Berkeley who might be able to help. A scientist who specializes in … fuck, help me out here, Ronan."

"She's a Wielder, and a doctor, specializing in a particular type of cellular regeneration that involves mRNA translation and atypical protein synthesis. Long story short, it might give us the breakthrough we need. As far as we can tell, Caleb didn't breach this arm of my research when he was torturing Lennie, so we should be good to go if I can just get up there to—"

"Grand," Dom interrupted, nodding heartily but clearly not interested in allowing Ronan to elaborate further. "Second, we need to solve our weapons issue. We need something more effective that can stand up to whatever the Wraiths are doing to fuck with our arsenal. Lennie is certain that there is a group of desert Knaves who have the weapons, or at the very least, the knowledge we need to deal with this new Wraith scourge."

And you can lead them, I thought to myself.

Dom's eyes flickered to me as if he could read my mind, then continued.

"And the numbers. Had we found more allied support yesterday—and been able to mobilize sooner—things might have gone very differently. I want to be sure that we've got the West Coast on lock for any and all support we can get. Not least of all because it seems to be one of Cassius's favourite playgrounds."

Based on the looks on the Knaves' faces, Dom had obviously touched a nerve.

"Sorry," Stuart said, "but there's no way in hell I'm going back out to the desert to see *them.*" Despite his tone, his accent remained comparatively breezy in contrast to the collective brogue of the Celts surrounding us. "I don't care how much they can help us; I'm never going back into that snake pit."

Stuart went on to explain that, after the Washington Knaves had found out about what had happened at Gertie's cottage in June, which was all too clearly a targeted Wraith strike practically on their doorstep, Stuart and Wren had attempted to recruit both the Death Valley and Los Angeles Knaves in response to the growing threat. While the L.A. Knaves had readily offered their services on a "needs-be" basis, when it came to the desert group, they'd been met with only venom.

"Sorry, Dom, we just can't help you there," Alanna said. It turned out that she and Shereen were leaving directly from breakfast to return Wren's body to her family, which was an extremely important task to be sure.

"I understand," Dom said, nodding gravely. This was clearly an unexpected change to how he had envisioned things, not having any Knaves other than Lennie along. But his leadership took it in stride.

"Let us know what you find out though," Stuart said genuinely. "I'm going to do my own research on the matter, if that's alright with you. The Oregon forge might hold answers we don't have in Washington as well. What happened with your sword ... well, Shereen will help me once she and Alanna have delivered Wren's body."

I wasn't sure if this was a command, assumed role, or just understood by Shereen now that Stuart was in charge. She didn't seem phased though and nodded peaceably in agreement. She was his apprentice after all.

Dom nodded several times before speaking again, pivoting gracefully. "That's actually a great plan. Thanks, Stuart. Lennie's *'all in'* for the desert mission, so we should be fine, as far as having a Knave to guide us goes. I spoke to him this morning; he's already sourcing us bikes for the trip, since apparently the road runs out by the end, and we'll be relegated to a dirt trail." He had a slight twinkle in his eye as he looked towards me.

Aha! I was right about the motorcycles leading back to Dom. I had also been wondering who he'd been texting frantically this morning after we got out of the shower, blindly assuming it was Ronan as usual. Once again though, I wasn't asking enough questions. Or perhaps Dom wasn't sharing enough. It was fair to say that he assumed I would go with him regardless of what he had planned. That much was obvious.

"Thanks, Dom. Good luck ... really," Stuart said, looking skeptical that we would find success in the desert but attempting to offer support nonetheless.

"We've got work to do with the Druids on our way back north," Lindsey said, nodding her head vaguely in the direction of the road.

Graham laughed. "I don't think the Knaves would welcome us very kindly out there anyway!"

Sean nodded solemnly. "I'm still recovering from the last battle. I need a break."

"Oh hey—Alanna and Shereen are taking my truck and the trailer. Is it alright if I jump in with you for the ride to Oregon then?" Stuart asked Lindsey, as if this was the most obvious solution.

Smooth.

"Of course," she said, equally casual. An extended pause punctuated her answer.

Feeling the weight of my compass in my pocket with sudden awareness, I was reminded of Bernie's words to honour the fact that Dom and I were both on our own paths, even if we were in a loving union throughout our shared journeys. In truth, my intuition was practically screaming at me that the motorcycle journey didn't involve *me* either. I needed to find out more about how my Bearing magic might influence the Wielders around me. If that meant going north with Ronan, then so be it. If I was being honest, this was a feeling I'd been secretly fighting for quite some time already. Weeks even. Ronan needed my help.

"Well ... it sounds like we're all going to have to split up for a time," I said, avoiding Dom's gaze.

"Julia's right," Ronan said, jumping in immediately. I ground my teeth. "We need to go speak to Dr. Bailey. The magic user at Berkeley."

"What do you mean 'we'?" Dom asked, glaring at Ronan.

I let out a long sigh. Ronan had pieced it together even more quickly than I had anticipated. "Dom, I need to go with Ronan to Berkeley. It's important."

I thought of the rivers I knew that with absolute certainty ran between us and felt a deep trust that we would be alright. There was no need for Dom to dam the flow if our paths needed to veer slightly apart for a time. This was the way of it.

A fleeting look of hurt etched across Dom's face before he rounded on Ronan, this pivot from his previous plans not nearly as graceful as the last. *"Ronan,"* he said, barely hiding the fact he was absolutely seething, "I thought we decided that Julia and I can't go to places we've gone before. We've *been* to San Francisco."

"Did you go to Berkeley though? It's not the precise location you were *then*, or am I wrong?"

Dom exhaled loudly through his nose and looked back to me. I couldn't quite decipher the look on his face, and it made me uncomfortable. "Are you sure?" he asked.

I nodded. "I'm sure."

And so, Alanna and Shereen would return Wren's body to her parents in Washington. Stuart, Lindsey, Graham, and Sean would travel to Oregon before venturing north to Canada. Eventually Ronan would join them too, once he and I sought out the research and answers he needed in Berkeley.

Meanwhile, Lennie and Dom would take to the desert.

CHAPTER 18

Dom downed a final swig of water before dragging the back of his hand across his lips in what could only be described as *mild* satisfaction. He felt dusty and dishevelled; the current length of his beard wasn't helping in the inescapable heat either. He should have at least trimmed his mustache before they left, but hindsight was something he couldn't afford to deal in. Besides, it still held Julia's musk on it, and he liked that.

"We need to keep moving!" Lennie shouted from across the desolate parking lot, his helmet already back atop his mouse-brown head. As if Dom had any choice in the matter, anyway. The man had been driving their pace relentlessly, even for someone deep in the throes of grief. Their brief pit-stop at the dilapidated service station hadn't been more than five minutes total.

Dom said nothing and slowly zipped his leather jacket before donning his own helmet. He was drenched in sweat, and his hunger was beginning to gnaw into his throat, but ultimately, he still had plenty of miles left in him if that's what it was going to take. When it came down to it, he appreciated Lennie's urgency, hoping it meant they would make the return journey with a matched expediency.

He kick-started his bike hard with a growling roar, grateful that Lennie had at least sourced an appropriate stallion for the trip. The brand-new Triumph Scrambler was robust enough to hold his frame comfortably while still able to tackle the unpredictable conditions ahead. He had also made sure it was well equipped for the voyage, efficiently packed with necessary supplies and plenty of water in two paniers at the back.

Plus, it looked cool as hell with a matte-green finish and gold accents.

Lennie had, unsurprisingly, chosen a jet-black sport bike for the journey, which couldn't be more different than his own. Crouched over the bike, Lennie's knees were bent at a strange angle and did not look comfortable; it left Dom to wonder if the miles were taking a toll on his body yet. Or maybe, he invited the discomfort. So far, he seemed to be tolerating the contortion. He had also relegated his supplies into a tiny backpack. Dom hoped Lennie wouldn't find himself thirsty at any point in their journey.

Suddenly, Lennie took off at great speed, kicking out a blast of sand and gravel behind him.

"*Fucker,*" Dom said, cranking his throttle and urging his own beast onward in Lennie's gritty wake.

Throughout the journey, their dusty path had narrowed steadily from six lanes at times across Los Angeles to what was now a single-lane highway disappearing into the low desert mountains ahead. His mind, however, still lingered far behind amidst the supple, moving California coastline; the ride into the endless expanse of Death Valley replicated, far too closely for his liking, his feelings around the growing distance between him and Julia.

Rounding yet another bend deeper into the vast desert, he thought of the curves of her body and arch of her spine as he'd said "goodbye" to her for the third time in twenty-four hours. The decision around their short separation had been abrupt and made him uncomfortable. He tried to recall her description of the groundwater and rivers from her personal map, the essential connectivity between them, but it provided little comfort. He shuddered in longing instead. Like the ocean, she was vitality in its purest essence. Lush and free, he'd drunk in as much of her as possible before setting off towards the Nevada border in the early hours of the morning, the expanding desert openly mocking his growing thirst to be by her side once more.

He forced himself to focus on the task at hand.

According to Lennie, they would know the entrance to the Knave Keep when they saw it. Or, in Lennie's case, *sense* it. Their muster point in Los Angeles had still been very clearly a warehouse, even after Dom had passed through its outer glamour. He assumed what they would encounter in the desert would be similar, the entry resembling an old mine or shallow cave, or perhaps just a simple recess in a wall of stone. It sounded an awful lot like finding a needle in a haystack, and so he would be relying on Lennie's intuition when it came to sussing it out.

This particular group of Knaves had become notoriously elusive, holing up in what sounded a lot more like a desert commune than an encampment of highly trained fighters. Perhaps both could be true at the same time. Dom had known countless warriors who knew only two things: fighting and fucking. He could hardly discriminate. Lennie was certain that, if they could meet Dom in person, they would be sure to join their cause.

"You're placing a lot of faith in me, Lennie," Dom had said when the matter was brought up again the evening before. "Honestly though, what does a group of self-exiled Wielders want from a thousand-some-year-old Irish prince with no magical ability?"

Lennie snorted. "Well, for starters, while *we* need their weapons, *they* need a leader."

"I'm no leader," Dom had replied. Unfortunately, he was holding his sword outstretched at that very moment—an old habit he tended to lean on before any sort of dangerous mission. Even when broken, the ancient sword gave him a distinct air of power by default. Noticing the bemused looks on both Julia and Lennie's faces, he had dropped his arms to his side, causing what was left of the sword to hit the floor with a ringing clatter as yet another piece of metal fell off. He grinned in spite of himself.

"Don't bring that with you, though." Lennie had said as he picked up the busted piece of metal and turned it over in his hand.

Julia had remained uncharacteristically quiet throughout his and Lennie's discussions around the logistics of the journey; Dom sensed she was attempting to stay out of his way on purpose.

But his thoughts were always on Julia.

"You could still come with me," he'd said after Lennie had left their room for the night.

Smiling somewhat sadly, she'd sat down on the edge of their motel bed, wearing a thin white towel and nothing else, showered and ready for sleep. The gash on her face was already healing nicely, but his mind had been focused elsewhere.

"You know I can't," she'd replied, letting the towel drop slightly. He had wondered for the hundredth time why motel towels were always so small. Not that he was complaining.

Dom wasn't the kind of man to beg for anything, except when it came to her. And in that moment, he had lowered himself onto the floor before her and took her cool hands into his own, kissing her long fingers softly, sucking on each of them in turn. This pose at her feet was becoming a bit of a habit, he had to admit. But thankfully, this time, he could continue on in his full worship. He'd moved his lips to her right knee before pressing her legs open and slowly trailing his mouth up her inner thigh.

"It doesn't feel right to leave you ... It goes against my entire nature ..." he had breathed.

"Dom, you have to go—" she'd replied, her voice catching as he approached her inner warmth.

But ultimately, he had a job to do.

Another unexpected challenge was the burgeoning envy he was fighting back that she would be travelling to San Francisco area with Ronan instead of him. Besides the obvious risk in re-visiting a past locale—his obligation to protect her as strong as ever—he was also unfathomably jealous of her and Ronan's trip together. It wasn't that he was concerned about anything romantic happening; it was simply not being in her presence. Vital mission or not, he should be there instead of that ungrateful bastard.

As he sat atop his motorcycle, an ancient frustration scorched his chest, borne from centuries of aching for her to return to his life. But then, like a moth to a flame, his mind flicked to their most recent parting instead.

Julia had responded to his affections emphatically as the sunrise kissed the horizon outside their motel window, the moans resulting from his worship etched into his recall forever. Indeed, she had made it *very* clear who ruled her heart by the time he'd left in the morning. His cock pressed against his jeans at the memory, which were already tight across his groin as he turned his bike around yet another curve. It was becoming plain that this entire journey was going to be wrought with discomfort and painful longing.

For fuck's sakes.

Taking a final water break before they were expected to reach their destination, Dom spoke to Lennie about the realities he anticipated ahead.

"You know they're going to want to test me. And that might mean doing some things that would make the others ... uncomfortable." Dom didn't mean anything totally unconscionable. And he certainly wasn't referring to infidelity. But he knew that people like this thrived on the fringe, where morals were grey, a place people like Ronan would not venture into.

In the end, it was probably for the best that both Ronan and Julia were far from here, no matter how badly he longed to have her by his side. He didn't need her divine presence distracting him from embracing his own shadows, and that would be a requirement from the Knaves for sure. Nor did he need Ronan's judgemental glares burning into the back of his neck throughout the ordeal.

Thankfully, Lennie understood. "Mum's the word. Unfortunately, I have no clue what those trials might be, though Wren—the Washington Knaves—have always just referred to this group as 'snakes.'"

Dom nodded darkly; he had never been a fan of snakes.

The final leg of their journey took them off the main road and onto a dirt trail that reminded him of a donkey path, narrow but not unpassable with the right vehicle. The sun was hot, and he had dirt between his teeth, made all the more notable each time he ground them together as he hit more bumps. Eventually, the path took them into a crevasse between two massive boulders, and then a steep rock face. Before Lennie even said it, Dom could tell this was the place.

They turned their bikes off and dismounted, with Lennie immediately walking forward to touch the stone and then cursing under his breath. He looked rough and ready for war, like he was ready to walk through hell and back if that's what it took to avenge his lover. This was a far cry from the pretentious British prick he'd grown accustomed to over the past several years. If not for the most recent circumstances, he might even say he liked the new version.

"My skin's itching. Can you feel it?" Lennie asked.

"Not the itching, no. But it feels ... uneasy."

"Precisely." He spit a slew of dirt from his own mouth.

Suddenly, the rocks before them shuddered and a large crack appeared in the stone wall.

"Apparently, it needed some kind of offering," Dom said with a wry laugh, and Lennie shrugged.

"I suppose it did."

The two men passed shoulder-to-shoulder through what was now a concrete-framed doorway built into the mountainside. Dom, broad in his command, and Lennie, roguish in his wit, made quite the pairing as they traversed the narrow passageway. Inside, the air was strikingly cool, a harsh yet welcome contrast to the beating heat of the desert outside.

Sooner than expected, the passage opened into a much larger chamber. The space itself was unexpectedly fleshed out in its engineering, despite the fact that the walls were made of chiselled brown and grey stone. He wondered if the bunker, for that was what it felt like, had always belonged to them. Regardless, he had no intention of sticking around long enough to get into the finer details. Something about this sect of Knaves made the hair on the back of his neck stand on end.

"Welcome, Lennie," a raw-looking woman said, though she only had eyes for Dom. "You've brought company."

"I have, and you know that. This is *Domhnall Mac Brien*," Lennie said, and Dom was surprised to hear him use this iteration of his name.

"Dom is fine," he said, his voice low.

Lennie snorted. "I told you; they already know who you are."

Dom heard soft whispers echo off the stone walls of the cavernous space: *"Is he really the World Ruler?"* A slight whistle. *"Well, if he is, I'd like to have him rule my world."*

Dom smirked. His suspicions were quickly confirmed.

They walked deeper into the chamber, but the Knaves kept their distance as he and Lennie moved into the belly of the beast. Dom couldn't help but feel like they were being circled, like there was pack of coyotes behind them. After all, this was *their* territory. Why should they get their backs up when, really, there was no way for Dom and Lennie to get out now unless permitted?

All around them, faces stared from dark recesses, leering. The woman who had greeted them first had all but disappeared without them noticing.

"I'm starting to see what Stuart meant," Dom said under his breath. Lennie's face remained impassive.

At last, they reached what appeared to be a massive stone altar situated atop a round dais. Around it, six pillars were stationed in a hexagon shape, their shafts carved with intricate and menacing designs all the way up to the ceiling. Dom kept his distance as Lennie approached and stepped up without fear. Dom felt curious but wasn't ready to approach it just yet; places like this could mean trouble.

"What is this?" Lennie asked, gesturing to something wrapped up on the altar. No one answered.

They were surrounded on all sides now. Dom quickly assessed the situation and noticed another door beyond where they stood, set deep into jagged stone at the end of the cavern. It looked older than the rest of the place, which was saying something.

Lennie drew his attention back to what was just before them. He was holding his hand up, eyes closed and muttering something. The Knaves all around them seemed to be holding their breath.

Then Lennie turned abruptly towards Dom. "It's bloody moonshine."

Before Dom's eyes, what had originally looked like a set of carved stone columns now came into focus as a complicated set of copper stills. The Knaves it seemed, apart from forging dangerous weaponry, were also running a moonshine operation, and quite successfully too by the look of it. This was no piecemeal set-up. He momentarily puzzled over the fact that they were apparently using one illegal operation to front another, but these people weren't the type to live within the law to begin with.

He grinned mischievously. "I've had a long ride. Is anyone going to pour me a drink?"

***

Apparently, Lennie's ability to expose the stills for what they were was a test to see if he and Dom were friend or foe to the operation—and they passed with flying colours. Almost like magic, the atmosphere in the cavern shifted spectacularly as the moonshine began to flow. Out of nowhere, a man as thick as a tree clapped Dom in the middle of his back before handing him a stiff drink in a short metal cup. Dom threw it back in one swig, knowing this was as much of a test as anything else. He had definitely tasted worse.

"Another," Dom said. The giant man nodded approvingly.

Lennie had all but vanished from his side. He wasn't entirely surprised, however. Lennie had done his job, finding the place and proving to the Knaves they weren't an immediate threat, and that was more than enough. Now it was Dom's turn.

Still, he scanned the hall for Lennie's current whereabouts, just in case, and saw yet another chamber door off to the side of the hall. It opened with an echoing *bang!* and Dom was immediately distracted, all thoughts of Lennie quickly forgotten. His nostrils were suddenly overwhelmed with the savoury, nostalgic tang of greasy meat being slow roasted over hot coals. He felt himself begin to salivate. To add insult to injury, his stomach growled loudly; he had underestimated how truly famished he really was.

The room was soon filled with countless Knaves of all ages and ethnicities clamouring for dinner, like spiders coming out of the cracks. This was an eclectic group—their most unifying feature being a penchant for tight leather—yet Dom could understand why they had been drawn together. These were the kind of people who thrived on the fringes of the world.

Rolling his shoulders back several times, Dom noticed the same raw-looking woman from their arrival approaching him yet again out of the fray. Her short-cropped hair was dark and glossy, and her skin lightly tanned. Upon closer inspection, he guessed her to be somewhere in her late-forties. They locked eyes as she peered at him dangerously over her own recently downed glass of hooch. His grey-blue eyes were in stark contrast to hers, which were almost onyx in tone. Scanning her figure quickly, he noted the tight camouflage pants she wore, and the thin, white tank-top that was clearly meant to accentuate her busty, albeit somewhat hardened, figure.

"You hungry, *World Ruler?*" she asked. Her voice lingered greedily on his prophesized name. The room was cold, and Dom was surprised to feel his face flush.

"I'm starving. Actually."

"Good. I'll have someone bring you some grub," she said, her Midwestern accent drawn out; she was obviously a transplant to the area, like everyone else. She turned away slowly towards the kitchen fires. He watched tolerantly as she moved with a deliberate swing to her thin hips; without question, this maneuver was meant for his eyes in particular.

Another test.

Minutes later, a pair of younger women approached, each holding a plate piled high with barbequed meat and two buns a piece. Neither brought utensils.

"Heard you were hungry, World Ruler," the first said, blushing at the sight of him.

"Dom is fine," he said once more, though this time somewhat apprehensively.

Ignoring him, the second one spoke quietly. "We thought we had better bring you two plates ... just in case you were *extra* hungry." The wink that followed the statement increased his unease. Were they trying to mock him or seduce him? He honestly couldn't tell. However, since he always thought more clearly with a full stomach, he pushed his discomfort aside and leaned coolly against the nearest stone wall, feigning non-concern.

Polishing off both plates of food within minutes, along with several more glugs of hooch that had appeared seemingly out of nowhere, Dom licked his chops in satisfaction. He didn't know how they were venting the smoke out of the mountain, but the food was certainly well-cooked. Leave it to a group of Wielding smelters and liquor-makers to have the intricacies of underground furnaces sorted.

The two women who delivered his meal had lingered just out of earshot as he ate. And as soon as he'd completed his meal, they approached and removed the plates from his grasp. They had plainly been assigned to keep track of him. He didn't like it.

"Drink, Dom?"

"Thank fuck," Dom said under his breath as he turned to see Lennie by his side; his return was more than fortuitous.

"I had expectations about what it might be like in here but, this *far* exceeds them," Lennie said, taking the words straight out of Dom's mouth.

Dom took the large metal tankard held out by Lennie and eyed the room with suspicion. How the hell was he going to win the allegiance of these rogue Knaves, who all basically looked like they either wanted to pummel, devour, or fuck him. Maybe even all at once. Meanwhile, Lennie's face bore a completely different expression, almost as if his eyes were glazing over, spellbound and ready to release himself to whatever might come next. Julia might have called it dissociating, but in truth, only a small part of Dom was surprised at the look; grief did strange things to a man.

The pair of women, who had moved closer once more, smiled keenly at Lennie. He grinned back, a bit like a madman, but they didn't seem to mind. Dom felt relief for both his own part and for Lennie's.

The dark-haired woman returned once more, waving the women away with Lennie tucked into their elbows, chuckling loudly at the scene unfolding. She was gnawing on some kind of rib with very little meat left on it.

"They'll take care of him; don't worry. He's one of us," she said, holding out her free hand to shake. "I'm leader here, for the most part. You can call me Glenys."

CHAPTER 19

Dom was pretty sure her name translated to something along the lines of "pure" or "holy" in Welsh, but he was far from fluent enough in the language to be entirely sure. However, he had strong doubts whether Glenys embodied either of these characteristics, so he kept this tidbit to himself and shook her hand politely. Her fingers were far warmer than he had expected them to be. He thought of Julia's hands, which were always ice cold within his own, but pushed the thought aside.

"We're all pretty uncertain about you," Glenys said, gesturing for him to follow. Lennie was completely consumed by the attention of the others, which had now grown to a group of at least six men and women chatting animatedly all around him. "But we knew of Wren. She was one of the good ones. It was a tough loss to our Washington kin. For all of us, really."

"Indeed," Dom said. He was surprised to hear her make a sentiment that referenced them all as a unified group; from what Wren had told him back in Oregon, and then Stuart at the diner, there was a stark divide. He took a deep swig of his drink. It was going down easier and easier with each draught, and he was suddenly concerned that they could easily slip something magically illicit in without him knowing. He looked at the drink and then at her, concerned.

She read his mind. "It's just straight moonshine with some pop. Don't worry yourself. Lennie on the other hand, well … they may give him something to take away the pain. But I think that's exactly what he needs, don't you?"

Dom nodded but said nothing.

Soon, another man joined them. He had black skin and a noticeably commanding stature. He appeared close in age to Dom, with a broad, friendly grin. "Glenys showing you the ropes I see?"

"No, not yet," she said, cackling a bit before making the introduction. "This is Booker."

Deciding to trust his instincts around these people, rather than his logic, Dom grinned impishly before speaking straight to Booker. "Is she always like this?"

Laughter ensued; these folks could definitely handle a bit of play.

"Watch yourself, Dom; she's a faster fighter than anyone I know. She'll either have you by your balls or shove a pair of throwing daggers into your kidneys before you even know what happened."

Dom laughed and finished off yet another drink. "I think my kidneys are already taking a beating this evening."

"And what about your balls?" Glenys asked, howling with laughter.

They walked for a time through the thronging mass of desert Knaves, which was growing in volume by the minute. What he'd initially assumed to be a place of reckoning for many, seemed very much a home for most. All around them people were drinking, eating, fighting, or laughing. You could practically smell the sex on the air, mingled with the strong scents of food and freely flowing liquor. Off and on, Dom could smell a strange metallic odour on the air, which he assumed was from the smelting fires.

"We do a lot of things around here, World Ruler. But working outside of our realm isn't one of them," Glenys said, nabbing another tankard from one of the many tables that had popped up across the once empty hall and handing it to him. He noticed she continued to refuse his real name.

Receiving the drink, Dom was definitely feeling the effects of the alcohol now, though he was still well in control. "Thanks."

"It's not that we don't believe in the greater *'cause'* you all speak about. We do. The Child of Rome is all of our enemy, and his reputation definitely precedes him. Or ... well, it's never really left him I guess," Glenys said, shrugging. Dom suspected she was sharply informed when it came to Cassius as well as the Prophecy, despite her casual, if not animalistic, demeanour.

"And then there's the Wraiths," Booker said, anger clouding his face. "None of us take kindly to them." Knaves seemed to all have a rabid hatred for Wraiths, no matter where they hailed from.

Glenys stared at Dom. "But don't get me wrong. We might be on the same side of that issue, but we also don't see eye-to-eye with the other Wielders, and how they handle these ... matters."

She was clearly referencing the Druids.

Booker wove his arm around Glenys's waist as she continued to slither through the crowd. She swayed into his arms freely as they dodged the increasing energy of the group. Clearly the two had an intimate relationship of some flavour. Dom also sensed Booker was a protective sort of man, even if Glenys was undoubtedly the most powerful woman in the room.

Julia might call him old fashioned, but Dom understood and respected that type of behaviour. A man had to defend what was his. His mind naturally wandered to Julia, but she might as well be on the other side of the world right now. He was deep into the lair and wasn't coming out without giving it all he had.

Winding their way through the crowds, Dom realized they were making their way towards the far end of the hall once more, towards the dais. He noticed with curiosity that the door beyond was now wide open. From this vantage point, he could only see darkness within. Before he could ask what lay beyond, Glenys directed him towards the altar.

Atop the polished granite surface, he discovered a freshly unwrapped two-handed long sword that had been covered he and Lennie had first arrived. It had been fashioned strikingly similar to the one he had left behind in L.A., only this one wasn't broken. But there was more to it; even he could *feel* its eagerness.

"How—"

"We have our way of knowing things," Glenys said, her voice heavy with mystery. "Just like hearing the Prophecy. We know what has been foretold, World Ruler."

Booker approached silently from behind and carefully lifted the blade, giving it notable reverence before handing it over to Dom.

"Did you make it?" Dom asked, directing his question to Booker but hardly daring to take his eyes from the immaculate weapon. He had spoken fairly extensively with Stuart about the process, or what Stu could share of it at any rate, and was deeply intrigued by the Knaves and their metallurgy.

"I did," Booker said. "And it should stand the test against the Wraiths. And most anything else I can think of."

Dom recalled that, while his old sword had practically disintegrated after contact with whatever the Wraiths were throwing in Los Angeles, the Knaves' weapons—though weakened—had fared far better. And that was *without* intervention. He wondered what Booker had done differently with this particular blade, though he didn't question it openly.

His creation was large—a great sword—and obviously designed with Dom's history in mind. The great Celt turned the longsword over in his hands several times before placing his fists firmly around the long hilt, which was wrapped tightly in a buttery brown leather. It was utterly perfect. Even the balance point landed precisely where he liked it, about four fingers from the cross. The blade itself bore the fluid carbon-swirl finish similar to those made by Stuart but boasted silver and dark grey instead of gold.

"It's incredible ..." He thought of Julia's small golden blade, imbibed with Wielding magic. "The colour though ... Aren't Knave blades usually gold?"

"Good question," Booker said, visibly appreciating Dom's interest. "There's two parts to it really. First, we don't make any of ours this big ... I won't get into the details, but that's a lot of gold-imbued ore. And second, you're not a Wielder anyway, so you won't need it."

Or deserve it, according to you, Dom thought darkly.

"It's not like that," Glenys said, seeming to read Dom's mind once more. "We were told you have otherworldly powers of your own, and those that are in the sword complement them." Dom decided then that he didn't like this particular trait of hers and wasn't entirely sure he trusted the latest shift in her tone either.

Looking down at his hands, he realized he was definitely feeling the drink now; he felt almost giddy. The room was also distinctly warmer than it had been upon their arrival, and he felt the sudden urge to shed his jacket. Inexplicably, unknown hands stripped the coat from his shoulders before he could finish his thought, but he maintained his focus on the invaluable blade before him. It might not have the gold swirl that was signature to Knave smithies, but it had plenty of other forces flowing through it. Somehow, he could almost feel the blade awakening something that lay hidden deep within his bones.

Intuitively, he began to swing the sword this way and that, losing himself in the moment as it arced brilliantly before him like silver lighting. It was light as air, yet still heavy enough that he could swing it with speed. It also didn't feel quite right in his hands. Not yet anyway. There was a resistance there, which he guessed was because *this* type of weapon would require its allegiance to be won. He wasn't sure how much time had passed in his attempt to connect with the sword, but when he stopped, he was surprised to notice the atmosphere in the room had changed significantly.

"Look at his face," someone whispered. "He's *enthralled!*" Laughter broke out.

"Shh!" Glenys said, slowly stepping back towards the amassed crowd behind her. "Now, if you will … You'll need to fight us to keep it. Gifts like that don't come for free around these parts."

Several voices jeered. "Come on, World Ruler. Show us what you've got."

"Fight us, World Ruler. Take the sword for your own."

Dom felt his own power growing, the force at the core of his being that he kept so well hidden … the one that ached to be released, which he was equally terrified of and enamoured with. The one that would thrust him into the role of a modern-day king.

Raw masculine divinity.

In spite of it all, he grinned, his white teeth bared. "Here?"

"No," Glenys said, her voice strangely amplified and reverberating against the stone walls. "In the snake pit."

Suddenly, Dom felt a rush of hot air blast out from behind the altar, the sort one would imagine emanating from deep within the earth. At least he knew where the dark doorway led now. He scanned the room for signs of his only ally in the place.

"Where's Lennie?" Dom asked.

Booker boomed out a laugh and jabbed his thumb somewhere behind them. The group parted slightly for Dom to see. Peering past, he noticed that the knaves had moved the tables, making way for cushions and low couches instead. From his vantage point, Lennie was visibly inebriated and *very* entangled with a group of Knaves, participating in an act that could only be described as carnal healing.

Glenys cackled. "I told you we would take care of him."

"Let's get on with it then," Dom said, blushing in spite of himself.

He followed Glenys and Booker through the door at the end of the hall. The others who weren't "otherwise preoccupied" followed behind, hissing and muttering in his wake. Descending a set of low, wide steps, he found himself facing a deep chamber dug into the stone. It reminded him of a Roman amphitheatre, only smaller, rectangular, and underground. All around its sides were *cavea*—seats carved out in rows similar to the wide steps they had just descended from the main hall.

Glenys gestured downward, her eyes even darker than before, if that was possible. "We'll meet you there. We've got to get our own weapons ready"

Dom said nothing and began his descent.

Reaching the bottom alone, he noticed that the sandy ground seemed to be emitting heat from below. Barefoot, it would be too hot to stand on. He tilted his neck from side to side, flexing his chest and rolling his shoulders back in turn. How many times had he prepared for combat in precisely this way? He thought of his father and his distinctive pre-battle rituals, and how similar they were in make and form. Cut from the same cloth.

The chamber was beastly hot, and his body was already drenched in sweat, though the fight had not yet even begun. He felt a sudden urge to remove his shirt. These weren't the kinds of people to fight within the proper bounds, whatever that was. He realized then, based on their fondness of their own weapons, shirtless was probably their preferred style anyway, so as to show any flesh wound. A point of pride, no doubt.

He also somehow knew intuitively that they would need to see the scars.

Dom set the sword at his feet momentarily and pulled his damp t-shirt over his head. It stunk like sweat, leather, and road dust, and so he tossed it aside more than willingly. The last time he'd been shirtless, it was in front of Julia in their motel room, where he had engaged in a wholly different conquest. A holy one. He felt his cock stir at the memory of her on top of him, riding hard and almost desperate in her need for him before they parted. Her unabashed thirst for his body and soul in those moments fuelled him for days.

The thought left his consciousness as quickly as it had arrived though, loudly interrupted by the sharp intake of breath by the Knaves surrounding him in the seats above the pit. With the golden hair of his broad chest now exposed to the chamber full of people, and many more who still were filing in, he was also now freely exposing the death-blow scars—the ones that proved he really *was* a reborn man.

An artifact from the Otherworld.

"The scars ... He's ..." said a voice nearby, somewhere between fear and admiration.

Another voice said, *"I've never seen anything like them!"*

"Look, there ... See? It comes out the other side," came the reply.

It would seem they were seeing something he wasn't, and he looked towards Glenys and Booker for guidance. They had just arrived at the ground level with him, weapons in hand.

Booker's mouth was agape, evidently speechless, and while Glenys's face remained impassive, her eyes were wide, plainly in awe. "It's ancient magic to read the wounds inflicted by a blade—a distinctly *Knave* brand of magic you might say, one that only a small group of us still possess—and yours ..." She brought her hand to her mouth before dragging it down to her throat and striding towards him. "Yours really are ..."

"Hundreds of years old," Dom said, finishing her sentence.

He suddenly realized that *this* was the tipping point, not the anticipated combat ahead. Anything after this moment, if he played his cards right, would only further secure their allegiance to the cause. And more significantly, to his banner.

But did he even want to take up the mantle?

"Scars created by flesh wounds don't travel with me," he said, clearly now in full command of the room. "But the death blows ... those remain."

All eyes were on him, but he looked to Glenys, their leader, awaiting permission to proceed. Not that he needed it, but the posturing seemed important.

"May I?" Glenys asked, unable to hold herself back. Dom nodded almost imperceptibly and lowered his head. Glenys reached out and held her hands just above the surface of his skin. She gasped and locked eyes with him. "This one …"

"Cassius, on the Cliffs of Moher in Ireland, around 1475, I think," Dom said simply. "Most are from him, you'll find."

She walked around him slowly, and he breathed deep, shoulders back. He felt colossal in that moment, a testament to the power that sang through his bloodline. His black jeans were filthy and his boots scuffed, yet he was every bit a king standing there before them all.

"The blows … there are just so many …"

"Hmm," he acknowledged.

She paused abruptly as sadness suddenly etched across her brow. "And this one?"

"Self-inflicted."

She stared at him. "All for the Sovereign?"

This was the first time Julia had been mentioned openly, even if only by her prophesized name. Like a midsummer breeze, the new Prophecy whispered off the hot stone walls:

With the Sovereign standing tall, the World Ruler too must bear his crown,
As the Sorcerer seeks to find the grail, spear in hand, to chalice he is bound.

To reveal the lost wellspring, the Sun and Moon must accept their fate.
When the Celt accepts the mantle, the Crone too shall find her strength.

For the earthen weapons masters, and tree talkers with open sky above,
Darkness reigns where light cannot, and from its root, the land will rot.

"All for *Julia*," Dom said. "Yes."

He then sensed an almost undetectable shift in the magic of the room; speaking her name aloud, the spell of the new Prophecy had now been well and truly invoked. The Knaves might not appreciate honour in the same ways Dom did, but they *did* understand the power behind a calling.

"For Julia," Glenys said quietly.

He had passed their actual test, and now it was his time to show them his true power.

Glenys and Booker stepped back to the edge of the pit, giving Dom room to warm up his new sword with more intention. Being that it was Knave-made, he had wondered whether, if he were able to win its allegiance, it would "sing" for him the way the others had. Based on the soft keening sound that was now emanating from it with even the slightest move, it seemed it likely would.

"I know you would rather live in a world where you can express yourself and your magic more freely," Dom said, speaking to them all now, his deep voice carrying easily up and out of the pit. "And in truth, so would I."

He braced his legs in a stride step and thrust the sword down from his shoulder, swinging mightily as he took a step forward. The resultant sound reminded him of a hawk's scream, its pitch echoing loudly against the surrounding stone walls. Dom knew the sword wasn't happy with him yet, but Booker nodded in approval.

"Like I said to the others ... We don't all have to get along. Not entirely. And no one is asking you to leave your—*this*—way of life. But what if I told you that it *is* possible to operate by your own will while still serving under the same banner?"

Glenys stared at him without words, her face more curious than concerned.

He dropped low then, dragging the blade swiftly around him in an impressive circle. He could almost feel the blade catching on the air as the magic within it attempted to keep up with his powerful motion, emitting a sputtering sound that reminded him of a dry log being tossed on a fire. Both he and the blade were coming to know one another. Dom finished the move with a powerful thrust high above his head, the sword screaming again as it had before.

He heard a collective intake of breath as he released the pose and let the sword hang loosely at his side, panting only slightly. He was only just getting started. His body and hands were slick with sweat, yet his grip remained true. "Don't you miss fighting out in the open? Real fights? Fought on real planes of magic against those Wraith bastards?"

There was a murmuring now.

"I don't need you to come now. And maybe I'll never need you to, gods willing. But if and when the time comes, won't you stand and fight? Won't you Wield your magic for something beyond the everyday bullshit of your lives?"

He could feel the tension in the room as sure as he could feel his beating heart. It was time to break this sword in properly and get on with the fun part: the fighting.

Dom let out a howl before really taking the sword through its paces with a series of spectacular, choreographed strikes across the stone floor. He had done this routine a thousand times before, yet this time felt like the most important iteration yet.

As he went through the process, Dom was flooded with memories of fighting alongside his father and brothers, all those years ago on Brian Boru's road to the high kingship of Ireland. He could remember practising for hours on end as a lad, repeated swings and blows against trees and rocks to get it *just right*. Just as his father had done. This skillset was not only an expectation in his family but also the rule. And while his father had needed to invent foes to get practice as a young man, the *Ard Rí* had always made sure there were plenty of fighters for his sons to practise against as they grew older.

Today's challenge was nothing new.

What felt different, however, was that today ... Dom could *feel* the power of his father's legacy humming though his body, an intense resonance he had believed long dead after so many years of self-denial. He was his father's son. That was the truth of it, for better or for worse.

But he was also the *World Ruler*.

He could choose which parts of his history he wanted to carry along and leave the rest behind. For as much as his father had been a hero, he could also be a right bastard. Hell bent and obsessed with power, absolutely nothing got in his way. Ever. Not even the wishes of his own sons and, in particular, the one son who'd only wanted to give his love to a wild pagan woman.

To his Julia.

And as he continued to swing the sword in a warrior's dance, it dawned on him that his father's storied legacy—the one he had silently resented for so long—was only that: a story. He could create his *own* story to pass down to his own children. Fuck, he already was! And with any luck, it would be one they wouldn't live to resent. He had spent far too long fighting the expectations of being his father's progeny, so long that he had almost forgotten the possibility of his own role as an ancestor. And now, he realized he had never wanted anything so badly in all his many existences: to be remembered for *being himself*. And to father children of his own with Julia.

Completing the complex set of motions and returning his thoughts to the present, he noticed that the sword was making a completely different sound now. He had no idea how long he had been going, but now the blade was indeed singing. But not like the Knaves' weapons did. This was unique: a low hum that was undoubtedly deadly.

Across the floor, Glenys was almost licking her chops for the chance to start the gauntlet. Behind her, Booker held a broad, menacing-looking dagger. Clearly, he was next in line.

Glenys raised her two golden blades high, grinning. "You ready, *Domhnall?*"

"As I'll ever be," he said, noticing her use of his name at last, teeth bared and ready for action.

Dom stepped out at last from the confines of the desert forge and into the early dawn light. The air was cool and tranquil on his skin, but he knew it wouldn't last. It was in their best interest to get on the road as soon as possible. Plus, he didn't fancy battling a hangover *this* bad in the heat any longer than necessary.

He had slept for maybe an hour or two, stretched out on one of the many long benches that surrounded the snake pit. At one point, he would have expected having to fight off sexual advances all night from the voracious Knaves. However, after showing his scars and devotion to the Sovereign, not to mention fighting off seventeen or more of their best fighters in several supernaturally charged skirmishes, he had been awarded perfect solitude.

His hands were raw and bloody, and his body cut and bruised. But his body, mind, and spirit felt whole. Frankly, he felt more like himself than he had in hundreds of years.

He was fairly certain that Lennie had missed the entire thing, having experienced his own version of physical transcendence, albeit one far more sexual in nature than his had been. Dom had found him curled up with several men and women in a pile of blankets and furs near the other end of the hall. The sight had reminded him of what it must have been like in ancient Roman brothels, and he'd felt a small pang of regret for having to wake Lennie after his undoubtedly visceral experience. The man had roused quickly, however, and dressed without a word.

Dom zipped his jacket shut before swinging his leg over his motorcycle. He wore his new sword tucked away in a finely made leather back scabbard that fit his broad form to perfection. He looked over to Lennie's bike and felt relief once more for his distinctly more comfortable ride. Where he expected Lennie to soon be sitting, however, remained vacant. Instead, Lennie stood frozen on the spot about five paces behind him, feet firmly on the ground.

"I think I'm going to stay here for a while," he said, eyeing Dom with a look he had never seen before. He also seemed to still be drunk, swaying slightly.

"We can wait for a time if you're not able to ride yet," Dom said, but he knew this wasn't the true reason behind Lennie's hesitancy to leave. The deep pain that he had been masking through distance, action, and (most recently) indulgence over the past forty-eight hours was finally beginning to seep through.

"It's not that," Lennie said.

"You don't have to explain yourself to me," Dom said with a grim nod as he put on his helmet.

Lennie instantly shot Dom a look of challenge but quickly relaxed, a dam about to burst. "Thanks."

Sparing Lennie his gaze, Dom kicked his bike to life.

"Dom—" Lennie said and strode the final steps to Dom's side. "You're the only one who knows …"

"About the orgy?" Dom said, laughing in spite of himself. "Don't worry about that. I won't tell anyone."

"No. Not that … Well … maybe that too," Lennie said, but he didn't blush. "I mean about what it means to watch your lover killed in front of your eyes … how helpless … how …"

Dom clapped his hand onto Lennie's shoulder with a slight nod. There were no words in the moment that could soothe the pain he was working through. To have it witnessed was all Lennie needed, and Dom felt equal parts grief and gladness for his ability to hold that space for his friend in such a way.

CHAPTER 20

I slept only briefly before waking from a roiling pit of anxiety churning loudly within my belly. Looking over to the generic black motel alarm clock, I groaned; Dom had departed only two hours ago, yet already I ached at the miles growing fast between us. In fact, I was surprised at how uncomfortable I felt with it, even though it had been my suggestion for us to split up in the first place.

I blew loudly through my lips before tossing my legs dramatically over the edge of the bed, deciding to assign my unease to the fact that I just wasn't used to being apart from Dom. Since releasing the tattoo magic—almost exactly one year previous—the whole "three-kilometre radius" theory rang truer and truer the farther he went. Our curses *did* bind us, after all. There was also the fact that I had almost been killed the last two times we'd been apart during any sort of "mission."

But at this moment in time, I was choosing to ignore that more sinister fact.

To my surprise, Dom had practically begged me to go along with him to the desert. Frankly, though, the idea of barrelling into the desert on the back of a motorcycle into a pit of disenfranchised Knaves sounded awful, regardless of any alternative. Even one with Ronan. It was hard to witness Dom in his desperation when I knew in my heart that this was the best thing for it; if mapping with Bernie had shown me anything, it was that the ebb and flow of our proximity was required to defeat Cassius once and for all.

Plus, it was only expected to take three days. Tops.

Following an uncharacteristically quick shower all by my lonesome, I stuffed the last of my things into my bag and headed straight for the door, making sure to tuck my compass into my jacket pocket. Without a second glance, I locked the oceanside motel room behind me; the plastic key-tag reading "Dolphin Motel—Room 205" dangled loosely around my outstretched finger as I descended the second-floor walkway towards the front desk.

Ronan was already waiting for me beside the truck. For how long, I couldn't be sure. He was dressed comfortably in what I knew to be rather pricy black hiking pants and a plain grey t-shirt that likely also bore an expensive outdoor label.

"Are you ready yet?" he asked as I approached from across the lot.

"Yes, Ronan," I said, fighting the urge to roll my eyes dramatically. I had resigned myself to staying calm and non-confrontational for the duration of our voyage, but at this rate, I wasn't sure how long my resolve would last.

"Grand," he replied and gave me curt nod before rounding the truck to the passenger side.

I crawled slightly gingerly into the driver's seat.

"Julia, is everything alright?" Ronan asked in concern as he hopped in on the other side in one swift motion.

"What? I'm fine," I said. I wasn't exactly going to tell Ronan that I was slightly sore from the several *enthusiastic* partings with my lover before he left. In fact, Dom had been so determined that he say a proper goodbye to me that he'd almost missed Lennie's early wake-up call altogether.

Ronan gave me a distrustful look before jerking his chin once towards the road before us.

It had been agreed that we would drive my truck north to Berkeley before meeting up with Dom and Lennie in Carmel in three days' time. Hopefully within the anticipated seventy-two hours apart, both parties would arrive with the necessary intel to plan our next steps. Ronan had been all business in the planning for our arm of the mission, which would have irritated me to no end had I participated. I had left him to it though, far preferring to spend my last hours with Lennie and Dom anyway.

"Did you like growing up in Victoria?" Ronan asked as we hit the rhythm of the road. It felt like a stiff conversation topic for two people who had been through as much as we had together, but at least it was better than talking about the weather.

"It was alright. I mean—I suppose it's like any city; it had good and bad things about it. Can't beat the weather though."

Fuck. I'd brought up the weather; this was already proving awkward.

Ronan nodded enthusiastically. "I really do love the West Coast. Honestly, you wouldn't catch me dead doing my research anywhere that gets below minus ten for more than a handful of days at a time." His accent was slightly airier than Dom's, no doubt the product of having grown up in modern-day Dublin instead of the countryside.

"You wouldn't like the Prairies then. It's like a meat locker out there eight or nine months of the year," I said, chuckling. "Okay, maybe that's a bit of an exaggeration. But when people are trying to justify that minus-thirty is bearable in the sunshine, you've got to wonder about their heads a bit."

He grinned as he relaxed more in his seat. "Domhnall doesn't love the cold either, does he?"

I shrugged; I didn't actually know entirely. "He runs hot, so I can't see it bothering him that much."

"He's a big baby when he does finally get a chill, let me tell you," Ronan said, and went off on some story about a time they had found themselves frozen to the core after a botched camping trip, the weather sleeting sideways, and with a broken-down truck.

"Duly noted," I said with a forced smile. A part of me felt slightly "set up" by Ronan in this telling—like he wanted me to know how well he knew Dom. But another part of me actually felt slightly wistful; Dom and I hadn't even spent enough time together in this lifetime to encounter any real snow or cold beyond the occasional coastal dump.

"Tell me about where you grew up. A while back, Dom mentioned I should ask you about your childhood if I ever had the chance."

He snorted. "Oh, did he really? What did he tell you then?"

I shrugged for what felt like the tenth time that morning. "Nothing too specific, just that you got into trouble as a teenager and were put into the military as a result."

"Oh, well there's a bit more to it than that. But the long-and-short of it is that I got into some dodgy magic as a teenager. Nothing *too* sinister though," he said, momentarily placing his hand on my leg. It was purely conversational, as if to provide me with some assurance that he wasn't dangerous, but it still felt a bit arresting. Ronan wasn't exactly the touchy-feely type. "But it *was* enough to cause my old gran to worry about me. She was a Wielder too—a Druid—though not nearly as practised as I was even by then. She used it more practically. I mean, growing up when she did in Ireland, it wasn't exactly easy to be a practising Pagan. She mostly used her skills to make sure her garden grew to her liking. That sort of thing."

"Sounds a lot like my grandma Gertie," I offered. I thought of her then, and the cottage, and how not too long ago, Dom and I had been talking about growing a garden of our own. Those types of realities felt impossible from where I sat now.

"Well, she did raise me, so we do have that in common. Though Wielding isn't as much of a hereditary thing as Bearing is. I mean it is a bit—but it doesn't have the same 'born into your power' kind of energy around it. You have to practise at it for it to mean anything."

I raised an eyebrow. "You literally can't go a week without telling me I need more practice as Bearer."

"That's a complete exaggeration! I would never say anything like that," he said quite seriously. And then his face broke into a brilliant smile as he tossed his head back in a barking laugh.

I gave him a smack on the arm, laughing along with him. Maybe this wouldn't be so bad.

"She's still around, your gran?" I asked, surprised that no one had told me Ronan's upbringing mirrored mine in this way. I now felt a surprising kinship to the man.

"Sheila? She sure is. Though she doesn't really remember who I am anymore," he said, somewhat sadly.

I gave the conversation a beat before speaking again. "Dom mentioned you had a grandfather in the picture at one point as well?"

"Oh, that old bastard! Murphy was his name, but he's long gone now. Dom's quite right to mention him though—he was the whole reason I ended up getting into the dark stuff in the first place. He had some old hand-written Druidry notebooks that I nicked one night when he was piss drunk. My friends put me up to it, but before we knew it, we were in the thick of it. Meeting in the woods every Saturday to try to conjure dark magics, trying to bring animals back from the dead. You know, teenager stuff."

"Oh?" I asked, momentarily taken aback. "That wasn't exactly my teenage experience."

"Don't worry, Julia, it wasn't like *that*. We never actually managed anything significant. I was the only Wielder in the group anyway, so I didn't exactly want to show them what I could *really* do. Mostly we just drank a lot of whisky and came home too late. Caused a fair bit of worry to our families though."

I wondered then what he could "really do" in the context of dark magic, but I brushed it off for the sake of the easy conversation that was being had. "Well, I was no stranger to underage drinking in high school, so no judgement here."

"The drinking was one thing. But when the other lads' parents found out we had been dabbling with 'Witchcraft,' well ... that was a *real* problem."

"Those damn Witches," I said sarcastically.

"What was funny, actually, was that for my gran, it actually *was* the drinking. She didn't want me ending up like my granddad. So, it was off to military college for me."

"It feels a bit counterintuitive for a Druid to be in the military. But I suppose you learned some good combat skills?"

"To be sure—you can't discount the training and discipline. Even if the rest wasn't really a great fit for me otherwise."

By now we had made decent progress down the road towards Berkeley, and I found myself actually shocked at how quickly time was passing. While my mind had wandered to Dom several times, Ronan was keeping the conversation topics interesting enough—and more importantly, away from his usual heavily laden research topics—that it could almost be called pleasant.

I didn't mind that so much, really.

"*Your* fighting skills have improved though, especially with Stuart's help," he said, and I felt my arm hair raise slightly. "I was really impressed with what you managed at the tower. Actually, in particular with what happened with Sean. I've never seen anything like it."

And there it was. Perhaps I had just jinxed myself with the briefest mental acknowledgement of civil conversation, but we were back to business before I knew it.

"You saw what you saw," I said, pulling my sweater sleeves down one by one as we rounded another curve. "I'm honestly not sure how I did it. Or if I could even do it again. I just … did." I tried to make Bernie's words come to me then—to share some sort of understanding with Ronan about how offensive Bearing magic is individual to the user and wholly intuitive—but the words eluded me.

He looked skeptical as his face hardened once more into the mask he had been wearing so often as of late. "We are going to need to understand what happened a little bit better if we're going to have a chance at stopping Kenzie. That's the point of this whole journey, isn't it?"

"I thought the whole point was to go see this friend of yours who knew about … what? Protein folding or something?"

"So, you *were* listening," he said. "And yes, that is part of it. But not all of it. We need to pinpoint a clearer understanding of how the continuity lines of magic work between Wielders and Wraiths. Bearers. The earth. And of course, *each other*. It is the key to everything."

He sounded slightly dreamy as he finished his sentence, which made me uncomfortable. "Continuity lines? Did you make that term up?" I asked, avoiding unpacking the way he'd said "each other."

"Well, if you must know, I did. Not that I can publish any theories like that in a research paper anyway. But my point is … well, there's just so much we *don't* know."

Yet I could tell there was plenty he *did* know. Even though I (likely) couldn't understand the science behind it, he made little effort to share it. "And let me guess … You intend to find out."

He nodded briskly, and we drove in silence for a few minutes. I sensed I was about to be interrogated.

"As for the fighting skills," he said, barely able to contain himself, "does Dom know about what happened with Sean? How you boosted him using your Bearing magic?"

"Sort of," I said. This honestly wasn't the direction I had expected him to go in, but I found myself wishing desperately he would have stuck closer to his expected lane.

"I see," he said, gaining stride. "And … might I *also* ask why Dom hasn't put time into teaching you any hand-to-hand combat skills? Don't let the Knaves fool you—they might be good with their specialized weapons, but they also utilize their magic to make it a lot easier. Dom, being the ancient bastard that he is, is the best of them all without even really trying."

"Well, you know Dom …" I found myself saying, and then regretted it immediately.

"I do. And I guess that's why I'm wondering—"

"Look, Ronan," I said, cutting him off, feeling the heat of anger rising throughout my body. "He *has* taught me combat skills plenty of times in our past. Probably more than he or I could even keep track of. But this time around, we're doing things differently. Dom and I … our story just isn't like anyone else's. So, we don't do things like other people." What I had wanted to say was that *I* wanted to do things differently this time. That *I* wasn't going to do them like other people. That *I* had to determine my own path and how *I* would unlock my own power. But after the debriefing with the Knaves and Druids after fighting at Cassius's tower, I didn't have the desire to clash with Ronan at that level.

"I get that, Julia, but—"

"Seriously, Ronan. It's not something you would understand," I said with a tone that was meant as a clear signal to let it drop.

"Dom is a bit of an odd duck. You've got your hands full there," he said in what I assumed to be a weak attempt to smooth things over.

"He certainly is one of a kind," I said, smiling tightly and trying with all my might to rescue this conversational disaster waiting to happen. Why the hell was Ronan trying to cross my boundaries like this about Dom, whose decision should have been final? This was new territory, even for Ronan.

He didn't return my smile. "It must be strange for you to be born 'in the now' though, and then find yourself entangled with someone with such a different worldview than your own. I mean, obviously Domhnall and I have had plenty of our own altercations around his more outdated ways of thinking over the years—not that it's his fault of course—but sometimes he's got a pretty archaic way of being, you know? And I don't have to go to bed with the man either," he said, his voice incongruously light considering what he was insinuating.

I hated his tone.

"Ronan, really? *This* is the conversation you want to have right now?" I asked, pumping the breaks on the discussion as I became increasingly aware of how trapped I was inside the truck.

Ronan nodded slowly, either unaware of or unconcerned about the line he was about to blatantly cross. "Do you ever feel like he expects you to act the way you used to, rather than like who you are today?"

I puzzled for a moment at his nerve, the evidence of the heat rising in my body now obnoxiously red on my cheeks. This was none of his damn business. "I may not have all of the memories he does, but my body remembers *just fine* the way it was for us. And the way it continues to be." I wasn't sure why I was even bothering to argue with the man, as he was clearly trying to push my buttons. The fact was that Dom and I were growing together this time around, fully aware of the dangers of being trapped in the "old ways."

How dare Ronan insinuate otherwise?

I thought of my lover then, somewhere far out in the desert. Hot and dry, stepping into some sort of Knave cave in an attempt to gather allies for our cause—the cause that hinged on so much more than when or where we were from.

I felt my blood boil.

"Honestly, Ronan? Do you realize how eternally, horrifically bound Dom is to all of this? Do you?" I asked, my voice teetering on threatening. "As for me, at least I get the privilege of some sort of normal life—whatever that means—before it all comes crashing down and I'm murdered. Dom doesn't get close to that much grace with his curse. He's always faced with responsibility. From the day he's reborn until the day he dies. He's always got to be one step ahead. For fuck's sake—the man hasn't had a proper rest in over a thousand years!"

Turning my gaze to the window in an attempt to hide the angry tears that had (unfortunately) arrived, I hoped desperately that this last statement would shut him up. Outside of the truck, the weather was turning in tandem with my own rising tide of frustration. To my left, I could see tall waves and whitecaps whenever we veered closer to the shoreline, and the rain was beginning to pour down in buckets.

We drove in silence for at least twenty minutes before Ronan's next words forcibly interrupted my thoughts.

"You're an immensely powerful Bearer, Julia. But you have no training or discipline. And it's not like Domhnall's memories wouldn't be useful in that aspect, if he were to tell you more." I had to ignore his jab at my apparently sputtering abilities but could at least pivot to his next talking point with genuine interest. I recalled then a conversation with Dom from several months ago around Ronan constantly digging for information about Dom's experience in their early years.

"Do you mean his knowledge about the Otherworld?"

"I do."

"Hold on ..." I said, pausing to contemplate what he was *actually* asking me. "Are you saying you think he's keeping some kind of secret from me? Not that what goes on between me and Dom is *any* of your business, of course."

"*Well?*" his eyebrows said, awaiting my answer.

I laughed loudly at the absurdity of his accusation, refusing to grace him with any sort of reply. Ronan's face remained impassive as he turned to stare down the road, rain pouring heavily as the wipers swiped violently this way and that. I was now struggling to divide my attention between keeping us safe on the road ahead and the increasingly inappropriate conversation unfolding in the truck.

At last, unable to help himself, Ronan broke the silence. "I guess I just wonder why he left you so *unprepared*. Knowing what he knows, that is."

"You mean up on the ramparts?"

I looked over, noticing absently that he had sprouted more grey hairs on his temples and in his beard than had been there even several weeks earlier. His face, however, was still unreadable. "Yes."

"You're still angry with him, aren't you? For putting you in that situation." I struggled to keep any form of accusation from my tone. I pulled the truck off the highway into a rest stop; I needed to get the hell out of the truck. Now.

Suddenly, Ronan's blue eyes were frantically scanning my face, desperate perhaps that I held one of Dom's hidden otherworldly confidences. "So, you don't think he's keeping you in the dark?"

I shook my head angrily. Dom might have secrets, but I knew they weren't anything to worry about. He was allowed his privacy, just like I was.

"For fuck's sake, Ronan! *Give-me-a-break!*" I said, my face fully red now. "He's not keeping anything from me! Sure, I used to be a lot more capable of defending myself, both physically and magically speaking. And sometimes he still thinks ..." And then I paused, momentarily running my fingers over the talisman around my neck. I felt a huge wave of gratitude for Dom's unwavering faith in my abilities. I dropped my hand and took a deep breath. "Well, I guess he simply *believed* in me that day. Up on the ramparts. Believes in me still, actually."

Ronan grimaced. "There's got to be ... He *knows* something! I just don't see the logic in keeping it from me."

"You wouldn't," I said, all the warmth leaving my body as fast as it had arrived as I stared harshly at Ronan. He said nothing and got out of the truck, trudging off towards the men's washrooms without his jacket.

Letting out an irritated sigh, I reached into the back of the truck to grab my raincoat, causing Bernie's compass to fall to the floor with a muffled thud. I twisted awkwardly and managed to retrieve it before Ronan saw it, placing it evenly on the palm of my hand. She had said that Ronan's path would run alongside mine, closer even than Dom's at some junctures, and no doubt this is what she meant.

At least it really *wasn't* a "Lancelot moment." Thank the Goddess.

I took a deep breath, steadying my own trajectory. The compass remained stock still in my hand, however, pointing quietly north towards Berkeley. Urging us onward. I hoped against all hope that that I was interpreting it correctly. I also desperately wished in that moment that I could talk to Dom, if only to commiserate over Ronan's strangeness this afternoon, but I knew that he would be unreachable for most of the weekend. Then I remembered that Lindsey had shared her number with me before we left the diner, saying, *"Text me if you need anything."*

I pulled my phone out and sent her a quick message:

> *Real talk, what is Ronan's deal?*
> *One minute he's totally friendly, and the next minute, it's the fucking Spanish Inquisition. We didn't always get along last year but at least found an understanding. This feels almost hostile …*
> *Send help lol.*

I didn't expect her to reply instantly, but it felt good to know that there was someone out there who might understand the nuances of our medical comrade other than Dom, who was more than likely unreachable right now.

Pocketing both the compass and my phone, I hopped out of the truck, locking it with a beep behind myself as I ran hastily towards the women's washroom. With the deluge pelting down loudly around me, I took pleasure in the fact Ronan would have to wait in the rain without a jacket until I was ready to return.

CHAPTER 21

We arrived in Berkeley to cloudy, albeit dry, skies. Being that it was American Thanksgiving, I managed to score a nearby parking spot on Oxford Street almost directly in front of the west entrance to the mostly empty campus. The timing of our visit was to our advantage for a number of reasons, but Ronan still shook his head and mumbled something about dumb luck. I ignored him.

The remainder of our drive had been expectedly tense, though not for lack of effort on my part. Something had been off about Ronan since his arrival at my birthday, and I was bound and determined to find out what the hell was going on with him. I did my best to keep things light, hoping he might share a bit more about what had been going on in his world to prompt such a character shift, but instead, he'd spent the majority of the time on his laptop and shrugging off any of my attempts at polite conversation. Apparently, the initial rush of social interaction between us had pushed him past his quota for the weekend.

Lindsey had offered surprisingly insightful support on the Ronan front though:

Let me guess, he's been buttering you up to try to get more details about your magic?

He gets so obsessed about the most ridiculous things. Imagine him doing the same thing ... but in the middle of being pumped in bed.
And he wonders why I left him. Haha.

Ronan had offered to take a turn driving at one point, but I'd politely declined; the last thing I needed was to be suddenly trapped in a truck under Ronan's scrutiny while he held control of the wheel. That being said, after our voyage, I was now completely wiped and had a strong hunch that Ronan would decline any suggestions to rest before we located Dr. Bailey.

Hopping out of the truck at last, I stretched my arms high above my head before silently stuffing my sheathed dagger into the inside of my jacket where no one could see it. Dom had made me promise that, no matter what happened, or how safe Ronan claimed the mission was, I would keep the weapon with me at all times, just in case.

I was pleased to discover that "Springer Gateway" would lead us past a dense eucalyptus grove before we approached the Valley Life Sciences building, only a few minutes' walk away.

"Do you mind if we stop there first?" I asked, gesturing towards the green space. "I feel like I need to take a minute to orient myself."

To my surprise, he agreed. "I figured as much. I'll need a chance to recharge too."

We soon found ourselves standing amidst some of the tallest trees in the area. Walking in peaceful silence along the footpath, I watched as Ronan gathered what energies he could by stopping to place his hands on several of the greats. I didn't need the physical touch and could simply bask in the thinness of the place. The pull of the tide only several minutes' drive away also kept me rooted in place.

Eventually we arrived at a small bridge over what was named Strawberry Creek. I could feel the groundswell here too ... a portal energy. In fact, I had a distinct feeling it was the kind of place where no sooner would you ask a question than you'd find the answer.

"So, can you tell me more about this researcher friend of yours?"

Ronan took a deep breath as he gazed upwards to the distant canopy. "I haven't actually met her in person. But she's been working on a crucial element that's missing from my own research and is a leader in the field. That, and she's a Bearer."

"Pardon me?" I stopped in the middle of the bridge. "Ronan, that's a *significant* detail to leave out."

He didn't have the sense to even pretend he was ashamed for lying to me. "To be completely honest, Julia ... I didn't think Domhnall would have let you come on this mission if he knew the truth. Especially after what happened with Agnes. I mean, look how he well responded to that."

I stared at him for a moment, unable to process the series of emotions passing rapidly through my psyche like daggers. He'd evidently developed a skewed sense of how things were shared between partners in their primary relationship, but that wasn't the foremost issue here. I was shocked at the audacity in keeping this from me, particularly after meeting Kenzie in Cassius's tower. This was *critical* information that I'd been more than entitled to, so much so that I almost felt betrayed.

Instead, he had chosen to force my hand, if only through the omission of choice.

"You're an asshole. And a hypocrite," I said simply and kept walking as I shook my head.

Ronan said nothing but followed several paces behind. We exited the grove and walked towards the back side of our targeted building.

"She's on the third floor," Ronan said, pulling out his compass. My own weighed heavily in my pocket, where it would remain for the time being; I wasn't ready to show it to Ronan just yet.

He held his instrument out before him and waited. "Looks clear."

Despite this, I closed my eyes momentarily and checked for myself without telling Ronan, though he would surely feel my reaching out. I was at least trying to be discreet, and perhaps even downplaying my abilities at this point. I recognized not only clear passage but a distinct lack of protection spells from someone whom I assumed would be of the mind to have cast them. Then again, what did I *really* know about other Bearers anyway? While I might have forgiven them for their failings, my heart still felt heavy at the thought of my mother and Gertie and how little they had done to prepare me for the realities of my gifts.

The wound from their inadvertent betrayal was still sore.

Still, my intuition *was* nagging at me, so I attempted to listen to it. "Doesn't it seem strange that there isn't *anything* guarding her or her work? I mean …"

Ronan's face was strangely placid. "Hmm … Maybe it's just not dangerous here."

I stared at him blankly for a moment but said nothing.

And what about the fact that your compass is literally doing nothing *while I'm clearly picking up on something unusual? How is that not a sign of danger?*

"You're right, though," he said, clearly responding to the look on my face. "We'd best be careful. It could be a trap." I really didn't like how he was speaking, with almost no inflection let alone any morsel of concern. Again, it put me on edge, and I wondered if there was even more that he wasn't telling me.

For fuck's sakes, what are we getting ourselves into?

Rounding the back of the immense concrete building, it almost came as a relief to feel the thin lines of Wielding magic now pulling and tensing all around us. Friendly or not, it was something. In this moment, it didn't feel particularly sinister. Plus, since Ronan's compass remained still in his outstretched hand, we could at least hope there were no Wraiths hidden about.

I pulled my out my own compass, deciding that my bitterness towards Ronan was no reason not to witness my own magic in motion. If my understanding of its use was correct, for me, the compass would serve as a barometer for what my inner magics were trying to tell me.

"Shit."

Where it had been completely still all day, pointing ever true towards Berkeley, I was surprised to discover that it was now spinning wildly, almost frantically in my palm.

"Where did you get that?" Ronan asked, unable to hide his surprise as he grabbed me by the arm and shoved me roughly into a small alcove. I didn't like how he then placed his body between me and the only escape route.

"Ouch! Ronan!" I glared at him, feeling the heavy presence of my dagger pressed against my ribcage but unsure if I could pull it out before he stopped me. Not that I should be needing it against him.

"Sorry. It's just … I've never seen another one like mine."

He released me slightly, and I took several measured breaths. He smelled like spiced aftershave and onions from the sandwich he had eaten earlier. "I got it from Bernie when we were in Big Sur. She made yours too, if you *must* know," I said, sticking out my chin slightly to fill the gap that had opened up between us.

"Looks like I'm not the only one keeping secrets today," he said, staring back at me, jaw twitching as he held back a wall of his own anger. Quickly though, curiosity got the better of him, and his eyes dropped down, heavy and full of intrigue. He took another step back, shoulders relaxing slightly. "Okay, I'll bite. What does yours *do* exactly? It's different than mine … obviously."

The two compasses, side-by-side in our outstretched hands, were acting in complete contradiction. While his was steady and heavy in his palm, mine was running wild and light as air. A part of me wanted to tell him to go fuck himself right there on the spot, particularly for the way he had treated me for the last several moments. However, I also felt a rush of fresh excitement to discuss the compass with another user.

"The way Bernie explained it, is that—for a Bearer, anyway—it connects to your inner sense of direction. 'Life path' kind of deal. She said it was a bit different for Wielders though … It's more objective-based for you, if that makes sense."

He puzzled over that, taking a step back and allowing me a bit more breathing room. "What do you mean by *objective-based?*"

I thought for a moment. "Well … If your life goal is to defeat, or like … *sort out* the Wraiths—how they work and all that—that's what it does for you. If I could guess, the fact that your compass isn't moving—"

"Means I'm exactly where I'm supposed to be?"

"Yeah, maybe. But there seems to be some nuances around that too." I stared at my own apparently malfunctioning compass. I had no clue what its current agitation meant, but it was likely important.

Ronan was silent for a moment before we started walking again.

"Interesting. Maybe that's how Dom was able to use it to find you. I've never been able to figure out exactly how he managed to use it for anything other than tracking Wraiths because that's all I ever really use it for. But it's obviously his life's objective to find you, so maybe …"

I suddenly felt a heavy weight in my chest and fervently wished Dom were here with us right now. His presence alone would steady me. At least I wouldn't have been stuffed into an alcove with a stormy Ronan blocking my way out.

"I'm not too sure about how it worked for him either, actually," I said. "A lot of what happens between us is unexplained: how our curses work, how we find each other time and time again … I mean, obviously the Prophecies aren't something we can trust for certain. And fuck, even Cassius always seems to orient to where we are." I shuddered from the lingering feeling of him always keeping tabs on my existence throughout history. "It's just … a lot of unknowns, I guess. And a whole lot of trust."

Ronan paused for half a beat and then took two long strides backwards, angling his body away from me in the same motion. "Julia? I'm sorry about earlier. It's not my place to comment on your relationship with Dom."

I looked at him for a moment before stepping forward and giving him a slight shove. While I couldn't deny the growing sense of mistrust I felt towards him—Ronan easily fanning the flames of *that* fire—there wasn't much to be done with it right now.

"Alright. I guess you're forgiven."

We entered the building from the back side and immediately began our ascent to the third floor. I hadn't noticed any elevators, but I assumed that Ronan would have opted for the stairs regardless. Druid things.

"What *exactly* are we hoping to find out here, Ronan?" I asked as we reached the last landing at the third floor.

"Well, there's a missing piece in my own research around how the Wraiths are able to effectively suspend their existence between life and death. It goes beyond the parameters of simple Wielding magic, or Sorcery for that matter. Something shifts in their genetic makeup. I … Well, I'm hoping that if I can gain access to Dr. Bailey's research, it might help me jog—"

Ronan was cut off by a loud crash that came from somewhere on the floor ahead of us, followed by more silence. We paused in unison, both listening and feeling for what might lie ahead.

MANTLE OF THE WORLD RULER

"I don't feel any Bearing magic here, Ronan."

"Well, you also couldn't feel Kenzie, so maybe ..." His voice trailed off. His comment wasn't accusatory though. It was just concern. Was Dr. Bailey okay? I held out my compass before me, which was still spinning uncontrollably.

Unfortunately, now Ronan's was too.

"Wraiths," he muttered under his breath. He reached into the inside of his jacket and pulled out a small pouch, the same kind we had used in the diner the day before to hush our voices. Soon, the stair landing was filled with the scent of fresh lemon.

I blinked several times; the strength of the spell was staggering.

"Do you think they knew we were coming?" I asked.

He furrowed his brow, thinking hard. "How could they have? Unless ..."

"Unless what, Ronan?"

"Well, it's possible that when Wren was being tortured, Caleb could have gained access to the locations of other magic users who were connected to my research. Through Lennie. I've always been so careful, but it's just that we still don't know what all—"

Another loud crash signalled that this cozy corridor catch-up would soon be coming to an end. "We've got to go," I said, turning and making for the stairs.

Ronan grabbed my arm aggressively once more, causing my neck to snap back in his direction. "No. Julia. We have to get in there and see what's left! What if something's happened to—"

"To what?" I barked, cutting him off. I felt my breath quickening, unsure whether the biggest danger right now was the Wraiths or Ronan. "To Dr. Bailey or her research? It seems to me you're more concerned with the data than someone else's life!"

I wasn't sure if I was referring to her life or my own at this point.

"Don't be ridiculous, Julia. It's likely just a few Wraiths. We can handle it," he said, his eyes looking strangely pleading before he stowed that emotion back behind his cool gaze.

I had never seen a look like this on his face before, and it unnerved me. "Okay but—"

Boom!

A loud explosion rang out from several floors below us.

239

"Looks like we're going to have to fight our way out," Ronan said, flexing his knuckles. Soon, a putrid odour clawed its way up the stairwell towards us. It looked like Ronan would be getting his way after all, and we would be visiting Dr. Bailey's lab regardless. Forward was the only way out.

I swapped the compass for my golden dagger, pulling it out silently from the recesses of my coat, daring Ronan with my gaze to challenge me for carrying it.

"Remember what Stuart told you about your blade aiming true," Ronan said as he pulled his own larger silver blade from a hidden harness he wore discreetly under his jacket. On the other side was a sleek black gun. I hadn't noticed it before and glared at him.

"Were you anticipating a fight?" I asked, eyebrows raised. When had he put that thing on?

"Possibly. Let's go!"

Ronan kicked the doors open dramatically, and we were immediately met with the stench of Wraith magic. He beckoned me to follow him to a lab located about halfway down a long corridor, which now had its double doors pushed wide open.

"In there!" he said as he braced himself against the Wraith magic that lined the halls, blade raised, scenting the air like a hound on the hunt.

Holding out my own dagger, I could feel it cutting through the magic as we raced towards the lab. There was at least one person inside, as far as I could tell. Maybe two. Behind us, loud voices rang up the stairwell.

Wraith Slayer was about to be put to use again.

Ronan charged into the lab before me. Two Wraiths stood at the opposite end, busy with a blatant act of destruction. I couldn't see their faces under their hoods, but I could picture their leers at the sight of us.

"Stop!" Ronan demanded.

The larger of the two Wraiths spoke. His southern accent thick and dripping with malice. "What, so you can gain access to what the Witch has been up to here? No. I don't think so."

The second Wraith smashed yet another bank of equipment onto the floor. The two were not looking for anything, just bent on destroying everything in sight.

Ronan let out a growl and charged towards the two Wraiths. I had no idea what he expected me to do in this moment, but I assumed flanking him was the appropriate tactic. And I was right. Just as Ronan made to dispatch of the first Wraith, the second jumped spectacularly towards him, sickle raised. I threw Wraith Slayer as hard as I could towards the catapulting creature. As the blade left my fingertips, I felt its magic torque into a hard spin forward. It homed in on its target and hit the Wraith square in the chest. A wailing scream emitted from the second Wraith as it crumpled to the floor.

"Julia, the doors!" Ronan barked as we heard loud footsteps approached outside the room.

I flung my hand backwards in an attempt to barricade us in. I had no idea if it would work, but seemingly, I managed to at least slow them down. Three or four Wraiths were now pounding on the door, unable to get in.

I looked towards Ronan again, who was standing over the dead body of the first Wraith. "Is any of this salvageable for you, or can we get the fuck out of here?" I shouted.

Chest heaving, Ronan began to scour through the remains of Dr. Bailey's research, muttering.

"Do you think they took her?" I asked, fighting back panic as I joined Ronan in his search for Goddess knew what.

"It's more than likely, since they were destroying what's left," Ronan said, emotion completely absent from his voice. What he lacked in verbal expression, however, he now made up for entirely on his face. He had a terrified expression that left me wondering if he was going to cry or scream.

"Ronan, we need to get out of here!"

"I need … just give me …" he said, pushing another desk aside with a crash of his own.

The Wraiths continued to pound on the door, and I could feel whatever protective magic I had conjured beginning to waver. Soon, it would crack.

I looked at Ronan, pleading with my eyes that we go, but suddenly, a vision of the future flashed before me.

I saw Ronan standing on an abyss of his own, surrounded by storm clouds and a strange white light. The look he wore was disturbing—far more disturbing than anything I had witnessed from him today. I was reminded ominously of the faces of fanatics and religious extremists as they charged headlong into conflict, firmly holding only their own beliefs in hand, martyred to their addictive obsessions. He looked manic. Beyond crazed, in fact. Ronan's inevitable war-with-self, which he had long mitigated through the rigid discipline of both his military and medical careers—and with his faith—was now colliding headlong with his forked path of destiny. There was no stopping him on this path, and he would do whatever it took to get the answers he needed. The lives of others, and himself, be damned.

Unfortunately, my brief hiatus from reality meant that I had dropped the protection spell.

Shaking my head as my vison cleared, I was met with the sight of Ronan charging across the room towards the doors, significantly outnumbered. What I had thought was only a handful of Wraiths turned out to be at least ten or fifteen of them.

Shit.

Fear rising through my chest like magma, I thought of my own precipice moment before reaching deep within to access the magic I knew would save Ronan's life. Without Kenzie there controlling the magical climate, I knew that this time I could draw on it easily.

Reaching inward, I felt my inner hearth grow from a pile of weakly stoked kindling into an unadulterated inferno of Bearing magic. I raised my arms in one half-moment and dropped them in the next, taking out the entire enemy force in one fell swoop.

It felt good—almost too good. And powerful. Like a dammed river being released after many months of retention. *Kill them dead*, as Dom had said. And that's what I did.

But then something happened that I didn't expect: Ronan hit the floor too. Hard.

"Ronan!" I shouted, frantically dodging the busted desks and equipment to get closer to my fallen friend.

"Yes. I'm … I'm alright …" he said, bleary eyed.

I landed hard on my knees at his side. His face looked tortured and disturbingly pale, as if he might pass out right then and there.

"What happened?" I asked, my thoughts still several steps behind me.

He grimaced. "Well done, Julia. That was magnificent."

MANTLE OF THE WORLD RULER

"Easy-peasy, lemon squeezy," I said awkwardly. Ronan gave me an annoyed sort of smile in response, and I felt the tension in my chest ease slightly; he couldn't be that injured if he still thought I was a blithering fool. "What do you need me to do?" I asked compassionately.

"What happened there, Julia? You ... *left,*" he said, ignoring my concern. "Did you have a vision about what happened to Dr. Bailey?"

I hesitated. "No. It was—Ronan, we can't talk about it right now. We have to get out of here before more of them come. I don't think you can fight like this."

He reached his hand into the inside of his jacket once more and pulled out a small vial of something familiar. It was the same liquid he had given Dom when we'd hauled him out of the battle in the spring.

"I'll be alright if I take this," he said before throwing it back in one swig. His face flushed instantly, and he made to get up without a moment's hesitation. "You'll have to drive us back though."

I stared at him for a long moment, picking up my dagger. *Obviously.*

Despite his quick rise to standing, he was wobbly. "Easy there, big fella," I said. He rolled his eyes obnoxiously. I was pleased to see he was still himself though, even as he leaned on me heavily for support. Thankfully, we didn't encounter any more Wraiths between the third-floor lab and my Tacoma. In fact, our exit went strangely unnoticed. How far had my "Wraith elimination" reached?

"Ronan. Did you ... Did I ..."

My head finally reached my truck. My neck was strained from supporting his unbalanced weight, but he didn't seem to notice or care.

"What are you asking me, Julia?" His tone was sharp. His cheeks were ashen, despite the elixir's helpful boost.

I needed to get us somewhere safe, and fast. However, even with adrenaline surging through my veins, I couldn't ignore the facts of what I had just witnessed. And when it came to Ronan, there was no point in beating around the bush. "Did *you* feel the effects of my magic when I killed them? Or was it something else?"

He was silent for several long moments. My stomach dropped deep into my abdomen; so, it *had* been my magic that had kicked him down. Fuck. Dom was going to be furious. Meanwhile, a lump of leaden concern filled the space in my belly previously occupied by my stomach. "Ronan ... what in the name of the Goddess have you been playing at?"

I expected him to snap back at me, but instead, his face brightened. "Julia. I think I finally understand how you do it!"

"Um ... Do what?" My head was spinning. I wished Dom was here to navigate this with me.

Ronan looked exhilarated now. "I ... Well, I've never been able to piece together the mechanics of it all, like how you're able to strip the Wraiths of their magic and send it back to the earth, and all that. In Los Angeles, your magic was blocked by Kenzie, so we didn't get to witness it in its fullness again."

"Just—stop," I said. I could practically feel my mind grinding in response to his erratic behaviour. We didn't have time to discuss this right now. We needed to get out of here before more of the Wraiths showed up. That said, I wasn't sure if the greater danger currently lay outside of the truck or now seated beside me in the passenger seat. Ronan looked completely unhinged, smiling like a madman, or perhaps someone who had just smoked a ton of weed.

I pushed my right foot on the brake and pressed the ignition, the truck surging to life. "Okay ..." I said slowly as I pulled the truck onto the road. "I think you might be going into shock a bit, Ronan. Let's get you out of here, and we can regroup somewhere safer. We can talk about this—"

"I'm fine, Julia," he said, both interrupting me and demanding my attention. "Honestly. Better than fine. What you did today ... It was incredible!" The look he offered me then wasn't only reverent, as his statement would suggest, but utterly euphoric. I had never seen him smile so wide.

I grinned in spite of everything that had just happened; it wasn't every day Dr. Ronan Gallagher smiled at you like that. "Thanks ... I think?"

"Oh, Julia, this is better than any research Dr. Bailey could have provided me with."

The brief moment of excitement I'd shared with him left almost as soon as it had arrived. I felt my chest tighten now at how casually he'd spoken of Dr. Bailey, who was very likely dead now, and at how quickly she'd been forgotten and dismissed. I also couldn't deny that Ronan had felt the pull of me killing the Wraiths. The same pull that had killed Malcolm.

"Ronan ... I'm not so sure about any of this."

Ignoring me entirely, he reached into the backseat and pulled out his laptop, along with a large notebook, and began banging away on the keyboard, that stupid grin still spread across his handsome face. His compass, now tucked haphazardly into the console cup-holder, was completely still.

I didn't bother checking mine; I didn't need to see with my eyes to know that my inner path forecast a total shitstorm ahead.

CHAPTER 22

Ronan and I arrived in Carmel two days earlier than anticipated. I wasn't complaining though. The return trip from Berkeley had been strangely exhausting, though thankfully shorter than our initial drive north. Between fielding Ronan's frenetic energy and excitement and processing what we had just been through at the lab, I could barely think straight by the time I put the truck into park at long last. It was well into the evening now, and my eyes were sore from driving in the dark.

More than anything, though, I needed space to myself to reflect. The past two hours in the truck alone with Ronan had almost been more than I could bear. Every so often, he would mumble something about the differences between Kenzie and my source magic, which would have been interesting if not for the fact that he was spouting half-finished thoughts and mutterings that clearly weren't meant for me. What was worse though was when he intimated something about the power of the connection *he* and I shared. I cut *that* one off directly at the stem with a hard glare.

The end of the road couldn't have come soon enough.

We finally checked ourselves into our separate rooms at the inn—the name not even mattering anymore—Ronan having called ahead to be sure someone would be at the front desk to help us. I positively ached to have Dom by my side. Without a word to Ronan, I took my room key from his hand and trudged swiftly down the first-floor hallway, turning to promptly close the door behind me with a *click* as if to ensure I would be left alone.

As expected, the room was luxurious with tasteful furniture. It even had a large window that I knew faced a blackened sea. Ronan's taste was one of his few traits I was actually grateful for. I let out a long sigh before tossing my things on the bed, my exhausted body promptly following with a loud thump. We could have been staying in an abandoned barn and I would have been happy to just sit still for a while. So, these accommodations made it all the more inviting.

I laid face down on the starch white linens for easily twenty minutes, groaning internally, and perhaps a bit externally, at both the high thread count and my current situation. Admittedly, it wasn't *so* bad. We had arrived safely at our destination, even if the mission itself hadn't gone entirely to plan. I was unharmed, if not a bit shaken up now that I finally had a chance to let my body settle. I wasn't sure if Ronan could say the same for himself though. He had clearly taken the significant blow of my magic hard, despite his protestations that he was fine.

The fact was that I had performed some fucking *spectacular* Bearing magic in Berkeley. And I had been completely in control to boot. But then why did I feel so strange about it? Lying now on the plush bed, I fought the sensation of knots tightening in my stomach and a heavy plate pressing down on my chest. *Hello, anxiety, my old friend.* Perhaps the feelings were mixed up with the fact that Ronan had been hurt in the process and the very worrying realization that came with it.

I felt guilty.

Reaching into my back pocket, I pulled out my phone to try to call Dom, if only for the imagined connection between us right now. I knew it was late, but it was worth a shot. However, as soon as the call connected, I was kicked straight to voicemail.

"You've reached the mobile phone of Domhnall O'Brien. Please leave a message, and I'll get back to you just as soon as I can."

My heart fluttered at the sound of his voice. "Hey, babe, it's me. Just checking in. Ronan and I ended up at the inn earlier than expected. Or later, I guess … It's nighttime. But everything's fine here. Don't worry. I … hope you're alright. Okay well, I love you. Bye."

Nice and awkward—well played, Julia. That didn't sound suspicious *at all*.

As far as the dead signal went, I wasn't entirely surprised—he *was* travelling to a desert cave. Even if they did have reception, it was sure to be confounded by complex Wielding magic. Still, that knowledge didn't help how fucking uneasy I felt inside at not being able to get ahold of him, on top of all of the other emotions I was carrying. I let out another sigh and wandered towards the window. Though I couldn't see it in the darkness, I took a moment to connect to the tidal energies.

Deep breaths, Julia. You can handle a bit of discomfort.

I supposed I could have texted Lindsey to complain about the weirdness that is "Ronan," but it just felt whiny when I thought about typing out the message. We were definitely becoming friends, she and I, but I didn't want to emotionally dump on her either. I tossed my phone onto the bed beside my compass, which was now completely still—whatever that meant.

What I *really* wanted was to get ahold of Dom and tell him what had happened, specifically, my side of things, and the choices I'd made leading up to the conflict, before Ronan spun his own manic tale. But that wasn't possible. Dom was still several hours or even days away and completely unreachable.

Taking myself back to basics, I opted first and foremost for a quick shower.

My armpits reeked with stress-sweat. I was anxious to wash the day, as well as any remnants of Ronan or Wraith magic, down the drain. I padded towards the bathroom and, pushing open the door, discovered it was even more grandiose than the rest of the suite.

Stripping off my clothes in peaceful silence, I turned on the tap, banking on the natural magic of the shower to deliver clarity of thought … or at least relax me enough to sleep tonight. After wetting myself thoroughly, I poured a small pool of fancy shampoo into my palm and lathered it quickly between my hands. Dragging my fingers through my tangled mane, I let out a moan.

The fact was that Ronan had put us both in immense danger in Berkeley, on several levels.

First and foremost, keeping Dr. Bailey's identity as a Bearer a secret from me should have been a massive, parachute-sized red flag. And, truth be told, I should have turned us around right then and there. It's what Dom would have done and what he would have expected me to do. And yet, I had continued, drawn in by the magic of our twin compasses and the bizarre thrall Ronan seemed to have on me when it came to his life's mission. Or was it something else?

Second, I *definitely* should have turned tail when we realized the lab's security had been breached, instead of wasting time arguing with Ronan and letting him stall me until we'd had *no choice* but to move forward. In hindsight, it was possible he'd used some sort of manipulation tactics on me; surely, he was a master at that sort of thing. And yet—once again—my gut was telling me that only *I* was responsible for the choices I had made in Berkeley.

Lastly, there was what happened in the lab. Ronan had delayed us enough in searching for Goddess knows what that we, or more accurately, *I* had been forced to draw upon my deeper magics to get us out safely. It could have ended so differently, and yet ...

An unbelievable thought passed through my mind. *Had Ronan set it all up on purpose?*

No. Surely not even he was that deceptive. I knew he practically lived and breathed his research, but he wouldn't put a friend in danger like that. Or would he? I thought about what he had said about Dom not preparing me properly for the dangers ahead, and the doubt he seemed to being trying to sow in me about Dom and myself. Was this Ronan's fucked-up way of trying to encourage me to dive deeper into my own magic? By proving that I wasn't capable? After all, only he and Lennie had *truly* witnessed what had happened up on the ramparts that day. It wasn't Ronan's place, and yet ...

I rinsed the remainder of the soap out of my hair, gave my body a quick scrub, and turned off the shower. That was more than enough thinking for tonight, especially in this state. I towelled off quickly, rooted through my bag for a pair of pajamas, slipped into them, and practically collapsed into bed. Shutting off the light, I poked a finger onto my cellphone screen, hoping that a message from Dom would be waiting for me.

But there was nothing.

I awoke the next morning at almost eleven. Well, officially. I had been up five or six times since about three a.m., the expected dreams and nightmares that followed any harrowing escape having arrived right on cue. Most of my dreams were of shrouded, unknown figures—Wraiths and the like—unseen faces haunting me from behind their heavily draped hoods. I still didn't understand why they bothered with costumes like they did, since they were Wielders just like the rest of us. Well, semi-dead Wielders, but all the same. They were mortal *enough* to dress like normal people.

There was one nightmare that had really thrown me though. It wasn't of Cassius—who remained mysteriously though consistently absent from my dreams as of late. It was of Dr. Bailey, or so I presumed. I saw her with a black cotton bag pulled over her head, being shoved roughly into an unmarked van just outside of the Valley Life Sciences building at Berkeley. I heard Kenzie's sugary laugh from the front passenger seat. I don't know how I knew, but it was plain that the van had taken off just moments before our truck arrived at Berkeley. I paused at the serendipitous timing, but then thought better of myself. As always, Cassius and my paths were set to cross in one form or another until we faced each other at last.

My dream didn't indicate what would become of Dr. Bailey, but I didn't need the answer. She was yet another Bearer now yielded to Cassius's darkest plans, and I knew next to nothing about her. What I did know for certain though was that, once again, Kenzie was harming her own kind.

I shuddered, despite the warmth of my blanket.

Rolling over at last, I grabbed my phone. One missed call and a text message.

The call, unfortunately, had been from Ronan. Though I could have let him know that Kenzie was part of things, I ignored his message entirely, not wishing to start my day with his voice nagging at my ear.

The text was from Dom:

> *Got your message. Back in cell-service. I'll be there as soon as I can. D.*

Instant relief flooded through my veins. Everything was going to be okay. Dom wasn't much of a texter to begin with, but I'd gotten what I needed from his message. He was finished with the Knaves, whether they'd agreed to help him or not. And now, he was on his way back to me, come hell or high water. While I had technically only spent one night away from him, it had felt much longer. And in reality, a lot had happened since we'd last spoken. Knowing Dom, it wasn't likely I would hear from him again until he walked through the door, but that was fine with me. I could keep myself busy until he returned

Suddenly, I was craving another shower. Last night, my mind had been preoccupied with Ronan and Berkeley. Today, it was filled with thoughts of Dom.

The walls of the shower were neatly finished with white subway tiles, all of which were immaculately polished and patently luxurious. Under the piping-hot stream of water, I quickly found myself fantasizing about what I was going to *do* with Dom once we were finally reunited. My nipples hardened despite the heat. Slowly, a vision slipped into my consciousness. I closed my eyes, hopeful that one of our steamier past forays would greet me—quite often, if the visions of our past weren't fearful in nature, they were *very* sexual.

This vision, however, seemed wholly new.

We were in a shower together, much like the one in which I was standing now. However, this one boasted an upper row of hand-painted tile with orange and blue flowers and leaves. A gecko scuttled by on the high ceiling, appreciating the moist air rising up from below. Before me, Dom's cheeks were flushed as he stroked back my hair, his own longing as clear as the water that cascaded down both of our bodies. The warmth of a sunburn rose from my shoulders, but I felt a more deeply heated longing in my root that was drawing my attention.

Sadly, the vision quickly trickled down the drain, and I was back in my hotel bathroom all alone. I completed its narrative with my own imagination; it was comparably lacklustre, though pleasurable. I was suddenly dying to know where we had been in my divination. It was rare for me not to detect even a semblance of familiarity with a vision, and so I concluded that this was possibly a future expression. I was itching to tell Dom about it. The location had to be tropical, like Mexico or Central America—perhaps it was even Spain!

I was surprised at how much I longed for his return, having spent so much of my life content in my independence. It wasn't that I wasn't comfortable in my own company because I *was*. It was just that I loved his companionship—mind and body—more.

Following a single rap on the door, Dom walked through the threshold at last. Eyeing his vast frame, I let out a huge sigh of relief; he was clearly exhausted and covered in road dust, but he was whole.

I had spent the last several hours in my softest loungewear, preferring to wait in comfort over greeting him in something sexier; Dom didn't care about such things anyway, so I wasn't sure why I bothered. Maybe it was just some old relic of greeting a returning hero in your best garb. Or maybe I just wanted to look good for him.

I grinned broadly at the sight of him. "Hey, you!"

He looked *very* sexy in his riding apparel, and I rose with excitement from my perch in the corner of the hotel room to greet him where he stood. Somehow during our time apart, I'd managed to forget how *big* he really was.

I reached up to kiss him, but he turned away.

"Hello," he said darkly before closing the hotel-room door behind him.

"Are you alright?" I asked, freezing on the spot.

"Oh, I'm *grand*," he said, pushing past.

I watched as he removed a brown-leather back scabbard from his shoulders, tossing it and what looked to be a brand-new sword onto the mattress in one swift motion. He then aggressively unzipped his jacket and threw it into the luggage rack at the end of the bed. Looking down, I noticed that his knuckles were swollen, covered with cuts and freshly blooming bruises. Upon closer inspection, his lip was also split.

"Dom, your hands … and your face … and that *sword!*"

"It's nothing," he said, reaching down to pull off his riding boots. It was clearly a struggle, with his hands as inflamed as they were. I leaned down to help, but he scowled at me. "I just ran into Ronan."

Shit. I had hoped I would get a chance to tell Dom what happened at Berkeley before Ronan did. Without a doubt, our two versions of the story would be vastly different.

"What did he tell you?"

Dom ran one broad hand through the waves of his sweaty hair. He looked like he hadn't showered or slept in days. Clearly, he'd lacked any opportunity for self-care. "I just rode for seven hours straight, Julia. I'm fucking exhausted. I need a shit and shower. Something to eat maybe. And then I want to go to bed."

This wasn't like Dom at all. What the hell was going on?

His minimal text had led me to think that the mission was complete, and he would see me as soon as possible. Early, in fact. I had taken this to mean that all was well. Plus, he was almost always thrilled to see me, if not relieved, regardless of the circumstances. My heart sank. "Dom ... *What* did he *say?*"

"Ronan"—he practically spat out his name—"said that you took a huge risk with your life and that you're both lucky to be alive, actually."

"That's not how it happened," I said flatly. It was sort of true, but there was more to it than all of that.

"But the funny thing was, Julia, he seemed *glad* for it. The fucking *look* on his face," he said, his mind clearly replaying the events.

"Dom," I said, still confused by his reaction and scrambling to catch up, "don't you want to hear my side of the story?"

Suddenly, there was a harsh knock on the door. It was Ronan. "Julia, are you alright?"

"Oh, for fuck's sakes," I said under my breath.

Dom turned and opened the door before I could get there. "Get out of here, Ronan! This isn't any of your goddamn business!"

Ronan's voice sounded strange. "Well, considering how you just greeted me, I wanted to make sure she's okay—"

"What happened to your *face?*" I exclaimed as I peered over Dom's shoulder. Ronan was holding a sopping-red facecloth to his nose, which was clearly broken. I had a firm suspicion that the perpetrator was also in the room.

I turned towards Dom, mouth agape. "Why—"

Dom let out a low growl in Ronan's direction, ignoring me entirely. "Are you implying that I would hurt Julia? *My* Julia?"

"You're clearly unhinged," Ronan said. "You can't blame me for being concerned."

To my surprise, Dom let out an indignant, barking laugh. *"Me?* You're the one who's delusional. Get the fuck out of my sight before I *really* hurt you."

I was in complete shock.

Sure, tensions had been high between Dom and Ronan over the past few months, particularly when it came to the divide between the Druids and Knaves, but this seemed extreme. Dom stormed into the bathroom and slammed the door.

"Ronan, what—"

"I didn't tell him anything he didn't need to know," Ronan said. A strange look clouded his eyes. "But I did tell him *exactly* how powerful you really are."

I stared at him for a moment. "You need to leave. Now."

Ronan turned away without another word, and I closed the door quietly behind him. Before I could turn the bathroom-door handle, Dom started the shower. I didn't have the heart to find out whether or not he had locked me out, so I dropped my hand and stalked towards the bed. I had been so anxious to tell Dom my side of the story, of the magic I had harnessed in Berkeley and how I had been able to access it so *easily*, but now I felt that same strange guilt about it all.

I took several deep breaths and tried to think with my rational brain. First things first, we needed food, not that I was remotely hungry now. Picking up the receiver on the bedside table, I called down to room service, ordering us each a beef dip with a Caesar salad.

"Did you want any wine?" the man on the other end asked.

"Uh ... sure. Thanks. A red and white," I said, panicking. Truthfully, I was doubtful that tonight was going to turn into *that* kind of evening.

I had only just hung up the phone when Dom joined me on the bed.

"I ordered food," I said with a small smile.

"Thanks," he said and picked up the remote to turn on the flat screen without even glancing at me. Dom *really* wasn't a television watcher, further evidence of how much of a tailspin his encounter with Ronan had apparently caused.

"Dom ... please. I need to tell you my side of the story. What happened and how we ended up in that situation in the first place."

"Of course," he said, mindlessly toggling through the channels.

I moved to sit directly in front of him, so he couldn't ignore me, and launched into my tale.

Dom maintained eye contact with me throughout, though he remained irritatingly impassive the entire time. He clicked his tongue in annoyance at several references to Ronan, and his lip twitched slightly when I told him of the control I had over my powers when I'd been thrown into danger. However, he gave me little in the way of being impressed or giving even mild assurance that I had done well to protect myself and Ronan under duress. Dom's eyes *had* shot up when I mentioned that I thought Ronan had experienced the effects of my magic. However, he offered little more than a growl in reply.

And after all was said and done, I shared what Ronan didn't know yet based on the dream I'd had: Dr. Bailey had been taken by Kenzie. Dom said nothing to this, which hurt me more than I expected. I let out a final slow breath. "So … that's what happened."

By divine timing, a loud knock followed by a voice came from the door, releasing us from the discomfort. "Room service!"

Dom hopped up and collected our meals, sharing few words and closing the door quickly behind him. "Wine?" he asked, sandy eyebrows raised surprise.

"I didn't know if you'd want any—"

"I'll pass," he said coolly.

"Dom, I promise I didn't know she was a Bearer. Or that Ronan might've had alternative motives. Honestly."

"I know you didn't," he said, and dunked his sandwich into the *au jus* so forcefully that it overflowed from the cup. He gobbled it back, barely tasting it, and soon I handed him the second half of my own.

"Are you sure?" he asked in reference to my sandwich.

"I am," I said simply, my shoulders dropping.

Once every morsel of food was consumed, he let out a low sigh. "You were this close to coming across Kenzie. Do you have any idea what could have happened to you if you had?"

I nodded. Of course, I did.

For whatever reason, he now couldn't bring himself to look at me. The last time we'd had a fight of any significance was when I had been taken by Cassius following our visit to Agnes Sweeney. I'd vowed then that we wouldn't find ourselves in this kind of miscommunication again. At least this time I didn't have the urge to run away. And I definitely wasn't in the wrong.

The rest of the evening consisted of pained conversation over late-night television until Dom dozed off around ten. I turned off the screen and shut off the lights, feeling disconnected and lonely; this wasn't how I had imagined our reunion at all.

At around three a.m., Dom began to stir.

Naturally, I had barely slept a wink. I was sitting with my knees pulled close while staring at the red dot of light glowing on the powered-off television. I wondered absently how many nights in a row you could be sleep deprived before you started to lose your faculties. I had spent the past several minutes allowing my eyes to go in and out of focus as the red dot grew larger and smaller within my field of vision. When my head began to hurt, I turned my attention towards the restless figure beside me.

Still blinking somewhat painfully, I watched as Dom tossed and turned through the lighter stages of sleep. He smelled fresh and clean, and I longed to caress him in a reminder that I was here and that we were in this *together*. Several times, he also reached out for me, unconsciously, but rolled over before settling into the comfort waiting there. I longed for his touch but found myself lost without the right words in the dark.

When he awoke at last, he gently curled towards me but didn't make physical contact. I reached out in response and gently stroked my fingertips across where I expected his cock to be, hoping for some—for *any*—connection.

"No, Julia," he said and gently pushed my hand away. In the dim light of the hotel room, I could see that the scowl on his face had softened significantly, though the shape of his brow still hinted at residual anger, even in the dark.

"Oh. I'm sorry," I said, slightly dejected.

"No, it's just ... I need to get the fuck away from all of this."

"What do you mean?" My stomach lurched. Did he mean away from *me*?

He reached out momentarily but pulled his hand back. "I just mean that we need to go away. The two of us. Away from the Knaves. The Druids. And fucking *Ronan*. Just ... to find some space to think. And ..."

I lay down beside him, concerned. "Did something happen in the desert?"

"It did, sort of. Nothing quite as significant or dangerous as what happened to you—not in the grand scheme of things anyway—but I realized a few things out there that I'm still trying to sort through." He paused for a beat. "What I really need is a break. I'm ... well, I'm at my limit. To say the least."

As always, Dom found the comfort of darkness the easiest place to express his truth. Even from across the mattress, I could feel his body relaxing slightly.

I swallowed before speaking. "I've been thinking about Mexico."

Dom snorted. "Mexico?"

"I know, I know. It's not Spain. But we haven't been there together yet." I shifted to a seated position once more. "Plus, it's close to both here and the shoreline. And ... I also think I had a Divination about it."

"Really?" He struggled to conceal a tone of surprise, his mood still grim. "Well, well, let's go to Mexico then. For Christmas."

Somehow, in all of this, I had literally forgotten about the upcoming holidays.

"Great."

I reached out tentatively towards him, and he gingerly took my hand into his own, wincing. His fingers felt swollen and tight around mine, and I kissed across each of his knuckles ever so gently. I still felt tightly wound, but the gesture allowed at least a slight release of tension.

"I know this isn't just from Ronan. Are you sure you're alright?"

"I am. And it's a really good story, but I want to do it justice," he said with a yawn. Apparently that was that, as he quickly settled back into what I assumed to be sleep, or at least pensive silence. I didn't feel particularly comforted by the conversation, but at least I was relaxed enough to drift off for a time.

CHAPTER 23

The late day haze further shrouded Cassius's glamoured form as he wandered slowly through the outer Medina, passively eyeing market stalls filled with perfectly poured cones of vibrant spices and hand-woven baskets. But he wasn't here to shop. He was winding his way slowly towards the *Djemaa El Fna*, the heart of Marrakech.

Cassius had, of course, visited the dense market countless times since its beginnings in the eleventh century, but it never ceased to impress. Even now. The sun was setting low, which meant that soon the musicians and street performers would begin warming up for the night ahead. In its prime, the market had been the haven of renowned storytellers, though those days had long since passed. Back then, it was a place where even he, The Child of Rome, could get lost for hours as the greats wove their tales deep into the night.

Sometimes, he lamented for the old days, not that the world had been any less convoluted than it was today. But power had held a different meaning in those times, and you could wield it with staggering magnitude without anyone questioning.

Wandering deeper into the old city, Cassius watched curiously as food stalls opened up around him along the outer edge of the square, not that he had the stomach for much these days. However, the market—with all its flavoured and visual splendour—would still serve as a perfect host for the more sinister consumption he had divined for later in the evening. But first, he needed to find what he was looking for.

In an attempt to beat the day's heat, which was unusually warm for this time of year, Cassius had spent the better part of the afternoon seated in his private hotel's *riad*—the shaded garden courtyard was the coolest place to feign enjoying cocktails. He felt nothing from the alcohol itself, but at least he could feel a slight burn as it travelled down his throat. Plus, sitting in the lap of luxury almost always calmed his turbulent mind.

The bartender, who seemed almost too eager to please him, was quick to regale him with stories about the region, nattering away incessantly for the better part of an hour. He had enjoyed the distraction for a time, sensing that the man had more than imported drinks in mind for the pair of them. But eventually Cassius grew bored. He had shut the man up with a harsh, cold glare. He had been to Marrakech hundreds of times before and could only tolerate so much small talk, no matter how interested the suitor. Cassius had left the man a significant tip though; he didn't need his reputation sullied by being referred to as cheap.

Arriving at the centre square at last, Cassius watched a man place a snake around the shoulders of a middle-aged tourist. She panicked and began digging frantically for her money belt, hoping to put an end to the experience through the deliverance of coin. He had never liked snakes, but he liked people even less, and so he laughed maliciously at the spectacle.

He was unaccustomed to the growing throng of people and felt his skin crawl anytime anyone brushed too close to him. Well, where his skin *would* be. Apart from his voyage to Louisiana to retrieve the map, and the brief stop to feed from Kenzie, it had actually been quite some time since he'd showed himself in public. Not that anyone here would recognize him, but the fact remained. It had been a hundred and seventy days since the summer solstice, when everything had changed.

It was high time for Cassius to start moving pieces into place.

In the past, he'd rarely focused on the passage of time. The days blurred together endlessly, only punctuated by the thrill of the hunt when the World Ruler and his Witch would show themselves once more. He had lived his life at the rhythm of a slow pulse. *Thump.* The Sovereign and the World Ruler arrived. *Thump thump.* They were gone. Repeat.

Now, however, he knew precisely how many days had passed since the summer solstice. And how many remained before the winter solstice arrived. He wondered absently if the date would serve any significance in their shared narrative but then thought better of it; the World Ruler's "birthday" was of no consequence to him. In fact, if all went to plan, the World Ruler's destruction would be the simplest of his many tasks ahead.

With the information Caleb and Kenzie had tortured out of those fool Knaves, he'd discovered the presence of a scientist working at UC Berkeley. She was a Bearer and was gaining too much ground in an area of research that might be used against him—a body of work that the Druid Ronan also seemed *far* too curious about. Ronan's time would come, of course. Cassius had big plans for him. But for now, the Bearer scientist would need to be extinguished. He wished he could travel to America to finish the job himself, savouring the sweet Bearing essence she surely carried. But he would let Kenzie torment her instead.

Cassius took deep satisfaction in Kenzie's active betrayal of her own kind. If anything, it was her only redeeming quality. Well, that and her inclination towards his particular brand of torture; she had been a good apprentice in that regard.

He took a deep swig of heavy night air and, bringing himself back to the task at hand, fought back the familiar bitter tang that consistently coated his throat. His cavernous hunger for power paled only in comparison to his unquenchable thirst for immortality. Time was running out, and he needed to source the book.

Before disintegrating, the map had provided him with four coordinates, the first set pointing directly to Marrakech. He had laughed then. But standing now in the very centre of the *Djemaa El Fna*, uncertainty rose into his chest—a most unwelcome sensation. He shoved it back down. What was *here* that would lead him towards the Codex's ultimate hiding place? He had theorized that each of the coordinates would combine to urge him towards the final location, an enigma waiting to be cracked by only the most cunning mind. And it only made sense that the first clue would be found at the very centre of one of the most magically charged places in Northern Africa.

The place oozed history, power, and *magic*. It had to be here.

A man leading a monkey on a leash wandered towards him through the thoroughly packed market. The monkey, wearing a shrunken sports jersey of some sort, hissed violently at the sight of Cassius. Its handler, who had initially borne a look full of predatory intent, was now suddenly afraid. Cassius leered. Animals always saw through his glamour, but he didn't fancy murdering a man and a monkey where they stood on the spot either. Not today. That would draw far too much attention.

He needed to reach out and find the source, or at least some sort of beacon that held the clue to his next steps. He ducked low, crouching down below the throng of people and rows of market stalls. This was the surest way to decipher what was simple Wielding magic and what was *more*. Disgusted by the very act of lowering himself in public, Cassius placed his hand on the dusted stone between his feet. Needs were what they were. The ground was warm to his touch, still emanating radiant heat from the day. His gold watch flickered in his view before he closed his eyes to the sensation.

Immediately, he felt the sheer concentration and vast magnitude the power of place was offering up through the stones. Countless years of magic had adorned the inner sanctum of the Medina. This came as no surprise, of course, though the intensity was admittedly staggering. Not for the first time, Cassius wished he was still able to gather Wielding magic the way he used to, siphoning it from the earth to fill the gaping hole that burned inside of him. This was a significant source. However, it had been years since this had provided him any form of vitality. Wielding magic was not enough for him.

No, it was only Bearing magic that fed him now.

His Wraiths were still able to take the magic from the earth, allowing them extended life and bolstered power. This also gave him a distinct advantage: having an army of semi-dead soldiers to face off against his much weaker enemies. But Wielding magic had its limits. Even sourced in the way they did it—through their shameless consumption—it was no recipe for immortality. It might buy them several hundred years of life, but it was far from indefinite. He had learned this hard truth long ago, when his body had begun to fail and he'd been forced to turn deeper down the path of Sorcery. This was something the Wraiths would never understand; nor would they dare try. Throughout the ages, he had effectively struck down any of his underlings who showed even the slightest signs of rising beyond their rank. There could be no usurpers. Only Cassius would reign supreme. The Child of Rome. Destined to be a God among men.

The tangle of magic around him was almost impossible to decipher with any surety. He could feel the presence of many Bearers in the square, but this wasn't new information. He intended to feed substantially tonight. He had already arranged at the hotel for a private entrance and disposal service; money and coercion could buy you *almost* anything.

Even here, Cassius was far above the law.

Pushing his hunger down, he caught a whiff of eucalyptus and fresh citrus on the almost non-existent breeze. At first, his mind went to the stalls nearby, where someone was surely brewing a vat of spiced tea or serving grilled food to patrons. However, he wasn't accustomed to smelling anything at all anymore, so he took pause. This was surely an enchantment.

Like a scent-hound on the trail, Cassius stood slowly, sniffing the air around him for clues as to the direction of his target. He guessed it was coming from some*one,* not a some*thing.* Which was all the better. If it was a Bearer, he would be able to kill two birds with one stone before the night was out.

Letting his Sorcerer's instinct guide him, Cassius found himself leaving the market square and returning to the cobbled passages of the outer Medina. It was dark now, but it had been a long time since he'd needed light to see. The further into the warren of streets he delved, the stronger the scent became.

"Reveal yourself," he said, casting his voice onto the air. Any magic user within fifty metres would feel his presence now. He had no interest in hiding his pursuit now; he was here for what he sought. And Cassius hated being kept waiting.

A crash sounded from a narrow alleyway to his left. Someone was running from him. He could almost taste the fear on the air. *Fool.* He turned his shoulders menacingly as he chased his prey through the narrowed veins of the city.

"You cannot escape me," he said placidly as he made a final turn down what was clearly a dead end. On the ground, huddled behind several wooden crates, he saw what appeared to be a bundle of discarded fabric. It was shaking. It was laughable, really, for Cassius could strip away any physical or protective spell with a mere flick of his wrist.

And then he tasted her power.

"Bearer ..." he said under his breath, practically salivating. Dripping and supple in her magic, this Witch would serve him well, even if she did not carry the information he sought.

She cast an arm into the air suddenly, sending a pulse of enchantment his way with a loud whoosh. It did nothing to unsettle him, however. These were the last-ditch efforts of someone whose power paled in comparison to his. She would not leave this alleyway alive.

He took a step closer.

"You are not welcome here, Sorcerer!" she said in modern Arabic.

Cassius was fluent in most of the tongues spoken in Morocco, Arabic being no exception. Languages were living things that changed, grew, and died throughout the ages. Far from immortal. However, he had learned early on that it was in his best interest to maintain some level of current fluency in most of the major languages of the world, regardless of their transformations.

He ignored her barb, diving straight to the crux of the matter. *"I am here because of an enchanted map. It is tied to a Codex. Do you know of such a thing?"* he asked, drawing air slightly through his teeth. It was of no concern to him if she knew the truth of his mission. She would not survive the night. Hand inside the breast of his jacket, he was struggling to hold his spear back from her core even now.

"I know not of what you speak," she said. He was irritated with the lack of fear in her tone, though he could still sense it on the air. Her face remained hidden.

"Do not lie to me, Witch," he said, venom dripping from his lips. No one lied to Cassius. Especially not Bearer whores. She shuffled under her robes, either unable or unwilling to stand before him.

"Rise," he said.

She pushed her hood back, revealing a deeply lined and sallow face. She was old—very old. And she was grinning infuriatingly at him from where she sat, wrinkles multiplying across her cheeks as she plainly refused to move.

This struck a *very* old nerve.

Rage filled every inch of his body as Cassius reached his right hand above his head, dragging her frail body violently into the air before him without physical contact; he would save *that* touch for the tips of his spear. Sheet after sheet of woven linen fell to the ground as he slashed his left hand up and down through the air, stripping her naked, further exposing her brittleness. Her weakness. It reminded him of plucking a pheasant following an especially lean season. Not much meat to be found, but hunger didn't discriminate when you are starved.

"The map contained coordinates leading me here. Right here, in fact ..." he said, sensing now a familiar magic seeping from her that had also been contained in the map before it had vanished. Her guard was failing, proving to him that she did, indeed, hold the answers he sought. *"You will not survive the night, whore. Give me the answers I seek, and I will make this quick ..."*

It was an untruth. When the rage overtook him, he took extended pleasure in the killing. Pulling his spear from the inner recesses of his coat, Cassius began to circle. Round and round and round again, falling into stride.

She bared her teeth to him and then began to laugh. *"Never."*

The insubordination of women was a plague the earth should have rid itself of long ago. Wrath like he had never experienced before exploded from his body as he drove his two-pronged spear into the bony ribs of the woman; he had other means of divining answers.

"Speak!"

The woman's face fell, her eyes growing dim almost immediately. She was powerful, or had been once, but had now reached an age where not even her Bearing magic would allow her to survive a blow such as this. Blood and drool dripped from her withered lips, which she now struggled to pull back into the foul grimace she had been wearing.

Instead, she spoke into his mind.

"You will not find the answers here, Marcus Cassius Longinus," she said, echoing laughter exploding like vitriol through his temples. She knew his name.

Cassius plunged his spear deeper yet, twisting it maliciously. His hand shook with force as he drove the cold metal further into her cracking ribs.

"Oh yes, we know of you. And we've been waiting for many centuries for you to come. My daughters and their daughters have fled the Medina as you have foolishly tortured me here. You will not succeed. The Codex isn't here ..."

Her laughter rose into a blistering cacophony before falling steadily as she began her passage into the Otherworld. Hunger mixed with fury as he used his spear for its second purpose, siphoning what Bearing magic she had left in her core. It was a surprising amount, considering her meagre form, but he took every last morsel of it. Savouring.

Pupils dilating, Cassius sunk down as her body clattered to the ground before him. The echoing laughter and sound of rattling bones sent him violently back to the Oracle's cave. He struggled to retain consciousness as the Sybil's milky-eyed stare re-entered his mind. Her face had haunted him for millennia and had visited him more frequently as of late. But she would not gain control.

He was Marcus Cassius Longinus. Akin to a God.

Staggering up from the ground, Cassius hastily wiped his spear on the linen sheets at his feet before tucking it into his jacket. There was no point in cleaning it properly, not now. It would spill the blood of several more women before the night was out. Dozens, if that's what it took to ease his wrath and hunger.

Then he would visit the next coordinate from the map: Ibiza, Spain.

CHAPTER 24

On the one hand, the small hotel room was sparse, noisy, and beastly hot. On the other, I had rarely looked forward to finding myself horizontal more than I did now. Even the stiff-looking mattress with its thin, scratchy green blanket seemed inviting after our tumultuous voyage south, and I couldn't wait to close my eyes at last and stretch out.

Due both to short notice and it being one of the busiest seasons of the year, we hadn't had a lot of options for flights or accommodations. Dom had also flat-out refused to ask Ronan or Lennie for help, their varied connections inevitably helpful in such situations, so we were stuck with what we got.

All we wanted was a vacation, just the two of us. Dom hadn't been picky on locale but had insisted that we stay somewhere popular enough that we would blend in as tourists. Protection through simple anonymity. There would, of course, be magic users wherever we went, but as tourists we should be under no immediate threat. Bonus points would be awarded to a destination with good food and sandy beaches. And so, we soon found ourselves in the heart of Puerto Vallarta, Mexico. It felt like our own version of a "fly-and-flop" vacation, only we were escaping much darker daily lives than the average traveller.

I wondered absently if Dom's plan was to spend the whole holiday avoiding talking to me by keeping his mouth full of a variety of Mexican delicacies, or if we would *finally* get to the bottom of what was going on between us.

"Do you think they're live?" Dom asked as he swung open the window onto our narrow Juliet balcony. He leaned out cautiously towards several heavy dark powerlines spanning dangerously close within reach.

I caught his arm firmly before he reached any further.

"Don't!" I said, and realized it was the first time we had properly touched in days.

He pulled away forcefully from my grasp, "I wasn't actually going to touch it."

I frowned. "Or me, apparently."

His look in reply bordered on anger before he turned away to silently rummage through his bag. We had spent the better part of the last two days in terminals and airplanes, and taxiing across hot tarmacs. Following that, we'd traversed by foot, rode a bus, and at last climbed into a cab towards our final destination. This meant Dom was hungry, tired, and in need of a shower.

Naturally, I felt similar. Not only was the travel physically exhausting, but my subconscious magic was working overtime to obscure our presence; my Bearing core desperately needed a recharge. I was also aching desperately to reconnect with Dom. I had assumed our talk in the middle of the night several days previously meant that words would soon flow freely between us once more.

Dom's behaviour since, however, spoke distinctly to the contrary.

"Is this how it's going to be the whole time we're here?" I asked his now naked back. I was reminded of the uncertainty between us the day I had released the tattoo magic and impulsively reached my hand out to retrace the memory.

"What should we do about food?" he asked, blatantly ignoring my question as he quickly threw on a fresh t-shirt.

I startled, pulling my hand back. He must have sensed the fragility of the moment as well. I felt sad and angry all at once, just like I had that fateful night in his apartment all those months ago. "Seriously, Dom? You've barely spoken a word to me in three days."

"I don't mind if you want to stay here and rest. But I'm going to need to find something to eat before bed. I'm starving," he said, again ignoring my call to action.

Since when would Dom O'Brien leave me alone in a strange place without any protection? I knew damn well his apparent willingness to abandon me had nothing to do with my ability to protect myself and everything to do with whatever it was he still needed to get off his chest.

"Now you're just being ridiculous. I'll have a quick shower, and then we can go," I said, cheeks flushing redder yet in the already warm room. I poked my head into the bathroom, noticing with disappointment that it definitely did *not* boast the decorated tiles from my divination.

"Well, we both know you're fine on your own, Julia." Dom spoke loudly so I could hear. "I don't want to give you the impression I think otherwise—"

"Oh, for fuck's sake," I said, facing him from the bathroom doorway. "Grow up, Dom!"

Then, after all the careful control and painfully polite conversation, he finally exploded.

"*Grow up?* What the hell do you think I've been doing for the past six months! Or maybe the last thousand *years!*" he yelled. "Do you think that's been easy? Meanwhile, you run off gallivanting on some magical quest and almost get yourself killed! Must have been a real laugh, fucking off like that with your new *adventure buddy.*"

"Is *that* what this is about? You're *jealous?*"

He refused me eye contact and made for the door instead.

All this time, I'd thought he was angry with me for taking a risk I shouldn't have, almost ruining our one chance at a new fate. I could understand *that*, but this was an entirely new angle I hadn't anticipated.

And frankly, it was ridiculous. And I'd had enough of biting my tongue.

"I'm sorry, wait ... Me? With *Ronan?*" I laughed loudly, if not a bit meanly too. "Dom, we talked about this back in Oregon. He's like a brother! Not even. More like a weird cousin or something."

He turned abruptly back in my direction, running his fingers though his hair as the built-up emotional pressure in his system slowly depleted. "Not *with* Ronan. I don't mean that. Or maybe I do ... *Fuck!*" he said, clearly frustrated with himself. "I know how stupid this must sound to you, but the way Ronan spoke about what happened, face alight with something ... a look I've never seen before. I just ..."

This was quickly devolving into an argument shared by a pair of teenage lovers, not ones who had been true to each other for over a millennium. Something still wasn't adding up.

"Don't you trust me?"

"Of course, I do!" he yelled, slamming his fists on the top of an old wooden dresser, its stubby legs protesting wobbly at this new assault. "It's not that ..."

I could vaguely hear the bustle of the street just outside our window, horns honking and music blasting from a street-food vendor just around the corner. An entire world existed beyond, but in this moment, ours felt wholly consuming.

Approaching him slowly, I was overcome with a strange sense of emotional *déjà vu*. "Dom ..."

"This is *exactly* why we were going to run away in the first place," he said, naming the feeling on my heart. "There's so much gravity between us. It literally hurts me when you step away. And then when I'm called to lead ... or forced to split my priorities ... I hate every minute of it ... the being away from you."

"Surely there's more to this life than *me*," I said with careful smile as I cupped his face with my hands, barely touching the surface of his heated skin.

His replying smile looked closer to pity than anything else. He then looked away. "The thing is, Julia. For me? There really isn't. You grew up in this time period, with your mind filled with endless distractions and possibilities. But my brain is still old. Very old ... even if my thought patterns are new. Every minute of every day, I feel drawn to be near you ..."

I knew him far better than to believe that this was a statement of control.

"But don't you *enjoy* the leadership? I mean, come on, Dom, you're clearly a natural. Everyone sees it."

His shoulders dropped, conceding to the truth at last. "Well ... I suppose that's what I discovered in Death Valley." He paused, looking me directly in the eyes. "It took so little of my own resolve to draw them in. To them, it probably seemed like a lot, but I had them eating out of the palm of my hand with minimal effort on my end. And ... I think I liked it."

I paused, feeling sympathy for the anguish that spread across his face. Yet, none of this came as a surprise. The Washington Knaves had made it plain that the mission would only be a success if the World Ruler showed his strength. And knowing Dom, he wouldn't have given up without trying absolutely everything. So, when Dom had texted me earlier than expected, saying he was on his way back, I knew full well what had occurred.

Well, almost.

"Are you going to tell me how that happened now, with the Knaves?" I asked, raising my eyebrows and eyeing his yellowing knuckles.

He grinned in spite of the tension. "Well … first, we got into some moonshine, and then they gave me the sword … and well … it sort of devolved into a mix of hand-to-hand and blade combat in a snake pit," he said, finishing the sentence rather quickly.

"Excuse me?" I said, mouth agape.

"Not a *real* snake pit," he said. "I don't think."

After the initial outburst, Dom went on to regale me with all that had occurred with the Knaves and the combat-gauntlet that had followed. Which, of course, he'd won. His prize was being able to call on them when needed, not to mention a fancy new sword. I knew it had been wrenching for Dom to leave the blade with Ronan, current circumstances notwithstanding.

"How could you have waited this long to tell me?" I asked, not sure whether I should be impressed or terrified, or burst into a fit of laughter. "That is literally *unbelievable.*"

"You're right," he said grinning. "I've been dying to tell you, actually."

"I bet," I said, smiling back, but his face grew serious once more.

"But then that's where the guilt comes in, you see. I watch you stand in your sovereignty, and all I want to do is be by your side—the spear to your chalice. It's honestly all I've ever truly wished for all these long years. To be honest … I'm not sure that part of me will ever change."

I nodded. "But with the new Prophecy …"

"Well, then I'm being asked to break myself into two. Because my heart will always be with you, wherever you are." He pulled me close. "How am I supposed to bear it? I've only ever known my own mythos, *to be your hero,* like you said."

His discomfort over the past several days was now making *much* more sense, though I still found it infuriating that he had bottled it up for so long. His anger with me was undoubtedly a projection of his own inner turmoil. "I know, Dom. But we're writing something new here. And we're going to have to learn how to operate divided sometimes." I placed one hand on his heart before looking up. "But we'll always find home in one another. Plus, you can't protect anyone, or truly *honour* their needs, without knowing your *own* needs first. That's what I've learned so far, anyway."

He let out a soft sigh. "Over one thousand years old and still a boy."

"Hardly," I said. "But it *is* a bit of an initiation. Or maybe, a coming of age."

"You *did* just tell me to 'grow up' pretty rudely," he said with a chuckle before kissing me on the forehead.

"I did," I said, feeling slightly embarrassed at my outburst. Then I thought about his confused jealousy. "And look … I can see how your mind wandered down the *Lancelot* path there … but honestly, there's nothing between me and Ronan."

He smiled, blushing in spite of himself. "I know, love. I told you. I'm just being stupid. I'm glad of the bond between you two. Really."

"I wouldn't call it much of a bond. Honestly … he gets under my skin most of the time."

"Mine too these days," Dom said, shaking his head.

An unexpected wind blew the shutters suddenly inward, carrying with it the canned music from the busy street below. Turning my attention beyond our balcony, I could smell the savoury fares of the local establishments drifting in as they catered to the supper crowd. The sun was nearly setting, and if I knew Dom, his stomach was practically screaming at him for sustenance.

In the past, we would have likely tried to fit in some steamy make-up sex, but one of the perks of our new life with its unfixed timeline was that, on rare occasions, we actually had the chance to pace things.

"Can I just have five minutes to wash my face and change my shirt before we go?" I asked, flapping my sweaty shirt away from my chest.

"Absolutely," he said, a genuine grin spreading across his full lips.

※

Several hours later, we found ourselves walking hand-in-hand along the Malecón, bellies full of delicious food and heads swimming from perhaps one too many margaritas apiece. In Dom's case, perhaps two. The sun had long since set, and so we found ourselves enjoying the colourful light displays and entertainment reserved for late-night visitors to the city.

As we waded through throngs of tourists and locals, I could feel other sources of magic passively press against me: gentle touches from Wielders, Bearers, and even thin places. The sensation was serene and effortless, like water over smooth stones in a trickling stream. I felt a strange thrill about acting like a tourist, like it was a forbidden treat to us in this life. I was also firm in my belief that my protective magic would continue to keep us safe out in the open while we ambled about without any particular purpose. It had to. We needed this.

Passing a popular shoreline sculpture of Triton and a mermaid, Dom suddenly scooped his arm around my waist and pressed me to its base. Even in the dark, I could see that his eyes had taken on a familiar inky hue, the surest sign of what would come next. And I welcomed it.

"Do you have any idea how badly I want you?" he asked.

I could smell the tequila on his lips as he raised my chin towards his own. Admittedly, I liked when he was loosened up in this way, particularly because his "old ways" tended to appear more freely.

"Right here, huh?" I asked, shamelessly playful.

He let out a low purr from somewhere deep within his chest. "Do you think anyone would notice?"

"Um, *definitely,*" I said, but that didn't stop me from removing any remaining distance between our heated bodies.

He grinned. "I miss it sometimes, you know. The old days."

I pushed my hips against his growing erection, slowly licking the salt off the skin of his neck, drawing him in with temptation. Teasing. "Did we just fuck wherever we wanted back then?" I breathed into his ear.

"You know what? We did."

I tossed my head back and keened like the siren I was. Of course we had.

His urges were getting the better of him now, a passionate combination of desire and stiff drink. He shoved one hand under my shirt, groping for whatever flesh he could find. The other hand rounded my back and gripped my ass. Hard.

"Okay, Tequila Don," I said, snorting out a laugh before rolling my shoulder out of his grip and slipping away from our position at the statue.

"Oh ho! You think you're funny, do you? Slippery little siren ..." he said, his accent thickening. He gave chase and quickly caught up to me, wrapping his capable arms around my waist once more.

I swooned appropriately. "Oh no. Triton. You've caught me. Help ... I'm a goner."

"You caught me long before I caught you," he said, growing suddenly serious. At this, I knew his mind was wading once more into the past.

"I have a seriously hard time believing that I could have *ever* resisted you," I said.

I kissed him forcibly, biting his lower lip with my teeth as his breath hitched. The change was subtle, but I knew Dom was hastily shifting gears from patiently playful to urgently wanting; it was only a matter of time before his need would drive us back to our hotel room. As usual, my own needs were a mirror.

"Believe what you like, Julia. But I've loved you since the first moment I laid eyes on you. And I've *wanted* you just as long."

"Oh really?" I asked seductively.

"Really, really," he said, rather drunkenly, in reply. "Haven't I ever told you—this cycle at least—about the first time I saw you? Surely, I have ..."

I knew he had, sort of. In bits and pieces over time for sure, but not in most recent memory. Frankly, any recollections of our past lives that he held close, like this one, seemed somewhat off limits. Protected. And assuming that the most precious ones were *also* those that kept him going when our rebirth cycles reached their toughest points, I had decided very early on to never push. After all, the collective memories of our past lives were as much a gift as they were an agonizing burden.

"Not in its entirety," I said. "Or at least, not this time around, I don't think, but that's alright." I shrugged it off. I was thoroughly enjoying the renewed comfort between us and was hesitant to dredge up any potentially difficult memories unless it was absolutely necessary.

"Did you want me to tell you the whole story?" he asked, somewhat tentatively. "It's a really good one ... and has a rather exciting ending, if I do say so myself."

"Only if you're sure," I said, suddenly desperate to hear more.

He paused for a moment and then smiled broadly. "I'd love to. I don't know why I've held this one so close to the chest, really ... Maybe I've just been a bit afraid of what you'll think of me."

CHAPTER 25

We settled onto a low bench together, looking out towards a deep black ocean. I could feel the tide's pull as strong as ever, and for the first time in days, or even weeks, I felt my body settle. Peace. I snuggled in close, eagerly awaiting more of the tale. "It can't be that bad," I offered.

He chuckled. "It's really not. Especially if you take it in context."

"How could I *not* take 'in context' a story from the eleventh century?"

"True. Alright. So, I was supposed to be training a group of farmers to use a Viking axe. You'll remember my father was rather fond of Norse weaponry, along with our traditional ones. It was a very fight-fire-with-fire situation, and was required within his ranks …"

I hadn't remembered that about his father but nodded anyway.

"In any case, I was standing in a clearing near where you lived then—in the-middle-of-fucking-nowhere just off the River Shannon—with a group of grumpy, farting old men, and their doubtful, skinny-arsed sons. They were having a hard time believing that any of this training was even necessary. You see, the worries of high kings often seemed rather suspect when you'd food and grain to harvest before the rains came. And I wasn't doing a great job of convincing them either, truth be told."

He was slurring his words slightly, definitely not atop his usual storytelling game. Not that it mattered really, I was too busy staring adoringly at the sparkle of reminiscence I could detect in his eyes, even in the darkness.

"I had just thrown up a prayer to God, asking for this godforsaken day to come to an end, and—lo and behold—there you were! *Just like magic*, walking down the path with a basket full of beeswax candles and onions, or something like, which I presumed you were going to be selling at the market. And me, well … I was sick and tired of trying to rally the group of fools before me anyway, so I happily wandered down the road behind you only a few moments later. One of the lads I was training offered a warning, something like, 'Stay away from that Witch-girl, Domhnall! She's trouble!' But I waved him off," Dom said, doing a hilarious impression of what the young boy must have sounded like, but in English. "You were *literally* the most beautiful woman I'd ever seen. Enchanting. All long limbs and auburn hair ablaze in the fall sunshine … I couldn't let you out of my sight."

I dug through my own patchy memories for any semblance of recollection of this day, but it was fruitless. "I'm sure you were equally as stunning," I said, shrugging.

"Hardly." He laughed. "My hair was a lot longer than it is now and usually quite scraggly, truth be told. But I still wore a beard, of which I was quite proud. I would have been around … twenty-two. A bit awkward in my bones still, I think. But you … Ah well, you were already *well* into womanhood." Dom's accent was thick as pudding as he lost himself in the memory for a moment.

I tossed my legs over his lap, placing my hands on the side of his cheeks as I faced him, demanding attention. "What happened next, Domhnall?"

He returned to the present. "Ah, well! You knew right away that I was following you, which in hindsight, was probably a really unfair thing of me to do. Big strapping lad following a young woman alone down an abandoned path. But in those times … well, it was different I suppose." He shook his head. "And I was rather brazen then and *well* aware that I was the son of the High King—"

I laughed. "No surprise there. I bet you had quite the ego."

"Yes, yes!" he said, deflecting my interruption. "I was debating what to say to you to get your attention, to introduce myself, when out of the blue, you turned and threw an onion straight at my head!"

"What?" I snorted.

"I kid you not! And you had good aim too. Hit me square in the jaw! I realized, after the fact, that there must have been some magic behind your throw as well—I wasn't *nearly* close enough for it to arrive with that much force! It fucking hurt!"

I laughed harder. "Good for me! No wonder I'm so good at throwing my dagger, all that practice tossing veggies."

"You would say that, wouldn't you?" he said, laughing too. "So, anyway, I yelled, 'Hey! What was that for!' as if I didn't know I was making you nervous. But you didn't look nervous, actually, you looked *really* angry. And powerful. I knew then that you really *were* a Witch, since the air around me was practically sizzling from your wrath. But somehow, that only made me want you more."

"You wanted me already?"

"Oh Julia ... You underestimate your own natural sensuality *and* the primal instinct of a young man *aching* for sex. Besides, I had been following you for a time by then—even the way you were walking while hauling that awkward basket was making my cock hard."

I ground my root where I knew his erection would be beneath his shorts. Bingo. "So, you've always been this lusty then?"

He groaned in pleasure. *"Julia* ... if you keep that up, I won't be able to finish my story."

"Can't I have both?" I asked, pouting. He thrust his hips once, reactively, before continuing.

"Anyway!" Dom said, his cheeks flushed. He was clearly losing patience in the storytelling as well. "I continued behind, eventually mustering up the courage to holler something along the lines of *'You're the most gorgeous creature I've ever laid eyes upon! Won't you let me walk with you for a time?'* You know, really acting the prince, and all that—and then you replied with something like, *'That's some fancy talk, coming from you. You're the most annoying creature I've ever met. Go away!'"*

Dom paused for a moment. "You spoke … Middle Irish back then, *An Mheán-Ghaeilge*, so the translation's a bit different than how I'm telling it. But that doesn't matter because you didn't mean it anyway."

"What—"

"You see, by now, you had this big, beautiful grin across your face—Yes! Just like that!" he said, smiling back at me in the present. "And I guess the fact that you hadn't managed to scare me away with your bewitched vegetables made you curious about me. Also, I don't think you actually knew who I was. Not by my face, anyway."

I put my arms around his neck, the sound of the Pacific Ocean waves crashing loudly behind us as I leaned in to give him a kiss. We couldn't be farther away from that time now, and yet, I felt as close to it as if it were happening in the present. Perhaps I was starting to recall my own experience. Dom was a wonderful storyteller, after all.

"It was hot that day, wasn't it?" I asked, reaching back into the memory, which was ever so slowly emerging into my psyche.

Dom startled and then beamed back at me. "Do you remember?"

"Pieces, I think …" It was feeling more and more familiar by the moment. "I can't explain it, but I feel like I know this part."

"Well, if this next bit doesn't jog your memory, I don't know what will."

I rocked back and forth a few times on his lap before closing my eyes, listening as intently as possible. He let out a low purr before continuing.

"You're right, it *was* hot! But by sheer luck, we'd also just come across a stream. Or maybe you knew it was there. Anyway, it wasn't very big but probably trout bearing, so big enough, as far as streams are concerned—"

I smacked him on the shoulder, "Oh my Goddess! Get on with it, you butt!"

"Just wait!" Dom said, teasingly, gripping my wrists. "This next bit is important."

I put my hands up in surrender as he let go.

"So, next you set your basket down in a dry place and wandered off the path towards the water's edge. I watched as you crouched down to scoop some of the fresh water into your mouth … and naturally, that was *unbelievably* erotic to my young mind. So, I followed you. To be completely honest, I was running on mostly hormones and instinct by that point, but you seemed patently aware of what was happening, making absolutely no bones about the fact that you were quite fine being alone in my presence. I was so used to being around God-fearing Christian women, and then there you were, resembling nothing of the sort ... enticing me to the water's edge like a well-maiden. Open ... alluring ... and dangerous. I was in *your* forest. That was when I realized I was also at a distinct disadvantage."

I searched my memory and could suddenly see him. Young and virile, if not a bit clumsy in his early manhood. He wore simple clothes, though the quality of the stitching and fabric gave away the fact that he came from wealth. A prince, indeed. "You've always been so fucking handsome ..."

I was pulled hard into a distant memory then.

I sat myself down by the river's edge before beckoning him closer. I knew he was nervous. I could practically smell it coming off his skin. My Bearing magic was remarkably attuned to all the living things around me, and he was no exception. I listened as a squirrel chattered somewhere in the distance, busily collecting stores for the winter. I knew an owl was asleep in a nearby tree, fully camouflaged from sight. In fact, compared to the many creatures quietly hidden in the forest, minding their own business, his essence had practically crashed into the place like a young stag in rut.

I had, of course, noticed him as soon as he started following me. And I knew immediately that he wasn't a magic user and so posed little threat to me, at least under the circumstances. This *was* my forest, and anywhere I led him ... well, he was there by my permission alone.

Admittedly, I'd been annoyed at the nuisance at first; I really didn't want to waste my energy deterring yet another man. But as soon as I turned to face him, something significant had shifted inside of me. Perhaps it was the amusing look of indignation from being hit with an onion, followed by his starry-eyed proclamations, but seeing him standing there on the path behind me, I had suddenly felt like I was like looking into a mirror of my deepest self.

Almost like ... like I was seeing what *home* looked like for the first time. Like I was looking into my future.

Lumbering down from the path, he joined me by the stream. Instinctually, I lay back onto the soft earth beside him, causing a look of shock to spread across his angelic face from above. It was cool there, a delicious contrast to the late day sun that had dogged us along the way.

"Would you like me to be yours?" I asked boldly.

"I … you …"

I giggled. "I think I'd like you to be mine too."

Domhnall Mac Brien, now eager beyond reckoning to experience the fruits of my body, practically fell on top of me as I pulled up my woollen skirts. That inky lust, so familiar to me in the present day, made its first appearance in his eyes then. There, in the wild forests of eleventh-century Ireland, I consented more than willingly to his advances as though my body had been waiting for him all of my days.

And it had been.

Thrusting his young frame against my own, I watched in real time as he fell madly in love. More than once, he pulled back to take in the view of my face below his, red cheeked and raw in my own freedom. It was almost as if he couldn't believe what was happening right in front of him. Was it real or an illusion placed upon him by the forest Witch he'd been warned about?

None of that stopped him, however.

He was so beautifully innocent and completely unabashed in his desire. Unbroken by curses or extended trips to the Otherworld, Prince Domhnall was, in his very essence, *pure joy*. He had exalted in his climax, and I too revelled in the divine love and deep *magic* being woven between us. I already knew then that I would never love another the way I would love him. Our connection was forged outside of the confines of dire threat or confounding Prophecy.

It was a whole and real love.

But what might have happened, had we been allowed to love each other as we wanted to then, we would never know. I opened my eyes and returned very much to the present.

"I didn't even learn your name before taking you by the waterside. But I suppose you didn't know mine either," Dom said, sobering slightly and looking into my eyes. "Oh Julia," he sighed, "it all comes back to how we felt about each other then—in that very moment—and ultimately why we were planning to run away together in the first place. There was no possible way for me to follow in my father's footsteps and still have room to love you properly all at once."

"Don't you ever regret it though? Stepping away from it all?" I asked, still lost between worlds.

"Now you're just talking crazy, love," he said and kissed me deeply. "I've never regretted it for a single moment. You saw what happened that day. How could I have ever left you behind?"

"You didn't think that I had enchanted you? That it wasn't real?"

"I don't think I would have cared either way, Julia," he said, nuzzling into my hair and breathing me in deep, just as he had then. "I was in heaven. Still am."

"And what about now? With the new Prophecy?" I asked, trying Goddess knows why to keep the conversation above the belt.

His breath grew heavy as he pulled me nearer still. "Isn't it clear yet that I'm of only one mind when it comes to you? All I want is to be as close to you as possible …"

My own breath faltered at the look of sheer need and devotion on his face. "Should we maybe go back to the hotel room?"

"I think we'd better," he said, standing up from the bench and taking me by the hand.

Maybe it was the drink or the transcendence of time and space we had just experienced, but the walk felt like it took no time at all. Soon we found ourselves in a dimly lit Mexican hotel room, practically tearing off each other's clothes. I definitely popped at least one button off Dom's shirt in the process and was unsure of the state of my bra as it was cast hastily onto the cool tile floor.

"Christ," Dom said, taking full measure of me. A poorly placed streetlight beamed boldly through the unshuttered bedroom window and directly onto our bed, all too conveniently lighting my naked body before him. "Honestly, sometimes I'm *still* not sure if you're even real."

With him poised above me, I raked my fingers first up and then down his thighs. They were damp with sweat and heated from more than the day's endeavours. Indeed, our shared need was palpable, having not met sexually, or even really physically at all, since before Dom had taken off into the desert.

"I guess you'll have to fuck me and find out," I said, feeling need overtake me.

His nostrils flared before he gave in fully to his masculine desire. Sliding his hand down his cock once before entering, he was as gentle to my welcoming body as he was hard. His body tensed over me as he lowered himself in. I moaned loudly into his ear in response, freely vocal in my pleasure.

And surprisingly impatient.

Urging his pace onward with every trust, I wrapped my legs tightly around his hips as I pulled him towards the depths of all that was *me*. We soon discovered the true quality of the bed, which was extremely springy and not at all comfortable. However, I revelled in the transfer of his energy into my own being as his pace eagerly quickened, bouncing underneath him in heated enthusiasm; it was difficult to believe we had been living in such dire tension only hours before.

Suddenly, he let out a grunt of desperation before leaning back. He jerked one of my legs over his shoulder while simultaneously pushing the other one down into the mattress. This had always been one of his favourite positions, deepening our shared sensation as he approached imminent climax.

"Good God, Julia," he said, pausing at what I knew was the crest of the final wave, "I'm not going to last much longer."

"Dom, *please,*" I begged, digging my heel into his butt as I slid myself as close as possible; I too was on the edge of release.

He groaned in submission to his own will and released into me, his rhythm faltering only slightly as he relinquished bodily control. I shook in reply before crying out into the night, blissfully lost in our shared orgasm.

Afterward, Dom collapsed with his full weight on top of me, a sign that he was still slightly inebriated. Already short of breath, my lungs released what oxygen was left. I felt no panic, however, revelling in the closeness and trusting he would roll away momentarily. Unexpectedly, Dom started to laugh. First a low rumble, it quickly transformed into a full-on guffaw. I felt its vibration transfer through my body just before he slipped out of me and rolled onto his back. I took an audible breath as my lungs drew in much-needed air.

"Oops," he said. "Sorry."

I knew exactly what he was finding so funny and joined in his mirth. "This bed is *terrible.*"

MANTLE OF THE WORLD RULER

He blew air downward onto his own body in a loud exhalation. "I mean, we've slept on worse, of course. But … yes. It's fucking awful."

The next day, we booked a new suite.

CHAPTER 26

Our second day in Mexico had been blisteringly hot, making our relocation all the more necessary. New accommodations, booked on even shorter notice this time, were even more expensive. And that was without considering the luxury of the place. The strong evening breeze provided immediate relief, however, whooshing past as we unlocked the front door to the tenth-floor condo. We had definitely made the correct decision.

I followed Dom through the entry way, which spilled into an open concept living room. Unlike our last accommodations—which had apparently been owned by a foreign travel conglomerate—this condo was owned and operated by a group of locals, and it showed. The space was neatly adorned with local art and well-made furniture, and its pristine fixtures spoke of a sharp attention to detail. In other words, it was fucking fancy.

Dom had been agreeable to whatever I chose, of course, but I had the distinct impression he was treading carefully, if not uncomfortably, around me still, despite our reconciliation the night before. Deeply emotional experiences took him time to work through, and I sensed that his trip into the desert and subsequent conflict with Ronan fell under this category.

Once inside, Dom immediately dropped everything he was carrying and headed for a cold shower. He didn't extend his usual invite. Not that I needed to join him, but it was uncommon for him to not even *hint* at bathing together. It was one of those ancient things about him; I figured he liked the ritual of it all.

With the heat of the day still radiating from my body, I padded into our corner suite's large bedroom with my suitcase and quickly unzipped it. My compass sat tucked safely in one of the side pockets, the arrow as still as stone. I took this to be a good sign.

The room was tastefully furnished, its bed looking infinitely more comfortable than our last one. A large balcony extended off the west side of the condo, providing ample view of the water. I could hear Dom turn on the shower one room over, humming low and peacefully to himself as he noisily climbed in. Hastily removing my own clothes, I felt only slight relief as I slipped into a short, thin, loose-fitting cotton nightgown.

I needed moving air on my skin, and so I made my way outside.

Standing alone at the edge of the railing, I cast my eyes across the vast Pacific. I cracked open a bottle of water we had brought from our last place, sucking back half of the contents in mere moments. Relief washed over me. The tide felt especially robust this evening, its steady pull creating within me a welcome sense of calm resolve. Here, I knew that Dom and I would *actually* have a chance to reconnect, and perhaps, reconcile more of what had happened over the past six months. And what might come next.

I took several deep breaths with my eyes closed. The coastal wind moved my hair gently this way and that. I opened my eyes to see the sun set magnificently beyond my vantage point. I revelled in the rapidly cooling air. Behind me, sheer white curtains danced along with my windswept locks, gently caressing the backs of my calves in turn.

Suddenly, I heard a clicking sound. Looking over my shoulder, I saw that Dom was holding my camera. Embarrassed to be caught out unawares, I called for a ceasefire. "Dom—"

"No. Don't," he said. "You looked so beautiful, just there."

He snapped several more pictures, effortlessly resembling a seasoned photographer. To my own surprise, I was up for the game and leaned against the railing. Tossing my head back vigorously, I allowed my auburn hair to truly greet the wind.

"Very nice," he said, snapping a few more. "I like your gown. Is it new?"

"This old thing?" I said coquettishly, swishing it this way and that. It *was* new—an impulse buy that afternoon as we'd killed time downtown waiting for our check-in. Dom was wearing only dark blue boxers. I eyed his muscular thighs greedily, immediately feeling a throb of desire bloom between my legs.

He snapped a few more shots. "I've got hardly any photos of you this time around," he said, growing in his creativity as he took several moody shots through the curtains. "Which is a problem."

"And what about photos of you?"

He laughed, turning the digital screen towards me. "You've shown me the photos on here already. There's *plenty* of me."

There was. Something about surviving past our anticipated expiry date at midsummer had made me anxious to document our life as much as possible. No doubt Dom had shared in this notion, gifting me the camera at an opportune moment. It felt slightly morbid, but instinctually, I wanted something of us to leave behind if this was truly to be our end.

The heat of the day had begun to settle at last, and my nightgown felt slightly damp on my cooling skin. With renewed comfort, I walked towards him seductively. "Do you like the condo?"

"I do," he said, taking several matching steps back and setting the camera down gently on the end table. Meeting beside the bed, Dom placed his hands lightly on my shoulders and slowly traced his fingertips down my arms. Goosebumps exploded across my skin. "You were right."

"Oh, was I?" Feeling suddenly brazen myself, I cupped my hand around him, stroking through his boxers.

His eyes widened as his erection stiffened. "Oh—"

"Do you know how much I need you?" I asked, increasing my effort as I drew my hips close. "How badly I *want* you?"

He groaned deeply, speechless. This perhaps wasn't my usual form, not in the past few lifetimes anyway. I thought of "talisman Julia"—the version of myself who had once sat upon a throne of pelts waiting hungrily for her Celt to return from battle. She was ancient and raw in her power, and I felt my Witch's fire stoke eagerly in turn; the erotic feminine within me was *begging* to be unleashed.

"Tell me ..." he said, his own deep vulnerabilities being slowly unearthed as his breath grew shallow. "Please."

"Tell you what?" I placed one hand on his chest as the other continued its rigorous work outside of his boxers. I kissed him briefly, open mouthed, before pushing him towards the bed. The cool white sheets received us willingly as Dom fell onto his back below me. He scrambled backwards on his elbows, flexing his core and pushing his legs so that his head landed on the pillows. I gestured for him to remove the barrier between us, and within moments, I was straddling him. I hadn't bothered putting on any underwear, which Dom quickly realized. He closed his eyes briefly, nostrils flaring as he took a deep breath of pleasure.

I spoke again, hovering just above him. "Tell you what, *Domhnall?*"

His eyes opened suddenly; I rarely used his full name. "How ... how badly you want me," he said, accent thickening. Mouth agape, he shifted his jaw ever so slightly as he traced his hands around my curves, as if he were now painting a picture instead of photographing one.

I took a deep breath of my own. "I want you so badly that some days I can't even think straight. I want you *so* badly ..." I said, raising my arms above my head and removing my nightgown. My breasts were now completely exposed to the coastal breeze pouring in through the balcony doors. I was feeling a wicked, erogenous pleasure simply at the sound of my own voice. "... that I would do almost anything to keep you near me. Just on the off chance that I might get to have you ... touch you ... feel you ... bring you inside me."

Dom moaned a deep baritone in reply. Slowly, he ran his hands up my sides and around my breasts. He flicked his thumbs across my nipples as I watched his jaw lock and unlock several more times as he focused on the sight before him. "I didn't know if it was still like that for you."

I paused, leaning back. "What do you mean?"

"That ... the desire was still so strong. I thought ..."

I knew exactly what he meant. Maturing love was new to both of us; it was natural to wonder if the life-and-death passion we shared could be maintained over the long term.

"It's ... deeper," I said and felt his entire body tense below me before softening once more.

"It is," he agreed, growing bolder in his own truth. "After all these years, I didn't think I could ever want you more than I had before. And yet ... the older you get ..."

We were having two conversations. One with our bodies, erect and moments from coupled surrender, and the other with our voices, vulnerable and desperate to be heard.

"Do I *look* old?" I asked, titling my head to the side. I had wondered more than once recently, and particularly since yesterday's exploration into memory, how the current version of me compared to the young woman he'd met all those years ago.

He thrust his hips and bucked me onto my side before meeting me face on. "I didn't say that. Not exactly. But I like ... this."

He started to kiss down my neck and across my chest. When he said *"this,"* I knew he'd meant the patient intimacy we were now exploring together. It was like we had never had the chance to truly slow down and enjoy one another. Sure, we'd always known how to be in the moment, but what would it mean if those moments weren't so fleeting?

"I like this version of us too," I said, bravely naming what we were both thinking. "I know we were once young and innocent—and intense—and I am glad we had those experiences. But this ..."

"*This* is something new," he said, finishing my thought. "And it's really exciting."

I suddenly felt an intense wave of knowing wash over me. "I think now's the time we hop into the shower together. The divination I had in California ... I think it was ... *now.*"

Dom narrowed his eyes playfully. "You know I love a good wash with you."

And indeed, it *was* the same shower I had seen in my vision, right down to the hand-painted blue and orange floral tiles and a resident gecko who scuttled off as soon as we turned the water on.

Dom entered the shower first and turned leisurely to face me. Seductively. He raised his arms high, draping them in casual grace, one hand over the curtain bar and the other braced against the decorative tile. This view gave me the perfect eyeline to the broadness of his chest and thickness of his legs, as his body's impressive X-shape leaned toward me, beckoning me in with its sheer stature ... and erection.

"That's not even fair," I said, eyeing him hungrily.

"What do you mean?" he asked, grinning slyly. He knew damn well how impressive he was. How fucking *delicious* he was.

I reached my hand down and began pleasuring myself before him; two could play at this game. He watched for a time, drinking in the show.

"Julia …"

"What?" I asked, eyes twinkling. That was enough teasing for tonight.

All pretence of patience washed away as soon as I stepped into the shower. After stroking my wet hair back from my face only once, Dom promptly lifted me up into his arms, grunting with the pleasure of exertion. I was his, and he meant to show me how powerfully he loved me.

Legs wrapped around him, I slid down his frame slowly and firmly onto his cock, our bodies slick under the trickling water as I let out a gasp of my own. Bracing one foot against an indent meant for a bar of soap and the other against the tap itself, my shoulders slammed against the cool tile as I began to ride him. If he'd meant to draw out the experience, plans quickly changed once we hit our stride. Dom drove into me with blind lust, the combination of want and need too strong for the both of us as we came simultaneously under the heat of the water.

Panting loudly and revelling in our shared bliss, I lost track of the foot braced on the tap and promptly kicked the hot water off, dousing us both in an icy spray.

"Jesus!" Dom howled, as he shuttled me out of the shower ahead of him. Even then, he was protective of me.

"Sorry!" I said, unable to contain my giggles. We towelled off together, fits of laugher bubbling between the both of us. This was unadulterated joy.

Afterward, Dom held me in bed, spooning me from behind while stroking my damp, unbound hair away from my neck and gently blowing on my shoulders. Although soothing, the resultant sensation was only *slightly* cooling. Though our harrowing escape from the icy shower had cooled us down temporarily, we were both now slick with sweat once more. It was difficult to discern where my body began and his ended at any point of contact between us, but it was plain that neither of us wished to be physically parted.

"Julia … there's something I want to ask you." The sun had long since set, with the spell of night now seeping in thickly around us.

I tried my best not to tense my pleasantly relaxed body. "Hmm?"

"I ..." He paused, clearly gathering himself, delicately running his fingers down my arm, making me shiver. "Well, I ... I want a baby—not now, obviously—but someday soon. I'd like to be a father ... to put a child inside of you. After the wedding maybe, and not if you don't want to, of course. I just ..."

I let out a soft sigh. Intuitively, I had known this conversation was coming and had hoped to prepare myself for it. I had instead shoved the notion to the back of my mind.

I could feel his entire body tense beside me as I rolled over to face him, slippery still in his arms. And in that moment, safely embraced and entwined with my lover, I decided at last to speak from my heart instead of my head. "I want a baby too, Dom."

He pushed his forehead against mine, barely breathing. "You do? Really?"

"I do. *Really.*"

A murmur emanated from his chest, entirely different than his usual resonance. He let out a long, slow breath. "Oh, Julia ..."

With that, we soon drifted off to sleep ... peacefully entwined.

"Well ... it might not be Ibiza, but it'll do just fine," Dom said as he stretched out on his blue-and-white-striped beach towel.

Despite his sentiment, he looked pleased as punch, having just procured some chopped pineapple garnished with chilli powder from a man pushing a cart down the beach. Now settled into our new condo, and with a renewed comfortability together, we made quick work of our intention to have a *real* vacation. Admittedly, I had expected Dom to grow impatient almost immediately with the lack of plans before us, but he had been surprisingly open to the pace.

"This is delightful!" Dom proclaimed happily in reference to his treat. "You sure you don't want some?"

"I'm good," I said. I had never been a huge fan of pineapple; it seemed to make my mouth burn more than most.

Dom quickly gobbled down the rest of his snack and rolled over onto his stomach.

"Everyone's staring at you," I said, eyeing Dom in his short black trunks that only served to further accentuate his immaculate form. A group of passersby, both men and women, had just practically fallen over themselves as he'd stretched and laid out his towel, though he had been apparently completely oblivious. "Mostly at your butt, actually."

"They are *not*," he said and reached to open up his newly purchased novel.

I eyed the long line of his legs from hips to toes; he knew damn well what a specimen he was, by modern standards, and wasn't fooling me for a second. "Are too."

"These shorts are perfectly in style and appropriate for the time. I researched it, like I always do. It's you, and that lovely ass of *yours*, that's catching everyone's eye."

"*Right*," I said sarcastically and kicked some sand at him before plunking down beside him on my own towel. "What book did you settle on, anyway?"

He leaned onto his side to face me, placing his head on his hand. "Oh, this? You wouldn't like it. It's science fiction."

"Who said I don't like sci-fi?"

"Julia, you pretty much only read historical fiction or romance. Or like ... psychology and self-help books. At least, that's all ever I noticed on your shelves at Gertie's. Correct me if I'm wrong?"

"You're not wrong. Although, the really smutty romance novels really *were* Gertie's." While I had enjoyed fantasy novels as a child, as an adult, I had always avoided anything that remotely touched on the paranormal, finding myself immediately frustrated by the lack of accuracy around what happened in the *real* magical world.

"Of course," he said, not sounding convinced.

Truthfully, I had barely made time to read at all over the past year, my mind all too often preoccupied with greater matters, namely "the cause." I felt like this was a reasonable excuse. However, the last book I had read for enjoyment likely *was* the one he'd witnessed me devour over the Christmas holidays. And it was a naughty one.

"Hey! And what about all the readings assigned by Professor O'Brien?" I asked, teasing him openly. "I'll have you know that those took up a lot of my time!"

"That guy was such a hard-ass."

I laughed and smacked Dom's bum. "He still is!"

I stretched my arms above my head and then pulled out a tube of sunscreen from our beach bag and started to apply it to my forearms.

"Would you like me to get your back again, love?"

"Sure. Thanks." I turned to face down the beach.

A parasail had just gone up over the water, and I watched for a moment as Dom arranged himself behind me. The sunscreen was warmed from the sun, and the combination of his hands and the warm liquid was soothing but for the bits of sand—though frankly, even that was fine. It truly was blissful to be here in the now with him in such a tangible, physical way. I thanked him when he was finished, and he peacefully rolled back onto his towel, diving into his book at last.

For my own part, I knew I still wouldn't be able to focus on any reading, despite our conversation. Instead, I pulled my sunhat over my face and closed my eyes, trying for a nap. My dreams the night before had been difficult, as usual, despite the relaxing way we had fallen asleep the night before. With the combination of that and the heat, I was feeling rather dozy.

I grinned broadly under the hat, thinking of what Dom had asked me the night before about making a baby with him someday.

I was surprised and overjoyed at how badly I wanted to; I had honestly never considered it being part of my reality before. But now? Frankly, it had been all I could think about since waking up. My mind waded in and out of what parenthood might look like with my ancient Celt, and I had absolutely no doubt he would make an amazing father. My own abilities as a mother were still in question, but I felt confident that, with him by my side, I could do anything. I started to doze off, imagining Dom cradling a baby and singing it to sleep at our home in Ireland. Then I was horrifically interrupted from my daydream by an image of Kenzie stealing the baby and taking off out of our bedroom window. I startled, my stomach lurching at the terrifying notion.

I peeked out from under my hat, but Dom apparently hadn't noticed my jolt; he still had his nose buried deep in his book. He now lay on his back, holding the book in the air above his face to block the sun, with his other hand shielding his eyes.

I had dreamed of Kenzie almost nightly in one form or another since she'd escaped in L.A., but this was a new level of intrusion. And it had likely come from my human mind rather than my mystical one. My heart sank. How could we bring a child into the world—this world—when we were still literally hunted just for being *alive*. I lay still for several minutes longer, sunny thoughts clouding over with darkness. Soon, I couldn't stand it anymore and pulled my hat off.

"Dom," I said, looking to the heavens as the familiar shadow that had haunted me throughout the past year returned, mocking the sun. "Do you really think *this* is it?"

He dropped his book on his face by accident. "Fuck," he said and then rolled onto his side to face me. "Sorry ..." He looked confused. "'*This?*' You mean life on earth, or this solar system, or ...?"

"You really do have your mind on science today," I said, laughing in spite of myself. "No, I mean, like ... is this *really* our last try to defeat Cassius? I know we always talk about it, but ..."

He furrowed his brows; we had likely shared this same conversation a hundred times since the summer solstice. "I really don't know. But I think ... maybe."

"So then how will we know when it's time to make a baby? What if we're hunted forever and never go ahead with it? The baby making?" Panic was rising.

"Oh, love. I'm so sorry. I shouldn't have brought it up," Dom said, looking both concerned and sad all at once. He slid closer and put and arm around me. "I didn't mean to make you afraid last night."

"No, no, that's not what I mean. Honestly. It's all I've thought about today," I said, attempting to reassure him, and rather bashfully, truth be told. "I actually caught myself thinking of paint colours for the nursery over breakfast! Can you imagine? Me!"

"I *can* imagine it, actually," he said, returning my shy grin with a special smile. I was instantly reminded of the day we'd gotten engaged in Oregon.

We had watched that family packing up at the end of the day, their children tired and disappointed about leaving, and Dom had looked on with the same sense of longing and care. A new family walked past us on the Mexican beach, engaged in a similar struggle with their three children. Evidently, difficult transitions to and from the beach were a universal constant.

"I just don't how we'll know. *When* we'll know."

"Well, you've got to get that thing out first anyway. So, we don't have to worry about it just yet," he said, gesturing randomly at my abdomen with his extended index finger.

"That thing?" I asked, raising my eyebrows. "You mean my IUD?"

"Yes, that," he said and kissed me on the top of my head. "We have time, love. I promise."

We sat for a while, looking out at the glimmering water. Then Dom's stomach growled, a clear signal that it was high time to wander back up the beach to find a restaurant.

CHAPTER 27

Our holiday thus far had been remarkably uneventful, though not particularly quiet. On the morning of the winter solstice, which I had cheekily dubbed Dom's "Tomb Birthday," we awoke to the booming din of construction outside our balcony. This had been a consistent pattern for the better part of our stay, as another large condo tower was going up just next door, but I hadn't yet grown used to it.

"Even on your birthday?" I rolled over and pulled a pillow over my head. As if the date would make any difference.

Dom laughed. "Even on my birthday."

He hopped out of bed exuberantly and headed for the bathroom. I expected he would return with coffee, as he had each morning before, and so I pulled the covers over my head to steal a few more minutes in bed. I supposed that, on his birthday, I should be making him coffee, but Dom didn't seem fussed about modern traditions when it came to himself.

Plus, coffee was life.

Within a few minutes, I could smell the rich and delicious scent of French press and pushed the covers back, aching for a cup. We were typically back at the condo by sundown after enjoying dinners out and last night had been no exception. Once "home," we would immediately find ourselves sharing wine or a cocktail on the balcony. One drink would lead to another, and we would tumble to bed relatively early, all things considered, but not altogether asleep.

It was a simple and divine rhythm.

And yet, time also blurred strangely on vacation with Dom. The days had been endless and blissful, but our next impending move was always on the back of our minds. The end of the month was fast approaching, and we would need to be on our way once more. We both agreed that staying in any place for too long without considerable protection was a risk, even though I was reasonably sure that my own subconscious defensive enchantments continued to work. Clues to that effect persisted, like the computer systems lagging or crashing any time we visited the condo's main lobby.

We'd had a few close calls with questionable Wielding magic, my own senses picking up jagged energy here and there. However, the American Knaves had assured us that the Wraith population was sparse in Mexico compared to the West Coast of the United States. So, I was more than likely just sensing other magic users up to no good.

But the fact remained we were effectively on the run until we could confirm a more accurate reading of both Cassius's and Kenzie's current whereabouts. After the cottage burned down, nowhere felt safe for any extended amount of time. I thought back to last spring in Ireland, when I'd felt like I was going to lose my mind at how stagnant everything felt. And how badly I had wanted to *do* something.

Now, I almost craved those quiet days. *Almost.*

We didn't have much planned for Dom's "birthday," though we did have reservations at what had quickly become one of his favourite restaurants downtown. For a gift, I had managed to pick up an English copy of the next book in the series he was reading—something about a conflict between Earth and Mars over mining for resources on the asteroid belt. Wasn't my thing, but he was loving it. I also bought us a bottle of what I assumed was fancy tequila (judging by its price), hoping he might tell me some more stories of our past before the night was out.

It was a recipe for another perfect vacation day with my lover.

"There are two emails from Lennie," Dom said, looking up briefly from his computer to take a sip from his third cup of coffee. Over a week had passed since his birthday, and unfortunately, Dom's vacation vibe was fast melting away.

Dom's laptop had remained tucked away in his bag for the past several weeks, with the pair of us only checking our phones intermittently for messages throughout our stay in Mexico. Of course, it came as no surprise that we'd been met with radio silence over the past several weeks; Dom had been explicit with our connections that they were not to contact us unless *"absolutely necessary."* However, since Christmas, I noticed him checking for messages with increased regularity.

Clearly, the directive had changed.

"Oh yeah? What do they say?" I asked, rolling onto my side and slowly sitting up. I had been stretched out beside him on the couch, staring dozily upwards at a leaf-blade fan as it turned round-and-round on the stucco ceiling above. We had stayed up later than usual the evening before, talking deep into the night about our hopes for our hypothetical future. Intuitively, we both knew it was only a matter of time before we would have to snap back to reality, so perhaps we were trying to hold onto our dreamy vacation for as long as possible.

"The first one is just an update of what everyone's been up to. Lennie's back in England, nose to the grindstone—coping no doubt—but he's seen Thomas and Peggy, so that's good," Dom said, dictating the essentials to me as he read onwards. "Sounds like they all spent Christmas together at Peggy's place in Cornwall. She sends her love. Says she has a gift for us—probably whisky—Oh! And that she would like to offer herself as our wedding officiant, if we would have her."

He looked up smiling, and I beamed back. "That's a generous offer!" I said. "What do you think?"

"I can't imagine anyone better for the job," he said, and continued happily scanning the message for important details. "Alanna and Shereen are still in Washington but sounds like *yer man* Stuart has crossed the pond to spend some time travelling in Scotland."

I chuckled. "Travelling, huh? And Lindsey?"

I had texted her a bit during our travels south, but we hadn't connected for a couple of weeks.

"She's in Scotland too," Dom said with a wink. "And Sean and Graham are travelling. Lennie can't list their location in the email, obviously, but I already knew they were going into deep cover. So, no news is good news."

I nodded, my smile fading.

A pang of guilt welled up inside me then, regarding our current whereabouts. Here Dom and I were, pleasantly on vacation—like a real vacation—while life carried on for the others, in some cases quite dangerously. On the other hand, I knew how badly we'd needed this break. It was imperative we had time to recharge for what would inevitably come next. Both could be true at once I supposed.

I also noticed that Dom failed to mention whatever Ronan might be up to in his relayed update, or perhaps Lennie hadn't said. Regardless, I didn't ask. "And the second email?"

"It's good news, I think," Dom said, though he looked visibly skeptical. "Apparently Ro— the Druids have found someone who can maybe help us take down Kenzie."

Yes, Dom was definitely avoiding talking about Ronan. I adjusted myself to look at his screen. "What? Where?"

"The Arctic Circle, apparently."

I stared at him, hanging on his next words.

"In Northern Norway," he continued, oblivious to my reaction. I watched as he slowly dragged his pointer finger across the laptop's trackpad and awkwardly clicked on an attached file; despite his best efforts to blend into the modern era, his relationship with technology continued to be a dead giveaway that he belonged to a different century altogether.

I muffled a laugh that had managed to escape by pretending to sneeze.

"Bless you," Dom said absently, his brows still furrowed at the screen.

The file expanded to show an area in the very, very far north of Norway near the Russian border. He rubbed his chin in contemplation as he scanned the map. The action created a soft scratching sound from his beard that was oddly satisfying to listen to, sending a pleasant tingling feeling across my head and neck. I leaned closer to the screen.

I knew he was not only considering the geography of the region but also wracking his brain for all he knew about the area and its history, which was likely a fair bit. Dom was absolutely voracious when it came to the consumption of history and politics, both past *and* present. Allegedly, this was something he shared in common with his (very) late father.

"The source is in Finnmark—or Vardø, more specifically. The larger city near there is called Kirkenes—though it's not very big either, truth be told. Small population. Very isolated."

I could practically hear his brain whirring now; he was back in the zone.

"Oh yeah?"

"It's been in the news fairly recently though because of a wall—well, more of a chain-link fence—that the Norwegians built along the Russian border ... to keep out undocumented migrants," he said, tutting slightly.

I hadn't heard of Kirkenes, or the border wall. However, I *had* heard of Vardø. It was famous, or rather infamous, among our kind for the mass Witch trials that had been conducted there during the mid-seventeenth century.

"Vardø. In January ..." I said, grimacing. "Shit, that sounds cold!"

"You've heard of it?" Dom asked, finally looking up.

"I have, actually," I said as my own eyes tracked longingly towards the balcony. A soft breeze was now trickling in through the open doors, warm and inviting.

Dom followed my gaze before letting out a soft sigh. "Lennie says we should be able to manage a flight up there from Oslo—instead of driving, that is. I can't imagine the roads are great in the dead of winter anyway. Plus, it's a *long* way. Several border crossings if we were to drive into Sweden or Finland ..." He let his voice trail off, not needing to finish the thought, as he focused again.

In my mind's eye, I pictured myself standing next to the Arctic Ocean with tempestuous winds roaring in from every direction. I shivered in spite of my currently tropical location. I looked from the map on the screen to his face, making a vain attempt to sound positive. "I mean ... at least it's coastal?"

"Hmm! You're right. That *is* something. But we'll have to get to Oslo first." And with that said, he dove immediately into his reply to Lennie.

Unwilling to sit and listen to him slam away on the keyboard, I collected both of our cups and wandered towards the kitchen. Dumping the last dregs of creamy-brown liquid down the drain, I watched it slowly swirl down into the abyss and tried hard not to see it as symbolic of our quickly devolving sense of peace. With the approach of New Year's Eve today, I had foolishly hoped we had at least one final day of quiet, but it was no use. Indeed, the visceral shift in Dom's energy from across the room already signalled loudly that it would soon be time to pack up and leave.

I quickly rinsed the cups and set them off to the side of the sink. Then, after drying my hands on a stark white tea towel, I wandered towards the fridge to consider making us breakfast. Inside, I found four brown eggs, a chunk of stringy white cheese that Dom and I both agreed was particularly delicious, and a full container of fresh salsa we had bought just the day before. Behind a bottle of overly sweet orange beverage, I fished out a small bunch of cilantro, an onion, and a half-sliced green bell pepper.

"You alright with omelettes?" I asked over my shoulder, and Dom grunted something that resembled *"Yes, please."*

I immediately set to work chopping up the veggies, followed by whisking the eggs with milk, salt, and pepper. When the pad of butter began melting in a cast-iron pan, I should have felt my hunger increase. Who didn't love the smell of butter melting and bubbling in a pan? However, it now seemed that my appetite had disappeared altogether. While I *was* slightly hungover, the real reason my stomach was turning was because my mind was attempting to digest what was to come next.

Vardø. It wasn't a place many Witches visited willingly, unless to pay respects to the dead.

Between 1662 and 1663 AD, the region had been gripped with a mass panic following the tragic sinking of a fishing boat in a winter storm at Christmas. Witchcraft had been blamed. Rumour and suspicions grew that a group of women, taking the form birds through the use of enchanted knot-work, had "worked with the devil" to pull the ship to the ocean floor. What followed were months of horrific investigations and needless torture, all of which involved women, men, and children alike.

Because of its remote location and how long it took in those days to receive directive from the king of Denmark and Norway to the south, Vardø had effectively operated as its own jurisdiction when it came to the trials. It had been gruesome, excessive, and a shockingly misdirected interpretation of justice. While I knew the country of Norway had more recently created a spectacular monument to commemorate the horrors that had occurred then,

I still felt a cold finger run down my spine at the notion of being isolated there, especially in the dead of winter.

What memories or visions would greet me in a place like that? I didn't think we had been there before, but that didn't mean I wouldn't encounter the whispers of my distant sisters who *had* been. If I had learned anything from spending time in places with past magical turmoil, it was that the traces left behind could wreak havoc on my system. Even if I wasn't in a place to receive and interpret them willingly.

In the end, I cooked one large omelette for Dom and promptly turned off the burner; I *really* wasn't hungry. I plated his breakfast simply, topping it with extra salsa and a sprinkling of cheese. Spying an orange on the counter, I reached for it and made to slice some wedges to add to the side. Dom usually did the cooking for the pair of us, but I felt I was at least a decent enough cook to procure what could be considered a solid breakfast, and he wasn't one to complain anyway.

He appeared behind me out of nowhere, and I jumped, causing the knife I held to clatter loudly onto the tile floor.

Dom scooped it up as quickly as he spoke. "I think we'd better make plans to leave as soon as possible. This sounds really promising!"

As usual, he was already hurtling plans into motion before I'd even had a chance to process anything at all. I tried not to bristle but felt a surge of frustration, nonetheless. "What sounds promising, Dom?"

"Fuck. Sorry, I really got into my head there, didn't I?" He traded me the knife for his breakfast.

"Dom, that place is—"

"Really magical. I know," he said, happily sucking on an orange wedge and eyeing his plate with glee.

"Bad things have happened there," I said, perhaps a bit more ominously than necessary, but I needed to get his attention. "I don't have a good feeling about this."

"But you haven't even heard ..." He finally paused at the look on my face. "Are you alright, Julia?"

I put down my knife safely this time and turned towards him. "Please, don't do this. This ... *thing* you do."

"What do you mean?" he asked innocently, his mouth already full of omelette.

I widened my eyes at him; he knew damn well what "thing" I was talking about. "Oh, come on, Dom. The one where you get all … hyper-logistics mode … and leave me out."

"Right. Sorry," he said, blushing. "Just … hungry." He swallowed hard before taking a series of breaths to slow himself down. "Okay. There is a Bearer in Vardø who knows about Kenzie and something about intel on Cassius too. She reached out to the Druids actually, and they think she is someone we need to visit with. In person."

My heart sank.

Once again, the Druids—or Ronan, more accurately—were meddling in Bearers' business without immediately consulting me. They were trying to help, but it was still insensitive as I was the only *actual* Bearer in our ranks. I let out a long breath through my nose, attempting to keep my annoyance at bay. It wasn't working.

Finally attuning himself to my energy at last, Dom shifted tactics. "Did you want to maybe sit outside on the balcony, love? You seem—"

I shot him a *"don't you dare tell me how I'm fucking feeling"* look, effectively cutting him off, before striding out towards the fresh coastal air. He was right, though. He followed, plate in hand.

She was there of course: the moon. Out of sight but pulling the tides with predictable vigour. I placed my hands on the balcony railing and closed my eyes to drink in the essence of her hidden magic. The sun too shone down with his own brilliance from above, kind and gentle on my aggravated face. I felt my body begin to relax as the tumultuous energies settled within my Bearer's hearth.

This was a good place, and I felt good here. I would be very sad to leave.

But we couldn't hide in Mexico forever. We both knew damn well that Cassius was out there, biding his time and searching for any means necessary to defeat us. I listened in irritation as Dom scraped up the last of his breakfast into his mouth, setting down the plate and the fork on the ground beside him.

After several more beats, I spoke up. "Besides the fact Ronan is an asshole and should have contacted *me* about this immediately instead of contacting you through Lennie, how do we know this lead, and this Bearer, are not some kind of trap set by Kenzie? Or even Cassius?"

"Well ... that's where it gets interesting," Dom said, rubbing his hands together and joining me at the edge of the balcony. "You see, this Norwegian Bearer—Solveig, she's called—has apparently been tracking Kenzie for years, unknowingly. Or at least the traces of her magic. Apparently, she's some sort of Diviner—"

"Ugh! ... Dom! Why didn't you tell me this in the first place?" I said, my outrage mixing strangely with a bubbling, unexpected injection of laughter. His mind really was a fixed machine when it came to strategy, archaic almost. It thought of how Gertie used to refer to situations where *"if you didn't laugh, you'd cry,"* but I wasn't entirely sure this fit the bill. Still, my instinct was to give him the benefit of the doubt.

"What do you mean?" He still looked confused.

"You were more concerned with the fact that the source was in Norway than that she was not only a Bearer but a *Diviner!* Oh, and one who can apparently pick up on Bearing magic around the world? Do you have *any* idea how significant this is?"

"I do ... and I said as much, didn't I?"

I raised my eyebrows for what felt like the tenth time in as many minutes. "Did you?"

"Okay, maybe not *that* clearly," he admitted, looking unsure whether I was going to lash out in anger or have a fit of laughter. Or both. Grimacing, he braced himself by crossing his arms and tucking his wrists under his neck, reminding me of a timid bird.

"Good grief, Dom!" My reaction to his expression and posture was a mingled attack of tickles and frustration as I pushed against his broad chest. "You are such a dick! You didn't say *anything!*"

We fell back together onto one of the lounge chairs on the deck, both laughing heartily as our bodies naturally entwined.

"I really am sorry, Julia. Does it help that I find it hard to communicate and work through the digital world at the same time? My brain gets all slow and overwhelmed. The fact of the matter is that I'm no good at it."

"I hadn't noticed," I said teasingly.

In truth, it was hard to be angry with him anyway. After all that we had worked through during the past weeks, it felt like such a waste of energy to fight with him about this. I could be patient today, especially when we still had another full day left in paradise. Also, the prospect of gleaning more knowledge from yet another Bearer lit a renewed fire in me. I was still digesting what Bernie had imparted to me but was already hungry for more.

We snuggled there for a few moments, with Dom pushing my hair back behind my ears and whispering something Irish into my ear that I didn't understand. I knew this meant his mind was wandering onto more sensual planes, perhaps in an attempt to make up for his blunder.

"Wait though," I said, sitting up. "I'm serious, Dom. We need to be careful up there. There is a *ton* of wild energy in the raw places of the world."

"Not to mention the political history of the location."

"That too." I let out a long sigh. "All I'm saying is that, if there are allies up there, there are also enemies."

"You're right," Dom said, nodding. "But what else is new? In all our years trying to defeat Cassius, when we don't find the danger, it inevitably finds us. I really think we've got to try."

"That and you're tired of sitting still," I said truthfully.

"Well, I think I can manage one final day of vacation sex," he said, grinning cheekily. "If I have to."

He then led me towards the bedroom without another word on the matter.

CHAPTER 28

Several days after receiving Lennie's email about Solveig, Dom and I found ourselves landing rather abruptly on the tarmac at Toronto's Pearson International Airport.

"Jesus, Mary, and Joseph!" Dom exclaimed loudly while gripping the armrests. A middle-aged woman in the row ahead of us turned around and glared at him through narrowed eyes, but he didn't notice.

"You okay?" I asked, squeezing his thigh in reassurance.

"I am," Dom said, relaxing his fingers only slightly. "I just can't seem to get used to landings like that."

Leaning to look out the window, I noticed the frosty-looking drifts of snow and ice that lined the runways on both sides, more than a bit of a change from Mexico or the California coastline.

"Looks cold," I said.

He nodded silently, still reeling from our rough landing.

Unfortunately for Dom, in just two days, we would be up in the air again, first boarding an international flight to Oslo and then another domestic one to Kirkenes. Following that, we would take a boat on the Barents Sea to Vardø.

Before we'd left Puerto Vallarta, we had strategically jammed all of our summer clothing and footwear, as well as any extra personal items we didn't anticipate needing, into a single hard-sided travel suitcase, which would be sent onward as unaccompanied luggage to Ireland. Morgan would take care of receiving the bag for us, Dom had assured me. He knew that, since I had practically nothing to my name after the cottage had burnt down, I might want to hold onto whatever I had left. I appreciated the consideration.

Both my compass and talisman, some of Dom's more important documents and notebooks, my camera, his laptop, a handful of between-season outfits, and our undergarments remained in our other bag. And, of course, the quilt. At this point, I wasn't entirely sure why I had been dragging the quilt across the world, but it felt wrong to leave it behind.

As for Dom's sword, Ronan had sent an email weeks ago confirming that he had safely brought the weapon into Canada and that it had been stored away for safekeeping. Dom had muttered something about Ronan "sucking up to him" when the email had come in but had left it at that.

Shivering as we exited the cab from the airport, Dom and I checked into a mid-range hotel in downtown Toronto. Unlike Ronan, he wasn't fussed with luxe accommodations when we were on a mission, just so long as it came with a decent bed and working bathroom. I had initially suggested we stay closer to the airport, but Dom had wanted to see "Toronto proper" while we were here, which I had obliged.

"I'm not sure I'm a fan of Canadian winters," he said as we entered our modest room at last.

"This isn't even that bad. Try a Prairie winter," I said, still chilled from the cold and rubbing my hands together.

Dom dropped our remaining bags at the foot of the bed and turned towards me. "No thanks. I'm an island boy, through and through."

I was reminded of the story Ronan had told me about Dom complaining about the cold on one of their camping trips. I felt a mingled sense of gratitude for now being officially privy to this detail about Dom as well as lingering resentment that Ronan had bragged about knowing it and for how much it bothered me.

"Speaking of coastal climates," Dom continued as he fiddled with the thermostat on the wall, "how are you feeling being so far from the ocean? This is the first time you've been this far inland for a while."

I paused for a moment, pushing my mixed feelings aside to sense the world around me. "I think I'm okay. I mean ... I don't feel particularly powerful right now, but I'm also tired from flying, so it might just be that. Besides, this is just a quick stop. I'm sure I can handle it."

After a hasty shower, we headed for the mall. We planned to spend most of the afternoon shopping for necessary gear for the journey ahead, but before that, we both filled a need to charge ourselves with urban conveniences. For me, this meant a chain-brand cheeseburger and fries, and for Dom, a massive Styrofoam container filled with chow mein, fried rice, and sweet and sour chicken. As he polished off the last morsels, I wasn't entirely sure I wanted to watch him consume a food-court meal in front of me ever again. My stomach hurt at the sight. *Where does he put it all?*

In addition to the necessary outerwear for our journey north, we fitted ourselves with more appropriate clothing for the northern climate. Naturally, Dom looked amazing in anything he tried on, demonstrating that he was every bit a "man of the woods" as he donned different thick woollen button-downs and sturdy khaki pants with re-enforced knees that made him look like he was about to go chop down a tree.

"I didn't think there were any trees as far north as Vardø," I said. "Being that it's above the Arctic Circle and everything."

He chuckled. "No, there aren't. What I should really be after is more of a fisherman's knit though. That region is still quite coastal—the North Atlantic Drift keeps the ice from freezing year-round, though I still imagine it's fucking freezing in the wind on land."

In one instance, when Dom was trying on an overpriced quilted flannel jacket, a store clerk had exclaimed so loudly that he should consider modelling for their next catalogue that it made other customers jump.

"*Seriously, though!*" they had hollered as we left the store.

Dom had declined gracefully, but (judging by the princely grin that had spread across his face during the encounter and the definite swagger he carried for the rest of the shopping trip) he had taken it as a compliment. For all his humble traits, Dom *was* a bit vain when it came to his looks.

Not that I was complaining or anything.

For my own part, and as flexible as I considered myself to be, it turned out I didn't particularly love scattering pieces of ourselves around the world as we jetted towards new locations on a whim. I was glad for the sturdy new wardrobe, of course, but I also felt unsettled. For all my wanderings throughout this life, what I *really* wanted was to put down roots with Dom in Ireland or in Canada. I honestly wasn't picky, I just wanted to be still. All of the talk about getting married and having babies had proven as much. I knew that, deep down, Dom felt the same; he was just better at coping with the unknown than I was.

I had received an email just before we left Mexico that Gertie's—or rather *my*—property had sold on Salt Spring for a considerable amount of money. Not that we needed the cash right now, but I was grateful to at least have that loose end tied up. We had come into some tricky dealings when it came to my power of attorney, but thankfully, Lennie had managed a workaround, as he always did. It was a final ending to a significant chapter in my history, and it felt good to contribute and bring something to the table financially, given the size of Dom's estate.

We were both almost comically sad to be leaving our truck behind on the West Coast. Shereen and Alanna promised to take good care of it until we returned. Ronan had sent a message that he'd delivered it to them in Washington, but once again, I was fairly certain Dom had denied him a reply.

"I'm going to miss that thing," Dom had said wistfully.

"Me too," I replied, smiling. "Our first pet together!"

He had shoved me playfully, but we both knew the sentiment around it was true. As for the motorcycle, Lennie had taken care of it as well, but I knew Dom was sad to leave it behind. Not that he didn't already own several of his own in Ireland.

Our "quick stop" in Canada was indeed just that. Before we knew it, we had arrived at Oslo Gardermoen Airport during the early morning hours of January seventh. Again, my protective magic seemed to carry with us as we travelled. If nothing else, it felt stronger than ever now that I had rested. My best guess was that it was similar to how it had worked on Salt Spring: Only those with whom I had intentionally shared our travel details were privy to my location. Or at least, that's what we hoped.

Much to Dom's satisfaction, this had been a smoother landing than our last. Disembarking from the plane, he informed me that it would remain dark for several more hours before sunrise, since we had landed at the 60th parallel. I knew this was the same latitude that marked the boundaries between the provinces and the territories in Canada, but truthfully, I had never actually been quite *this* far north before. At least not in this lifetime anyway.

Meanwhile Vardø, our final destination, sat above the 70th parallel. There, they were still in the winter period referred to as the "polar night," which would extend for several more weeks yet. I had a hunch that, between the time change and distinctly different geographical location, I was in for a doozy of a time when it came to sleep.

We had two seats booked on a domestic flight departing for Kirkenes later that morning from the same airport, which meant we wouldn't need to stay at another random hotel. Rather, we could spend the several hours hanging out in what was arguably the least stressful airport I had ever encountered.

"Look at the plant installations on the walls!" I said excitedly.

Together, we walked slowly between the international and domestic terminal areas, discovering more of the newly refurbished airport's rounded and arching wood ceilings throughout. Apparently, it had been designed for comfort and ease of travel, the design giving it a modern and natural flare all at once. So far, so good.

And then, before we knew it, we were off again.

We arrived in Kirkenes from Oslo in a little over three hours from takeoff to landing. From here, if we were to *drive* to Vardø, it would take us approximately another three hours. However, the roads were known to be unpredictable in the winter months, not so much due to snow—though there was plenty of that—but because of the wind, creating unexpected and immovable snowdrifts along the way.

Instead, we would travel by boat. Dom was far more comfortable aboard seagoing vessels than up in the sky, even in inclement weather. Thankfully though, the forecast was clear for the next several days, which would hopefully make for easy passage.

"I'm looking forward to seeing the area from the water!" Dom had exclaimed during our taxi ride from the small airport.

"Even in the dark?" I asked, looking out the window. The polar night was indeed in full effect, which would have felt extremely strange, if not for the fact we were already jetlagged anyway.

Dom laughed. "Even still."

During a quick search about the area, I had stumbled upon a website for a snow hotel, an extremely popular tourist destination of the region. However, while I was curious about it, I figured it might be a bit of a stretch for Dom. For all of his apparent toughness, it was plain he really wasn't keen on the polar climate.

Instead, we checked into a hotel on the water for the night where, after setting our alarms for the morning, we collapsed into a heap and fell asleep almost instantly.

A distinct lack of dawn greeted me as our alarm went off, and I rolled over to find Dom still in a dead slumber. I instantly regretted setting our alarm so early; I stretched my legs and wandered to the small window to open the blinds. No light came in, so I switched on a small lamp in the corner of the room, mimicking the morning sun. Our room faced the Barents Sea, yet it was difficult to see a whole lot beyond the immediate coastline. That didn't matter though; I could already feel the immense power of the region all around me.

Vardø had apparently gotten its name from a combination of the words *"wolf"* and *"island."* It might have felt foreboding if not for the surprising ease I felt now that we had returned to the coastline. No ... "ease" wasn't the right word for it. More like a sense of rightness, of being welcome. Undoubtedly, the power of place was exceptional here, and being a Bearer, I was privy to its magnitude. I could only imagine how I would feel when we crossed the water to the island of Vardø.

Still standing by the window, I contemplated the day ahead of us.

According to Lennie, Solveig Olsen lived directly in the township of Vardø. Admittedly, I'd had concerns that, being a Witch, she might have isolated herself in the outskirts of the community on some frosty embankment, but that didn't seem to be the case. In fact, she appeared to be deeply embedded within the community as a scientist and vocal climate activist, as well as a regular at the local pub. According to one archived blog post Lennie had uprooted, she was also known for making incredible *Skillingsboller*, a Norwegian cinnamon bun.

Dom had delighted at that detail in particular.

"You alright, Julia?" Dom asked groggily, as if sensing that my thoughts had drifted to him. I watched as, breathing in slowly through his nose, he stretched out on the bed, accidentally kicking his covers onto the floor in the process.

Taking stock of my own body, I was surprised to discover that I actually felt significantly recharged, despite all of the travel and time changes. "I am actually. There's *so much* magic here!"

"Hmm ... Well, I'm glad you're adjusting," he said, rolling onto his side and beckoning me back to bed. "I feel like I've been hit by a truck."

I wandered towards his side of the bed to collect the discarded blankets. "You don't have to get up just yet. We still have time." I sorted out the tangled mass of sheet and duvet.

He raised his eyebrows at me and looked down towards his groin. "Oh, I'm up."

"It *must* be morning then," I said, snorting.

Then I dove onto the mattress, the bedding flowing like a cape behind me as I cocooned us for another few moments together alone.

A little over an hour later, we were packed up and making our descent to the main floor to seek out breakfast. The Norwegians we encountered below, both in the lobby and in the restaurant, were pleasant, happy people, and seemingly unaffected by the potentially depressive elements of the polar night.

"I'm not sure I could get used to it," I said, sipping back a delicious cup of coffee. Like our hotel room, the restaurant faced the sea, though with wall-to-wall windows allowing for what I assumed would be an incredible view year-round.

"Maybe not now, but if it was all you'd ever known, and the generations before you ... well, I think you'd adjust just fine."

I thought of all the adapting Dom had been required to do throughout each of our regenerations and figured he knew better than anyone what it would take to acclimatize to adverse conditions. "You're probably right."

At the table next to us, four Swedish travellers were chatting away animatedly while eating bowls of muesli on porridge. Based on the pamphlets and maps laid on their table before them, they were headed out snowmobiling for the day.

"That looks interesting," Dom said, reaching his neck to peek at what they were up to.

"Snöskoter!" said a woman wearing a puffy blue vest with a cozy-looking sweater underneath, noticing Dom's curiosity.

"Grand!" he said, before turning his attention towards the breakfast buffet; frankly, I was surprised he had waited this long.

While he was away, I pulled out my phone to double-check our itinerary for the day, simultaneously slugging back the remainder of my first cup of coffee of the day. Before long, Dom returned with a heaping plate of food. Thick slices of rye bread, a chunk of *brunost* cheese, some whipped butter, and several slices of thinly shaved ham piled haphazardly together.

"I might go back for some cereal once I'm finished," he said to no one in particular and immediately dove in.

I had opted for something *à la carte* and was soon served an open-faced smoked-salmon sandwich on the same rye bread with a thick layer of herbed cream cheese spread in between.

"I think we'll need to be at the quay close to midday," I said, scrolling for the email Lennie had forwarded with our electronic tickets as I noshed on breakfast. Dom nodded in acknowledgement, his mouth too full of bread and cheese to speak. We ate together peacefully as the day grew slightly less dark.

Making our way to the quay at last, we noticed that the temperature was in fact milder than we had expected, thanks no doubt to the Atlantic current.

"I think the thing is, though, that it doesn't really get all that *warm* up here either," Dom said, hoisting our bag over his shoulder as we boarded the ship.

"Well, maybe not ... but I bet climate change is biting into that."

I thought of the increasingly intense weather we had been experiencing over the past decade on the West Coast of Canada; no doubt Norway was similar in its own way.

"Perhaps a question for Solveig!" Dom said in reply. "Lennie says she will pick us up on the other side. She drives a yellow Mini Cooper apparently, so we won't be able to miss her."

I chuckled. For some reason, I had been expecting something a little more rugged—or understated. I looked forward to seeing my great Celt trying to squeeze in and out of such a vehicle, though it would likely be a tight fit for me as well.

Aboard the M.S. *Kong Harald* at last, we began our adventure on the Barents Sea, steaming our way towards the island of Vardø. Spectacularly, we managed to be on the water during what the locals referred to as the "blue hour." This was a time of day when the sun lingers just below the skyline, creating a luminous effect off the sea and across the snow.

"I've heard of the golden hour, but this is something else," I said, wowed.

"Absolutely incredible," Dom said, wrapping his arm my waist. We continued to peer out of a portside window for several moments in awed silence. Standing this close, he smelled like fresh air mixed with a hint of the scented soap from our hotel room—something like gardenias. Maybe it was the magic of the place, but just then, I might have swooned for real if not for his arm wrapped firmly around me.

"I love you," I said, feeling suddenly swept up in the romantic magnitude of both the place we had found ourselves in and our wild life together.

"I love you too," Dom said sweetly as he turned towards me. Then he cocked his head. "Um ... Are you alright, Julia?"

"What do you mean?"

"You look a little ... not quite pale but ... almost iridescent." His eyes widened suddenly. "You're glowing."

I looked at my hands, and they didn't look any different than usual, other than the slightly blueish evidence of poor circulation. "I'm not seeing it."

"I can't quite explain it—but then again, I've never really been able to explain *you* either," he said, his mouth spreading into a brilliant smile. My chest swelled at the thought of how I might have exuded magic like this in my past lives, just as I was now, attuned to the sea and my lover. Knowing me for as long as he had, he was clearly used to this sort of stuff. So much so that now he almost seemed amused as he pulled the hood of my jacket up over my head to hide whatever was going on with my face.

"Hark who you're calling 'unexplainable,' World Ruler!" I said playfully in reply. His lack of concern over my strange state did, in fact, settle me. We found an isolated set of seats, lest someone else notice my current luminosity with less ease. And thankfully, once the blue hour passed, so did my strange glow, but I knew we would have to keep an eye on it in the days to come.

Along our voyage, we passed several summer encampments, a lighthouse, and apparently, a World War II torpedo bunker, Rødberget, which was nestled into a seaside cliff. Frankly, it was pretty much impossible to see any of it in the dark, but we took the word of a pamphlet Dom had collected as we boarded.

Nearing Vardø at last, we could see the outline of the Globus II radar stations looming high above the town, which was lit up below like a coastal Christmas village.

"What are those for?" I asked, relying as usual on Dom's proclivity for researching the hell out of anywhere we went.

"Radar stations," Dom said, leaning towards me conspiratorially, "and apparently, they're meant to be looking for 'space junk,' though most think they're really meant for monitoring the Soviets!"

"I bet," I said, feeling like I'd been suddenly transported into a Cold War novel. "I don't think anyone calls them 'the Soviets' anymore."

"Alright, Russians," he said and tapped his nose.

We found Solveig Olsen leaning on the driver-side door of a sunshine-yellow Mini Cooper, smoking a cigarette. She waved emphatically as we left the quay. Dom approached first and shook her hand enthusiastically for slightly longer than necessary. I wasn't sure if this was just him being his usual outgoing self or a strategic move to allow me extra time to assess the level of magical threat. In truth, I had felt her magic long before I could make out the details of her smile, but I appreciated Dom's protective stance.

"It's so wonderful that you've come," she said, her Norwegian accent fainter than I had expected.

"Thank you for meeting us here," Dom said as he shifted awkwardly with the larger of our two bags slung over his shoulder.

Unlocking her trunk with a button on a round key fob, she gestured him towards the back of the vehicle. "Well, it wouldn't be very good manners for me to invite you halfway across the globe and expect you to walk the final leg of the journey through the snow!" She tossed the cigarette butt to the snow and ground it out with her heel. "Nasty habit, but I just can't seem to kick it."

I continued to linger slightly behind Dom as he loaded the bags, locked in a silent conversation of my own with the northern Witch. Just as surely as she could feel me, I could also feel her, Bearing magic jabbing ever so slightly. However, I didn't get the sense that she was feeling threatened in the least. Unlike Agnes's magic, which had whipped and lashed me upon its inspection, Solveig's felt warm. Curious. Not every Bearer had such a strong quality when it came to their presence, but in the case of Solveig, it was hard to miss.

"Kenzie feels different, doesn't she?" Solveig said, as if reading my mind and cutting right to the chase.

Peering past my hulking Celt's frame, my eyes widened, I asked, "What do you mean?"

Stepping past Dom in two long strides, she smiled and took my hands into hers. She wore thin black-leather gloves and a long, red puffy down jacket with a fur collar. I guessed her to be about fifty years old, give or take.

"I mean, she feels different *than the rest of us,*" she said, raising her eyebrows.

Come to think of it, Solveig did feel somewhat *like* me, but it was hard to explain the sensation. The look on my face must have signalled confusion, or at least marked effort, as she waved her hand dismissively. "It's not important now, but it will be soon. Come," she said, gesturing with her thumb up the road. "I've reserved us a table at the pub!"

Dom chuckled. "You need reservations on an island this small?"

"You'd be surprised," she said happily. "First we will eat, and then we can go to my place to talk more privately afterward."

We nodded in agreement and set forth without another word.

CHAPTER 29

I'm not sure what I had imagined a Norwegian climatologist—who also happened to be a Bearer—might be like, but Solveig Olsen was an absolute delight. She was warm, interesting, and unquestionably hardy. She also wove fabulous tales and so got on with Dom famously. At one point, the pair were positively in stitches while Dom recounted an incident with a bull when he was around fourteen, involving him being covered head-to-toe in mud and cow shit in a rainy field, trying to coax the animal back to the other side of the fence to no avail. Solveig had apparently spent her summers on her cousin's farm in the south during her youth and was very familiar with cows.

"He wouldn't budge for days. Hours and hours of the great beast just chewing slowly and looking at me like the complete fool I was. I could have sworn the bastard was taking the mickey out of me—'Look at this child, thinking he's the big man around here. I'll show him a thing or *twooo* …'" Dom's eyes were twinkling as he did his best impression of a cow's accent from the eleventh century. "But of course, it was *my* fault he'd strayed in first place. I was being reckless, you see … chasing after one of the neighbour's daughters—showing off how strong I was lifting the stones like a big man. And then I didn't reassemble a stone wall on one side of my father's land holdings. So, you know I didn't *dare* return home without the bull. My father would have flayed me alive!"

Solveig snorted loudly into her beer.

"But the fat lump just wouldn't budge! Even now, I'm fuming just thinking about it."

I laughed as well, though I felt a bit sorry for this younger version of him. "Couldn't you have offered him some nice grain or something?" I asked practically.

"Or, I don't know, maybe a good hard shove?" Solveig asked, laughing.

"You think I hadn't tried that?" Dom asked, tears streaming down his face in mirth. "Two days! *Two whole days* I sat in that fucking field. On the second night, my pride finally broke, and I slept curled up next to the beast. And I cried!"

I pictured a young Dom then, just as stubborn as the bull. Poor kid. "And no one came to help?"

"No, of course not. Anyone who cared enough would have deemed this a lesson I needed to learn for myself. There's an old saying, something along the lines of, *'You don't buy or sell a moiled.'*" I knew from previous stories that the Irish Moiled was a type of dual-purpose cow in Ireland that dated back to before Dom was a lad. In those days, cattle were currency.

"They're extremely precious now," he continued, "and they were even more so back then. But this fella, by the time we got out of the field, I was about ready to give him away. Even if that meant I'd lose my head," Dom said, grinning.

"How did you get him to move in the end?" Solveig asked.

"I woke up on the second morning to him practically trotting towards the fence. A cow had wandered up to the other side, you see. A *lady* cow. And just like that, he hopped over the stone wall like a bloody show horse to join her and the others on the other side of our field."

"Typical," I said, laughing.

"I always wondered if someone hadn't taken pity on me and sent her my way. I don't know why I hadn't thought of it myself, to be honest."

"A young man's pride is hard to shake even under the direst circumstances," Solveig said sagely, though with a distinct twinkle in her eye.

"Especially when I was just as much of a fool for love as the bull," he said, laughing.

I smiled fondly at Dom then. As always, I loved his retellings of his youth.

When it came time to leave, I was far from shocked as the pair of them squabbled about who would pay.

"Well, Dom, since I'm practically old enough to be your mother in *this* lifetime, this meal is on me," Solveig said. She had taken our explanation of the curses, Prophecy, and general history like a champ. Another perk of spending time with magic users was that we didn't have to fight to explain our circumstances.

Fully warmed with food and drink, Dom and I squeezed our lengthy frames back into Solveig's small car, and she drove us to her house, a bright-yellow rectangular dwelling with white trim located only a few blocks away. The fact that it matched her car was not lost on either of us. Many of the houses in Vardø were painted with similarly bright colours though, with the sides of some of the warehouses and commercial buildings even decorated with street art. Earlier, upon our arrival to the port, I had chuckled at a large building that had "Cod is Great" painted onto its side in bold capital letters; first impressions were that it was a small yet vibrant community.

"Normally I'd walk. But who wants to haul luggage through the snow in the dark!" Solveig said.

"True," Dom agreed. "But easier than dragging a bull through the mud." The laughter continued. He was clearly in his element. For me though, there was a familiarity between the Norse Witch and me that could only be described as kinship: like an aunt, or distant cousin, or perhaps even a lost sister. We didn't need to exchange words to find comfortability. We just *were*.

It felt good to be near another Bearer once more.

Entering the home, Dom and I were soon ushered towards one of the two low couches in Solveig's sitting room as she made to busy herself in the kitchen. Plunking himself down, Dom crossed one leg over the other and braced his arms across the back of the couch, gesturing for me. I tucked myself in close, appreciating his sturdy nature for what was probably the millionth time.

"Are you doing alright, love?" Dom asked, kissing the side of my head.

"I am. I know we haven't really touched on anything important yet, but I have a good feeling about this."

The inside of Solveig's home was clean and bright. The walls had been painted white, which helped immensely to lighten the space in contrast to the long dark of the region. In keeping with the overall theme, the floor was also finished in bright wood. I was quickly beginning to understand the practical elements of Scandinavian design. However, there was also a distinct climate-activist-meets-Witch energy to the space as well. Clearly, this was where she lived and worked, both vocationally and magically.

Solveig returned with a tray of coffee and a variety of yummy-looking pastries. *"Solskinnsboller,"* she said, smiling as she gestured towards a cluster of delights that looked like cinnamon rolls with a custard filling and vanilla icing. "Named to celebrate the return of the sun. I usually make *skillingsboller*, but I thought you might enjoy these, even though we're a touch early for it." She looked out the window towards the darkness. There was also some sort of almond cookie, as well as what looked like small, rolled, crepe-like delicacies.

Dom leaned forward in anticipation.

"So ... where shall we begin?" Solveig said as she sat down on the opposite couch, adjusting her tray on a simple teak table that occupied the space between us.

Dom spoke up. "We had hoped you might—"

"We need to find Kenzie," I said, cutting to the chase. "She can't go on like this."

Solveig raised her eyebrows. "Oh, I agree, Julia. But we'll need to be careful. From what Lennie's told me about what happened in Los Angeles and the loss of the Knave Wren, and then, with what happened in Berkeley with Dr. Bailey ... Kenzie's far more dangerous than I originally sensed. It's ... I think it's a good thing I reached out when I did."

It was plain that Solveig was in the loop when it came to Lennie's current intel. While I hadn't yet sensed anything sinister in Solveig's motives, it was good know that if Lennie was sharing this type of information with her freely, it meant he'd done the legwork to confirm she was fully on our side. I let out a slow breath, relaxing.

Meanwhile, Dom leaned forward, focused now, any signs of relaxation from earlier in the evening quickly dissolving. He attempted to hide the change by casually reaching for a cookie, but I knew the tension in his body was immediately ratcheting at the mention of Wren.

"Don't worry, Dom," Solveig said, already attuning herself to his nature. "I didn't say there wasn't a way. We just need to make sure we stay protected

319

in the process. Set firm boundaries and move forward with care," At that, she poured us each a coffee, and Dom settled slightly.

I was grateful to have Dom with me. Bearer or not, when it came to devising offensive logistics, there was no one else I wanted by my side. That being said, it would also likely change the dynamic of the conversation if I wasn't careful. I needed this discussion to stay firmly within a Bearer-to-Bearer context if I was to stand a chance at truly understanding the threat Kenzie posed to us.

"I can't explain it," I said, "but something felt wrong with her when we found her at the top of the tower. I mean ... it's not like I've been around very many Bearers—in this lifetime anyway—but any that I *have* encountered always have a sort of ... *depth* to them. And in that depth ..." My voice trailed off; unable to put the concept into words, I swirled the last of my coffee around at the bottom of the cup.

"In that depth, you can feel how connected we truly are," Solveig said, finishing my thought with a knowing smile.

"Yes ... right," I said, sipping the last of my coffee and setting the cup down between us. "But when it came to her, she felt rotten almost. For the lack of a more obvious example, almost like a sick branch on a fruit tree. Fungal and dark."

Dom breathed out slowly through his nose. "It sounds like the Bearing family tree needs some pruning."

Solveig's smile faltered incrementally. "Possibly."

"It's more complicated than simply tracking her down though, isn't it?" I asked. "I mean, she's obviously aligned herself with something, or *someone*, immeasurably dark. We all know that." I watched as both Solveig's and Dom's faces darkened.

"Yes, and it *is* complicated," Solveig said. "While she's not exactly hiding herself—like most other Bearers have been forced to do—looking for her comes with its own risks."

Silence fell between us for several moments as we pondered what the repercussions of seeking out Kenzie might look like, and what we might uncover if we turned over the wrong stones while unprepared, such as Cassius himself.

"But there's also something else," I said, breaking the silence and staring deep into Solveig's eyes. I felt a hot anger well up within me. "This ... what Kenzie has done ... is betrayal."

Solveig paused for a moment, and an eerie calm spread across her face. She looked older now, and I wondered if I had misjudged her age. Or perhaps, she had wanted it that way.

"As I'm sure you've noticed, Julia, there is a lot of source magic up here."

Dom looked confused at the conversation's sudden detour, but I felt relief at last; we were about to uncover the real reason we had been invited up here. By now, I was used to the cryptic ways that Witches knit their teachings, and I knew that what would come next would prove priceless, regardless of whether I understood it just yet. Bernie had taught me that much, and so I had no doubt Solveig would do the same.

"We all bring our own gifts into this life. And—if all goes to plan—these gifts knot and tie themselves into the collective, ultimately aiding in the betterment of humanity. Bearers, Wielders, and regular folks alike." She nodded towards Dom.

In my mind, I could almost hear him saying something like *"Who are you calling regular?"* but he kept his mouth shut.

"To me, it's almost like a great weaving or a tapestry," she continued, gesturing towards a large wall hanging I hadn't noticed before, almost as if it had been magically concealed. Dom swore under his breath, confirming my suspicions. "We aren't separate from one another. Not really. Nor are we separate from the earth."

"Or the sea," I said.

Dom spoke quietly, staring intently at the tapestry that had revealed itself before us. "Or the sky."

Red, blue, green, yellow, and various shades of brown threads came together to create a stunning, immersive set of four images. The hanging had definitely *not* been there before, or at the very least, it had been obscured until it needed to appear. There was a subtlety with which Solveig had curated and woven magic into her own house. It made me wonder what else I had perhaps missed. I would have to pay closer attention.

"It bears similarity to some of the more famous pieces from Norway's 'age of tapestry,' if you were to look them up," Solveig said in a slightly mocking tone, "at least in the colourways. Though I must say, ours are far more interesting when it comes to the actual content."

I rose to peer more closely at the piece, with Dom following closely behind me. I could feel his breath on my neck as he too inspected the weaving further.

In one section, birds circled what were clearly women mounted on horseback. Depictions of the birds' vibrant feathers were plaited in and out of view, intermixed with flowers to create a thick border. In another, more women in wooden boats paddled across a dark ocean, a handful of stars and a bold yellow moon cast boldly across the night sky above. The border around this part was a thick rectangle as well, though this one contained what looked like rolling waves. The third section depicted women standing along a shoreline in traditional dress, holding out offerings of welcome. Behind them, something resembling stalks of grain filled the background, spilling into another solid border. The last image was as yet unfinished but contained what looked to be far more modern implements.

"Is that the beginnings of a bicycle?" I asked, surprised.

Solveig smiled. "This weaving has been passed down through the generations in my Bearing family line. Mother to daughter. Witch to Witch. We've always considered it to be sort of a symbol of our connectivity to the other Witches in our lineage. Our power. We add to it with each generation."

My face dropped. I thought of the quilt, which lately had felt like something I was simply hauling from country to country to no real end—a reminder of past lives but not really providing me with any future clarity. Bernie had tried to give me reassurance about this, but in truth, it hadn't stuck.

"Are you alright, Julia?" she asked, pausing in her telling.

"I am. It's just … I have a quilt that I've apparently added to slowly throughout my many lifetimes. I've never been able to decipher it, in terms of its purpose, but it follows me from life to life. And up until recently, I had thought that maybe it was just a symbol of the past that I needed to let go of. But in listening to what you're saying now …"

"Perhaps it's a symbol of the many ways you have woven and worked yourself towards your own future throughout your history. Like a confirmation of who you are and where you come from. Isn't that something?"

I looked at her in appreciation. "Thank you."

"It's just one woman's opinion," she said with a flick of her hand. The tapestry disappeared. "It's why I study what I do, though. And *where* I do. Not only am I allowed the privilege of living in a place that offers an almost infinite access to raw, wild magics, but it also lets me consider the greater impact of our individual actions on humanity as a whole." She laughed at what she clearly deemed to be a grandiose statement. "Well, that and the fact that there's a state-of-the-art radar station here that I've learned to use to my advantage."

"But I thought magic and technology didn't—" Dom started as we moved back to the couch, but I grabbed his arm. *Just wait, Dom.*

A tiny smirk appeared at the corner of Solveig's mouth, and she continued. "One of the ways I have honed my Bearing abilities is to tap into the collective magic of the world to locate other Witches throughout the world. I'll explain it in more detail to you both tomorrow when we visit the radar station, which—you're right, Dom—isn't something that would usually be useful to most Bearers. A little science never hurt anyone though, and if anyone was going to use it to their advantage, it needed to be me. Sometimes, it just identifies concentrations, but at others, actual individuals."

"That would be a dangerous tool in the hands of Cassius," Dom said.

Solveig grimaced. "Indeed."

"But that doesn't explain how you were able to connect with Lennie," I said. "Surely, he's almost impossible to find. Plus, he's a Wielder." Dom nodded.

"Well, that was a bit more of a reverse circumstance," Solveig said. "Lennie actually found me prying around. It wasn't exactly how I meant to connect initially, but it worked out well for all of us in the end, wouldn't you say?"

"Sometimes," Dom said wistfully, "I trick myself into thinking that it's merely dumb luck that Julia and I manage to find each other each time. But at others, I am almost certain it's due to a greater power than all of us."

She nodded kindly, beaming at the pair of us. "Without a doubt."

Dom leaned forward and refilled both of our coffees. I reached for another cookie but didn't put it in my mouth. "I hope he was kind to you. Lennie can be a bit …"

"He was cautious, but we sorted ourselves out quickly," she said, finishing my thought. "It's actually been your friend Ronan that's been the challenge. I was probably getting three or four emails from him a day for a while there."

Solveig subtly swirled her wrist in the direction of our coffee cups and tendrils of steam curled up in reply. I would have missed her reheating the liquid had I not been paying closer attention to her movements. She was clearly proficient and had no qualms with semi-regular Wielding.

"He's tenacious," I offered.

Dom scoffed. "That's one word for it."

"The thing is," Solveig said, "Ronan's not wrong in his concern, or his suspicions, even if it seems to be bordering on obsession."

"The bastard is rarely wrong about things," Dom conceded. "But the question is, do you *agree* with him?"

"I do."

I looked between the pair of them, not quite keeping up. "What? What is it?"

CHAPTER 30

Subtly at first, Solveig's demeanour changed before us. So far, she had presented as almost predictably warm, but now, she was working herself into visible agitation. She stood abruptly and paced once towards the kitchen before turning on her heels and returning to where we were still seated on the couch. Dom tensed but didn't stand as I continued to stare at Solveig in open confusion.

"There's more to it than even Ronan knows. It would seem that Cassius is using Kenzie as some sort of live source—a magical conduit, perhaps—but connected through her inner Bearing magic."

My jaw slackened as Dom ground his teeth together loudly.

"How is that even possible?" I asked. My mind was jerked back to the musty auditorium in Leeds; I knew full well that *had* Cassius managed to gain access to my magic, he would have drained me completely. To the death. In fact, I don't think he could have stopped himself.

"Ronan has filled me in on your theories about his … spear. Is it true that you hadn't seen anything like this in prior regenerations?" Solveig asked.

"No, we haven't," Dom said, filling in the blanks for me. "He's used plenty of other horrific … *implements* … to kill me and to torture Julia before killing her too. But nothing like this."

Dom stared at his hands, trying to keep his own control in check as Solveig wandered silently towards the front of the room and stared out the window into the darkness at nothing. After a moment, and still facing away from us, she started to speak.

"Well … it would seem he is gaining control—or restraint—over its uses now. Honing it, if you will. And he's using Kenzie as practice."

In shock, I stared at the back of her head.

In all of the nightmare visions that had followed my own experience with the spear, none of the girls I witnessed had survived. In fact, their deaths had been a major impetus in drawing Cassius's forces to the north coast of Ireland in the first place; too many people were dying on our behalf. But now—if he could *siphon* off Bearing magic without actually killing the Witch herself— what might that mean for the future of our kind? For me? Suddenly, my own future felt a lot darker, as did the possible outcomes to this life. There were things worse than death.

Dom, who I would have expected to blow up into a full panic at what I assumed would be a similar realization, remained eerily calm. His hands remained still, palms down and spread wide across his knees. However, his knuckles pressed white. His breath had slowed considerably, and he stared down at them almost forcibly. I wondered whether he was going to speak or faint.

"Dom, are you alright?" I asked, turning towards him, peeling his hands off his lap and pulling them into my own in an attempt to break the spell.

"No, I'm not," he said quietly. He looked up at me, his eyes cold with fury. "I know what he's doing. Or trying to do … If he can figure out how to tap Kenzie's magic without killing her, then he can try do the *exact* same thing to you. He knows you have exceptional magic now—a depth of magic beyond his wildest dreams—and he wants it. He wants you."

Solveig slumped down onto the couch.

"But why would he need to keep me alive?" I asked, momentarily surprised at my own flippancy towards my mortality.

"My guess?" Solveig offered. "Because he requires a continuous source."

Dom and I both stared at her in astonishment, and she continued.

"Well, if Ronan's research holds true—his theory that the more the Wraiths *take* from the world, the deader they become—then Cassius is likely in the same boat, only he needs something a bit stronger. Or at least he *demands it* … being who he is. He needs a source of *infinite* magic, just for him."

She was staring at me. I had almost forgotten for a moment that Solveig was a scientist, and likely had no trouble following along with Ronan's line of thinking while forming her own theories concurrently.

Dom nodded, keeping up. "Of course! He's been killing the Bearers to take their magic, but that only goes *so far* and requires a fair bit of effort as well. Not to mention the fact that Bearers are almost extinct throughout the world. Or in hiding. His source has been quickly diminishing and proving harder and harder to locate." I could almost feel the heat rising from him as spoke. "And I know Cassius. He'll *never* work harder for anything himself than is absolutely necessary."

Dom stood then, struggling to contain the anger boiling within his veins. I looked at Solveig, momentarily concerned that Dom's mounting intensity might be unsettling to her. However, she looked entirely like him, her fists clenched and lips tight.

"Exactly. I am glad to see you sense the gravity of this situation, *World Ruler.*"

Dom stared at Solveig then and swallowed deeply. He nodded once and excused himself awkwardly to go to the bathroom, slamming the door perhaps a bit louder than was necessary.

Solveig turned towards me, tempering her own distress as she spoke. "He's going to need to face it one way or another."

"Face what?"

"Oh, come on, Julia. Surely you know."

I stared at her.

"Cassius wants you for himself. Beyond the source magic. A trophy."

"*What?* How can you know possibly know that?"

"Well, you already knew that the original Prophecy had been passed down through generations of Witches. You don't think the latest version hasn't reached our ears? I might not be a proper Diviner, but that doesn't mean I'm not in with them. *'As the Sorcerer seeks to find the grail, spear in hand, to chalice he is bound.'* Do you know what that might mean?"

I wracked my brain through the fragments of Arthurian legend and stories of the Holy Grail. "Uh … not exactly. But there are a lot of interpretations of the quest for the Grail, aren't there?"

"There are," Dom said, and I jumped; I hadn't heard him re-enter the room. "To some scholars—and this is a simplified explanation—the spear represents the masculine, and the chalice the feminine. The divine balance, and together… the rumoured key to immortality."

"Or so it's been speculated," Solveig clarified, a consummate scientist.

Dom continued, impulsively shifting into what I recognized as his professor's stance. "One tale, in particular, tells of the Fisher King. Essentially, his kingdom—which guarded 'The Holy Grail'—had become barren because the spear, meant to protect the chalice, seriously injured him while being stolen from his court. There's a lot more to it, but the kingdom became a wasteland without the spear to pair with the chalice. No Grail, no life."

I nodded. Dom had referred to himself as the spear and me as the chalice before, but I had never really inquired what it meant beyond what I assumed to be the physical characteristics of the items. Sometimes Dom's antiquation showed.

"There are *obviously* many ways to unpack that—all of which have been hotly debated, and heavily Christianized throughout the centuries. And then there's the likely Celtic origins which—"

I coughed.

"All I'm saying is, even though the new Prophecy refers to Cassius's spear as separate from the Sorcerer, based on his need to murder and harvest Bearers … I'd venture he sees himself as not only Sorcerer but also as the spear. And Bearing magic is the chalice," Dom said. "He thinks if he can bring the two together, he will become immortal."

"So then … why can't he just use *Kenzie* if he needs a chalice?" I asked, almost spitting her name. "She probably thinks she's important enough."

Solveig let out a slow breath before replying. "I think, deep down, he believes it needs to be you. The purest, strongest source of magic and true expression of the Divine Feminine. Kenzie is neither of those things."

It's true; she wasn't. As Dom had said, she was becoming a branch on the family tree that desperately needed pruning.

Dom placed his hand on my shoulder, and I closed my eyes.

Dom and I planned to spend the next day working with Solveig, with her explaining how to access and locate other Bearers around the world through our innate connectedness. She assured me that the lesson wouldn't take us long, and then Dom and I could be on our merry way back to Ireland. I had the distinct sense that, while she was enjoying our company well enough, she also knew our presence up here had the potential to draw unwanted attention her way. She had a good thing going up here, with the blend of magical and scientific work she was doing, and didn't need Wraiths nosing about where they weren't welcome.

Or worse … Cassius. The magic she was harnessing would surely be something he would want access to. Imagine him being able to map all of the Bearers around the world for himself! I had tried to assure her that the protective spell I'd cast around me and Dom had held true thus far, but the reality was I couldn't make it an actual promise. Bearing magic was tricky like that. Not to mention the fact that we literally had no idea where Cassius actually was at this point in time.

Lennie stayed in touch while we were in the north, both with us and with Solveig. The pair of them were working on a relationship in which she might be able to provide him with her own brand of intelligence, and vice versa. It seemed to be going well enough. In our emails, we were updated (albeit vaguely) on the details of Graham and Sean's current reconnaissance mission. They had recently followed a lead into Northern Africa, but the trail had grown cold. Ronan too had made his needs plain, sending multiple emails addressed to me *firmly* requesting that I speak with Solveig and enquire about any and all information she had that might connect to his research.

"The bastard just won't let us rest," Dom said, shaking his head after a third email landed in his inbox that morning. I said nothing; my feelings around Ronan's persistence were already well known between the two of us.

We turned our attention towards our day with Solveig.

"Though individually sourced from within," Solveig said, forging on in the face of my weak assurances about our innate protection and reminding me of Gertie's teachings, "Bearing magic still remains part of the greater collective." Well, that part was new. I had always assumed we were connected through our shared histories, but to think we were connected by more than that was an interesting prospect.

"One of my areas of personal curiosity is trying to determine if our dwindling numbers might lead to a decrease in our individual powers. In other words, as Cassius destroys more of us, collectively speaking, will we become weaker individually?"

I contemplated what she was saying, rolling the idea around in my head, but then my intuition took over. "I don't think so, actually. I mean, I think as long as there is even one of us still standing, the strength of Bearers will remain."

She smiled at me, with only a hint of pity on her face. "Spoken like the Sovereign."

Dom, however, looked immensely proud.

For her part, Solveig had somehow managed to find a way to use her Bearing magic in conjunction with the radar station to reach outwards—like a Send but on steroids.

"Obviously you're not going to be hanging around a radar station all days of the week," she said as we crunched through the snow. "But if I show you how I manage it, you can take the concepts and apply them to something in your own life. You've mentioned the tide being important?"

"It has been ... but it's a lot like the radar station in that way. Like, I'm not always *near* the shoreline."

"We travel a lot," Dom said resignedly before cocking his head in thought. "What about using the rivers? Like Bernie showed you?"

Solveig looked towards me for my response. I thought about it for a moment before answering.

"I think maybe ... it's the *wells.*" I thought back to Peggy's teachings about the connection to our inner world through the wells, and it was almost as if I had always known this to be the way. Whether they were physical wellsprings from which water and magic overflowed, or more profound and elusive thin places, Peggy had emphasized these were streams all leading back to a single source. A conduit between all magical users. That was where my power came from, as well as my connection to the Otherworld.

Dom nodded in consideration. "There's certainly plenty of connection between the lost wells and the aspect of sovereignty." I stared at him in surprise. "Oh, come on, Julia. I've heard and read most of the Celtic legends. I might actually be able to help you here!"

I gave him a playful shove. "I didn't say you couldn't."

With the help of Solveig and her headlamp leading the way through the dim daylight, we at last reached the closest point we could to the Globus II radar station without trespassing.

It was absolutely massive.

"It's a bit ironic actually," Solveig said as we joined her, "using something so militaristic as a tool when you're a Bearer."

"Militaristic?" I asked from my place at her side.

"Well, you don't actually think they use this only to track space junk, do you?" She laughed.

"No, I suppose not."

"I mean, you didn't hear that from me, of course," she said with a chuckle and then continued more seriously. "Do you both understand the basics of how radar works?"

"Yes," Dom said, nodding.

"Not entirely," I said at the same time, surprised at his answer. But then, I supposed he'd probably done his due diligence around these types of things long, long ago.

"Shocked again, Julia!" Dom said, chuckling. "You've really got to give me more credit."

I always thought of that scene from *Wall-E*, when the captain learns about pizza for the first time, when I imagined Dom's acclimation periods. More accurately, of course, Dom had probably just read about radar in books; it wasn't exactly new technology. And it was important for him to have a knowledge of surveillance and all things military.

I felt slightly embarrassed for my own lack of knowledge. "Honestly, it feels like just another one of those modern things I take for granted. Radar just ... *is*, you know?"

"You've got to be careful with turning a blind eye to these types of things, Julia," Solveig said, speaking as a scientist now. "Radar is one thing, but how do you think the world has ended up in this climate predicament? So much of what we do every day creates toxic by-products."

"You're right." Suddenly flooded with guilt, I had the strangest urge to apologize to Solveig, I guess for my own supposed climate-destroying transgressions. But I realized how ridiculous that would be.

"It's of no concern," she said, patting me on the arm, perhaps recognizing the unnecessary guilt. "Essentially, a radar station emits microwave energy—the same as cellphones or the microwave in your kitchen—and the long waves bounce off things. When they do, and find their way back, the distance between the station and the object is measured, as well as the object's size."

I nodded, vaguely recalling the concept from high school physics.

"And so, you use the same waves to locate other Bearers?" Dom asked, keeping up.

"Essentially. I almost piggyback on the waves to allow myself to reach out further. There is a reason Bearing magic interferes with regular cell signals, though it's too complicated to explain fully now. The best explanation I can give you is that it's *interference*. Bearing magic and most other signals hamper one another, but how badly they interfere depends on what frequency a Bearer might be on. Or how strong they are. In your case, you interfere with almost *any* signal. For me, I just needed a source consistent and strong enough that I could experiment. Rather than cancelling out the waves, I amplify them—superposition!" Solveig said, beaming at her own cleverness as she gestured towards the radar station. "And then, by 'riding the waves,' I can seek out other Bearers and their signals."

"Kind of like when you can sense a Bearer in the room," I said, "only way bigger."

"Yes, exactly. On top of some small talent with divining, I've always had a knack for 'feeling out' Bearers in more than just the same room. It's my own special gift as a Bearer, just like *yours*, I think, is your divining magic. I felt you when you landed in Norway two days ago. Mind you, I was also waiting for you, so I was somewhat attuned, but even still. There aren't a ton of us left in the world, so someone like me *would* notice when someone as powerful as you is near."

"As powerful as me?" I muttered, realizing too late that I accidently said it out loud.

"Yes, Julia. As powerful as you," she said, suddenly very serious. "And don't think Cassius can't sense that power either. No offence, but you're oozing with it."

"He's always had a knack for showing up almost exactly where we are," Dom said. "It's why you've not asked us to say any longer than we have."

She didn't reply, but the unspoken words were more than enough.

CHAPTER 31

Cassius slid his cellphone slowly into his breast pocket, barely able to contain his rage. It was fast approaching the end of January, and he was no closer to finding the Codex than he had been his first night in Marrakech when the haggard market Witch delivered him nothing but a dead end. He'd rid the Medina of any scourge she had associated with, feasting on Bearing magic and the place as a whole. After all, there was no point in going all the way there and not taking advantage of the convenience. Following an equally fruitless trip to Ibiza—though he had fed there too for several weeks—he needed some good news. Unfortunately, Kenzie had failed to deliver.

Though Kenzie had successfully captured the scientist in California as planned, she had also tortured her extensively over the past two months. That was expected, of course, but Cassius had given Kenzie explicit instructions *not* to kill the Bearer. He needed her, especially if he was going to leverage the Druid Ronan when the time came. The scientist was a hostage he had planned to use to his advantage.

And yet, the little psychopath had killed her outright. He would deal with Kenzie later.

His hands shook with a combination of scarcely concealed ire and freshly stolen Bearing magic as he strode forward to exit his jet. The only benefit to his stop in Ibiza had been the plenitude of young flesh—remnants of which now lay bloodying the plane's floor behind him. Otherwise, it had been an utter waste of time, with the Bearer he'd sought having left the island a decade ago.

It was an abandoned post, identifiable only by the long-stagnant map magic left behind.

He was starting to believe that the coordinates were not actually clues to an enigma at all. Instead, it was a series of potential red herrings, set specifically to deter anyone who sought out the Codex. Someone like him. It certainly *felt* that way, considering how his rage was boiling over. As infuriating as it was though, it did make sense. The map had clearly fallen into weak hands and so had likely come from similar origins. Some fool didn't have the power or aptitude to destroy the Codex, so they had hidden it, hoping the map's staggered coordinates would be enough of a deterrent or perhaps allow for advanced warning to move or hide it elsewhere. Three or four hundred years ago, this strategy might have been effective enough, but with access to modern air travel, it was pathetic. Even with lingering in the previous two locations, "enjoying" himself, he should still come out ahead. He had to.

And indeed, it was only a matter of time before he cinched the noose. Someone held the answers, and he would catch them *very* soon. The fact that the trail had gone cold only reinforced to him how easy it would be.

Worthy of note was that each of the four coordinates corresponded to an ancient walled city. He wasn't sure how he'd failed to register the fact before; perhaps his hunger was at last starting to cloud his judgement. No. That wasn't true. He just didn't consider walls the same way others did. What were walls and borders to a man who'd faced no boundary he couldn't cross?

At the time of the map's creation, these walled cities had likely served as an additional protective barrier from those seeking out the Codex. They would be heavily populated, obscuring its presence. Cassius had spent *plenty* of time in Ibiza in the past (as he had in the streets of Marrakech); he was well acquainted with the trade routes and hub cities of the Old World. Ibiza's Renaissance wall was only a small part of the island's varied history throughout the ages. These types of fortifications had held no meaning to him then, and they certainly didn't now. Not to mention that in the modern era "walls" held a completely different meaning anyway.

Landing in Carcassonne, France, under the cover of darkness, Cassius stepped onto the tarmac and strode smoothly towards a BMW with blacked-out windows that was waiting for him. It was cool and rainy outside, though not wet enough to warrant an umbrella. He glowered at the trembling man who attempted to offer him cover as he approached the rear door of his car, baring his teeth as an added threat. Night was the natural realm of a Sorcerer, and he would spare no one any kindness as he moved through the inky evening.

The vehicle was armoured—an added layer of protection required for this particular locale. Cassius wasn't particularly well liked in France and never had been. It was one of the few places people actually recognized him and paid any attention to his activity. The French were a proud people, and those in the know didn't appreciate how much of their real estate and pieces of history he owned. It was not the everyday man he was concerned about but the true power brokers. Men who thought they were like him. So, he was used to needing additional security while in the region. After a near miss in the nineties, he had taken matters into his own hands and invested in a permanent security corps that always accompanied him while on French soil and guarded his many properties while he was away.

A worthy investment to protect what was rightfully his.

Since he had landed directly at the airport just outside of Carcassonne, the trip wasn't long to the walled city itself. Despite his annoyance at the lack of forward movement in his greater plans, Cassius was *almost* beginning to enjoy the familiar nature of the locations he'd visited thus far. It felt like it had been ages since he had actively chosen to do something unknown to him; it exhilarated him as much as it angered him. He'd also been on steady ground, magically speaking, as these sites were ripe with Bearers ready for the picking. Ancient places always were, and he was grateful for not having needed to rely on Kenzie over the past two months.

His mind soured at the thought of her.

He purposely looked out the window instead and took in the view. How often had he spent time in this area, so visibly kissed by the many powerful influences of Rome? The impressive high stone walls and arched bridge shone like the sun as they gradually approached the ancient fortress, lit up with artificial light even in the increasingly heavy rain. Though, generally, he no longer had a sense of smell, Cassius could almost recall the raw odour of livestock gathered by the many traders along the route and the earthy scent of petrichor as the dust rose off the cobblestones from fresh rain. It was fertile ground here for trade and magic, and always had been. All of humanity knew it, magic or no.

Though sentimentality didn't exist in his mental framework, familiarity wasn't something he rejected—familiarity in the places he'd graced before he could maintain absolute control. Indeed, the reason he had left the final coordinate for last was precisely because it was unfamiliar. He hoped he wouldn't be forced to go there.

Control, especially now, was paramount.

Over the past two millennia, Cassius had limited his seat of power mostly to Europe, though he had invested his energy in certain sections of the Middle East and North Africa, which had of course been utilized on the many Roman trade routes throughout history. It only made sense that he continued with tradition. Finally, in the past several hundred years, he had extended his influence into the New World. With so many Europeans colonizing the North American continent, including the Witch, it had only made sense. And while he had since developed many place holdings and corporations throughout the United States, why he had chosen Los Angeles as the head of his American branch had been simple: He preferred to exist in warmer climates. And always had.

After all, he was The Child of Rome.

The car reached the gateway into Old Town at last, slowing to a halt at its entrance. Though it was exceptionally difficult to navigate the ancient streets in a vehicle, he opted to travel on foot for a different reason altogether. His business was his own. And though it wasn't far-reaching to explain his reasoning for the visit—not that anyone would dare question—he couldn't risk anyone finding out what he sought. If anyone else knew of the existence of the map, let alone of the Codex, these locations might serve as dead giveaway.

He needed to be careful. Which was something Kenzie seemed completely incapable of. Once again, he pushed the little bitch from his mind. He would deal with her indiscretions later.

Once his driver took off, Cassius pulled his black cloak tightly around his shoulders and began the slow walk through the gate, his feet leading him naturally towards the inner streets of the fortress. Much like the previous two locations, the power of place was significant here, magnetic, expansive, and almost explosive, which made sense. Over generations, magic had implanted itself into the very stone, creating a complex symphony of enchantment throughout. He felt strong where he stood, even though he couldn't effectively access the Wielding magic all around him, and hoped that his heavy consumption on the plane would be more than enough. Bearing magic seemed to be entering and leaving him like sand though an hourglass these days.

Time was running out.

The book *had to be* here. This place was as familiar as the back of his hand. And he *knew* his destiny was to possess the *Codex Druidicus*. The new Prophecy had made it true. He just needed to scent the right trail.

Reaching down to palm the wet stones, Cassius shuddered as an especially potent gust of Wielding magic shot through his creaking bones. His rotting ligaments and muscles strained at the unbridled force, but he held strong. Then he waited. Bringing his breath to almost a standstill, he used his senses to reach for signs of the magic attached to the map.

And there it was.

Lavender and ... Was that thyme? In Ibiza, the empty house of the escaped Bearer had smelled strongly of Mediterranean pine and juniper. Distinct and overpowering. Nauseating. He couldn't help but think it was being employed specifically for him. A mocking lure juxtaposed to the scent of his rotting flesh, which he denied despite knowing full well its stench.

He felt his heart rate quicken, wrath boiling barely below the surface.

His cloak billowing behind him, Cassius followed the scent around the curve of the fortress's inner wall, onward until he finally came to a staircase. Rain was pouring down so heavily now that he could barely see several feet ahead of himself. Still, the scent of lavender and thyme grew heavier yet with each measured tread, heady and overwhelming. These particular stone steps led to the ramparts and then to the towers. Having spent many seasons here throughout the ages, he knew it intimately, and despite the oppressively floral odour, Cassius felt excitement growing in his body.

This was the end of the line. The Codex was nearly in his grasp.

Crossing under a high archway into a round tower, Cassius stopped in his tracks, tossing his hood back, ready to declare his victory. Suddenly, he felt his entire frame start to sway. There was a Bearer here alright. A dead one. He cast his gaze to a bloodied blade lying just beyond her outstretched palm on the stone floor. It would seem her death had come by her own hand, based on the slashes across her forearms. She'd meant to make it quick. But she had also drained her own magic in the process.

Cassius strode forward, white rage blinding his thoughts. He reached down, his jaw so tense he thought it might crack. The blood pooling around the Witch was still slightly warm despite the cold air; her death had been recent. How had she known he was coming? He hadn't been in Carcassonne for more than an hour, his surprise arrival being part of the plan. He placed his hand just above the cooling torso, sensing. Perhaps there was still some Bearing magic within? He had never successfully siphoned it from a dead body, but perhaps …

Shaking violently, his craving overtook him as he reached through his cloak and into the inner recesses of his suit coat. He drew his spear out, twinned blades menacing in the gloom, and slowly shunted it into the Witch's freshly deceased form. For a brief moment, he thought it might work, but that chance flickered away almost as soon as it had come.

He stood then and slowly backed away, his feet soon treading the slick, familiar ground without a clear destination as he attempted to collect his unspooling thoughts.

So, he would need Kenzie after all.

She was lucky he hadn't ordered her killed immediately after he'd hung up the phone earlier. It would have been justified. However, if he was going to make the journey towards the final set of coordinates, not to mention maintain his needs while there, he would need a consistent supply. It was more than an insurance policy now. It was survival, and he hated the realization.

Unlike the past three locations, which were familiar—not to mention chocked full of Bearers just gallivanting about as if their lives weren't in any sort of danger—the final coordinate was going to prove far more difficult to breach successfully. He wasn't welcome in that country; he knew that much. And hadn't been for *many* years.

But that had never stopped him from procuring what he needed before.

He pulled his phone from his pocket, dialling Kenzie.

She picked up immediately. "Cassius? I—"

"Silence!" he said viciously. "I've changed my mind about your life. I require you. We're going to Russia."

Cassius sat silently in his seat as the jet took off jerkily down the runway. He'd only just finished sipping a gin martini, which was good fortune or the entire drink would have landed in his lap. He would have the pilot dispatched when they reached their destination.

He had originally planned to distract himself during the flight by reading the latest reports from the many arms of his empire. He'd received daily updates from all of his generals for as long as he could remember, in one form or another. In the past, he'd had people do this part of the job for him, if he wasn't feeling inclined, but with the stakes being what they were now, he couldn't afford any more mistakes. In any case, technology made it easy.

Admittedly, he'd taken the situation in Carcassonne poorly, lashing out violently throughout the lower township and killing at will. He didn't discriminate between Bearers, Wielders, and ordinary humans. It had been a long time since he'd lost control like that, but he'd been furious at being thwarted, and it felt *good* to kill. Unfortunately, he'd left quite a mess behind him, not to mention draining any magical stores he had gained in the process.

But he had people for the clean-up or, at least, to stage some sort of tragedy.

He'd been forced to wait in France for Kenzie to join him, which had been agony as the hunger pangs clawed terribly at his throat. Even so, the look on her face as she'd climbed into the plane's cabin was so pathetically remorseful that he'd almost killed her just to put a stop to it, hunger be damned. But he was starving, and he needed her.

He choked back the memory of what had followed in disgust.

With the jet now firmly in the air, Cassius flicked his thoughts between reports and the news of the day. Staring at his laptop, he found any sort of attention proving to be a struggle; he'd only just replenished his supply and already his thoughts were filled with hunger.

Kenzie lay at his feet, breathing heavily. Her hair was embarrassingly askew, and she had a dreamy, almost ecstatic look on her face. He was correct: She *did* get some form of sexual pleasure from the act. In the end, he'd made the bitch beg for him to take her magic, which she'd probably liked. She was truly twisted in the head. As for Cassius, well, it had been a long time since he'd felt any sort of thrill in the consumption of Bearing magic, Kenzie's included. No, the real euphoria came from imagining himself forcing Julia to beg him to take her magic in the same way. Or screaming for him to stop. Either was acceptable. And all the better if the vision included the World Ruler watching him do it.

His heart gave a deep thump at the thought.

"Cassius?" Kenzie said, pushing herself off the floor.

Bright red blood was dripping from her naked torso, which he supposed she wanted him to remedy. He had the ability of course to turn some of the recently acquired magic back towards her and stitch up the wound, but he still wasn't convinced he was pleased enough with her to keep her alive. He also wanted to keep her wounded a little longer, to reinforce her place.

"Yes, Kenzie," he said, not looking up.

"Wh-what are we doing in Russia?"

Cassius silenced her with an icy glare. She winced, like some sort of beaten dog, and then he thought better of himself. She *was* keeping him alive after all. He owed her some form of courtesy. For now, at least. "You know better than to ask questions," he said, holding his palm out passively towards her.

Kenzie shuffled towards him desperately, pushing her side into his wrist. The sensation of her touch turned his stomach. He released the tiniest bit of magic her way, sufficient to stem the internal bleeding but not enough to remove the pain. He pulled his hand away and wiped it on a starched white napkin. She looked momentarily disappointed, but he wanted her to remember his presence inside of her. Perhaps next time she would think twice before taking liberties with his captives and killing them.

"When we arrive in Russia, you will stay in the jet."

"Don't you want my h—"

"No, Kenzie. I do not need your help for anything more than what you are doing for me behind closed doors. And it will stay that way, until I'm ..."— he paused, roping her in darkly—"satisfied you've met my needs sufficiently."

Her lips contorted into a strange smile, quivering as she spoke. "Yes, master."

"And if at any point during this mission I tell you to leave the country without me, you will go," he said. On second thought, he wouldn't kill the pilot just yet.

"But—"

He shot her a look that ended the conversation. Kenzie nodded, blinking back tears.

"Good. Now clean up this mess and get out of my sight," he said, gesturing to the blood on the floor. She scurried off to gather cleaning supplies without another word. She could have cleaned it up with her magic if she'd had enough left, but she didn't. Kenzie was clearly deluded; he knew that much. But again, needs were what they were. And she'd served a purpose thus far.

Before they landed, he would need time to collect his thoughts ... to plan and then create a contingency plan. He'd never ventured to expand into Russia, for business, pleasure, or otherwise. Nor had he needed to. There was an unspoken understanding between him and the elite men of the world. Much like it was with those that held seats of power in the East, there could be many empires under the sun, so long as they did not get in each other's way.

Plus, none of them were immortal, like Cassius was. Not even close. Despite their boastful proclamations, they could only ever extend their lives. Maybe stave off death. But he would always have the upper hand and could take it if needed. He sensed that, on this trip, it may very well be required. He was to visit the *Smolensk Kremlin*, with its red-brick walls and towers looming high. And there, at last, he would source the Codex. Surely, they would give it over without a fight—there was no way anyone could fathom what it really was, and money was something he could easily provide in transfer.

And if they still didn't budge, he would slaughter them all.

CHAPTER 32

Dom wove his warm fingers between my much cooler ones as we settled in for the two-and-a-half-hour flight between Oslo and Dublin. I knew he still wasn't much of a fan of flying, so I was grateful we had managed to secure a direct flight back to Ireland on short notice. Frankly, after all the effort it had taken to get up there, I was surprised at how quickly we had been ejected from the north. Though kind about it, Solveig had made it plain that our visit was over.

"At least we had a decent meal before we left," Dom said, using his free hand to press the silver button on the armrest, pushing his seat into the reclined position. Solveig had treated us to *fårikål*, a traditional stew made with mutton and cabbage. Dom had absolutely devoured the meal, but I hadn't touched it, likely because of my unease around what we'd learned about Kenzie and Cassius.

But there was still so much we didn't know.

"Do you think you'll sleep?" I asked, but I already knew the answer.

"Not if you don't want me to," he said, already stifling a yawn.

I smiled at him; some things never changed. "No, it's fine. I have a lot on my mind, and I wouldn't mind some time to process things before we touch down. I have a feeling Ronan is going to be like a bug on fly tape as soon as we get back."

"Fly tape?"

"Yeah, those super sticky coils used to catch flies in the summer." I thought of the time a feral cat at Gertie's cottage had accidentally got one plastered to her fur. Gertie would never have left one hanging outside, far too concerned with accidentally catching bees or other helpful pollinators, so it likely belonged to an uninformed neighbour. It was an absolute nightmare trying to remove the sticky strip from a yowling, hissing cat. We were both scratched to ribbons by the time we'd finished. However, she was freed.

"Ah, like a fly in ointment," Dom said, bringing me back to the present.

"Sure ... anyway, what I am trying to say is that Ronan isn't going to let me rest for long before pressing me for details. I could practically feel him breathing down my neck as soon as Solveig started talking about Cassius's plans for Bearers. For Kenzie ... and for me."

Dom shifted his neck into what I assumed was a comfortable position and closed his eyes. "I think you're probably right."

Before long, his body grew still, presumably asleep. Meanwhile, I was left to my own dark contemplation. Much like when I'd visited Bernie, what I had discovered visiting Solveig left me with as many questions about my own magic as answers. In order to locate Kenzie, I would need to tap into the wells somehow, since this seemed to be where my power source originated and a clear thread that connected us as Bearers, even though Kenzie was poisoning the well for the rest of us.

The other challenging discovery was that clearly Cassius had been active over the past several months since he'd gone "dark." We knew he had contact with Kenzie—that much was obvious from the evidence Solveig had uncovered through her searches—and we now suspected he was siphoning off her Bearing magic to feed himself. A part of me wanted to believe she was being forced into it, as I was reminded of the not-so-distant memory of Cassius's spear embedded into my rib cage. How could anyone endure that by choice?

I gagged at the thought, forcing down a regurgitation of the acidic coffee I had foolishly chugged before boarding the flight; some mistakes were smaller than others. And indeed, the fact that I had not stopped Kenzie then and there in the tower in L.A. had been a *big* mistake. Dom knew this fact now too, but he had thankfully remained silent when Solveig let us know the depths to which Kenzie was willing to go to betray all that was good in the world.

By giving herself, and her magic to Cassius.

As was apparently now customary, Morgan had left a car waiting for us at the Dublin airport. Instead of a spritely sports car though, this time it was Dom's green Land Rover. Chilled from being overtired, I couldn't wait to switch on the heated seats and stare out the window while Dom drove us home.

I yawned loudly as he stowed our bags in the back of the vehicle. "You know what I'm looking forward to most tomorrow morning?"

"Breakfast?" Dom said dreamily, pulling me into a hug and kissing my bedraggled hair; as always, I felt disgusting after flying, but he didn't seem to mind.

I laughed, looking up into his tired eyes. "No. I'm looking forward to the sunrise."

"It's January, Julia. The nights are still fairly long, all things considered. And it could rain at any minute."

"But the sun *will* rise," I said, stepping away from him and turning for the passenger door. "And that's something."

His fingers reached for mine, lingering for a second.

"The sun will rise," he repeated finally, and let go. There was something in his tone that left me wondering if he didn't have more on his mind than he was letting on. It almost sounded like a lament.

The sun will rise, with or without us.

"Are you alright?" I asked, buckling my seatbelt as we pulled away from the curb. The airport was busy, despite the late hour. I watched as artificial lights flickered across Dom's face, both streetlamps and headlights from oncoming cars. They strobed the concern that lay plain across his brow.

"Of course, love," he said, giving my thigh a squeeze but not inviting further conversation.

I'd spent the entire flight agonizing over everything we had learned during our visit with Solveig, and it was more than likely he'd done the same. Only for him, it had been done under the guise of sleeping. He tended to do that, folding his arms over his chest and becoming as still as stone as he worked his way through his muddied thoughts. There was no way my body could

345

manage something like that; when I was anxious or thinking through things, I became positively fidgety. I respected the strength of his mind but worried that he was once again holding too much in. He did have a bad habit of that.

We arrived back at *Caisleán na Spéirmhná* close to midnight. The drive had been quiet, with Dom encouraging me to sleep more than once. I'd kept him company, however, as I had never been able to sleep in cars for more than a few moments anyway. We hadn't talked, but the quiet company had felt important as we'd wound our way closer to home.

The January air was cool on our faces as our boots crunched across the drive towards the front door. I noticed immediately that lights were on within, which I supposed wasn't a surprise. Just like delivering the SUV, Morgan would have also prepared the house for our arrival. However, it seemed like far more rooms were illuminated than were necessary.

"Why are there lights on at that end of the house?" Dom asked aloud, his thoughts following a similar trajectory to mine.

"Morgan?" I asked, and he shook his head.

Dom's pace quickened as he took the front steps in one stride. I couldn't imagine there being a sinister reason for the manor house being so awake at this hour, but it was still unusual. Opening the door, we were surprised to hear voices coming from the sitting room. Thankfully, they were instantly familiar.

Ronan and Lennie. And they were fighting.

"I'm telling you right now, this is a terrible idea," Ronan said angrily.

"You would say that, you git," Lennie said, and I could practically hear him rolling his eyes in Ronan's direction.

Despite what felt like a bit of an intrusion, to have guests in our home before we'd even arrived there ourselves, I laughed at the familiar bickering regardless. Dom cleared his throat loudly, making our presence known. The pair in the sitting room grew silent. Then two flushed faces appeared in the doorway, grinning in spite of themselves.

"You're back!" Lennie said. Ronan smiled, though he looked tired.

"We are. And so are you, apparently," Dom said, gesturing towards their unexpected presence in our home.

"Sorry, Dom, we needed somewhere to crash while I helped Ronan," Lennie said, the words sounding unnatural coming from him. A year earlier, I couldn't have imagined those words coming from Lennie sounding casual and familiar. Yet now, it made complete sense. Plus, with everything we'd been learning during our visit with Solveig, it was logical that Lennie and Ronan would convene under the same roof while sharing information. Safer than sending things online, especially after what had happened in L.A.

"So, what's a terrible idea?" Dom asked, an eyebrow raised in reference to their argument. He was apparently used to people dropping into his house at unexpected times, even if he wasn't here. I admired his ability to pivot.

Ronan strode forward to take our bags from us. Though his eyes looked dark, his voice sounded light enough. "Lennie wants to throw a party."

"A party? What for?" I asked, surprised as I set my bag down on the ground before Ronan could take it from me.

Within minutes, we learned that Lennie had been leaning heavily on the Knaves over the past two months as he worked towards locating Kenzie and Cassius. They had also been integral in his healing.

And, it seemed, they wanted to party.

"Some of the Knaves will be in the area this coming weekend—Stuart included. He and Lindsey have been travelling about the U.K., actually, and when I told them you were going to be back soon, well … they've been itching to see you!"

I felt a brief pang of guilt in my belly. I had effectively dropped my budding friendship-by-text with Lindsey over the past weeks. However, I also knew she would be busy with Stu and equally understood what pressure we were under, so she likely wouldn't mind.

"There are other Druids in the area who would likely want to come too," Ronan conceded, looking towards Dom. "If we *were* to throw a party."

I also looked at Dom, trying to get a read on his feelings around the suggestion. No doubt we were both tired from months of travel and craved a rest. I wasn't even sure I was keen on having Lennie and Ronan here at the moment—though Dom seemed alright with it—let alone a house full of Wielders. Still, companionship might also be what I needed right now.

I was met with a flash of brilliant white teeth framed by a mischievous grin. "Oh, I think that sounds grand," Dom said. "A party is *exactly* what we need to blow off some steam. That is, of course, if it's alright with you, Julia?"

I looked between Dom's knowing smile, Lennie's anticipation, and the miserable look pulling on the edges of Ronan's face. I wasn't exactly sure what Dom meant about "blowing off some steam." I certainly didn't feel like I had any extra steam in my tank. But he may have had his own reasons for agreeing to the gathering—group cohesion or something like that. I leaned into that trust, a smile growing on my own face.

"Alright then," I said, taking his hand into mine. "But right now, I just want to go to bed! And no more yelling in my house!" I pointed at the other two men with my free hand, not altogether jokingly.

"Agreed," Dom said, and with that, he turned his back on Lennie and Ronan. In the past, he would have likely joined them for drinks well into the evening, not because he was obligated to but because that was just the kind of person he was: a social creature to a fault. However, I sensed he wasn't up for playing referee tonight.

I followed him quietly up the familiar stairs towards our shared bedroom this time around. We had stayed in the larger middle suite when we'd been here at the end of the 1960s—or at least, so Dom had told me. My memories of that time were still so patchy, even with the photos and clothing he had saved, tucked carefully into two boxes under our decades-empty bed. It had been a bittersweet telling when he'd first taken me in there, sharing that he had slept in there when he was first reborn this time around, but it had been agony between the grief and the loneliness. So, instead, he'd moved himself into another room down the hall while he'd waited for me to resurface once more.

It was *our* room. And I couldn't wait to melt into the sheets beside him.

Reaching the door at long last, we soon collapsed into bed and slept solidly for almost twelve hours straight. We had missed the sunrise, of course, but it rose nonetheless. In spite of everything

---

Over the following week, Dom and I settled seamlessly back into the usual manor-house rhythm. A little over one year ago, I'd arrived in Ireland wide-eyed and terrified of the magics I might encounter within Dom's home. Packed with relics and dripping with memories, it had felt unpredictable, causing constant unease in my belly. Now, however, it felt more like a warm hug. Familiar magics, both old and new, surged from the place, and I felt myself almost immediately begin to settle after so many months on the road.

We had essentially been on the move since we'd left Salt Spring Island over half a year ago. It felt good to be *home*.

However, there were a few slight adjustments.

Lennie had taken to spending his working hours in Dom's study rather than his bedroom while we were away. Dom and I gathered that, since the loss of Wren, he'd likely felt lonelier than he had on previous visits. Dom didn't mind, however. Lennie usually wore noise-cancelling headphones and stuck to himself. He even typed quietly, especially compared to Dom. As for me, I was grateful for Dom to have someone else to talk to besides me; without Ronan to confide in over the past few months, I sometimes felt like he might actually talk my ear off.

"You're sure it's alright we have a gathering here?" Lennie asked one afternoon when the three of us were in the study and Ronan was nowhere to be seen. "It *is* your house, and … I can't help but feel like you agreed only because it would piss Ronan off."

Dom looked up from something he was reading on his own laptop, feigning complete innocence. "What would make you think that?"

"Just a hunch," Lennie said, grinning. "But the Knaves can be—"

"I know how much they like to party, Lennie. It's fine," Dom said, returning a knowing wink.

The dynamic between Lennie and Dom had changed drastically since their voyage into the desert, likely more than either of them had anticipated. In fact, when Ronan had handed Dom his sword upon our return to Ireland, it was to Lennie that Dom's eyes had darted with appreciation and understanding. The sword, and that experience, had changed them both.

"Has Ronan been like this the whole time?" I asked, looking somewhere towards the upstairs.

"He has. We were only here a few days before you arrived, but I've really only seen him in the late hours of the day, after he's hit his limit with work and put back a few drinks before coming down."

"Sounds like you guys have swapped styles, less the drinking," I said, stating the obvious as I set my coffee cup down. It was perhaps a bit of a social overstep, naming it out loud like that. But Lennie didn't seem phased. When I'd first met Lennie, he'd mostly been a recluse. Meanwhile, Ronan had put his best efforts forward to demonstrate how comfortable he was at Dom's estate. Showing off, in fact.

Dom's eyes returned to his screen before affirming my suspicions of his real reasons for agreeing to the gathering. "The party will be good for him. He's wound up like a fucking top."

"That's one way to put it," Lennie said, shaking his head. And then he smiled. "Plus, the party will be good practice for when you finally have your wedding. I assume you'll host it here?"

I had wondered what Lennie's perception of our upcoming nuptials might be, treading lightly around the subject whenever it was breached. I had worried it would dredge up an uncomfortable grief for him, which it might yet, I supposed. In this moment, he seemed to be expressing enthusiasm around the event. He was even smiling.

"Soon, we hope," Dom said, looking at me fondly. And then his face clouded over. "To be completely honest though … I'd hoped we would have sorted the Kenzie problem first."

"Be careful what you wish for," Lennie said, his features darkening now. He put his headphones back on without another word, leaving me and Dom sitting in uncomfortable silence.

♥

"I'm just going pee!" I said to no one in particular and wandered dreamily out of the sitting room and towards the smallest bathroom off the hallway near the kitchen. I could still hear indie rock music from the late noughties blaring loudly behind me as I padded down the hall—one of Lennie's playlists from his university days—and smiled contentedly to myself. It had been a long time since I had attended a party like *this*. Not to mention that the Knaves brought an electrically charged energy that reminded me, sentimentally, of the raucous social gatherings from my early twenties.

I tipsily wiggled my hips to the bassline from a familiar song before closing myself into the washroom. After quick relief, I made for the kitchen to look for a snack, where I unsurprisingly found Dom picking through some of the roast-beef leftovers from dinner with a knife and fork.

He looked up, grinning broadly. "I followed you from the sitting room. And then I ended up here. Go figure. Sandwich?"

"I thought you might," I said, smiling back as I dragged my hand across his butt and joined him on his other side. "Yes, please."

I watched in silence as he diligently topped two white buns with thinly sliced beef and red onions. He slathered mine with extra horseradish and mayonnaise, just the way I liked it. I took in the sight of his muscular forearm, crushing pepper on each bun, with hunger—literal and physical.

"I saw you dancing down the hallway. Did you know that song?" Dom asked before he leaned and gulped back his entire sandwich in two hearty bites before I had even picked mine up.

"I did! I know a lot of them actually—Lennie and I are close to the same age, don't forget. I think we must have been into similar music back in the day." I realized how silly it sounded referencing a time in my recent history as "back in the day" but was pulled from my thoughts by the look on Dom's face. He looked sad. In my inebriated state, I wasn't entirely sure if it was because he was already done his snack or something else entirely.

"What's wrong?" I asked and took his hand in my snack-free one. It was slightly calloused and expectedly warm.

"Oh, it's nothing really. I just get sad sometimes to have missed your twenties this time around. I think we would have had a lot of fun together."

I chewed thoughtfully as I polished off the rest of my own bun almost as quickly as he had; I was hungry too. "While on one hand I think you're probably right, on the other, well … I was a bit of a mess to be honest. I'm not sure you would have been very proud of me all the time."

"I find that impossible to believe," he said and leaned in to sloppily kiss me. He tasted like raw onions, beef, and beer. Pulling away, he spoke again. "I think sometimes I'm actually jealous of other people's nostalgia."

"What are you talking about?" I asked, wiping his spit off my lips with my sleeve. "You have more nostalgic memories than anyone I know."

"True … but there's a lot of tragedy woven into them too." He suddenly stabbed a chunk of beef with his fork and shoved it into his mouth. "I guess I just mean like … the carefree days of your twenties—university classes and kegs, and all that. I just realized tonight that I never really had that … not in the conventional sense anyway."

Dom's manners around eating and talking tonight were reminding me of a version of him from a *long* time ago. I fought back a laugh out of respect for his sad sentiment. "But what about all of those stories you and Ronan have from Cork University? Or, I suppose, that wasn't technically a typical experience. What about in past lives? Surely you chummed it up with peers somehow? I mean, the Druids, they had to have thrown some weird parties."

"Well, there was that," he said, staggering slightly as he barked out a laugh.

"Okay, Dom, how drunk *are* you? You're all over the place right now. I'm having trouble keeping up."

He then ran his hands down my hips. "All over the place, am I?"

"Yes, you are, which I suppose is a pretty accurate portrayal of how these types of parties went … Well, for me anyway."

"Hmm … This part too?" he asked and pressed himself against me just as Ronan wandered into the kitchen. Spotting us entangled next to the beef, Ronan snorted loudly, grabbed another several bottles of wine, and headed back to the party without another word.

"He seems to be doing alright," I said over my shoulder, laughing.

"As expected," Dom replied, looking smug.

"Did you want to go upstairs?"

He raised an eyebrow. "What about somewhere else? You know … keeping in the spirit of inebriated youthful dalliances."

He stumbled through the last three words, and I giggled. "Where do you propose then?"

Dom poked his nose towards the larder. "What about in there?"

"In the pantry?" I shouted. *"Absolutely* not."

"No, not in there, silly. Downstairs! In the cellar …" he said mysteriously, raising an eyebrow and flashing his white teeth.

As far as I knew, the cellar was only used to store spare weapons and dangerous Druidic implements. "Sounds like a good opportunity to get blown up," I said.

"Ah, you're probably right," he said, seemingly resigned to what could only be a more boring location, at least according to the playful slump in his shoulders. He took me by the hand and led me out of the kitchen and down the hall towards the main staircase. Several sets of Knaves and Druids I didn't fully recognize were entwined in the hallway, and we hadn't seen Stuart and Lindsey for at least an hour.

"What was in that *beer?*" I asked, and Dom shrugged happily; he didn't seem to care. A door slammed somewhere above us, no doubt tied to a fit of passion between two or more of our party guests.

"That better not be the door to our room."

Dom laughed. "They wouldn't dare."

He was right. Even though the party had reached a scale far beyond what we had anticipated, the level of respect for Dom, and the home we'd made here together, was still evident. Nothing had been broken, yet everyone seemed to be thoroughly enjoying themselves. I thought back to a bush party I had attended during my summer on the Prairies, where a barbeque had literally been launched into an above-ground pool, and somehow that had only been minor compared to the other damage that ensued.

This was peanuts in comparison.

Dom pulled me out of my reveries and into the cool dark of our bedroom. His breathing was audible, rasping slightly as his drunken passion mounted.

"Now ... where were we?" he asked and immediately began to strip. Despite being very inebriated, he maintained impressive body control.

I followed suit, though far less gracefully. "I think we were talking about how *I* used to act in my twenties."

"Ah. Right ..." he said, approaching me smoothly as our eyes adjusted to the dim room.

"Well, I know, you don't want me to tell you about all of my discarded ex-lovers," I said, hiccoughing, "and there were quite a few of those." I suddenly realized I had spoken out of turn; the statement didn't sound *nearly* as humorous out loud as it had in my head.

Dom fell silent for brief moment. "No, I don't want you to tell me about that," he said softly.

As always, the challenge with mixing alcohol and passion is that the conversation can shift from romantic leanings to hurt feelings at lightning speed. I panicked. "Dom ... I didn't mean that. There weren't that many, truly. And it was a long time ago ... I don't know *why* I said that."

I had no idea why I felt so insecure all of a sudden. Likely, it was mostly the alcohol, with a healthy dose of attachment wounding for good measure.

"Julia, please ..." Dom said, pulling me close to make his meaning quite plain. "It's none of my business. But can we talk about something else? Like how badly I want you in my bed right now?"

I took a steadying breath. "Yes."

Of course, youthful nostalgia had its place, but adult parties, and more importantly, mature love, were *far* more enjoyable in the long run.

The nightmare wasn't particularly clear or long, but it was startling enough to wake me in the middle of the night, tangled in our covers and thrashing. Dom, having indulged in food, drink, and sex following the Knave party, struggled to rouse himself enough to help. I stilled him with my hand—there was nothing he could do, since the vision made so little sense to me anyway. We could discuss it in the morning.

After a few beats, Dom rolled over into a rumbling, still-drunk slumber.

What I had seen was a room full of dead people—dead adult *men*, to be exact. That fact stood out with significance because most of my visions of Cassius's carnage involved young Bearers in lonely hotel rooms.

In this one, Cassius stood as the lone survivor in the centre of a large hall, arms outstretched and covered in blood from polished shoe to pinstriped chest. His face was hidden, but I could almost feel his wrath through the dream as he slowly cleaned the blood from his fingers with a soiled handkerchief. This group of men had made him *seriously* angry.

I could glean little from Cassius's surroundings to pinpoint where exactly he was. But if I had to guess, it wasn't anywhere near us. There was a distinctly Old World vibe to the furniture and finishings, oddly ornate and significantly dated. Gold-trimmed chairs lined the edges of the room, their red-velvet upholstery disguising the sheer volume of the blood that had been spilled at the hands of the Sorcerer.

Once those same hands were satisfactorily clean, Cassius moved from the room like a ghost, leaving yet another trail of bodies in his wake.

And that was all I saw.

CHAPTER 33

Besides my brief-yet-graphic nightmare, the next two months passed by without a single sighting of Cassius or Kenzie. Not that I was complaining exactly. Since Graham and Sean had lost track of him—or rather, the long trail of bodies he'd left behind—at the beginning of the year, there hadn't been a single scrap of news. This meant that, while we wouldn't be able to fully rest until they were located, or more specifically *defeated*, we also got to experience the immense relief of being still for a time.

To just breathe.

I was overjoyed to spend yet another early spring at the manor house, as this time around felt wholly different. I was constantly reminded of where we had been roughly twelve months previously, when Peggy had nudged me towards the lost wells, and just how lost I had been. I still felt disoriented in some regards—being hunted by a dark Sorcerer had that effect on a person—but at least I was aware of my own path now. The wheel of the year was remarkable to witness, and I felt instant gratitude to greet another February and March with Dom by my side.

We'd spent the better part of the last *many* months stuck in airports or sleeping in unfamiliar beds; apart from the weekend party unwinding with the Wielders, I was still thoroughly and frayed. Dom was too, though he showed the strain less than I did.

No matter how mentally exhausted he was, he seemed to always have boundless physical energy to burn. Whether he did that by regularly checking our perimeter defences on his daily runs or going over combat strategies with whichever Druid or Knave was rotating through that week, Dom had remained thoroughly active since our return. I felt sure that, between the existing enchantments on the manor house and my own subconscious protective spells that seemed to extend to anyone who was around me in any place I called home, we were relatively safe for the time being, without the addition of all the safety checks and battle practice.

Still, Dom had insisted he stay in peak physical condition. Something about the time he had spent with the desert Knaves had stuck with him. The rigours and hardness of his old training habits had re-emerged, possibly more than was necessary.

"Are you sure you've got to go?" I had asked him early one foggy morning at the beginning of March. "It's so spooky out."

He had laughed but continued to pull on his joggers and pullover. "And when exactly do you think the bad guys come out?"

I dove under the covers, hiding from said bad guys. I'd expected him to dive under the bedding behind me, but when I re-emerged, he was gone.

I hadn't felt nearly as inclined to follow such a rigorous training schedule, though I *had* been joining Dom for routine dagger practice and on some of his shorter jogs when the mood struck. I had also become much better about connecting with my Bearing magic each day, mostly through meditation or regular visits to the wellspring. Our time on the West Coast, so close to (and in) the ocean, had taught me that frequent exposure was necessary to connect to myself. A positive result of this activity was that the tangled magical energy I had once felt around the manor house was almost non-existent now. That was a definite plus. A negative was that I still hadn't managed to hone the skills Solveig had taught me well enough to locate Kenzie.

More than once, I travelled down to the wellspring and returned empty handed. I wondered in part if this wasn't because of the sheer mental exhaustion I felt; perhaps I didn't really *want* to spring into action and find her just yet, which made me feel guilty. However, knowing what we did now about Cassius feeding off her, it was likely that, wherever he was, so was she. And if *that* were the case, he would likely be shrouding her from any attempted sight anyway. Solveig had relayed that she hadn't seen her as of late either, which was concerning.

In fact, even my nightmares had been cleared of Cassius's usual sinister Bearer-murdering activities, which likely meant he was getting precisely what he needed from her. While I was deeply grateful that there were likely fewer Bearers currently being harvested by him, and the fact that I was sleeping *far* better than usual, it was repulsive to think about Kenzie giving her inner magics away to him in such a way.

It was an utter betrayal.

Late on the afternoon of the spring equinox, which fell on March twentieth this year, Dom and I found ourselves in the sitting room, chatting about nothing in particular. We had spent the morning outside, preparing and turning soil over in what would hopefully become a small veggie patch off the back of the house. Dom was determined that we get to plant at least some kind of garden this time around. I agreed wholeheartedly.

With dirt under my nails and my body settled from the day's tasks, I began to doze off on the couch while Dom nattered on about something Lennie had sent him about cryptocurrency; Dom apparently wasn't a fan of the idea.

We both jumped when his cellphone went off.

"Speak of the devil," Dom said into the phone, and I waited for a few moments as he and Lennie exchanged their usual greetings.

"What do you mean he's been in *Russia* this whole time?" Dom said loudly into the receiver. He rolled his eyes once and then snorted, placing his hand over the receiver to speak to me. "Apparently Lennie isn't even allowed in Russia. Not well liked by Russian authorities, so he's had to find other means to collect the intel. *That's* why it's been so hard to find him."

"Figures," I said, unsurprised. My mind instantly went to the countless Russian oligarchs who were undoubtedly in line, or in competition, with Cassius.

"Where is Kenzie though?" Dom asked, quickly growing impatient with Lennie. Some things never changed.

I wandered anxiously over to the buffet across from us in the sitting room and fiddled with some of the barware situated on top. I wasn't really in the mood for a drink but thought Dom might be after this call.

"England!" Dom yelled. "You're fucking kidding me! What's she doing in *England?*"

"All done feeding Cassius?" I suggested as I gagged audibly. Dom shot me a look; this really wasn't the moment for jokes.

"For *fuck's* sakes!" he said into his phone, slamming his fist down on the arm of the couch and causing the bag of beef jerky he'd been snacking from to cascade to the floor. Thankfully, it was empty. "And where are *you* right now?"

Several moments passed, during which I assumed Dom was receiving a lecture from Lennie about location privacy over the phone or some other modern concept that apparently eluded him, at least according to Lennie.

I turned my mind towards a group tally.

Several days after the January house party, the unknown Knaves and Lennie had disembarked once more for an undisclosed amount of time, presumably to visit other allies on their European tour. Their *actual* destination and the members of their group had remained vague, however. As far as I knew, Alanna and Shereen had remained in Washington, though Lennie had invited them more than once. They said they would come for the wedding hopefully but had business to attend to in Washington. Stuart and Lindsey, meanwhile, had set up camp in Scotland for the time being and weren't part of the travelling party. Apparently, Stuart had made a connection at a forge in Scotland and was "conducting research." As far as the other Druids went, Thomas and Peggy had mostly stayed in England since our return, though they had surprised us with a visit several weekends ago. Sean and Graham were still AWOL, as far as we knew, which was apparently a good thing.

Regrettably, Ronan had elected to stay with us instead of joining the others. He had resigned from his position at UBC, or so he told us, so he was effectively unemployed for the time being. He hadn't seemed particularly disappointed though, and after the Knaves left, he even began to emerge from his room somewhat more frequently, evidently preferring their absence. Still, he hadn't been fully himself, which was causing Dom undue stress. Even now, Ronan was nowhere to be seen. It was probably for the best though; Dom needed time to think without his friend glowering at him.

He ran his free hand through hair several times before speaking again. "Fine. I get it. And how quickly can you gather everyone together?" Another pause. *"Grand."*

Hanging up the phone with some difficulty, Dom stood and rolled his shoulders back several times. I handed him a glass of whisky, which he threw back with enthusiasm before speaking once more.

"She's in England,"

"Yes, I gathered as much."

He gave me a withering look. "The problem is that Lennie's lost her again. She came through Heathrow this morning, but she's disappeared off the map again. Sean and Graham have apparently gone off book trying to find her though."

"Off book?" I asked, thoroughly perplexed. "Wait. Are Sean and Graham back ... um ... *online?*" I had no idea what the correct term was for this circumstance.

Ronan spoke suddenly from the doorway, causing us both to jump for a second time. "They're back in England too? Sean and Graham? They lost track of Cassius months ago and have been tucking tail ever since—"

"Is Lennie in England too?" I asked, interrupting Ronan and looking to Dom.

Dom exhaled loudly through his nostrils. Despite being the one who had taken the call and had the answers, he was frustrated that *we* weren't keeping up. *"Yes,* they're all in England. Somewhere. Lennie's hopeful Sean and Graham have dropped out of contact again because they have a lead on Kenzie. He says it's likely they will turn something up within the next several hours."

Ronan wandered across the room to pour himself a drink. He looked visibly ill today, and I wasn't entirely sure that whisky was the right medicine for Doctor Gallagher.

"So ... what's the plan then?" I asked, eyeing Ronan warily as I sat down in my usual spot empty handed.

"For now, we wait," Dom said, spreading his long fingers across his thighs as he leaned back on the couch. "Lennie's going to gather everyone together at a safe-house—Stuart and Lindsey are coming down too—and then I don't know, but we'll have to be ready to act quickly when the time comes."

I looked at him with concern.

"Our allies are completely capable, Julia. We have to trust they can pull this together with us over here."

Ronan snorted but said nothing as he stared at Dom, who was blatantly ignoring him.

"That's not what I'm worried about," I said, "but what does capable *mean*, exactly?" I was trying to decipher the unspoken conversation going on between Ronan and Dom while keeping up with everything else going on, but no one answered me.

As was usual these days, the undercurrents between the two Celts were far more tumultuous than what the two were showing on the surface; they still hadn't really reconciled.

Dom's phone went off several more times. As he checked his messages, I looked out the front window for a moment towards where I knew the closest wellspring existed, beyond the copse of trees. I felt a sudden pull from deep inside.

"Maybe I can try what Solveig taught me again," I said quietly. "The need feels greater than usual."

Ronan raised both dark eyebrows as Dom looked up abruptly from his phone. "Do you think you could give it a try? Lennie's apparently already got us booked on a flight out of Galway tonight. Just in case." He poked the screen once as if to prove the fact.

"Uh … yes, I suppose so. Wait—fly out tonight? Doesn't that feel a bit … hasty?"

"The lad's bound and determined to catch her within the next twenty-four hours or die trying. Especially since she's separated from Cassius. This might be our only shot. And I have to say, I agree with him—well, not the dying part—but …"

A familiar, mournful look crossed Dom's face as we both recalled the loss of Wren, and its effect on Lennie. I too wanted Kenzie snuffed out, but my hatred for what she had become didn't override my wish for the safety of my friends, or my lover. It could be a trap.

"I understand," I said, somewhat reluctantly. "Let's give the wells another shot first."

Ronan rolled his eyes but didn't object.

MANTLE OF THE WORLD RULER

Within the hour, I found myself marching across the grounds towards our hidden wellspring, Dom and Ronan in tow. I knew that Sully and Mags were with Morgan, but Oisín, of course, trailed along behind Dom like a ghost. The sun was low now, with the air cooling steadily towards evening. I felt the hair on the back of my neck raise.

"Do you think you'll be needing anything from us at all, Julia?" Dom asked as we made our way closer to the familiar copse of trees.

"No. But I do think it'll be good to have a lookout. I'm not one hundred percent sure if I'll stay ... well, *present*, during the experiment."

Admittedly, I was hopeful that if I could locate Kenzie somehow using Solveig's method, it would buy us some time for a more rational plan. Both Lennie and Dom had personal axes to grind. Big ones. It was understandable, but I worried that this was spurring things on faster than was necessary. And I also wasn't keen on taking a risk when it came to any of our lives for the likes of her.

"What exactly do you plan to do here, Julia?" Ronan asked as we reached our destination. He dropped his bag down to the earth, evidently having felt it necessary to bring protective pouches and medicaments for our small journey. However, if any part of the Druid within him was curious about what I was about to do, it was being overridden by some other, far more grumpy entity standing in its place.

"Ronan ..." Dom said irritably, effectively silencing his friend. The pair had instinctively stopped in their tracks several paces behind me where the land sloped upward towards the manor house, and I was grateful for the space. It also happened to be the last dry patch of grass, which was maybe the real reason they'd halted.

"I'm just hoping for a little luck," I said to no one in particular and wandered closer to the wellspring on my own. I had yet to achieve what Solveig had taught me in Vardø, so I was leaning into the trust around her theories; my own untrained, wild abilities; and the urgent need to locate Kenzie, now that we knew she was separated from Cassius.

Admittedly, it was asking a lot.

Pushing back the green woollen hood of my jacket, I knelt carefully onto the damp earth surrounding the edge of the wellspring. The knees of my jeans were instantly soaked, but I had the sense that this would only increase my chances of success, as if it were part of the ritual. Before me, several pools of groundwater swelled up gradually from the earth, bubbling gently as they rose from their subterranean streams.

Welcoming me back.

Dipping only my fingertips in at first, I carefully felt for any of the signs of the connectedness Solveig had primed me on. As instructed, I reached into my Bearing core, seeking out the heart places of those who shared my lineage ... the hidden Witches of the world, who laid in wait for their own calls to destiny. I attempted to dial in, riding my own frequency as I visualized connecting to the land, not working against the signals but *with* them.

And I felt nothing. *Fuck.*

This was as far as I'd ever made it when coming here: a healthy connection to the wellspring but never more. I thought of the new Prophecy, considering the line specifically referencing the lost wells.

> *To reveal the lost wellspring, the Sun and Moon must accept their fate.*
> *When the Celt accepts the mantle, the Crone too shall find her strength.*

Surely, Dom and I had accepted our fate, hadn't we? Or at least, we were damn well trying to. We'd done what we'd needed to do when it came to separating—he to the desert and me to Berkeley. It was possible Dom still hadn't *fully* accepted his role as the World Ruler, but from what I could glean about his time in the desert and beyond, he was a hell of a lot further along than when we'd first heard the new Prophecy.

As for me, my abilities might be growing slowly, if not unpredictably, but I *was* feeling stronger every day. I'd learned in Big Sur that *how* my Bearing magic would manifest came down to me and what I wanted, a matter of both intuition and intention. And what I wanted right now was to locate Kenzie.

Come ON ...!

Throwing caution to the wind, I plunged my hands entirely into the frigid water, begging for help from all those who had gone before me. I called loudly from my innermost centre outward through the wells and heard the echo across the realm. I thought of Bernie, and the vision she had created for me of my path—the past, present, and future ... the rivers that connected all of us, and the power of the tides.

The world seemed to pause around me. No birds sang, and no wind brushed on my cheeks. I could sense Dom and Ronan behind me, but they too were completely still within my shadow. I held my breath, hoping, wishing ... And then at last, I felt a shift.

At first, the vibration was only slight, almost like I was shivering, but it wasn't coming from within. Then I felt a growing energy running through the water at my fingertips and up into my arms, pulsing through my being with increased intensity. Through the water, I could already sense countless Bearers throughout the realm, some quite near, others very far. My breath caught as I began to take in the vastness of the threads connecting us all, the greatest, most immense weaving of all. In my mind's eye, I could almost see a web of nodes—evidence of our innate connectivity. It was almost more than I could fathom.

Looking up all around me, I saw that individual droplets of water were fast forming into a thick globe, swirling violently and much more solidly than any of the glittering crystalline droplets I had accidentally created in the past.

This time, it felt intentional ... and powerful.

"Julia!" I heard Dom cry out from the slope.

I knew I must be completely obscured from their view now, but that was precisely as it was meant to be. This was my connection to the wells and mine alone. I had this in the bag.

I steadied his worries with a quick Send. It was almost effortless and came from my heart. I guess practice did make perfect—either that or I was learning not to fight my own magic anymore and to just let it come as I needed it.

"Dom, I'm fine."

He fell silent, and I felt rather than saw his body calm in response. Beside him, Oisín rested his head on his paws.

At a distance, however, I still could sense Ronan's agitation as he muttered something ancient under his breath. He was attempting an incantation. Suddenly, I felt laughter rise to my throat, but it wasn't my own.

"He's trying to talk to us," a twinkling voice said.

"But it's not the Druid's time," said another, bright with laughter.

"When will he ever learn?" a third uttered, as if to shake its head in jest.

Strangely, the voices were actually speaking through me—with the lost voices of the wells. Ancient Bearers, perhaps, women and Witches of old. Somehow, I knew that they represented something far older and far greater than any being I had encountered in any of my lifetimes. These were the inhabitants of the Otherworld. Soon their laughter died, and they quickly began telling a vivid story of loss: Kenzie's story.

The first voice spoke. *"He's used her. Poisoned her. And he will soon discard of her."*

Another voice replied, sounding fearful. *"This isn't going to end well for her ... but there's no turning back from what she's done."*

The third sounded angry. *"He already knows too much ... You have to end this."*

"Where is she now? How can we stop her?" I asked, then paused to rejig my question, surprised at my own compassion. "Can we ... help her?"

"You must strip her of her magic, before he learns the truth."

"She's made her choice; it cannot be helped."

"Bring her under your power. The rest is destiny."

"Strip her of her Bearing magic? Bring her under my power?" I was starting to panic at the thought. "How is any of that even possible?"

As much as I hated Kenzie, I hated the idea of removing another Bearer's agency more. In fact, at this point, I felt like it would be easier emotionally to kill her outright. Stripping her of her magic felt like sacrilege.

The first voice spoke quietly. *"We'll give you the gift. Just this once."*

The second added sweetly, *"You bear the strength for this, young one."*

The third, with love, said, *"We believe in you."*

Hot tears streamed down my face at the fresh pain of knowing what I must do next. I also wept for the love *they* bore for me. I could feel the voices surround me, soothing gently as the agony of what must come next settled into my reality.

I was held. And always had been.

"What will happen to her ... after?" I asked through my sobs.

There came no answer, but I felt something heavy land somewhere in the middle of my chest, and hot metal around the back of my neck. Looking down, I saw that I now wore a stone amulet. Something like obsidian. It was smooth and round, bound together by what looked like hot copper wire, which burned my flesh. However, the amulet cooled rapidly once in contact with my skin, the metal of the gem's casing and chain around my neck turning dark black to match the stone.

I knew then what I would have to do.

Reaching out once more towards the wells, searching for those who had spoken through me, I found that the connection was severed. Soon, I could feel the orb of water thinning around me until finally it resembled only a light mist. Turning around, I saw Dom sitting placidly on the grass, waiting as he always did for me to return.

Ronan, meanwhile, was nowhere to be seen.

"Hello, love," Dom said, getting to his feet. He loped down the hill towards me to help me up.

"How long was I gone?" I asked as I got to my feet. I was completely soaked and no doubt would soon feel the damp sinking into my bones.

"Not long," he said. "Thank you for the Send though. It made waiting a lot easier."

I nodded, placing my slightly shaking hand on the newly placed amulet. It was still warm to the touch, a bold contrast to my chilled body. "It didn't really work like Solveig thought it would, but ... I know how we can defeat Kenzie now, once we find her."

Dom looked down at the stone before giving me a knowing glance in return. "A gift from the Otherworld."

I gave him a curious look, eager to find out if his experiences had been anything like mine, but just then, Ronan came crashing through the thicket from the north. Apparently, he'd been circling it on repeat since I'd gone under cover.

"I told you he was weird about the Otherworld," Dom said under his breath.

"Julia! What did they tell you?" Ronan asked, guessing correctly what had happened. Or perhaps he had sensed their presence. Either way, this felt like a full three-sixty from his moody skepticism earlier.

I contemplated for a moment telling him what they had said about it not yet being his time, whatever that meant. But then my intuition, and the overwhelming urge to be somewhere warmer, overrode any such thought patterns. I understood now why Dom had been so hesitant to share any of this type of thing with Ronan; it just felt misguided, almost like it would bring him bad luck ... ill fortune. I also knew I couldn't show Ronan the amulet.

"I know how we can defeat her," I said, feeling my body shivering more violently with each passing moment, chilled and suddenly on the brink of exhaustion. "But it can't involve killing her."

"Well, that's not very helpful if we still have no idea where she is!" Ronan said, not bothering to contain his frustration.

Dom spoke then, looking up from his cellphone with a mingled look of surprise, anticipation, and fury. "Actually, *we do.*"

CHAPTER 34

Running his hand through his hair once more, Dom looked from Julia to Ronan and then back to Julia as urgency flooded his system. He felt hot and cold all at once, his mind spinning as he waited for the call to go through. Infuriatingly, the phone still rang several times before Lennie answered.

"You've got her then?" he shouted as soon as Lennie picked up. Dom was still standing on the slope between Ronan and Julia, but his body and mind were already poised and ready to spring into action. Before him, Julia was shivering like a leaf, soaked from head-to-toe from her recent transcendence. A voice at the back of Dom's thoughts was urging him to get her inside as soon as possible. Still, he persisted with the phone call. It was of the utmost importance that they knew the facts. Fast. "How did you manage it?"

"Graham and Sean. The bloody bastards … *They did it!*" Lennie replied, sounding like he was still in shock himself.

Dom learned that, between the last time he and Lennie had spoken and Julia's soggy convergence with the Otherworld, Sean and Graham had successfully tracked, captured, *and* effectively incapacitated Kenzie in Gloucestershire. Lennie's best guess was that they had intercepted her on the way to one of Cassius's known estates in the county, where she'd likely been waiting for him. But Lennie still didn't have all the details of *how* Sean and Graham had actually managed it. Not that it was entirely important right now. However, the general belief was that, since she was not currently under protection—Cassius still being in Russia—they could keep her subdued for a short time without being hunted too viciously.

Those circumstances were bound to change. And quickly.

"Do you have a safe-house you can take her to until we arrive?" Dom asked as he, Julia, and Ronan headed back up the slope, in an aggravatingly slow pace, and across the grounds towards the manor house. He would have liked to make the trip at a sprint and gathered details once he had his desk and computer in front of him—no doubt Lennie would be sending details soon—but Julia seemed to be struggling with her drenched clothes and shaking limbs, so instead, he wrapped his arm around her, silently hoping it was just the cold affecting her and not some other force she was struggling with.

Lennie continued on the other end of the line. "That's the problem. We don't. Sean has her stuffed into an enchanted box in the back of an unmarked van on the side of the road right now—don't worry, she's not conscious for any of it, and there's plenty of air; he's made sure of that—though I don't know what kind of state she's in. But there are Wraiths crawling absolutely everywhere. We're stuck for now."

"*Yer man* Sean's got a dark side it would seem," Dom said to Ronan out of the side of his mouth. Ronan didn't look the least bit surprised.

"Dom, there's another problem," Lennie said, pulling Dom's attention back towards the conversation at hand. "I'm just not sure we can bring you and Julia into the country safely right now, not with any expediency, anyway. It's what they will be expecting. And my intelligence says that they are watching every access point with increased security. I'm guessing that means they've already noticed she's missing. That *Cassius* has noticed."

"What do you propose to do with her then?" Dom asked, hesitant to hear the answer. In truth, he was concerned Lennie would soon take matters into his own hands regardless of what Dom said, when this was clearly, as Julia would put it, "Bearers' business."

"Well ... I *propose* we kill her outright. Obviously. After we torture some details out of her. I can get to them within the hour and do it myself," Lennie said, his voice strangely detached and dripping with malcontent. "Frankly, Dom, the only reason we haven't killed her yet is out of respect for your leadership. And the fact that she's Julia's kin. We thought it prudent that it be your call. But with that being said …"

Dom recognized the profound rage he could hear growing in Lennie's voice; he knew it all too well himself. A deep, dark part of him wished he could hop on a plane and kill Kenzie himself, using only his bare hands as he tore her limb from limb. He had developed an almost unhealthy thirst for revenge over the years—having your lover murdered or tortured in front of you repeatedly throughout the ages had that effect on a man. However, those same years of experience had also taught him that this type of revenge was just that: unhealthy.

Besides, Julia had expressed that there was another plan, directly from the source. He knew better than to dispute the Sovereign or the command of the Otherworld (and in that particular order too).

"You can't kill her," Dom said flatly.

"What? Of course, we're going to kill her!" Lennie exclaimed.

"It's not that I won't let you, but that you can't. Julia's found another way to deal with her," Dom said, the strength of command growing in his voice; this wasn't up for discussion.

Lennie spoke low, spitting the words through his teeth. "Let's just say, for argument's sake, that we can somehow connect the two of you with Kenzie. What then?"

"I told you, Julia's found another way. She's got this. You have to trust me," Dom said, doing his best to sound calm. They had reached the manor house at last, and he was anxious to get Julia inside.

There was a pause on the other end of the line.

"Lennie …" Dom growled.

"Fine. We'll bring her to you. But this is on *your* head if she escapes." Lennie hung up without another word.

Just then, Julia collapsed into a heap on the entranceway floor before them. Dom immediately launched himself to her side as Ronan followed suit, looking quite worried himself, and he knew then he wasn't alone in hoping this new plan wasn't a colossal mistake.

By the grace of the gods, Julia remained unharmed.

The combined effect of the intense magics she had encountered down at the wellspring bringing deep chill to her bones, followed by the strain of the walk and the sudden heat of the manor house had effectively driven her into what she had dubbed a "forced shutdown." Blearily, she had described it as if she had "just downloaded some new software from the Otherworld" and needed to restart her system before she could actually use it properly. "Or something."

Surprisingly, Ronan had laughed at this statement as he took her pulse where she lay in Dom's lap on the middle of the entrance floor. "That's a creative way of stating that your body went into shock, darlin'."

Dom was slightly arrested by the tone of affection he heard in Ronan's voice. But he chose to ignore it.

Julia smiled at the pair of them before leaning back into Dom's lap and closing her eyes, taking several deep breaths. "I'm alright, boys. Don't worry. *I've got this.*"

Dom appreciated her echoed sentiment to what he had told Lennie on the phone only minutes earlier and brushed her hair back affectionately. She was so breathtakingly beautiful, even now with her hair askew and smelling like damp wool and bog water. Dom was darkly reminded of the last time the three of them had found themselves in this same position. That was when Cassius had shoved his "Spear of Longinus" into Julia's ribs just before they had discovered her on the floor of the auditorium in Leeds, covered in vomit and blood. Thankfully though, this time she seemed completely sound, random computer references notwithstanding.

And in that instance as much as now, Ronan had been unwaveringly loyal to the pair of them. He felt a surprising rush of gratitude for his friend's steadfast care.

"Let's get you upstairs into the bath," Dom suggested but looked to Ronan for his confirmation that this was the correct course of action.

"A bath is a good idea," Ronan said. "Not too hot though. Warm it up slowly. And then I suppose we will need to prepare for their arrival. How did you say they were getting here?"

"I didn't," Dom said, helping Julia to her feet. She made a noise that sounded a lot like *"blegh,"* but he was pretty sure she was just being her usual silly self in the face of adversity. She still seemed slightly unsteady, but he would have no trouble in getting her upstairs; he would throw her over his shoulder if he had to.

Ronan shrugged at the both of them and turned heel towards the kitchen. No doubt, while he and Julia got themselves sorted, Ronan would be delving into the Druid stores in the cellar under the kitchen for anything that might keep Kenzie subdued and contained long enough for Julia to work her magic. Gods willing.

Dom switched on the light in their shared bathroom, guiding Julia in with a gentle hand on her lower back. He was afraid she was going to fall again, though she seemed steady enough. She was unusually quiet as she slowly stripped off her clothes, accepting his help when her soggy jeans jammed around her legs. This was hardly the moment for sex. He knew that. Yet, his body had other ideas as she peeled off the layers, a deep ache forming in his lower abdomen, throbbing all the way from the base of his cock through to his backside. Removing her t-shirt and bra in one movement, she briefly exposed her pert nipples to him before turning towards the bathtub, cranking on the tap.

His chest pounded in brazen want, but then he froze. The amulet, which she had shown him only briefly after her visit to the wells, had burned harsh marks into her skin where it lay.

"Julia …"

She turned to him slowly once more as the steam rose behind her. Even now, she looked like a goddess. "It's alright, Dom, really. I'm *alright*."

Her skin was all shades of flushed—pink, red, blue, and purple—as she stepped into the bath. He was reminded strongly of past versions of her—the ones where her body had experienced far harsher day-to-day realities. Taught and strained, scarred and worn, she'd always been remarkably beautiful but also hardened by each of the repeated lives she'd lived. Much like he had been, though arguably he'd been lucky to be reborn as a prime version of himself each time. It felt unfair sometimes, that she had to endure an unpredictable lifetime before he arrived.

"Your skin …" he said, kneeling down beside the tub, unsure what to do with the information presenting itself before him.

"Don't touch it. It's—"

In his mind's eye, he'd grown accustomed to Julia's body in the now—well fed and clear skinned. Supple like a fresh peach. She wasn't marked with many scars, apart from a few childhood scrapes and Cassius's spear, though he knew all too well that not all wounds were visible to the naked eye.

"It will scar," he said, matter of fact as he dunked a washcloth into the warm water.

"I know," she said.

He wiped her arms gently, carefully avoiding the burnt flesh around her neck and chest. Once they'd dealt with Kenzie, he would have Ronan attend to the burns properly; it wasn't lost on him that she'd not shown Ronan the amulet yet.

"Dom, you're staring at me," she said, looking up at him from the bath with those big, beautiful eyes.

"You can't blame me, love. You're a vision."

She smiled, but it didn't reach her eyes. He could tell that the weight of the dark amulet was heavy on her shoulders. He wondered what type of strings had come with its gifting and whether the voices in the Otherworld had told her of the stakes. He didn't dare ask though. Julia seemed to be straddling worlds even from where she sat, a precarious balance he knew all too well. She deserved this moment of peace.

He reached into the water and took her hand, kissing the engagement ring he had placed on her finger. "I am so proud of you."

She pushed her forehead into his hand, silent words flowing between them. But then his phone went off. Standing slowly, Dom dried his hands on a soft towel before turning his back to her to check his messages. It was from Lennie:

It's go time.

It turned out Kenzie would be arriving by helicopter. Lennie had worked his *other* magic and procured a private charter on demand. However, when it came to who would be *paying* for the flight, Lennie made it plain that the astronomical cost would land squarely on Dom's shoulders. He had agreed without argument.

Dom absolutely hated the idea of bringing Kenzie to Ireland, let alone anywhere near their home. Yet, it seemed like the safest course of action, particularly when it came to taking advantage of both the enchantments of the estate and Julia's own subconscious protection spells that she wove anywhere they went. The last thing they needed was a horde of Wraiths descending on them. Not to mention that Julia worked best when she felt most connected to water or wells and a sense of place.

"Are you absolutely sure you can maintain the integrity of Kenzie's container *and* perform the ritual at the same time?" Ronan asked Julia as the three of them drove cross-country towards the landing site. They had piled into Dom's older Land Rover; he owned two, but this one was far sturdier for the cross-country job. Ronan had scoffed, preferring the newer, flashier model.

"I'm sure," she said, sounding irritated in the passenger seat. Dom didn't blame her. Ronan had asked some iteration of the same question at least ten times over the last hour. She pulled out her compass and placed it on her knee. It was completely still.

Dom had no idea what that meant, but he felt his own protectiveness growing around her. "She's got this, Ronan," he said over his shoulder to where Ronan sat bouncing around in the back. He didn't bother containing his frustration. "We just need to make sure she isn't interrupted."

And indeed, they would have their hands full on that front.

Due to the nature of helicopters, landing it safely would require an open and ultimately *exposed* place. This made sense from a completely non-magical viewpoint, of course. However, they would be dealing heavily in magic if this was going to go off without a hitch.

Even though the entirety of the estate was protected on some level, there were simply more opportunities for breaches the further they got from the house. The "security system," at least to Dom's best understanding, worked like a spiral with the house at its core. Therefore, the further you got, the weaker the defences were. The Druids had "installed" it when he'd bought the place, weaving it into the earth itself so it was self-sufficient, and it had proven impenetrable so far. However, the field in question was located across the estate, away from the manor house, which was definitely outside of the tighter protection spiral and so would need reinforcement.

And then, of course, they had to consider the situation from above as well.

In order to actually land, Ronan would need to create a precise rift in their defences just long enough for the helicopter to touch down temporarily and then take off again, the rift sealing firmly behind it. All of them had been in complete agreement on this front. Before they even *considered* approaching Kenzie in her container, they needed as much protection in place as possible.

There could be absolutely no possibility of escape.

It would require precise timing, but Dom knew that if anyone could pull it off, it would be Ronan. The plan was that, as soon as they arrived, Ronan would work to further fortify the area from Wraiths, and Dom would help Julia prepare for what she had to do next. Because of the helicopter's night-time arrival, they also brought floodlights and a generator, to briefly mark their location.

Julia had said she required only the cover of darkness.

They heard the helicopter before they saw it.

Julia pressed her head firmly into his chest before the pair of them walked to the edge of the field, well clear of the landing zone. "Dom, please forgive me for what I'm about to do," he thought she said, though it was hard to hear her.

Puzzled, Dom spoke loudly over the growing noise. "Forgive you for *what?*"

She shook her head once, clearly not wanting Ronan to overhear. "Just know that this is what *they* have commanded. It's … it's just what has to be done," she said, barely audible over the ever-growing *chop, chop, chop* from above.

"Of course, love. I trust you entirely," he said, taking care to express the sentiment clearly on his face as well, just in case his words were lost in the noise.

Julia returned his gaze, though her eyes were dark. He couldn't tell for sure, but she seemed to be shifting somehow. Like an ancient power was seated inside. She didn't look afraid. Not exactly. What was striking, however, was how much *older* she looked—and not in the sexy aging-into-your-thirties way he had been enjoying over the past year either. This was wholly different. Even since they had left home, something had changed in her demeanour. It had been gradual at first, but now that he looked at her, he could easily see the physical strain on her body. She was moving almost as if her life was being drained before his very eyes.

"Julia, that amulet …" he began to say, but he knew she wouldn't hear him. He regretted not voicing his concerns earlier while she'd still been in the bath.

He felt fear coldly grip his chest. What unnamed cost had this amulet brought with it? If she didn't use it against Kenzie, would the same magics be turned against her? This version of Julia wasn't as versed in the Otherworld as her past selves, let alone in comparison to what *he* knew about that place. Along with the fear, he now felt a disgusting rush of guilt in his chest for all he had neglected to share with her about it. Dealings with the Otherworld rarely came without consequence.

But there was no time for that now.

The helicopter was now in sight, blinking its red and green lights.

Immediately upon their arrival, Ronan had busied himself with protection incantations and what looked like about twenty-five different pouches, which he hurled this way and that. The entire field smelled like a bloody potpourri before he finally threw up his hands, out of both pouches and ideas.

"It's the best I can do," he had said, joining them on the sidelines.

Looking up, Dom swallowed deep. What would be would be.

Dom nodded gratefully while Julia threw him a quick thumbs up. At least she still retained some part of who she was. His silly fiancée. With the three of them now standing at the edge of the clearing, it felt like they were awaiting the arrival of a supernatural bomb, which would need to be dismantled quickly before it inevitably detonated. He didn't like the feeling at all.

Lennie had texted him about fifteen minutes before with the basic logistics. Kenzie was still being held in a container, which Dom imagined to be something like a shipping crate. On the helicopter were Lennie, Sean, Graham, and as it turned out, Stuart and Lindsey as well. He hadn't realized they'd made it down in time, but no doubt Graham had called in Lindsey

375

as soon as they knew they were about to make the catch. Dom felt relief at this. Stuart and Lindsey would be immensely helpful on the ground if things turned and a hoard of Wraiths arrived. Frankly, he hadn't seen a better pair of fighters in years.

He turned his attention towards Ronan, who was now staring at Julia with a look of deep concern and suspicion. She, meanwhile, was standing with her chin to the sky, her eyes closed, and her arms extended slightly downward beside her.

A power stance if he had ever seen one. Sovereign. Goddess. Queen.

Ronan turned his dark gaze on Dom, shouting, "What exactly does she plan to do to Kenzie?" There was a knowing in Ronan's eyes that Dom didn't like. Dom jutted his chin out slightly, throwing daggers with his gaze. *Back off.*

Realistically, Ronan probably suspected the same thing he did: Julia had been given some sort of weapon from the Otherworld to stop Kenzie once and for all. But whereas Dom respected that Julia might have to dabble in a grey area in order to do what she must, it was quite likely that Ronan didn't share the same viewpoint. The bastard spouted morality like a fountain. Even though he was quick to lecture everyone else, he could have taken the same criticism.

But right now, the last thing Julia needed was Ronan down her throat about something.

"This is a Bearer's concern, Druid," Julia said suddenly. "You may not interfere."

Dom realized the words she'd spoken were actually inside his head—actually, both of their heads, based on the look of complete surprise on Ronan's face. The voice both was and wasn't hers and sent a chill down his spine.

Dom gritted his teeth then, looking up. The helicopter was landing.

"What now?" Lennie asked, not bothering to contain his anger.

The helicopter was already flying off into the night, dangerous package and passengers having been delivered safely.

So far, so good.

"We cut the lights and form a protective circle," Ronan called out. "Dom and Julia will be on the inside, with the ... the box. The rest of us need to maintain an external container. Once that's in place, Sean will release his hold and step back into the circle. Julia will take over the container then."

"How will Julia be able to see what she's doing?" Lindsey asked.

"She'll be fine," Ronan snapped. Lindsey rolled her eyes.

Dom turned his gazed towards Sean, who was still maintaining magic around the wooden crate; Dom had been right, they had boxed her up like useless freight. Now though, even in the near darkness, it was obvious that the act was coming at great cost to Sean. They needed to get on with it.

Lennie, Stuart, Lindsey, Graham, and Ronan took several paces back, leaving Dom, Julia, and Sean standing beside the box. Dom wished Thomas and Peggy could also be here, rounding their number from eight to ten, but there hadn't been enough time to gather them. It was likely they would make it by morning though, and he was glad for that; he had a sense Julia would need support following the ordeal.

Ronan raised his hands and began to recount something very similar to what Peggy had done before their battle at the castle, calling in the four directions and elements in succession. A low glow filled the space, emanating somehow from the five Wielders in the outer circle.

Indeed, Julia would have no problem seeing at all.

"Are you ready, love?" Dom asked quietly. Sean didn't look like he would be able to hold on much longer.

"I am," she said aloud. Her voice sounded strange, somehow reverberating through his chest. An echo of the ages.

She was working on another plane indeed, calling in the lost voices of the wells.

Dom nodded to Sean, who dropped his hands and stepped backwards, making the surrounding number six. Julia stepped forward, hands outstretched. The night air around them was completely calm, yet Julia's hair blew back behind her in an unseen wind. She looked utterly transformed.

Dom stood protectively about three paces away, legs braced and sword raised. If Julia's magic fell and Kenzie made a move for her, he would skewer the traitor in her tracks before she even noticed. And if *he* fell—which was extremely unlikely—then the ring of Druids and Knaves would take care of matters squarely. Assuming nothing attacked from the outside, of course. But so far, the grounds seemed quiet. Morgan was somewhere in the distance with his shotgun and Oisín and would sound the alarm.

Dom watched as Julia lifted the heavy lid off like it weighed nothing at all.

Kenzie's voice spoke from within, and she projected outward as she gathered her faculties. "Where the fuck am I? You stupid bitch! He'll come for me, *and* you!"

"You're under our power now," the voices speaking through Julia said. "Cassius will not come for you here."

In hearing these words—as if a spell were cast on the air making it so—Dom knew that, indeed, no one was coming for Kenzie.

"Who's there?" Kenzie spat angrily, but Dom could sense she was afraid.

"Six Wielders …" Julia's voices said. "The World Ruler … and the *Sovereign*."

"I can hear … others," Kenzie said, any sense of fight waning in her awareness of the powers that surrounded her.

Julia didn't reply.

Out of the corner of his eye, Dom could see Lennie shifting on the spot, ready to spring at any moment. Yet, he maintained his position in the circle. Dom reworked his thoughts—if he fell, then Lennie would surely do the job of dispatching the dark Bearer before anyone else even got close.

Kenzie stood, her chest barely reaching the top of the crate. She was a slight woman, barely five feet tall and probably weighing about as much as Oisín. Yet the damage she had inflicted had been irreparable.

Julia waved her hand, and the four wooden sides of the box fell to the ground.

"Kenzie Clarke," the voices spoke through her, "you have broken the laws of our natural order and of our people. You have betrayed the countless women who came before you, fought before you, to maintain the magic of our Bearing lines."

Kenzie began to shake, attempting to access her own magic without success. Dom noticed red marks around her wrists where bonds must have been tied pointlessly at some point; Kenzie required something stronger to contain her. She dropped her hands. Julia was now in complete control, and she would not escape.

"But worst of all," the voices said, "you have betrayed yourself." In this utterance, Dom could hear Julia's voice strongest of all.

Dom shifted the grip on his sword slightly, anticipating whatever Julia might do next.

She paused a beat, stepping an arm's length from Kenzie and forcing her gaze up towards her with her outstretched magic. Hand reaching, Julia cupped her hand under Kenzie's jaw. Dom felt his body tense at their contact.

"We forgive you," the voices said. He did not hear Julia's voice this time.

Kenzie began to sob as she fell to her knees.

Julia stepped forward, removing the heavy amulet from around her own neck. The black stone at its centre was dark and, somehow, pulsing. Like a *heartbeat*. Even from where Dom stood, he could see and feel that this was not an entirely wholesome piece of jewellery.

Darkness reverberated within its core.

Relief washed over Dom now that the amulet wasn't around Julia's neck. Out of the corner of his eye, Ronan's jaw dropped. Wisely, Julia hadn't shown him the amulet; no doubt he would have immediately noticed the darkness it bore within. Still, the circle was maintained.

Julia stepped forward, the wind encircling her now at a dizzying speed, pulling with it the strings of light magic from the Wielders on the outside. Kenzie, who now seemed to be utterly frozen, looked up at Julia, eyes filled with terror. Gently—far more gently than Dom would have imagined—Julia placed the amulet around Kenzie's neck. Her screams were horrific and filled with agony. The stone sizzled as it sunk beneath her skin, searing inward to her Bearing core.

Suddenly, the wind stopped, freezing everything and everyone in place. Kenzie tossed her head and body back like a bow.

The stone was gone.

It was an awful sight to behold, and to feel: a Witch being stripped of her magic. Dom heard gasps from the circle around them as Kenzie writhed in pain on the ground. Dom now understood why Julia had asked his forgiveness beforehand. However, he did not believe she needed any forgiveness. It was an insane notion. This had to be done.

And then, something happened that Dom had not anticipated.

"I forgive you too," Julia said at last, the voices of the wells no longer in her utterance. "But unfortunately ... he will not."

Those final words were felt like shattering glass around the circle of Wielders. It obliterated the spells that held them bound in the circle. All the enchantments around them had been extinguished as Julia stripped Kenzie of her magic. Yet, she was still alive. Kenzie would be returned back to her master, allowing him to finish the job once and for all.

To some in the circle, it was likely a cruel choice, leaving her to either turn herself in or be hunted by Cassius for the rest of her life. But to Dom, it was the most humane thing Julia could have done, relieving them all of the darkest job of all.

And he was proud of her for it.

CHAPTER 35

The next several weeks passed slowly. After what I had done to Kenzie, I spent most of my time in bed recuperating, with very few visitors and a quite a lot of napping. And though my boredom was quickly becoming insufferable, I really *was* quite incapacitated. Wearing the amulet, along with the ancient magic it had carried, had taken a huge toll on me in the end. Dom had rightly suspected that this was one of the undisclosed consequences of having dealings with the Otherworld. He knew it well, as he would sleep for days after his regeneration.

"They didn't tell you though, did they?" Dom asked. "About the cost." It wasn't really a question at all. It was a statement of fact. He traced his fingers along the pink scar in the middle of my chest, a souvenir from wearing the amulet, and looked sad.

"No … It's almost like it was an insurance policy to make sure the work was done. Not that I needed it … There was no way I was letting her continue to harm other magic users in that way."

"You did what was required, love. I'm just sorry it's been so hard on you, and your beautiful body."

He kissed the centre of my chest, and I let out a long sigh.

Externally, Ronan had cleaned my skin as best as he could but had flat-out refused to speak to me throughout the process. Dom had likely threatened to thrash him within an inch of his life if he didn't strictly perform his doctorly duties after Kenzie had been stripped, but he had done so in enraged silence. However, I didn't care at the time if Ronan didn't wish to speak to me or what he thought of my actions. After the amulet had been removed, I'd felt strangely like I was aging backwards to my normal age, which was both awkward and painful.

It was agony and had taken hours to complete.

For many days, I hadn't felt up to conversation with anyone but Dom. Even Peggy, who had come as quickly as she could after learning of our experience with Kenzie, had agreed that what I needed was rest and time. Quiet. Still, it had been a delight to see her again, even though there was little she could do in the way of magical ministrations. Her presence was always soothing to Dom and me. She had returned to England shortly thereafter to her growing grove of students. Since Malcolm's passing, she had taken her role within her community more seriously than ever. In light of what had happened in Northern Ireland, she had pledged that the world needed more trained Druids, and that she would be the one to make it happen.

Happily, she'd left Thomas behind to help Dom out with anything he might need done on the estate, or otherwise, so that he could focus on my needs. Dom and I suspected that Peggy had actually left Thomas there to keep an eye on Ronan—it was plain to everyone that the man was on the brink of a personal crisis—but it was not something that had been spoken aloud. Dom appreciated Thomas's presence, nonetheless.

Naturally, Dom had taken beautiful care of me, his intuitive connection to my needs an obvious blessing.

"In sickness and in health," he had happily said one afternoon as he brought me a fresh pot of tea and a pile of smutty romance novels he'd collected for me from a local used bookstore.

Unlike when Cassius had speared me, and Dom had blamed himself for my wounds, this time, he could tend to my needs without much guilt. Between his attuned understanding of my bodily needs and the complexities of Otherworld, he was the perfect nurse. I also had the sense that he wanted to keep me tucked away so he could keep me to himself for a while. Undoubtedly, the experience had frightened him, even if he had stood beside me, spear to my chalice. He'd made love to me countless times since the event, each time quiet, gentle, and tender, as if reaffirming my connection to the world we shared together.

That part of my healing had been pure bliss.

However, my recovery and Dom's heaping affections weren't the only reason I was still lingering in bed perhaps longer than I usually would have. I was also hiding in my room, at least somewhat. Tensions remained high among the group, and everyone needed time to cool off.

Lennie, for one, had been outraged that we planned to send her back out into the world alive.

"She could still murder *other* people!" he had exclaimed after all was said and done. "She's *still* a psychopath! What if she doesn't go back to Cassius and instead just starts going after innocents?"

"Julia is certain she will return to Cassius," Dom had said calmly, and that had been about the extent of Lennie's outrage towards me. At least outwardly. The space Lennie gave me after was likely due to Dom intervening, pushing him towards his own healing that needed attending to, rather than coming after me in anger. In the end, we suspected Lennie knew that it had been the right thing to do.

Ronan's anger, however, was palpable throughout the manor house. With nowhere to go, he had remained on the estate, locking himself in his room, and refusing contact with anyone but Thomas and Lennie. And even that was sparing.

"Ronan's *really* not happy with you. Or me actually," Lindsey had said after she, Stuart, Graham, and Sean had returned Kenzie to England the day following the event. Her accent was as thick as toffee while she sat on the edge of my bed and complained about her ex-boyfriend. It was something I had noticed about her: The angrier she was, the thicker her brogue. "But don't listen to that asshole. What you did will have kept the balance in the natural world, and I told him as much too."

"I bet that went well," I said, scoffing.

Apparently, Ronan had refused to join them on their mission, which had ultimately enraged her. He had a duty to follow, as far as she was concerned. Adding fuel to the fire, Lindsey had then told him that she'd agreed wholeheartedly with my choice, which had apparently sent him into his own tailspin. I had never witnessed Ronan in full anger, probably because Dom almost always pushed him back into place, but apparently the fight between Lindsey and Ronan had been pretty brutal, ripping open a deep wound between them. I was glad for both of their sakes that their relationship hadn't lasted. It was a terrible pairing to have that much conflict.

Stuart, who had wisely steered clear of the entire entanglement, had agreed with my choice too, though I hadn't been sure if he was just agreeing with Lindsey—at least until he'd poked his head into my bedroom right before they were about to leave the manor house for Scotland once more.

He'd gotten straight to the point, speaking frankly about his stance. "Honestly, Julia. Wren would have wanted it this way. She wouldn't want Lennie, or any of her friends, to become murderers. I know we kill Wraiths when we fight them, but that's almost … Well, there's some level of accord there. We're engaging in battle on equal footing. It's not like we go out and hunt Wraiths for the sake of killing. Not entirely. But to slaughter an unprotected and outnumbered woman outright … Well, I know Wren wouldn't have been alright with it. Not under that circumstance. Those weren't the kind of odds she would have favoured. What I'm saying is … she would have been on your side … if she were …" He let his voice trail off.

"Thanks, Stu," I had said, and he smiled silently before backing out of the room once more. I got the impression he was fighting back tears and didn't want me to see. With that affirming knowledge in hand, however, I felt somewhat reassured that I hadn't incidentally created a massive rift in the group.

Well, in the whole group anyway. Ronan was clearly on the other side of a gaping canyon.

At first, I thought his dark mood after the fight must have been because he didn't agree with the ethics behind stripping Kenzie of her magic, but since the rest of the Druids had all agreed that it was the most humane course of action, I realized it couldn't be that. Well, not *only* that. No doubt we were leaving her to death by the hand of Cassius, but that was between her and her master.

We had all agreed on *that* part.

Yet, it was plain that something else was bothering him about the whole thing. I tried to shrug it off, as undoubtedly, it would take all of us time to heal after the ordeal. *No one* would be the same after witnessing what I had done. And honestly, I almost couldn't believe it myself—the fact I had been used as an instrument of the Otherworld's bidding—though the more I ruminated on it, the less I felt like I had been used, more like I had been an extension of my kindred.

Despite what anyone said and the fact I was shying away from direct confrontation with our allies, I knew I was right. None of them knew the burden the Otherworld had placed on me: It would be either me or Kenzie. That was the cost of the solution to stop her. But more importantly, *they* had demanded that balance be restored. That Kenzie's magic cease serving Cassius. And I agreed with them. But that didn't equate to death. Taking Kenzie's life was not something I had been bidden to do, and she would have to face the quantum of her choices.

Still, the nightmare had come, confirming the very real consequences of my actions.

About a week after the Druids had returned Kenzie to England, I woke to Dom speaking to me in familiar, soothing tones. His hand rubbed my chest.

"Julia, it's alright … I'm here. You're safe …"

It wasn't often that Dom woke me from nightmares anymore, understanding them as simply part of my divining makeup; I usually sorted my way through them myself. This one, however, was bad enough to cause him concern.

"He's killed her," I said, wiping cold sweat off my brow. "It's done."

Dom was silent, pulling me into a firm embrace. I could almost feel the relief shudder through his bones, but I knew he would never admit how badly he himself had craved the revenge.

"You should tell Lennie," I said, my lips quivering.

"It can wait until morning," Dom said, stroking my hair. "For now, let me hold you."

I leaned into him then, sobbing.

For all the misguided thirst for power Kenzie held, and the darkness and betrayal she had curated through her doings with Cassius, she was merely the product of a much, much darker mechanism. He had used her, abused her, and then cast her away, just as men like him always did. She was the perfect candidate—a poster child for the very system that was actually destroying her. Pitting women against other women had been used as a means of control for ages. Sprinkle a bit of mental instability into the mix, and there she was, caught in the snare like so many before her.

She had been primed and readied for self-destruction.

In the dream, I'd witnessed her begging at his feet and seen the disgust on his face while she grovelled. She had gone back to him in Russia, I assumed, judging by the unfamiliar buildings beyond the window of the dark room they occupied. I was unsure if he was now allowing me the Sight, or if I could see what was happening because of the connection I had shared with Kenzie. Regardless, the sight was grim as he raised his hand once, snapping her neck just as she had snapped Wren's.

I felt his rage—rage for this experiment being thwarted. She was nothing to him, yet we had delivered a significant blow. The fight against Cassius was far from over.

After several long moments, I spoke again.

"You need to talk to Ronan. He's so angry with me. With all of us. And I'm worried he'll go off the deep end this time."

"I know. His mood swings are getting out of hand."

"That's not quite what I mean," I said. It was more than mood swings Ronan seemed to be experiencing. Sure, he was pissed that I had made a morally grey decision. I could live with that. But I sensed Ronan's discontent went far deeper. What I had done to Kenzie, and what the Otherworld had "gifted" me, was information he would *kill* to have ... details he seemed to be literally dying to know.

It fed directly into his obsession.

"I feel like he's constantly on the edge of wellness and madness," I said, finally speaking what was weighing on my heart. "He needs someone to talk to that isn't me. And probably not Thomas or Lennie either. He's so ... unstable. Which is ..."

"So *not* Ronan?" Dom offered.

"Dangerous," I finished.

"Don't worry, love. I'll get it sorted."

MANTLE OF THE WORLD RULER

Several days after the nightmare, when we felt I had healed physically and settled emotionally, enough to leave my bedroom den, Dom endeavoured to make some kind of peace with Ronan.

Ever since the incident in California where Dom had regrettably—or maybe not so regrettably on his part—broken Ronan's nose, tensions had remained high, despite their outward show of getting along. I had *thought* things were repairing over the past months in the manor house, but after what had happened with Kenzie, the fragility between them had been exposed once more. Ten-fold. Ronan was flat-out refusing to speak with me and avoiding Dom at all costs.

I wasn't sure how Dom planned to get through to Ronan, though I had no doubt that using force was on the table as much as anything else right now. Still, I felt a tiny bit of tension leave my shoulders as I watched the pair of them walk out the front door and towards the horse-barn-turned-garage Dom kept.

From what I understood, Dom planned to take Ronan off-roading in the same old Land Rover we had used to drive to the helipad. Usually reserved for cross-country treks and estate maintenance, it was as rough looking as the landscape, and a pretty brutal ride. Not that I had been paying much attention on the night I had exacted the Otherworld's bidding. What I did know was that it wasn't Ronan's favourite mode of travel and suspected that Dom's reasoning for taking that particular vehicle out must have been intentional. Besides, there were few people who could say no to Dom when he demonstrated this combination of charm and power.

I watched from the upstairs bedroom window as the two departed down the road, bumping along, and recalled a conversation we'd had several months before about Dom's special skill.

"I hate to do it," Dom had said when I teased him about his ability to get others to do just about anything he wanted. Well, anyone but me.

"I think, as long as you're *aware* that you're doing it, and only use your powers for good, then it's okay," I had said, chuckling at his unusual superpower.

"I suppose, Julia. But sometimes, it almost feels *too* easy," he'd replied, apparently not finding the same humour in it that I did.

"Good thing you have me to push back! Keep you humble," I'd said, tickling his belly.

He had finally laughed then. But it was true that I *did* have some sort of special immunity. Not that I didn't find him incredibly charming, but I always knew when he was working to control the situational and emotional climate around me. The incident with the engagement ring after the summer solstice had taught me as much, and he hadn't tried any of that bullshit on me since.

Now, watching the lads head down the gravel drive, I felt a pang of sadness. What if Dom wasn't able to reconnect with Ronan? To reel him back in? What if this didn't work? Who else did he have to talk to? Lindsey had expressed that this was precisely why their relationship had failed; Ronan was like an impenetrable wall when it came to his own demons, unwilling to receive support or seek out professional help. Apparently, he was *"enough of a professional to treat himself,"* Lindsey had quoted back to me, shaking her head in disgust.

I watched as Dom aggressively veered the SUV towards a large puddle. It created a massive splash, and I could only imagine the effect on the vehicle's occupants. Watching them disappear out of sight, I was then reminded of stories of women trying to induce labour by driving on rough backroads and made a mental note that maybe, someday, I might need to take a ride in the Land Rover to bring on my own labour.

I sighed and, turning away from the window, headed towards the kitchen to make a pot of tea and find something to eat.

I found Lennie and Thomas in Dom's study.

Lennie was working away on his laptop as usual, headphones on and hyper-focused. He had returned from being "away," which had meant Dom had sent him somewhere to deal with his grief alone. I wasn't sure if that had meant solitude in the countryside or a week spent in Amsterdam, but upon his return, he seemed more whole.

Thomas was sitting on the floor while playing a game of Solitaire on the coffee table. Oisín was fast asleep beside him, resting his head on Thomas's lap. The rest of the Druids and Knaves had returned to their own corners of the world for a time, rather than returning to our place immediately. Everyone needed some time to regroup before the wedding. It was early April now, and we planned to have it at the beginning of May.

However, it was nice to have some company right now. I assumed it would take time for my magical levels to return to normal, as well as for the aftereffects of the Cassius nightmare to abate. But until then, I honestly didn't want to be alone, unless I was tucked into bed, sleeping or fucking Dom. The night before had been expectedly rough on the sleeping front, and I was tired.

I snatched Dom's laptop from his desk and streamed a movie on my lap while dozing off and on. It was an older film about a family who moves into a castle, and the father, who is a writer, cannot defeat his writer's block due to his grief.

As the afternoon wore on, so did our hunger. Determining that it would likely be just us three for dinner, since we had heard nothing from Dom or Ronan since they'd left, Thomas elected to go start cooking something, and I joined him. We decided on toasted bacon, lettuce, and tomato sandwiches. Nothing fancy. And we could toss any leftover bacon in the larder in case Dom or Ronan wanted something simple to eat when they got back.

"Do you like living in a house this big?" Thomas asked, pulling out a cast-iron frying pan and placing it on the gas range. It soon sparked to life, and he began adding individual strips of bacon.

"Well, I haven't really lived here for long. But … it really *has* grown on me," I said truthfully. I pulled out a wooden cutting board and a sharp knife to begin slicing the tomatoes and lettuce—Dom wasn't someone to tolerate blunt knives in his kitchen. "It's completely different from the homes I lived in growing up. So, I don't have much to compare it to."

"Me either. I grew up in council housing, so it was always a tight squeeze. Didn't make for a very easy childhood," he said and then chuckled unexpectedly. "You could probably fit ten or fifteen of my homes into this place. Or more!"

"Same," I said, shaking my head at the fact that I now called a castle my primary residence.

Lennie joined us then, no doubt drawn to the kitchen by the smell of fried bacon. "Hello! Anywhere I can help?"

"You could toast the bread," Thomas offered, and Lennie set to work.

"We were just talking about our childhood homes," I said. "Both Thomas and I grew up in much smaller ones than this."

Lennie smiled. "Mine was decently large, and definitely detached—which is something in itself I suppose—but nothing like this. I was away at public school most of my childhood though. Dorm rooms and the like."

The linguist in me delighted in the stark contrast between Lennie's posh accent and Thomas's distinctly Scouse one. Thomas was from near Liverpool, so that made complete sense. As for Lennie, I knew that his accent reflected his public-school education. It also made it hard to pinpoint exactly *where* he was from, his practised elocution eliminating hints of social class or region.

Soon enough, we were sitting down to our simple meal in the kitchen. Oisín was pleased for any breadcrumbs offered, mostly by Thomas. I missed having Sully and Mags around too, but they had apparently bonded quite closely with Morgan over the past year, and it was in everyone's interest for them to continue staying down in Morgan's cottage.

However, Oisín would always be Dom's dog; if Dom was home, so was he.

With our impromptu dinner consumed and dishes done, we waded into the sitting room; Dom and Ronan were *still* nowhere to be seen. I thought I had heard gravel on the drive earlier when I'd gone to the washroom, but it was possible that it was only Morgan out on maintenance. I padded across the carpet, past my favourite loveseat, and peered out the Georgian window closest to me. The sun was now sunk deep into the skyline, threatening to go dark within the next ten or fifteen minutes.

Oisín whined impatiently at my side.

"Where are they?" I said quietly before pulling out my phone. No messages. I sat down heavily on the plush couch. I didn't have anything to worry about really. But the fact remained that I felt safer when Dom was near.

Surprisingly, Lennie joined me on my narrow perch, offering a resigned smile. He also seemed concerned about the two Celts' whereabouts and took up the same vantage point over the driveway. Across from us, Thomas sat down heavily on the low mid-century couch. "I guess what I meant before was that I didn't have any privacy in my home," he said.

"What do you mean by privacy?" I asked, momentarily distracted from my concern about Dom's whereabouts. "I mean, you said it was small, but was there more to it?"

"Everything I did, they knew about," Thomas said, letting out a long sigh.

"So like ... surveillance?" Lennie asked. "That's awful."

"No, not like that. Well ... sort of actually. They might have if I had actually resisted. But realistically ... I just told them everything they wanted to know. That was the expectation," he said as he looked down. He swirled his glass once but didn't take a drink. "It was just easier that way."

I recalled my own relationship with my mother, her preference for me to mirror her needs rather than express my own. "I get that."

Thomas looked up. "Do you?"

I tensed, smiling tightly. "I do."

Lennie scanned out the window once more before continuing. "Didn't it make you angry?" he asked Thomas, all the while reading me correctly by not pressing the matter my way. "Their control?"

"Well, yeah ... but I was rarely allowed to be outwardly angry, so—"

"Allowed? Isn't it a rite of passage for teenagers to get bloody angry and act out? Shout at their parents? I mean, I sure did," Lennie said, though not without compassion. "I always thought that was just part of growing up."

"I think it's called *enmeshment,*" Thomas said, stiffening. "I didn't have my own feelings. Or I did ... but wasn't allowed to express them. Anything upsetting that came up for my parents—which was common—was everyone's to feel. Usually, it was my father's rage. Or my mother telling us how to feel, act, and behave so we wouldn't cause problems by adding fuel to the fire ... *his* fire. I guess what I am saying is that my feelings were never solely *mine.*"

I felt my heart rate quicken and face flush, the all-too-familiar feeling of walking on eggshells suddenly brought to mind.

Thomas didn't notice my discomfort and continued onward. "It was like everyone had a role in our house. My younger brother was the peacekeeper, which explains why he's spent most of his adult life doing mission work overseas—my family are also staunch Christians, which doesn't help the insular nature of everything—but really, I think he just wanted a reason to escape the madness. That was a viable excuse for him."

"Did you have any other siblings?" Lennie asked; he was an only child.

"Yeah. An older sister. Of course, she could do no wrong, but I also think she had an undue amount of pressure put on her to be perfect. I never actually envied her, not really. I mean, she had the looks, of course—my father's pride and joy! But last I heard, she'd also developed a considerable drinking problem, no doubt to cope with the mountain of obligations placed on her by my parents as they age. I'm sure she's still there though. She was always terrified of my father. And lacked confidence to step out fully on her own, just like my mother."

"That's tragic," Lennie said, finishing his drink.

"And me? I was the family scapegoat. So, you can imagine how *that* went."

I let out a low whooshing sound from my lips.

"Julia, are you alright?" Lennie asked, turning to face me.

I felt a deep pang of sadness; there were years where all I wanted to do was please my mother so that *maybe* she would be happy and settle in to a life that was enough, instead of always searching for the next best thing.

But she never did.

"I'm sorry," I said. "It's just that a lot of this resonates with me. Maybe not the enmeshment part but having a parent's needs outshine your own. That was *definitely* part of my story. I went through a lot of therapy in my twenties to work through it all. Honesty? I think it's a large reason why my magic has always been so … unreliable. I'm still figuring out how to push past the mental block of not getting to know my authentic self during those crucial years of childhood development. Emotional abuse and manipulation have a lasting effect."

"They do." Thomas nodded, momentarily lost in memory. "When I finally broke free and saw it for what it was—that I would have to choose their needs or my own—I was *very* angry. Lost. Depressed. Honestly, most days I didn't even want to be alive."

Thomas looked down to his massive feet, his eyes brimming with tears. Lennie and I both remained silent, allowing the feeling to be held safely between the three of us. Witnessing it, despite the discomfort.

"But that's also when my Wielding magic emerged," Thomas said thickly.

I cocked my head; I had falsely assumed it was just Bearers whose magic could be suppressed by grief, but of course, Wielders would be destined to the same fate.

"I mean, it was chaotic and unpredictable! But it was there. And then somehow … I came across Peggy and Malcolm at a LARPing weekend. They were participants in the festival. I … I don't even know how it happened that I got so lucky—that they *just happened* to be seeking apprentices. Or so they told me. But frankly, they saved my life."

"Those two always had a knack for being in *exactly* the right place at the right time. Or at least, that's what my parents always said," Lennie replied, leaning back and looking towards the ceiling.

Lennie rarely spoke about his parents. It was my understanding that they had been Druids, and friends of Peggy and Malcolm, but that Lennie had clearly followed his own path. His cool exterior had always prohibited me from asking about them, yet somehow, it felt important now.

"What happened to your parents, Lennie?" I asked. "If that's okay to ask?"

"Sure. Actually, no one really does anymore. It was a long time ago," he said, smiling simply. "They died on a mission. In between the last time you and Dom were … *together* … and this time. About fifteen years ago. You think Ronan's bad about privacy and pushing for Druids to act alone. That generation of Druids? They were like MI6 on steroids … Well, magically speaking anyway."

Thomas frowned slightly. "Aren't you in MI—"

"I never actually saw their bodies," he continued, blatantly interrupting Thomas. "Malcolm identified them, actually. I was away at school. But it was clearly death by Wraith. And it wasn't pretty."

"I'm so sorry," I offered.

"Nothing to be sorry about. They knew the risks, and they were on the right side of the issue as far as I'm concerned. The Druids wanted it hush-hush, of course, which was the challenging part … I had to go back to school and tell everyone that they'd died in a car crash. I felt like fucking Harry Potter—very cliché for a young boy who'd never felt like he fit in to begin with. *Of course,* I had dead parents."

Thomas looked sorry, but I nodded in understanding.

"I've always had the sense that one of the reasons they actually died was because of all the secrecy," Lennie said. "If they'd had more support, others working with them on the mission ... maybe it would have gone differently."

"Actually," Thomas offered, "after a couple of drinks one evening, Malcolm once told me that their deaths have always been a blemish on the Druidic order's *most wholesome* record. Something had gone wrong that night—like it shouldn't have happened—but I could never get him to tell me the whole truth." He waved his hand in the air.

"Well," Lennie offered with an audible sigh, "I did find out the truth in the end. Perks of being me." He leaned forward once more, seemingly disappearing into memory. "And my assumptions were correct."

We sat in a continued silence for a time, digesting the truth Lennie held. It wasn't our place to press for details, but it was obvious there was more that could be shared. The burden he carried was lifelong.

Before long though, Thomas spoke once more. "I think so many of us come from damaged places. Not just our individual homes, but ancestrally. I feel like our generation is the first to sort of consider the lasting effects of all that trauma and seek out change. Or at least, that's how I feel."

"I think you're right," I said, recognizing how this affected my entire history, beginning in the eleventh century. I had been attempting to face and heal my own demons for the better part of a millennium. Dom too.

It was time for change.

We were startled out of our contemplations as Oisín bounded towards the door, greeted by Dom and Ronan.

"Hello, everyone," Ronan said, looking perkier than he had been in weeks.

Lennie hopped up to pour a round of drinks, but I knew he was also offering his seat to Dom.

"What have you two been up to?" I asked as Dom settled down beside me. He smelled like fresh air, as well as something distinctly skunkier.

I cocked my head in surprise.

"Ah, we've been back for a little while now. We were just outside having a good chat about things," Dom said, gazing at me with a slightly sheepish grin. I had wondered what he was doing in my side of the armoire that morning, and now I knew. He leaned close and spoke only to me, "Hope that it's okay I helped myself to your stash, love. Thought it might ... make a difference."

I chuckled. "Of course."

Funnily enough, I had managed to source an eighth of Morgan's weed before the whole situation with Kenzie had unfolded. He apparently needed it for his arthritis and other medical reasons. Cannabis wasn't legal in Ireland yet, but apparently, he had a "prescription." Dom had also let it slip that some of Morgan's relatives had less-than-legal gardening pastimes; it was far more potent than anything from a dispensary.

"Is everything okay though?" I asked Dom quietly.

"Yes, quite *grand* actually."

Across the room, Ronan was grinning from ear to ear; I realized then that I had never seen him consume anything mind-altering other than whisky, wine, or beer. Or perhaps bloodsbane. I shuddered at the memory.

"What have you all been up to?" Ronan asked as he took the drink Lennie handed to him.

"Sharing family stories. Not really happy ones, though. More like commiserating over our disappointing childhoods," I said, shrugging.

"Everyone's got their story," Ronan said and plunked himself down beside Thomas, who was now free of tears. Ronan's eyes lingered on mine for a moment, and I recalled what he had shared with me about his childhood on the way to Berkeley.

"What about you, Dom?" Lennie asked as he decided on which armchair to sit in. "You must have the most interesting childhood story of all!"

"Oh. Well, probably. But it's a bit of a tale …"

CHAPTER 36

It was decided that we would have our wedding on Beltane, at the beginning of May. All had remained quiet since my nightmare about Kenzie's murder, which for better or for worse, meant that we were relatively safe for the time being.

Or at least we hoped.

Dom and I had agreed the guest list would be kept small, not only for our safety but also to keep it as intimate as possible. I knew that he was the kind of person to extend the invite to absolutely everyone he'd ever met—and really, once anyone connected with Dom, they *did* feel like family—but it was really more our style to keep things close to the vest these days. I also didn't want anything super traditional; however, Dom had made a few things plain when we started planning in earnest.

"I want to see you walk down the aisle," he said. "I've dreamed of it … well, for a very long time. I … need that."

I smiled. "I bet you have, and I don't mind it. I want to see you there too. But I'm going to walk myself there, not be ferried by Ronan or something stupid."

This had always been my plan; growing up without a father figure and with a mother who could at best be described as broken, I knew that if and when I did marry someday, I would lead the charge on my own.

"I think that suits you just fine," Dom said, and I could tell his mind was wandering to the image once more.

"Since we are making requests," I said, bringing him back to reality, "mine is that we still spend the night before it together. I have no interest in some bullshit pretending I'm a virgin. Plus, I sleep better with you in the bed *with* me."

Dom barked out a laugh. "I can confirm, that indeed, you are *not* a virgin. Besides, we both know it was *my* virginity that you stole all those years ago anyway."

We had just finished a steamy midday shower session followed by a solid romp in bed and were feeling wholly content in our sexual connection. Our bed had always been a haven in which we found our way back to one another, and I had no interest in removing that part of our day for the sake of stupid tradition.

"If I recall correctly, it was both of our virginities."

Dom brushed his lips on my shoulder, reminiscing about our moment by the riverbed that had occurred over one thousand years previously. "I remember it like it was yesterday."

"Oh, I bet you do," I said, giggling.

He rolled his eyes before propping his head on hand. "Will you wear a traditional wedding dress?"

"I can if you want me to."

"It's your choice," he said, and I knew he meant it. However, I knew he would also love to see me in a real wedding dress finally.

"I will."

"You're supposed to say, 'I do!'" he said, diving on top of me in the bed, apparently looking for more.

The night before the wedding arrived before we knew it, and I found myself sitting in the kitchen, armed with pruning shears and floral wire.

"You should really go to bed," Lindsey said, yawning wide. "Big day tomorrow."

She, Stuart, Alanna, and Shereen had all arrived the week before to help with preparations. Once Dom and I had agreed the wedding would take place, all of a sudden it was happening *very* quickly, and we needed all hands on deck.

She wasn't wrong either; the hour *was* growing late. I eyed the kitchen clock and saw that it would be midnight in five minutes. After rubbing my eyes for what felt like the tenth time in as many minutes, I finally conceded defeat. "Ugh. You're right."

"As for me, if I trim one more stem, I might keel over!" Lindsey tossed a pair of secateurs loudly onto the table. Alanna jumped.

We had spent the better part of the evening transforming an assortment of flowers and greenery into bouquets, wreaths, and garlands. My suggestion of a wedding with a nod towards May flowers had somehow morphed into a full-blown theme, but it was too late to turn back now.

"We'll add the more sensitive flowers to the garlands in the morning. But you don't have to worry about that," Alanna said; Shereen had already tucked herself into bed hours ago.

I stood up and stretched my arms above my head. The effects of the wine shared between the four of us only hours previously had long since dissipated, though I felt groggy and thick-headed anyway. "I'm going to go find that lover of mine."

"Isn't that bad luck the night before?" Lindsey asked with a wink. Alanna rolled her eyes.

I let out a sarcastic "Ha-ha" and left the two of them behind in the kitchen to finish up. Oisín followed silently behind, dutiful as ever. The hall was cool. I dragged my fingers slowly around the photos and artwork adorning the textured wallpaper as I sought out Dom. I knew he would still be awake somewhere in the house.

I reached out with my inner compass—something I had been honing as I had gotten to know Bernie's compass better—and could feel he was still somewhere nearby, but that was about it. Guessing correctly, though, I found Dom tucked away in his study. He was sitting alone at his desk pouring over a stack of paperwork. I knocked gently on the doorframe before entering so as not to startle him.

"Julia! Is everything alright?" he asked, setting down his pen and rising to his feet. Clearly, I had startled him anyway.

"Of course. But I'm ready for bed I think," I said as I stepped down towards him into the room's sunken central area. The study still bore its signature fragmented energy, but most of it felt merely ancestral these days. I watched as Oisín settled himself happily by the dying embers of the fire, noticing several empty whisky glasses on the low coffee table as my eyes swept the room. "Everyone's gone to sleep?"

"They have," he said as he walked around the desk and held his arms out to me. "Come here."

My heart leapt at his offer of embrace; even now, I found myself overcome with a sense of homecoming any time we connected. His face, however, looked strange.

"Dom, are you okay?"

"If you can believe it, I'm feeling a little bit nervous about getting married tomorrow," he said, releasing me momentarily and pulling me towards the couch and onto his lap instead.

He smelled strongly of whiskey and cigars; evidently Morgan had joined the lads for a drink as well. Knowing this, I was surprised at his nerves. "Really?"

"I just ... well, you know. This time just feels so different ... with *everything.*" He gave a slight shrug and waved his hand dismissively. "But we've talked about this before. I'm just feeling such a strong urge to get it right. But that's foolish. I know it's going to be wonderful."

I nodded in agreement. "I'm not super keen on standing up there with all of the attention either."

"It's not that, Julia," he said, shaking his head. "It's just ... I've never really thought of what it *means* to be a husband. Over the long term, you know?"

"Well, I'm not looking for a traditional marriage in the 'patriarchal sense,' if that's what you're getting at." I pretended to shove off of him to escape.

He caught my wrists. "And *I'm* not looking to have you obey me or anything—not that you would anyway!"

I bit him playfully on the shoulder but let him continue.

"It's more like ... I want to do right by you. And myself. But I don't know what that looks like yet, officially."

"Of course, you don't," I said, leaning back and taking his face between my hands. "But that's the fun of it: the journey. We can't know what's coming next. Not really. But we get to find out together."

He pulled my hands from his face and kissed the top of each one in turn. "You're right. You're always right."

"See? You're going to make a great husband," I said in jest. He beamed back at me innocently.

I looked over his shoulder at the pile of papers on his desk. "What are you working on?"

Dom blushed. "Oh, those. I was hoping you wouldn't notice … but I suppose now's as good a time as ever to show you. We *are* getting married tomorrow, after all."

He winked before leading me by the hand towards his oak desk. On top stood a stack of what appeared to be handwritten letters. He picked them up gingerly, and I noticed that the top sheet bore his tidy script.

"What are these?"

"Some are letters, and others are stories," he said, holding back the stack momentarily. "I've written them throughout our history, but very few of the originals were in English, let alone modern English. So, I've been transcribing some of my favourites for you. As a wedding present."

I glanced up at him and then towards the volumes of journals and parchment he'd always kept stacked on the shelves throughout the room; I knew there was an absolute treasure trove of his own documented history spread throughout the space, which was largely why I always felt so uncomfortable in here. Dom's mementoes, while less threatening than before, still posed a risk for unexpected transcendence.

My right hand hovered just above the stack. "Do you think—"

"I'm not sure," Dom said, reading my mind. "That's why I wanted to wait."

I had no way of knowing what the effect of touching the paper might have as far as visions were concerned, but something in my gut told me this was safe; Dom had created these in the *now*. Holding my breath, I took the stack of paper into my hand and was pleased to find that nothing major came crashing into my psyche. I could feel Dom's essence all around me, and the love he had poured into the task, but that was about it.

He grinned, evidently pleased. "There are some great stories in there. About us and some of our more colourful friends as well. It's ... it's time I shared more of them with you."

"Dom, this is brilliant!" I said, tears filling my overtired eyes.

"And the letters—some of them are correspondences I thought you might find interesting—but most of them are actually *love* letters."

"Love letters?!" I said, squealing with sudden excitement, despite how exhausted I felt.

"I went through a real Romeo phase, embracing my inner Renaissance man," he said, puffing his chest. "You're going to enjoy those ones, I think. I hope the translations turned out alright though. It's a bit tricky with all the tenses."

I set the stack down on the desk and wrapped my arms around his neck. "It's perfect."

He kissed me deeply before stifling a massive yawn. "I'm so glad."

"Mm," I said, before catching his yawn and turning it into my own.

Dom wrapped his gift up in what could best be described as a leather folder and tucked it under his arm before placing his hand on my lower back. "Shall we go to bed?"

"Please," I said and staggered towards the door.

Oisín looked slightly harassed to discover that we were now leaving the room. He had aged a lot over the past year and was likely nearing the end of his days earthside.

"Come on, old boy," Dom said affectionately, scratching his hound behind the ears as he trotted gingerly past. "I've got a beautiful woman to marry tomorrow."

Dom and I woke first to a completely still house. It would be a while before anyone else got up to prepare for the day, and we quietly relished our moment of alone time in the early dawn.

"Today's the day," he said, lying on his side and grinning at me. His face still held remnants of sleep, and he looked as serene as a king in the thin morning light.

"It is," I said as I rolled to face him. Over his expansive frame, I caught a glimpse of his gift to me sitting on the bedside table. I put my hand under my head and rested on my elbow. "I got you a present too, you know."

"Oh Julia, you didn't have to do that," he said, furrowing his brow.

I yanked my pillow out from under my head and smooshed it into him. "Don't be silly."

"You're the one being silly," he said playfully before shoving the pillow back in my direction.

I tucked it under my head once more before speaking. "Don't you want to know what it is?"

He held out his broad palm towards me, waiting. "Of course, I do."

"It's not *inside,*" I said, dragging out the last word as if stating the obvious. "And it won't fit in your hand either."

He raised his eyebrows groggily. "What is it then?"

"You'll have to come outside with me to find out," I said, grinning devilishly.

"I'm not ready to leave our bed though," he said. He reached around to my behind and scooted himself closer. "It's awfully nice right here."

I ran my fingers through his golden chest hair, revelling in the closeness between us. "Then I guess you'll have to wait to find out."

He let a barking laugh before pulling the sheets over both of our heads. "Fine then, bossy one. And what will we *do* while we wait?"

"I've got a few ideas."

He purred in welcome.

The second time, we awoke to the clatter of a positively bustling home. A series of loud raps on the door signalled that our cocoon of solitude had at last been breached.

"For fuck's sakes, hold on a minute," Dom said grumpily as he pulled on his joggers and a t-shirt before poking his head out the door. It was Ronan. Apparently, the rental tent wasn't going up as planned, and they needed another set of hands to "erect it properly."

I snickered immaturely from the bed. Ronan gave me a withering look from over Dom's shoulder before striding back down the hallway. Dom grinned at me before planting a big kiss on my cheek and heading out the door after his best man.

Effectively alone but for Oisín, who was still snoozing away on the rug after his late night, my attention was drawn towards the stack of paper on the bedside table. I pulled the package onto the duvet top, deciding that now was as good as a time as any to explore my gift; ultimately, I was hoping to postpone my descent downstairs as long as possible.

Undoing the leather tie and folding back the cover, the first item on the stack turned out to be a letter dated yesterday:

> *Dearest Julia,*
>
> *It's the night before our wedding, and I'm currently sitting alone amongst stacks of old letters and stories I've prepared for you over the past few weeks (I'm also a touch drunk, so I apologize if this isn't terribly legible).*

I paused, laughing a puff of air through my nose; his cursive was still miles ahead of my own chicken-scratch attempts at "proper" handwriting.

> *It's been a real trip down memory lane, as you can imagine.*
>
> *But what's struck me most is a common theme among the documents, a theme that centres around the timeless power of our love, and the otherworldly draw that's always existed between us.*
>
> *I've never actually told you this before, but the truth is that the negotiation I made in the Otherworld that "first time" really was "until death do us part," or something of the like. The Druid's curse was only ever supposed to work once for me, while yours had the potential to go on indefinitely, which of course, I couldn't fathom at the time.*
>
> *So, I am forever bound to you in these lives because of being just as stubborn as you always say I am. I hope you'll forgive me for*

tethering myself to your destiny in this way; that I made this choice without you has sat heavily on my conscience all these many years.

I am hopeful that, in reading these translations, you'll see that the love shared between us has always been bright and true. And please know, I have absolutely no regrets in my decision to forfeit my own "proper death" to be reborn with you each cycle. It has been my greatest blessing.

What looked like dried teardrops stained the last few lines.

Anyway, with that said (and my conscience clear), there is nothing I want more than to grow old with you in this life. I would be lying if I said I wasn't the least bit nervous about tomorrow, because I am. Terribly nervous actually. Because somehow everything in this life is new again. Each breath I draw is deeper, each heartbeat stronger. And my love for you knows no depth.

Yours in this life and the next.

Domhnall

I reread the letter several times, tears of my own streaking the white paper. I hastily wiped my eyes on the back of my arm and held the letter to my chest. I had always assumed the rebirth element of his curse was tied to those first Druidic incantations, assuming that the Druids of old had access to the same complicated magic that existed in that original grimoire. But instead, it had been a negotiation Dom made that had ensured I had the best chance at overcoming my plight.

I let out a deep sigh and turned over the letter. There was a small post script:

P.S. Don't tell Ronan that I had the balls (or the stupidity) to negotiate in the Otherworld. He won't like it, especially after what happened with the black amulet.

MANTLE OF THE WORLD RULER

I laughed in spite of the dark reference.

I was slowly beginning to understand the magnitude and complexity of Dom's forays into the Otherworld—being that I had recently had one of my own—and could also understand why he would choose to guard that knowledge. I knew now that it *was* a dangerous thing he had done, negotiating in that way, but "they" must have known he was here to serve a greater purpose.

Further, while I might not remember all of my past lives, I knew without the evidence of the translations that his choice had undoubtedly been the right one; we were destined to be together. Why else would the fates have allowed such a bending of the rules?

I lay back on my pillow with my hand on my heart.

Blessed indeed, the stubborn ass.

After luxuriating in Dom's eternal and otherworldly proclamation of love, I decided it was high time I took a shower and headed downstairs for something to eat. Lindsey had demanded that I take the morning for myself, saying, "It's the one day you actually get to be a real princess, so you'd better damn well act like one, missy."

I had shot her a childish look in reply but appreciated her urgings.

It was never meant to be an overly formal affair, so I attempted to adhere to her instructions simply because I liked a slow start to the day. Also, the ceremony wasn't until late in the afternoon anyway. Following the formalities, we planned for a long-table dinner followed by bonfires and a party. The tent, which apparently was still being wrestled with since Dom hadn't returned to me, was to mitigate the looming forecast of rain.

I was in my housecoat, towelling my hair, when suddenly another knock came at the door, but this time it swung open in response to a solid *boom* on its other side. Before I could react, there was Dom, positively vibrating.

"Julia!" he beamed. "What have you done?!"

I stared at him, confounded by his open accusation mixed with a look of positive glee that was spread across his face. And then it dawned on me. *Shit.* "You found it then?"

"Stuart and Lennie both tried to stop me from going in the garage, but—"

"You know how he is, Julia," Lennie called from the hallway, "say one thing and he does the other,"

"Sorry, Julia, I tried!" said Stuart as he arrived panting, several steps behind with Lindsey at his side, laughing heartily at the whole scenario.

"Get dressed!" Dom said, still beside himself. "We're going for a drive!"

"Alright, give me a minute, you nut!" I said, laughing. The others took off downstairs, but Dom lingered in the doorway. "You can go back down if you want. I'll catch up."

"Oh, it's alright, I'll wait ... you sneaky little Witch," he said, grinning through his teeth.

I smiled as I pulled on my jeans. "Speaking of sneaky ... I read your letter."

He glanced to the bedside table and then towards the bed. "Oh."

Clasping my bra, I walked over to where he stood, tense and holding his breath by the door. "Thank you," I said simply and pulled him into a hug that I hoped would put the rest of the words I wanted to say into one tidy, unspoken package. His body eventually relaxed in reply, and slowly the excited vibrations resumed.

"Can we go now?"

"Yes, we can go," I said, and threw on a plain white t-shirt before Dom dragged me by the hand downstairs and out the front door.

The 1973 Datsun 240Z was still sitting in the garage where we had left it, in all its metallic-green glory. Dom, ever the collector, had missed out on decades of nostalgia for vehicles he'd never known. This was one he had talked about on and off. I knew little about the Datsun, but it was clearly the right choice, and something Dom would never have treated himself to.

"How did you manage it?" he asked.

I poked my chin towards Lennie and Stuart, who were grinning innocently from the doorway.

It had been a bit of an ordeal, locating and then procuring this specific model under such a tight timeline, but I'd also had some of the best and brightest working on my side. I wanted to be sure it was drive ready so that Dom and I could take it out for a spin on our wedding day, and the boys had pulled through magnificently.

"Well, you've been giving me the gears about me not spending 'our' money, so I figured when we finally *did* get married, officially, I would start big."

"It's incredible."

"Stuart was trying to convince me to go for a …" I paused, making sure I got it right, "1966 Aston Martin DB5, but I didn't figure you meant for me to spend *all* of the money," I finished, chuckling.

"Maybe a bit over the top," he agreed, laughing as he elbowed Stuart.

"Might be nice for the pair of you to go for a drive while we get things ready," Lennie said, and Stuart nodded enthusiastically.

Dom was almost vibrating now. "Don't have to tell me twice! We'll be back in"—he paused for a hurried moment, thinking—"a little over three hours!"

"Perfect!" Lennie shouted as Dom turned over the loud engine, waving us off.

"Where are we going? Is it safe to travel that far from home?" I asked, though I placed my full trust in him for whatever adventure lay ahead.

"I think it's worth the risk today of all days, don't you? Besides—we are safe." He said the last three words without any levity.

I nodded. He was referring to the scrupulous security measures our friends and allies had spent weeks implementing. The protection and surveillance stretched well beyond the estate and far out into the countryside. If any threat emerged, our allies would know about it immediately. Dom's serious pause could have threatened the joy of the moment, but it didn't. In truth, I felt as light as a feather and freer than usual from the nagging fear we both carried each day. We were safe; at least for today.

"Let's go!"

Dom and I took off like a shot. Content and free.

The next three hours were spent on the best drive of my life. We travelled along what was called "The Connemara Loop," which took us through some of the most gorgeous country and seaside views I had ever experienced. This had apparently become a regular stress-relief route for Dom this time around, before he had finally located me in Canada. I wondered why he hadn't brought me here before but was reminded of how careful we always had to be, *especially* when at home. We never strayed far from our strongest magical boundary.

The forecasted rain had also somehow held off—thank the Goddess. This was a blessing in itself, not because of our upcoming nuptials but because I didn't think Dom was ready to dirty the paint job just yet.

"Couldn't ask for better weather," he said, beaming at me as we rounded the top of the scenic loop and turned for home.

I smiled back at him. "What was that thing about Irish people being *really* lucky?"

He winked before reaching across the car and squeezing my hand. Truthfully, he had been in some of the brightest spirits I had ever encountered as we laughed and loved our way blissfully through the countryside.

The day felt enchanted.

"One second ... I need to piss," he said, breaking the spell. I laughed as he pulled the vintage car over into an unassuming rest stop. It was more of a gravel pull-out really, with no bathroom in sight. Dom wasn't afraid to bear it all to the wind to relieve himself though—another one of his old habits that I was discovering as part of his modern life. I noticed that he placed himself such that the wind wouldn't carry anything towards the car.

I waited patiently inside, since I knew he wouldn't take long.

Suddenly, he appeared at the passenger side, crouching down and knocking, so I rolled down the window. "Can I help you?"

"Did you want to take a turn driving?"

"I didn't think you'd want to share it with me yet," I said, teasing as I poked my head out. He leaned down and kissed me slowly, lingering on my bottom lip as he braced his hands on the top of the doorframe. This went on for several minutes, the heat rising quickly between us.

Then he suddenly pulled away, smiling. "I *can* share ... if you'd like."

I cocked my head, considering. Between my mediocre stick skills and needing to drive on the wrong side of the road, I didn't feel like it was a risk I was interested in taking today; we needed to get back home and married in one piece.

"How about I take us on the next one?"

"Deal," he said, straightening. My breath was heavy as I watched him stride slowly around the front of the car. He dragged his hands seductively across the shimmering paint, pausing to take it all in.

"I must be the luckiest man alive," he said, finally sliding into the driver's seat.

"Because of the car or ..."

"Yes, Julia, *all* because of the car," he said, perfectly deadpan. After a moment, he broke into a barking laugh.

"Alright, alright," I said, laughing too. My face literally hurt from smiling so much. "But tell me truthfully ... Did I do alright?"

"You're just fishing for compliments now, love. You know the answer," he said, leaning across the car and pressing his forehead into mine, breathing deep. I expected his eyes to take on their usual inky hue, but there was something else to them today—something infinite. "I love you more than the world itself, Julia ... more than the ocean and the sky. Today, and every day with you ... it's heaven."

Dom pulled me into another passionate kiss, and I responded in kind, weaving my fingers through his wavy blond air. It was longer than I'd seen it in quite some time, and I liked having something I could grab onto in moments of passion. His hands trailed slowly towards the warm place between my thighs and up my shirt simultaneously. The usual magnetic energy between us felt thicker than ever as I pulled back to look at him with heavily lidded eyes. I felt a mixture of lust and magic crackling across my skin.

"We should probably get back," I said, not meaning what I said.

Dom was about to speak—something equally as seductive I expected—but then his phone sounded. Glancing down at it momentarily, he read the text message and looked suddenly concerned.

"What is it?"

"It's from Lindsey," he said, straightening up. "She says, '*In no uncertain terms can Julia be late for getting ready for this wedding, Domhnall. Bring her home, now!*'"

I laughed, enjoying his attempt at mimicking her Scottish accent. It was pretty good. "Oh boy ... I think you might be in trouble." Admittedly, we *had* been gone a bit longer than expected.

Dom feigned shock. *"Me* in trouble? What about you?"

"I'm not the one driving," I said, putting my hands up innocently.

He shook his head with a grin as he buckled his seatbelt. "Well, I for one am not interested in getting on the wrong side of Lindsey today."

409

"Me neither," I said, wishing we could continue what we had started. I could see the outline of his erection though his jeans and let out a sigh. "We'd better go."

Frankly, I dreaded the idea of being apart from Dom at all today, even for the hour or so it would likely take for me to get ready. That being said, I also wanted today to be special for him. He had waited a *very* long time to marry me properly, so the rituals needed to be adhered to—at least to some extent.

"How close are we to home?" I had no idea where we actually were.

"About twenty minutes," he said, pulling onto the road.

"Step on it!"

CHAPTER 37

Dom and I returned mid-afternoon, only slightly later than planned, thanks to his speedy driving. However, upon our arrival, I was practically dragged out of the car by Alanna and Shereen as though I were seven hours late. Lindsey and Peggy followed along gleefully in our wake.

"Just hold on, you guys. I need to give Dom my ring!" I said, already feeling swept up in their energy. I wriggled the Claddagh off my ring finger, where the point of the heart had still been pointing outward. When I wore it next, it would be pointing towards me.

"Where's *Dom's* ring?" Shereen asked, ever mindful of the details.

"Upstairs," I said, feeling slightly overwhelmed. Our foray into the country had left me on an unsteady footing when it came to arrangements.

"I'll grab it once we're up there," Peggy said, easing my concern. "You have nothing to worry about, dear."

Lindsey hollered back to Dom, reminding him that he was no longer allowed near his bride until he saw her the altar. "And don't you dare try anything!"

He leaned back against his new car, tossing his hands up in surrender. "I promise. I won't."

"You've got to have *some* element of ritual here, Julia," Peggy said in her singsong voice as I was scooted onward. I'd missed her so much over the past

411

year, and it was such a blessing to have her returned to us again for a longer span of time.

"Peggy's right," Lindsey said, naturally on her side. "Plus, I do think Dom really wants to see you just appear there in the moment. You know?"

I felt my heart begin to race as we reached the bottom of the main staircase; our friends had really gone all out. Along the railing, from top to bottom, was an exquisite garland, twirling along with a mix of colourful spring flowers and jutting bright with greenery. It reminded me of something from an episode of *Downton Abbey*, where one of the three Crawley daughters gets married.

Quickly, we reached the landing and turned towards the centre bedroom. I liked the idea of bringing some joyful energy back into the space. It was also the largest bedroom in the house, which would give our party more room to get ready.

Pop!

"Champagne, Julia?" Alanna squealed, reaching for glasses.

"Absolutely," I said in Dom's accent, and with a fit of giggles, the ladies set to work preparing the bride.

I was glad for the cool bubbles as they tingled on the tip of my tongue, keeping me in my body as my nerves attempted to take over any rational thought. Today, I was marrying Domhnall O'Brien, and I would soon be Mrs. O'Brien. Admittedly, the name reminded me more of a Sunday school teacher than who I really was—just Julia—especially since I had never actually been to church. But I did like the idea of leaving my paternal name behind. Embracing the person that I chose to be with Dom felt right. It was the right choice for *me*.

In the end, I'd opted to wear a two-in-one dress that had been hastily ordered over the internet. Not the most mindful choice perhaps, but something about this particular gown had spoken to me. Of course, since this wedding had been a bit spontaneous in its planning timeline anyway, it had also appealed to me because it had been shipped quickly without effort or need for much alteration—at least, not anything Peggy couldn't handle. I also liked the idea that I could remove the outer layer for the party that would follow the formalities.

The inner layer consisted of a full-length satin chemise dress in a soft champagne hue, with a low-cut back and thin spaghetti straps. The front was cut tastefully while accentuating my figure. Coupling this was an overlaying pearlescent mesh gown embroidered with flowers and leaves in shades of pink, gold, and green; we were certainly sticking to the May theme here. It had a simple boat neck, dolman-style sleeves with velvet cuffs at the wrist, and a three-foot train. A synched waist with a matching velvet tie pulled together a wide keyhole at the back, mixing modern and old fashioned in the most singular way.

I had no doubt that, once everything was pulled together, Dom would be floored when he finally saw me.

"Simple makeup, I think," I said, and the others nodded approvingly. I planned to keep the palate simple: warm blush with a pink lip and just a touch of mascara. I wanted to look as natural as possible but also didn't want to fade into nothingness in any pictures. I was only marrying once in this lifetime, after all.

"I have some setting spray you can use too, just in case you try to sweat it off during the dance ... or *something,*" Lindsey said with a wink, handing me a small, frosted bottle.

"Yeah, yeah. We already consummated the marriage this morning, so we're ahead of schedule," I said with a chuckle.

Alanna let out a whistle. "I don't know, Julia. I see the way Dom looks at you on a normal day. But as a bride? He might combust!" she said with a cheeky grin. "Should we wager how long it takes before Dom drags you upstairs? Think he'll let you stay for the dance?"

Shereen gave her a smack, though she was also cackling. "He's not some sex-craved teenager, Alanna!"

"You don't know, Dom," I said, finishing my champagne. If not for Lindsey's texted interruption to get us back on time, we likely would have hooked up again in Dom's new car on the side of the road. His hunger for me seemed insatiable. Not that I was complaining or anything.

"Hurray, hurray, the first of May! Outdoor screwing begins today!" Gertie's voice twinkled in my mind. I smiled at her memory, the cheeky old thing.

"Well, I know him better than the whole lot of you," Peggy added, "apart from his bride of course!" Her pleasant smile turned slightly wicked as she raised an eyebrow. "And our Domhnall has *always* been rabid when it comes to Julia. You should have seen them in the sixties! Like a pair of bloody rabbits! I wager you don't even make it upstairs!" she said with a howl.

The others rolled with laughter as I tossed my hand out in denial, though I knew she wasn't wrong. "I'm *not* placing any bets."

Our afternoon gathering felt a little bit like a mini-bachelorette party, and I enjoyed the intimacy of the women around me. The four of us continued chatting, Lindsey working on my hair while the others put the final touches on their own outfits.

"And you're *sure* you want to keep your hair down?" Lindsey asked, Scottish accent singing through the room.

"It *has* to be down. With the flower crown," I nodded, certain. "We can pull it up for the dance." Shereen had spent the entire afternoon crafting the crown while we'd been away and was as hell-bent as I was on its role in the ensemble.

I leaned into the mirror as I pushed my hair behind my shoulders. Lindsey had been fussing with it for a while now but threw her hands up eventually. Tumbling in heavy waves, its weight was already thwarting her efforts to give me the illusion of a tighter curl. "Ah well, Domhnall likes you a bit wild anyway!" she said, chuckling.

I rolled my eyes as Shereen moved in to place the crown. Pinks, greens, and creamy yellows stood out brilliantly against my auburn hair. The effect was positively ethereal, and I didn't even have my dress on yet.

Rising to my feet, I crossed the soft carpet barefoot and stepped behind a white paper screen that had somehow been procured for the day. I slipped easily into the first dress, feeling every bit the goddess. Next came the sheath, which required some help, so I stepped out instead to a collective sigh. With the help of my "glam squad," as Lindsey had dubbed them, the ensemble was finally complete.

I stood, eyeing myself in the mirror, at a loss for words.

"Magnificent," Peggy said, beaming. "Domhnall will be speechless, and that's saying something when it comes to him!"

I laughed before turning around to take her hands into my own. "Thanks, Peggy. It means so much having you here today … And for you to be marrying us as well."

"No crying!" Alanna chimed. "Lean forward if you have to, and blot your tears with this Kleenex." She shoved the tissue into my hand sternly.

Indeed, I wondered how I would keep myself from going full waterworks when I saw Dom at last. I wasn't someone who dissolved into tears typically, but today seemed destined for the extraordinary.

The ceremony itself was going to be held in front of the lake—weather permitting—with a natural wood altar and arch constructed by Thomas from wood from Peggy and Malcolm's home garden back in Cornwall. It was Thomas's wedding gift to us, which he'd finished over the past month as he visited.

"It's almost time," Shereen said, eyeing her watch. I was still so honoured that she and Alanna had made the trek to Ireland for the wedding, Goddess knew they had enough on their plates in Seattle with the growing Wraith insurgence to the south.

I pulled out my new pair of green velvet flats. Their simplicity would offer me great comfort during what I hoped would be a night filled with fun and dancing.

"Don't forget the six-pence!" Peggy shouted and quickly shoved a silver coin into my left shoe. Shereen and Alanna looked confused, while Lindsey reacted like this was perfectly normal.

"How do you feel?" Alanna asked me as she took Shereen's hand affectionately into her own.

I took a moment to look inward. My Bearing hearth was crackling away merrily inside. Steady and sure. I felt comfort knowing that I had *technically* done this before, or at least something like it, though I couldn't remember the details with clarity. Dom was right though, something felt different this time around. Not that it was a bad thing.

"I feel fantastic," I said, a bit surprised at how calm I actually felt.

"Wonderful," Peggy said, and the five of us headed out of the bedroom and towards the stairs for the next stage of waiting.

I could hear the sound of a traditional pipe band as we settled into the sitting room. Oisín was lying in the centre of the rug, no doubt stationed there by Dom to greet me.

"How many people did you end up inviting?" Shereen asked, scratching the large dog behind the ears as he rose slowly to greet us.

I peered out the window at the gathering crowd, noting that Dom was nowhere in sight. "Oh, you know Dom. He's got more friends around the world than the average person."

"Something around fifty was the final count," Lindsey said. She and Stuart had worked together with Lennie and Ronan on security and, frankly, knew better than I did. She looked serious then. "Don't worry, Julia. No one is going to ruin your day. We'll make sure of it."

I wasn't worried. In fact, I had a strong feeling that my own Bearing magic was humming at such a significant frequency that I alone could keep everyone safe from Wraith threats, simply by means of my own protective magic.

"Well, if you're feeling ready, Julia, I'm going to head down to the altar and find your Domhnall. I'll send someone up when its time," Peggy said. She wore a lovely set of silver robes and some cheeky matching boots that reminded me of Janis Joplin.

"Sounds great," I said and sat down on the low couch in my usual spot. Lindsey poured me a short glass of whiskey from the sideboard, which I took gratefully.

"Where were the guys getting ready?" Shereen asked.

"In the garage, I bet. Dom won't want to part from his new baby," Alanna said with a laugh. Apparently, while we were out driving, they had enjoyed a vibrant description from Stuart of Dom's initial reaction to its discovery. A part of me wished they would have filmed it, but perhaps it was a happy moment meant for our friends to savour more than it was for me. After all, I got to *keep* the thing, and its sexy driver to boot.

The four of us chatted merrily for a time, peacefully enjoying the late afternoon sunlight as it poured through the tall Georgian windows. As always, a small part of me struggled to believe that I had found myself in this situation at all.

Queen of my own castle. Today *truly* felt like a fairy tale, with everyone looking the part.

MANTLE OF THE WORLD RULER

Alanna and Shereen were both dressed neatly in black slacks and blouses that complimented each other perfectly. Shereen's delicate floral top with soft pinks and oranges reminded me of a sunset; it paired beautifully with the deeper hues of Alanna's ocean-coloured shirt. They also wore their blades. Alanna's heavier dagger was placed in the centre of her back in a sleek black holster, while Shereen wore a more delicate blade at her hip. I didn't think it was for protection so much as for ceremony, but you could never be too sure with the Knaves. Lindsey meanwhile wore a form-fitting charcoal midi-dress with an open back that showed off her best assets. Frankly, she looked like a million bucks, fierce and sexy. Stuart was in for it.

The forecasted rain had continued to hold off through the late afternoon, though I was glad to have the option of the tent regardless; I didn't want the dance to be ruined by an unexpected shower.

"What did Dom get you for a wedding present," Lindsey asked, swirling her own glass before throwing the whiskey down the hatch in one shot. "Stuart said he wouldn't tell anyone what it was."

I smiled but chose to keep it simple. "He wrote me some love letters and a few stories."

A collective "aww" filled the room just as Thomas appeared in the doorway.

"Well, I don't get that response very often," he said with a chuckle. He was wearing a handsome set of smart-looking green robes. "Peggy says five minutes, Julia. You look beautiful by the way."

I felt heat rise to my face at both the announcement and the compliment. I was definitely nervous now.

"Thanks, Thomas," I said before tossing back the remainder of my drink just as Lindsey had done.

I was nervous, knowing I would soon be walking myself down the aisle. Since I had always imagined it that way, I knew that wasn't really the root cause of my nerves. I think they centred more around the attention I would be facing from so many people at once, and perhaps a small fear that I might make a fool of myself in the process by tripping on my dress or something.

"You're going to do great," Shereen said quietly with a squeeze on my arm before she and Alanna left to take their seats.

"I'm going to go find Stuart quick before I take my place," Lindsey said after giving me a big hug. "See you at the altar."

"Maybe it'll be you next," I offered, and she rolled her eyes dramatically before heading down the drive and towards the lake. Alone now, I stood in the entranceway to *Caisleán na Spéirmhná*—the home Dom had named after his love for me—and peered out. It was a life I had never expected ... and one I was now prepared to fight tooth-and-nail for.

In the distance, I could see two banks of folding chairs with the aisle clear in between. I wasn't entirely sure what the point of the set up was, as we were actually having a more traditional Druidic ceremony. Peggy had walked me through the rhythms of the ritual already. However, I knew that Dom really wanted to keep some of the more traditional Christian traditions in the mix, for the sake of his own history. He wanted to see me walk down the aisle.

I couldn't quite see him yet from my vantage point, though I could see Ronan standing and chatting with Peggy so I presumed Dom must be nearby. Thomas and Lennie stood there too, a few feet away, and my heart ached for the pain this day might bring up for Lennie. For now, he seemed happy and relaxed, and I hoped the day brought him peace as much as anything else. I watched as Lindsey joined the grouping, towering over Lennie in her heels and ignoring Ronan entirely, at least based on her body language.

Then at long last, I caught a glimpse of Dom's golden hair in the late afternoon sunlight. Immediately, I was engulfed by the scent of sea and sunshine and felt the connection between us tighten dramatically.

Intuitively, I spoke to his thoughts with a Send. *"I'm coming."*

With his frame still slightly obscured from my view as he chatted with Ronan, I could only see the top of his head as he turned towards the house: *Send received.*

He must have said something to Peggy then, since the music stopped, shifting to a slower, traditional Irish song. I felt a cold nudge at my hand and realized that Oisín had arrived at my side. I still had no idea how the hound knew where to be and when, but I was immensely grateful for his presence. I gave him a quick scratch and gathered my bouquet from a vase by the door before stepping out into the low sunshine.

I barely registered the loud crunch of gravel below my feet as I crossed the drive and floated onto the front lawn. I could see Oisín's tail out of the corner of my eye, swishing happily as he ran ahead, but my focus was entirely on the ethereal pull between myself and my ancient lover. What I had worried about before, the staring faces or making a fool of myself, melted away as I traversed the slope between our castle and our union. The otherworldly promise Dom had made all those years ago was felt deeply within my own body, and I finally understood the depth of what had been woven between us during all of these iterations.

Our guests rose to greet my arrival at the back of the aisle, but I only had eyes for Dom. He stood tall and proud and positively *beaming* from the other end of the aisle. I smiled back at him, a wellspring of joy surging inside me as several "oohs" and "ahs" rose from the crowd. I was likely emitting more than a little bit of a magic glow, but I was in safe company.

Dom wore a green and brown flecked tweed waistcoat with a simple cream linen shirt underneath. His sleeves were pushed up casually, adjusted for the unexpected heat of the day. On his bottom half, he wore a smart pair of dark green trousers and simple brown shoes. He had also pulled his golden locks back with a hair tie, tidy waves gathered at the back of his head in a stylish knot. I noticed that he'd also tidied his beard as his smile radiated at me with perfectly white teeth. The overall effect had him looking like he had walked straight off the pages of a trendy bridal magazine.

He was dazzling.

I began my slow walk down the aisle but could sense in Dom's body language that he could barely stand the wait. The man who so often seemed to be made of stone was shifting back and forth uncomfortably until I held my hand out to him, beckoning him to join me. He strode proudly to greet me halfway, at my side in life, both physically and spiritually, as we approached our nuptials together. I could hear several people sigh to my right and another "aww" from somewhere to my left. I thought then of my inner map and compass, as Dom took my hand in his, and felt the strong current of togetherness that rushed freely between us.

"May there be peace to the north, south, east, and west!" Peggy called as we approached the altar. Peace did indeed fill my body in what felt like an endless wellspring of joy and ancient magic.

Peggy beamed as we settled ourselves under Thomas's magnificent wood creation. Dom's fingers gripped mine tightly as we awaited the ritual of our Druid-meets-traditional wedding ceremony.

"Welcome everyone," Peggy said, her voice ringing out, filled with gladness. "Please, form a circle around our dear friends Domhnall O'Brien and Julia Harrison, who are here in our presence to be witnessed in the sacred rites of marriage!"

Quicker than anticipated, our guests moved into the outer circle. I wondered if Peggy had coached them to do this or if most were familiar enough with the basics of pagan weddings that it was second nature. Dom smiled at me, delighting also in the feeling of our friends and chosen family gathering around us in a protective circle of love and kinship.

"We are gathered under the Beltane moon and call to our ancestors in acknowledgement of all they have passed on to us, both in spirit and in blood."

My mind wandered to Dom and my "activities" on the Beltane moon a year ago before the dark portents. I blushed at the memory.

Next, Peggy held her right hand to the sky, holding up a short dagger that I recognized as her personal athame, while her left hand pointed gracefully towards the ground. She walked clockwise, drawing energy from both the air and earth to form an inner circle around us.

"Let us consecrate this sacred space! Breathe deep from the earth below, this ancient land that tells the stories of our lineages. Or in this case, the many tales of Dom and Julia's countless lives together." Soft laughter rippled through the greater circle. "Take a deep breath from the air, pulling from the beautiful canopy of sky above us, with sun and moon high above."

I couldn't exactly *see* the line of magic that she drew, but I could definitely feel it humming around us. It felt safe, like a warm hug of held space.

Peggy then grabbed a small silver cup from a low ledge on the altar. I recognized it as a chalice used for consecrating the space with water. East, south, west, north, and back to the east once more, we watched as she flicked the water all around. At the completion of her circle, my magic caught hold, pulling the droplets from the cup and forming a glittering globe around us. This was an enchantment everyone could see as it sparkled into a light mist around us, drifting off into the cool spring evening and out of sight.

People clapped, and Dom leaned close, speaking low. "You still don't know you do that, do you?"

"No clue," I said, speaking low and winking. I knew exactly what I was doing, though it wasn't something I could explain fully yet; ever since the events at the well, I felt a surer connection to my magic growing by the day.

Peggy chuckled and told me just as quietly, "Please don't ignite us with this next one, Julia." She then consecrated the space with fire, using a thick incense stick and speaking to the light of the hearth and heat of the flame. With divine timing, the angle of the bright orange sunset caught Dom from behind, casting his otherworldly character into the spotlight like some sort of anointed prince of the sun. He had always been pure sunshine to me, both in sense and vision, but never more so than now.

Our guests let out an audible sigh.

"Wonderful. And with that, we will call on the four quarters," Peggy said, extending her arms to our friends, "Quarter masters, please step forward."

I watched as Thomas, Lennie, Lindsey, and Ronan took several steps towards the centre, each one smiling brightly towards where we stood as they took their positions in the four directions. Beyond Lindsey, I could see Stuart's loving grin as he faced us, and I watched as his gaze slowly travelled from us towards Lindsey's back, a different type of adoration spreading across his brow. It made me smile; it really would be their union we witnessed next, and I didn't need the Sight to know as much.

First, Peggy led Dom and me towards Thomas, who spoke from his position to the east. Raising his hands, Thomas spoke with a booming voice, far more confident than I'd ever heard from him before. "Spirits of the east—of air, sky, and spring—I call upon you!" Silence followed as a bird resembling a small hawk flew overhead, and I was unsure if it was in fact real or imagined. "The gateway to the east is open!"

Several Druids in the crowd shouted, along with Peggy, *"The gateway to the east is open!"*

Peggy spoke alone then. "Do you, Domhnall and Julia, promise to support each other not only through times with soft breezes but through the winds of change and gales of challenge?"

"We do," my groom and I answered as his hand squeezed tight. As always, his warm grasp and presence at my side were infinitely steadying in any storm.

Next, Peggy led us to the south, where Lennie stood. He wore a slick black suit, which highlighted his warm skin against the surrounding greenery. He wore his dual blades in holsters under his arms. I noticed he also wore one of Wren's smaller blades at his waist. A part of me was surprised to see him stepping into the role of Druid today, when he was so clearly a Knave, but I sensed it was in healing practice towards the memory of his parents, and in honour of the brief friendship Wren had shared with Dom and me.

"Spirits of the south—of summer, fire, and heat—I call upon you!" Lennie said, his voice not nearly as loud as Thomas's, though it carried plenty of power behind it. In the distance, a mighty stag bounded out from a copse of trees and then disappeared as it ran off into the sunset.

Our guests chimed. *"The gateway to the south is open!"*

"Julia and Dom," Peggy said then, "do you pledge to care for each other both when the flames are stoked and when they sputter to the smouldering coals?"

I felt my bearing hearth roar at the words and closed my eyes momentarily to listen to the fire within. The answer was there: My love for Dom would never go out.

"I do," I said, confident in our shared destiny.

Dom—who seemed to be having a similar internal conversation—called out with pure conviction half a second later, "I do."

We were led towards Lindsey next, who stood to the west. Our newest friend lifted her chin confidently as she spoke. "Spirits of the west—of autumn's wisdom, running rivers, deep contemplation, and the pull of the tides—I call upon you!"

I could feel the moon above me, silently sending her loving encouragement.

"The gateway to the west is open!"

"Domhnall and Julia, will you embrace the ebb and flow of life's tidal flow, combining your dreams and desires as you travel together arm-in-arm throughout this life and onto the next?"

I felt a chill go up my spine. I knew she meant onto the Otherworld, but the incidental reference to our repeated life cycles also bore significance. I looked up and watched Dom's jaw flex several times as he processed our shared reality. This was yet another one of our truths: The pain that we, and Dom in particular, carried was as deep as the ocean. The strength it had taken to re-enter each life with full awareness towards the potential loss was truly his greatest challenge. And even now, we truly didn't know if this was our final cycle.

Yet our shared love was also his deepest pride. And mine.

"We will," we said quietly in unison.

At last, we were led to Ronan. His smile was smaller than the others' had been, though not without love. "Spirits of the north—of winter, stone, and iron—I call upon you," he said, his accent soft and steady as he lifted his hands to the north. I could see a great sadness in his eyes, but it had nothing to do with our union today.

In my mind's eye, I sensed a great black bear wandering quietly in the trees beyond, shadowed and alone in its quest. Solemn in its purpose.

"The gateway to the north is open!" called our guests for the final quarter.

Peggy rose to her greatest height, arms outstretched. "Julia and Domhnall, do you promise to work together through times of ease, as well as when immovable challenges arise, when it seems that all hope is lost and there is no way forward? Will you stand together?"

This question I knew neither of us needed to contemplate. It had always been this way. Together we were as unyielding as the night, as sure as solid stone. "We will!"

Everyone cheered as Peggy led us back to the altar, the quarter masters returning to their places within the outer circle.

"Wonderful! And now, with your witness, we will guide this dear couple through their handfasting and exchange of rings!"

The next few minutes drifted past as if it were a dream.

Facing Dom at last, we clasped both hands and gazed into each other's faces. His grey-blue eyes, with their immeasurable depth of soul, were rimmed with sparkling tears of joy. I felt hot tears gather in my own as I beamed back at him, blinking. I recalled what Alanna had said about leaning forward to blot them but knew that Dom would love me regardless, tears, smeared make-up, and all.

Peggy wrapped a colourful rope around our joined hands and spoke to the sun and moon, the earth and sky, and so on. I recognized an old prayer, an Irish one about the roads rising to meet you, but I could barely take any of it in. The words washed over us like a wave, blending together as she fasted and unfasted the length of entwined fabric around us, declaring us united as one. Cheers and applause erupted from the circle around us.

I swayed on the spot slightly, the magnitude of this moment on the verge of overwhelming me.

"I'm here, love," Dom said. "It's just you and me now."

"I know," I replied, steadying my breath.

The crowd quieted, and we prepared to speak our vows and exchange rings. Dom had wanted this tradition, and I wanted to be here with him in it. While I'd struggled to actually listen through the handfasting, distracted by the weight of the moment, my centuries-old lover now had my complete and utter attention.

Smiling right into the depths of my soul, he stared deep into my eyes as tears pooled in his beard. "Julia … I vow to honour and love you for as long as our souls are intertwined and beyond … My sovereign. My queen. Forever." He pulled the Claddagh ring from his breast pocket and slid it onto my ring finger, its point towards me now at last. For once, the coolness of my hands was a benefit, as the ring didn't get stuck.

My turn came, and all fear of being watched melted away. It really was only us now. "Domhnall, I vow to honour and love you … to the end of our days and through whatever comes next … The sun to my moon. The spear to my chalice … My whole heart."

Peggy handed me Dom's ring, a plain gold circle. I struggled slightly to place it on his much warmer hands. He laughed and helped it along with a sweet smile.

Peggy spoke. "With these rings, as the representation of the circle of our year, the natural world, and of our lives … you may kiss the bride!"

Dom leaned in and pushed both hands into my hair, kissing me hard. I kissed him back in kind, and the crowd cheered and whistled loudly. Surprisingly, he continued on, demanding entrance into my mouth with his tongue, tasting deeply of our shared love and desire. I obliged for a few moments, forgetting where we were, and then pulled back, blushing crimson. He looked completely unashamed, the light in his eyes brighter than I had ever seen.

"Naughty," I said.

He shrugged. "My wife has cast a spell on me. Not my fault."

MANTLE OF THE WORLD RULER

Dom wrapped his arms around my waist, pulling me close like he would never let go. We swayed there together for a time as the sun ducked low in the sky. Around us, I could hear Peggy proceeding to close the gateways with the help of the quarter masters, but I only had eyes for Dom.

He was my anchor to this world, and I to his.

CHAPTER 38

With the formalities completed, it was at last time to eat, drink, and be merry. Although generally Dom was sucked into the vortex of social engagements very quickly, he remained stuck to my side after the ceremony.

"You make the most *gorgeous* bride, my darling," he said as he brushed my hair back and kissed me behind the ear. "Standing there at the end of the aisle. Mm … Well, I'm of a mind to whisk you away right here and now, guests be damned."

Mead and champagne were currently being passed out in waves, and based on the already growing crowd, the full expression of celebration would soon be at hand. I wondered how long it would be before people would be wearing their neckties around their heads, but perhaps that was just a Canadian thing. We hadn't even eaten dinner yet.

I giggled at Dom's predictability before taking a big sip from my own glass. "You do know that the gals have a bet going, right?"

"A bet? What about?" he asked, eyes sparkling. I had a feeling he knew exactly what kind of wager had been made.

"Well, Alanna thinks you'll drag me upstairs before the dance."

"Oh, she does, does she?"

"She does. But Peggy thinks you won't even bother taking me upstairs; you'll just find somewhere nearby, and we'll fuck like bunnies."

MANTLE OF THE WORLD RULER

He laughed heartily and feigned surprise. "As though I lack *any* self-control! Well, I doubt that. And besides, we can't abandon our guests."

"No, we can't," I said, rubbing my body close to his.

"My wife is a tease," he said, nostrils flaring.

I liked hearing him call me his wife. "And my husband is insatiable."

"Is that a compliment?"

"It could be." I giggled. "I'm also looking forward to the party though."

He nodded in agreement. "Me too. But later …" he said low into my ear. "I'm going tear that dress right off you."

"Well, the outer layer will come off for the party; it's a bit fancy for my taste," I said, looking down and playfully ignoring his directness. Frankly, I was surprised at how lusty the whole scenario had made him. But I supposed this was a day he had dreamed of for a long time.

"Oh? I think it suits you. Brings out your eyes," he said, placing his fingers under my chin and gazing at me fondly.

My eyes were a rather nondescript hazel, and so I doubted this to be the case. I eyed him speculatively for a moment in reply; then I felt a naughtiness of my own well up from within. "Tell you what. I'll need help getting it off anyway … So, maybe we can sneak away to the garage later, between dinner and the dance. And while we're at it, you can show me more of that sexy car your *wife* bought you," I said, winking at him.

He threw his head back in a booming laugh, evidently satisfied with my idea. "Deal."

A passing tray of appetizers briefly stole his attention, and he shoved several different canapés into his mouth in quick succession, groaning in delight. I helped myself to a cracker with what looked smoked salmon in cream cheese with an onion sprig on top. It was delicious, and so I took another. We then wandered hand-in-hand towards Ronan, Lennie, and Peggy, who were also sharing food and drink.

"Hello, you two!" Peggy exclaimed.

"Lovely ceremony," Lennie said with a smile. I could still detect sadness in his eyes as he looked around the space, missing Wren, but he did seem happier than he had in a long time.

"You look beautiful, Julia," Ronan said, taking my hands into his with a kiss. They were cool like mine, which felt slightly uncomfortable. Unlike

427

Lennie, who seemed to be slowly improving in his wellness over time, Ronan seemed more haunted by the day. Even at an event as special as this, something about him just seemed off.

I tried to ignore the vision of the lone bear I had seen during the ceremony while he had been speaking.

Dom clearly sensed the shadow that hung over him too, shifting uneasily onto the balls of his feet to peer out over our guests. "Julia, we should probably continue saying hello to everyone."

"Hmm …" I said, giving Peggy a knowing look. She too had expressed concern for Ronan and hoped to reach him at a more spiritual level while she visited. However, she knew as well as anyone how stubborn he could be and wasn't holding her breath.

We made our rounds, chatting with familiar faces and some new to me as well. I recognized several of Thomas's friends from the final battle, and it was good to see that they were keeping well.

"Great ceremony!" Thomas said as his face blossomed into a wide grin. His scar had healed well but still created a certain level of distortion to his expression. I felt a pang of guilt about it, but he had assured me on many occasions that he wore it with pride.

"I'm the luckiest man in the world!" Dom said, wrapping his arm around me. The resultant maneuver caused me to slop champagne onto his pant leg, but he laughed it off. "Not to worry. Shall we carry on, my darling?"

I blushed. This newest term of endearment seemed to be coming out of nowhere, and I wondered if it stemmed from some other time in our past lives. We mingled for another half an hour before everyone eventually migrated towards dinner. It was being served family style across a single long table, just as Dom had requested. It reminded him of the days of old, and he loved the idea of our guests being able to dig in as they pleased while sharing in open conversation.

Dom and I seated ourselves at the centre, with Ronan on his right and Lindsey to my left. We eyed the platters placed before us hungrily, and Dom patted his stomach in excitement. The main entrées consisted of salt-baked whole trout, roast spatchcock chicken, and a beef sirloin with chimichurri sauce. There were also trays of assorted roast vegetables, mushrooms, new potatoes, salads, and dinner buns, and plenty of wine, mead, and cider for all. Frankly, the caterers had outdone themselves.

"Oh God, I'm starving," Dom said, unsurprisingly.

Ronan seemed to be remaining in decent enough spirits, and the two men were chatting happily about a trout-fishing trip they had been on together shortly after they'd first met.

"As usual, Domhnall made the whole thing into a competition," Ronan said with a smile to me.

"You know that's a lie. It was *you* who made it into a competition," Dom said, scoffing as he gave my thigh a soft squeeze, a reminder that he was still right there beside me, despite the escalating boasts.

Across the heaping platters from us were Lennie, Peggy, and Thomas, seated shoulder-to-shoulder and laughing along with the pair of Irishmen. On our other side, Lindsey and Stuart were chatting animatedly with those down the table from them, including Alanna and Shereen. Sean and Graham were seated at the end, both men growing louder and redder in the cheek with each glass of wine.

I didn't invite anyone from my old, pre-Dom life to the wedding, mainly for reasons of risk and safety, but also … What could I possibly say to explain such a gap in both our communication and circumstances? Still, it left me feeling slightly sad. I had no biological family left, so it wasn't exactly a surprise to feel a hollowness there—anyone in my situation would experience some level of associated grief. But my mind also wandered to Virginia, Becky, and Dave, along with some of the other friends I had spent time with most recently while in Vancouver and at UBC. They had been good to me during that stage of my life, and I was grateful. Unfortunately, considering our reality, it just wasn't practicable to drag them into what could potentially lead to disaster.

At the very end of the table, I could see Morgan in rapt conversation with some of the more trustworthy locals Dom had invited to the dinner portion of the night, all of them donning their Sunday best. Apparently, each had been connected to Dom's estate-keeping throughout recent history and knew him to be a good man, despite some of the more unique company he kept. I also knew that the old boys were a dead shot with a rifle and each had brought a small arsenal with them, at Morgan's request, to keep the grounds safe this evening. It was my understanding that they would disperse onto the property once the dancing started, keeping an eye on the borders while the rest of our party let loose. Morgan had insisted upon it, citing it as his wedding present to us, and Dom wasn't the kind of man to decline that kind of offer. Morgan was loyal through and through, so this was as much a sign of respect as it was a gift.

Some of the Knaves who'd joined us at the house party earlier in the year were at both the ceremony and supper, apparently by Lennie's request. In truth, I wasn't really familiar with most of them. Dom, however, knew each of them by name and treated them like old friends. I had a hunch that the real reason Lennie had extended the invite was because Dom had instructed him to line up a small legion of magical fighters for the day. Just in case. And in the end, Dom had a point. Including a group of Knaves really was the easiest way to ensure added safety for the group, as well as the promise of a great party.

"You're not regretting that you didn't invite any of the Knaves from the desert, are you?" I asked Dom when his attention returned to me sometime between dinner and desert.

"Oh, God no! This definitely isn't *their* type of party."

"What? We aren't raunchy enough?" Lindsey asked, catching onto the conversation.

Stuart laughed from the other side of her. "I don't think it's a matter of being raunchy so much as you not serving moonshine in a dank cave followed by a half-naked basement fight club."

"You *knew* that might happen when Dom went there?" I asked, surprised.

"Not that exactly, but stuff like that is always a possibility with those snakes," Stuart said, though his voice didn't sound unkind. "They love a good brawl, the less clothes the better."

Lindsey raised her eyebrows as Dom shook his head with a rueful grin. He'd just finished a second helping of dinner and was content and well satiated. "I'd like to say that I'm used to tackling the unexpected, but that was a bit of surprise even for me."

"I bet," Lindsey said.

"I'm sure we will have plenty of fun tonight though," I said reassuringly, "even without a blade gauntlet."

"Especially without a gauntlet," Stuart said. "I'd rather not have to pull any weapons tonight."

I eyed the pair of blades crossed neatly on his muscular back. They bore significantly more intricate handles than some of the others I'd see him use in the past, though I knew their purpose wasn't only ceremonial.

I gulped, reminded once more of the threat we faced each day and would until Cassius was defeated.

However, the evening chugged on with neither sight nor sound of trouble. Plenty of food and wine was enjoyed across the board, followed by a tantalizing strawberry tart and a mini-Oreo cheesecake platter, as requested by Dom. *"What? Oreos are one of the best inventions of the modern era!"* he had said in pre-emptive reaction to my disdain. In the end, his perseverance had won out.

The general atmosphere was both loving and wholly familiar. Just as we'd hoped. And soon, our plates were cleared, and attention turned towards the bride and groom—us—for a round of toasts.

Glasses were topped with champagne and uncorked bottles of mead were placed along the table for anyone who wanted some. Traditionally, the drinking of mead was related to the "honeymoon"—the period of time during a full lunar cycle when the bride and groom would be supplied with a month's supply of mead to consume. I liked the idea of it, yet while I enjoyed mead, I couldn't see myself drinking it regularly for thirty days straight—though I had no doubt Dom would try to convince me otherwise.

Lindsey stood to kick off the toasts. She clinked her glass with a dessert spoon and waited for the crowd to hush, which happened quite quickly. I think a lot of the people in the room were slightly afraid of her.

"I haven't known the pair of you for long ... though that's not saying much, as I don't think any of us have really. You two are both *really* old!" Laughter rippled down the table.

"Hey, I'm not as old as he is!" I shouted. Dom wrapped his arm around me, kissing me on the cheek before whispering something naughty in my ear about devouring my *"ripe young flesh under the full moon."* I elbowed him promptly in the ribs.

"Yes, yes ... But while we've only been friends for a short time, I have witnessed first-hand the devotion, adoration, and *passion* you share. Anyone who knows you can feel the love in the room whenever you're together. It's palpable ... and a delight to behold! So, to keep this short and sweet, I raise my glass to your endless love. Past, present, and future!" With that, Lindsey tossed the rest of her drink back.

Dom leaned in and kissed me, and we both took big swigs of champagne.

Next came Ronan. He had known Dom best and longest during his friend's most recent rebirth, and Dom had been adamant that he speak. Ronan had dragged his feet slightly, citing his not having felt like much of a friend to anyone over the past year. But Dom had threatened him with kicking him out of the house, so in the end, he'd obliged.

Ronan cleared his throat, smiling down at Dom and me. "Would you look at these two!"

Someone wolf-whistled.

"In all seriousness," he continued, "when I first met Dom, I was seriously skeptical that he had all his screws in place"—more laughter erupted along the table—"and if you know the man as well as I do, you'd know he most certainly does not!"

Dom laughed heartily as he rubbed his hand down my back. I leaned in, looking up at our dear friend.

"Dom's love for Julia was evident from the moment I met him. No matter what we did, she was always on either the front or back of his mind. I shit you not; we could be camping in the middle of nowhere drinking beer, and I would catch him with this ... *strange* look on his face. It wasn't sad. Not really. It was the kind of look that reminded me of when you make a promise." I felt my eyes begin to tear up. I had never heard anything like this from him, always assuming he was secretly (or in some cases, not so secretly) resentful that Dom had finally found me.

Ronan continued. "And really, that's what it was. Dom had made his promise to her—the woman he loves more than the moon and stars and sky. More than life itself really. The promise that he would come back for her. It's hard to grasp a love like that when you've only lived one short lifetime." He sighed. "I admit that when Julia came back into Dom's life, I was perhaps a little bit salty—"

"More than a little bit!" Dom said, patting his friend's back playfully.

"Alright, I was fairly salty, but hear me out. Dom is the kind of friend who gives you his all, and I had foolishly worried that when the love of his life returned, he would lose interest in the world we had shared together. I am a bit of a lonely man you see, so this was frightening."

I blinked several times, shocked at Ronan's vulnerability. What was this all about?

"But then … I met you, Julia. And I realized I had gained not only a friend but something akin to a sister. Another member of our chosen family—the missing piece, in fact. Because without Julia, there is no Dom. Not really. And the transformation that occurred when you joined us was incredible to behold. Largely because *yer man* here could finally let off some of his … bodily frustrations."

"Careful, Ronan," Dom growled. I threw my face into my hands, feigning embarrassment.

"I mean, in a way other than fighting, of course," Ronan said, winking at me. "But despite the constant threat we all live under, the true Dom was released when his soulmate came back into his life. He loves you so, so much, Julia … but you already know that."

"I do," I said, nuzzling into Dom affectionately.

"Grand. So tonight, I would like everyone to raise a glass to the chosen family Dom and Julia have created through their union. They are the glue that binds us all together … and the promise of a world and future filled to the very brim with love!"

Everyone cheered loudly, and Dom stood to embrace Ronan in a massive bear-hug. The friends stood like that for a while, and I knew there was a great deal unspoken flowing between them. Next, I offered Ronan my own hug, whispering, "Thank you," into his ear.

"I meant what I said," Ronan said as he smiled back sweetly. The sadness that had plagued his expression remained, but I also sensed a little bit of hope growing too.

Ronan sat down, and Dom and I were left standing. It was our turn to speak.

"Alright, everyone, I'm going to keep this brief," Dom said, and Lennie rolled his eyes dramatically while Thomas let out a belly laugh. "No, no, I promise. Julia won't thank me if I keep her from the dancing for too long."

I gave him a playful hip-bump as he laughed, truly together in the joy of the moment.

"But we wanted to thank you all from the bottom of our hearts for being here. Not only tonight but for gracing us with your friendship throughout this lifetime. You are a rare bunch, and we couldn't imagine facing everything, or *anything*, without you all by our sides."

Dom raised his glass, and I followed suit. "Thank you!"

Dom's loquaciousness was well known to the attendees, so the brevity of his thanks spoke to its depth.

Speeches complete, our guests dispersed for a much-needed break throughout house and grounds. And apparently, I wasn't the only one who was glad Dom had opted to keep it quick.

Smiling cheekily, he pulled me close and whispered into my ear. "I've got something to show you."

"Oh?" I said, still feeling flushed from the food, wine, and sentimentality. "It doesn't happen to be a certain *car*, does it?"

"You know what? It does!" he said as took me by the hand and marched me away from the tent, his face filled with glee.

The air bore the crisp bite of early evening, and I felt myself shiver slightly at the shift. We would gather for the dance once the tables were removed and the sun was low enough to turn on the twinkle lights under the tent. I *had* planned to remove the outer layer of my dress upstairs during this time, as well as grab a warmer wrap, but I liked Dom's suggestion to sneak off into the garage better.

Just like during the ceremony, and almost every moment since, I had his full attention, with him only looking over his shoulder once to holler jokingly to Lindsey and Stuart that he needed to have a private word with his *wife*.

"Looks like I'm in trouble!" I said, shrugging playfully. Truthfully, I was looking forward to a private moment with just the two of us, if only just to breathe in silence together.

We approached the horse-barn-turned-garage and slipped into its quiet darkness alone.

During our previous life cycle, in the 1960s, the barn had been tastefully converted to store his new collection of cars and motorcycles. This time around, to add to its comfortability, he'd renovated it further to include a small lounge area with seating and a large television. He had also integrated an array of modern gym equipment, and it had quickly become a haven away from the house over the past decade when the memories became too much. Admittedly, I had always avoided the place out of reverence for its sanctitude to Dom.

I turned my back and closed the door with a soft click. And then I locked it.

"Julia," he said, his voice a low purr. I turned towards him and noticed a visible shift in his posture as he swiftly let his guard down in front of me.

"Hello, husband," I said, smiling seductively.

"Can I help you take your dress off?" he asked, cheeks flushing.

"Not just yet. Let's go over there," I said, gesturing towards the lounge. He moaned slightly but followed me obediently towards the far end of the barn. Along the way, I dragged my hand seductively across the hood of his new wheels, offering him a sultry wink over my shoulder.

"You're just teasing me now," he said.

"I know."

At last, I stood in a pool of fading light and turned my back to him. I set my flower crown gently aside before letting out a soft sigh. I feigned reaching for the clasps myself, but it was merely an invitation. He placed his warm hands over mine before gently undoing the outer catches himself. Job done, he carefully removed the sheath, caressing my shoulders and arms as he pushed the gown towards the ground.

Goosebumps rippled across my skin, and I turned towards him. "Thanks."

"Is this what you're wearing to the dance?" he asked, now eyeing the inner dress from the front.

My chest was heaving slightly with anticipatory breath. "I was going to. Why?"

An all-too-familiar inkiness welled in his eyes. "I just don't want to damage it if you have plans for it later," he said, taking a handful of the garment into his fist and lustfully pulling me towards him.

I could feel his erection hard against my hip. "I do … have plans …" I said, barely completing the sentence over the roar of my own rising tide.

"Me too," he said, breath ragged.

Contrary to both his physical and verbal tone, he gently removed the chemise from my shoulders, letting it cascade over my hips and onto the floor.

I wore only a simple blue-lace thong underneath. At the sight of my bare chest and skimpy underwear, he was thrown into frantic attempts to remove his own clothes. A button skittered across the floor as he tossed his vest aside, and I helped him pull his linen shirt over his head, meeting him hungrily with a kiss as his arms were still being pulled from his sleeves.

"Oh God …" he said, forcing his pants and underwear to the floor, then kicking off his shoes and stepping free. "Do you have *any* clue what you do to me?"

The sight of his naked body was utterly magnificent. I kicked off my own shoes and hopped up into his arms, wrapping my legs firmly around his waist. "I think I have a good idea."

Dom carried me towards the couch, using his arms to protectively cradle my body as he drove us toward the leather surface below. He didn't even bother removing my underwear, forcing the gusset aside to thrust into me at long last.

Now at a loss for words, he simply groaned.

I arched in welcome, breathing my pleasure into his ear and urging him onward with my heels; I knew he would be making quick work of his adoration, and I meant to encourage it.

"I've been waiting for hours," I said.

He gave me a wicked grin before increasing his tempo.

Again and again, we met as both heat and friction amplified between us. He smelled like fresh air and beard oil and tasted like Oreo cookies. I breathed in his deliciousness, releasing a sudden moan as he angled deeper into the place that made my knees go weak. Within moments, my body erupted into a powerful orgasm, with his own climax following shortly thereafter.

Collapsing on top of me a few moments later, he let out a soft chuckle. "God … I'm sorry that was such a quick ride!"

"Well, we do have guests to attend to," I said, nuzzling fondly into his neck. Darkness had fallen completely during our moments indoors, and the dance couldn't start without us. I kissed along the left side of his neck several times and felt the gooseflesh rise all the way down his left side. The right, however, remained smooth.

Pushing himself off, he shuddered involuntarily before wandering naked towards his gym. "I've got fresh towels over here."

We proceeded to clean ourselves up as best we could, though the state of my hair would be a dead giveaway of the frivolity that had taken place.

"Did you want me to run up to the house and get you anything?" he asked tenderly as he pulled his pants on.

"Hmm, maybe," I said, eyeing myself in the gym mirror. "Although, maybe, Lindsey's thought of that."

Dom chuckled. "Unless Stuart has distracted her."

"That's true," I said, pulling the sheath dress back on. "I was hoping to wear my hair up though. And I had a shawl as well."

Dom pulled the hair tie from his own locks. "Here! I want to wear mine down anyway," he said with a grin. He tousled his waves and yet somehow still managed to look like a model. "Let loose and whatnot."

I laughed. "Alright, that solves one issue," I said, eyeing my own situation with less ease. Letting out a long breath, I made several attempts to pile my hair on top of my head in a fancy knot but couldn't manage to get it quite right. I looked up to discover that Dom had disappeared to the other end of the garage and was now digging around in the trunk of one of his other cars.

"What about this?" he hollered.

I ran my fingers through my hair several times and pulled it into a loose bun at the nape of my neck. Good enough. "What about what?" I asked, padding down the centre of the barn towards him.

He re-emerged holding a thin blue blanket. "Will this do? You're going to be cold."

I took it into my hands and turned it over several times. It was delicately woven from what felt like soft, luxurious cotton. I wrapped it around my shoulders immediately. "It's perfect."

The shawl I had upstairs was not nearly as cozy, and I had a feeling the evening would be much cooler now that the sun had finally set.

Together, we left the garage and stepped out, only to discover all of our guests, holding sparklers, whooping and cheering, and creating a lined pathway towards the tent.

"Do you think they know what we were up to?" I asked, blushing.

"Absolutely," Dom said, grinning wide as he led me to the dance.

♥

Ready for a break, I left Alanna and Shereen dancing with Thomas and some of the others. I smiled as I passed by Lindsey and Stuart, who were huddled intimately beside one of the tables, hands and legs intertwined. Looking out from the cover of the tent, I could see Dom regaling a group of Druids and Knaves with some vast tale beside one of the bonfires, much to their collective enjoyment. No doubt it was about a past life, or so it seemed, based solely on the animated arm movements he was making in his signature broad stance.

Leaving him to it, I wandered over to the bar to refill my drink before finding somewhere to sit down. My shoes *had* been comfortable, but still, my feet were sore. Dom and I had taken our first dance to a traditional song he had promised was special to our history. And indeed, it kindled memories of sunny days with him, holding hands and tickling our toes in swift river water. It didn't strike a specific vision, per se, but I could feel the sentiment behind it, like a layering of all of our love throughout countless lifetimes.

After that, music ranging from traditional Celtic to sixties rock to nineties pop blared out into the night. I had a blast dancing with Lennie and Thomas in particular to some of the popular numbers from our youth. Dom looked at me like I was crazy when I sang all of the words to several Spice Girls hits. He then surprised us as he crooned the entirety of "Pretty Woman," announcing it as the song from our "first date, this time around." He had a gorgeous voice, and I planned to encourage him to use it more around me. During the dance, I saw a side to Dom that I rarely did—just like our first date—and I vowed then and there that we would stick to our promise to party the night away in Ibiza someday. He was just so fucking fun to be around!

A night lunch was set out for guests to enjoy nibbling on their own, so I opted to fill a plate and sit down for a moment to rest. As I eyed the assortment of buns, cheeses, and deli meats, a warm hand suddenly enveloped my own.

I smiled and turned towards my husband. Leave it to Dom to home in on me ... and the *food*.

He smelled strongly of beer and wood smoke now. "Are you having a nice time, love?"

"I am," I said, leaning into him peacefully. "Are you?"

"Of course. Though I'm starting to feel a bit tired," he said, not looking the least bit sleepy.

"Mm ... I bet," I said, smirking. "My feet hurt too. Perhaps a snack and then we'll head up to bed?"

"Sounds divine," Dom said as he shoved a slice of cured meat into his mouth with a wink.

A handful of guests were still dancing and enjoying merriment in the tent, but most had gathered around the bonfires or were currently migrating towards the food.

"Have you seen Ronan?" Dom asked, looking concerned.

"No, but I assumed he wouldn't have liked watching Stuart and Lindsey dancing together." The pair of them had since disappeared, though I had a feeling *they* were in absolutely no danger.

"No, I think he's actually fine with it. There's something else though. While we were getting ready, he wasn't fully *present*, if that makes sense. It feels like he's almost acting."

"His speech was so genuine though. Vulnerable," I said.

"That's what I'm worried about. It was almost ... *too* vulnerable."

"Hmm ..." I said as Lennie appeared to our right, filling his own plate with food.

"I'm famished," he said.

"Any idea where Ronan went?" I asked him.

"He went to bed a while back. Said he wasn't feeling well." He turned and stared at the both of us, stone serious. "Honestly, I'm still quite worried about him."

"We are too," I said, nodding. Dom remained silent, deep in thought.

With his plate now full, Lennie wandered back to a group of Knaves. Dom finished piling his own plate, stacking several slices of meat onto a bun with turkey, salami, and mayo-mustard.

"Do we need to announce our exit?" I asked, chucking a few olives into my mouth.

"No, we'd never get out of here then," Dom said, and so we opted for the "Irish exit" instead.

It was beginning to rain heavy droplets, which I took as a sign that our timing was perfect. I assumed the partygoers would either migrate under the tent or into their rooms. Either way, we were headed inside. Dom and I skipped up the hill towards the front entrance, hand-in-hand.

"Oh, that's better," I said as we reached the dry front entrance. Dom let me enter the house first, and I felt the softness of his fingers run down my back, grazing the top of my bum before crossing the threshold himself.

"I have the most beautiful wife in the world," he said fondly.

I rolled my eyes dramatically, never having been great at taking compliments. "I'm sure all new husbands say that."

"Shouldn't they?" he said, closing the door behind us. "Besides, it's the truth."

In any case, I was fairly certain that I *did* have the most gorgeous husband around. "Likewise!"

The entrance hall was deserted, so we quietly made our way upstairs without being noticed by any partygoers. Reaching the top of the landing, I realized I was feeling slightly strange. A bit woozy in fact; perhaps the exhaustion of the day was catching up to me.

"Julia, are you alright?" Dom asked as I swayed on the spot slightly.

"I think so …"

He grabbed me by the elbow and directed me carefully into our adjoining bathroom. "You look like you're going to be sick!" he said, concern spreading across his face.

"It's just …"

Cassius's face was fully engulfed by the shadows of a sinister looking hood. He was crouched, almost frozen, at the edge of a pool of still, clear water, one of his hands braced solidly on the ground. The only signs of life were the faint clouds of respiration on the air.

It was cold wherever he was, though not frozen.

In all of my visions of him throughout the past year he had been shrouded, veiled from the sunlight and wholly unclear. They had also been few and far between and had *never* shown him like this. Never in action. On a mission. It was as if I were now witnessing him from above, and I knew that this was in *real time*.

My eyes registered a slight movement, with him glancing once at his gold watch before rising to his feet. Slowly, he drifted through dense green woodland, clearly in search of something. Underneath his cloak, he wore typical business attire, a black pinstriped suit with patent-leather shoes. It all looked expensive and wholly out of place for whatever forest glen he was haunting.

As he approached a hollowed-out tree, I could almost taste his anticipation in my own mouth. He was salivating, his need for whatever was hidden there tinged with the taste blood and iron. I abhorred the reality of this intimate connection, the one I knew that we'd shared throughout my many lifetimes and, more specifically, since he had speared me last spring.

Cassius knew of it too, and I wondered if he *wanted* me to see what he was experiencing now or if he was so wholly focused on his task that he had let his guard down, unknowingly allowing me access to him. I surmised it was the latter, knowing how closely he guarded his secrets.

Bending carefully, Cassius reached into the hollow and procured something small and rectangular. It looked to be wrapped in some sort of deerskin or other animal hide. He stood, turning abruptly towards a clearing where dim light was managing to trickle down through a deep canopy.

His pace quickened.

Arriving at what resembled a stone altar, he brushed dirt and filth from the small package, untying the leather bands that encircled it, keeping it shut. With steady hands, he removed the wrappings, exposing the item within. I felt a stab of familiarity rush though my body as I watched him hold the book up into the air with sheer reverence.

I knew this book.

The *Codex Druidicus*. The book from which I had dictated dark magic to viciously scrape Dom's memory tattoo into his pristine back.

And the book we had vowed to *never* let fall into the wrong hands.

CHAPTER 39

I found myself braced over the toilet during the aftermath of the short, vivid vision. At least we were alone. Dom instinctually directed me into the bathroom before all hell broke loose in my mind.

Through the waves of heaving convulsions, night lunch, and undigested alcohol, I sputtered out to Dom what I had seen. Cassius in the forest, finding the package, and at last, unwrapping what I'd immediately recognized as the *Codex Druidicus*. Dom's hand, which had been compassionately rubbing my back throughout, stilled. He stood abruptly, clearly not knowing what to do with his body as terror slashed across his beautiful face.

All I could think was that at least the vomiting had been minimal. So, that was something. I was also pretty sure I was going into shock.

I leaned back on the cool tile, hoping the worst of the stomach upset was behind me as I steadied my breath. I needed to stay in my body. I needed to *think*. Dom was fussing around the bathroom, visibly fighting back an unfamiliar panic. It wasn't like him to lose his head in situations like this, and it frightened me.

"I'm fine, Dom, honestly," I lied, pushing back the glass of water he had now shakily offered me for the fourth time.

"You're not fine," he said.

I didn't reply.

Dom continued to look concerned, placing the glass on the bathroom counter with a low growl. "Leave it to that bastard to ruin our wedding night."

I stared at him, eyes brimming with unexpected tears. "It's ruined?"

"Oh, no ... It's not *ruined*, not like *that*. But ... fuck! This is bad, Julia. Do you have any idea what Cassius could do with that book in his hands?"

"Well, it *is* in his hands," I said, bordering on delirious, "so I guess we—"

"I'm serious, Julia! What kind of timing is this? Today of all days? Do you think he wanted you to know he's found it? Do you think he knew? We've got to warn the others ..."

He was spiralling.

"Dom, stop. We don't even know if he *knows* what today was for us. It could just be a random chance that I had the vision now. And I only threw up because of the booze." I was making excuses now, downplaying what was obviously a *serious* blow to both our future plans and our safety.

Dom raised an eyebrow skeptically and reached for the glass of water again, this time downing it himself. "Nothing is random with Cassius."

I groaned, resigned to the disappointing truth of our shared destiny.

Dom pulled out his cellphone and began texting furiously. I was relieved that he was gaining control of himself again because I was pretty sure I was only moments from falling apart entirely. A reply came immediately, and he looked temporarily satisfied.

He crouched down beside me. "I'll need to ... make some calls. I'm worried about security. Will you be alright if I step out for a minute?"

"Sure," I said, slumping further down onto the cool marble floor in resignation. "I'll wait right here."

What must I have looked like, mind and body poured out, utterly empty on the bathroom floor? I was still in my sheath dress, which I had miraculously avoided puking on. It was, however, quite wrinkled, which I supposed was a strange thing to care about given the circumstances.

Dom ran his hands through his unbound hair. "I won't be more than fifteen minutes, love. Twenty, tops."

"Don't go too crazy interrogating guests, Dom ... It's probably just a divine coincidence."

Dom mumbled under his breath something that sounded like, *"I've had enough of these divine fucking coincidences ..."* before kissing me roughly on top of the head.

He stood abruptly and left the room, closing the door with a quiet click behind him. The fact that he'd left me splayed out on the bathroom floor instead of transferring me to the bed made it clear that he was even more worried than he was letting on. Immediately, I heard him talking to someone just outside the door; it sounded like Stuart had been stationed as my guard. I didn't hear Lindsey, however.

It looked like Cassius was ruining more than just *our* evening.

For fuck's sakes.

Resisting the urge to march out and send Stuart away, and instead trusting Dom's leadership in the moment, I slowly stood up and looked at myself in the mirror. The dark circles under my eyes that followed most visions had yet to appear—or else my makeup had stayed on as well as we'd hoped thanks to Lindsey's setting spray. I pulled my hair out of its low bun and scratched my scalp soothingly.

What the fuck were we going to do?

I eyed the shower—so often a place where I could gather my thoughts—but thought better of it. I was still quite dizzy and didn't want to fall. Perhaps Dom would join me in there before bed. I was exhausted from both the day and this latest vision.

My stomach turned slightly; I couldn't shake the feeling that Cassius had just taken a major step against us in our fight. Bigger than even we knew. And suddenly, a wave of regret and doubt washed over me, second guessing everything we'd done in the last several months. Had it all been a waste?

Leaving the bathroom, I padded quietly over to our bedroom window. Peering out, I could see that Dom had called off the party. I felt a wave of sadness as the last of the lights were shut off. It was a dark ending to what had been a brilliant day. I removed my dress and tossed it over an armchair in the corner of the bedroom, opting for a plush bathrobe instead.

Still feeling slightly woozy, I crawled into bed to wait for Dom to return, hoping the room would stop spinning before then as well. There was nothing we could do to combat Cassius right now. Dom would take care of security, and then we would sleep on it. Or at least that's what I told myself.

True to his word, Dom was back within twenty minutes, just as I was beginning to doze off. "Shit, sorry," I said, slightly startled.

"Oh love, keep sleeping. We've had a long day. You must be spent."

I smiled at the sight of him. Thankfully too, the room was now solid before me. "But we still have to consummate our marriage, Mr. O'Brien."

He let out a barking laugh, which surprised me, given the circumstances. "And what were we doing earlier, *Mrs. O'Brien?* I'm pretty sure I already bedded my new wife in our garage while our guests congregated a mere twenty metres outside the door."

"Oh yeah," I said, yawning into the back of my hand with a giggle. *"That."*

He unbuttoned his vest and shirt and lay them over my dress on the chair, followed by his pants. The sight of his almost naked body roused me further, but I also found myself curious about what sort of protocols he had enacted while downstairs.

"Is everything okay with security?" I asked, gesturing towards the house at large.

"It is," he said, his tone reassuring as he crawled into bed beside me. "I've had some additional guards posted about the place, just in case, though Lennie is positive everything is secure. Ronan too. They will both be on patrol tonight though, along with Sean and Graham, and several others."

"I feel bad …"

"Why on earth would you feel bad?" Dom looked legitimately confused. "Or do you mean you're feeling sick again?"

"No, I'm feeling a lot better. But … shouldn't we be helping out? It's not just *our* safety that matters, but everyone else's too."

Dom smiled at me, but I could detect a slight hint of pity woven into his grin. This was the kind of smile he gave me when I wasn't fully understanding the facts because I was too busy caring about other people's feelings or what they thought of me.

He collected himself before speaking, the pity smile melting away. "Besides the fact that it's our wedding night, Julia—which is more than enough of reason on its own—sometimes … *sometimes*, I need to delegate. This is my home. And it's my job to be in charge. That's the deal. I'm the …"

"The *World Ruler?*" I finished with just a hint of cheek, my eyebrow raised.

He blushed. "Don't make fun of me. It's hard to explain. Leadership is a fine balance. I actually have to *lead* sometimes … and …"

"I'm not making fun! I get it. The team captain has to act like a captain. It's a system. I get it. *Really,*" I said, pushing him onto his back before climbing on top of his hips; his erection was already solid below me.

My breath caught in my throat.

"Well … we all know who *I* answer to," Dom said, jaw clenching as he looked up.

I leaned forward and began to kiss his neck. Nuzzling. Nipping. Hungry. What was it about being in imminent danger that made me so aroused? I expected him to ask if I was alright, if I was sure I was feeling up for this, but instead, Dom responded in kind, grabbing at my breasts almost ferociously. He also knew the deep need for proof that we were still here on this earth. Alive, together.

"You just married me for my boobies, didn't you?" I asked, as usual wishing to break the tension of what I'd seen in my vision with laughter as much as passion.

Startled, he laughed incredibly hard then, a deep belly laugh that I could feel all the way into my core.

"So, what if I did!" he said, eyes twinkling. "Why *else* do you think I keep coming back for you?"

I laughed along with him as he flipped me onto my back, gazing into my soul.

Miraculously, I was no longer woozy from the earlier vision, his return to my side a wholly grounding tonic. Fuck, I loved this man! Time and time again, he was the one. Not even a dark vision from Cassius was going to ruin this night. Not if we had anything to say about it. *This* was the tenderness of having known each other for such a long time. Just because our moments had been broken up over a millennium, and just because I didn't always remember the exact details of each existence in my most recent births, that didn't mean there hadn't been a culmination of intimate, joyful vulnerability over the ages.

We had been together for *years and years*, after all.

I knew the trust between us so deeply in my bones that it made me ache sometimes. Ache for him and ache for us and the future we dared to plan for ourselves. Cassius be damned. He would rue the day he tried to ruin our wedding night with his sinister plans. Sure, he had the Codex, but tonight … *tonight* was for us. Our dreams. And our realities. And our bodies—our finally-aging-together bodies—crashing together again and again until we shook with pleasure.

And so, staring straight into the face of imminent threat, we consummated our marriage for the second time, just to make sure we got it right.

Then, in a massive fuck you to Cassius, we drifted into the deepest, most peaceful sleep of our lives.

The following morning, we found Ronan in his bedroom with the door wide open. This was a significant change from how buttoned up it had been as of late, which was oddly concerning. He was lying on the floor, staring at the ceiling, with his arms outstretched amidst a mess of papers, textbooks, and several sleek silver laptops. An abundance of occult items, tinctures, and Druidic implements were also scattered haphazardly about what was usually a religiously clean room. Lying on his back, he was wearing the exact same clothing he'd had on the night before. I noticed a large cocktail-sauce stain on his breast pocket and that his hair was sticking up in several different directions.

"Knock-knock," I said. He didn't move. "Can we come in?"

"Why not?" he said, distantly.

"Ronan, everyone's so worried about you. Have you even slept? Why didn't you come downstairs for breakfast?" I asked. Dom and I had joined the others hours earlier, displaying a unified front against the most recent details of Cassius's master plan.

"I'm so close … so *close!*" He lifted his head and then slammed it back on the floor. A stack of discoloured books fell off his bedside table with a clatter. They looked dark and dangerous.

Ignoring the growing mess and concern in my still tender belly, I took a deep breath and walked towards him, hands on my hips. "I understand that Ronan, but this obsess—"

"Julia! Don't you understand? If I can solve this, we can defeat Cassius once and for all!"

"I don't think we can defeat him without eating or sleeping, you dope," Dom's voice resounded from the doorway. He was holding a tray containing four slices of toast and a massive mug of coffee.

"You can keep the good-cop bad-cop routine to yourselves," Ronan said. "I *know* this isn't fucking healthy." He sat up. "But what Julia saw? The Codex!? I'm almost out of time! And I just *know* I've got the answer here somewhere!"

Dom must have filled Ronan in on the details of my vision when he'd taken his twenty-minute hiatus the night before. I wished I'd had the intuition then to warn Dom not to burden Ronan with the details, especially when it came to the types of dark magic we knew to be contained in the book. Between the mounting exhaustion and intense fixation, Ronan was now bordering on delusional.

"Is this what you did the whole time you were on patrol last night?" Dom asked. "Ruminate yourself into a tizzy like your old gran?" He was shifting tactics and attempting to appeal to Ronan's more jovial side; their friendship *did* usually contain a fair bit of laughter.

Ronan flat-out ignored him.

"Is there any way we can help?" I asked, sinking down onto the floor beside him. A glint caught my eye from this vantage point; his compass lay strewn across the room, shattered as if it had been thrown violently against the wall.

I gulped. This was bad.

"The Druids have helped where they can. But none of them have the scientific knowledge that I have …"

"Isn't Lindsey a vetere—"

"She's already said she's not interested in helping," Ronan said shortly.

Dom bared his teeth at me, as if to say, *"Okay don't ask about that one."* Then he sat down beside me, and the three of us eyed the single cup of coffee.

Ronan waved his hand dismissively at the hot drink, irritation spreading across his brow. "Shouldn't you two be, like, eating breakfast in bed or something this morning instead of being here with me?" He poked a piece of toast once and then lay back down, looking queasy.

"We've got the rest of our lives for that," Dom said, laughing darkly and snagging the slice for himself.

Ronan glowered at him from the floor.

"Give yourself a break, man," Dom said, crunching loudly. We were meant to join the others within the hour for a meeting regarding Cassius's recent discovery. And to set plans in motion. "We need you *whole,* Ronan. Not this ... shadow self."

"Shadow self?" Ronan echoed, laughing almost cruelly. "You don't know the half of it."

"What do you mean?" I asked, legitimately concerned. I took his hand in mine; it was ice cold. "Have you been—"

"Of course not. I mean ... some spells have pushed my limits, sure. But I've been careful," he said, looking deep into my eyes with something that vaguely reminded me of empathy. Or maybe it was pity. His voice dropped. "It's the nightmares. I keep seeing myself with—No. It's not important. I'm just so fucking tired ... but when I *do* sleep ... I ... never mind."

He pulled his hand away, and I had the strangest sense he was trying to tell me something but was too afraid—far too afraid. In any case, he didn't need to because part of me already knew. I had known since we left Berkeley when I'd felt his pull to the darkness, proven by how my magic had affected him.

Dom looked uneasy, still stuck on the fact that Ronan had been meddling with dangerous magic. "Christ, man! You do remember what happened to Malcolm, don't you? He took too much without returning the balance—I mean, I know he knew what he was doing, but ..."

"But then I accidentally killed him," I said flatly.

"Well, if you need to kill me at any point in time, you will, won't you?" Ronan asked, eyes growing dark. "Not strip me of my magic like Kenzie. You'll need to kill me outright. Don't let Cassius do it."

"What in the name of God are you on about?" Dom asked as he stood up, visibly frustrated now with his best friend.

"I mean ... if something goes wrong, you'd kill me before ... before I—" Ronan interrupted himself, pushing himself up to a seated position and staring at me directly.

"I won't let them take you," I said, uttering the exact words Ronan had said to me on the precipice. There remained an understanding between the two of us, the same magic that had connected us during the battle all those months ago.

"I'm so sorry, Julia," he said. "I don't think we can stop what's coming."

Suddenly, I felt my eyes roll back as I was overcome with another powerful vision, the mysterious bond between Ronan and me coursing harshly through my veins. For a split second, I felt myself slumping towards the floor but was long gone before I could brace for impact.

In my mind's eye, I found myself standing several paces in front of a small white-washed cottage. It reminded me of the ones you see on all of the touristy postcards and guidebooks for travel in contemporary Ireland. It was much older than Gertie's modern home—Goddess rest its burnt-down soul—but newer than the memory of Grianne's modest hut from the eleventh century. Yet it remained intensely familiar ... Another version of my grandmother's cottage from another lifetime perhaps?

Standing quietly on the spot, I continued to ponder exactly where I was—or *when*. I still wore my modern clothing—the same sneakers, blue jeans, and plain white t-shirt I had donned before visiting Ronan in his bedroom—but I had the distinct sense that this wasn't a present-day rendering of reality.

Before me, a low stone wall lined a bare kitchen garden. Beyond that stood a rectangular dwelling with a steep thatched roof. It boasted only two small windows that I could see, although I supposed there might be four or five, if there were additional ones I couldn't see on the far side. I vaguely recalled something Dom had told me about the "Window Tax" in the early 1800s in Ireland, which had effectively levied a price on the homeowner if they had more than six windows. *"Utterly ridiculous,"* Dom had said, scoffing at the lunacy. My best guess was that this building was about two hundred years old.

The front door of the cottage banged quietly on its hinges, the subtle sound catching my attention only slightly.

Bang. Bang.

Taking several steps forward, I passed the outer stone threshold and could feel my arm hair raise almost imperceptibly. There was magic here, so this had to be home … But then why did it feel so strange? I took a moment to find my bearings, feeling out for any unseen foes or otherworldly messengers. Meanwhile, the sky above me was growing steadily darker. Strangely, the air remained calm but for the slight breeze causing the door to call out to me more loudly now.

Bang. Bang. Bang. Bang.

I didn't feel afraid. Not entirely. But I did sense the need for caution as I explored the property further. As far as I could tell, I was unaccompanied. I took several more steps closer to the door before looking up again. The clouds continued to roil, slightly disorienting me as they loomed and swirled ominously overhead.

I froze. Did they have tornadoes in Ireland?

I felt fear rising now at the notion of sheltering from the oncoming storm alone. Where was I? And where was Dom? Was this a real memory or some sort of distorted, terrifying vision?

Bang. Bang. Bang. Bang. BANG!

The door slammed tightly shut against the eerie pre-storm backdrop, jolting me back to my senses. It seemed the cottage had grown tired of waiting for me to listen, and frankly, I was quickly understanding why. There was unfamiliar magic in the air now … dark magic. I could feel it creeping in all around me, the growing tempest more than a simple meteorological phenomenon for sure.

I needed shelter. *Now.*

Instinctively, I walked around the cottage towards a sort of root-cellar type of structure that I spotted further out back, its door nestled deep into the unassuming hillside. It would have to do. Between me and the door stood a stone well. I eyed it curiously as I passed by, not daring to stop for more than a moment.

Then out of nowhere, both wild and domestic animals started to gather around me at a startling rate as I approached the hillside haven, from both land and sky, clambering to get inside the tiny space. Indeed, it was the strangest thing to see a mother hawk jostling her young babies to safety directly beside a rabbit and her kits, their mutual goal of shelter overriding the natural order of predator and prey. Above, another hawk keened loudly.

Who was I in this divination? Fucking Snow White?

Everything seemed to be moving in slow motion as I waded through a sudden sea of fat golden chickens towards my destination, a lone rooster standing guard watchfully as I passed by his flock. I quickened my pace as best I could, but it all felt dreadfully slow.

A pair of black cats were pawing impatiently at the door latch when I finally arrived, hissing in my general direction for not moving fast enough to let them in. A small fox peered at me from the hill above the entrance, tilting its head ever so slightly in wonder: *"What are you waiting for?"* A great owl hooted from a low tree nearby, clearly in agreement with the fox.

Okay—this *definitely* wasn't a memory. Not entirely anyway. I certainly couldn't talk to animals. Not in *any* of my lives. But what did it all mean?

Still unsure about the symbolism of the animals, I opened the door. The creatures all scurried inside, the gathering completed by three large dogs that charged past me, catching my hands as they swept by, as if in thanks.

And then just as quickly as they had all arrived, they were gone.

I stumbled slightly as I ducked to enter the cool, windowless space. Utterly alone. There was no food stored on the shelves, no sustenance or promises for another day. Just darkness, the smell of cold, damp earth, and a few crumbling clumps of dirt. If I were being honest, as my eyes adjusted, I realized that the space resembled a tomb more than a root cellar, famine rather than feast.

I felt bile rise to the back of my throat. Starting to panic, I immediately regretted my decision to hole up in the darkness. Why had the animals led me in here?

I peered out of the opening and watched in horror as a thick, black, seemingly enchanted tornado touched down from the sky, just beyond the cottage. I shut the small door with a flick of my wrist, far too afraid to watch. Instead, I crouched shaking in the corner like a frightened child. I had been absolutely terrified of tornadoes when we had lived on the Prairies as a small girl—they were my worst nightmare, even though they weren't terribly common. I shook violently in my hiding place, hot tears streaming down my face.

Outside, I could hear the cottage being ripped and torn to pieces, the thatch being spread violently across the surrounding countryside like seeds sown by the wind, the sound of its howling almost unbearable at its peak.

And then everything went silent. I hoped against hope that the storm had passed just as quickly as it had arrived, and that my hole in the hillside had done its job, thanks to my animal friends.

Wrong.

Without warning, the rickety door between me and the outside world was torn off with a crash. Through the small opening, a dark, twisted cloud rolled in, beckoning to me like an evil finger crooked towards itself. Thick and dark as acrid smoke, it reached into my hiding place, the tornado's tendril, searching for the small, frightened girl hiding there. I pressed myself against the back wall, hardly daring to breathe as I turned my face away and pressed my cheek against the cold earth. Noticing my movement, the finger of darkness shot down my throat, filling my lungs with hot, smoky air. And then I lost consciousness again.

Now, I was in a deeper divination. A vision within a dream.

Here, I saw Ronan standing in a dark chamber, hair significantly greyed, handsome face brutal and haggard. While the thatched-cottage vision had seemed a skewed version of the past, this one appeared to be of the future. My perspective had changed too—whereas, at the cottage, I had been able to move under my own steam and participate, in this place, I was merely a witness from some unspecific perspective I couldn't decipher.

Ronan stood before a boiling cauldron of some kind of viscous tar. Beside his station was a book. The *Codex Druidicus*. It was flipped open to a page spattered with dark marks, the existing Latin script harshly contrasting Ronan's smoothly added notations.

A hand rested on his shoulder. The hand of death. Rotting with stretched sinew and hollowed bone.

Then I heard a familiar voice. "There's no turning back now." Cassius's laugh filled my ears as I gasped audibly from somewhere within the transcendence. The noise from my own throat brought me back to reality with a jolt.

Well, back to the root cellar reality at least.

I was still swaying on the spot, lungs full of obscurity and unable to breathe. With all my might, I forced myself to exhale. I watched as the smoke left my lungs, half as dark as it had been when it entered, and then began to dissipate ... until it was as though it had never existed in the first place. As my eyes once again adjusted to the root cellar, I found that it was still empty.

MANTLE OF THE WORLD RULER

The storm outside had largely subsided, but what lingering, charring darkness had it left behind within me?

Intuitively, I ran out of the cellar door and towards the well, which was miraculously still intact. I grabbed a shredded rope and pulled and pulled until a small wooden bucket appeared, clear water sparkling brightly within. I drank deeply, feeling the cleansing water cool my scorched lungs. Yet, I was still unfathomably thirsty, as each desperate gulp purged more evil from my chest.

Then I heard three familiar voices on the wind:

"This is his fate, young one."

"You cannot fix this for him."

"It is not yours to fight."

Instinctively, I kept drinking until I felt the absence of evil within my body at last.

My belly full of healing water, I fell back onto the grass beside the decimated cottage and closed my eyes, unsure of where or when I would wake next.

CHAPTER 40

"Julia!" I heard Dom call out from somewhere in the distance. "Wake up! *Please!*"

He was on one knee, shaking me vigorously, when I finally came to and found him leaning over me, looking terrified. I looked into his eyes only momentarily, orienting myself hastily before turning towards Ronan. He was lying on the floor where I had seen him last, unconscious.

I couldn't help but notice that no one was shaking *him* awake.

"Julia, what happened? Are you alright?" Dom asked, placing his hands on my face and drawing my attention back towards him. He looked frantic, and I could only imagine what my body had done during such a spectacularly horrifying set of divinations.

"Dom …" I said, barely able to speak. My throat was on fire, but this was important. "Is Ronan alright?"

Suddenly, Lindsey and Stuart were in the room, followed by Lennie, Thomas, and Peggy close on their heels.

"What's happened?" Lindsey demanded, visibly shocked at the sight of Ronan unconscious on the floor. She immediately went into action, dropping to her knees beside him and checking his pulse. From my proximity on the floor, I could have sworn I heard her mutter something about him being a fool.

"He passed out as soon as Julia fell," Dom said, still regaining his bearings. "Honestly, I've not had much of a chance to assess the situation."

He sounded scared and agitated, reeling once more.

"He's breathing," Lindsey said. Stuart knelt beside her, unsure of what to do next.

While I wanted to explain to Dom about what I had seen, I felt oddly attuned to Ronan's state, like we were linked somehow. And I needed to know what the hell he had done.

Shereen and Alanna stumbled into the room next, still in their pajamas, gleaming gold blades in hand and ready for battle. Graham and Sean were nowhere to be seen, but I assumed they were outside somewhere, still on patrol.

"We heard Dom yelling from downstairs!" Shereen said, chest heaving. Alanna swung her blade through the air menacingly in search of unseen foes.

At this commotion, Ronan began to stir. Ignoring everyone else, I pushed Dom's hand aside and crawled towards Ronan through the detritus of his room. Lindsey and Stuart stepped back to join the others nearer the door.

"Ronan," I whispered, "what have you *done?*"

He stared at me, eyes wide, pleading for my silence without words.

I felt myself begin to shake as the shock of the vision caught up to me. Had he seen the same one I had?

Dom's mouth was agape as he looked back and forth between the pair of us. I watched as he opened and closed his jaw several times. Then he finally found his voice. "What the actual *fuck* is going on here?"

I held my hand up to silence him. The others in the room barely moved an inch.

"Ronan," I said, "what have you been meddling with? And who knows about it?" Of course, what I was really asking was whether *Cassius* knew about it.

Ronan's face went ashen. "Not here. Not now. I can't ..."

Dom let out a low growl. "Everyone ... *out!*"

I knew he didn't mean me or Ronan. But Dom also wasn't the kind of man to subject his best friend to an impromptu tribunal before he had all of the facts. I watched as Lennie ushered the others out; the World Ruler's word really was law. I heard the group silently move down the hallway and downstairs, where I assumed they would settle in the sitting room. Surely a meeting would convene as soon as Dom had a clearer picture, and they would be fully armed with questions.

Several moments passed as I watched Dom slowly inhale and exhale. I managed to get my shaking under control as best I could, while Ronan looked like he was going to be sick.

"Can someone *please* tell me what's going on?" Dom asked through gritted teeth.

I kept my focus on Ronan still, who looked frailer than ever. I swallowed hard. "Have you … Ronan, did you *know* Cassius sought the Codex?"

He nodded imperceptibly. Dom's eyes grew wide, and I could see raw, lethal anger burning there.

"And your research … Is there a connection?" I asked.

Ronan pushed up onto his elbows and then rolled to his side so he could seat himself properly. A strange look came over his face, as if there was no life left behind his eyes, and then he spoke the truth very quickly at last. "Yes."

Dom released a guttural sound—the sound of a man wholly betrayed. I watched as Dom stood up and stormed towards the windows. He slammed his fist on the frame once, causing the glass to shudder, though thankfully it didn't break. After several heaving breaths, he returned to stand directly in front of Ronan, fists clenched, ready for blood.

Ronan did not meet his gaze. Instead, he put his head into his hands and began to sob. "I'm sorry I didn't tell you."

"How could you?" I asked, stealing the words I knew were stinging like acid on Dom's tongue. "If you *knew* Cassius was looking for it—or that it still existed—we might have tried to find it ourselves first or … or something. *Anything*. I don't know …"

Lips tight, Ronan looked at me, sitting on the floor beside him, and then up towards Dom. "I—"

"What, Ronan?" Dom almost spit the words at him. "You thought you could handle this on your own? That you had the right to keep something like this from me? Or from Julia? I thought she was like a sister to you. Isn't that what you said yesterday?" He wasn't bothering to contain his contempt. His voice was choked, like he was struggling to keep himself from either screaming or crying. "How could you do this to us?"

"I didn't mean to ... It wasn't my intention." Ronan looked and sounded uncharacteristically timid. "I've been so careful. Especially since what happened with Wren. I've kept it all offline ... I don't know how he could know what I've been doing. But then ... then the nightmares started."

"Nightmares?" Dom scowl only deepened.

I squared my shoulders, preparing for the worst; Dom's anger was surely going to blow after this. After a deep breath, I spoke up. "In the vision I saw"—Ronan looked at me, his eyes widening in horror that I would speak the truth out loud—"Ronan was standing at Cassius's side ... with the Codex. It was open to a page near the end, and they had created some kind of ... concoction. And—"

"Enough, Julia," Ronan said, his voice desperate. "Please!"

I was afraid to hear the answer to what I had to ask next. "How long have you been having these nightmares, Ronan? How long have you known he sought the Codex?"

There was a long, horrifying silence before he finally answered in a voice that seemed wholly broken. "Since you went to Norway."

My heart sank, and I felt like leaving my body entirely. How could he have kept this from us? How could he honestly have thought that this was something he should keep under our radar?

"I know," Ronan said, his mouth quivering. "I know, but I couldn't know for sure that it was real. I can't Divine. I don't ... I don't have the Sight. They were just dreams ..."

I was more exasperated with him than I had ever been. "That doesn't mean Cassius didn't want you to know! He's a Sorcerer, Ronan!"

His excuses just weren't adding up to any sort of reason to lie to us like this. My mind returned to the new Prophecy, something I hadn't thought about for a while, and I was immediately drawn to its final lines:

> For the earthen weapons masters, and tree talkers with open sky above,
> Darkness reigns where light cannot, and from its root, the land will rot.

"Oh fuck, Dom ... *the Prophecy.*"

I watched his mind work for several moments before his anger spilled over at last. "Fuck you, Ronan! Fuck you and your sneaky *bullshit* excuses! Fuck your foolish pride! You have no idea the *darkness* that is contained in that book! *And* what it's going to take to keep everyone safe now that he *has it!* Julia and I have seen its magic! First hand! It's *beyond* sinister! *You've put all of our lives at risk!"*

At that, Ronan's back straightened, and he glared at Dom. "Put *you* at risk? I don't fucking believe the words coming out of your mouth! Do you have *any idea* what I've been trying to *do* here? What I've been trying to *stop from happening?!"*

I shook my head in disbelief. "How, Ronan? How the fuck are we supposed to know that when you've been, you've been *hiding everything from us?! …* Maybe if you would have told us the *truth …"*

I didn't know how to even finish my thought, struggling between feelings of hurt, anger, and even a strange compassion for the shell of a man Ronan had become. I was reminded of the words that had been whispered to me from the Otherworld: *"You cannot fix this for him."*

Dom spoke then, his voice suddenly cool and calculated. "Julia, we need to leave. If I stay in this room any longer, I'm going to do something I regret."

He held his hand out to me, and I rose to my feet, swaying slightly from the effects of my second harsh vision in less than twelve hours. I needed to lie down.

Ronan looked to me. "I'm so sorry, Julia."

"Don't you dare speak to her!" Dom snapped.

I gave Ronan a pitying smile and followed Dom out of the room, closing the door quietly behind me. From the hallway, I heard Ronan crying out, howling on the floor where we'd left him.

"How could he? How … I can't …" Dom was pacing almost frantically in our bedroom, angry and hurt. "He *knew* that Cassius was seeking the Codex! He *knew!"*

I was lying down on our bed, the room spinning.

I didn't have an answer for him since I was feeling equally as confused and betrayed. What part of Ronan had honestly thought it was a good idea to keep this information from us? Even if he *hadn't* thought the nightmares were real—which based on the look on his face this morning, I knew was a blatant lie—he *still* should have told us. Any information pertaining to Cassius's whereabouts, magical clues or otherwise, was infinitely valuable information and critical to our very survival. And what was he "trying to stop from happening" anyway?

And then the truth hit me like a ton of bricks: This was Ronan's fate. He had proven to us that we had no control over what he did. The choices he made. And now there was no stopping what had been set into motion.

"Dom," I said, my voice a hushed whisper, "I don't think there's anything we can do for him."

He paused midway through running his fingers through his hair, which was now standing on end, his arms flexed behind his head. He looked huge standing there. Powerful. Yet the look on his face was shrunken into anguish. "Did *they* tell you that?"

Attuned as ever, and wholly aware of the realities of our cursed existence on this plane, Dom had guessed correctly. Ever since I'd visited *them* at our wellspring, their message to me had been that Ronan was on his own path, with his own fate. Hell, even Bernie had expressed as much. I thought of Ronan's broken compass and the state of his room ... his person. These were not just things he had brought on himself. He'd chosen them.

His path truly was his own. And my intuition was screaming that we had to let him go.

"Yes. *They* told me that," I said, pulling the covers up, wishing to drown myself in the feather comforter. I hated the idea of leaving our friend to fall apart. I hated the notion of having to discern when it was time to step away and let someone face their demons alone. "And I think they're right."

"I don't accept it," he said, striding over to the bed beside me and sitting down.

I stared into his eyes, deep pools of sadness mirroring my own. "I'm sorry. We have to."

"I refuse," he said, his hands shaking. I reached out and took them into my own, my chill countering his warmth. I grasped his wedding ring, spinning it around his finger absently. It looked good there.

We needed to focus on the promise of our future.

"Dom … we *need* to keep our attention on stopping Cassius. If he does have the Codex, we have far bigger problems than dealing with Ronan."

"Then why do I feel like Ronan is our biggest problem right now?" Tears were gathering in his eyes.

"Because you love him," I said. "And because that's what family does. But family also has to know when to let someone go. He's made his choices, and he has to live with them. Just like we'll live with ours."

Dom motioned that he wanted to lie down beside me, and I lifted the covers up so he could burrow beneath them. Once there, he took the position of little spoon with only slight hesitation. Wordlessly, I wrapped my arms around him, kissing his back gently and trailing my fingers along his muscles and the scars on his body—a body that had seen so much in its many lifetimes. Too much. He had loved his friends so deeply and had lost so many to the annals of time. The burden he carried on his shoulders, his mantle, must be infinitely heavy.

Facing away from me, I could soon feel him crying in my arms and encouraged this with soft caresses. I wasn't afraid of his vulnerability. Nor his pain. I was here for him no matter what and always had been, wedding ring or no.

I had no idea what was going on downstairs, whether or not they were waiting with bated breath or had dispersed to cope in whatever way suited them. But they would have to wait until Dom was ready to face the world again.

Right now, my king—my husband—needed to be held.

We at last descended the stairs towards the sitting room later that afternoon.

Dom had cried silently for the better part of an hour before finally drifting off into a heavy midday nap. Grief was exhausting, and I had a sense he was mourning more than just Ronan's betrayal but the many people and lives he had lost along the way throughout our history. He'd had to let go of so much. Too much. And it broke my heart to see him this way.

"Gather the others," Dom said to Lennie as we passed him in the hallway, his voice level, revealing none of his emotion from earlier.

Lennie nodded without a word, and before long, all of us crowded into the sitting room, with Ronan as a notable absentee. I wasn't sure if Lennie had avoided calling Ronan down or if Ronan had declined the invitation. It didn't matter because Dom did not intend to include Ronan in our next steps.

I settled onto the low couch beside Lindsey, still shaky from my divination. I would need to rest again soon, but I needed to be here to support Dom as he set his plan in motion.

Once the room was quiet, Dom launched into the details without hesitation. "It is imperative we locate Cassius *now*, whatever the cost. He has come into possession of a very dangerous magical book. The *Codex Druidicus*. Julia and I have had experience with it in our past," he said, grimacing, "and it is truly wicked, full of dark Wielding magic stolen from the ancient Druids. If he were to enact even the simplest incantation from its contents, all of us could be in grave danger."

"You mean more than we always are?" Graham said. Sean elbowed him.

Dom nodded gravely.

"How do we know he has it?" Stuart asked.

"Julia's had a clear vision. And Ronan has … also come across proof of its possession."

Even now, Dom was protecting Ronan's integrity.

"Do you think he found it in Russia?" Lennie asked, but the question answered itself.

Silence fell across the room just as the sun ominously dipped behind a cloud. I noticed that the air pressure also seemed to be dropping as we spoke; my temples throbbed, threatening a headache. A storm was coming—more than just the weather system accumulating outside.

"We need to find him," I said, pleading to the group with my eyes. "The new Prophecy, we think it refers to this. It's … We have to stop him before it's too late."

"What do you need us to do?" Lindsey asked without hesitation, looking back and forth between Dom and me, loyalty plain on her face.

"We need to revisit all of his usual haunts. The ones we know about: Los Angeles, Vancouver, his London tower … the works. We need to look for any unusual Wraith activity that might indicate they are preparing for his arrival at any of these places. Now that he has the book, he will feel invincible, but that doesn't mean he won't be setting up his security detail. He will want an army around him. And in that, we can hopefully catch him out."

"And how do you suppose we actually *get* the book from him, once we've penetrated his gathered forces?" Sean asked, sounding skeptical.

With his shoulders set in determination, Dom replied simply. "We fight."

First, Dom dispatched the Los Angles Knaves, along with a core of desert Knaves, to gather intelligence in the region. He was concerned that the two groups wouldn't mix all that well, but that wasn't as important as the mission. "The L.A. Knaves know the area best, but Glenys and Booker from the desert know *me*. They understand that I wouldn't ask unless it was significant. And I trust them to get this done. There are several Conventos in the area that need attending to anyway, so I'm sure they will enjoy themselves regardless."

I nodded. I was somewhat glad not to have met Booker and Glenys yet. Not knowing what they looked like made it easier to avoid picturing what they did for fun. It was late, and Dom and I were sitting alone in his study. I was nursing a scotch by the fire, scratching Oisín between the ears and trying to pretend the end of the world wasn't imminent.

"And what about Washington or Vancouver?" I asked, yawning into my glass. It smelled strongly of peat, and I felt like it grounded me to the earth somehow—that, or it was simply doing an excellent job of calming my nerves.

"Alanna and Shereen are already on a flight there. They've sent word ahead and are working with the Oregon Druids too, so the entire coastline should be covered. There's been significant Wraith activity in the area recently, so that's another place we will need to keep tabs on." Dom sounded tired. He had spent the better part of the last forty-eight hours swinging things into motion, and only now was he was able to catch me up. Meanwhile, I had spent much of the last two days resting, the double-whammy visions taking their toll.

I felt useless, but it was the cost of my gift.

"And then Sean and Graham will be stationed in Vancouver. The Wraith concentration around there seems to be significant as well," he said, his brows gathering together in concern. Something about Vancouver felt noteworthy to me as well, though I couldn't place my finger on why. Maybe I was just homesick. "I've tasked Lindsey and Stuart there too, as they can be a bridge between the Knaves and Druids in the area."

"Right. And England?"

"Lennie is already there, and Thomas and Peggy with him. As soon as we get information of any flights out of Russia towards any of his usual destinations, he will let us know. I wonder how we'd be able to catch Cassius in the air now, when we've failed to manage it countless times over the past year. But again, I have to put my trust in our friends that they can do their jobs and fulfil their roles."

Even if Ronan had done otherwise.

"Dom?" I said, looking at him where he sat in the armchair across from me. His face looked like it had aged several years since our wedding day. It was hard to imagine that, less than a week ago, we had been joined in wedded bliss, and now we were fighting against the knowledge that Cassius had obtained a book that could potentially destroy us all. "Are you alright?"

He pondered for a moment. "No. Not really."

I stood, wandered over to where he sat, and placed myself onto his lap. Taking his face into my hands, I kissed his mouth softly, tucking a wave of his blond hair behind his ear.

"I ..." he began, before catching himself, *"we* finally got a taste of the life we've always dreamed of and now ..."

"And now ..." I said, unable to finish the sentence either. I snuggled into his chest, listening to his breath and to his heart.

It was late. I closed my eyes, wishing to preserve this moment of safety and intimacy, and drifted off to sleep.

Zzz. Zzz. Zzz.

Zzz. Zzz. Zzz.

I startled as Dom's cellphone abrasively vibrated across the study's coffee table. What time was it? The coals in the fire had burnt down to nothing.

Dom shifted beneath me, and I reached to pass his phone to him.

"Hello?" he said groggily into the receiver. After a moment, his face dropped. "Thank you, Lennie."

I looked at Dom, fearful. "What is it?"

"Cassius is on the move. The Wraiths too. He's on his way to Vancouver."

Less than a week after the discovery of Ronan's betrayal, we found ourselves standing in his room once more. It smelled like he hadn't showered or left the space since we'd been there last. I watched as Dom's jaw clenched repeatedly, chewing on the words he was about to speak.

He spat them out finally. "You can't come with us to Vancouver, Ronan."

"What?" Ronan looked like he'd just been slapped.

"You can't come with us to Vancouver. You're too much of a risk. If it's true that you have some sort of key or … *connection* to the magic Cassius is seeking through the Codex, we can't have you there. The Knaves will surely agree with me. The Druids … well, once they have the facts—"

"Dom, please. You can't seriously plan to face Cassius's Wraiths in open battle without me! Have you lost your mind?"

Dom walked towards the Georgian window and spread his arms high and wide between the deep frame, pressing out as hard as he could. "The answer is no. I won't say it again."

"Julia?" Ronan said, turning to me. "Please?"

"Dom's right," I said, though I felt a strange unease about the decision.

On the whole, Dom *was* correct. Ronan had been messing with some seriously risky magic, and if Cassius knew about it, we were in deep shit. Especially if he had plans for Ronan. Not to mention the fact that Ronan's apparent obsession with the Codex had caused him to keep it a secret from us. For *months*. But on the other hand, it was a divination that we had seen, not necessarily a truth. If I had learned anything this far in my magical life, especially when it came to prophecies and portents, it was that nothing was sure until it played out in real time.

"I'm serious! I can help over there," Ronan said, standing amidst the filth of his room. "I know it looks like I'm not coping, but—"

"Don't make me comment on the state of this room, Ronan," Dom said, his eyebrows raised. "Please. It's hard enough asking you to stay behind."

With that, he exited the room. Ronan looked humiliated.

"Ronan——"

"I don't need your pity, Julia," Ronan said, turning away.

I left without another word. I had nothing else to say to him.

CHAPTER 41

Time was up. We were leaving for Vancouver in several hours, whether we liked it or not. Lennie's intelligence had confirmed that Cassius was indeed there, as well as a massive Conventos of Wraiths that was growing in numbers by the hour. We had no idea what his motivation was, apart from what the Prophecy told us. We didn't even know if he would stay in Vancouver. However, he had the Codex, had purposely sought out a metropolitan centre, and crucially, had telegraphed to us where he was. Dangerous trap or not, this might be our one and only chance to stop him before he unleashed real darkness into the world and on crowds of helpless, unsuspecting people.

We needed to go. *Now.*

Dom had called upon the Knaves in the south, futilely hoping that many of them would come. Alanna, Shereen, and their core group would be able to cross over for sure, so that was positive. But when it came to Glenys and Booker—who had offered their support, along with a handful of their number—there was no promise they would make it in time. Mobilizing a group like that on short notice, not to mention crossing the border when many of them were "wanted," was hard at the best of times, let alone within a small window of time.

Still, they had promised to try their best, as they had pledged themselves to the banner of the World Ruler.

MANTLE OF THE WORLD RULER

"Dom, are you absolutely *sure* this is the right thing to do?" I asked as we climbed into his SUV. I was concerned we were rushing into the situation. But then again, I had also come to mistrust the construct of time altogether, so what was "rushing" anyway? Living this life with Dom meant that we existed in a state of constant vigilance. Was it really a surprise that we'd only been married a week before our hand was forced, potentially marching us towards our death?

Dom raised an eyebrow at me. "I am. You are you aware, I hope, that you're the *only* person I'd ever tolerate questioning my command so openly?"

I let out a huff as I slumped into the passenger seat. I think he'd meant it as a playful compliment, but I was out of patience. "Dom, I'm being serious."

"I know, love. But you and I both know what that book means in his hands. We won't have long once he has a chance to start trying it out, even if the magic within it is volatile. You might not remember entirely what the book was like, but I do. It's … We have a duty to stop him from using it."

I hated that he was right—that even with our love and plans and everything we'd promised each other at the altar, we were still beholden to Cassius. It had been a dream to think we could get away with joy so easily. I was fucking sick and tired of The Child of Rome taking up room in my life—in my marriage. I wished I'd never heard the new Prophecy at all. But I had, and that meant our friends were in grave danger if we didn't stop Cassius from using the Codex.

We had to do whatever was necessary.

♛

Dom and I landed in Vancouver late at night, our sense of time getting thoroughly messed up. But what else was new?

"I've been thinking about the animals in your vision," Dom said blearily as we piled into a black Lexus that had been arranged by the Druids. Sean was driving, with Graham in the passenger seat as co-pilot.

"Oh?" I said, not having expected this line of conversation.

"Well, it's just that they might be important. At least, in old Celtic mythology, animals are very relevant. For example, the *seabhag*, or hawk. Did it cry out?"

469

"Uh … the one in the sky did. The mother on the ground didn't though."

"If I remember correctly, the hawk symbolizes far-memory and a need for a clear head. To be decisive on the journey, so you aren't thrown off course."

"Well, *that* shoe fits," I said, yawning as we took off down the road. "What about owls?"

"Well, that one's a little trickier. I think owls can see through people's falsehoods. Unmask foes."

"Hmm …" I said, not sure about that one. "What about the cats and dogs?"

"Dogs are always a good thing, I think. Loyal, with great tracking skills. I'm always glad to have dogs in my dreams. Cats are a little more mysterious. Back in the day, they were far wilder than the dogs were, so perhaps there was a little fear there. I mean, have you met a feral cat? But they were also viewed as protectors, especially in a conflict."

"Well, the cats were almost guarding the cellar, and then the dogs almost ushered me in."

"Sounds about right," Dom said, nodding. "That's a good thing."

Sean and Graham couldn't help but join the discussion.

"What else was there?" Sean asked.

"Well, there were a flock of chickens, and a rooster—"

"Ah, well, I think dreaming of a cock," Sean said, laughing at the surprised look on Dom's face, "or *coileach,* is a good thing, too. A crowing rooster scares away the ghosts of the night. It's a powerful creature for driving out darkness and negativity."

"Maybe dreaming about the other is alright too," Graham said, laughing loudly.

"Are we done with the cock jokes, lads?" Dom asked, but he was chuckling along with them.

I rolled my eyes. "There was also a rabbit. Oh, and a fox, who was conversing with the owl."

"Wow!" Sean said. "That was quite the dream, wasn't it, Snow White?" I chuckled silently. He wasn't wrong. It was one of the strangest divinations I'd ever had. "I think foxes are good at watching others while staying unwatched themselves. If it was talking to the owl, maybe they were trying to determine who was false and who was true."

Dom nodded. "Perhaps. Hares can be good though, I think. They can be connected to divination, which makes complete sense for you. Boudica used a hare before her last battle with the Romans actually."

"Didn't she keep it up her dress?" Graham asked.

Sean replied stoically, "And then she died, but not without a sturdy cause."

"Well, that doesn't exactly bode well," Graham said, keeping his eyes on the road.

I felt a chill go down my spine. "I don't think I like animal symbology all that much."

"Dom?" I asked, pulling the covers close to my neck. The air conditioning in the hotel room was cranked on high when we'd arrived and hadn't yet warmed to a comfortable temperature. "When we have sex, why does it always feel like it might be the last time?"

He laughed darkly. "Because it might be."

"I want our last time to be as old people," I said, sadly, "in our own bed."

"You know, it's kind of funny. Do normal people with regular lives think about the last time they might have sex? Or only the first time?" Dom asked and then grew serious. "But me too, love. I wonder about that a lot too. Though I still have hope that we *will* be old and grey the last time we come together."

We were set to approach Cassius's Vancouver stronghold sometime within the next few days; how quickly we would strike depended on what our intelligence came up with. As far as we knew, our arrival in Canada had gone undetected. For tonight, we were stationed in a bland hotel near the airport, while our allies arrived. Handfuls of Druids and Knaves were still on their way to the city, which would unfortunately draw more attention. Just as the Wraith's gathering was a giveaway, soon ours would be too. But our hope was to trickle them in and then amass as late as possible.

Tossing his bag and sword aside, Dom dove under the covers to join me. "It really *is* fucking freezing in here."

We had attempted to order room service upon our late-night arrival, but all they were offering was ramen in a Styrofoam cup or ripple chips with a dip that I suspected was just sour cream mixed with French onion soup mix—not exactly the after-hours menu I had hoped for but it was what I should have expected.

Dom ordered three cups of soup though, while I went for the chips and dip.

"Warm me up," I said, my teeth chattering slightly. It wasn't only the room and lack of sustenance that was giving me chills. I was completely exhausted.

"Not exactly the honeymoon we had in mind," he said, pulling me close. "And I'm sorry for it. Don't worry. We don't have to have sex tonight. I know you're tired."

I snorted. "I know we don't *have* to. But I also don't want to die on this mission without having you inside me one last time," I said frankly. He didn't flinch.

This was how it was.

Almost instantly, his temperature began to rise. "Well, one thing I *do* know is that you've always been incredible at telling it like it is."

"I know," I said, surprisingly turned on myself, despite how heavy my lids felt.

Suddenly, a knock came at the door.

"That'll be your soup," I said, rolling my eyes. "Right on time."

"And your mystery dip!" He wiggled his eyebrows at me before hopping lithely out of bed. Before heading to the door, he jumped up and down several times, shaking each leg out to sort out his growing erection.

Within moments, Dom returned with two trays of what was essentially pantry food served on crisp white napkins.

"They left it on the ground outside the door. Dinner … is served," he said, dragging out the last few words with a pretentious French accent.

I giggled. "Not much of a last supper."

"Indeed," he said. And plunked down beside me on the bed once more.

With the heat of passion between us momentarily quelled, we each nibbled quietly on our food, the salt content alone almost driving us mad for water within minutes. However, once our bellies were full and thirst moderately quenched, we tucked back in under the covers together.

It was good enough.

"Let's try this again," Dom said, and pulled me close once more.

"I have no idea what to expect," I said, worries rising to the surface. In the coming days we would attempt to steal the Codex from Cassius, a risk that could cost us our lives. I was terrified.

Dom put his warm finger over my lips and spoke. "We never do. But just know that I'll protect you with my life."

I felt myself caught somewhere between tears and elation. So few people knew a love like this. In this moment, no matter what happened tomorrow, I knew that I had been blessed in this life and all those that had come before it.

The sheets were still cool, but Dom's warm body now provided more than enough heat on top of me to take off the edge. How many nights had we made love under the stars, warming each other in some abandoned barn as we travelled the long road in attempt to rescue our destinies from the hands of a raging Roman lunatic? Despite the fact that it seemed we were only repeating our clash with the Wraiths in Ireland from last summer and each cycle before, this felt different. Yes, our hands were forced, but we still were choosing to *be here*. What was more, I had a quiet confidence building about my own abilities—one that I wasn't even fully sharing with Dom, just in case it slipped. But still, it was there.

I leaned into Dom, and his lips tasted like salt and artificial chicken seasoning. "You taste like *Itchiban*," I said, giggling. "This feels like high school."

I felt a strange nostalgia surge within me for the many meals I had prepared for myself as I slowly learned independence in this most recent iteration of my existence—a reality that truly felt like a lifetime ago.

He chuckled, pulling me towards him as he leaned back onto the pillows. "Well, I never went to high school, so I wouldn't know."

"What were you like when you were sixteen?" I asked playfully, wrapping the covers around me as I straddled his waist.

"Awkward as hell. You should be glad you've always known me as a man."

In one swift move, he somehow had me flipped onto my stomach, proving that he not only had incredible body control but the strength to match it too. He could have me in and out of any position before I even knew what was going on. This was partly because he knew me so well, but also because he was just that impressive in bed. I was reminded of when we'd first "met" again two autumns ago; Dom had always kept things dynamic between us.

Whiplash, indeed.

I pulled one knee up as the tone of our interaction quickly shifted from playful to serious.

"I *am* glad to know you as a man. Now, please … make love to me." I was tired of waiting. I wanted him to fill me.

He purred. "With pleasure."

I arched my hips upwards as he started slow, digging his knees into the mattress as he gradually buried his cock deep inside with each careful thrust. The position was a physically intense one to start in, and we both groaned with pleasure when he was finally fully sheathed. He paused momentarily, and I knew we both wanted to feel this love as deep as possible.

"Oh, Julia …" he said, and we were off.

I didn't think I would ever tire of sex with him and wished for a long life ahead of us to test out my theory that he would only get better with age. But if this *were* to be the last time, we would make it unforgettable.

There was no certainty what tomorrow might hold.

The next morning, we were picked up by Sean and Graham once more just outside the hotel. We were apparently being taken to a Druid safe-house in Kitsilano, which sounded pretty swanky considering how "modest" the Druids claimed to be.

"Wow! Kits? Really?" I said, not bothering to hide my surprise.

"It's old money," Sean said simply, and I didn't doubt his word. No one talked about it, but the Druid network over the years had been wise, investing in many different ventures, most often property. Dom wasn't the only one with the benefit of time and foresight.

"Is everyone else already there?" Dom asked.

"Mostly," Graham said. "Stuart has connected again with the Washington Knaves, and so he'll be bringing them from wherever they are once we have a plan. Lindsey's with him too." I wasn't surprised. I doubted that they would be parted for any reason anymore; it was how I felt about Dom. "Lennie and Thomas are at the Druid house though. Peggy too."

I was surprised to hear Peggy had come in the end, but no doubt, she knew the stakes and would be here in whatever capacity might be the most helpful to us.

"So, Ronan's not coming?" Sean said. It wasn't really a question. Graham followed Sean's statement with a noncommittal grunt. They weren't disputing their leader's choice.

Dom remained silent, however. Resolute. I wove my fingers through his with a squeeze.

I knew it was a decision that had been eating away at him ever since we'd told Ronan he wasn't welcome on our mission, an admittance that he had become too much of a liability.

Frankly, we couldn't be sure of what he would do when the Codex was within his reach. And late last night, Dom had finally voiced the same fears I was carrying within my own heart: that Ronan had kept the Codex a secret from us because he wanted it for himself. It sounded ridiculous when you put it into the context of the Ronan we thought we knew. But in reality, this new version of Ronan seemed hell-bent on understanding the darkest complexities of Wraith magic, regardless of the consequences.

Regardless of the cost.

I didn't tell Dom in exact detail—because it was more of a sense than a solid truth—but in the vision, Ronan hadn't seemed too concerned with the role he was playing at Cassius's side. He'd seemed almost resigned, accepting of his part. He looked tired, but he wasn't fighting either.

I stared out the darkened window as we travelled north towards Kitsilano. Nostalgia seeped from my bones as we drove further into familiar territory. As we crossed West Broadway, I felt my mind pull west towards UBC. Then my heart tugged to the east, where the road would lead me eventually back to my old neighbourhood, South Main. Looking at the clock, I wondered what Virginia was up to now. She was probably already at work, pre-portioned lunch in hand and ready to take on the world. Doing good in the "everyday."

I hated that I'd had to leave her, and my old life, behind. But ultimately, it had been for the best. I simply wasn't the same person I'd been before. Both literally and figuratively. It was hard to imagine the reality of this life—the one where I was armed with the very real knowledge that I might die at any moment—existing in the same universe as the one I used to inhabit. Of course, I wouldn't trade this existence with Dom for anything, but it was a wild reality nonetheless.

I shielded my eyes as I peered out the window, having forgotten my only pair of sunglasses back in Ireland. The sun was bright as buses, cars, and bicycles scooted by, their occupants traversing the gorgeous stretch between Downtown Vancouver and the UBC campus, completely unaware of the threat that currently loomed over their city.

Before long, we pulled up to a red three-storey house located several blocks from Kits Beach. The Druids had obviously been savvy in their investments, and I was impressed. However, I dismissed my thoughts as we pulled into the driveway and swiftly opened the car doors. I was in shock. Easily seen through the windows, and even spilling onto the veranda, were hordes of Wielders.

"Ah, looks like Stuart brought the Knaves over after all," Graham said, sounding pleased.

"I don't think so," Sean said. "It's just more Druids."

"Aren't you worried you'll all be seen?" Dom asked, but he didn't sound particularly concerned. He sounded excited.

"The house has the usual enchantments around it. Nothing to worry about," Graham replied.

Sean strode towards the steps, greeting what were apparently familiar faces before climbing the rise and heading inside. We left our bags in the trunk, unsure if we would be staying here (or anywhere) tonight. Once again, I was reminded of our grim reality.

Many had come to the call of Dom's banner, and from the sounds of it, even more were still expected to arrive before the day was out. Graham explained that several safe-houses throughout Vancouver and the Lower Mainland were accepting Druids and Knaves alike in preparation for whatever happened next.

They all understood the importance and threat of what Cassius had planned *"for the earthen weapons masters, and tree talkers with open sky above."*

Yet something was sitting uncomfortably with me.

Dom continued to look pleased at the number of Wielders who'd come, and he turned to me for a similar reaction. "It's incredible, isn't it?"

I wanted to agree, but instead, my stomach dropped. In the chaos of everything—the wedding, followed by multiple debilitating visions and a hasty return trip to Canada—I hadn't even considered that I should reach out to Solveig to see if she could possibly help me locate some Bearers, even if only to warn them to stay safe with Cassius on the move. I had sworn after the battle with Cassius that I would work harder to locate my missing sisters.

Concern spread across Dom's brow. "Julia? What's wrong?"

"Nothing really. I just ... I should have contacted Solveig. Maybe she could have helped us find some Bearers who might have wanted to fight." While I knew that most of the world's Bearers were in hiding, for fear of being found by Cassius, my heart still held out a distant hope that maybe some of them would've come.

Lennie appeared on the steps before us, looking haughty. I wondered if he was irritated at being in a house full of Druids, when he was so obviously a Knave.

"Interesting you should say that, Julia," he said. "I had the same thought. Unfortunately, though, Solveig is gone. Forced into hiding. Apparently, Wraiths crossed over into Kirkenes through the Russian 'wall' not long ago. If I were to guess, Cassius was in the far north when he finally located the Codex, and then word came of the Bearer in the north with an exceptional power. A useful one too. So, he moved in. Her work wasn't exactly secret to the local Wielder and Bearing community. Someone was sure to let slip she was up there eventually."

Or else we'd drawn his gaze north by way of our strange connection.

I didn't like the tone of Lennie's voice though. He sounded self-important, like he was glad to know more than we did about Solveig's situation.

"I feel like this is something you should have told me," I said through gritted teeth, trying to gain my composure as we climbed the steps towards the front door. I could feel my Bearing hearth igniting and becoming increasingly dangerous. Several Druids gave me startled looks, no doubt picking up on my sharp edge. But I didn't care. My heart hurt for Solveig. I hoped she was alright and had found safety in time.

"Julia, she's safe," Lennie said. "She told me, in code, before she disappeared. And I know what you're thinking. But as much as I know you want Bearers to fight, when it comes to Cassius, it's infinitely more dangerous for your kind. Not to mention the fact that Bearers don't exactly gather in groups like this anyway."

Dom tensed. It wasn't the right thing to say, especially when I'd just found out Solveig was currently being hunted simply because of who she was.

"The time will come," I said, cutting Lennie off at the pass, "when Bearers will mean the difference between life and death. And in case you've forgotten, in *your* case, it's already happened more than once."

It was a low blow, and I knew it. Yet the words held a strange weight after I'd uttered them. Almost a portent.

Dom raised his eyebrows towards Lennie, letting him know that he'd deserved that, before following behind me, a supportive hand placed on my lower back.

The only consolation to the interaction with Lennie was that it had been good to see that he was acting more like himself. We needed his cunning (though insolent) mind fully intact if we were going to greet any sort of victory on the other side.

"Dom, what exactly are we doing here?" I asked tentatively as we stood in the entranceway. Suddenly, being faced with a house full of unknown Wielders felt overwhelming. "I don't feel like I'll be much help here."

"We're here to talk battle plans. That's all," he said, before fully sensing my discomfort. He pulled me up onto an empty staircase and took my face into his hands. "Julia, listen to me. You're the most important person here. You don't *need* other Bearers to lead. You're the Sovereign! You're here because you deserve to be. And that's enough."

I had the impression that the message was meant for him as much as for me. We both had our roles to play in this life. In this war. And we needed to rise to the occasion.

CHAPTER 42

We were seated in the main-floor living room, which was delightfully cozy, with plenty of soft couches and blankets throughout. The gathering looked more like an afternoon house-party than a meeting to discuss how we could separate Cassius from the Codex. The group had been more than welcoming, quickly quelling any discomfort I held about joining in.

The group naturally congregated around Dom as he prepared to deliver his speech. He was wearing a simple pair of blue jeans with his riding boots, along with a black short-sleeve tee. It was almost obnoxiously casual, given the reason we were gathering today, but the people here knew Dom. He didn't have to earn their respect; he already had it—previous late-night antics of his notwithstanding.

I'd learned while we waited for the meeting to start that this was where many of the Druids in Vancouver lived and worked. Apparently, Ronan had even called this place home over the past several years. This meant that Dom had been a regular visitor, not only for work but for social calls as well. While I was slogging away to complete my degree, I had often wondered where Dom had gone on weekends. Now, I knew.

This new detail was solidified with an amusing story of Dom visiting Ronan several years previous and partying with a group of uncharacteristically boisterous Druids. Three sheets to the wind long before the night was done, they had proceeded to wager on who among them all could race to the ocean, strip down naked, fully dunk themselves in the ocean, and then race back the fastest. The funny part was supposed to be getting their clothes back on with frosty limbs. It had been December, and the prospect was (admittedly) stupid, but they knew that. What Ronan and Dom hadn't anticipated, however, was that their guests would steal the pair's clothes as a joke before jumping in themselves, forcing the pair of Celts to walk back, buck naked, in the cold.

"Don't you sometimes think you're too old for stuff like that?" I asked, snorting back giggles. I could see the pair of them, looking like complete loons as they slogged it back to the house.

"I *am* old," Dom said, proudly. "And I blame the rum."

And Ronan.

I felt a pang of sadness that he wasn't there offering his side of the story, no doubt blaming Dom for the entire debacle. However, Dom seemed happy enough in the retelling even without his "brother" there, so I didn't worry too much. Maybe this separation would be okay?

"Did you get caught?" Lennie asked, drawing my attention.

"My lips are sealed," Dom said, leaning against the mantle as he waited for the meeting to commence. "But I will say, that's the last time I ever tried to bribe a police officer without my pants on."

"And what about the first time?" Peggy hooted. She, more than anyone, always enjoyed Dom's hijinks.

The laughter carried for a time before finally fizzling out. Soon the light-hearted conversation—so familiar that it almost hurt—was replaced by more serious topics. As was usual with Druidic gatherings, they gracefully balanced the light with the dark. We'd enjoyed the happy element, and now it was time to deliver the grim. Dom stood before everyone, his body language now giving way to the seriousness of the event and sombre nature of our purpose.

Once everyone was paying attention, he spoke, his jaw set and shoulders back. "As you know, Cassius has come into possession of a very dangerous book—a volume containing the worst type of ancient dark Druidics—that could mean the difference between life and death for magic users as we know it."

"Okay, wait," a woman said; she was seated in an armchair by the window. "Before we start, why have we—*actual* Druids—never heard of this book before?" I was surprised to hear someone interrupt so soon, but she seemed to be the type to do so, reminding me of Gertie's neighbours on Salt Spring Island.

"Because it was supposed to be hidden forever," Dom said gently.

Silence fell once more. If the room hadn't been so jam-packed, I was pretty sure Dom would have begun to pace, demonstrating his power by casting an even wider net with the spell of his words. Instead, he leaned his forearm on the fireplace mantle, his bicep flexing. It had a similar effect. He was a dominating presence.

"Julia and I have encountered the book once before. And we—along with some of the strongest magical minds at the time—had it hidden so that the likes of Cassius could never find it. We were never told its final hiding place so that it couldn't be traced back to us and we couldn't be used to gain access to it. As far as I know, there was a series of complex coordinates placed onto a map meant to deter anyone from searching for it. And then the person who placed it in its final hiding spot ended their own life immediately after so that the secret died with them. After all that, you can understand why we kept its existence a secret."

I didn't know this last fact, and Dom looked towards me apologetically for delivering the information so late. It was a horrific thought, and I hated that yet another person had died for our cause. Again, I was reminded how much responsibility Dom carried on his shoulders for all of us.

"Forgive my ignorance, but why didn't you have it destroyed back then?" Lennie asked, and I noticed Dom's jaw twitch.

"You can't just destroy a book like that," Peggy replied, stepping in to support Dom. Many in the room nodded at her words, also understanding the intricacies of how volatile grimoires could be. But others continued to look confused. "They become almost a permanent earth fixture upon their creation," she continued. "All of the dark magic contained within the pages effectively makes them a magical bomb. Dangerous to use and even more dangerous to dismantle. It's so different than our magic ... our oral tradition. Where our magic is inherently balanced, this is only subtractive. Destructive. And so, unfortunately, hiding it would have been the only safe bet."

A wizened-looking Druid clucked in agreement. "Some incantations are never meant to be written down."

I thought of the effects of the *original* grimoire once more, and Grianne's burning cottage. I was lucky to have escaped at all, regardless of the cursed life I'd led.

"Right," Dom said. "And so now Cassius has it in his possession. We can assume he's keeping it on his person, which makes things difficult, though not impossible. We just have to find a way to get ahead of him."

The room fell silent, and I knew I wasn't the only one who couldn't fathom how we could possibly "get ahead" of Cassius without countless lives being lost. It was, admittedly, poor wording relative to the task.

A timid voice spoke up. "But … what kind of magic does it *actually* contain?" The question had come from a teenage boy, his curiosity getting the best of him. He was sitting between two adults I assumed were his parents. One of them shot him a look of annoyance while the other looked to Dom, clearly also wishing to hear the answer.

I stood then, feeling called to speak. Dom shot me a look that said I didn't have to expose myself like this, but he didn't interrupt. "My recollection of the book isn't strong. But I *have* performed one spell from it, long ago … In essence, I carved my memories onto Dom's back using a technique drawn from dark practices … rooted in ancient Druidry."

A low, collective gasp followed, but no one interrupted.

Darkness reigns where light cannot, and from its root, the land will rot.

"I know what you're thinking," I said. "How could someone on our side use a book like that? But magic isn't so black and white." I knew these modern Druids likely didn't hold the same belief, but if my fresh dealings with the Otherworld had taught me anything, not to mention Ronan's recent descent, it was that we were nothing without our shadows. Real magic was grey, ever shifting between choice and consequence.

Magic always came with a cost.

"Dom and I found a need to use the Codex to …" I couldn't bring myself to continue and looked to him for support.

Dom nodded, consenting to share our truth for me. "Together, we decided to have Julia Wield dark Druidics to carve our memories—or more accurately, *her* memories—into my flesh so that I could carry them with me through the Otherworld, and the rebirths, and return them to her when needed." He flexed his back, an old habit. "We were … desperate."

When he put it like that, this book sounded like it had the potential to make or break lives with the flip of the page. And in truth, it did.

"And that was one of the simpler spells," I added. "I'm sure of it. A one-to-one kind of ritual."

Dom nodded again. "But we know the book contains magic beyond anything we've seen as well. Grand scale," he said, spreading his arms wide. "Mass effect."

"No wonder Cassius sought it out," Thomas said. Many in the room nodded grimly.

"And that's why we need to get it back from him," Dom replied.

Sean and Graham smiled darkly, evidently ready for whatever it was going to take to separate The Child of Rome from the *Codex Druidicus*. Ideally, we would kill Cassius and destroy the book in one swift move. But since both were so volatile, we had neither the resources nor predictive ability to determine how to achieve that without losing our entire force. Especially on the short notice we were working with.

Cassius had managed to survive for nearly two thousand years, a powerful Sorcerer in his own right, with or without the book. But with the Codex, he was sure to grow his power at an exponential rate. Who could know what new adaptations he might garner from the tome.

We needed to remove it from his grasp. And quick. But how?

※

The next several hours were spent going over details of Cassius's Vancouver property holdings, in particular, the one we thought was his primary: his gargantuan coastal mansion. We also poured over plans for any Conventos the Druids and Knaves had knowledge of. Stuart and Lindsey were performing the same steps at another location, regularly checking in with Lennie and Dom over the phone with updates, cross-referencing whatever we found out. It was like a series of cogs in a machine that was working to solve a complex problem.

A Wielder hive-mind.

"Sorry," I said, "tell me again: *Where* is the big one?" The hair on the back of my neck was standing up in anticipation of the answer. For some reason, it wasn't sinking in.

Dom patiently pulled a map towards me, pointing at the south side of UBC, literally a ten-to-fifteen-minute drive from where we were stationed now. And minutes away from where we had landed in Vancouver, just across the Fraser River from the airport. *"That* is Cassius's stronghold."

Apparently, he owned a multi-million-dollar property on Southwest Marine Drive with its own three-hole private golf course, tennis court, and swimming pool. It was the kind of house one might come across never knowing who the owner might be, but you'd be certain they were in the "one percent."

And you would be right. I gagged slightly. "S-seriously?"

"Seriously," Lennie said, shoving his laptop towards me to give me a better picture of what we were dealing with. The mansion—a Tudor revival-style monstrosity—looked like something out of a movie. I thought of Gertie's small Tudor cottage and forced back a sick laugh; Cassius really *was* obsessed with me.

His estate was also practically a stone's throw from Totem Field Studios, relatively speaking, where I had attended some of my linguistics courses. The Child of Rome had practically been my next-door neighbour. Too often, it had felt like we passed each other like ships in the night—Cassius and I—my enemy always lurking in the shadows, inches away but just out of reach. Whether it was destiny or fixation, I was growing tired of being proven correct about all the ways our paths had crossed. Anger and urgency spurred me onward, easily keeping up, as Dom and Lennie bickered about possible next steps.

As the sun began to set, however, we were all hitting a wall. Many of the larger group had retired to their own corners for the evening, seeking sustenance and connection—a chance to recharge before whatever challenges lay ahead. Only Dom and I were left now, working away in our small corner. Even Lennie had tagged out for a short break.

"I just don't see how we're going to get anyone close enough to take it from him, even with all of the information we have here. Cassius will just kill them on the spot! And if we send a large force," I said—gesturing randomly as I pushed back from the many sets of plans, practically cross-eyed from how many times I'd poured over them—"too many will die."

Dom looked exhausted, lines of frustration etched permanently into his brow. He squeezed the bridge of his nose for several moments before releasing a long sigh, rolling his shoulders back in ritual habit. "There is a solution."

"Can you tell me what it is then? Because *none* of this feels right," I said, huffing as I slumped onto the low chair beside him. I'd been pacing for the last half hour—with far too much coffee and not nearly enough food—while Dom had become strangely still. Frozen.

"Well, we know one thing for sure: It won't be *you* going in," he said, in a tone far too casual for the body language that accompanied it. He stood abruptly, almost knocking over a lamp in the process, and turned away. For a man normally as graceful as a cat, it was unnerving. Almost as if a magnet was forcefully repelling him from my side.

I jolted at his quick movement, sensing the sharp shift in his demeanour; small stones were about to kick off an avalanche. "Obviously, Dom. And I wasn't volunteering myself. But—"

Dom turned fast towards me, his eyes jerking to meet mine as he blinked back tears. "No! You are far too precious."

I felt a distant rumble within my Bearing core, my mind flickering to the rocks on the road Bernie had shown me all those months ago and to the natural rivers that ran between Dom and me. "I'm just—" I stopped mid-thought, a sudden realization dawning. "Wait. You don't think *you'll* be going in, do you?"

He said nothing. Instead, he looked away.

"No!" I squeaked, barely containing my shock.

He took off towards the stairs. His movements were stiff but rapid, working hard to contain what was erupting from deep within. I knew in my heart that he was struggling, caught between the role he played in our life together and the mantle he had accepted as World Ruler; the tension between those two roles was agony for him.

The avalanche had begun.

Frozen for only an instant, I balled my fists as he reached the bottom of the stairs, his back towards me still. I stomped towards him and chased him up towards the second floor.

This was *not* happening.

"Don't you fucking dare, Domhnall O'Brien!" I hissed, but I knew already that my anger wasn't going to be of any help.

Reaching the upstairs hall, I collected myself as quickly as I could, hoping to talk some sense into his thick Celtic head. If that didn't work, I'd resort to tying him up. Surely, Lennie and the others would help.

"Dom, stop!" I said, on the landing between flights, and caught his solid shoulders at last, demanding he turn towards me. "You aren't playing the hero on this one. Absolutely not. There has to be another way to do this."

He looked at me, but I couldn't read his expression. I knew, somehow, that it had been many centuries since he'd made a choice like this, and the look tearing across his face made that plain: aguish beyond any of my living years.

"Dom, listen to me. I know I said that our rivers were going to ebb and flow from each other, and all that ... but not like *this!* Never like this ..." I felt my shoulders begin to shake.

Dom pulled me close, wrapping me in his solid embrace, a place of safety I was never willing to let go of. When he spoke, his voice was gravelly. "Who else is going to be able to even reach Cassius without being immediately killed, Julia? I'm literally the only one here who—"

"I can do it," an Irish voice said behind us. "Am I too late?"

We turned together to see Ronan standing at the top of the stairs, kitted head-to-toe in his best fighting gear. Bracers and all.

CHAPTER 43

"Conflicted" couldn't *begin* to describe how I felt about Ronan being used as bait. I had been forced into that same role once before, and it had almost meant the decimation of our entire army. Yet, the look on Dom's face when he saw his general standing at the ready—ready for battle (and providing a solution), even after he'd been told he wasn't welcome—had sealed the deal before there was any room for further discussion. Dom had immediately pulled his friend into a firm embrace, hot tears pouring down his face in unabashed gratitude for Ronan's arrival.

Ronan looked relieved as he peered over Dom's shoulder towards me, a slight smile spreading across his lips. I stood there staring stupidly and blinking back my own muddled tears. "Um … This is a nice house you and the Druids have here, Ronan," I said awkwardly.

They both laughed. I sighed.

As much as I wanted to share in Dom's relief, I felt a sickly concern growing in my belly. Dom wanted so badly for his friend to be well, to be the man he remembered, but something told me—or rather, screamed at me—that we needed to proceed with extreme caution.

He might technically still be *our* Ronan, but he was not fully okay at the moment either.

Naturally, the lads—Dom, Ronan, and Lennie—immediately settled into a complex plan that involved Ronan crossing into enemy territory once

Cassius's Wraith guard had been stripped back. I watched as the three of them resumed their usual patterns: Dom overseeing with seasoned authority, Ronan providing detailed tactics, and Lennie barking at them anytime their suggestions showed the hint of any flaw. It was a relief to see the three of them working together again, just like old times, even if the gnawing worry in my gut was becoming a distraction.

Lindsey and Stuart checked in periodically, acting as field captains for the different Druid and Knave groups lying in wait. Sean and Graham were integral to the attack on Cassius's mansion, though they were more focused on the "force elements" of the plan than the tactical stratagem. Their intensity brought a grounding realism to the task that the lads sometimes lacked; however, the stakes were high, and it was no time to be messing around. The pair had apparently devised a demolition package that would not only serve as a distraction but also an escape plan if needed.

"And then ... *boom!*" Graham said, spreading his fingers wide, his eyes lit up. Sean grinned and flexed his arms tight across his chest.

Dom nodded, his face awash with appreciation and apprehension in equal measure.

Peggy and Thomas also joined in the discussion, though Peggy headed to bed fairly early into the proceedings. She would never admit it openly—not wishing to dispute Dom's choice—but I had the distinct impression she hadn't aligned with Dom's initial decision to ask Ronan to sit this one out. But besides that, she also didn't look entirely well. Perhaps it was just the strain of things. It was a lot to take in, after all, in a very short period of time.

Eventually, I also took my leave, feeling woozy from the efforts of the day. Assuring Dom that I simply needed a breather, I tiptoed into the empty kitchen and was happily met by several dozen tins of assorted tea.

Goddess, I loved the Druids.

Fingering though the options, I chose a sleepy-time blend and quietly put on the kettle to boil. Years ago, a therapist had taught me to focus on "front brain" tasks during times of stress. Rituals that kept me grounded in my body were a solid choice when my body was kicking into fight or flight. However, I wasn't sure if what was coming—a literal fight for our lives—could be combatted with a mere tea ritual.

Waiting for the kettle to boil, I tried and failed miserably to keep my worried thoughts at bay.

We already knew that Cassius likely had designs on Ronan, being that he had tasked Caleb to torture the information out of Lennie and Wren, as well as the fact that Kenzie had captured Dr. Bailey, another direct link to Ronan's work. Not to mention the vision both Ronan and I had shared; he was bound to Cassius now, though we didn't know yet to what extent. So, it really was likely that he stood the best chance of getting close to the Codex without a fight. Not that tricking Cassius was something any of us believed was possible, but if Ronan could just get *into* Cassius's inner sanctum, then we could hopefully cause enough of a distraction to also get him out.

Since Ronan's return, however, I'd desperately attempted to avoid thinking about it. I wanted to believe, beyond a doubt, that he would stay true to our cause. Yet every time I looked at him, I couldn't help but draw up the image of him standing at Cassius's side, resigned to his purpose and unflinching. With how strange he had been acting lately—really, since our road trip to Berkeley—I found it hard to trust the man unconditionally anymore. But still my belief persisted that Ronan's loyalty to us, and to the cause, would overrule any underlying motives of his own.

I shuddered, halting the thought in its tracks as the kettle began to whistle.

I redoubled my efforts to focus on the task at hand and eventually felt my body and mind calm as I slowly went through the steps of preparing a piping-hot cup of tea.

It was midnight by the time I poked my head into the conversation once more.

"So, where are we at?" I asked. To my own surprise, I'd almost dozed off in the kitchen chair and felt supremely groggy as I re-entered the war room.

"We've got it sorted, finally," Lennie said. Ronan nodded in agreement, giving nothing away.

Dom reached towards me, cheeks also flushed with exhaustion yet looking surprisingly at ease. "I was just saying that we've already had Druids stationed around Cassius's property for the past several days, ever since he returned.

Their groups will be in charge of drawing out the majority of his Wraiths before we arrive, leading them away from the mansion."

"Okay," I said, looking around and noticing that the group had dwindled. "Wait. Where are Sean and Graham?"

"They've just left to do some more reconnaissance tonight," Dom said. "They'll be the ones entering the building with Ronan, and so they need to be the most familiar with it."

"Tonight," I said, yawning. "That means …"

"We attack at dawn."

I leaned into him, fighting the growing trepidation in my mind as my sleepy body fought to catch up. I swayed on the spot, feeling clammy all over.

I opened my mouth to speak, but Lennie took over. "Once the Druids flush out the majority of the Wraiths, the Knaves will then draw the larger Conventos northwest, even further away from his property. And another group of us will block the opposite direction with magical and physical barriers—Alanna and Shereen have already volunteered their corps for the blocking. This way, we can direct the Wraiths towards UBC."

"UBC?" I asked, shocked. Though I supposed the trajectory of Southwest Marine Drive *would* naturally funnel them there, I felt a surge of protectiveness towards my alma mater. "Why there?"

"Because it's closed down for the long weekend, and it's only summer school anyway. There shouldn't be many people there, and so there will be less chance of civilian casualties than any of our other options." Lennie's voice was almost robotic. Perhaps this was how he got past the fact that many lives *were* going to be put into danger by the plans he'd helped create. Although I suspected he was right about our options, I wasn't sure I liked it.

Instinctively, and as usual, Thomas acted as a peace-wielding buffer. "Peggy and I will have a group of allies waiting on campus—sort of a backstop to keep any Wraiths from filtering too closely to the general population. We'll do what we can to create an enchanted barricade using Wielding magic. We just need to get the Wraiths away from Cassius's mansion long enough for Sean, Graham, and Ronan to isolate Cassius and take the Codex."

I let out a levelling breath. "Okay. And where will the rest of us be?"

Dom answered. *"We* will be with Lindsey, Stuart, and Lennie, just outside the barrier of Cassius's mansion, in case they need backup." He wrapped his arms around me, securing me to the spot.

"Right," I said, forcing my brain to think of who else was left. "Have you heard from Booker and Glenys at all?"

Lennie shook his head. "No, but that doesn't mean they aren't coming."

"What do you mean?" Thomas asked.

Lennie rolled his eyes. "It means that the desert Knaves will have a hard time crossing the border in the *conventional* way. I'll make sure they have the information they need though. If they can make it across, they will."

Dom nodded in agreement, their strange relationship with the desert Knaves being one that only they seemed to understand.

Ronan, meanwhile, had remained silent through most of the discussion. I chose to assume this was because he was both tired from travel and focused on catching up as best he could, rather than anything darker coming into play as the night wore on.

It wasn't lost on me that he was avoiding my gaze, however.

Was he still as concerned about the vision as I was? Regardless, as far as the Codex went, we would still have to deal with Ronan's potentially dangerous draw to the book once it was safe in hand. That detail *couldn't* be ignored or forgotten, even if it wasn't being articulated in the drawing of these current plans.

We eventually adjourned for the night, each of us hoping to cobble together at least a few hours of sleep before we loaded up at five a.m. Unfortunately, I was now wide awake with a head full of concerns.

"I don't like the idea of Ronan having the Codex either, Julia," Dom whispered as he closed the bedroom door behind us. "But what other choice do we have?"

I shot him a stern look. Dom *knew* the other "choice" we had—according to him at least—so I didn't bother answering. His walking headfirst into Cassius's lair wasn't an option I was willing to entertain.

"Okay, let me rephrase that," he said. "We are stuck with this choice now, whether we like it or not." We both began to strip for bed.

I kicked off my shorts, halting the rest of the process and heading straight for the window instead; we'd been given a small guest room on the third floor, which was going to be extremely stuffy unless we could get some air flowing. It reminded me of the apartment I'd shared with Virginia back at university. It was stuck, but I knew *exactly* what to do.

"I suppose," I said, jerkily yanking the window's handles back and forth until it began to wiggle slightly, "once Ronan *does* come across the Codex"—I turned my body, causing one elbow to bend upward at an awkward angle, and pulled harder on the handles—"it's better that he battle any potential demons by our side than all alone." With a final grunt, I got the window opened at last.

Victory!

Dom paused, staring blankly at me for a second. "Absolutely. Though, I'd prefer if Ronan didn't have to battle any demons at all."

Revelling in the fresh air spilling in across the back of my legs, I watched as Dom stripped his t-shirt off, his hair catching a bit in the process, tussling it deliciously askew. I bit my lip. "I know that. But I don't think that's what's on the table here exactly. We need to make sure Sean and Graham are aware of his … his *risk*. And Lennie too. We need to keep Ronan contained until we can sort out what his relationship actually *is* with the book. He can't be left to deal with it alone."

Ideally, once Ronan had the Codex in hand, we would relocate him and a Druid guard to a safe-house until further instruction. What Ronan didn't know was that the guard would be focused as much on him as on the Codex.

But that was a problem for a later time; we couldn't get too far ahead of ourselves.

"You're right. I'll make sure they know," Dom said, sadness momentarily stitching his brow before he shook it off. He continued slowly stripping down, apparently clueless to his distracting physique. Either that or he was playing me like a harp. "A part of me still wishes Ronan wasn't here at all. But the other part …" he said, removing his jeans to expose long, muscular thighs, "it's complicated."

MANTLE OF THE WORLD RULER

Dom was right. There were a lot of conflicting emotions swirling around in the ether tonight, particularly under this one roof. Not least of all, the two completely separate conversations we were having right now.

Trying to hide my waning attentiveness to the more serious conversation at hand, I scooted into bed and pulled the covers up to my neck, which reminded me more of an unzipped flannel sleeping bag than a duvet. I pushed it off immediately, feeling hot and bothered.

"What's on your mind, love," Dom said, climbing into bed beside me. He turned to his side, resting his head on his hand and looking unbelievably gorgeous. We had only four hours before we needed to be up again. Why was my brain so primitive sometimes?

"Well ... I guess I'm just wondering if we've been conditioned," I said, turning on my side as well, facing him. My boobs immediately fell out of my tank top.

"Conditioned how?" he asked, staring at my nipples and proving my point.

"Like, why the sex is *so* good? Because here we are again. About to have sex for possibly the last time ... again."

Dom jerked back playfully. "Oh, are we?"

"Come on, don't tell me you weren't staring at me opening that window in my underwear."

"Okay, you caught me," he said, cheekily.

I ran my lips along his collarbone, breathing into him. "But seriously. I'm desperate for you. It's like an automatic response or something. Imminent danger lies ahead, and I just want to fuck. Isn't that so strange?"

"I ... I don't think it's strange at all," Dom said, his breath catching. "It's actually very ... 'original-Julia.' You've always been like this, love. Hate to break it to you. Plus, I think it's the only way we'll get you to fall asleep tonight, so needs being what they are ..."

I snorted at his last statement. "So practical, Mr. O'Brien. You surprise me."

He let out a low groan. "I'm nothing, if not surprising."

In the early hours of the morning, we loaded silently into the unmarked cars and took off for Cassius's compound. According to our intelligence, he was definitely home. Along with about eighty Wraiths. Give or take. No big deal or anything. I felt slightly delirious at the prospect and caught myself wondering more than once if Cassius actually slept. Did he own a coffee maker? No, he seemed too removed from humanity for caffeine. Did he eat perfectly crafted smoothie bowls like one of those weirdos? That seemed a better fit.

Dom held my hand, his warm palm offering its usual assurance. We had a plan, and we had to try. At least that's what he'd told me before we'd finally drifted off to sleep: *We have to trust that it would work.* Again, it felt like a projection of his own fears. Had Ronan truly regained his trust?

A part of me seriously doubted it.

Lindsey and Stuart were riding along with us in a massive black SUV. It reminded me of something the U.S. president would ride in. I wondered absently if it was bullet-proof. I knew Dom had brought them in the same vehicle as us for protective duty, in case something happened to him. Protection for *me*. In the event of a crisis, Lindsey would call upon the Druids, and Stuart the Knaves, and they would get me the hell out of there.

And, of course, they were both incredible fighters in their own right.

"Dom, I don't want you going in there," I said quietly. "I mean it. No matter what. We can try something else if this doesn't work."

He said nothing but gave me a light squeeze. It didn't make me feel better.

We would be stationed just out of sight. Once the Wraiths were agitated and moving south, Sean, Graham, and Ronan would leave Lennie's vehicle and enter Cassius's property from the south side. Lennie would remain outside, at the console in the back of their SUV, from which he would dismantle any electronic security Cassius might have and direct contact with all of the other moving parts of the assault. His role was an infinitely important one when it came to keeping our forces organized. Or at least, that's what Dom told me.

I knew both Dom and Lennie would rather be in the action right now, but they had vital roles of their own to fill.

Our driver parked us on what looked to be a maintenance road connecting the estate to the greater golf course beyond. We watched as Lennie parked slightly closer to the property line, as he would need to be within a certain range.

Then everyone fell silent.

It was a strange sensation, almost a cocoon of active denial around what was about to happen. Outside of our SUV, I could hear the early scales of birdsong, a warm-up for the dawn chorus. Feeling soothed by this simple aspect of nature, I dared to reach out with my Bearing magic towards the house in which Cassius was likely sleeping. I was met with what felt like a fuzzy wall of magic; no doubt his Wraiths had placed protective enchantments around the compound.

There were Wraiths out there alright. Loads of them. And I suddenly worried that they could potentially feel my presence as well. Of course, the Druid transports had their own Wielded protections around them, but the fear remained.

At my feet were the bare essentials of our life. The quilt was tucked neatly into a bag, along with several changes of clothes for the both of us, my camera, talisman, and any potentially necessary documents. I tried not to think of the circumstance when we might need this simplistic escape kit, but Dom had insisted we bring the essentials with us just in case.

I looked over and watched as he closed his eyes, transporting himself undoubtedly to a distant memory from long ago. I noticed more and more that he did this in moments when he sought calm. Often, I wished I could spend time within his head, where memories of our past lay dormant, ready for him to page through them when the moment was right. I knew he also carried within his mind the dark chapters we had experienced in our past. However, I was learning more and more these days that there truly could be no light without darkness.

"What are you thinking about?" I asked quietly. Stuart and Lindsey were engaged in their own private conversation in front of us, which involved a lot more whispers and touching than ours did.

His eyes opened slowly. "You."

"Me? What about?"

"I was thinking about this one time ... I don't even know what year it would be. A long, *long* time ago. You were walking through a garden, and your hair was gleaming in the sunlight as you picked these bundles of little yellow and white flowers. The air smelled like fresh grass and honeysuckle. You stopped to put your hair into a braid, delicately tucking the flowers in through each plait, and then you pulled it over your head and said, *"Look, Domhnall, a crown!"* A goddess on earth. I was sitting on a sharp stone on the edge of the garden, polishing my blade or something uninteresting. But I remember it so clearly because you were …" He paused, catching himself. "Well … it's not important. You were really beautiful that day is all. It's one of my fondest memories."

It sounded like a glorious day, but he had obviously not finished the thought. "What were you going to say?"

"Are you sure you want to hear?"

I frowned, puzzled. "Was I naked or something?" Surely that wasn't a big deal, though it would be kind of funny if he selectively chose to peruse nude memories of me in times of stress.

"No, love. You were *pregnant,*" he said, sounding unsure of whether this was something that would upset me.

"Oh. I see. Um … How far along?" I asked. I wasn't actually sure how I felt about it.

"You were just starting to show. Maybe, oh … five months? It was the farthest you'd ever made it along. Remember, we found each other earlier then. So, there was more time to … Well, it was back when you still remembered me."

I understood why he had chosen that particular memory. It was one that signified a promise of our future together. Something he'd always wanted and had longed for more than anything else. To grow old together, with a growing family around us.

He was reminding himself why he needed to stay alive today.

"Dom, I'm really serious. You can't go in there after Ronan. I want to—"

Stuart's phone pinged loudly. "It's Alanna. The Wraiths are moving. It's almost go-time."

All of us craned our necks towards Lennie's SUV, where Sean, Graham, and Ronan stood and silently prepared themselves in the waning darkness. I'd never once asked Dom what Sean and Graham did for a living, other than being Druids, but now it was clear. All three of them wore military garb and looked perfectly primed for tactical ops. They were natural-born soldiers.

MANTLE OF THE WORLD RULER

"How long do they have?" Lindsey asked. She looked more concerned than I'd ever seen her, but these were her people in there too. Even Ronan.

"Ten minutes, give or take. If they aren't back within that amount of time …" Dom hesitated. "We leave."

Next came the longest ten minutes of our lives.

CHAPTER 44

The coarse wool of Ronan's jacket chafed harshly around his neck as he, Sean, and Graham exited the SUV just outside of Cassius's property line. Ignoring the discomfort encircling his throat, he took several desperate gulps of the damp morning air. The sensation was staggering, especially in comparison to the near suffocation he'd felt only moments before.

Mentally preparing themselves for battle along the way, they'd spent the majority of the trip in concentrated silence but for a *slight* moment of tension in which Graham—being the bloodhound of a man that he was—had almost sniffed out Ronan's teetering resolve.

"You with us, Doctor?" Graham asked in his heavy Scottish brogue. He'd apparently noticed the shift in Ronan's impeccably schooled features, and that wasn't acceptable. Ronan had become a master at obscuring his true feelings over the decades, but the mask was slipping more and more the closer he got to the Codex.

"Of course," Ronan had replied simply, flexing his jaw almost imperceptibly.

If he weren't so logically bound, he would have sworn he'd *felt* the Codex's presence growing as they got closer to their destination. As if it were calling out to him. Perhaps it was the other way around? But that wasn't possible. Not whatsoever. Even in the magical world, Wielders didn't have that kind of ability at such a range. Bearers? Sure. Sorcerers? Maybe. Not Druids.

Air *in*. Air *out*.

Sean and Lennie hadn't seemed to notice Graham's question as they pulled up to the perimeter, and so Ronan forced himself to breathe through the growing ache he felt in his palms and the conflicting alarm bells screaming in his ears. Sweat trickled hotly down the back of his neck, the war in his body now almost unbearable. The fact was that Ronan now lived for the Codex—his need for it had become as essential as breathing. And that very longing filled the blood that coursed through his veins, oxygenating the cells with ever-increasing vigour as it reached his heart, naming his greatest wish.

He continued to breathe through the waves of panic. As always, the profound craving ebbed slightly with each shaky exhalation.

Air *in*. Need.

He could definitely feel its presence now—practically taste it. The source of his deepest longing ... his most overwhelming need.

Air *out*. Want.

He knew what he should do ... what he *wanted* to do. Each breath out reminded him of his longstanding loyalty to the allies he'd sworn to protect years ago—back when he'd first embarked on his path as a Druid. His kin had welcomed him with open arms, despite his difficult past and the violently militaristic years that would follow. He'd always struggled to keep to the light, but both Druidry and medicine had made it significantly easier for him to keep afloat.

At least until he'd seen what Julia had done on the top of the battlements. That act—that seemingly simple wave of raw Bearing intuition she'd expressed—had changed *everything*.

Ronan thought of Dom and Julia: Dom, a soul brother in the truest sense of the word, and Julia, someone who had been cast into the fire repeatedly, only to emerge ripe with optimism. And both of them still holding room in their hearts for people like Ronan. Not only were they the epitome of what was good in the world but for some reason ... they loved him, in spite of everything he'd put them through. They were his family, or the closest thing he'd ever had to one.

Would the deafening roar of need that was ruling his mind and body actually betray them?

His chosen family?

499

He wanted to believe in the good in himself—that when it came down to it, he would choose his friends over his unrelenting lust for the Codex and the answers he so desperately sought. Still, it was one quandary, among many, left unanswered. But this one would be answered soon; would he choose himself or his friends?

Air *in*. Air *out*.

Ronan forced himself to the present moment as Graham and Sean readied themselves to his right, drawing their weapons and assessing the current situation at lightning speed. The pair were trained soldiers, at least in the modern sense of the word. With their abilities as Wielders added to that, they were positively lethal. But they were also expendable … when it came down to it.

And they made no bones about it.

"We stick to the plan. Ronan reaches Cassius, whatever the cost," Sean said, locking an elongated blade to the under-barrel of the semi-automatic rifle he would be wearing across his back. Modern firearms weren't exactly practical in a magical battle—nor were traditional bayonets—but Sean had found the specialized weapon useful on more than one occasion in their many raids over the years; Ronan wasn't about to question it now.

"The three of us are coming out alive, with the Codex. *That's* the plan," Graham said, lifting his fist to his chest, which also held his heavy battle axe, its sharp silver edge glinting only slightly in the early dawn light. Ronan was familiar with Graham's usual pre-battle bravado. The man was as big as a tank and would be about as hard to take down, but no one was infallible. He was simply the kind of man who entered a battle with zero doubt in his own capabilities. The Scot grinned back at the pair of Irishmen. "Or we die trying. Right, lads?"

Sean nodded his head with a grin, sharing the same twisted keenness for the impending battle ahead. These two *knew* the stakes; it was Ronan who was the wildcard here. And he had the gnawing sense that, while he had been asked to "do the job," no one actually trusted him to carry it out as planned.

He mentally cauterized the oozing feeling and went over his arsenal instead.

For his part, Ronan also carried a gun—a jet-black pistol with a silencer—but he knew it wouldn't be used today. Instead, he would wield his dagger, bracers, and other Druidic skills to fight towards their target: Cassius. But more importantly, the Codex.

Ronan looked down at his watch. Thirty seconds to go.

Air *in*. Air *out*.

He quickly eyed the second SUV, containing Dom, Julia, Lindsey, and Stuart. And then the one he'd arrived in with Lennie, who was still inside behind his countless screens. For a brief moment, he wished that Lennie—or better yet, Dom—would also be joining them as they fought their way inside, but he knew better than to entertain such an irrational want. They needed Lennie's technical skills in the SUV more than his abilities with a blade. That was just a fact. As for Dom, well, they didn't need him playing the hero and getting himself killed after all he and Julia had been through. He was far too important to the cause, and in truth, to Ronan. And then there was Lindsey. Ronan felt compassion for her in the moment, hoping she would have a chance for a happy life with Stuart—the fact that he didn't particularly like the man was irrelevant, and not a nearly a good enough reason for the Knave to risk his life today.

No, Ronan was the only one for the job. If only he could just—

"Go!" Graham roared, taking off at a sprint with Sean directly on his heels. Ronan raised his dagger and followed at full speed behind the two Druids.

Five Wraiths stepped onto the main path from behind a hedgerow to their left. They seemed surprised to discover intruders, which gave the Druids a slight upper hand. Sean, who was double-wielding short daggers, besides the artillery on his back, took two Wraiths out in one sweeping motion. Graham swung his axe in graceful but powerful arcs around him. They fought seemingly together, in the way only two men who had done so with regularity could do, and took out the other three combatants in quick succession.

"Keep going!" Sean hollered from the ground, where he had landed briefly, slipping on some blood, as Ronan skirted past the still-falling bodies and sprinted towards a set of double doors on the back side of the mansion. This was their targeted entry point. Ronan recalled the detailed plans the lads had already outlined with him even before his arrival in Vancouver, with Dom, as always, making certain the maps were detailed and memorized to the nth degree by every member of the mission.

Ronan knew exactly where he was headed.

But just as he hit their first barrier—marked by the flashing red security scanner—two hulking Wraiths stepped in front.

"Fuck," Ronan muttered under his breath, raising his dagger. He needed backup.

Lennie's voice simultaneously chirped in Ronan's earpiece. "Three, two, one …"

The light turned green.

At that instant, Graham and Sean charged up behind him, their footfalls thundering on the gravel walkway—any hopes of arriving undetected had been lost. The Wraiths lunged towards them, arms outstretched and ready for battle.

"You're not going anywhere," one said, leering at them.

"The fuck we aren't," Graham answered.

Following his intuition, Ronan ducked to his right, letting the two Druid berserkers coming from behind roar past him and into the Wraith guards. Slipping past the fray, Ronan unlatched the recently unlocked door with ease before stepping inside.

The unlit hallway was currently empty, though the stench of Wraith magic—and something far more sinister—occupied the passageway in an almost unearthly manner. He gagged slightly before pressing onward. For an instant, he thought of the face Julia would be making if she were there, her tongue lolling out as she tried to make light of how awful the stench really was.

Air *in*. Air *out*. Don't give in.

The floors under his booted feet were a glossy slate grey, with the walls above covered in dull white plaster. Over half a dozen nondescript doors lined the hall, each framed in dark wood. The original structure of the Tudor-style mansion was old but had apparently been retrofitted to accommodate Cassius's needs, or more specifically, to house his security detail off the back. The allies knew that Cassius wasn't going to share a living space *with* the Wraiths, so entering through their confines had felt like the most logical, unanticipated approach.

Thankful once again to the ancient Celtic bastard's obsession with memorizing maps, Ronan continued to the third door on the right—the easiest way to reach the core of the house.

Slipping through the door, still apparently undetected, he continued towards the heart of the manor. He would have no way of knowing if Graham and Sean were still on his tail until they caught up to him, but there was no time to wait. Lennie had only promised them ten minutes of security clearance before the mansion itself went into lockdown, trapping them inside. And that was the last thing they needed.

No. This mission was *his* to complete.

The soft echo of a door closing behind him, followed by the heavy breathing of two men, told him that all three Druids were still on the hunt.

Ronan turned and raised an eyebrow to the lads, both roughed up but mostly intact. A strange mix of relief and trepidation filled him.

"Onward," Sean panted, nodding.

Graham grimaced as his shoulders heaved slightly, and the three of them took off at a silent trot.

They were moving into the original body of the house now, where the simplistic grey and white finishings gave way to greater luxury. Heavy wood panelling lined the dim passageway now, where soon they came across another secured door. Thankfully, the panel light was already green.

Lennie was a bloody genius.

Graham stepped forcibly past Ronan, keeping him behind. The Scot's massive frame blocked the view into the next space. "Looks clear," he said, lifting a muscular arm and beckoning them onward. Ronan followed second, with Sean abnormally tight on his heels.

If Ronan didn't know any better, he'd swear that they were suddenly sticking closer to him than was tactically necessary. Had they been given different instructions to the original plan? Keep a close eye on Ronan once the Codex is in sight? He knew his allies—Dom in particular—had been uncertain in his ability to help on the mission. After all, Dom had tried to leave Ronan behind in Ireland in the first place. But even so ... this seemed extreme.

Ronan was a man of his word, wasn't he? He'd proven as much!

Air *in*. Air *out*.

Your friends care about you. Don't be paranoid.

The three Druids continued to the first staircase. Ronan looked down at his watch. Five minutes had already passed. They were almost out of time, and they hadn't even reached Cassius, let alone the Codex.

Noises came from a room to the right, and soon a dozen or more Wraiths wandered out, too casually to indicate they'd been actually surprised. Those whose faces could be seen beyond their hoods were grinning maliciously. They had *definitely* not been surprised.

"Hello, boys," Graham said. "I take it you've been expecting us?"

What followed was pandemonium.

Before anyone could jump forward, Graham detonated several small pouches that he pulled from inside his jacket. Small explosions crackled in quick succession as thick smoke quickly filled the space. The Wraiths pressed forward in a semi-circle meant to close on the three of them in a pincer motion. However, the Druids had seen this formation before and were familiar with one another's rhythm; Ronan and Sean leapt backwards, and Graham leapt to the side. Caught off guard, some of the attackers clashed with each other and fell upon themselves. Those that didn't collide with their own tried to engage the three men. But they were already upon them, ready to counter.

Sean launched himself away from Ronan and into the smoke, while Ronan remained huddled close to the wall and started shuffling to the other side of the room, though not without lunging occasionally to strike at Wraith robes as they appeared amidst the swirling smoke. These particular pouches weren't meant to cause damage—just to disorient and confuse, which they were doing sublimely. Almost shockingly effective. The larger bombs were being saved for their escape, should they need to blast their way out through the walls. Ronan stomped blindly, but unimpeded, over several disoriented bodies as he hurled himself from the wall and towards the staircase that led to Cassius's main office—the most likely location of the Codex.

Behind him, the sounds of flesh gnashing and wood shattering rang through the halls. He hoped it was the sound of Graham slamming Wraiths into the walls and not the other way around. He heard Sean swear loudly, followed by the clash of metal.

He pushed onward, noticing that no one was on his trail, neither Wraith nor Druid.

There was no time to waste. Ronan plucked the earpiece out—Lennie's voice still crackling—and let it drop from his fingers as he trotted towards the last door on the west wing of the hallway: Cassius's office. He took several steadying breaths. Now that he'd been separated from his group, this felt too easy. Where was everyone?

Air *in*. Air *out*.

MANTLE OF THE WORLD RULER

Ronan approached the door, which stood suspiciously half-open. A quick glance at his wrist told him he had just over three minutes to go before Graham detonated them all the hell out of there.

Steadying himself before the final move, the last lines of the new Prophecy haunted his thoughts:

> *For the earthen weapons masters, and tree talkers with open sky above,*
> *Darkness reigns where light cannot, and from its root, the land will rot.*

Stepping through the threshold, Ronan saw Cassius seated at his desk. There was no book in sight, but he could feel it.

Air that was shared with the codex filled his lungs.

Air *in*. Air *out*.

Soul crushing *need* …

A silvery voice sliced through the air. "Hello, Ronan … I've been expecting you."

CHAPTER 45

I found myself grinding my teeth, the waiting having quickly become almost unbearable. Lennie had Dom on the walkie-talkie, relaying what he knew in real time—which wasn't a whole hell of a lot. We couldn't truly know what was going on inside until the group returned, but Lennie was able to keep us abreast of what the rest of the Knaves were up to at least.

"They're still attempting to clear the south road," Lennie snapped. "Awaiting the signal from Graham inside."

I knew that Graham and Sean would have been cutting through the house with Ronan to clear his passage. Hopefully, there were only a handful of Wraiths left inside, making the job easier, but there was no guarantee. When Ronan reached Cassius, he would offer himself to him—a part of the plan that made me feel especially sick. Then, once Ronan was within reach of the book, he would give a signal, and Sean and Graham would detonate a series of both magical and regular bombs, hopefully causing enough chaos that the three of them could escape with the Codex in hand.

It was *possible* Cassius would give chase, but he'd never been the type to fight himself unless he absolutely had to. In fact, according to Dom, it had been years since he'd actually seen Cassius engage in any form of combat.

If he didn't kill or capture Ronan on the spot, it wasn't likely he would follow.

I watched as Stuart's stopwatch passed the nine-minute mark. Dom clenched his fists one at a time, his breath rasping in his throat. Sweat was running down my back.

The remaining seconds ticked away until none were left, and then we heard the explosion.

BOOM!!

Before the smoke had even cleared, movement came from the house. It was definitely Ronan, followed by Graham, hauling an unconscious or possibly dead Sean over his shoulders.

"Step on it!" Dom shouted, and our driver took off. He was a Druid with a long beard who I had never seen before. We watched as Ronan, Graham, and (a hopefully still-living) Sean almost fell into the back of Lennie's SUV, and then it took off after us with similar gusto.

Lennie's voice crackled over the radio: "We've got it!"

With a crunch of gravel and skidding tires, we blasted towards the main road. When we got there though, we found that it was still blocked to the south. Our driver had to slam on the breaks so hard I lurched forward. The Knaves' handiwork had fractured and splintered the asphalt into something that resembled peanut brittle. I assumed it was some kind of elemental magic that reshaped the road's foundation from below.

"Fuck!" Dom shouted.

Once the Wraiths around Cassius's stronghold had been pushed back, the plan was for our allies to clear a path for us to the south, so we could get to the airport, but it looked like things hadn't gone that way.

Now we would have to head in the opposite direction, towards UBC and the fighting.

I could see Dom's fingers flex subconsciously towards his sword, which lay sheathed at our feet. My own blade, tucked carefully at my shin, began to vibrate in anticipation. I had never managed to make it "sing," per se, but I'd definitely formed some sort of connection to it over the months it had been in my possession. And I noticed it now.

I pulled my compass from my pocket. It was spinning madly. Made sense. I felt completely disoriented. I wondered darkly whether Ronan's would have been perfectly still, had he not destroyed it in some fit of anger or despair.

Preparing to leap into battle, I was checking each of my own armaments, just as my companions were. I had the dagger, the compass, and my own power. I still felt a solid, albeit somewhat shaky, confidence that I could handle whatever the circumstances required of me.

Whatever that might be.

"Where are we going to go now?" I asked Dom.

Assuming we'd been able to reach the airport and the helicopter meeting us there, our plan had been to send Ronan, Lennie, Sean, and Graham off to an undisclosed location with the Codex until we could forge a plan to either hide it or destroy it. We would follow later when the battle was over, and the coast was determined to be clear.

"We'll have to reroute the helicopter," Dom said, his mind running a mile a minute. "There has to be somewhere on campus where it can land. Assuming we can get to it."

And indeed, as we approached the UBC grounds, it was clear that the Knaves, Druids, and Wraiths had been locked in a terrible battle. Bodies were strewn everywhere—clearly a fight to the death had been taking place in our absence.

Our driver slammed on the breaks once more, just shy of Thunderbird Stadium. We could go no further except on foot.

"Everyone out!" Dom said, picking up his sword as we hopped out. Our driver took off towards the fight ahead without looking back.

Ahead, the road was completely blocked with debris and flooded with water. The same to our right down West 16th. It looked like something had exploded underground, causing a water-main break.

"That will be Glenys and Booker's work," Lennie said, breathing hard as he splashed towards us from his group's hastily parked SUV. "Their crew got here right as the fighting started and got to work. I asked them to make it difficult for the *Wraiths* to get anywhere in their cars on the UBC end of things, but this isn't exactly what I meant."

"It worked well enough though," Graham said as he joined us. "We're stuck."

I looked around for his comrade, dreading what his absence might mean. "Is Sean—"

"He'll survive. But he won't be fighting again today. He's safer in the SUV for now."

So, we were already down one of our best fighters, not to mention one of Ronan's helicopter escorts. Dom and I had both agreed that it was imperative the man be chaperoned every moment he had the book in his possession—we didn't dare try to separate him from the Codex at this point in case it spooked him somehow and caused him to take off with it.

At the thought, Dom startled a bit, looking around nervously for Ronan. His shoulders relaxed only slightly when he spotted him hurrying towards us, the Codex clearly tucked into the inside of his coat, confirming our suspicions: He had absolutely no intention of being parted from it. His were eyes strangely alight with what I took at first to be urgency.

"Did you see Cassius?" Dom asked Graham, as yet another water main exploded somewhere in the distance.

"I think Ronan did, but then Sean got hit in the blowback from the explosions, and we had to make a break for it."

Dom's eyes were still on Ronan, who spoke next. "Everything went exactly as planned."

Other than Sean getting hurt and all of us being shunted into the middle of the battle, I thought but chose to keep it to myself. I knew what he was saying. They'd gotten inside, retrieved the book, and gotten out again largely in one piece, just as the plan had dictated. He was giving me no reason to think anything different, so I wasn't sure why I felt so uncomfortable with the glint in his eyes. I hoped it was just adrenaline from the mission. After all, he had just stolen something from the most dangerous Sorcerer in the world, and more importantly, he'd brought it back to us.

Lennie's phone went off, and he held it up to show us the new location for our rendezvous with the helicopter. It was *way* across campus.

"Grand. Let's go!" Dom shouted, taking off on foot.

Lindsey was by far the fastest runner of the group. She jogged ahead down the West Mall, a road spanning the length of campus, checking for threats with her long "dagger" raised. In reality, it was more of a short sword really, which made her seem even more impressive to me. As we progressed, Stuart kept pace easily behind her, and I wondered if they had taken anything to help themselves along. Even with the added adrenaline rush of our situation, I was already dog-tired before we'd made it a kilometre towards our target.

Dom stuck closest to me, with Ronan, Graham, and Lennie trailing in our wake. How he managed to run holding a sword that large was a mystery to me, though a miraculous one, but then again, Dom had always taken his fitness very seriously. Meanwhile, my breath was ragged. We pushed on.

The combat had clearly moved on ahead of us, as we continued to pass the bodies of Wielders and Wraiths alike as we turned down Agricultural Road, following the trail of violence like breadcrumbs. Any Wraiths that weren't already "killed dead" were dispatched properly by our corps along the way and left to disintegrate in the grass, while any allies we passed were told to hold on and wait for help. Even I was forced to use my blade at one point, when a Wraith emerged and reached out at me from the bushes.

"*Fuck ... OFF!*" I'd yelled as I drove Wraith Slayer harshly into his neck.

Dom had laughed. Warfare was utterly bizarre.

Connecting finally to the Main Mall—and approaching the area large enough for a helicopter to land—we could see more of our allies engaged in hand-to-hand combat, though they were shrouded. Druid-pouch smoke obstructed our line of sight as we rushed towards our friends to offer aid. In and out of an enchanted fog, golden Knave blades arced, their keening sound whistling like birdsong through the early morning air. Massive oaks towered above us, seemingly oblivious to the human plight below.

Entering the fray, we saw Alanna and Shereen fighting back-to-back as four massive, hooded Wraiths closed in on them, sickles raised and poised to kill. Stuart let out a growl and sprinted to join the fight, with Lindsey following immediately on his left. I watched as the pair of them worked in unison, together with Alanna and Shereen, to push the dark figures back. Lindsey's blade seemed to have some unusual properties itself, and I wondered if Stuart had custom-made it for her.

I didn't have much time to think, however. In the distance, I saw someone I assumed to be Glenys streaking through the air with two long blades and driving them into the back of a distracted Wraith. She was lithe, if not a bit leathery, and definitely reminded me of a pit viper, attacking as she did with such precision. It was both impressive and terrifying. Around her fought ten or more Knaves I didn't recognize, apart from Booker, who was as large and

MANTLE OF THE WORLD RULER

strong as Dom had described. He used a sword remarkably similar to Dom's as well, only it was a brilliant gold.

"Hey, Dom!" Booker's voice boomed out, notably pleased to see our arrival. "It's been a while!"

Dom grinned as Booker ran his sword through two Wraiths at once; the Knaves were surrounded by at least twenty hooded figures but seemed to have things well in hand.

From what I could tell, we were making good time, but we had to keep moving. Leaving our allies behind, we continued down the Main Mall. Ahead of us now, I saw Lennie, Graham, and Ronan charging towards the new landing spot for the helicopter, its coordinates having once again been confirmed by Lennie's phone.

"We just need to hold the Wraiths off long enough to get Ronan, the Codex, and the others off the ground!" Dom shouted towards me. "Then you can kick ass!"

We had to wait till they were clear of the area, at which point, I would attempt to use my Bearing magic to bring an end to the battle, taking out the rest of our enemies in a single sweep. *Killing them dead.*

If I drew the Wraiths' stolen magic from their bodies *too soon,* it might take Ronan down in the process. That was one of the consequences of the dark magic we now knew he had meddled in, but even so, opting to wait had been a very hard choice, knowing that some of our allies would almost certainly die in the battle while I held back.

It was a risk that several of us—Ronan excepted—had agreed was worth it, since he would be the key to us removing the Codex from Cassius's grasp in the first place. Not to mention that he undoubtedly knew more about the book than any of us at this point, which could prove vital to keeping it from ever falling back into the Sorcerer's hands. We simply couldn't risk killing him in the process of destroying the Wraith forces. We had to wait a little bit longer. But I was running out of steam.

"We have to flank them until Ronan and the others are in the air!" Dom yelled, pointing in the direction we needed to run.

"What about Lennie? He's supposed to go with them!" I shouted. He had veered off from Graham and Ronan, who were still sprinting for the landing site, to fight a group of Wraiths who had suddenly attack from their left.

511

"He's got his hands full!" Dom yelled. "Keep moving!"

We had just about reached the larger plaza where the helicopter would land, passing the Buchanan Building, in which I'd had countless classes during my time at university. Being here felt surreal, no longer fighting for my degree but for my very survival.

I shook my head, focusing on our mission.

Without warning, I felt as though I were being squeezed from all sides with almost suffocating force, unable to move forward. Some sort of magical barrier was being placed around us, barring us from getting through to the spot where the helicopter was now attempting to land.

Chop. Chop. Chop. Chop.

Something felt vaguely familiar about this magic ... It smelled herbal and earthly ... I shook my head, attempting to gain my bearings.

"Julia, what is this!" Dom yelled from somewhere behind me. Looking back, I could see that he'd been stopped by the same force I was. He kept trying to push forward, his shoulders lowered and straining, but he couldn't progress. Up ahead, closer to the landing pad when he'd been caught by the barrier, Graham had actually dropped to his knees in his efforts to break free and finish the mission, letting out a howling grunt of frustration.

Ronan, however, passed through without any issue and charged forward, sprinting for the helicopter at full speed.

"What—"

Before I could make any sense of this, a series of blasts went off all around us, aftershocks reverberating loudly in our ears. Helpless, I watched as the helicopter crashed into the ground, followed by another grand explosion.

And then everything went black.

CHAPTER 46

"Julia!" Dom hollered from somewhere unseen, coughing loudly. "Where are you?"

My ears were still ringing from the blast as I came to. I must have only blacked out for a couple of seconds, though, because the air was still filled with falling debris from the explosion.

"I'm here!" I coughed. "Are you okay?"

I heard Dom grunt as he heaved a massive hunk of concrete out of his way to reach me. "I'm fine. But what the hell just happened?"

Like me, he was covered from head to toe in dust from the blast. He knelt beside me and rubbed his eyes several times in an attempt to clear them, but it only made things worse. *"Ah! Fuck!"*

"Here, let me," I said, my head pounding violently as I crawled towards him. I turned my sleeve inside out before carefully wiping away the debris. The second I was done, Dom pulled me into his arms, hugging me tight for a moment. That had been a seriously close call.

"That wasn't Glenys and Booker, was it?" I asked.

Dom shook his head. "No, that was *way* bigger than anything Lennie asked them to do. Whoever did that, they meant to take out the helicopter."

The chopper, which we could scarcely see through the dust-clogged air, was a broken, smoking husk on the ground. We didn't have time to wonder about the pilot before we heard pounding footsteps approaching from behind. It was Lindsey and Stuart, panting but significantly less filthy than we were.

"Where's Ronan?" Dom yelped, realizing suddenly that he hadn't reappeared after the explosion. "He didn't reach the helicopter! I saw him—"

"We thought he was with you!" Lindsey said, breathing heavily, her sword still raised. Stuart wordlessly took off at a run to search the surrounding area.

"No," Dom growled. "The last I saw he and Graham were about twenty paces ahead of us. There was a force, and then—if that bastard got himself killed!" He pushed himself up off the ground.

"Dom, wait ..." I said with sudden understanding, my voice raw from the dust and debris. "It was *him* ... *He* blocked us from following him. I ... I could smell it. It was *his* magic. It didn't stop him. He passed right through and ..." I let my voice trail off as I tried to face what this meant.

Dom eyed me for a long moment as his anger with Ronan rose to a fever pitch. *"I'm going to wring his fucking neck! We need that book!"*

Lindsey cursed under her breath simultaneously. "We *need* to get the hell out of here! Where is he?" Looking around she called out for him. "Ronan?! ... You fool! Get back here!"

"Where's Graham?" I asked then, my breath catching as I remembered that he had been ahead of us, even closer to the explosion. Just then, a moan came from somewhere beyond another pile of rubble, and I saw him rise to his feet. He was badly bloodied but alive.

Stuart returned then, shaking his head. "Ronan's not here. Not at the crash site and not anywhere nearby."

"Maybe he's circled back?" Lindsey suggested, but her hope was faltering.

"You aren't *listening!*" I said to the group in frustration. "He was trying to get *on* the helicopter! *Alone!*"

Lennie appeared a few moments later, looking a bit dazed, followed closely by Shereen, Alanna, Glenys, and Booker. Strangely, after the most recent series of explosions, the Wraiths seemed to have disappeared.

"Something's not right," Lennie said. "I feel—"

In that instant, a hot wind rushed at us from all directions, sending the still-settling dust swirling upwards into the sky. On its heels came an acrid smoke, roiling and black as night, smelling like burning flesh and freshly smelted iron ...

Like death.

I saw again the image of Ronan and Cassius before a vat of boiling pitch-like liquid ... from which had rolled the same acrid smoke—smoke that had filled my lungs in that vision, choking me.

Smoke that would lead to Ronan's potential destruction.

Seeing the look on my face, Dom's eyes widened, and he looked to the others.

"RUN!!"

Together, we bolted down Memorial Road, skirting along the side of the Buchannan Building and towards Brock Hall, climbing over and around several concrete blockages—reminding me eerily of the barriers on the "map" Bernie had created for me, though these had clearly been created by the series of explosion Cassius had set.

We had thought the desert Knaves had been keen on blowing things up, but they had nothing on The Child of Rome when it came to civic destruction.

"Fuck!" Graham roared, realizing he had just led our charge into a dead end.

"He's trying to trap us with that smoke!" Lindsey yelled, assuming correctly that this was Cassius's work.

"What *is* it?" Alanna asked, panting as she wiped her face. The air around all of us was growing warmer by the minute, as though we were surrounded by flames. None of us said it, but we could feel the smothering effect of that smoke; it was blunting our magic even at a distance. It wasn't hard to imagine what would happen if we were to touch it.

Ronan's voice then called from thirty feet above us, on the rooftop of the Brock Hall Annex. "You should probably go," he said emotionlessly, in a voice that travelled farther than it should have.

We had finally located our friend, but looking up, I saw that he had changed.

"Ronan!" Dom yelled. "What the fuck are you doing up there?! Get down here! Now! We have to leave!"

"I can't," Ronan said, looking directly at me with an oddly imploring look in his eyes. He held one hand inside his jacket, clutching the *Codex Druidicus*.

"Bullshit you can't!" Lennie cried out, his eyes darting around for a fire escape or any other way for his friend to rejoin them. "You've got to move!"

None of this was right. Despite the group's apparent denial, I knew with absolute certainty that Ronan wasn't trapped up there. The height of the rooftop would be no obstacle for him. Despite his words, he hadn't meant he "couldn't" come down. He'd meant that he wouldn't.

I had to try to reach *him.* The *real* Ronan I believed was still alive somewhere inside this other person he had become. And it would soon be too late.

I stopped moving and forced every inch of my body to just be still. Closing my eyes, I felt my way outward towards him with my mind. With my magic. It took only a few seconds to find him and then connect with him, almost like building a bridge between our thoughts, suspending it with my power. As desperate as I was, this Bearing skill came to me with shocking ease.

As carefully as I could, I spoke to him in his mind: *"Ronan … please … Just let me help you. Nothing can be this bad …"*

I reopened my eyes when I heard his physical voice above me, though I maintained our mental link. "You can't help me anymore, Julia."

His voice sounded so strange. So … foreign. I knew then that his need for the Codex had overwhelmed him, the man he had been now lost in its depths.

"I won't let you be taken," I replied, pouring as much compassion into my words as I could.

Dom was looking back and forth between us, frustrated in his confusion, nostrils flaring. "What is he playing at?"

Ronan was staring down at me, teeth clenched and shoulders stiff. He was clenching his free hand into a fist so tight that I could see blood dripping from it. He could have collapsed the connection between us at any time but chose not to, even though he was physically struggling. Holding on a little longer.

Perhaps the Ronan we knew *was* still in there …

"If you won't come with us, then let me … let me end it," I said finally, unable to make myself phrase it differently but certain he would understand. *"Just like we promised."*

We had a pact, he and I … Neither of us would let the other be taken by the darkness, no matter the cost.

I placed those words in his mind as gently as I could, hoping that within them he would feel the love we all felt for him, and the sorrow I felt at the thought of having to end his life in order to save him.

Hot tears covered my cheeks as I raised my hands, ready to hold up my end of the bargain we'd made in his bedroom, which felt like a lifetime ago now. I would end it ... stripping the magic from him just as I did with the Wraiths, killing him in the process. It wouldn't take long. I didn't even think it would hurt him as much as the pain of his own betrayal, which he surely must be feeling in this moment.

For a brief moment, he looked like he might've said yes. But then another figure appeared to his left, from somewhere unseen, a hood low over its face, obscuring from view the decaying flesh and sinew I knew lay underneath. Immediately the mind-bridge between Ronan and I collapsed, and I was alone in my thoughts once more.

Cassius didn't speak, but we could soon hear his self-indulgent laughter on the air all around us as the black tendrils continued their creeping approach on all sides.

"I have to go now," Ronan said. I could see his jaw shifting slightly now, choking back tears as he settled into his resolve. "I need the answers the Codex holds."

I realized then that, faced with no hope of escape, Ronan would go with Cassius rather than give up the book. He was giving himself over, just like the vision had foretold.

"Ronan, no!" Dom yelled, his voice ragged and crazed in desperation. "Julia! Someone! *Do something!*"

Try as they might, our allies' magic had been rendered useless by the impending cloud of dark smoke. I couldn't access any of my Wielding sources either—with the haze surrounding us, there was no way to tap into the earth. What would happen when it actually reached us?

Despairing for Ronan and desperate for us all, I reformed the bond and shouted into his mind, *"I can still remove this burden from you! My Bearing magic is intact! Please ... Please, let me bring you peace!"*

Ronan looked way, not daring to remove his hand from the Codex at his breast.

Based on the violent retching and hacking coming from the others around me—and the churning nausea in my own stomach—I knew that whatever darkness had been unleashed today would surely kill us all if we didn't get out of here. And fast. I used my Bearing magic to pull all the water I could from a nearby fountain to try to create a shimmering globe to surround my friends, trapping the last remaining fresh air inside with them and hopefully buying them some time.

My efforts might as well have been a joke.

Cassius laughed as the water droplets collected, slashing down my attempt with a slow swipe of his arm. "I have you to thank you, Julia," he said. His voice was like frosty air through the charring smoke, but it was far from soothing. "For helping bring Ronan—and all of his intellect—here. For *believing* in him. I'll be seeing you *very* soon."

In that moment, I realized that the two of them must have communicated somehow when Ronan had entered the house. An actual conversation of some sort had occurred between them during that brief encounter, and this was its outcome.

Fear clouded my every thought as I reached into my Bearing core, attempting to do something, *anything*, to stop our friend from being taken by Cassius. I thrust my hands skyward; I would pull down the clouds if I had to, but The Child of Rome was having none of it. This time, he threw his arm up more forcibly and shielded himself and Ronan, showing us all that he had powers beyond my own. And then he turned, put his hand on Ronan's shoulder, and guided him away from the ledge, the two of them simply walking away. Together.

The next moments passed like a VHS tape stuck in slow motion. I remembered feeling Dom's vice-like grip on my arm as he dragged me down yet another boulevard in an attempt to escape, only to be faced by a wall of roiling doom at its end. I could detect the eerie cry of our friends' voices on the air, merging together in an audible blur as they called out to one another in the smoke, seeking asylum from the darkness Cassius had unleashed. In that moment, I lost all sense of action in a crushing awareness that the weapon we now faced was bigger than we could have ever imagined.

I froze on the spot, shaking my head in a desperate attempt to bring things back to regular speed.

"Julia, we've got to keep moving!" Dom cried, his urgency snapping me back into place.

"It's like it's trying to infect me from the outside," I said, my panic rising. As he was neither a Wielder nor Bearer, I knew he couldn't understand, but I could *feel* the effects attempting to seep in through my pores.

"Then can you try to block it out from the *inside?*" Dom asked, his eyes flashing at the startled look I gave him in response. He didn't seem nearly as affected as I did. In fact, out of our whole group, he was holding up the best.

This weapon was aimed solely at magic users.

"Maybe," I said. "I think so …" I focused on my inner Bearing magic, imagining myself producing a protective shield around me, just as I had done subconsciously throughout the last year as we'd travelled the globe. A cool sensation spread across my skin, and I instantly knew that I had managed it. "I've got it!"

Dom nodded, attuned and ready to fight onward. "Grand. Now, let's go!"

Behind us, I could hear Stuart calling out to the others, urging them onward. I spun around only to see him he hit the ground, crawling on his hands and knees as the smoke lapped at his heels. Lindsay was desperately attempting to drag him onward, but her own strength was rapidly failing.

The Wielders around us were weakening, stumbling more badly with each moment that passed, forcing Dom and me to support them as we sought out any kind of refuge.

"They aren't going to make it unless we find transport," Dom called to me as he struggled under the weight of his friends. "They can barely walk!"

I can boost them! I thought then. *Just like Sean in Cassius's tower.*

"Dom! I have an idea!"

Accessing as much of my Bearing fire as possible, I pushed my energy outwards towards our allies in the hopes that they would be strengthened by it. The effect—though not dramatic—was immediate. Our group suddenly began to move faster, pushing away from the smoke and towards the edge of the campus. We could barely see with all the ash raining down on us, worsening with the approach of the rolling clouds, but I knew the UBC grounds very well and led the charge.

By the grace of the Goddess, Sean had somehow regained consciousness and arrived with one of the SUVs just as we reached the edge of campus.

He must have backtracked and found a way around all of the rubble, but it had almost been too late. He had blood running from his ears, and his nose looked badly broken, but by sheer grit, he had managed to deliver us an escape route. We would never have been able to outrun the ever-expanding smoke on foot.

We all threw ourselves inside—Graham taking over in the driver's seat, as Sean had collapsed to the floor between it and the passenger seat before we'd gotten to him, unconscious once more—and took off, tires screeching down the road towards some unknown destination. Lennie sat up front, frantically attempting to contact anyone we might know who had survived.

"Sean and I didn't make it all the way to Cassius's office with Ronan," Graham offered, his voice breaking. "I have no idea what happened in there."

"No one blames you," Dom said, and I knew that he meant it. And that we all agreed.

Silence followed.

It was clear we couldn't go back to the Druid safe-house in Kitsilano; it was far too close to the smoke. We had no idea how far it would reach or how long it would take to dissipate. We could hope for rain, but the skies ahead were uncharacteristically clear.

We had to get out of the city.

I looked around the vehicle at the eleven of us, crammed into a space much too small for such a grouping. Lindsey was actually on the floor with Stuart, holding his head in her lap; he was unconscious, though he seemed to be breathing. She was petting his face gently, tears running silently down her own. Booker and Glenys were tucked into the back, faces pressed together in what I took to be sheer gratitude to be alive. I watched as Booker tucked Glenys's short hair behind her ear, speaking to her softly. Dom had told me he was uncertain of the parameters of their relationship, but it seemed clear to me that they were deeply in love. Alanna and Shereen were squeezed in beside Dom and me with their eyes closed, holding each other's hands so tightly that their knuckles were white.

Dom's arms had been wrapped protectively around me since we'd landed in the SUV—with a vice-like grip, to be damned sure I didn't leave him. I felt myself beginning to fall apart inside, as the adrenaline began to wear off, and was thankful for his sturdy frame around me.

How many others had made it out alive? Thomas and Peggy were nowhere to be seen during the battle, but we could hope that, between Thomas's determination and Peggy's savvy, they had found a way out long before the smoke arrived. I couldn't bring myself to imagine how many of our allies, alive but injured, had been unable to drag themselves from the smoulder.

"Peggy!" Lennie hollered into his phone, causing Dom to jump beside me. "Where are you? Where's Thomas?"

The entire SUV waited with bated breath, and then Lennie hung up the phone, speechless.

"Well?" Dom said, voice cracking.

"They ran for the ocean. It seems the smoke can't cross over bodies of water. She's with Thomas. At Wreck Beach …" His voice trailed off, looking up the location on his phone. They had clearly run in the exact opposite direction we had, but thankfully, it had resulted in safety.

"And how many others got out in time?" Dom asked, clearing his throat and bracing for the worst.

"Not many," Lennie said, shock hardening his face.

Not many.

Despite our attempt to remove the Codex without excessive losses, we had been faced with a catastrophic failure. Even if Ronan had escaped with the book alone on the helicopter, it would have been a far better outcome than this. Now, Cassius had not only the Codex but a shattered version of Ronan who was so hell-bent on finding answers that he had left his humanity behind along the way.

"I don't think he made the decision until he had the book in hand," I whispered, so quietly that only Dom could hear. "I just don't think he meant to …" I could feel his body tense even further as my voice trailed off, locked tight and not willing to let go of what just happened.

"Dom …" I whispered again. "Breathe."

"We can't … I can't talk about this now," Dom said quietly through gritted teeth. I knew he wouldn't be able to release his anguish until we were alone, and that wouldn't be until we found somewhere safe to hide. Not only was he going to have to contend with Ronan's betrayal but also the fact that his most recent leadership decisions had led to so many lives lost—or so he would see it.

"Where should we go?" Graham asked, a question directed at no one in particular. Sean seemed to be struggling to regain consciousness again, while Lennie looked like he might shatter into a thousand pieces.

Everyone in the SUV was on the brink of falling apart, if they weren't already doing so.

"We need to split up," I said.

At this moment, I was fairly certain I was the only one with clear thoughts. Perhaps it was merely the aftereffects of the smoke on them, but I sensed it was also more than that. The Wielders, who found strength and safety in numbers, had just been proven that their strategy was now wholly ineffective, if not outright dangerous.

They'd been rendered useless by whatever Cassius's noxious haze had contained. And this was only his first strike against us using the Codex.

Dom cleared his throat. "Julia's right. We all have targets on our backs, and we can't stay together. At least not right now. I know it goes against what you ... what *we* know ... but we have to disband."

I could hear the anguish in his voice as he spoke. Everything he'd work for over the past year, bringing the different camps together, attempting to create a sense of unity under one banner, was falling to pieces around him. I squeezed his hand as silence cloaked the SUV for several more minutes.

"Your truck is parked near the airport," Alanna said, the first of the group after Dom and me to regain her composure. She fished the keys out of her pocket and handed them to me. "We can hitch over the border with Booker and Glenys."

Glenys nodded from the back seat. Undoubtedly, the desert and Washington Knaves had forged a bond today, probably the only positive in an absolutely horrific day.

Lindsey spoke next. "Stuart and I ... we'll be fine. Just drop us at the Knave safe-house. We can go from there and get in touch when we can." Stuart still hadn't risen, but he seemed to be stirring more as time went on.

"Sean and I will round back to help Peggy, Thomas, and the others," Graham said. "I know we need to be on the run, but we can't abandon them. We need to get as many of our own out of the city as we can."

Dom nodded in silent agreement. He knew Sean and Graham were the kind of fighters to die for their cause if necessary. If anything, it was their preference. Dom wasn't about to argue with them over how they attended to their own business.

"And you, Lennie?" I asked. He had remained uncharacteristically silent through the disbursement planning. I noticed he held his left hand squeezed so hard on his cellphone that its hard case was buckling. "Lennie?"

His voice came out like ice. "I'm going to track down that bastard if it's the last thing I do."

This time, we all knew he wasn't referring to Cassius.

I climbed into the Tacoma's driver's seat, readjusting the seat to accommodate my long legs. Dom, who had bravely held up his resolve until now, looked positively ashen. He placed his hands on his knees, palms down, and through a distant memory, I recognized the rhythm of him schooling his breath, desperately trying to keep it together before collapse.

"Dom ... are you going to be alright? We can find somewhere to rest for a bit before we take off," I suggested. I had no idea how I was still functioning after everything that had happened, but I wasn't about to question my own resolve in this moment. I had to get us out of here.

"No, love. Our priority now is getting you ... us ... into hiding. Cassius might have taken Ronan, but we know that you're still his intended target." His voice was slow and strangely devoid of emotion. I knew he was fraying at the edges as we spoke, no longer able to hold it together.

Lindsey had quietly voiced concern about Dom before she and Stuart made their way into the Knave safe-house. Stuart had roused enough to stumble inside, but she'd paused on the threshold. "Keep an eye on Dom, Julia. I've ... well ... let me just say, Ronan has a weirdly profound effect on the people he loves and ... it can turn your mind awfully dark for a time when he fucks you over."

I nodded, understanding what she meant. I had always assumed that it was Ronan who suffered when their romantic relationship had ended, but clearly, Lindsey had faced her own shadows in the aftermath as well.

"Where are you taking us?" Dom asked from his side of the truck as we took off down the road. It was terrifying to see him so frozen ... and without solutions. But I also couldn't blame him. He had placed his utmost trust in Ronan, something not every human had the privilege of holding, and he'd just witnessed it blow up in his face.

I wracked my brain for possible locations before answering. I honestly hadn't thought that far ahead. My only thoughts were that it had to be somewhere surrounded by water and away from what had just happened in Vancouver.

"I think we'll stay in Canada but go east to the mountains. Find a lake somewhere. How's that sound? You ever stayed on a houseboat?" I asked, my levity poorly timed as usual.

Dom nodded once, before leaning against the passenger door. In the same motion, however, he also reached his hand across to me, resting it heavily on my thigh. He would be alright. He just needed time.

Reaching the Trans-Canada Highway at last and heading east, I wondered absently if the explosions would be chalked up to a gas leak or even domestic terrorism. Surely, they would have to find a way to explain the crashed helicopter, as well as the mass destruction to the university's infrastructure. I could only hope there were no civilian casualties, but we wouldn't have those details for a while. Peggy, Graham, and the others would do their best to care for our own, those who remained, and that was the best we could do right now.

Thankfully, our essentials kit had come along with Sean in the SUV when he'd rescued us. So, we had the most important things and could get quite far before needing to buy much else. Dom and I needed to slip into the night.

And so, we did.

CHAPTER 47

Cassius's mansion, 5:30 a.m.

"What are you talking about? *Expecting* me ..." Ronan said, white knuckling his blade.

While Ronan's words and physical actions were plainly defensive, Cassius could practically taste the man's desperation. Like all Wraiths in their early days, his sickened essence betrayed him.

"Come now. Let's not pretend you haven't shared the visions with me," Cassius said calmly from behind his desk. Oozing charm. His glamoured hands were spread neatly on the polished-oak surface, his fingers tapping down, one-by-one, in a slow rhythm, demonstrating his lack of concern. He had expected a confrontation like this now that he'd re-emerged visibly, though he was surprised to see that the World Ruler hadn't pushed his nose in further. Particularly when he knew the Celt was currently sitting in an unmarked vehicle just outside his property line.

"I need answers," the Druid said. "I'm taking the Codex."

"Is that so?" Cassius asked, a false smile on his lips, his teeth bared.

Ronan nodded, and Cassius was surprised to detect something other than fear in his eyes: pure, solid resolution. He had to give the Druid credit. That quality alone was worth more than gold to a man like Cassius. Few men these days possessed it: the grit to do whatever it took to achieve an ultimate agenda. He could find good use for this skill.

"And what makes you think I have it in my possession now?" Cassius asked, curious more than anything about what the Druid had learned of the book already and whether that knowledge had come from the dreams they shared or somewhere else.

"Because ..." Ronan faltered momentarily, and then his eyes widened. "Because I can feel it in here with us."

"Intriguing," Cassius said.

This was getting *very* interesting. Initially, he had planned to kill the Druid on the spot for daring to trespass, soothsaid future together or not. He had no time for allies of the Sovereign. Instead, Cassius rose from behind his desk, circling it and moving towards the man. Ronan didn't step back, keeping his eyes locked to the space Cassius had just occupied. Subtly searching for the book, no doubt. Cassius slowly approached him. The Druid stood several inches taller than him in his military boots.

"How many minutes are we at now, before your friends detonate their bombs?" Cassius drawled, stopping directly in front of him. The Druid didn't look him in the eye but flinched slightly.

Yes, fool. I knew all about your plans to attack me this morning.

"How long, Ronan?"

He spoke quietly. "Approximately two minutes."

"Excellent. Then I'm going to make you a deal." Cassius spoke low now, almost intimately. "I'll let you walk out of here with the Codex. And I'm even going to give you a head start to get away with it too. You can try to escape. But if ... *when* ... I catch you, you come with me. Willingly. This is the only way you'll *ever* get a chance to read the Codex ... and unlock its secrets."

Ronan's eyes locked on his finally, and Cassius chose this moment to let his glamour drop, exposing the truth of his rotting flesh, the horror of his existence. He was beyond ancient, and yet still, he lived.

Recoiling, Ronan tried to speak, his voice shaking, "I ... I don't ..."

Codex in hand—coupled with the sudden and overpowering sense that the Druid who stood before him was vital to his mission—Cassius knew that here, in this moment, he was the closest he'd ever been to achieving true immortality. Negotiations were over.

"Otherwise," he said with cruel certainty, interrupting the Druid's pitiful attempts at a response, "I will murder *each and every one of your friends,* starting with the World Ruler." Anger and starvation burned in his core. "I'll take great pleasure in killing that one, although … I've lost track of how many times I've done it already." He cocked his head as he stared up into Ronan's eyes. "Julia, however … I'll go slow with her and make it last … savouring every morsel. I always remember every moment of killing her …"

The Druid's jaw ticked, and Cassius knew he was quickly putting together the fact that the survival of all of them depended upon his agreement to this offer.

"Do you agree to my terms?"

Ronan shifted on the spot.

"I'm not hearing an answer, Ronan. Tick-tock …"

"I …"

Cassius reached into his suit jacket, magically drawing the Codex forward from its recesses. He was a master at cloaking things, and the book—just like the Spear—hadn't left his person since he'd gained possession of it.

Ronan's eyes glazed briefly as he stared at the Codex and then lit vividly from within. "You have a deal."

Cassius grinned maliciously before handing the book to Ronan's waiting hands. "Ten seconds …"

Ronan shoved the book into his coat, turning on his heel just as the explosions began.

Boom!

Boom, boom!

"I'm looking forward to doing business with you, Ronan," Cassius said, before setting his own plans into motion.

ACKNOWLEDGEMENTS

Thank you to the first readers of The Lost Wells Trilogy for your support, and for loving Dom and Julia as much as I do. Your encouragement has been the fuel to boost me through the chaos of writing and publishing on *so many* occasions.

Becky, your enthusiasm around the story is unparalleled. Thank you for diving into the first draft after the girls went to bed; I know the days (and nights) of motherhood are long, and I appreciate the depth of your support immensely.

To Margot—the Lindsey to my Julia—thank you for being a sturdy long-distance sounding board through all stages of this journey, and for always talking me off the ledge of self-doubt. I appreciate your unwavering belief in my abilities more than you know.

Love to Francine for being an irreplaceable friend along the path. This life's journey can be rocky, but it has been a gift to have you by my side. I am proud of the women (and writers) we have become, and excited for the adventures—and charcuterie boards—that will come next!

A Dom-sized hug to Dalyce for your spiritual counsel throughout this process, but also for being that cozy sweater kind of friend. It is such a warm comfort to have you in my life. And to Anna, for the peace and magic you bring. I'm manifesting that perfect witchy forest-cottage in your future.

To Alecia, thank you for sharing your Divine Feminine power, and for transporting me (and Julia) down the California coastline with such rapturous joy. Bernie would be so proud of all you have achieved this year—I am fortunate to be creating alongside you.

Thank you to Melissa and Jessie for getting your hands dirty in the final formations of MotWR—your proofreads came at the perfect moment. It's such a blessing to have bookish friends like you!

Thank you to James for the translation help from overseas.

And big hugs to Kristy, Erin, Fiona, and Shoshone for cheering me on!

To Finn, Lucien, and Stephanie for your unwavering care of our children over this past year—thank you for the peace of mind and love you continue to extend to us and our boys. More is more.

And to our sons: the wild boys who sprinkle the magic of childhood into the everyday. Thank you for always being game to come along for book deliveries, even if that childhood magic often translates into crumbs and sand spread throughout my vehicle's interior.

But most importantly, my deepest appreciation is to Scott—we did another one babe (and survived)! Go us. I can't imagine travelling through this wild life with anyone else, and I am endlessly grateful for the space you provide for me to create and be my truest self. You are the spear to my chalice. Thank you for being my home.

Thanks to Britt Low at Covet Design for yet another jaw-dropping cover. And to Matt Gladman, Arianna Augustine, and Ashley Marston for the film and photo magic—your creative collaboration during the birth of my books has become an integral part of my process. And thank you to Danielle Cunningham for your continued marketing savvy and friendship over the last year.

Thanks to everyone at FriesenPress for your continued support in bringing these books to life. To Carly Cumpstone and Emily Perkins for making it happen. To my editors, Janet Layberry and Gisèle Plourde —your investment in this story has been one of the happiest outcomes. Thank you for your enthusiastic support and all that you have taught me so far. I am stoked to bring you Book Three. Let's finish this beast!

KATE GATELEY

With a B.A. in Linguistics and a B.Sc. in Physiology from the University of Saskatchewan, KATE GATELEY has always been fascinated by history, Celtic Ideology, ancestral memory and generational wounding, and the "Divine Feminine," and those personal studies continue to influence every aspect of her life, on the pages of her books and off.

When Kate published her first book, *Tides of the Sovereign* (FriesenPress 2022), Book One of the *Lost Wells Trilogy*, she knew that it was only the beginning of a story she has always wanted to write—one with heart and meaning that was actually worth sharing. Continuing now in Book Two, *Mantle of the World Ruler*, and beyond into the next volume still to come, that story has grown far beyond what she could ever have imagined … into something that she dearly hopes can one day find—and deserve—a cherished spot among those volumes of both contemporary fantasy and historical romance that so inspired her growing up.

Kate currently lives, and writes, on a small farm in the Cowichan Valley on beautiful Vancouver Island, with her amazing husband, two incredible sons,

an adorable dog, several barn cats who don't earn their keep, and some decidedly ungrateful chickens ... all of whom are very dearly loved.
Look for book three of the *Lost Wells Trilogy* ... coming soon.

To connect with the author, go to:
www.kategateley.com

Printed in Canada